BETWEEN

A MODERN FAIRY TALE FOR THE DISCERNING
DEVIANT

L. L. STARLING

Illustrated by
REBECCA MORSE

WICKED FABLES PRESS

To Peter, my very own wizard from Wisconsin, who makes lovely things happen.

To my Mother, who is still the most magical person I've ever met.

PART I

THE WITCHES OF OLD MIDDLETON

OR: How Sasha's life was turned upside down by accepting the wrong job

PROLOGUE

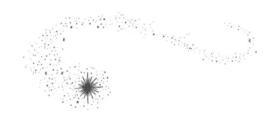

SOMETIME IN THE PAST (TUESDAY, OCTOBER 30TH TO BE SPECIFIC...JUST BEFORE LUNCH).

SASHA PIERCE STARED AT THE MANGY UNICORN SWAYING DRUNKENLY BESIDE her car and sighed. When she had informed her friends and loved ones that she planned to take a teaching position in Old Middleton—a village cradled deep in the woods of Wisconsin—they warned her that the place was bound to be a little old-fashioned ("Quaint," said one, with a knowing smirk); a little isolated ("Just imagine the peace and quiet!" said another, with forced cheer); and exceptionally dull ("You can brush up on your quilting ... and your jam-making ... and your alcoholism," said another still, with a sympathetic pat on Sasha's shoulder).

Regrettably, no one had warned Sasha that Old Middleton was a supernatural hotspot—a gateway between this world and several fairy tale realms. If they had done so, then the unicorn trying to head-butt Sasha's car in the school parking lot would not have been so unexpected.

Nor would the goblins—currently being chased around the Old Middleton Elementary School playground by a small mob of first graders wielding safety scissors—have come as quite a shock.

And the brownies—who were gleefully stealing shoes and leaving irate, barefoot children in their wake—would have been as unremarkable as the oak leaves scattered around Sasha's boots.

But no warning, no matter how well-meant, could have truly prepared

Sasha for the sorcerer, who lounged indolently on a branch high in the village's oldest oak tree while his creatures wreaked havoc on her work-place. Dressed in sinister black armor and a showy cloak comprised entirely of shadows, the sorcerer watched the chaos unfold below him with a smile on his infuriatingly handsome face—the kind of smile typically worn by pyromaniacs skipping toward a fireworks factory with a flaming torch in each hand.

Unfortunately, that smile was soon directed at Sasha.

"Fine," she said wearily to the man in black. "You win. I'll do it. Just call off your unicorn—that car cost me a fortune."

Fairy Tale Chaos at Old Middleton Elementary

1

ONCE UPON A TIME …

ONE WEEK AND TWO DAYS EARLIER (WHEN SASHA'S LIFE WAS RELATIVELY NORMAL AND CONTAINED 100% FEWER DRUNK UNICORNS)

"WE ARE LOST. AND DOOMED."

Sasha gripped the steering wheel a little more firmly and tried to peer through the torrential rain buffeting her windshield. In this weather, it was hard to determine whether the blurry shape that had suddenly appeared in front of her was another vehicle or if she had veered off the road entirely and was now hurtling toward a tree.

Her passenger's announcement was doing nothing to increase their chances of survival.

"Not helpful, Lyla," Sasha said sternly as she slowed the car and squinted ahead. "Besides, 'doomed' is a little extreme, don't you think?" Much to Sasha's joy, the blurry shape appeared to have taillights and was now well ahead of her. She gave the accelerator a tentative prod.

Lyla, however, was not as jolly. She smoothed the roadmap out across her lap and studied it yet again. "I thought it was rather accurate. Let me spell it out." She held up her hand and began to count off the doom indicators on her fingers. "One—we're in a torrential storm, that could quickly turn into a Biblical-grade flood. Two—we're in a car without heating—"

Sasha groaned. "For the hundredth time—I can't put on the heating because it steams up the windshield. Do you want me to crash into another vehicle?"

"Does that other vehicle have heating?" Lyla pointedly pulled down the sleeves of her cream-colored sweater. "As I was saying—we are in a car without heating. If the flood doesn't kill us, we'll freeze to death, leaving some passing hitchhiker to find our popsicle-like corpses."

"Thanks for that morbid visual," Sasha said dryly.

Lyla ignored her. "Three—we have no cell phone coverage, so not only are we stuck using prehistoric methods of navigation"—she scowled down at the map—"but we can't call for help or, more importantly, pizza and wine. Four—we're in the middle of nowhere, which means no one can hear our cries of distress. Five—we're trying to find a village that we've never been to before and we'll probably want to leave it as soon as we arrive. And six—it's almost midnight, the time when doom is most likely to occur. See?" Lyla wiggled her fingers in Sasha's peripheral vision. "*Doomed.*"

Sasha disregarded the wiggling fingers and carefully maneuvered the car around a fallen branch. "Glass half-empty, Lyla. Our car is wet, but we're dry. We're wearing warm clothes, so we aren't cold. We aren't lost, we're just temporarily displaced … in what is probably Wisconsin. And there's still at least an hour until midnight. We're definitely not *doomed.*"

Lyla gave her friend a stern look. "Catastrophes make you unforgivably perky." She sniffed and began to pull her long hair into a ponytail. "What you fail to realize is that *this* is how most horror films start; two attractive, single women—one of whom is blonde …" She paused to wrap a tie around her hair, giving it a decisive shake.

Sasha laughed. "We both know that you're a redhead."

Lyla waved her hand dismissively. "Stop putting facts into my story. As I was saying, two attractive, single women—one of whom is *currently* a blonde —are driving along a dark highway during a storm. Any minute now, our car will break down, and we will be besieged by Midwest serial-killers."

"Or farmers."

"Farmers *are* serial killers, except their victims are more cow-like. Or chicken-like. Or vegetable-like."

Sasha rolled her eyes. "Instead of planning our gruesome deaths, could you please try to figure out where we are? I feel as though I'm just driving around randomly here." She spared a glance at the gas station map in Lyla's lap. "You have a master's degree—navigating a map should be child's play."

"I have a master's in *psychology*, not cartography. The skills aren't trans-ferable … unless you want me to probe the map about its deep-seated anxiety issues." Lyla sighed in frustration and looked back down at the well-creased map. "I have no idea where we are. I'm not even sure if we're still in the United States. The last time I looked, we entered Wisconsin and were never seen again. We are in the midst of an Ordeal."

"We are not in the midst of 'an Ordeal.' This is just a temporary setback. Stop being such a pessimist."

"I'm not a pessimist. I'm a realist, and so are you. And, in this situation, it is realistic to assume that something is about to happen to us."

Sasha eased her little red sports car around a corner, careful to leave plenty of space between herself and the vehicle in front. "I'm beginning to suspect that you *want* something to happen to us."

Lyla shrugged. "Nothing death or dismemberment related. I *do* want something fun to happen to us, but that's doubtful given that we're heading toward a village in *Wisconsin*."

"Cheer up! It could be one of those fun villages that have a dark and terrible secret. Or one where everyone is part of a nudist cult."

Lyla perked up. "You think so?"

"No, I don't."

Lyla sighed the sigh of the long suffering. "Tell me again—what possessed you to take this job? If you're aiming to get us killed, you could have done that back in New York in a more glamorous setting. Something with less doom and farmers, and more martinis and male models." She groaned. "See what I left behind for you? Over-priced alcohol and *man-flesh*."

"You also left behind your doctoral dissertation. *And* all those classes you signed up to teach this semester. *And* that conference you were supposed to be attending in—"

"Let's never speak of that again," Lyla interrupted firmly. "We were discussing *your* poor life choices, not mine."

"Really? I'm ready to switch the spotlight to you and talk about why you've suspended your enrollment." Sasha glanced at her friend. Lyla was staring resolutely ahead, her shoulders rigid. The sight made Sasha distinctly uneasy. "A topic you've been avoiding for the entire trip."

"You make it sounds so ominous."

"It might be." Sasha spared Lyla another glance but couldn't make out her friend's expression in the dark. "You're not telling me anything."

"I wish it was interesting enough to be ominous. I'm simply taking a well-earned break from my degree ... that may last for the rest of my life. *You*, however," Lyla said in a rush before Sasha could reply, "appear to have taken leave of your senses entirely by choosing to teach kindergarten in the middle of nowhere. Especially when you could be teaching children who are old enough to appreciate sarcasm in a fun city, like New York or Las

Vegas or New Orleans or a city in any state other than Wisconsin. So, tell me again—why are we here?"

Sasha's hands tensed around the wheel. *Why indeed,* she thought, the leather creaking in protest beneath her palms.

Though, even as she began to second-guess herself, she heard *it*—the impatient little voice that seemed to be permanently camped somewhere in the back of her mind.

Keep moving, the little voice whispered whenever she became complacent with her life.

Where's the challenge here? it goaded as soon as she settled into a new routine.

Surely there is something more, something better *to be savored just around the corner,* it whined the very moment she contemplated setting up a home base.

Frankly, Sasha was quite sick of that little voice. That little voice had prompted her to leave a perfectly adequate—if somewhat bland—relationship to backpack across Australia until she was exhausted and flat-broke, even though all she wanted to do was turn around and go back home.

That little voice had led her to take up fifteen substitute teaching positions this teaching year alone—and it was only October.

That little voice had led her straight to where she was right now: lost on a slippery, dark road, searching for a remote country village in the middle of the night with her best friend—and possibly heading toward a stereotypical death by rural serial killer.

Just as she was starting to feel a little morose about allowing an auditory hallucination to dictate her life-choices, Lyla's voice broke her reverie.

"Hey, what does that sign say? Does that say *Old Middleton*? Or does it say *Yak Disco*? It's difficult to tell with all this rain."

"Yak Disco? *Really*?" Sasha peered at the sign as best as she could through the downpour and promptly gave up. "You're right. It could be either. Whichever it is, we're following it."

"Bring on the yaks!" Lyla whooped.

Sasha eased her car around a sudden series of twists and turns that drew them deep into what appeared to be a small forest.

"*Doomed,*" Lyla said, watching the trees suspiciously.

To Lyla's credit, the forest did look particularly sinister and possibly even doom-ish.

Not that Sasha would admit it.

"Not doomed," Sasha corrected firmly, as they emerged unscathed from the trees ten minutes later and found themselves on the outskirts of a village. Miraculously, the rain eased to the point where there was only a smattering of raindrops against the windshield. Sasha was determined to see this as a good omen.

"Looks like we're here," she said.

The road was deserted, so she stopped the car in front of a large, wooden sign that stood at the entrance to the village. A black cat crept out from the shadows and sat beside it, its tail curling protectively around one of the wooden posts.

"*Old Middleton*," Lyla read. "*Welcome to the Gateway Village.*"

Sasha frowned. "Gateway to what?"

She leaned forward over the steering wheel and tried to see past the sign. The village beyond was silent and still, lit only by the twin rows of streetlamps and the strands of fairy lights festooned between them. The lights reflected off the wet cobblestones, making it appear as though the street was awash with silver and gold.

"Well," Lyla sniffed, "it clearly isn't the gateway to a wild nightlife or debauched adventures. Then again, it could refer to *that*."

Sasha peered through the windshield toward where Lyla was pointing. There, on what appeared to be a stone platform, was an immense, sandstone arch. Soaring, ornate columns held the arch aloft, giving it the appearance of something strong and steadfast. Even at a distance, she could tell that it was old, possibly even ancient—the last vestiges of something grand and glorious that had once towered above this small village. Although the night was overcast, the arch seemed aglow with starlight, glimmering faintly in the dim light.

"Maybe," Sasha said. "It certainly looks like a gateway."

Abruptly, Sasha's entire body shivered violently. She lurched forward, grabbing the steering wheel tightly for support. But then, just as quickly as the shaking began, it stopped.

Lyla eyed her incredulously. "What the *hell* was that? Did someone walk on your grave? Or are you finally going to admit that it's cold in here?"

Sasha shook her head. It was not the cold that had moved her like a ragdoll in her seat. It was not the cold that had set her heart racing and caused goosebumps to scatter across her skin.

It felt more like dread.

No, that little voice in her mind whispered gleefully. *Anticipation*.

Sasha blinked, dumbfounded. "That was strange."

"It's all strange," Lyla said, frowning at the cat who stared back at her with disdain.

Sasha opened her mouth to explain about the voice, but Lyla suddenly yawned.

"Let's find the boarding house and get into a nice warm bed," her friend said, rubbing her eyes. "I'm exhausted."

Watching Lyla yawn made Sasha yawn and the odd moment passed.

"Sounds like a plan," Sasha said, determined to ignore the entire episode. "Just read out the address, and we'll be there in a flash."

~

"AND THERE WILL BE NO LOUD NOISE-MAKING OF ANY DESCRIPTION. NOR will you be coming in at all hours of the night like *flibbertigibbets*. There is a very generous curfew—11:59 p.m. *on the dot*. And although Headmistress Dean has arranged for your accommodation personally, you *will* observe the curfew, or you will be removed from the premises *immediately*. Is that understood?"

"Yes, Miss Adeline," Sasha and Lyla said obediently.

Miss Adeline's Boarding House for Genteel Young Women of Unimpeachable Reputation was a grand, Queen Anne style mansion painted a delicate shade of duck-egg blue with cream trim, located just off Main Street. The boarding house was as fiercely preserved as any museum piece: its antique furnishings and gilt-edged mirrors were polished to a high sheen; its many rugs were beaten to the point where dirt actively feared to settle within a three-foot radius of the ground; and all of its fireplaces were gleaming and, inexplicably, soot-free. The entire house smelled of beeswax polish, oatmeal cookies, and oddly enough, *secrets*.

Miss Adeline, the owner of this august establishment, was a tall woman of indeterminable age and terrifyingly good posture. She wore a calf-length, gray woolen skirt—the scratchy kind—and a crisp, white blouse with a multitude of tiny buttons that led, arrow-straight, to a point just beneath her chin, making her neck appear impossibly long. Both garments had been pressed—each pleat, each seam—with a precision that bordered on the fanatical. Her gray hair was braided and wrapped around her head like a steel coronet, and her keen brown eyes were perpetually narrowed in suspicion behind round, iron-rimmed glasses.

Overall, her appearance was both charming and fear-inducing, like a baby seal wielding a machine gun.

As Miss Adeline paced back and forth in front of her new guests, Sasha suppressed the urge to squirm, and smiled up at the older woman, hoping to appear proper and presentable. That hope was dashed when she glanced up at the mirror above the fireplace and caught sight of her reflection. Her dark curls were a windblown mess, tumbling to the waist of her rumpled, forest-green peacoat, and getting hopelessly tangled in her scarf along the way. Her cheeks were still flushed the color of stewed tomatoes from the effort of lugging her bags into the house; and her blue eyes were tired and ringed with shadows. She looked exhausted and bedraggled—maybe even a little feral. To make matters worse, the pink chaise lounge that she was sharing with Lyla was so low to the ground that Sasha's tall frame was folded practically in half, her chin an inch away from resting on her knees, her elbows jutting pointily at her sides.

I look like a human accordion, she thought wryly.

She glanced at Lyla and noted, with considerable relief, that at least *one* of them looked somewhat genteel. Despite the long hours spent in a cramped car, Lyla had emerged relatively unscathed: not a strand of her pin-straight, blonde hair was out of place, nor was there a wrinkle in her cream-colored coat. Moreover, thanks to her short stature, she was able to sit on the tiny, sunken chaise without resorting to human origami. She looked as calm and composed as one could look while sitting on structurally unsound antique furniture that belonged to a terrifying geriatric.

As if hearing Sasha's thoughts, the springs of the old chaise let out an ominous creak. Lyla looked up at the mirror and caught Sasha's eye.

Doomed, Lyla mouthed.

Miss Adeline cleared her throat.

Sasha quickly turned her attention back to their hostess and tried—as hard as she could—to radiate charm, manners, and unimpeachable morals. Surprisingly, it must have worked because Miss Adeline stopped pacing, apparently satisfied by the behavior of the two women sitting awkwardly below her. She clasped her hands—covered in gray, crocheted fingerless gloves—tidily before her and cleared her throat.

"No pets," the older woman continued, "*particularly* dogs as they are noisy and have been known to perform lewd acts on one's leg."

Sasha bit her bottom lip to hold back a laugh.

"And there will be no"—Miss Adeline's small mouth pursed in distaste as if she was sucking on a pickled egg—"*gentleman callers* hidden in your room under any circumstances."

"Yes, Miss Adeline," Sasha said obediently.

"What if they hide in the bathroom instead?" Lyla asked.

Miss Adeline and Sasha turned to Lyla, both wearing identical incredulous expressions.

"I beg your—" Miss Adeline began.

"Or in a closet?" Lyla persisted.

Sasha cleared her throat meaningfully.

"Yes, Miss Adeline," Lyla said, sighing.

Miss Adeline's eyes narrowed to mere slits. She opened her mouth to speak but then stopped, her attention suddenly drawn to the misshapen pillow beside Lyla. Sasha watched in surprise as the older woman snatched up the pillow and began to beat it violently into shape.

"I feel like I'm sixteen all over again," Lyla whispered to Sasha from the corner of her mouth.

Sasha nudged her in the ribs, which sent Lyla into a coughing fit.

Miss Adeline spun quickly toward Lyla. "You aren't diseased, are you, girl?"

"No, Miss Adeline," Lyla spluttered. "Just a little thirsty."

Miss Adeline sniffed and returned the tortured pillow to its place. "I'll send for tea as soon as we are finished. Now, where was I?"

Sasha and Lyla exchanged looks.

"Ah ... dogs," Sasha said.

"*Lewd* dogs," Lyla added with considerable relish.

Miss Adeline nodded sharply. "No dogs. No gentleman callers. No gallivanting."

"Got it," Lyla said. "And the Wi-Fi password ... ?"

"No Wi-Fi," Miss Adeline said.

Lyla paled. She turned to Sasha, her hazel eyes wide with horror. "No dogs. No gentleman callers. No gallivanting. *No Wi-Fi.*"

Sasha shrugged helplessly.

Miss Adeline gestured to the far wall. "You will find postcards at your disposal in the writing desk."

"Well, thank goodness for that," Lyla said. "I was starting to regret not bringing my carrier pigeon."

"No pets," Miss Adeline said.

Sasha looked down at her lap and bit her lip.

"As I was saying ..." Miss Adeline resumed her position before them, her eyes narrowed behind her glasses. "These are the rules of my boarding house. If you are unable to follow them, I suggest that you leave immediately for the nearest hotel."

"Which is located where, hypothetically speaking?" Lyla asked.

Miss Adeline lifted her pointy chin. "The next town over. Do you wish for more specific directions?"

"Ye—" Lyla began.

Sasha promptly nudged her friend in the ribs once again.

"No, Miss Adeline!" she said hurriedly as Lyla started coughing anew. "Headmistress Dean"—she glared meaningfully at Lyla—"my new employer, *the person who will be signing my paychecks,* said that you were a close, personal friend of hers—"

"Gotcha," Lyla said between coughs.

"—and could not recommend your boarding house highly enough." Sasha tried to smile winsomely at Miss Adeline but felt her lips shape into something lopsided and a touch hysterical. "We're delighted to be staying here."

"Delighted," Lyla spluttered.

Miss Adeline pursed her lips. "That remains to be seen."

Ominously, the old grandfather clock in the corner chose that moment to strike midnight, its chimes strangely discordant in the sudden silence.

"May we go to our—" Lyla began.

"*Shhhh!*" Miss Adeline hissed, pressing a bony finger to her lips.

Lyla mimed buttoning her lips shut and folded her hands primly in her lap.

Miss Adeline nodded approvingly and turned toward the clock, apparently waiting for it to complete its chimes.

Sasha bit her lip again, trying not to smile. She attempted to distract herself by letting her gaze drift aimlessly across the rose drawing room, as Miss Adeline had referred to it. From what she could see in the dim lamplight, there appeared to be an alarming amount of pink. The drawing room's opulent rose-patterned wallpaper and plush, dusky-pink velvet couches made Sasha feel as though she was sitting inside her grandmother's jewelry box. There was also a considerable amount of clutter: every available surface was either covered in a lace doily or displayed a porcelain figurine or, in some unfortunate locations, featured both simultaneously.

Sasha firmly believed that no room needed six porcelain shepherds, all of whom looked far too intoxicated to tend to livestock.

There were also far too many paintings—*disturbing* paintings—in ornate, gold frames. Sasha could not decide which was worse: the portrait of the extremely unattractive child in a pink pinafore holding an even more unattractive dog; or the portrait of the foppish young man standing beside a rather lascivious-looking donkey. The lamplight threw odd shadows across the artwork, making it appear as if the subjects were moving. As Sasha watched, the girl and the foppish man seemed to frown at her suspiciously. The donkey, however, gave her an approving leer.

Sasha shuddered and turned her attention to Lyla and noticed, with some alarm, that she was asleep. She nudged her friend, who woke up with a start.

"Yes, Miss Adeline," Lyla said automatically, catching herself before she fell off the chaise.

Miss Adeline turned away from the clock and looked over at Lyla, puzzled. "What did you say, girl?"

The last chime of the clock died away.

Sasha put her hand over Lyla's. "We were wondering, Miss Adeline, if we could skip the tea and go to bed. We've been traveling since very early this morning."

Miss Adeline gave a reluctant nod. "Very well. I can see that you're almost dead on your feet. I'll get Martha to bring up your bags."

She crossed over to one of the many side tables, her footsteps muffled by the thick, dusky-pink rug, and picked up a small, silver bell. Within seconds of ringing it, the door to the kitchen swung open.

A thick-set, broad-shouldered woman in a pale blue dress, sensible black shoes, and starched white apron emerged. She paused in the doorway and assessed the newcomers with a frank, dark-eyed stare that made Sasha squirm.

Whatever she saw must have amused her; she snorted quietly to herself and shuffled over to Miss Adeline's side.

"You rang?" the woman—Martha, Sasha presumed—asked Miss Adeline, her tone as dry as unbuttered toast.

Miss Adeline smiled approvingly. "Would you see to Miss Lyla and Miss Sasha's luggage?"

Martha gave a sharp nod, her short, iron-gray curls barely moving, and shuffled toward the front door. Sasha and Lyla shared a horrified glance.

"Really," Sasha said hurriedly, "we can get our bags."

"We insist," Lyla said. She sprung up from the couch and promptly bent over, clutching her leg. "*Agh*, my damn leg—"

Miss Adeline slammed her hand down onto the side table, causing a figurine of a dancing goat to rattle alarmingly across the surface. "*Language*, Miss Lyla! There will be no foul language in this boarding house."

Lyla froze. "Ah ... my *darn* leg?"

Again, Miss Adeline slammed her hand down onto the table, the dancing goat now teetering precariously near the edge.

Lyla lifted an eyebrow. "My *dashed* leg?"

Miss Adeline lowered her hand. "*That* I will allow."

It may have been a trick of the light, but the goat looked inordinately relieved

So did Lyla. She exhaled in a rush. "My dashed leg is asleep." Grimly, she tried to massage the circulation back into her limb.

Sasha stood cautiously, wincing as her cramped muscles protested the movement. "I'll get the bags."

Before she could move, she heard a bang followed by a creak and an oddly muted scraping sound. The women turned and saw Martha shuffling past with their luggage. She had placed the four suitcases into one big pile and was gamely dragging them, inch-by-torturous-inch, across the floor.

Sasha crossed to Martha's side as quickly as her own numb limbs would allow. "Please, let me——"

Martha slapped away her hand. "I have this under control! Girls today," she muttered, dragging the luggage another inch, "always know better than their elders. I went through a war, dash it!" She yanked on the bags. "I once defended myself against an enemy soldier in my nightgown with only an egg whisk!" She moved the bags another inch.

Miss Adeline smiled proudly at the irate woman. "Martha is very capable of looking after your luggage. Let me show you to your rooms."

Ramrod straight, she walked past the heaving, wheezing Martha and began to climb the impressive staircase.

Sasha and Lyla shared an incredulous look.

"How is Martha going to get the bags up the staircase?" Sasha whispered to Lyla.

They both looked at Martha. She had moved the luggage a whole two feet.

"The *two-flight, circular* staircase!" Lyla squeaked.

"This ends now," Sasha said grimly.

The women turned and walked resolutely back toward Martha.

Sasha reached for one of the suitcases. "Sorry, but we insist."

Martha rapped her soundly across the knuckles.

"*Ouch.*" Sasha looked down at her hand in shock. "That really hurt!"

"It was meant to," Martha said. "I told you that I could do it without your help, and I will."

"You can't take us both," Lyla said, snatching one of the luggage handles. "Hey!" she cried as Martha slapped her hand away, too.

"Let me do my job, dash it! I've got this!" It sounded like a battle cry.

"I believe you." Lyla looked down at her hand. "I take it back——you have *way* more upper-body strength than you should for a woman your age."

Martha snorted. "You have no idea."

"But——" Sasha started.

"No buts!" Martha said, grabbing the luggage once more and pushing it across the floor.

"Leave Martha be," Miss Adeline commanded.

Sasha and Lyla looked up; Miss Adeline was staring down at them from the top of the landing.

"And no dawdling!" she called down.

Sasha and Lyla took one last look at Martha, who was now muttering something about miniskirts and rationing and quickly followed Miss Adeline upstairs.

~

To Lyla's great amusement, their room was just as terrifyingly kitsch as the rose drawing room. There were two white, wrought-iron single beds covered in pink and mint-green handmade quilts, and far too many matching throw pillows. Porcelain knickknacks—shepherdesses appearing to strangle sheep with their crooks, and cross-eyed china cats licking bowls of milk—were scattered on every available surface. An antique alarm clock, crowned with twin brass bells, guarded the nightstand.

"It's like a time capsule," Sasha said, staring at the lacy, pale green lampshades in awe.

Lyla gingerly ran her fingertips across the rose-print wallpaper. "Yes, it is. And just like any time capsule, it should be sealed shut for the good of humanity and never opened again."

Sasha looked up at the ceiling, where plaster roses clustered around the blush-tinted light fixture and smiled. "I love it!"

"Of course, you do." Lyla sighed and headed toward the adjoining bathroom. "Do you think there's modern plumbing? Or will we have to fetch our water from a nearby stream?" She paused, her hand on the doorknob, her eyes widening. "Quick! Check under the bed for chamber pots."

"Chamber pots?" Sasha laughed and sat on one of the beds. "In this century?" But then the bed creaked alarmingly under her weight as if to remind her that this particular piece of furniture was *not* made in this century and could be hiding all manner of historic, chamber pot-like objects beneath.

"Right," Sasha muttered, quickly crouching down beside the bed. "Chamber pots." She pulled aside the bed skirt and peered into the darkness beyond. "We're all clear."

"So far so good." Lyla turned the doorknob. "Now, let's hope that there's plumbing; I want to freshen up before bed and I'll need more than a tin tub and a rag on a stick."

To their great relief, there was a rather lovely and fairly modern bathroom, complete with running water, a modest shower, and an antique, claw-foot bathtub.

As tempting as the bath looked, Sasha was too exhausted to do anything but slip into bed. Although it tended to squeak every time she shifted, the sheets—fringed in lace and needlepoint bluebirds—were crisp and clean and smelled of lavender, and the comforter and pillows were filled with real duck down. Sasha felt as though she was lying on a cloud.

"This," she announced, stretching out her arms across the sheets, "is *heavenly*." With a happy sigh, she sat up, picked up her hairbrush from the nightstand, and attempted to wrangle her unruly hair into submission.

"I'm still trying to figure out if I find this place horrifying or hilarious," Lyla said, as she climbed into her bed. "Right now, I'm voting for *horrifying*. Look at this!" She snatched her phone off the nightstand and held it up toward Sasha. "Barely any reception and no Wi-Fi. Which means no Internet, Sasha. *No outside world*!"

"Well, I won't miss it; I hate being so dependent on technology. It'll be nice to be gadget-free for a few weeks. Very retro of us." Sasha winced as her brush snagged a knot in one of her curls. "We'll fit in nicely with our new room."

"Look at you—so gleeful in the face of the apocalypse. I should have known better than to complain to you; you barely use your phone, you Luddite." Lyla's eyes narrowed. "You're going to use those postcards, aren't you?"

"Yes!" Sasha said, laughing, as she began to braid her hair. "I'm going to send one to everyone I know. My parents are going to love it."

"They really will, those lovable weirdos." Lyla shuddered. "Don't worry, old friend," she whispered to her phone, and placed it reverently back on the nightstand. "I will find a way to bring you back to life."

"It's only for three weeks. You'll survive."

"Will I?" Lyla gave her phone a fond pat and sat back against her pillows. "Three whole weeks without the Internet, *and* no staying out late, bad language, or men—that's four of my favorite pastimes outlawed. Talk about deprivation." She sighed deeply. "And I won't even have a lewd dog to console me ..."

Sasha paused mid-braid and looked over at her friend. "You look utterly miserable. I don't want you to be miserable, especially since you've come all this way to keep me company. Do you want to look for somewhere else to stay?"

"And potentially anger your new employer by fleeing her friend's boarding house in the dead of night?"

"You're my number one priority. I'll think of an excuse to tell them both." Sasha peered out the window. It was storming again, the wind throwing the rain against the glass in harsh, staccato bursts. "Though, if we're fleeing, I'd prefer to do it in the morning. Preferably after a large breakfast."

"You're so *practical*. But, no—I vote we stay. I like a challenge." Lyla rubbed her hands together gleefully. "And just think of all the anecdotes we'll have by the time we leave!"

"I'll bet you ten dollars that Miss Adeline expels you—and your salty language—from the boarding house long before the end of my contract."

"Possible, but unlikely. Haven't you noticed that we seem to be the only ones here?"

Sasha had noticed. The boarding house was eerily quiet; she could hear every creak, every rustle, every footstep. "Well, given Miss Adeline's welcome speech, is that really all that surprising?"

"True. For someone in the hospitality industry, Miss Adeline is surprisingly inhospitable. She reminds me of my childhood nanny ... what was her name?"

"Which one?"

"The one who told me I was too deviant to amount to anything."

"Which one?"

Lyla frowned. "You're right, that doesn't narrow it down. The one with the gray hair and the unhealthy fondness for chocolate pudding cups and punitive discipline."

"Oh. Nanny Phelps."

"*Nanny Phelps*! That's it! She was just like Miss Adeline, posture and all. Oh, the flashbacks I'm going to have!" Lyla shuddered. "But I digress— Miss Adeline can't turn away customers; you can't operate a boarding house with substitute teachers alone. And I doubt there are many genteel women with unimpeachable reputations seeking accommodation in Old Middleton."

Sasha snorted and resumed braiding. "Well, it's not like *we* meet the entry requirements."

"*Thank goodness* for that! Then again, maybe Miss Adeline is independently wealthy, like me, and she merely runs this place as a hobby to fund her crochet habit."

Sasha laughed. "Clearly, that's the most plausible explanation."

"I will say"—Lyla paused to yawn—"that being in a genteel ladies' boarding house with you, my childhood friend, seems like something right out of *Anne of Green Gables*. Or one of those black-and-white films about two young women going out into the world, seeking adventures and jolly-good-times."

Sasha grinned and wrapped a hair-tie around the end of her braid. "You said most of those films were horror films."

Lyla stilled. "You're right. Any moment now, Miss Adeline is going to burst into the room and smother us to death with her crochet shawl. Or she'll send Martha to do it."

"Great. I'll rest easier now. Thanks for that."

Lyla settled more comfortably into her pillow. "Let's hope Martha is the assassin; we'll be able to hear her coming for at least an hour before she strikes."

Despite their repeated, unsuccessful, attempts to assist her, it had taken Martha almost fifteen minutes to haul the suitcases up the staircase. She had been muttering angrily to herself the entire way.

"I'd rather take my chances with Miss Adeline." Sasha mock shuddered. "Martha is *fierce.*"

"True. How she manages to be fierce while wearing an apron is beyond me."

"She said she'd been in a war—which one do you think she was talking about?"

"My guess would be the Trojan War." Lyla looked down at her hand and shook her head, bemused. "Seriously, that woman has the hand strength of a Spartan warrior."

Sasha grinned at her friend. "And on that bizarre note ..." She placed her hairbrush on the nightstand next to her sketchpad and switched off the lamp. " 'Night, Lyla."

" 'Night, Sasha. Sweet dreams."

There was a terribly awkward pause.

"Damn—I mean, dash—I mean, *sorry,*" Lyla said hurriedly. "*So* sorry. I'm exhausted and not thinking ..."

Sasha carefully smoothed the coverlet over her lap. "It's fine, Lyla. I'm fine with it now—you know that."

And she was. Mostly. Although Sasha had not dreamed since she was five years old, she had given up on wishing it otherwise and had decided that she was better off without them.

Mostly.

But Lyla knew better. "I'm sorry," she repeated. "It was completely insensitive to—"

Sasha could hear the guilt in Lyla's voice and cut her off immediately. "You? Insensitive? Never."

"You mean *always*."

Sasha laid down and rolled onto her side. "Go to sleep, you."

"By the way ..." Lyla's tone was deliberately light in the darkness. "If Martha strikes tonight, you'll be the first to go. The perky blonde is usually the heroine of the film. Just saying."

The pillow hit Lyla square in the face.

~

DESPITE HER REASSURANCES TO LYLA, IT WAS NOT THE THREAT OF Martha's possible assassination attempts that kept Sasha awake long after Lyla had fallen asleep, but rather the daunting task of falling asleep itself.

For Sasha, it was a tragic and somewhat tedious fact of life that she appeared to be unable to dream. For the past twenty-five years, she would fall asleep ... only to awaken in a vast, dark space—a vacuum where her dreams should have been, fantastic and bright.

The cause of her lost dreams was a mystery to Sasha. Childhood appointments with baffled sleep doctors had yielded very little information about her condition.

("We're almost fifty percent certain that your brain isn't broken," they explained cheerily, with the help of a sock puppet, while her parents looked on, horrified.)

Nor did she know how to fix the situation. All the remedies she had tried—therapy sessions, sleep clinic visits, mindfulness exercises, meditation, sedatives, herbal teas, hot milk, and a voodoo ceremony in New Orleans after too many novelty drinks on Bourbon Street—had led to naught. Instead, she was left metaphorically, and sometimes literally, twiddling her thumbs in the absolute darkness of her subconscious mind until her alarm clock chimed away in the early hours of the morning.

"Right," she whispered, psyching herself up for what lay ahead. "Bring on the darkness."

Sasha closed her eyes and allowed herself to fall into the endlessness of her usual dreamless state. But, for the first time since she was a child, the darkness lifted, and suddenly, she was *elsewhere*.

She found herself standing on a hillside, looking out across a vast plain. Above her, the sky was on the cusp of true night, a dusting of stars just becoming visible above the violet-hued horizon. A playful breeze brought the scent of something sweet, something sharp, something *familiar*: bruised cloves and burnt honey and a coppery tang that tickled her nostrils.

Looking down, Sasha almost jumped in surprise; in the fading light, the ground beneath her feet seemed to glow gold, the dust of the plains glittering across the pale skin of her feet like pure sunshine. Something about that soft, golden dust made her heart pound, made that restless voice in her head positively bristle with excitement.

"I know this place," she whispered, watching her red-polished toenails disappear under the glittery dust. "But from where?"

Without warning, she felt an odd sensation in her midsection—almost as if a fisherman had cast a hook behind her navel and was reeling her in. She lurched forward, her hands outstretched toward the ground to halt her fall.

But instead of landing on the sand, she found herself on her mattress, wide awake and blinking in the pale light of dawn.

Sasha sat up, breathing heavily.

"What. The. Hell?" she whispered. "That was a dream. *A dream*! Lyla! Lyla, *wake up!*"

But even as she turned toward her friend, the memory of the dream—if that was what it had been—began to fade away.

Sasha sat very still, just in case moving around shook the last fragments from her memory, and tried desperately to recall what she had seen.

"I was on a hill?" she whispered, eyes closed, trying to see the images again in her mind's eye. "I was standing in … dirt? No, dust. No, that's not right—"

The images were fading.

"It was night? No! Dusk—I think? I—"

Fading.

"I remember sinking … and stars—"

Fading.

"There was something familiar—or was it strange? Oh, I can't—"

Gone.

"No! *No*! Come back! *Agh.*" Sasha groaned and fell back against the pillows, defeated. "Dash it."

At that moment, a noise reminiscent of a herd of mating llamas blasted through the room. Both Sasha and Lyla lurched upright.

"*Agh!*" Lyla yelled, still half asleep. "What's happening? Who's being tortured?"

Sasha turned to the old-fashioned alarm clock on the nightstand. Desperately, she pressed every possible button and knob, and slapped at the bells, until with one last, tortured wail, the sound ceased.

Lyla stared blearily at the clock, clutching her chest. "That was an *alarm?*"

Sasha rubbed her eyes and sighed. "Yes."

"Who sets a damn alarm for *6:30 a.m.*? I told you this place was nefarious."

"Language, Lyla. Plus, it's Monday; you're supposed to get up early during the week."

"You are far too judgmental for *6:30 a.m.* on a Monday. Hang on—did you call me? Before the alarm?"

Sasha rolled her eyes and pulled back the covers. "Yes. You're impossible to wake up."

"It's my best quality." Lyla yawned luxuriantly. "What did you want?"

Sasha closed her eyes. Nothing. She remembered nothing. She was surprised by just how disappointed she felt. How was it possible that she still held out hope?

"False alarm," she said, her voice thick with more than sleep. She opened her eyes. "I thought I had dreamed, but I must have imagined it."

Lyla paused, hands stretched above her head and turned to her friend. "Are you sure?" Her tone was a little too casual.

"Yes. I thought …" Sasha shook her head. "I can't remember a thing. False alarm."

"I don't remember all my dreams. Forgetting doesn't mean that you *didn't* dream. The dreaming itself is the important bit."

Sasha's breath caught somewhere in her chest. Wishing for a dream did not make one appear—she was not going down this path again. She quickly swung her long legs out of bed and stood up.

"I'm sure I was mistaken. It was probably just something I was thinking about before I was completely awake."

Lyla lowered her arms slowly. "Fair enough." Her tone was very careful. Sasha could feel the weight of Lyla's gaze as she crossed the room. "Where are you off to?"

Sasha took a quick look out the window and nodded, satisfied at the blue skies beyond. "I'm going for a run." She had not gone running in days and the inactivity was making her feel positively twitchy. "It'll give me a chance to check out the village."

And outrun my feelings … as usual, she thought dryly.

"But isn't it still raining?"

"Nope. It looks like the rain has cleared up."

Lyla squinted at the pale sunshine pouring in through the curtains. "How can it be sunny? It was supposed to rain for days. Hang on—don't you have a meeting with Principal Dean?"

"*Headmistress* Dean," Sasha corrected. "And not until ten."

"Why is she a headmistress and not a principal? This isn't a boarding school in jolly old England."

Sasha shrugged. "It's a private school founded in the nineteenth century—it's bound to have its quirks."

"A likely story." Lyla rubbed the sleep from her eyes. "Plus *headmistress* sounds so severe: it makes me think of after school detentions ... and time-out corners ... and stern spankings administered with a wooden paddle." She paused to yawn, her mouth stretched comically wide. "Did you know that corporal punishment is still legal in private schools in Wisconsin?"

Sasha stared at her friend. "You know the oddest facts."

"Yes, I do; thank you for noticing. Do you think Headmistress Dean is a strict disciplinarian—the elementary school version of a dominatrix?" Lyla clutched her pillow to her chest, her grin positively gleeful. "*Oooh*—do you think she has her own monogrammed paddle?"

Sasha blinked. "I certainly hope not." The last thing she needed was a monogrammed paddle-wielding employer. "I guess I'll find out at ten. In the meantime, do you want to go for a run with me? I'd like to check out the village."

"You're the runner, not me. I would rather drink bleach."

Without warning, the alarm went off again.

"*Agh!*" Lyla howled. "Okay, okay. Turn off that demonic clock, I'll get ready."

As Sasha battled the alarm clock for the second time, the dream fragment slipped from her thoughts and disappeared like a sigh in the breeze.

THE CHARMINGLY SUSPICIOUS VILLAGE
OF OLD MIDDLETON

MONDAY, OCTOBER 22ND

"I DON'T TRUST THIS PLACE," LYLA ANNOUNCED DRAMATICALLY AS SHE finished the last of her cranberry scone.

The two women sat at a table outside the bakery, eating pastries and drinking coffee in the mild sunshine. After Lyla had successfully argued that running on so little sleep constituted a form of torture likely outlawed by the Geneva Convention, they had decided on a brisk walk down Main Street in search of breakfast instead.

"What do you mean?" Sasha asked, taking a sip from her coffee cup.

Lyla pulled her phone out of her bag and placed it on the table in front of Sasha accusingly. "Look at this—still barely any coverage. Which means no access to the outside world—"

"Aside from landlines, computers with non-Wi-Fi Internet access, post-cards, letters, cars ... I could go on ..."

Lyla waved her hand dismissively. "Old Middleton is hiding a sinister secret." She looked around, her eyes narrowed. "I don't trust this place."

"How can you say that? It's gorgeous!"

Lyla nodded, her ponytail bobbing agreeably. "Yes, it is. It's practically perfect, and that's precisely the problem. Behold!" She gestured to the side-walk. "Charming cobblestone streets." She pointed to the buildings surrounding them. "Genuine, nineteenth-century storefronts complete with original signage." She pointed to a small, fluffy dog tethered to a post outside the bakery. "Delightful Pomeranian puppy wearing an adorable fall-themed sweater." The dog tilted her head to the side and frowned at Lyla. "It's all *too* wonderful. It feels like a film set. Or an elaborate front for a Mafia money laundering scheme."

"Mafia? In Old Middleton? Do you even hear yourself?" Sasha placed her cup back on the table and shook her head. "Be as suspicious as you want. I *love* it."

Lyla sniffed into her coffee. "Yes. *You* would."

Sasha looked around the street, wondering how the quaint, old village had failed to enchant her friend. Sasha had been to pretty places aplenty, but Old Middleton was more than just a collection of charming buildings —its history was almost tangible. Bronze plaques commemorating historic landmarks were scattered all over the village, attached to centuries-old houses and storefronts, old clocks and even older wells. Everywhere she turned, there were vestiges of the past—like the iron shoe-scraper on the doorstep outside the bakery; and the sandstone horse-trough outside the fire station, now filled with bright-orange dahlias.

Looking down the street, Sasha could imagine horse-drawn carriages clattering down the cobblestones, and candles lighting the black, wrought-iron streetlamps that stood like sentinels before each shop. She positively itched to sketch Main Street: to capture the way the narrow stores leaned against each other as if gossiping about those passing in the street below; and the sugar maples, with their fall foliage of red and gold, that lined the street like a row of flames.

It was too much to explain to Lyla. Instead, Sasha merely gestured to the street around them. "Seriously, what's not to like? I can't wait to come down here with my sketchbook." She tried to visualize how she would bring the scene to life on the page. "I take it back—pencils won't do the fall colors justice. This is crying out for oils. And it should be on canvas ... something big so there's some scale." She felt a familiar wave of excitement as the piece began to take shape in her mind. "Do you think there's an art supply store around here?"

Lyla waved away her question. "*Pfft.* You artists are all so superficial; you're too easily seduced by a pretty façade. And for the record, I didn't say that I didn't *like* it. I just don't *trust* it."

"I felt like that when I first moved here from Chicago," a husky, female voice rasped from behind them.

The two women started. Sasha turned toward the voice and was initially blinded by white. One of the baker's apprentices stood behind them, dressed in a baggy white uniform that covered her from neck to

ankles, and a matching floppy, white cap that concealed her hair. All that
was visible was her face: a tanned oval with deep-set brown eyes framed by
thick, black brows; a bold nose that was slightly askew; and a wide mouth
tilted to one side in a wry smile.

Looking first over her shoulder to see if anyone was listening, the
apprentice leaned toward the two women conspiratorially.

"Everyone was so nice," she whispered. "I thought they were trying to
lull me into a false sense of security—you know, so they could eventually
sacrifice me in a cornfield during a harvest-themed, pagan ritual."

Lyla looked up at her admiringly. "That's exactly what I was thinking!"

The apprentice grinned. "You must watch a lot of horror films set in
rural towns, too."

"They're the best kind," Lyla said.

"We should hang out," Sasha said.

The woman laughed. "Yes, let's. Us non-geriatrics really should stick
together—there aren't many of us in Old Middleton. Well, if you don't
count the tourists."

She put down the dishes she had cleared from the table behind them
and wiped her hands on her apron.

"I'm Ellie," she said, holding out her hand to Lyla and then to Sasha.

"Nice tattoo," remarked Lyla, pointing to Ellie's left wrist. "Unusual. I
haven't seen many white tattoos."

Ellie gave her an odd smile and turned over her hand to reveal the
mark on her inner wrist. It was a simple design—two broken, concentric
circles that framed a triangle—but the white ink made it stand-out, stark
and lovely, against Ellie's tan.

"They're more common in these parts than you'd think," Ellie said.

"Does it have a meaning?" Sasha asked.

Ellie looked down at her tattoo with that same odd smile. As she shifted her hand, the sunlight hit the tattoo in such a way that it made the mark shine pale gold, almost as if there was glitter caught beneath her skin. "Fire. Nothing all that exciting. But at least it's not a butterfly, right?"

"I have a butterfly tattoo," Lyla said matter-of-factly.

Ellie looked horrified. "I am so—"

Sasha nudged Lyla with her elbow. "She doesn't. She's more the mosquito or praying mantis type."

Lyla made a show of rubbing her arm. "Do you *sharpen* your elbows?" She paused mid-rub and considered Sasha's words. "Praying mantis, huh? An insect that eats its mate after sex? That's actually pretty apt."

Ellie grinned. "We should definitely hang out." A harried-looking man sitting at a neighboring table waved his hand, trying to get Ellie's attention. "I've got to go. I'll catch up with you later."

"Bye!" Sasha and Lyla called out.

"I think she's our kind of people," Lyla mused, watching Ellie deal with the irritated customer.

"Agreed. Come on." Sasha pulled on her gloves and stood up. "It looks like the shops have finally opened. I want to explore."

"Of course, you do," Lyla sighed as Sasha hauled her to her feet.

"Admit it," Sasha said as they passed cheery pots of orange and gold flowers set up outside each store, "it's lovely here."

"And yet, oddly sinister. I mean, how many gargoyles does one town need?" Lyla pointed toward the rooftops. Sure enough, smirking creatures carved from stone—some with wings, others with horns—peered down at the women from almost every building.

"They're *charming*," Sasha said firmly. She frowned at one leering gargoyle who had a stubby finger lodged firmly up his nostril. "*Charming*."

"Uh huh."

"And so is the Village Hall. Just look at it!" It was a gorgeous, peony-pink confection of a mansion in the Victorian gothic style, surrounded by topiary hedges and late-blooming roses. "How could a place with a *pink* Village Hall possibly be suspicious?"

"Yes … but look how pointy the roof is." Lyla gestured to the hall's conical tower. "And it has a weathervane on top. It's like it's daring you to be impaled."

"You're just looking for problems. Why can't you just admit that this place is lovely and enjoy yourself?"

"Because it's too lovely to be true! Show me some litter, or a rat-filled dumpster, or a pile of burning tires, and I'd feel so much better. Oh, look— it's a trolley, the most charming way to travel."

Lyla frowned as a green and gold trolley rattled past, the driver cheerily ringing the bell. "That's the last straw." She looked up at the sky and shook her fist. "I'm onto you, Old Middleton. I *will* find out all your sordid secrets!"

Sasha watched the fist-shaking and shook her head. "You know, being grumpy is terrible for the digestion. I bet—oh!"

A red maple leaf drifted toward them in the breeze.

With a triumphant cry, Sasha snatched it from the air and presented it to Lyla. "Here, make a wish—it'll make you feel better."

Lyla looked down at the leaf in Sasha's outstretched hand and sighed. "Are we really going to have this discussion again?"

"Apparently so," Sasha said cheerily, still holding out the leaf.

"Leaves do not have the power to grant wishes. Wishing on leaves isn't a *thing*."

"Of course, it's a *thing*." At Lyla's skeptical look, Sasha shrugged a little defensively. "It's a thing if we believe it's a thing, and *I* believe it's a thing."

"Well, you'd better lawyer up. I bet *legitimate* wish granters—shooting stars, fairy godmothers, Santa Claus—will sue you if you start this leaf thing up."

"It's a free wish. Are you really at a point in your life where you can turn down a free wish?"

"Well, when you put it like that …"

Lyla took the leaf and, ignoring Sasha's broad smile, held it up in front of her. "Okay, leaf, I wish for cell phone reception and Wi-Fi access. Oh! And an attractive male limber enough to hide undetected in Miss Adeline's laundry closet until I need him. And—"

"Hey! You aren't supposed to ask for more than one wish—you'll overwhelm it!"

Sasha lunged for the leaf, but Lyla quickly moved it away.

"Don't mind her," Lyla said to the leaf. "She just doesn't know your true potential. Fine, forget the other wishes, this one is the real one: I wish that Sasha would be offered a teaching position in Tahiti—effective immediately."

"Right." Sasha snatched back the leaf and put it in her pocket. "No more leaf wishes for you; you can't be trusted."

"It's the *leaf* that can't be trusted. I can't help but notice that we're still in Old Middleton. The leaf is a fraud and should be reported to the appropriate authorities."

"You made a terrible wish—I'm glad it didn't work." Sasha linked arms with Lyla and pulled her into a brisk walk. "The longer we're in Old Middleton, the more time you'll have to fall in love with it."

"The longer we're in Old Middleton, the more likely we'll be sacrificed to a pagan god in a cornfield," Lyla muttered.

Nevertheless, she allowed Sasha to lead her down the street.

In a blatant attempt to buy their way into Miss Adeline and Martha's good graces, they decided to stop at the florist. To Sasha's delight, it was owned by two of the sweetest old women she had ever met.

"We're twins!" giggled one as she wrapped up their bouquet.

"Can you tell?" asked the other, as she handed Sasha her change.

"It's a little difficult to miss," Sasha said with a smile.

The two women were not only identical in appearance, but they also wore identical periwinkle dresses. At first glance, the only way to tell them apart was by their aprons: one wore an apron patterned with violets, the other with daisies.

"Who is the eldest?" Lyla asked.

"Why, that would be Violet," said one, with a cheeky twinkle in her eye, pointing to the sister wearing the violet-print apron.

"Oh, hush now." Violet patted her sister's hand. "We both know that *you're* older, Daisy, by a whole seventeen minutes."

Sasha and Lyla waved goodbye to the twins, who were now arguing over who was taller.

They passed an eclectic array of shops: a shoe repair store, where they could see the cobbler mending a pair of boots from the front window; a shop selling candles of every shape and color; a confectionary, where a freckled young man in a white uniform was carefully dipping red apples into a vat of freshly made caramel; a grocery store, its window decorated with bunches of blue, orange, and yellow corn; and a shop selling a dizzying array of homemade condiments. As they passed, an employee handed them samples of sourdough bread covered in tart cherry jam.

But it was only when they reached the bookstore—The Sleepy Cat Book Emporium—that Lyla finally became excited.

So excited, in fact, that she began to drag Sasha toward the door.

"Oh, no, you don't," Sasha said, digging in her heels and stopping their progress.

"But ... *books*," Lyla said yearningly.

She grasped the store's brass door handle, cunningly fashioned to look like a cat, and began to open the door.

"No." Sasha pulled her friend bodily away. "If you go in there, you won't come out again until next week."

Lyla deflated. "True, but ... *books*. And look—a cat! A *sleepy* cat, just like the name!" Sure enough, there was a lush, black cat in the store window curled up like a queen on a purple velvet cushion. "How can I resist that? *How*? I'm only human, dammit!"

"But resist it you must—at least while I'm around." Sasha looked down at her friend's wistful expression and threw her arm around Lyla's shoulders. "In five minutes or so, I'll have to go back to the boarding house and get ready for my meeting, and you will be free to do whatever you want. You'll be waist-deep in books and sleepy cats before you know it."

"True. Hear that, cat?" Lyla turned to the queenly feline. "Soon, you will be mine!"

The cat lifted her nose in the air and deliberately turned her back on Lyla.

Lyla pressed her face against the window. "You *will* love me."

With a last, longing look at the bookstore, Lyla allowed Sasha to lead her onward once more.

"Is it just me or are you bossier than usual this morning?" Lyla asked, as they passed the fire station where a Dalmatian was sunning himself on the front step. "You're almost yanking me down the street."

Sasha grinned. "I'm not bossy—I'm *driven*. I'm on a mission."

"To do what? Invade a neighboring country? Topple a foreign government?"

Sasha paused. It was a good question. Ever since she had set foot on the street, she had felt energized—no, *electrified*. She could not wait to explore, to discover everything she could about Old Middleton.

Which, now she thought about it, was rather odd; she couldn't remember the last time that she had felt this exuberant about walking down a street.

Sasha frowned, but continued down Main Street. "I think the coffee here is stronger than what I'm used to drinking at home. Or it could be the sugar from the pastries."

"True. You did eat four of them." Lyla shook her head. "I'll never cease to be amazed by just how much you can eat."

"I'm very tall. There are a lot of places where I can store it all."

"Whereas I am short, and everything gets stored on my hips. *Ooh*, look at the pretties!"

Lyla stopped in front of The Well-Dressed Vixen Boutique. She pointed to the flouncy cocktail dresses and delicate silk pumps adorning the mannequins in the window. "Do you think I could wear one of those outfits around the boarding house?"

"Sure! Miss Adeline would probably be thrilled by how genteel you looked."

"I've never looked genteel before," Lyla mused.

As they watched, the owner of the store approached one of the mannequins and draped a string of creamy pearls around its neck. Dressed in a tight, pale-orange pencil skirt and an even tighter, matching cashmere sweater, the woman reminded Sasha of a slightly overripe peach. Her short, red hair was artfully arranged; and her makeup applied in bolder colors and heavier strokes than what was probably needed outside of a beauty pageant.

Seeing Lyla and Sasha, the store owner sashayed over to the door in her sky-high pumps, her coral-coated lips stretched into a broad smile.

"May I help you?" she asked, her words tinted with the barest hint of a Southern accent.

Sasha shook her head. "Ah, no. Thanks. We're just window-shopping."

The store owner's smile dropped. She eyed each woman shamelessly from the tips of their boots to the tops of their heads, noting their worn jeans and nondescript coats along the way. By the time she had reached Sasha's hand-knitted hat, she was already turning away.

Lyla's eyes narrowed.

"Though," Sasha said quickly, "you have some lovely dresses in your window."

The store owner reluctantly turned back. "Thank you. I just got those in."

She started to turn back toward her shop but hesitated, as if weighing her options. Finally, she pasted on a fake smile and turned to Sasha. "I'm Felicia DuPre."

"I'm—"

"I know who you are," Felicia interrupted, glancing down at Sasha's gloves. "The substitute teacher ... and her *friend*."

Felicia had the dubious talent of making even pleasant words such as "friend" sound distasteful and possibly even a little sordid.

Lyla's eyes narrowed even further.

Before Lyla could reply, Sasha took her arm. "Right. We'd best leave you to get on with strangling those mannequins." She gestured toward the pearls. "I'm sure we'll see you around."

Felicia looked down at Sasha's gloves once again. "Possibly a lot more than you'd expect."

Sasha also looked down at her gloves, puzzled. They were just gloves. "Ah ... okay. Sounds great."

"I'm choosing to end this conversation now," Lyla said cheerily, leading Sasha away.

"Y'all come back soon," Felicia called after them. Her tone was so lacking in authenticity that it was practically the vocal equivalent of a fake tan.

"Well, that was charming," Sasha said when they were back on the sidewalk. "What was all that about?"

"I think Felicia figured out that we're not the cocktail dress-wearing types and dismissed us accordingly. She certainly didn't think much of your gloves." Lyla looked away, her attention catching on something across the road. "*Ooh.* Come on."

She grabbed Sasha's arm and dragged her across the street.

Sasha looked up at the store window and her earlier sense of anticipation—briefly doused during her interaction with Felicia—burst back into life. She smiled at the store name, written in winsome gold cursive surrounded by a smattering of small, gold stars.

"*Stardust and Brimstone: Potions and Spell Shop,*" she read aloud.

"Spooky! I approve. It reminds me of all the occult shops in New York."

Sasha peered up at the dragon gargoyle that sat, wings spread wide, above the door. "Don't you think an occult shop is a little out of place in a Midwestern village?"

"No more than we are. Frankly, I think they're out of place in New York, too." Lyla shrugged. "Maybe it's a tourist trap. Or maybe—as I keep telling you—the people of Old Middleton are all part of a cult ... and that cult requires potions and spells. Either way, I'm going inside."

"No, you're not." Sasha pointed to the opening hours listed on the door. "It doesn't open until midday on Mondays."

"What?! Not good enough! The shop should be accessible twenty-four hours a day to meet all my occult needs."

"Well, according to the sign, it stays open late in October. I guess most occult-shop customers are nocturnal."

"Very vampire-friendly. Still, I am extremely displeased by this turn of events." Lyla pressed her face against the window. "It's too dark in there to see much."

Sasha peered through the glass and grimaced. "You're right."

The shop was small and dim and *waiting*, with lots of shadowy alcoves where secret rituals and rendezvous could take place. Sasha could just make out wooden shelves, some filled with leather-bound books, others covered in squat, glass jars. The soft, morning sunlight caught on a display case close to the front window holding all sorts of oddities: antique ostrich feathers in shades of blush and gray, gathered in a vase like faded flowers; crystal balls —some cloudy, others clear—held aloft by delicate silver stands; packets of tarot cards arranged in teetering piles on a sapphire velvet throw; and fat, white pillar candles sitting in puddles of old wax.

Lyla pointed to the window display. A large cauldron filled with bubbling pink liquid sat on the floor, surrounded by glittery red hearts suspended from the ceiling. Tiny brown bottles hand-labeled *Love Potion* covered the floor. "Are we short on love potion?"

"I think we're good." Sasha noticed the sign on the cauldron. "*Potions and Pills for all of your ills*," she read. "Cute."

"We'll have to come back here and buy some Bitch-Be-Gone to put in Felicia DuPre's tea."

"Language, Lyla."

Lyla rolled her eyes. "Please, it's the only vice I can exercise in this place."

"Give it time. Speaking of time ..." Sasha reluctantly moved away from the window with all its exotic delights. "I'd better get back to the boarding house and get dressed."

"Well, be sure to give these to our cruel overlords." Lyla handed the bouquet to Sasha. "Let's hope flowers thaw their ice-cold hearts." She brushed a stray petal off her sweater. "If they fail, we'll have to resort to industrial-strength heaters and ice picks."

Sasha carefully arranged the bouquet in her arms. "If you're not at the boarding house when I return, should I send a search party to the bookstore? Or will you be gallivanting elsewhere?"

"Send them to the bookstore; I have a black cat to charm."

"Right, search party to the bookstore. Got it."

"For the record, I'd like my search party to consist of tall, broad-shoul-dered men, preferably with Nordic good-looks. Shirts optional. Many thanks in advance."

Sasha laughed. "You want me to wrangle up a group of shirtless Nordic men in Old Middleton? That seems optimistic."

"True. But a girl can dream. See you!"

Lyla waved a cheery goodbye and walked briskly toward the bookstore.

Sasha frowned at her friend's departing back. "Dream."

And, just like that, for a tantalizing second, Sasha remembered her dream fragment from the night before. She remembered the plain stretching before her, and the sensation of sinking into silk-soft gold dust, thicker than glitter. The feeling was so real, so *familiar*.

She was *sure* she had seen that place before last night.

"Ha!" she crowed, heedless of the fact that she was in the middle of a busy sidewalk. "I did dream! I knew it! *I knew it!*"

But once again, the dream fragment slipped away before she could examine it more closely.

"No!" she wailed, covering her face with her hand. "Are you *kidding* me? What the hell? Why can't I—you know what? *Fine.*" She dropped her hand and lifted her chin, ignoring the stares of several passers-by. "Be that way. I *will* remember. I *will* conquer this."

With her head held high and her arms filled with flowers, Sasha walked away, determined (and painfully hopeful) toward the boarding house.

3

WHERE THE MONSTERS ARE SMALL AND HAVE DESIGNATED NAP TIMES

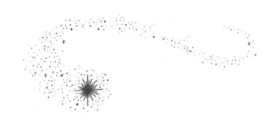

SASHA SAT ON THE SERVICEABLE, BUT ODDLY LUMPY COUCH IN THE WAITING area outside Headmistress Dean's office and tried not to let nerves get the better of her. She adjusted the skirt of her demure, green wrap dress, made sure that her black ballet flats were still polished to a high sheen, and fiddled with her lucky bead necklace—an impulse buy from a stall in Bali— until it lay flat across her chest.

Then she went back to being nervous.

Get a grip, she told herself sternly. *It's not as if you haven't done this before. Many, many, many times before ...*

And then, just like that, a familiar feeling began to emerge from behind her nervousness: a sort of restless energy that made her want to stretch, made her want to stand, made her want to run back down the hall, and out the door, and then down the street, and run, and run, and run until she was far away from here.

Until she was somewhere else.

Oh no, she told herself firmly. *Not again. Don't you* dare!

But the feeling did not listen. Instead, it unfurled within Sasha, like a vine seeking the light, and pushed outward toward freedom, dragging her along with it.

Sasha wanted to wail with frustration because she knew—she *knew*— from bitter experience that this was just the beginning. First, there would be the restlessness, making her feel itchy and unsettled. Then, that insistent voice in the back of her mind would start whispering, prompting her to search for the next teaching position. Nothing close to home, mind you. Oh, no—that little voice would push her to travel further and further away, seeking-out somewhere new, somewhere different. Then, as soon as she settled down in this new place, the entire process would start all over again.

She had hoped this time would be different. Old Middleton was odd and charming, and she *liked* it here. Instead, the restlessness had set a new record, arriving sooner than ever before. Worse still, it was laced with something new: that odd sense of anticipation she had felt the moment she had driven into the village.

Stop it! You like it here, she reminded herself, trying to push down the restlessness, trying to regain control.

Sasha quickly reached into her bag. Pulling out her day planner, she opened it to the last page where she had carefully pasted a map of the United States. Red pen dots were scattered over the surface of the map, signifying all the places that Sasha had visited and worked. There were so many dots that the entire country appeared to be infected with a particularly virulent strain of measles.

Sasha pulled out her red pen and carefully drew a dot over Old Middleton.

See? she told the familiar restless feeling. *Now it's official—you're here. And you had better like it because Old Middleton is home for the next three weeks.*

"Ms. Pierce?"

Sasha started and looked up; a harried-looking woman wielding a clipboard stood in front of her. She wore a hesitant smile and a mousy-brown suit that just so happened to match the mousy-brown shade of her hair—scraped into a neat bun at the back of her neck—perfectly. Her brown eyes were frantic behind dark-rimmed glasses, and her long string of pearls was caught on her clipboard.

Sasha stuffed her planner and pen hurriedly back into her bag. With a deep breath, she stood up and pushed her feelings down *hard*.

"Just Sasha is fine," she said, holding out her hand.

The woman relaxed a little. She pulled her pearls free of her clipboard with a frustrated sigh and took Sasha's hand.

"Welcome! We are so happy to have you here at Old Middleton Elementary. I'm Esther Carter." She shook Sasha's hand limply, then quickly dropped it. "I'm ... well, I'm whatever the school needs me to be. This morning, I'm the acting Headmistress."

Sasha smiled reassuringly. "Lovely to meet you."

"I wish we were meeting under better circumstances; I'm afraid we're in the midst of a small ... chaotic patch. Several of our staff have come down with the flu—" She paused, looking over Sasha's shoulder. "Speaking of which—you should be home, Poppy, dear!"

Sasha turned. Leaning limply against the doorway was Poppy: a pale, miserable, wheezing, woman, who smelled—most regrettably—of menthol and martyrdom. She coughed weakly, the sound throaty and wet, and clutched a small pile of manila folders against her hunched chest like a shield.

"I think I'm dying," she gasped. She carefully eased herself from the doorway and into the room, dragging her feet with every step. "I know I've said it before, Esther, but this time—" She paused to sneeze, the tip of her nose cherry-red. "This time ... I mean it." She pawed at the cuff of her rust-colored sweater until a crumpled tissue emerged and lifted it weakly to her nose. "*This* is the end."

Esther moved to clasp Poppy's shoulder but quickly stepped back when the sick woman began to sneeze uncontrollably. "Oh, Poppy! This, too, shall pass." She reached into her pocket and handed a clean tissue to the ill woman. "And it shall pass even sooner if you're home in bed."

"Thank you." Poppy stashed the new tissue in the old one's place. She looked down at the folders in her arms. "But I promised the Headmistress that I would file these—"

"I can do that for you. The Headmistress thought you'd be home sick; she certainly didn't expect you to be here, doing her filing."

Esther held out her hand for the folders. For a long moment, Poppy simply stared at Esther and clutched the folders even closer to her chest.

"You won't get better if you don't rest," Esther said gently.

Reluctantly, Poppy handed Esther the folders, defeated. "Fine then—I'll go home."

"Hang on a minute." Sasha rummaged through her bag and pulled out a small bag of cough lozenges. She held them out to Poppy. "Here, try these. They taste like dirty oranges, and you'll regret ever putting one in your mouth, but they'll stop that cough in its tracks."

Poppy took the bag with a hesitant smile. "Thanks ...?"

Sasha grinned back. "Sasha Pierce. Substitute teacher."

"Where are my manners?" Esther said with a groan. "This is Poppy Mange, Headmistress Dean's assistant."

Poppy sniffed. "Assuming I survive this." She stared blearily at Sasha through blood-shot eyes and leaned toward her.

"Leave this place," she whispered. "I think it's cursed."

"Ah ... thanks?" Sasha said, not quite sure how to respond.

"Home, Poppy," Esther said, exasperated.

Poppy turned around and slowly dragged herself from the room, coughing all the way.

Esther waited until Poppy was no longer in earshot before tsking sympathetically. "Every October, without fail, flu season sweeps through Old Middleton Elementary. It's typically over quite quickly, but poor Poppy seems to have caught the worst of it." She grimaced. "Unfortunately, everyone seems to have come down with it at once; we are *so* short staffed. To make matters worse, Headmistress Dean has been called away on official business. She should be back this afternoon, but she asked me to apologize for not being here personally."

"Oh, that's fine!" Sasha tried to contain her relief. "Would you like me to come back tomorrow?"

The older woman fiddled with her pearls. "Actually, I was hoping ... I'm so sorry to ask you this—and please feel free to decline—but since we already have your paperwork on file, I was wondering if you would mind starting a day early? Just for this morning; I can fill in after lunch. We found someone to mind your class, but she's ..." Esther grimaced. "Well ... you'll understand when you meet her."

Sasha gave her another reassuring smile. "I'm more than happy to start; I haven't got anything planned for the day."

Esther almost seemed to deflate with relief. "Wonderful, wonderful! Thank you so much—you have no idea how grateful I am! I'll give you a quick tour and then show you to your class."

She beckoned Sasha to follow her and set off down the hallway. "I wish I had more time to introduce you to everyone before you started. But you'll meet the other teachers during lunch."

They moved through the school at a rapid pace, with Esther briskly pointing out amenities. The school—housed in a converted mansion that once belonged to "one of Old Middleton's founding families," Esther announced proudly—was beautifully maintained with excellent facilities. But it was clear that it had been designed to educate many more children than were currently enrolled; several of the classrooms were empty, and others seemed sparsely populated.

"As you will soon see," Esther said with a sigh, "we don't have many elementary-aged students in Old Middleton anymore. The truth is, we don't have many students at all, even though we waive tuition fees for the local children. When the building was first built, Old Middleton was the largest village in the area. Back then, it was just called 'Middleton.' But over the years, the nearby towns grew and not surprisingly, our citizens moved to where there were more job opportunities. They renamed one of the other towns 'Middleton,' and this became 'Old Middleton.'

"Nowadays, Old Middleton tends to attract a much older, retired crowd. Not to mention the tourists." Esther threw back her shoulders and straightened her spine. "Nevertheless, we pride ourselves on our history and the quality of education we provide. And thanks to our generous alumni, we are never short of funds.

"Ah … here we are!" She stopped beside a green door. "This will be your classroom. Ready?"

Sasha took a deep breath. "Right. Let's do this."

Esther gave her a slightly uneasy smile and opened the door.

Although the school was a converted mansion, the room was a standard classroom, complete with all the features Sasha had come to expect from a kindergarten class. There was a whiteboard at the front of the room decorated with a brightly colored alphabet; teeny-tiny furniture that made Sasha feel like a clumsy giant; and the usual selection of toys stacked tidily in the corner. There was also a small fish tank, where two goldfish—one black, the other the standard orange—swam in lazy circles around a miniature purple castle. The classroom even smelled familiar, the mingled scent of pencil shavings, waxy crayons, and the sharp, citrus tang of industrial-grade floor cleaner heavy in the air.

With some surprise, Sasha noted that the class consisted of only four children, one of whom was standing in front of his peers, his nose running defiantly, as he told the class about his weekend. The remaining children sat cross-legged on a red mat the shape of an apple, looking up at the boy in horrified fascination.

"And that's the last time I'll ever eat my ear wax," the small boy with the drippy nose said rather proudly.

"Good work, Mason," a woman's voice responded dryly, as his peers clapped. "A story with a moral. Be sure the rest of you learn from Mason's unfortunate experiment. Now, sit down Mason and let someone else trigger our gag reflex with a story about their weekend."

Sasha took a moment to locate the source of the voice; it was coming from one of the tiniest, most ancient women Sasha had ever seen. Not much bigger than the children she was teaching, the white-haired woman sat on a chair in front of the class, her black ankle boots swinging high off the ground. Her pale face was liberally wrinkled, but her ice-blue eyes were keen and bright. As she eyed Mason, her thin lips twisted into a sarcastic smile.

Esther beckoned Sasha to enter the room. "Hello, class," she said brightly to the children.

"Hello, Ms. Carter!" the class responded.

Esther smiled an overly wide smile. "I'd like to introduce you to your new teacher, Ms. Pierce."

"What? Another one?" Mason asked, rubbing the back of his hand across his nose.

Esther retrieved a tissue from her pocket. "Yes," she said, handing it to Mason. "Another one. Can we all say hello to Ms. Pierce?"

"Hello, Ms. Pierce," the children responded warily.

"So, *you're* the new one," the tiny teacher said. She eyed Sasha up and down with keen amusement, then abruptly turned her fierce blue gaze toward Esther. "It's about time you got here," she muttered none too quietly. "I've had more than enough of Mason's adventures with his bodily excretions."

"It came from my ear," Mason clarified. "And it was *not* tasty."

Esther shot the woman an exasperated look. "*Thank you*, Mrs. Landshome, for minding the class." She turned to the children. "Shall we say goodbye to Mrs. Landshome?"

"Goodbye, Mrs. Landshome!" the class responded enthusiastically.

"Whatever," Mrs. Landshome mumbled.

The old woman hopped down from the chair in a surprisingly spritely manner and shuffled out of the room as fast as her little legs could take her, leaving the smell of liniment and, oddly enough, whiskey in her wake.

"Well, class," Esther said, turning her back on the doorway, "I'd like you to be on your best behavior for Ms. Pierce. She has come all the way from New York to teach you, so mind your manners."

And then she was gone, leaving Sasha alone with four strange children who were staring up at her in ominous fascination.

You don't know it yet, she told the class wordlessly, repeating the pledge she gave to all her students, *but I am going to take* such *good care of you*.

"It's *so* wonderful to meet you all!" she said, crossing the room until the toes of her black ballet flats touched the edge of the apple rug. "I hope that we'll get to know each other very well over the next three weeks."

Mason, his nose still running, raised his hand.

"Yes?" Sasha asked, smiling encouragingly.

"You're really tall. Are you a giant?"

"No," she said. "You're just really, really short." Nevertheless, she sat down in Mrs. Landshome's abandoned chair, halving the distance between herself and the four staring children.

The boy nodded. "That's a fair point. I like you."

Sasha's lips quirked. "Thanks! You have excellent taste in substitute teachers." She turned to the rest of the class, smiling as broadly as physically possible. "If we're going to spend three weeks together, we should get to know each other, right?"

The children nodded solemnly.

"So, how about we go around the room and you each tell me your name and one thing that you really, really like? Let's start with you— Mason, isn't it?"

Mason paused in his attempt to jam Esther's tissue entirely up his left nostril. "My name is Mason, and I really like destruction. And chaos," he added thoughtfully.

Sasha blinked. "Ah ... thank you, Mason. And how about you?" She gestured to the girl sitting beside Mason.

The girl cleared her throat. "My name is Joanna, and I really like my hair." She patted her long, blonde braid in a manner reminiscent of petting a horse's mane.

"You have lovely hair, Joanna," Sasha said in her most solemn tone.

Joanna nodded. "I really do."

Sasha smiled encouragingly at the girl sitting cross-legged beside Joanna with the serious brown eyes, and rows and rows of tiny black braids across her scalp, each finished with bubblegum-colored beads. "And you?"

"My name is Kaytie," she said confidently, straightening her posture. "I haven't found anything yet that I like *a lot*. I like some things *a bit* ... like cake and my dog. But not a *lot*. My mom said I should learn from her mistakes and not settle."

"That's good advice," Sasha said, nodding slowly. "I also like dogs and cake. And what's your name?" she asked the last student.

The red-haired boy shrugged. "Bryce."

"And what do you like?"

He shrugged again. "Stuff."

"You can't say 'stuff'—that's more than one thing," Mason said. "Stuff could be everything."

Bryce huffed. "Fine, then. I like stuff and bananas. The *whole* banana," he clarified.

Joanna looked scandalized. "The skin, too?"

Bryce nodded. "It's crunchy and chewy at the same time."

"*Ewww!*" the rest of the children screeched.

Sasha shuddered. "Thank you, Bryce. Bananas are ... yellow, I guess."

She looked around the room. "No one said that they really liked the gold-fish." She pointed to the fish tank. "What are their names?"

The children's faces lit up.

"The gold one is called Fish Stick," Kaytie said.

"And the black one is called Aluminum Foil," Joanna piped up.

"Very creative," Sasha said. "Let me guess—you picked the names?"

"Yep," Mason said.

"They are the best names ever," Bryce said.

The other children nodded in agreement.

Sasha suppressed a smile. "Well, do you have any questions you want to ask me before we begin?" Joanna raised her hand. "Yes, Joanna?"

"What happened to our last teacher, Ms. Fletcher?"

Before Sasha could answer, Mason raised his hand. "Did you have to fight her for this job? With a sword?"

"Ah … no. I didn't," Sasha said. "When you're a kindergarten teacher, swords aren't usually part of the interview process."

Mason raised his hand again. "What about in Viking times?"

"Maybe," Sasha conceded. "But not in modern-day Old Middleton. I'm not sure what happened to Ms. Fletcher," she said, trying to steer the conversation back to less pointy topics. "I can ask Headmistress Dean when I meet with her this afternoon. Anything else?"

Bryce raised his hand. "Can you also ask her what happened to Ms. Gonzalez?"

"*And* Ms. Chandra," Kaytie added.

Sasha heard the distinct sound of warning bells. "Sure. I'll ask about all of them."

Extensively, she thought to herself, wondering why so many teachers had left the school without saying goodbye to their students.

Unless the students were the reason they had fled …

"Any more questions?" Sasha asked hurriedly, keen to move on to a new topic.

Mason raised his hand once again. "Are you a witch?"

Sasha blinked. "N-o. Why do you ask?"

Mason stared at her incredulously. "Old Middleton is full of witches, didn't you know? There's like, lots and lots and lots of them."

"But only women," Kaytie clarified. "Men can't be witches."

"And children can't be witches," Bryce said.

"Or pets," Joanna added.

"Well," Sasha said, "that seems a little discriminatory. Who told you that the village is full of witches?"

"Everyone knows," Mason said loftily. "My Dad said it's in the history books and on the Internet and everything."

"And they told us about the witches when we went on the village tour," Bryce said.

"It was a special field trip with the Women's Historical Society," Kaytie added.

"It was at night!" Joanna said excitedly, her braid swinging as she bounced on her knees. "We got lanterns and everything."

The other children nodded with fiendish delight.

"That sounds appropriately spooky," Sasha said. *And dangerously flammable*, she thought, but kept that to herself. "For the record, I'm not a witch. I can't do magic, and I don't have a broomstick."

Mason waved his soiled tissue in the air dismissively. "You don't need a broomstick. Mrs. Landshome is a witch, and she drives a Volvo."

"Well, I drive a Mustang, and that's a bit conspicuous for a witch." Sasha decided to end the conversation as quickly as possible before the children kick started their own witch trials. "But I can draw a witch—a very, very scary witch. How about we draw witches for Halloween and use them to decorate the classroom?"

"Yay!" the children cheered.

"Great!" Sasha said, relieved. "Go and sit at your desks, and we'll begin."

"I'm drawing Mrs. Landshome in her Volvo," Mason announced as he made his way to his seat.

Sasha tucked a curl back behind her ear and smiled. It was going to be an interesting first day.

~

WITH THE HELP OF HER CLASS, SASHA FOUND THE STAFFROOM DURING lunch. As a substitute teacher, she expected very little interaction with her colleagues; in her experience, no one wanted to get overly attached to a colleague who would not be around for long. So she was pleasantly surprised by the warm greeting she received when she walked into the room.

"Come in, come in!" Esther beckoned. "Shae baked a cake to celebrate your first day. It was only supposed to be a welcome cake—we didn't expect you to work today."

Esther gestured toward a woman around Sasha's age who was wielding a cake server with great gusto. Shae wore a fuchsia sweater dress that brought out the warm undertones in her russet brown skin and made her stand out like a spring flower amongst the faded fall colors worn by the other teachers. Her black, corkscrew curls were pulled back in a matching fuchsia headband, revealing pink-and-gold tassel earrings that bobbed and swished with each turn of her head.

"Hope you like strawberry layer cake," Shae said, cutting Sasha a large slice.

"Who doesn't like strawberry layer cake?" Sasha looked on in delight as Shae handed her a generous piece of cake topped with thick, pale pink frosting. "It looks absolutely delicious! It was so kind of you to go to all this trouble."

"I thought you could use the sugar." Shae grinned slyly as Sasha took a forkful of cake. "After all, you have Mason Barnes in your class."

The other teachers groaned.

Sasha paused, the bite of cake halfway to her mouth. "Is he really that bad?"

"Mason isn't … *terrible*," Esther said, hesitating a little too long for Sasha's comfort. "He just has a few odd notions—"

"And he's very forceful in the way that he puts them across," Shae finished.

Sasha relaxed and resumed eating. She could handle odd notions expressed forcefully—after all, she was best friends with Lyla.

"Well, I guess he'll keep me on my toes," she said, taking another bite of cake.

"That child will either save the world or blow it sky-high," Mrs. Landshome muttered. "I'm placing a bet each way."

She reached under her skirt and—to Sasha's surprise—pulled out a silver flask.

"Want some?" the old woman asked Sasha, screwing open the lid. She took a long pull and smacked her lips in appreciation. "It's aged twenty years." She wiggled the flask enticingly.

"Ah—" Sasha began.

"Gussie," Esther interrupted. She gestured wearily at the flask. "We discussed this, and you agreed—no drinking on school property."

Old Mrs. Landshome frowned, her myriad wrinkles cascading down toward her chin in a sort of fleshy domino effect. "Doesn't sound like something I'd agree to." She held up her hand to stave off Esther's next comment. "And before you get your panties in a bunch, I'm only drinking because I'm done for the day. And I've earned it … damn kids and their earwax." She saluted Esther and took another long drink.

"*Gussie,*" Esther entreated.

"Fine, fine," the old woman spluttered, reluctantly screwing the lid back on the flask. "As if I'd do anything to endanger the children." She paused. "Even the terrible ones. Do you want me here again tomorrow?"

Esther glanced at Mrs. Landshome's flask, her mouth pursed tight in distaste. "Possibly ... we'll have to see if the flu strikes anyone else down. I sent Poppy home."

"Poor Poppy." Shae shook her head, her earrings swinging madly. "She seems to catch everything going around."

Mrs. Landshome snorted. "I tell you, that gal is a walking disease. Burn everything she's touched and then salt the ashes for good measure."

Sasha watched—equal parts enthralled and horrified—as Mrs. Landshome flipped up her skirt and slipped the flask into a blue lace garter located high on her pasty, white thigh with ease born of long practice.

Sasha had a sudden flash of insight: if she continued substitute teaching for the next twenty years, she would probably become Mrs. Landshome, flask and all.

The prospect was not entirely unpleasant.

"I'm afraid that Headmistress Dean is still away," Esther said to Sasha, still eyeing Mrs. Landshome as the old woman arranged her skirt back into position.

"*Still?*" Mrs. Landshome asked, reaching for her fork.

"She sends her sincere apologies," Esther continued, ignoring the old woman, "and will meet with you tomorrow afternoon after school."

Sasha quickly swallowed her mouthful of cake. "That's absolutely fine. I hope everything is okay."

Mrs. Landshome snorted.

"I'm sure everything is *fine,*" Esther said firmly. She smiled at Sasha. "That means you're free to go. I can take your class for the rest of the day."

"Are you sure? I don't mind staying."

"We'll be fine," Esther said. "Why don't you spend the rest of the day getting to know Old Middleton?"

"If you're interested in seeing the village, I'm giving a Twilight Tour on behalf of the Old Middleton Women's Historical Society," Shae said. "We meet at the Village Hall at six."

"Do you have lanterns?" Sasha asked, remembering what her class had said earlier.

Shae laughed. "Yes. They add to the atmosphere."

"Sounds great!" Sasha said. "I'll bring my friend, Lyla; I bet she'd love to know more about the village. She'll have a fantastic time."

～

"I AM HAVING A TERRIBLE TIME," LYLA ANNOUNCED, AS SHE TRIED TO adjust her scarf without dropping her lantern. "Plus, I think I'm choking."

Sasha rolled her eyes and put down her lantern. "Here, let me." She rearranged Lyla's cream wool scarf so that it was less lethal. "And how could you be having a terrible time? The tour hasn't even started."

"I know, but I'm already close to hypothermia." Lyla shivered. "I should have paced myself."

In hindsight, it was probably not the best night for a twilight walking tour of Old Middleton. The temperature had dropped during the afternoon, leading to a frosty evening. An icy wind was merrily scattering leaves around their feet, and sneaking into the gaps between scarves and collars, chilling slivers of exposed skin.

But Sasha did not care about the weather. How could she, when she was about to walk through a village by *lantern light*? She adjusted her rainbow-colored knit scarf and looked up; there were fairy lights festooned between the lampposts, and stars peeking out from behind the clouds. Wood smoke spiced the crisp, night air. In the distance, she could hear the hoot of an owl.

It was utterly enchanting.

She breathed it all in and shivered with anticipation.

"Where is your sense of adventure?" she asked Lyla, linking their free arms together.

"In my other coat. The warm one." Lyla huddled closer to Sasha. "You have the overly cheerful demeanor of a woman who remembered to wear thermals."

"Yep!" Sasha said with a laugh, "I'm always prepared. Now *shh*—it looks like we're about to begin."

"Damn you and your thermally warmed limbs," Lyla muttered.

The two women turned toward the front of the group where Shae stood, waving her arms to get their attention. She seemed impervious to the cold weather: she wore no hat or gloves and only a light coat in a bold shade of blue. Across her chest was a red satin sash that read 'Tour Leader.'

"Welcome!" Shae said. She frowned up at the sky as if personally affronted by the stormy skies. "Given the weather, I'll be limiting the tour to Main Street. Nevertheless, a warm welcome to Old Middleton, whether you are staying for a while …" She smiled at Sasha and Lyla. "Or just passing through." She directed her smile at a woman in a navy polka-dot coat and her husband, who—despite the darkness around them—was happily snapping photos of the Village Hall.

"And welcome back to our tour regulars." Shae smiled wryly at two teenage boys: one tall and lanky with feathery, matte-black dyed hair; the other short and frail, with bleached blond hair that fell stubbornly over his eyes. Both were dressed in head-to-toe black and wore an impressive amount of eyeliner. "Lucas, Travis, this is your … what? Third tour this month?"

"Fourth," Travis said.

"Aren't you all toured out?" Lyla asked.

"We like to support local cultural initiatives," Lucas said, brushing his blond fringe out of his eyes.

"And we like lanterns," Travis added.

Shae raised an eyebrow. "Right. *That's* why you're here. Does your mother know where you are?"

"Sure does," Travis said. "She's parked over there."

He and Lucas waved toward a blue sedan on the other side of the street. The woman inside the car waved back half-heartedly.

"Okay, then," Shae said, clapping her hands. "Let's get started before the temperature drops further—"

"Further?" Lyla gasped.

"—and make sure that you hold your lanterns high! The exercise will help you ward off the chill."

Lyla hoisted up her lantern and turned to Sasha. "The only way this flimsy lantern could ward off the chill was if it was filled with lava. Or bourbon. Or lava covered in bourbon. Oh, how I long for lava covered in bourbon …"

"Maybe later, if you behave," Sasha said.

Shae set off down Main Street at a brisk pace, her tour group shivering behind her.

"Although officially established in 1858," she began, "it is believed that Old Middleton—then named simply 'Middleton'—was actually founded much earlier."

"How much earlier?" the woman in the polka-dot coat asked.

"*That* is the subject of vigorous debate," Shae answered. "Some local historians believe that it could be as early as the end of the eighteenth century. What *is* known is that the original settlers were four families: the Lennoxes, the Carters, the Godwins, and the Deans—"

"And they were running away from the Salem witch trials, right?" Travis interrupted.

"Because they were all witches, yeah?" Lucas added eagerly.

Shae shook her head, her tassel earrings swinging merrily "It's always the witches with you two, isn't it?"

"We like to support local practitioners of the alternative arts," Lucas said.

"And we like their outfits," Travis added.

Shae's lips twitched. "*Right.* Well, as you both know, that's only a theory. It's much more likely that the families settled in Old Middleton because the land was free territory and unwanted by the local indigenous tribes."

"Because it was cursed?" Lucas asked hopefully.

Shae snorted and adjusted her sash. "No, because it looked uninhabitable." She gestured around her. "All of this was once forested wetlands. It took a lot of work to turn this land into a village. But the land was very fertile, and the surrounding forest not only provided protection but plentiful hunting. *That's* most likely why they chose to settle here."

"Yeah, the witch theory is better," Travis said.

"It really is," Lyla said.

"Much more interesting," the woman in the polka-dot coat agreed.

"I guess so," Shae acknowledged with a laugh. "Irrespective of whether or not the four founding families were witches, or had been accused of witchcraft, it is said that Old Middleton became a haven for those escaping persecution from witch trials across the country."

"Go founding families!" Lyla said.

Shae grinned. "To mark the founding of the village, the four families planted five oak trees—"

"The Elders," Travis interrupted.

"Known as the Elders," Shae said, nodding to Travis. "They planted one in each corner of Old Middleton and one in the center—which is now the playground of the Old Middleton Elementary School—where it still stands today."

"Oh!" Sasha whispered to Lyla. "I'll have to visit it tomorrow when I go to work."

"Get its autograph for me," Lyla whispered back.

"The Elders are said to protect the village," Shae continued. "You'll find that most of the villagers carry an Elder leaf in their pocket or wallet as a protective talisman."

"I've got five," Travis said. "You can never have too much protection."

"Bring me back a leaf from that school tree," Lyla murmured to Sasha. "No—make it a branch. I need all the luck I can get."

Sasha squeezed Lyla's arm. "I'll bring you back the biggest branch I can carry."

Shae gestured to the street around them. "Unfortunately, the village that you see today bears little resemblance to the one built by the Founders. In October 1861, the village was beset by several natural disasters, including a terrible fire—"

"*Fire*," Lyla said longingly, huddling closer to Sasha.

"—which destroyed Main Street and most of the surrounding homes. The disasters displaced many of the citizens, but those who remained rebuilt the village, creating the Old Middleton you see today. When the founding families fixed or rebuilt their homes, they decided to give them in trust to the village. The Dean Family mansion became the Old Middleton Elementary School; the Lennox Family mansion the Village Hall; the Carter Family mansion became the Boarding House for Genteel Young Women of Unimpeachable Reputation—"

Sasha and Lyla exchanged looks.

"—and the Godwin Family mansion became the Old Middleton Finishing School for Young Women."

"Huh. I wonder if I'm finished?" Lyla whispered to Sasha. "I mean, are people looking at me and thinking, '*Hmm*, that Lyla could use some finishing'?"

"You are the most finished person I know," Sasha said loyally.

"You can still see remnants of the original village," Shae continued, "such as the cobblestone streets and the horse troughs. A few of the original structures also survived, including this clocktower, which was built by Peabody Lennox."

The group paused in front of an imposing stone clock tower that stood in the center of Main Street. Sasha peered up at the clock and frowned. Even by lamplight, she could see the deep crack that marred the surface of the clock face, running from the twelve and ending just beside the seven.

"Is there something wrong with the face?" she asked Shae.

Shae nodded. "It's damaged, possibly by a lightning strike. But it's only cosmetic; it still keeps excellent time. Another original structure is the old village well."

The group moved down the street and stood before a squat, stone well set outside the candy store, its wooden bucket swaying in the wind.

Shae patted the rim of the well fondly. "Also built by Peabody Lennox, the well is no longer functional. But legend has it that if you throw a penny into the well and make a wish, the wish will come true. Shall we give it a try? Everyone huddle around, I have pennies for everyone."

"Ah, a *legitimate* source of wishes," Lyla said, with a sly look at Sasha. "What if you throw two pennies in the well?" she asked Shae, as the tour guide handed her a penny. "Do you double your luck?"

"Woah," Travis said. "Never thought of that."

Shae handed a coin to the woman in the polka-dot coat. "Good question. I don't know."

"We should try this out," Lyla said. "For science."

She pulled out her wallet and, rummaging around, managed to find extra pennies for everyone.

"You know," Lucas said, as Lyla handed him a second penny, "if this works, it will revolutionize all well-based wishes."

"You're a pioneer," Travis said to Lyla admiringly.

"Yes. Yes, I am," Lyla said, pleased. "Thank you for recognizing that."

"I have no idea what I'm going to wish for," the husband of the woman in the polka-dot coat said, as Lyla offered him a penny. "I've already got everything I need." He patted his wife's arm fondly.

"Oh, what a lovely thing to say!" Sasha said.

"Disgustingly wonderful," Lyla agreed. "I'm taking back both of your pennies."

"Okay," Shae announced, "make a wish and, on the count of three, drop in your pennies. Ready? One—"

Sasha closed the pennies tight in her fist. She looked up at the few stars that remained amongst the gathering storm clouds and closed her eyes.

I wish I could dream again, she wished to the entity responsible for granting two-penny well-wishes.

"Two—"

Please, she begged.

"Three! Now, throw them in!"

Sasha opened her eyes and let the coins slide from her fingers, listening to the muted splash as they hit the surface of the water.

Thunder rumbled in the distance.

"Well, that's not ominous at all," Lyla said, looking up at the sky.

Shae also looked up and grimaced. "I think we'd better skip ahead to the question portion of the tour."

"But you missed the best part!" Travis said.

"The best part?" Sasha asked.

"The part where all the men disappeared, and the village was cursed," Lucas said.

"What?" Lyla shrieked. "Men disappeared? There was a *curse*?" She looked up at Sasha, her expression gleeful. "There was a *curse*!"

Shae shook her head wearily. "As I told you boys before, most of that is just speculation."

"I love speculation," Lyla said. "Tell us more."

Shae hesitated.

"Come on, dish out the dirt," the woman with the polka-dot coat said.

Everyone else nodded eagerly.

"Fine," Shae said. "But take this with a grain of salt, okay?"

She beckoned the group closer. Everyone happily obliged until they were clustered around Shae in a tight circle, their lanterns illuminating the tour guide in cheery, gold light.

"There is some evidence," Shae began, her voice low and secretive, "very sketchy, mind you—that on Halloween night in 1861, something happened to the male citizens of Old Middleton."

"What, to all of them?" the husband of the woman with the polka-dot coat asked. He looked warily around him.

"No, only to twenty-five of them," Shae said.

"What do you mean 'something happened?' " Sasha asked.

"They disappeared," Travis said, his voice a spooky whisper. "Into thin air."

"Awesome," Lyla whispered.

"All we know—from what remains of Old Middleton's historical documents—is that the men went missing," Shae explained. "What happened to them is open to speculation. Some believe that they succumbed to an illness. Others think they joined the Civil War effort, which had just begun a few months before."

Lyla whistled. "That's a lot of man-flesh to misplace. Hang on, Halloween night in 1861? Isn't that the same year as the fire?"

"It is," Shae said. "In fact, the two events happened right around the same time. It's quite possible that the men died during the fire or the floods that followed. Or they may have relocated after the disasters."

"Leaving their wives and families behind?" Travis asked incredulously.

"That would be irresponsible," Lucas said. "The answer is clearly witchcraft."

"I agree," Lyla said. "Excellent deduction, boys!"

Shae shook her head at Lyla. "There's no need to encourage them; Travis and Lucas are doing a wonderful job of fabricating history all by themselves."

"I like to encourage curiosity and deviant thinking in youngsters," Lyla said.

"Two very important qualities," Sasha said.

"Thanks!" Travis said. "We like to be encouraged."

"Several women in the village were blamed for their disappearance though, weren't they?" Lucas asked. "And people accused these women of being witches."

"They were acquitted," Shae said firmly. "What happened remains a mystery to this day."

"So ... what about the curse?" Lyla asked.

"There is no curse," Shae said.

Lyla turned to the teenagers. "Travis?"

Travis's eyes lit up. "It's said that, after the men disappeared, Old Middleton was cursed so that all marriageable men leave, die, or disappear from the village. Maybe as a punishment—on account of what the women did to their menfolk in 1861."

There was a tense silence.

"Come to think of it, I haven't seen that many men around ..." Sasha mused.

"And certainly none that were marriageable," Lyla said. "Unless you've stashed all the hot, marriageable men in a barn somewhere ..."

"We haven't," Travis said.

"That wouldn't be feasible," Lucas said. "Or legal."

"Then Old Middleton is definitely in the middle of a man-drought," Lyla said.

The woman with the polka-dot coat sidled closer to her husband and took his arm nonchalantly.

"Old Middleton isn't cursed with a man drought," Shae said. "It only *feels* that way." She looked up at the sky and grimaced. "Let's move onto question time, shall we?" Thunder rumbled once again, closer this time. "As quickly as possible."

Travis held up his hand. "Are there still witches in Old Middleton?"

"As I told you during the last tour, I very much doubt it," Shae said.

Lucas raised his hand. "But ... what about Rosa?"

"Who's Rosa?" Lyla asked.

"She owns the magic shop." Lucas raised his lantern toward Stardust and Brimstone on the other side of the street. "She makes all sorts of potions and spells: love potions, luck potions—"

"Truth potions, and something to help you do well in exams—" Travis continued.

"—and spells for harvests, and solstice rituals, and elixirs to cure ailments," Lucas finished. "She fixed up the wart on my big toe. Do you want to see?"

"Yes," Lyla said.

"*No,*" Shae said firmly, before Lucas could take off his shoe. "Not again. Boys, Rosa isn't a witch. She's a naturopath, which is why she's interested in herbal medicine. She also dabbles in a bit of jewelry-making. Before that, she was a chiropractor. Next question?"

Lucas held up his hand. "How—"

"Before you ask, Lucas, I have no idea how someone goes about becoming a witch," Shae interrupted. "I don't think it's something that you can just learn, like algebra."

"Just as well—I'm terrible at algebra," Lucas said, dejected.

Travis patted his shoulder consolingly. "It runs in the family."

Lyla raised her hand. "A non-witch-related question: why isn't there cell phone coverage here?"

"The witches are hiding the village," Travis answered matter-of-factly.

Shae gestured to the other members of the tour group. "And you can see how well that's going."

"We came from Idaho!" the woman in the polka-dot coat said.

Her husband smiled proudly. "Sure did! Our state slogan is: Great potatoes, tasty destinations."

Lyla nodded approvingly. "Gotta love carbs."

"The reason for the poor cell phone coverage is dull, and it involves geography," Shae said. "We're a long way from the nearest cell tower. On top of that, we're in a valley, surrounded by a forest. Both diminish cell phone signal."

"Sure," Lucas muttered. "*That's* the reason."

The wind began to pick up, curling around the tour group.

"Any other questions?" Shae asked, trying to hold down her sash as it flapped frantically in the high winds. "This will probably be the last one."

"The stone gateway at the entrance to the village," Sasha began, surprised to find herself speaking, "is it part of the original village?"

"Ah … the Middleton Gateway! Yes," Shae said, smiling widely, "it was part of the original village."

"What was it? Originally? It looks like it was part of something very large."

"And fancy," Lyla added. "Almost *too* fancy for a village."

Shae hesitated for a moment and then shrugged. "Historians speculate that it was part of an entrance to the village that was never completed."

Sasha's eyes narrowed. There was a little too much hesitation *before* Shae's answer, and a little too much nonchalance *during* her answer, and far too much fidgeting with her sash *after* her answer. There was only one explanation for such behavior.

Shae was lying.

"But—" Sasha began.

Suddenly, lightning lit up the sky around them, far more effectively than any lantern. Fat, icy raindrops began to fall as thunder cracked, too close to the small group for comfort.

"And that concludes our tour," Shae shouted above the storm.

The wind roared through Main Street, scattering leaves and tour group members in its wake.

Sasha and Lyla fled back to the boarding house—Sasha laughing while Lyla cursed—leaving their lanterns behind.

As the storm began, their pennies settled on the bottom of the well—a well far more ancient than any of the tour group could have imagined—and *waited*.

~

THAT NIGHT, SASHA DREAMED OF THE HILLSIDE AGAIN.

"Yes!" she crowed, spinning around. "I'm dreaming! I'm *dreaming*! Look at me go!"

She inhaled the scent of cloves, burned honey, and copper, holding it in her lungs for as long as she could while she stared up at the familiar, stormy sky.

"Okay, it appears I'm having the same dream again." She frowned down at her feet, which were sinking—yet again—into glittery sand. "I'm not that imaginative, am I?"

Thunder boomed behind her.

"That's not a complaint," she said quickly, "just an observation. Speaking of observation, I need to remember this when I wake up."

She gazed out across the plain, trying to find landmarks that would be particularly memorable. But there was nothing distinctive in view—no strange rock formations or oddly shaped trees.

"Not helpful," she told the plain sternly, shaking her head.

Taking a new approach, she looked over the landscape as if she were going to paint it, noting the strange, green tint to the twilight sky and the exact shade of gold of the hillside dust beneath her feet. Finally, she reached down and sifted the gold dust through her fingers, trying to commit the sensation to memory.

"Come on, Sasha—remember!" she told herself fiercely as the fishhook sensation began behind her navel.

"Remember!" she chanted to herself as she floated skyward. "Remember! Remember!"

∾

"REMEMBER ..." SASHA SLURRED, LURCHING UPRIGHT IN BED. BREATHING heavily, she looked around her dawn-tinged room and tried to get her bearings.

"Remember ... remember?" She frowned. "What was I supposed to remember?"

"Milk," Lyla mumbled in her sleep, "chicken, sassafras, abs, why—hello sailor!"

Sasha glanced over at her friend, who was sprawled on her stomach, her limbs hopelessly tangled in the blankets. "What are *you* dreaming about?"

Lyla began to snore softly.

Sasha shook her head and then peered down at her hands, confused. She rubbed her fingertips together.

They felt gritty.

She knew there was something—a memory, a thought, an idea—that wanted her attention; it was teetering on the very edge of her subconscious, so *close* yet tantalizingly out of reach. Something to do with the sensation between her fingertips ...

Something ...

Nothing.

She sighed, frustrated, and rubbed the sleep from her eyes.

"The only thing I have to remember is my meeting with Headmistress Dean after school," she told herself firmly.

But she knew that wasn't it. Whatever she was supposed to remember made her heart beat faster and her blood *thrum* with exhilaration—it was definitely not her meeting with the Headmistress.

With a groan, she pulled back the sheets. "This place is getting to me," she muttered. "Probably too much fresh air."

She pushed back an irrational surge of disappointment and looked at the alarm clock; it was almost time to wake up. With another groan, Sasha rose from the bed and stumbled off to get ready for her morning run, determined to put her strange mood behind her.

If Sasha had looked back, she would have seen gold dust suspended in the air like dust motes, glittering in her wake.

4

WHERE THE TRUTH IS DECIDEDLY OVERRATED

BY THE TIME SASHA ARRIVED AT HEADMISTRESS DEAN'S OFFICE AFTER school, she had long forgotten about her odd morning experience. She was exhausted, her temples were beginning to throb, and her right eyelid was twitching.

Mason had lived up to his reputation, peppering her with questions all day. These included queries about the nutritional value of earwax, and whether conjoined twins have one soul or two. After Sasha read the class a story about a family trip to the circus, Mason stood on his chair and made an impassioned speech about the mistreatment of circus animals. He then scampered onto the bench with his drink bottle and attempted to liberate Fish Stick and Aluminum Foil from their tank—all to the enthusiastic cheers of the other children.

He refused to come down until Sasha proclaimed the fish tank an honorary sanctuary city, and the fish "free citizens" of Old Middleton—as opposed to oppressed aquatic lifeforms forced to perform for the sadistic enjoyment of humans.

He insisted that Sasha shake on the deal to make it legally binding.

"Do you want me to draw up a formal contract?" Sasha asked wryly, as she shook his tiny hand.

"I trust you," Mason said, his grip surprisingly firm and his expression solemn. "And I know where you work."

As she left her classroom for the day, Sasha half-hoped to run into Mrs. Landshome and her silver flask.

Esther, sitting at an antique roll-top desk outside Headmistress Dean's office, waved Sasha in with a smile. "The Headmistress is just finishing up some paperwork. Go right in—she's expecting you."

Sasha gave her the most enthusiastic smile that she could muster and peeked through the office doorway.

Sure enough, Headmistress Dean was bent over her desk, signing documents. At first glance, she looked like the sort of woman typically cast as the benevolent grandmother in 1950s sitcoms: all rosy cheeks and dimples, white hair artfully arranged in a cotton-candy cloud high on her head, and ample curves encased in lavender cashmere. She was humming a merry little tune to herself as she signed a stack of documents—a tune that sounded suspiciously like a breakfast cereal jingle.

Sasha felt herself relax: this did not look like a woman who owned a monogrammed paddle. She knocked on the doorframe.

Looking up, Headmistress Dean greeted her with a smile. "Why, welcome, welcome, *welcome!*" she said, standing.

Before Sasha could react, the Headmistress had crossed the room and gathered Sasha up into a fierce hug. "It is so lovely to meet you!"

"Ah ... it's lovely to be met?" Sasha sputtered from amidst cashmere-covered flesh and a cloud of lilac scented perfume.

The Headmistress laughed—a laugh reminiscent of bells chiming, or birds twittering, or something equally high-pitched and cheery and somewhat improbable for human laughter—and released Sasha. She stepped back, holding Sasha's hands in a firm grasp, and looked her up and down. "You're a pretty thing, aren't you?"

"Thank you?"

"And so tall!"

Sasha sighed. "Yes."

The Headmistress's eyes narrowed, and Sasha caught a glimpse of steel in her merry-blue gaze. "Though, a little thin. Not to worry ..." The steel was gone once more, suffocated in merriment. "We'll fix that in no time."

Sasha suddenly knew how Hansel must have felt in the gingerbread house.

While she contemplated the prospect of being fattened up for possibly nefarious purposes, the Headmistress turned Sasha's hands over and stared at the bare skin of her wrists. The older woman frowned, clearly perturbed. But then quickly recovered, her smile bright once more.

"Is something wrong?" Sasha asked, looking down at her wrists.

"Oh, not at all. It's just that I've noticed a trend amongst you young-sters." The Headmistress bent toward Sasha conspiratorially. "Tattoos on your inner wrist." She said it as if it were a glorious secret just between the two of them. She leaned back, her blue eyes twinkling. "I enjoy looking at the designs. My assistant, Poppy, has a purple butterfly on her wrist! Can you imagine?"

"I'm trying," Sasha said, though it was difficult to picture dour, diseased Poppy with a colorful insect tattooed anywhere on her body. She looked down at the pale, butterfly free skin of her inner wrists and shrugged. "Well, sorry to disappoint—no tattoos for me."

"Never say never! Sit, sit, and we'll have a chat, shall we?" The Head-mistress released Sasha's hands and beckoned her toward a chair.

Sasha, still a little disturbed by the inspection, sat gingerly on the offered chair. She waited patiently as Headmistress Dean arranged herself behind an antique desk that looked as though it had been brought over on the Mayflower.

The Headmistress moved her paperwork aside and smiled kindly at Sasha. "First, I'd like to express my gratitude: it was very good of you to step in and take the class yesterday morning. I assure you that it was only due to extraordinary circumstances; it's rare for so many of us to be away at the same time—flu season is such a nightmare." She shuddered. "Of course, the children were well supervised." Her smile faltered. "I'm sure you met Mrs. Landshome ..."

"Yes." Sasha nodded slowly, trying not to smile. "She seems very ... experienced."

Headmistress Dean pursed her lips. "Well, that's one word for it." She folded her hands primly on the desk before her. "Let's get all the business-talk out of the way first, shall we? As you know—since you've started already—the position is for a kindergarten teacher. Your contract is for three weeks but there's the option of extending it for the rest of the school year. Of course, that depends on how well you fit into Old Middleton."

That was new, Sasha thought. Contracts were usually extended based on need and performance.

Odd.

Speaking of odd. "Headmistress Dean—" Sasha paused. "I just real-ized that we haven't been properly introduced ..."

Headmistress Dean's smile froze. "You *could* call me Penelope." Her tone, however, suggested that Sasha could not.

Sasha decided to try it anyway. "Penelope—" she began.

"But," the older woman interrupted, a little more forcefully than required, "staff members—particularly the new ones—address me as 'Headmistress.' It has *always* been so at Old Middleton Elementary. A mark of respect, you see?"

"Oh … of course," Sasha said with a polite smile. "*Headmistress*—"

The Headmistress nodded approvingly.

"—I heard that the three previous substitute teachers left suddenly—"

The Headmistress waved away her concerns with a flick of her well-manicured fingers. "All three young women had to leave because of personal reasons; it was certainly nothing to do with the class itself. You'll find that the children are dears, though Mason Barnes can be a little … spirited."

Sasha's lips quirked. "*Spirited* is an excellent way to describe Mason."

Possessed was another, Sasha thought to herself. Still, she wouldn't be bored while he was around.

"Even so," Headmistress Dean continued, "I'm sure you'll have them in hand in no time." She handed Sasha a manila folder stuffed with documents of various colors. "Inside, you'll find all the information you need about Old Middleton Elementary and the lesson plans for the next three weeks. They'll probably be very similar to those you've used in other schools, except for a few local tweaks."

"Tweaks?"

"Tweaks," Headmistress Dean said firmly. "Old Middleton is very proud of its history and traditions." She leaned back in her chair and preened. "As both Headmistress of Old Middleton Elementary and a direct descendent of one of Old Middleton's four founding families, I have made it my mission to educate our youngest citizens about the village's glorious heritage. After all, my family founded this school."

No wonder she looks so at home behind that desk, Sasha thought with a smile. "Really?"

The Headmistress nodded, a proud tilt to her chin. "*Really.* And from the day it was founded, there has always been a member of the Dean family on staff, often as Headmistress."

She gestured to the wall behind her, where a row of portraits stared down at Sasha from their ornate frames. Some, Sasha noted, had the Headmistress's dimples; others, the same proud tilt to their chin. All of them looked down at her with a variation of the Headmistress's twinkly smile.

"I can see the resemblance," Sasha said. "It's wonderful that you've continued the tradition."

The Headmistress beamed. "It is an honor to follow in their footsteps."

Sasha peered up at the portraits and wondered what it would be like to have one's life so tightly entwined with a place.

Would I still want to run away? she silently asked the smiling women.

"And it's so lovely to be reminded of their legacy each day," the Headmistress continued, interrupting Sasha's thoughts. "Why, all I have to do is look around me! One of my ancestors planted that tree." She gestured out the window toward a handsome oak in the middle of the playground. "It's one of the oldest trees in Old Middleton."

Sasha leaned forward and tried to get a glimpse of the tree through the window. "Oh! Your ancestor planted one of the Elders! I heard all about them during the Twilight Tour." She made a mental note to pick a leaf for Lyla and herself when she left the meeting.

The Headmistress beamed. "I'm *so* glad that you've taken it upon yourself to learn about the history of the village! It speaks very well of you."

Sasha smiled at the unexpected praise. "Ah … thank you."

The Headmistress placed her hand on her chest. "I, myself, am the Vice President of the Women's Historical Society. We all take turns hosting the tours."

"My friend and I enjoyed the tour very much." Sasha surreptitiously crossed her fingers under the desk, lying a little on Lyla's behalf. "We found it very atmospheric." Technically, Lyla found it cold, but Sasha figured that cold still counted as atmosphere, and uncrossed her fingers.

The Headmistress gave another pleased nod. "Given my family's place in village history, it would be lax of me *not* to care about preserving the past. Don't you agree?"

"Of course," Sasha said. "I'll try my best to do your tweaks justice."

"Wonderful! Be sure to read that folder through and let me know if you have any questions." The Headmistress clapped her hands together. "Now, enough of business—let's get to know each other better."

There was a knock on the door.

"Enter," the Headmistress called out. "Impeccable timing as always, Esther."

Esther blushed under the praise and entered, pushing a brass tea trolley. She placed the trolley beside the Headmistress and quickly left the room, sending Sasha an encouraging smile as she walked away.

"Wow," Sasha said, staring at the cream and gold tea set. "An actual afternoon tea."

Headmistress Dean looked over the contents of the trolley, pleased. "I find that you can say anything over a cup of tea." She began to pour the steaming liquid into two cups. "How do you like your tea?"

In the packet, never to be opened, Sasha thought unhappily. In her experience, tea looked and tasted like grass clippings soaked in dishwater.

Instead, she said, "Milk and sugar? Please?" *That sounds appropriate,* she thought to herself.

"Cookie?" The Headmistress handed her a cup and offered her a gilt-edged plate of sugar cookies with pink sprinkles.

"Thank you." Sasha selected one and took a polite bite. It was delicious, as were the tiny egg and cucumber sandwiches that the Headmistress set out on a plate before her. Even the tea was palatable. As she sipped the warm, fragrant brew, Sasha began to relax, her anxiety about the meeting fading away.

"So, what do you think of Old Middleton?" the Headmistress asked.

Sasha swallowed her bite of sandwich. "I've only been here for a day. So far, it seems wonderful."

She washed down her sandwich with a long sip of tea. It was starting to grow on her, with its faint hint of orange peel, and an aftertaste of something familiar that she could not place.

Headmistress Dean stirred her tea, careful not to touch the sides of the cup with the teaspoon. "And how are you finding Adeline's boarding house?"

"It seems lovely. Though, I don't know if I'm sufficiently genteel, or if my reputation is unimpeachable enough, to stay there." Sasha paused. "I can't believe I said that aloud."

The Headmistress laughed her tinkling laugh. "I doubt many of the guests fit the bill, but it's such a lovely old name, isn't it?" She pushed the cookie plate closer to Sasha. "Have you had a chance to look around the village? Oh! That's right—you did the tour."

"Well, thanks to the storm, we didn't get to tour the whole village." Sasha selected a cookie from the plate. "We only toured Main Street."

The Headmistress watched as Sasha bit into her cookie. "And what did you think of Main Street?"

Sasha finished her bite and took another sip from her cup. There was a strange, sweet taste on her lips that was neither sugar nor spice. Her tongue felt oddly loose. "It's charming! The buildings are beautiful. The architecture, the leadlight windows—*everything*! The gargoyles ..."

Sasha's eyes fluttered shut. Behind her eyelids, she could see the stone creatures leering and grinning at her in startling clarity.

"Yes, the gargoyles," the Headmistress said. "Aren't they fabulous? What *else* stood out?"

Unbidden, an image of the old gateway—gold and imposing—came vividly to Sasha's mind.

"The Middleton Gateway ..." she began.

"The Gateway? What about the Gateway?"

Sasha opened her eyes. The Headmistress was staring at her encouragingly. *Eagerly.*

"It's ancient, isn't it?" Sasha found herself saying.

"Yes. Yes, it is," Headmistress Dean cooed approvingly. "What else?"

"The ... the ... old well." In her mind's eye, Sasha saw the well in vivid detail. She could visualize every stone, every crack. She could even hear the creak of the rope as the bucket swung back and forth in the wind. "We threw pennies in there ... two pennies each ... and made wishes. The well seemed so old ..."

"You're quite right. The well is *very* old."

"You can sense it," Sasha said. "This whole place—you can feel how old it is. There's a sense of history and yet ..." She paused, trying to put her feelings into words.

"And yet?"

"And yet ... the atmosphere of the village isn't stodgy or still or tired. It's—it's—"

"Electric?" the Headmistress suggested, her expression oddly intense.

Sasha found herself nodding. "Yes! *Electric*. Like there's a current buzzing away beneath the village. And somehow, you can—you can *feel* it under your skin. Like static electricity only sharper. *Shinier.* Strange, but—but it feels familiar somehow ..."

Sasha blinked—she hadn't realized that she felt that way. She licked her lips; that sweet, cloying taste seemed stronger now. The throbbing in her temples had eased, replaced by a feeling of lightheadedness that made the world seem oddly unfocused.

"You know ..." She placed her fingers against her temples, her skin overly warm beneath her fingertips. "I think I may be coming down with that flu that's going around."

The Headmistress stared at her, alarmed. "Why? What are you feeling?"

Sasha dropped her hands. "I thought I was getting a headache, but now—now, I'm feeling a little ... foggy."

"Oh! You poor thing." Headmistress Dean pressed her hand against her chest, sympathy personified. "That won't do—why, you've only just got here! We need to fix you up. Do you know what's wonderful for the flu?"

"Hardcore cold and flu drugs?"

"*Tea.*" The Headmistress picked up the teapot and began to refill Sasha's cup. "Especially this one. A friend of mine created this special blend just for me. It's full of all sorts of wonderful things." She pushed the cup closer to Sasha. "And best of all, it's blended right here in Old Middleton. Drink up! It truly is the best medicine."

Sasha sincerely doubted that boiled leaves were any match for pharmaceutical interventions, but she took the cup anyway.

"Thank you," she said, raising the cup to her lips. "This is the nicest tea I've ever had." She took a long sip.

The Headmistress watched her carefully. "So, why did you decide to trek so far from your family to work with us?" Her smile slid away. "Or are you all alone in the world?"

"Oh, no! I have family."

"You ... you do?"

Sasha took another sip of her tea. "Oh, yes. Just parents, though. No siblings."

Headmistress Dean tsked sadly. "Such a small family! Why, you're *almost* alone in the world."

"Hardly," Sasha said with a laugh. "I have a big extended family. Loads of relatives."

"*Hmm* ... perhaps not so alone after all."

Sasha blinked. "Sorry?"

The Headmistress smiled quickly—a smile that was mostly lipstick and very little sentiment. "That's ... wonderful! Having lots of relatives," she clarified.

Sasha nodded slowly and took another sip of her tea. "Not to mention Lyla—she's practically a sister to me. It's Lyla—my friend, Lyla—who's the orphan." She paused, wondering why she had said that.

The Headmistress's gaze turned speculative. "*Lyla* is the orphan. Well, I'll have to meet her." She pushed the plate of sandwiches closer to Sasha. "It must be difficult to be so far away from your family—or is it? Families can be so *trying*."

"Not mine," Sasha said, taking another sip of tea.

The Headmistress's eyes widened. "No? You get on well with them?"

"Very. My parents are fantastic. The only problem—"

The Headmistress leaned forward. "Yes?"

"—is that they are adventurers. Ever since they retired, they've been traveling pretty much non-stop. Right now, they're in Marrakesh—no, that's not right. I think they're still in Casablanca. Yes, Casablanca; they're in Marrakesh next week ... and then onto Egypt for Christmas and New Year. At least, I *think* they'll be in Egypt for Christmas ..."

Sasha's brow furrowed. Why was it so hard to remember? She shook her head. "Anyway, they travel a lot. And I travel a lot, too, so I rarely get a chance to see them face to face. But we're in contact as much as possible: phone calls, emails, texts, postcards ..."

Headmistress Dean sat back in her chair and folded her arms on her desk. "Oh. Wonderful."

Sasha noticed the Headmistress's sudden distance and her overly polite smile and wondered if she had said something wrong. "Is that ... is that a problem?"

"Oh, no!" The Headmistress leaned forward, animated once more. "Not at *all*. It's just that we're so isolated in Old Middleton; most of our substitute teachers only apply because they don't have family ties. We'd have a better chance of keeping you if there was less pulling you away." She pushed the plate of sandwiches even closer to Sasha. "It's wonderful that you get on so well with your family. Being away from them must be so hard! And if Lyla is your only friend—"

"Oh, no—she isn't. I have lots of friends."

"You *do*?"

"Oh *loads*," Sasha said expansively, happy to chat about her friends. "Lyla thinks I have too many but—"

"Does Lyla have many friends?" the Headmistress interrupted.

"Ah ... no. Not really."

The Headmistress drummed her fingers against her desk. "*Interesting.*"

"Lyla is a *fantastic* friend. The *best*. But she thinks that friends are a lot of work, so you should only have one ... or two at most, just in case the other one is on vacation. I don't think that's right, do you? I think you can never have too many friends. I *love* making new friends and I—oh, I'm sorry. I'm rambling," Sasha shook her head, trying to clear the odd, light-headed feeling that was becoming stronger and stronger. "This isn't like me. I'm—I'm—"

She raised her hand to her temple—only to realize that she was holding a cucumber sandwich with the same hand. She stared at the floppy bit of bread and cucumber accusingly. "I don't remember taking this sandwich."

The Headmistress Dean smiled. "Well, it certainly didn't climb into your hand all by itself."

"No, I guess not." Sasha placed the sandwich carefully on her plate but kept an eye on it, just in case it moved of its own volition.

"You'll have to invite Lyla to join us for afternoon tea sometime this week," the Headmistress continued, ignoring the sandwich debacle. "Old Middleton is more than a village—it's one big family. I want her to feel welcome. What does *she* think of Old Middleton?"

Sasha was still eyeing her sandwich suspiciously. "She thinks this place is a mafia-run drug den that needs more dumpster rats and—oh my good-ness!" She placed her hand over her mouth. "I am so sorry. I have no idea why I said that. I *really* think I'm coming down with the flu ..."

The Headmistress reached across the desk and patted Sasha's hand reassuringly. "It's quite alright! Really, dear—I'm sure that you're just tired. And besides, your friend is entitled to her opinion." She pulled her hand away from Sasha's. "As wildly incorrect ... and mildly hurtful ... as that opinion may be."

"*Thank you,*" Sasha said hurriedly, grateful that the Headmistress was taking everything so well. "I—I'm feeling quite exhausted." She shook her head again, trying to clear it. "I'm sorry I keep babbling."

"Nonsense! I want to hear everything about you." The Headmistress reached for the teapot and refilled Sasha's cup. "Here, have another cup of tea."

"Thanks." Sasha looked down at her empty cup, puzzled; she could not remember finishing the last cup.

"But tell me," the Headmistress said, placing the teapot back on the trolley, "did you leave someone *special* behind?"

Before she could stop herself, Sasha found herself answering, the words slipping from her lips unchecked. "No. I was dating someone—Todd—but we broke up earlier this year. He wanted to settle down, but I wanted to travel and see the world."

"Oh, what a pity! But if two people care for one another, then surely they can make things work—even long distance."

"Caring wasn't the problem. Sex, on the other hand—" Sasha slapped her hand over her mouth. "I'm so sorry," she said between her fingers, mortified. "I have no idea why I keep saying these things. I haven't even told Lyla about that, and she's my best friend—"

"Not to worry," the Headmistress tittered. "It's just us girls. Besides, you're just tired. Everyone's a little loose-lipped when they're tired. And, as you said, you're probably coming down with the flu."

Sasha gestured to the teapot. "Unless you spiked the tea to liven up the meeting." She smiled half-heartedly at the Headmistress, trying to diffuse the horror of the situation. But then she remembered Mrs. Landshome and her flask and wondered if the old woman had passed the tea trolley on her way home.

Headmistress Dean's eyes widened for a moment, and then she laughed. "Oh, heavens, no—there's no need to spike the tea! I had Esther put a potion in your cookies."

At Sasha's shocked look, the older woman laughed even harder. "I'm joking, my dear. It's just a little joke we locals make. By now, I'm sure you've heard that the village has a history of witchcraft; you've been on the tour."

"Y-es," Sasha said, eying the cookies warily. "And Mason Barnes mentioned it on my first day. He said that all the women in Old Middleton were witches."

"Well, *that's* a stretch. Can you imagine me on a broomstick?" The Headmistress laughed again, clearly tickled by the idea. "Still, the witch-craft rumors keep the tourists coming, which is good for the village. Us locals usually make fun of it ... or play along." She offered the platter of cookies to Sasha. "Have another cookie. They're potion-free. Promise."

Sasha noticed the Headmistress's clean plate and untouched tea and frowned. "Aren't you having any?"

"I try not to eat between meals." The Headmistress placed a hand over her belt and sighed. "The problem with having an hourglass figure is that the sands *shift* over time, if you get my meaning. But that's not something you'll have to worry about for a long time. Go ahead and finish that cookie."

Sasha looked down and blinked. She was holding a cookie—a cookie that she could not remember picking up. She licked her lips, the taste of sugar and spice thick on her tongue and tried to focus past the fuzzy feeling that had settled over her mind like a fluffy blanket. "When did I pick up this cookie?"

The Headmistress blinked. "Why, just now. Don't you remember?"

Sasha most certainly did not remember. She looked down at the cookie, then at the Headmistress's concerned expression, and inwardly groaned. She was *definitely* coming down with the flu and making an absolute fool of herself in front of her new employer in the process.

"Right," she said with a tight smile. "Of course. Just now. Cookies."

She had to leave as soon as possible, she realized, before she started stealing the teacups or dancing on the desk.

Sasha placed the cookie in her jacket pocket as nonchalantly as possible and stood up.

"Well, on that note, I'd better go. Lyla is waiting for me by the old well on Main Street. We're going to buy food for dinner. I love cooking! I was planning to make—" She shook her head; she was babbling again. "It was a pleasure to meet you," she said firmly, "and I am sorry for—well, *every-thing* I said during this conversation. I'm not usually so ... so ..."

"So?"

"Flu-encrusted—I mean, *addled. Flu-addled.* Not encrusted. Or crusted. Or crusty." Sasha closed her eyes, mortified. "I'll just stop talking now."

The Headmistress pouted, her hand fluttering to her throat. "Oh, but we were just getting started! There's so much we still need to discuss. For instance, I'd like to learn more about this Todd fellow of yours."

The odd thing was that Sasha *did* want to keep talking—almost desperately so.

"He's no longer mine," she blurted. "He's dating an anthropologist. He 'accidentally' sent me a photo of them holding hands at some party. I think he wanted me to be jealous, but all I could think about was how manipulative he was being, and how that poor woman would now be subjected to Todd's subpar sexual—*I am so sorry!*" Sasha bit the inside of her cheek to stop herself from saying anything more.

I'm going to be fired, she thought, horrified, *and thrown out of the boarding house for demonstrating that I'm not a genteel young woman of unimpeachable reputation.*

Thankfully, the Headmistress only laughed. "Well, well. I *so* love girl talk! And I rarely get a chance to have it."

Sasha merely nodded, too afraid to open her mouth.

"Now ..." The Headmistress settled back into her chair. "Why not tell me about your hopes and dreams? Particularly your dreams."

"What dreams?" Sasha asked, before she could stop herself. "I haven't had a dream since I was five years old. But I threw two pennies into the well and wished—" Sasha pressed her hand against her mouth. "I have to go," she mumbled against her palm.

She turned on her heel and started walking toward the door.

The Headmistress stood up. "Are you absolutely certain that you want to leave, dear? Surely you want to tell me all about your hopes and *dreams*."

There was something about the way the Headmistress said the word *dreams*. It felt compelling, almost hypnotic.

Suddenly, Sasha could feel the glittery sands of her dreamscape beneath her feet.

She could feel the breeze on the hillside moving through her hair, carrying that spiced, burned honey scent.

Remember.

Remember.

Remember!

Sasha's eyes widened.

She remembered.

She remembered her dream!

She turned back in shock, her heart racing. The older woman was watching her carefully, the expression in her bright, blue eyes eager and knowing.

"You will find," the Headmistress said gently, "that I am an excellent listener."

Sasha opened her mouth to tell her everything … and stopped.

I'm making a terrible, terrible first impression, she realized with a sinking heart, *and talking about my dreams is only going to make it worse.*

She had to leave *now*.

"Lovely to meet you," she whispered, and turned toward the door, desperate to leave this nightmare of a meeting behind.

"Don't forget your folder!" Headmistress Dean called after her.

Sasha stopped. *Damn. Foiled by paperwork.*

She turned back and retrieved the folder, avoiding the Headmistress's gaze. "Thank you."

"Are you sure you don't want to talk about your *dreams?*"

Once again, the dream fragment flashed before Sasha's mind's eye, as clear as if she were back on the hill once more. She *had* to leave.

"Yes! *No!* Sorry! Gottagetdinner."

Sasha turned and hurried—as quickly as her light head would allow—out of the office, waving a sloppy goodbye over her shoulder to Esther as she went.

Then, with a deep breath, she made her way through the long halls and down the twisty staircases, out the grand entrance way, and through the ornate, wrought-iron gates until she found herself—to her great relief—in the parking lot.

As she fumbled with her car keys, she had the distinct impression that someone was watching her. She looked back at the imposing school building, but the windows were empty.

"Great, now I'm hallucinating," she muttered to herself. "Which means that I'm in no condition to drive." She patted the hood of her car. "Sorry, sweetie—you're staying here tonight."

Squaring her shoulders, she began the short walk to Main Street where Lyla, and lots of lovely flu medication, awaited.

~

"You owe me," Lyla called out, as Sasha approached the bench beside the old well. "And it's not because you're late—though, you are." Lyla put aside the book she had been reading and took off her reading glasses. "I've been here so long, I swear this bench and I have started to become one." She grimaced and wiggled on the hard seat.

"Sorry," Sasha said faintly, and sat carefully beside her friend.

"But I digress," Lyla continued, scooting over to give Sasha more room. "You owe me because I went to the library today and found out that Old Middleton *is* the single woman capital of America—adjusting for population size. Apparently, single women outnumber single men four to one. And I know what you're thinking: 'Those aren't *terrible* odds, Lyla! Surely, we have the upper-arm strength to each fight off three other women!'

"But, *no*—it gets worse. Eighty-six percent of those single men are over sixty-five. *Over sixty-five,* Sasha!" Lyla punctuated the point by poking the air vigorously with her glasses. "You've dragged me to a technology-free village in the Midwest where my only chance of scoring a date is during a field trip to a nursing home." She shook her head, her blonde ponytail swinging wildly behind her. "I don't care what Shae said—Old Middleton is *definitely* cursed.

Sasha rubbed her temples and waited patiently for Lyla to finish her rant.

"And before you say it," Lyla continued, "that isn't a rumor or an exaggeration; it's a *fact* based on government gathered statistics that were conveyed to me by a reputable source—a librarian, who just so happens to have blue hair. Not that I could verify this alleged fact. The library has the

Internet, but it's the Internet from 1998. It took fifteen minutes just to load the homepage. I swear I could feel my cells aging during the entire process."

Lyla placed her glasses back in their case, closing the lid with a *snap*. "Finally, I gave up. I was forced to resort to old-fashioned methods to research this place." She gestured to the book she was holding. "But, research it *I will*. Soon, all of Old Middleton's sordid secrets will be mine. You hear that?" She turned to a jack-o'-lantern sitting on the ground beside the bench. "All your secrets will soon be mine!"

The jack-o'-lantern looked up at Lyla with a gap-toothed grin, refusing to divulge a word.

Lyla *hmphed* and turned back to Sasha. "So, as I was saying—you owe me. Your next substitute teaching position had better be in a place where men outnumber women two hundred to one, and the Internet speed is off the charts. Which, now that I think of it, is probably Silicon Valley. Do they need substitute teachers in Silicon Valley? Or are all the classes taught by robots? Hold up ..." She peered more closely at Sasha. "You aren't speaking, you're rubbing your head, and there is a slice of cucumber on your chest." Lyla peeled the wayward sandwich filling off Sasha's dress and flicked it onto the ground. "Are you okay?"

Sasha looked down at the cucumber and groaned. "No. Not really. I think I'm coming down with the flu. There's one going around the school."

Lyla slowly sidled away from her. "There's always a flu going around the school; children are ridiculously diseased. How do you feel?"

"Strange. A little lightheaded. But the worst bit is that I seem to have no control over my mouth." Sasha groaned and covered her face with her hands. "I made the worst impression on the Headmistress. I wouldn't be surprised if she fired me overnight."

Lyla marked her place in the library book and closed it. "Why? What could you have possibly said?"

"I told her that the sex between Todd and I was terrible."

Lyla dropped the book onto the pavement.

"*See?!*" Sasha stared down at the book and shook her head in disbelief. "I can't believe I said that to you in *public*. I was going to wait until we got back to the boarding house."

Lyla's expression was an unholy mix of horror and glee. "Wait ... You told the Headmistress—your *new boss*—that the sex between you and Todd was terrible?" She blinked. "Hang on—the sex between you and Todd was terrible? ... Actually, that doesn't really surprise me. He was such an earnest do-gooder, wasn't he? *And* he had a terrible sense of direction.

Frankly, neither of those qualities bodes well for a wild and fulfilling sex life. Plus, *Todd* is hardly the name of a sex god, is it? It's so brief, so bland, so lacking in vowels—"

"Lyla, please focus. I need your help. First, with the flu. Then, with fixing the mess I made because of the flu."

"Don't worry—we've got this." Gingerly, Lyla laid her hand against Sasha's forehead. "You don't feel warm." She snatched her hand back and wiped it on her jeans.

Sasha rolled her eyes. "It's the flu, not a flesh-eating virus."

"As far as you know." Lyla pursed her lips thoughtfully. "Maybe you're just hungry. Low blood sugar can make you feel lightheaded."

"Does it also make you share sex secrets with your boss?"

"Maybe. Who knows? The human body is a complex organism."

Sasha wished that the answer to her dilemma was something as simple as low blood sugar. "No. I just ate. The Headmistress gave me afternoon tea with cookies and sandwiches."

"*Pfft*—that's just sugar and cucumbers. What you need is something substantial, like a steak." Lyla stood up from the bench and offered Sasha her hand. "Let's get you a steak; it'll give you the energy to fight your flu."

Sasha took Lyla's hand. "The Headmistress said that tea was good for the flu."

"Tea drinkers tell such lies. It's a cult, I tell you." Lyla helped Sasha to her feet and picked up her library book. "You know what's also good for the flu? Rum. Lots of lovely rum. We'll get you some steak and some rum, and you'll be back to your old self again."

"Sure, if I was originally a pirate." Sasha allowed Lyla to lead her down the street. "Just get me some cold and flu medication, okay?"

Lyla steered her toward the grocer and ushered her through the door. "Fine, fine. All the drugs you want—after your steak and rum."

Exactly four minutes after entering, Sasha and Lyla hurried out of the store, Sasha's hand firmly over her mouth.

"Well," Lyla said, blinking, "that was an interesting conversational gambit on your part."

"I am *so sorry!*" Sasha cried out from behind her palm.

Lyla glanced back at the shop. "I guess we won't be buying food from there today. Or any other day when the man in the green sweater is working."

Sasha removed her hand from her mouth. "That poor old man. He looked so devastated."

"It's his fault for asking your opinion about his sweater. Which, for the record, *did* look as though it was made out of moldy lettuce. But I guess he didn't expect someone to tell him that in so many words."

Sasha also glanced back towards the shop, utterly mortified. Through the window, she could see the man in the green sweater staring back at her. He shook his head at Sasha disapprovingly.

"See what I mean?" Sasha wailed. "I keep saying inappropriate things! I can't stop myself." She lifted her chin. "I'm going to march back over there and apologize again." But before she could even step toward the store, Lyla grabbed her arm and dragged her away.

"You've already said sorry—a lot. He needs time to heal ... and possibly rethink his fashion choices."

"But we won't be able to shop there again!"

"Sure, we will," Lyla said, her tone soothing. "Tomorrow, I'll explain to the nice, fashion-challenged man that you were drunk. Or delirious. See? Problem solved. Let's buy some bread and cheese and have sandwiches for dinner tonight, okay?"

"Fine," Sasha sighed, as Lyla led them into the bakery.

Precisely nine minutes later, Sasha and Lyla ran out of the store, Sasha's hand clamped over her mouth like a vice.

"Wow," Lyla said, staring at Sasha. "I always thought that small talk was bland and overrated, but you just elevated it to strange and spicy heights."

"What's *wrong* with me?" Sasha wailed from behind her palm. "We can never return. Ever. *Ever.*"

"It's true—we may have to swear off carbs for the rest of the trip. But, for the record, the baker seemed genuinely amused while you recounted your lackluster sexual adventures with Todd."

Sasha groaned.

"Though, he *was* a little taken aback by the hand gestures you were using to illustrate your points. I guess he'll think twice about asking people about their day in the future."

Sasha shook her head frantically. "I've traumatized that nice man! Not to mention his poor customers: they were in there for baked goods, and I gave them sex charades."

"It was a nice bonus for them."

Sasha's eyes widened. "Oh, no. Those sweet, old ladies from the florist shop were there! What must they think of me after what I said? *After the sex charades?*"

Lyla shrugged. "They probably think you're very flexible."

"You're not helping, Lyla!"

"It's not as bad as you think." Lyla linked arms with Sasha and led her friend over to the bench, where she helped her take a seat. "Everyone in that shop was an adult. Odds are that they've all done far more sexually deviant things than what you were explaining. Well, maybe not that nun..."

"*Agh!*" Sasha cried and buried her head in her hands. "When word of this gets out, I'm going to get fired. I'm supposed to be a role model, a pillar of the community, an educator—"

"And what you said was very educational. Even I learned a thing or two."

"I'm *so* fired."

At that moment, Daisy and Violet walked by their bench.

"Ladies," the twins said, with sly, matching smiles.

"Ladies," Lyla responded with a prim nod.

Sasha looked up and gamely tried to smile at the florists but gave up as soon as they passed.

Abruptly, Daisy turned back and gave Sasha a thumbs-up. She then quickly walked off with her sister, both ladies giggling madly.

"See?" Lyla said. "All good. Daisy approves of your deviant display."

"Hey!" a voice called from behind them.

Sasha and Lyla turned to find Ellie hurrying toward them, a white paper bakery bag in her hand.

"Here," she said, giving the bag to Sasha. "On the house. It looks like you're having a bad day."

Sasha cringed. "I am so, so sorry—"

"Are you kidding?" Ellie grinned. "That's the most fun I've ever had in the bakery. Visit us any time ... especially when I'm working."

"Ah ... thanks?"

Ellie winked at the women and ran back to the store.

"Thank you!" Lyla called after her. She took the bag from Sasha and peered inside. "Your sex charades just scored us free pastries. And you thought nothing good would come of them ..."

Sasha buried her face in her hands and attempted to merge with the bench. "We are never visiting the bakery, ever again." She looked up at her friend from between her fingers. "Could you please go and get me some flu medication? I can't trust myself to speak to strangers."

"Sure." Lyla handed her the pastry bag. "And after that, let's go home. Surely Martha has something in her pantry that we can borrow for dinner. Gruel, perhaps. Miss Adeline looks like the type who would enjoy a meagre bowl of gruel."

Sasha's shoulders sagged in relief. "Thanks."

"Don't mention it. You just stay here and relax."

Lyla began to leave, but then stopped abruptly.

"You know ..." She tilted her head, looking closely at her friend. "You don't look as though you have the flu. You're not flushed, you're not sneezing or coughing, and you don't have a temperature. You're pale, but you're always pale, so even that's normal. You're just lightheaded and can't stop telling people what you think. That doesn't sound like the flu to me."

"No? What does it sound like?"

"Me, actually. I'm like that most of the time. In fact, it sounds like you have a terrible case of *bluntness*. But given that bluntness is not a recognized medical disorder ..." Lyla shrugged. "I have no idea what's wrong with you. You're not acting like yourself, that's for sure. But the flu?" She shook her head, clearly puzzled. "I don't think so."

Sasha leaned back against the bench and sighed. "Maybe ... maybe I'm just tired. All the packing and driving and worrying—maybe it's all caught up with me."

"No." Lyla sat down beside her. "I know you. When you're tired, you speak slowly, you forget your keys, you buy bourbon instead of milk—" At Sasha's incredulous look, she shrugged. "Okay, that was me—*I* bought bourbon instead of milk the last time I was tired. But, you—even if *you* were tired, you'd never tell your new boss about your dismal sex life with your ex-boyfriend, even if the topic of discussion was Dismal-Sex-I've-Had-With-Ex-Boyfriends. Or chastise elderly grocers for their poor sweater choices—not *you*, Miss Congeniality. And you certainly wouldn't perform sex charades for a baker and a sister of the church ... well, not while sober. You're far too concerned about your professional reputation. When did this all start?"

Sasha rubbed her eyes with the heels of her hands and tried to pinpoint the exact second when everything had gone terribly wrong.

"During my meeting with the Headmistress," she said eventually, "while we were having afternoon tea. Speaking of which—I need something to get the taste of that tea out of my mouth." She opened her handbag and began to rummage around for her gum.

Lyla stilled. "What kind of taste?"

"Some kind of spice. Cinnamon? Nutmeg, maybe? I don't know." Sasha reached further into her bag, pushing aside her wallet and a few loose graphite pencils, wincing as the edge of her day planner poked the back of her hand. "I can't figure out if it was in the tea or the cookies. I don't think it was in the sandwiches—oh! Here it is." She took a stick of gum and offered the pack to Lyla. "Do you want some?"

Lyla ignored the pack and simply stared at her. "Why don't you tell me all about your afternoon tea with the Headmistress."

"Okay," Sasha said, slightly unnerved by Lyla's sudden seriousness. She chewed her gum and thought back to her meeting. "The first part was just business—lesson plans, and so forth."

"Hang on—were you lightheaded before you went into the meeting?"

"No ... though, I was tired. And I thought I was getting a headache."

"Were you saying strange things before the meeting?"

"No." Sasha shuddered, thankful that she had not spoken her mind during Mason Barnes's quest for goldfish liberation.

"Okay. What happened next—after the business stuff?"

"Esther came in with afternoon tea, and the Headmistress started to ask questions about my life—about my family and friends." Sasha frowned, remembering the conversation. "She was surprised that I had so many people in my life. Most substitutes only take this job because they don't have many ties. Oh! That's right—she told me to bring you to afternoon tea."

"Why?"

"Because you're a quasi-friendless orphan and—*oh, my GOD.* I am so, so sorry, Lyla!" Sasha reached over and grabbed her friend's hand, completely mortified. "So, so *sorry!*"

Lyla shrugged. "Why? That's a succinct and accurate summary of my life—and it's also something that you would never say to me. Which is both interesting and worrying."

I'm so sorry, Sasha mouthed, too scared to speak it aloud.

"Stop worrying about me. You're the one going through an Ordeal." Lyla squeezed her hand. "What else happened during afternoon tea?"

Sasha cringed. "I babbled on and on about nothing. After I mentioned Todd again, I tried to leave."

"Did she try to stop you?"

"Yes! How did you know? She wanted me to stay and chat. And the weird thing was that *I* wanted to stay and chat. I wanted to tell her all about my life. But I was too worried about what I was going to say next, so I left. Do you think I had an allergic reaction to something I ate or drank?" Sasha grimaced. "I can *still* taste the spice, even with the gum. Could I be allergic to the spice?"

Lyla shook her head. "An allergy wouldn't make you say strange things; it would make you break out in hives or make your tongue swell. Did the Headmistress drink or eat the afternoon tea?"

"No. She was watching her figure."

"Ha! A likely story! I *knew* this place was nefarious." Lyla took Sasha by the shoulders and turned her until they were face to face. "This is going to sound preposterous, but I think she put something in your tea."

Sasha stared at her friend incredulously. "Are you *nuts?*"

"I know, I know—it sounds crazy. And yet, here we are, sitting on a bench after running away from a bakery thanks to your lewd finger puppetry."

"But—" Sasha stopped abruptly, a memory trying to make its way through her mental haze. "You know ... when I started to say all those strange things, I asked the Headmistress if the tea had been spiked. And she laughed and said that she'd ordered Esther to put a potion in my cookie."

Lyla's eyes widened. "You mean, she admitted to drugging you?!"

"No." Sasha shook her head. "She was joking. She said it was a common joke around here ... because of the witchcraft rumors."

Lyla raised an eyebrow. "They casually joke about drugging women around here?"

"Yes?" Sasha threw back her head and groaned. "I don't know. What I *do* know is that it's highly unlikely that my new employer drugged me during a routine first meeting. I can't believe that she would do that."

"Would it be more believable if she'd drugged you during your second meeting?"

"Don't be pedantic. What I mean is that there's no reason for her to drug me. What would she gain from it?"

Lyla dropped her hands from Sasha's shoulders and sat back against the bench. "Give me a minute, and I'll think of something appropriately shifty." She drummed her fingers against the armrest. "If only we had some of that tea, we could test it out ..."

"I don't have the tea. But"—Sasha reached into her pocket—"I kept a cookie."

Lyla's eyes lit up. "You kept a spiked cookie? Way to think on your feet during a potential drugging!"

Sasha looked down at the little sugar cookie sitting innocently in the palm of her hand. "We don't know that it's spiked."

"Exactly! That's why we need to test it."

Before Sasha could stop her, Lyla snatched up the cookie and popped it into her mouth.

"Are you *nuts?*" Sasha screeched. "What if it *is* spiked? After I ate a cookie just like that one, I said terrible, secret sex things to strangers. I don't want that happening to you."

Lyla swallowed the remains of the cookie. "I say terrible secret sex things to strangers all the time. That's pretty much my way of meeting people."

"But you're not a guinea pig. We should have taken the cookie to be analyzed."

"Where? In the forensic lab in the basement of the boarding house? Or the CIA lab down the street?"

Sasha groaned. "We can't have it analyzed, can we? What was I thinking?"

"You, young lady, have been watching too many crime shows on prime-time television."

"You're right. I hate it when television gives me false expectations of reality." Sasha stared at Lyla, looking for any outward signs of cookie spiking. "Are you feeling anything?"

Lyla frowned. "Nothing. How long did it take to work on you?"

"Assuming that the cookie *was* spiked? Not long."

"Let's give it a little while longer."

They sat back and waited.

"Anything?" Sasha asked five minutes later.

Lyla shook her head. "Maybe I ate the placebo cookie."

Sasha sighed, both disappointed and relieved. Disappointed, because she still did not know the cause of her behavior. Relieved, because at least her new employer was not a substitute teacher-drugging psychopath.

"But," Lyla said, "I'm not experiencing a weird aftertaste. It's just a sugar cookie—no spice. I think the tea was the culprit, which means we're off to the doctor." She stood up. "We can't test the cookie, but we can test *you*."

"What?" Sasha asked, as Lyla hauled her to her feet. "*I'm* getting tested?"

"Yes. For drugs. For the flu. For everything." Lyla looked around the street. "Where did you park?"

"At school. I didn't trust myself to drive."

Lyla's face lit up. "Which means I get to drive."

"No," Sasha said, shaking her head slowly. "You're not driving my car."

"Oh, relax—it'll be fine."

"You've had an accident almost every time you've gotten behind the wheel."

"Yes, but they're usually small ones."

"You knocked over your mailbox. Twice."

"It provoked me."

Sasha rolled her eyes. "Please, can we take a cab?"

"Have you seen any cabs in Old Middleton? I haven't. And I don't think the trolley goes all the way to the medical center."

Sasha's shoulders slumped in defeat. "Fine. But drive slowly, and if I say pull over, pull over."

Lyla rubbed her hands together gleefully. "This truly is a day when dreams come true."

Dreams.

Sasha stopped and grabbed Lyla's arm. "Wait." Amidst the bakery and the sweater dramas, she had forgotten to tell Lyla about her dream. "There may be something else going on here."

"What do you mean?"

"I had a dream, Lyla! *A dream!* Well, two dreams, actually. Last night and the night before."

Lyla's eyes widened. "Are you sure? The other day you said you didn't—"

Sasha nodded frantically. "Yes, I know what I said. I *did* dream, but I kept forgetting them. The Headmistress asked me about my dreams and the way she said it ..." She closed her eyes, hearing the Headmistress's voice.

Why not tell me about your hopes and dreams? Particularly your dreams.

She opened her eyes. "I remembered."

"But—but that's wonderful!" Lyla drew Sasha into a fierce hug. "Congratulations! And what was this twenty-five-years-in-the-making dream of yours?"

Sasha opened her mouth to tell her ... but there was nothing to say. The dream memory had disappeared once more.

"*Agh,* I can't believe this!" Sasha buried her face against Lyla's shoulder. "I can't remember. Every time I try ... it ... it disappears." She lifted her head and looked Lyla in the eye. "But I *did* dream. And, for a moment— when I was with the Headmistress—I could remember it all."

Lyla patted her on the back. "Don't worry. It'll come back to you. Just let it go for now."

"But, don't you see, Lyla? Maybe the lightheadedness, the babbling— what if it isn't a drug or the flu? What if there is something wrong with me? With my brain?"

"Then we'll get it fixed," Lyla said firmly. She released Sasha and took her arm. "Come on—we're off to the doctor. The doctor will have all the answers."

~

"I CAN'T BELIEVE THAT THE DOCTOR HAD NO ANSWERS," LYLA SAID TWO hours later, as she closed the door of the Old Middleton Medical Center behind them and headed for the car. "It was all so anticlimactic."

"How could you say that?" Sasha asked. "She gave me a clean bill of health. That's not anticlimactic at all. That's the best possible scenario!"

"Technically, that's true. But it answers none of our questions. Your drug test was negative—"

"Which is a good thing."

"—but they only tested you for a limited number of drugs. What if the Headmistress used something that wasn't on the list? Which, incidentally, is what *I* would do if I were a Headmistress hell-bent on drugging my substitute teachers."

"I'm sure the education system is heaving a sigh of relief that you aren't planning on becoming a Headmistress."

"Never say never." Lyla pulled the car keys from her pocket. "Let's get back on topic. Apparently, you don't have a concussion—"

"*Also* a good thing."

"—but we won't know if your brain is truly broken unless you have an MRI—"

Sasha snorted. "Thanks for putting it so colorfully."

"—which the doctor thought was unnecessary—"

"Because I had no other symptoms, except the dreams—"

"And she had no idea what to make of that. So, her only explanation for your adventures was exhaustion, which I don't buy."

"Only because you want it to be something more exciting. Here, give me the keys." Sasha held out her hand.

Lyla clutched the keys possessively to her chest. "No way. You feel light-headed, remember?"

Sasha blinked. "Not anymore. I feel fine."

And she did. Somewhere between the bench and the waiting room, Sasha had begun to feel more like herself. The world, which had felt muddled before, was now sharply in focus. She was back in control and so incredibly relieved that she almost felt like crying.

Lyla peered at her closely. "Do you really feel fine? Or are you just terrified of my driving?"

"Both." Sasha grinned. "But mostly, I feel fine. No lightheadedness."

"No desire to blurt out fashion tips or sex secrets?"

"None. Thank goodness."

Lyla frowned. "Come to think of it, you didn't say anything strange or crotch-related in the doctor's office."

"That's true." Sasha thought back over their time in the waiting room. "I started feeling better about an hour ago." Even the strange taste in her mouth had faded away.

"Huh." Lyla's eyes narrowed. "Let's see."

Without warning, Lyla threw the car keys at Sasha, who snatched them effortlessly in mid-air.

Lyla whistled. "Nothing wrong with your reflexes."

"Told you!" Sasha said gaily, as she opened the door and climbed into the car. "Now, let's get something to eat before I pass out from hunger."

Lyla paused, her hand on her seatbelt. "But—"

"We can puzzle this out in the restaurant."

"Okay," Lyla said. She stretched out her seatbelt and clicked it in place. "It's a plan. And on the way, you can tell me more about the terrible sex between you and Todd. I refuse to know less than the baker."

"Deal," Sasha said and started the car.

"Let's sum up," Lyla said, tossing the remains of her pizza crust onto her plate. "After consuming afternoon tea with the Headmistress, you began to make inappropriate comments, and spilled deep, dark sex secrets—"

"I don't think they qualify as either deep or dark," Sasha interrupted.

"True. Let's amend that: After you consumed afternoon tea, you spilled shallow, beige sex secrets—"

Sasha rolled her eyes.

"—to strangers. However, your drug test was negative … for the limited set of drugs tested. And whatever caused your behavior—whether flu, drugs, or exhaustion—wore off within two hours. Which leads us to where we are now"—she gestured to the center of the table, where an electric candle jutted proudly from the stem of a raffia-covered *chianti* bottle —"eating pizza by candlelight in an Italian restaurant that appears to have been decorated sometime in the seventies and never touched again."

It was true. Luigi's Pizzarama was a shrine to seventies-era, Italian restaurant décor. Luigi himself had selected the wine-bottle centerpieces, the cheery, red and white checked tablecloths (made of the best quality plastic that money could buy), the maps of Italy that hung on the exposed brick walls, and the saucy photograph of an Italian starlet that he had personally taped to the cash register. His decorative flair had culminated in the ceiling, where bunches of fat, purple plastic grapes hung festively above the heads of his patrons, scattered amongst fairy lights and waxy, green vines.

It was like eating in a plastic vineyard.

"I like it here," Sasha said, looking up at the grapes. "Though, I'm not sure about the music."

The women turned toward a small stage at the back corner of the restaurant where a four-piece band—*Polka Fever*—was vigorously playing original polka compositions at a volume that required you to scream politely at your dinner companion.

"Agreed," Lyla said. "I have nothing against polka music, but I don't think it's good for one's digestion. To return to the matter at hand, I think we need to acknowledge a few truths. As strange—and as unlikely—as it may be, we have to seriously consider the possibility that the Headmistress drugged you."

Sasha picked up her red plastic cup, stalling for time. At Lyla's pointed glance, she sighed. "It seems so implausible."

"It does. But it's the only explanation that truly fits the evidence." Lyla tilted her head, watching her friend closely. "I know you don't want to admit it."

Sasha took a long, slow sip of her soda. Lyla was right: she was not ready to acknowledge the possibility aloud, even if it appeared to be the most likely scenario.

The consequences would be devastating.

Lyla's eyes narrowed. "I know that you're trying to stall for time by taking the longest sip of soda ever consumed by a human—"

Sasha defiantly kept sipping.

"—but it may help if you say it aloud. Go on. Say it. Say—"

Polka Fever triumphantly played their final note.

"—the Headmistress of Old Middleton Elementary is a drink-spiking psychopath," Lyla yelled into the sudden silence.

Sasha spat her soda across the table.

For one excruciating moment, everyone around them appeared frozen in time, Lyla's words echoing boldly across the restaurant.

Then, everyone moved at once. The band members lowered their instruments and stared at Lyla in disbelief; the diners turned toward the two women, their forks suspended halfway to their mouths; and Luigi himself stood up from his chair behind the cash register to get a better look at Lyla, the ends of his bushy mustache twitching incredulously. Even the saucy Italian starlet appeared to be staring at Lyla, her pout now more shocked than sultry.

"…is the name of my death metal band," Lyla improvised gamely.

An awkward silence ensued.

The leader of *Polka Fever* cleared his throat. "A shout out to a fellow band, *The Headmistress of Old Middleton Elementary is a Drink-Spiking Psychopath.* Can't wait to hear your work." He nodded politely to Lyla. Sasha covered her face with her hands. "Our next song is called 'Goat Whisperer.' "

The music began once more. The diners slowly returned to their plates of pizza and pasta, and Luigi went back to counting his money. The sultry starlet, however, continued to watch Lyla suspiciously from her frame.

"I don't think I can handle running away from another shop today," Sasha said, wiping her mouth with her napkin. "And I *really* like this place."

"It'll be fine." Lyla passed her another napkin. "The rollicking strains of 'Goat Whisperer' will purge the incident from everyone's mind."

Sasha stopped cleaning and listened. She winced. "You're probably right."

"So, stop avoiding the subject—what do you think?"

Sasha dabbed soda off the tablecloth, again stalling for time. Part of her wanted to believe that her adventures today were due to exhaustion and put it all behind her. The other part—the more suspicious part—knew that her behavior had nothing to do with exhaustion and wanted to solve this mystery … even if it meant fleeing from a possibly psychotic Headmistress in the dead of night.

The suspicious part won.

"Right." Sasha balled-up her wet napkin and placed it on her plate. "Let's just say—for the sake of argument—that I *was* drugged by the Headmistress—"

"Excellent start," Lyla encouraged.

"Why did she do it?" Lyla opened her mouth to respond, but Sasha raised her hand, stopping her. "And don't tell me that she's the head of a drug syndicate or a human trafficking ring—"

"But all those missing substitute teachers!"

"Let's be realistic."

"Fine," Lyla huffed. "But those are two of my best explanations." She took a sip of her drink, her expression thoughtful. "Okay. What if she drugged you as a way of getting past your self-presentation tactics?"

"What do you mean?"

"I mean, what if she drugged you to find out the *real* you? You wouldn't be able to lie or put up a professional front. You'd be your true self."

"So … she drugged me as a way of finding out what I was really like?"

Lyla nodded. "Maybe she justifies it by thinking that she's protecting her students from unscrupulous characters."

"I … *guess* that's possible." Sasha thought back over her meeting, remembering the sweet, older woman who listened to her so avidly. "Or it could have been an accident."

"Accident? How can you drug someone by accident?"

"It could have been a bad batch of tea. The Headmistress said that a friend of hers blends it especially for her. Maybe the herbs were off, or moldy, or contaminated …"

Lyla studied her friend. "Okay. We'll consider that explanation—especially if it makes you feel better about pursuing the 'you were drugged' line of argument."

"It does." *Please be an accident,* Sasha thought desperately.

"Something you're not considering is that *Esther* prepared the afternoon tea. So, *she* would have been the one to put the drug—or potion, in the Headmistress's own words—into your tea."

Sasha's eyes widened. "I didn't think of that."

"Well, you're lucky I'm here to do your thinking for you. Esther may have worked alone." Lyla leaned over the table, beckoning Sasha to do the same until their foreheads were almost touching.

"Or, they may be in it together," she whispered. "It could be a school-wide conspiracy!"

Sasha groaned. "This is sounding more and more ludicrous by the minute."

Lyla leaned back, her attention caught by something behind Sasha's back. "You know, I'm not sure *why* the Headmistress and … or … Esther drugged your tea, but I think I know someone who can tell us *how*. Hey!" she called out. "Teenage males!"

Sasha turned around. There at the counter, collecting a stack of pizzas, were the two black-clad teenagers from the Twilight Tour.

"Teenage males?" Sasha shook her head. "Their names are Travis and Lucas."

"That's right! Hey, Travis! Lucas!" Lyla called out, waving. "Remember us?"

"Yeah!" Travis said, coming over to their table. "I remember you."

"It's the double-penny wish woman!" Lucas said, following close behind.

"I like that," Lyla said. "I'm going to get that put on a t-shirt." She gave the teenagers a bright smile. "We noticed during the tour that you guys seemed to be experts on all the witchy goings-on in this town."

The teenagers puffed out their chests, proudly.

"It's in our best interests," Travis said.

"We don't want to leave or disappear once we're of marriageable age," Lucas added. He shrugged. "Whenever that is."

"The average marrying age for men in Wisconsin is twenty-nine," Lyla said. "So, you guys have plenty of time."

The teenagers grinned widely. "*Awesome*."

Sasha stared at her friend. "How do you know the average marrying age for men in Wisconsin off the top of your head?"

Lyla shrugged. "I dated a guy from Wisconsin once, remember? Bob? John?"

"Sebastian," Sasha said, shaking her head.

"Right! *Sebastian*. He was a Wisconsin trivia buff. I also know that Wisconsin banned the use and production of yellow-colored margarine from 1895 to 1967."

"We don't take kindly to non-dairy spreads around here," Lucas said.

"They're imposters," Travis added. "Why not just eat butter?"

"Fair point," Sasha said.

"Speaking of strange things to ingest," Lyla began, "we were wondering about the potions you mentioned during the tour—the ones from the spell shop. Have you ever tried any?"

The boys shook their heads.

"Rosa has a strict 'over twenty-one' potion purchasing policy," Travis said.

"Plus, she says they're for novelty use only," Lucas added, pushing his fringe from his eyes.

"Which means?" Sasha asked.

"That they don't work," Lucas said. "She says they're just for the tourists."

"Oh," Sasha and Lyla said, deflating.

"But ..." Travis looked furtively around the restaurant and then beckoned them closer.

Sasha and Lyla exchanged looks and leaned forward.

"Rumor has it," Travis whispered, "that last year, someone spiked the punch with one of Rosa's potions at the Senior Prom down at Fitchburg High."

"What kind of potion?" Sasha whispered back.

Lucas quickly scanned the room again before leaning toward the two women. "A *truth* potion."

Sasha kicked Lyla's foot under the table.

"Truth potion, huh?" Lyla asked nonchalantly.

"And what happened?" Sasha asked less nonchalantly.

"Everyone started telling each other what they *really* thought about each other," Travis said. "You know—all their secrets."

"Lots of fights broke out," Lucas said.

"And then a fire," Travis added. He shook his head. "Poor Fitchburg High."

"Poor Fitchburg High," Lucas echoed.

Lyla's eyes narrowed. "Are you sure they didn't just spike the punch with alcohol? Because all that chaos is pretty typical when kids drink alcohol. Or when I drink alcohol."

"True," Sasha said.

The teenagers shook their heads.

"Truth potion," they said, simultaneously.

"Fair enough," Lyla said. "Thanks a lot, guys."

"Anytime," Travis said.

"We're happy to answer all your occult-oriented questions," Lucas added.

"Nice boys," Lyla mused, as she watched the teenagers leave the store with their pizzas. She turned back to Sasha. "Uncontrollable truth-telling, hey? Sounds familiar."

Sasha nodded slowly. "It does." She pulled a few dollars out of her wallet. "Are you up for a fact-finding mission?"

"Of the occult variety?"

Sasha placed her money on the table. "Yes."

Lyla picked up her napkin and quickly wiped her hands. "Let's do this!" she cried, slamming her napkin onto the table. She looked down at the crumpled paper ball and frowned. "Possibly with a little less aggression."

"Yes," Sasha said, looking at the napkin. "Let's keep this civilized."

5

THE SECRETS OF STARDUST AND BRIMSTONE

"As much as I like fact-finding missions," Lyla whispered to Sasha, "remind me to plan a fireman-finding mission or a male-stripper-finding mission for the future. Facts are great, but they don't have abs."

The two women were standing in the book section of Stardust and Brimstone, trying very hard to act casual. At any other time, Sasha would have been excited to explore a self-proclaimed occult shop, particularly late on a suitably spooky October night. She would have been delighted by the shadowy, candle-lit corners and the glowing crystal orbs tucked amongst smudge sticks and sleek, black feathers. She would have exclaimed over the fragrant bunches of dried flowers and herbs hanging from the rafters amidst glittering fairy lights; and pored over the glass cabinets filled with silver charms—perfect replicas of foxes and wolves, ravens and stars—and chunks of purple amethyst as big as her fist.

But she was here on a mission; her attention was focused solely on the mason jars filled with powders that lined the shelves, and the bottles of potions stacked neatly around the counter. The moment she entered the shop, she *knew* they were in the right place; the smell of herbs and the sweet, cloying scent of spices that perfumed the air reminded her of the aftertaste of the afternoon tea.

Sasha grabbed Lyla's sweater and pulled her down behind a bookshelf.

"If this goes well, I will happily join you on an ab-quest," she whispered. "But right now, I need you to ask Rosa about the truth potion."

Sasha peeked over the shelf and looked toward the counter. A woman

—Rosa, she assumed—was polishing a crystal ball with a red felt cloth and talking animatedly to another customer. Rosa, Lyla had been happy to note, looked the part of an occult store owner. She wore a turquoise silk caftan that floated around her like ocean spray as she moved. Her silver streaked, black hair was gathered into a thick braid and decorated with tiny, silver star clips and turquoise ribbon. Bracelets studded with semi-precious stones in a riot of colors were entwined around her wrists, and several rings set with gemstones—fiery opals as big as quarters, bubblegum pink tourmaline, and peach colored moonstone—glittered madly in the candlelight whenever she moved her hands. She was radiant and mysterious ... and completely oblivious to the fact that two women were plotting against her in the 'Spirit Guides and You' section of her store.

At least Sasha hoped that she was completely oblivious.

"The quicker you go, the quicker we get to the bottom of this," Sasha whispered to Lyla, wanting the whole matter over and done.

"Got it," Lyla whispered back, removing herself from Sasha's grasp. "Are you sure that *I* should be the one to talk to Rosa?"

"Yes. Because she might be in on the conspiracy to drug me." Sasha cringed. "Wow, that sounds paranoid. And a little insane. And also, a little narcissistic."

"Yes. Yes, it does. Lucky for you, I'm a psychologist, so I'm qualified to deal with all three. Well, I will be ... assuming that I ever get my thesis submitted, but let's never speak of that again." Lyla cracked her knuckles. "Stay here. I'm going in."

"Act natural!" Sasha hissed, as Lyla sauntered in an unnatural fashion toward the counter.

Sasha stood up slowly and pretended to browse the books around her, making sure to keep the counter in her line of sight. She picked up the closest book, opened it to a random page, and stealthily peered over the top. Lyla was standing at the counter, scanning the rows of potions and pills, while Rosa finished packing the crystal ball for the other customer.

Suddenly, Rosa looked up and caught Sasha's eye. Panicked, Sasha ducked behind her book, picked a place on the page at random and began to read.

"... in some cases, a dream may be a portal to the mind—a manifestation of our fears and insecurities. In others, a dream may be a message—a portent of things to come ..."

Sasha frowned. "This seems too coincidental. Are you trying to tell me something?" she asked the book.

The book, unsurprisingly, was silent. Nevertheless, Sasha quickly scanned the rest of the page, hoping to find something that related to her recent dream experiences.

"May I help you?" a woman's voice asked from directly behind her.

Sasha jumped and dropped the book. "Ah … no. I'm just browsing. And dropping, apparently—I'm so sorry about that." She bent down to retrieve the fallen book. When she looked up, she found herself caught in Rosa's amused, brown-eyed gaze. "If it's damaged, I'll buy it."

"Oh, no—it's my fault for startling you. Here, let me …"

As Rosa reached for the book, her bracelet—a tangle of turquoise strands and chunks of rose quartz—fell away, revealing a delicate, white-ink tattoo on her inner wrist.

Sasha stared at the small, white triangle surrounded by two broken, concentric circles for a long moment before realizing that she had seen the same tattoo before—on Ellie, the baker's apprentice.

Not quite *the same,* Sasha amended, looking at the design more closely. In Rosa's tattoo, the triangle had been turned upside down and bisected neatly by a small, horizontal line.

How odd, she thought, *that two such different women would choose almost the same tattoo, and have it inked in white on the same wrist. Perhaps it's a popular design in Old Middle—*

Sasha's train of thought skidded to a halt. In the flickering shadows of the store, the tattoo suddenly began to move, to *ripple,* the circles appearing to spin around the triangle, while the entire design turned a glittering gold—

Rosa turned her wrist sharply and the bracelet fell back into place, covering the mark. "I'll put that away for you."

"Put what away?" Sasha mumbled, staring at the hint of gold beneath the blue and pink stones of Rosa's bracelet.

"*The book.*"

Sasha tore her gaze away from Rosa's wrist and shook her head, trying to clear the strange vision.

"Sorry," she said, handing Rosa the book. "And thanks."

To Sasha's dismay, Rosa simply studied her for a long moment, her expression thoughtful "Forgive me for saying so, but you look tired. Problematic dreams, right?"

Sasha stared at the woman in surprise. "How did you know?"

The shopkeeper held up Sasha's book: *Dreams and You.* "Call it a hunch."

"Oh." Sasha smiled weakly. "Right."

Rosa turned to the shelf and placed *Dreams and You* back where it belonged. "Many people who move here find that their dreams become a little fantastic in the beginning."

Any dream would be fantastic after living twenty-five years without one, Sasha thought to herself. "Why is that?" she asked instead.

"Some say that the energy of Old Middleton 'awakens' people to their True Self—to their purpose, their destiny. It's not surprising that their dreams become a little strange as a result."

Sasha raised an eyebrow. "What do other people say?"

The older woman smiled widely, the corners of her eyes creasing into small starbursts. "Others would say that any big move is a stressor, and dreams are the mind's way of dealing with this stress."

"That sounds more plausible."

"It does, doesn't it?" Rosa laughed, her teeth startlingly white against her olive skin. "You probably need some time to settle in. Give it a week—you'll be sleeping like a baby."

"How did you know that I was staying here—that I wasn't a tourist?" Sasha asked, following Rosa toward the front of the store.

"It's a small village, Sasha Pierce. A new teacher and her friend"—Rosa gave Lyla a cheery smile as she passed—"driving across the country in a shiny, red sports car is big news here. Everyone knows who you are."

"So much for anonymity," Lyla said, giving Sasha a meaningful look.

"Apparently so," Sasha muttered.

"This is the wrong place to be anonymous—for better or worse. So …" Rosa stepped behind the counter and leaned over the wooden surface. "What brings you ladies to my shop?"

"We heard about Stardust and Brimstone during the Twilight Tour," Sasha improvised.

Lyla nodded, playing along. "It comes highly recommended by Travis and Lucas."

Rosa laughed. "Lovely boys. They'll be running the Twilight Tours in a couple of years."

"I don't doubt it," Sasha said. "We were hoping to take home some potions. As souvenirs."

"Of course! Which ones?" Rosa gestured to the charming display of bottles and boxes arranged around the counter.

Lyla eyes lit up. "We'll take the lust potion, and the love potion—"

Sasha raised an eyebrow. "We will?"

"We're in a magical potion shop," Lyla said. "As if we wouldn't take the love and lust potions. Hang on, do they work?" she asked Rosa. "Will they give me the sensual charms I need to enthrall the masses?"

Sasha grinned. "You have those already."

Lyla patted Sasha's arm. "Thanks! But think of how much *more* enthralling I'll be with these potions!"

"That's not how potions work," Rosa said, as she picked out the potions from the display. "Potions—*real* potions—merely enhance pre-existing feelings. So, a lust potion will only enhance any lustful feelings you're already entertaining; it won't create them. Same with a love potion." She placed the bottles in a navy blue, paper bag printed with gold stars. "You can't use a potion to bend someone to your will unless that person *wants* to bend and is already in position—so to speak."

Lyla stared forlornly at the bag. "Well, that's disappointing. So much for turning all the men on earth into my love slaves. I guess I'll just have to go back to my original plan and take over the world using manipulation and strategic military coups."

Rosa picked up a green bottle. "May I suggest a luck potion?"

"Yes," Lyla said, delighted. "You may. I'll take it. And the potion that helps you do well in exams."

"Excellent choices." Rosa picked up a purple bottle and placed it in the bag.

"How does a truth potion work?" Sasha asked, spying the bottles of Truth Elixir beside the love potion. "Does it work like a love potion, where you can only tell the truth if you want to?"

Rosa shook her head. "No. A real truth potion contains ingredients like primrose, which promotes the disclosure of secrets. It'll work, even if you don't want to tell the truth."

"So … you would, what? Just … blurt out the truth?" Sasha asked.

"Well, there should be a little more finesse to it. A real truth potion will make you *want* to talk, and what you say will be what you truly think and feel. It will be from the heart."

Sasha's own heart sank. It sounded very much like her experiences. "Oh."

"You keep saying a *real* potion," Lyla said. "Aren't these real potions?"

Rosa looked around the shop. Seeing that her other customers were otherwise occupied, she leaned closer to the two women.

"No, not really," she said, her voice low. "They're watered down versions of the real thing. You'll get an inkling of what a real potion can do, but that's all. The placebo effect does the rest. Can you imagine the chaos if I sold real potions?" She paused for a moment, lost in thought. "Poor Fitchburg High …" she muttered finally, shaking her head, her long, black braid swinging behind her.

Sasha and Lyla exchanged a look.

"What happened at Fitchburg High?" Sasha asked.

Rosa blinked. "Oh—nothing. Nothing!" She cleared her throat and smiled politely. "Anything else?"

"We'll take the truth potion, too," Lyla said. "I'll use it in my quest for world domination."

"Watch out, world!" Rosa placed a bottle of Truth Elixir into the bag. "Now, this is the point in the transaction where I remind you of your ethical and moral responsibilities toward your fellow citizens. These potions are better when self-administered, to help you gain insight into your own thoughts and feelings. Do not use them on others without their consent."

The two women nodded solemnly.

"The directions are on the labels—make sure you use each potion as directed, especially the Truth Elixir. Just use four drops of that one."

"What happens if we use more than four drops?" Sasha asked.

"You'll probably hear something you don't really want to hear. Secrets are usually secret for a reason." Reaching under the counter, Rosa pulled out a small, navy blue silk pillow covered in stars. She waved it at Sasha. "Something to help you sleep?"

Sasha shook her head. "Thanks, but I don't need—"

"To help you dream, then. It's a full moon tonight—the perfect night to dream. Why not try it?"

The perfect night to dream. Sasha's heart gave an odd flutter. "Well then … I'll take it. Thanks."

Rosa placed it into the bag with the rest of the purchases. "Oh! Before I forget …" She pointed to a wooden bowl on the counter, filled with red and gold leaves. "Be sure to take an Elder leaf. They're wonderful protection talismans."

Sasha and Lyla eagerly took a leaf from the bowl. "Excellent," Lyla said, placing it in her wallet. "I wanted one of these."

Rosa handed Lyla the shopping bag, while Sasha placed a few notes on the counter.

"Let me know how it all works out for you," Rosa said, taking the money with a smile. "But in as little detail as possible when it comes to the lust potion." She made a face. "You'd be surprised by just how much information people are willing to share."

"Tell me about it," Lyla said, shaking her head. "You can't even go into a bakery nowadays without someone telling sordid tales. And don't even get me started on the sex charades ..."

Sasha glared at her friend. "We will keep our sordid doings to ourselves." Involuntarily, she glanced over at the Truth Elixir. "This time," she muttered under her breath.

Rosa smiled. "Good."

"Thanks for all your help," Sasha said as they headed for the door.

"Sweet dreams!" Rosa called after her.

Sasha paused. Unbidden, the image of her feet sinking into gold dust came to mind so vividly that she almost gasped.

"Let's hope so," she called over her shoulder.

"ROSA SEEMS NICE," SASHA SAID, AS SHE SAT DOWN ON HER BED, THE FRAME creaking loudly in welcome.

"Well, she didn't try to drug you, so she's officially the nicest person you've met here so far," Lyla said, sitting opposite on her bed.

"*Allegedly* drugged me. Let's give everyone the benefit of the doubt." Sasha looked over at the Stardust and Brimstone bag perched on Lyla's pillow. "Even if the evidence suggests otherwise."

"Goody two-shoes."

Sasha watched as Lyla unpacked their purchases, neatly lining up the bottles on her nightstand. "I can't believe that you wanted lust and love charms. What are you? Fifteen?"

"I *wish*. I was so thin back then."

Sasha looked at her petite friend's curves and rolled her eyes. "Please. Not after all the fuss you made in your teens about wanting cleavage."

Lyla laughed. "Point taken. I approve of my cleavage."

Sasha picked up the luck potion. "Maybe we should give the luck and exam potions to Travis and Lucas as a 'thank you' for helping us out."

"You're going to traffic potions to underage boys? I *so* approve. Though, hang on, Miss Rule-Stickler—what about Rosa's over-twenty-one potion policy?"

"I doubt they'll terrorize the village with placebo luck charms."

"You're right." Lyla placed the two luck potions back in the bag and pulled out the starry, blue dream pillow. "I believe this is yours?"

Sasha took the pillow from Lyla. She brought it to her nose and inhaled. "*Mmm*, this smells lovely." She took another deep breath. "Lavender and jasmine, maybe? Something minty, too. And ..." She took another sniff. "Something that smells like chai."

"Throw it to me." Lyla caught the pillow and brought it close to her nose. "Star anise, I think. And there's something that smells like pizza spice."

"That doesn't sound very mystical."

"But delicious smelling, nonetheless." Lyla tossed the pillow back to Sasha. "Are you going to use it?"

Sasha placed the pillow on her nightstand in between the figurines of the placid shepherdess and the cross-eyed cat. "After today's adventures, I'm a little hesitant to use a bunch of herbs given to me by a strange lady."

"Speaking of which ..." Lyla handed Sasha the Truth Elixir. "Smell this and see if it reminds you of your afternoon tea."

Sasha screwed open the lid of the innocuous little bottle and took a tentative sniff. "It smells similar." She carefully placed a drop of the elixir onto her fingertip and lifted it to her mouth.

Lyla watched on, bemused. "I give you an A-plus for commitment."

Sasha rolled the liquid around her mouth. "It tastes very, very similar to the afternoon tea." She turned the bottle around, trying to find a list of ingredients. "It's a pity it's Truth Elixir; it's quite tasty."

"Trust old ladies to drug you with something delicious."

"*Allegedly* drug," Sasha answered automatically. But she had to admit that the evidence was stacking up. She carefully replaced the lid on the bottle. "But it's not a *real* potion, remember? According to Rosa, these are just herbal placebos."

Lyla took the bottle from Sasha's hands. "There's only one way to find out."

〜

Eighteen minutes later, the two women sat at the kitchen table in Miss Adeline's mint-green, 1950s style kitchen, staring at Miss Adeline's third-best teapot. An empty teacup sat, waiting, beside it.

"Is it ready?" Sasha asked, peering into the teapot.

Lyla shrugged. "I have no idea. I've never made magical tea before. In fact, I've never made *tea* before. If you think about it, a teapot is just like a Japanese bathhouse for tea leaves. There they are, just having a spa day, not aware of the terrible fate that awaits them—"

"What are you *doing*?"

The two women started. Miss Adeline swept into the kitchen like a queen, her maroon velvet dressing gown buttoned up to her chin. Matching slippers peeked out from beneath the hem.

"Making tea," Sasha said, gesturing to the teapot and cup.

Miss Adeline assumed her favorite interrogation stance: hands clasped primly in front of her, feet braced shoulder-width apart. "And *why* are you making tea at this time of the night?"

"We were thirsty," Lyla said.

"For tea," Sasha added.

Miss Adeline raised an eyebrow. "And why is there only one cup?"

"We each only wanted half a cup," Lyla said.

Sasha inwardly groaned. "Do you think it's ready?" she asked Miss Adeline quickly, before the older woman could reply.

"Is the water brown?" Miss Adeline asked pointedly.

Sasha peered inside the pot once again. "Yes."

"Then it's ready. Take out the leaves, or it will become dark and bitter." Miss Adeline turned sharply on her heel and headed for the door. "Dark and *bitter*."

"She would know," Lyla said under her breath. Sasha kicked her under the table.

Miss Adeline paused and looked at the women over her shoulder. "Be sure to return everything to its proper place." She pursed her lips. "And don't burn down my kitchen."

"Yes, Miss Adeline," the two women said obediently.

Miss Adeline nodded, seemingly appeased, and swept out of the room, just as regally as she had entered.

They were silent as they listened to Miss Adeline's slipper-muffled footsteps ascend the staircase. When they heard the door to her bedroom creak open and then click shut, they exhaled in a rush.

"I don't know why, but I always feel so guilty when she's around," Sasha said.

"She has a gift," Lyla said. "Was it just me, or did she look like a villainess in a gothic novel?"

Sasha grinned. "All she was missing was the candlestick."

"And the mad husband in the attic. Though, knowing Miss Adeline, she'd also have one in the basement. He would be her second-best mad husband—you know, for everyday use. The first mad husband would only be used for best." Lyla gestured at the teapot. "Let's get on with it before she unleashes her madmen upon us for dirtying her china."

"Right." Sasha placed the strainer onto the teacup and poured the tea, careful not to spill any on the tablecloth. "I think that's all we have to do. We made tea, we added four drops of Truth Elixir, we—"

"Oh. That reminds me." Lyla removed the Truth Elixir from her pocket. She opened the bottle and poured what appeared to be a table-spoon of the copper-colored liquid into the cup.

"What are you doing?!" Sasha shrieked, looking down at the cup in horror. "Rosa said no more than four drops!"

"For *placebo* tea. It's watered down, remember? For Truth Tea, we may have to up the dose." Lyla picked up the teaspoon and gave the cup a brisk stir.

Sasha stared at oily, copper film clinging to the sides of the cup and grimaced. "That is way too much for a small teacup."

"The occult isn't an exact science." Lyla placed the spoon back on the saucer and looked down at the cup, pleased with her handiwork. "That should be nice and truth-y."

Sasha leaned forward and inhaled; the scent of spices gently wafting from the cup was *very* familiar. "Right. Let's do this." She wiped her sweaty hands across the thighs of her jeans and reached for the cup.

But before she could pick it up, Lyla slapped her hand out of the way.

"Are you kidding?" Lyla held the cup out of Sasha's reach. "We need to do this scientifically. You've already been contaminated today—by a potion or some weird, child-borne disease—and that may compromise the test. *I'll* drink it."

Sasha shook her head vehemently. "No. No way. You shouldn't be—*No!*"

Lyla threw back the contents of the cup and swallowed. "*Please*, you don't always have to be the hero. *Ergh*, that was disgusting."

"The potion?"

"No, the tea. How do people drink this stuff? It tastes like boiled dirt." Lyla shuddered delicately. "Ingesting nature is for peasants, I tell you."

Sasha looked closely at her friend. "Anything?"

Lyla licked her lips. "Give it a minute."

They sat in silence for a few moments.

"The taste ..." Lyla began. "Now I can taste something *more* than the tea ... and it's ... delicious. Something—cloves, maybe? No, it's not that strong. Is it cinnamon?" She shook her head. "Not quite, but ... it's ... it's something familiar." She peered into the cup. "I feel rather relaxed and—" She licked her lips. "My mouth feels weirdly loose."

Sasha's eyes widened. "Yes! *Yes*! Mine did, too. Should I start asking you questions? Something simple maybe, to ease you into it?"

Lyla nodded slowly. "That sounds like a good idea. Ask away."

"Right." Sasha looked around. "Ah ... what do you really think of Old Middleton?"

"I think it's getting progressively more interesting with each cup of tea."

"And what do you think of Martha?"

"I wouldn't be surprised if she had a dark past as an underground Mexican wrestler." Lyla settled back into her chair. "Now, get me to divulge a secret. Ask me something I wouldn't tell you unless I was under the influence of a truth drug."

"Right. How about—? No ... not that. Oh! Okay, what is the—" Sasha shook her head. "No, that won't work; we've already talked about that. Dash it! We should have prepared for this ..."

Lyla bounced on her seat impatiently. "Hurry! We don't want it to wear off."

"Right! Right ... ah ... okay—where is the strangest place you've ever had sex?"

Lyla rolled her eyes. "I said something I wouldn't answer unless I were under the influence of a truth drug—I'd tell you that over breakfast. Come on! Do better! Hurry!"

Sasha threw her hands into the air. "This isn't as simple as it sounds! I've known you since we were kids. I already know most of your secrets; I was there for most of them. It isn't easy to find something you wouldn't talk abo—" She stilled and stared at her friend.

"Lyla," she began quietly.

Lyla's eyes widened. "Oh, no—"

"Tell me—"

"Not that!" Lyla hissed.

"—why aren't you enrolled this semester?"

"Dash it." Lyla groaned. "Can I answer the sex question instead?"

"No. You can tell me that over breakfast. Why aren't you enrolled?"

"Agh. *Fine."* Lyla slumped in her chair. "I'm having second thoughts—

no, third thoughts … No, make that fourth—well, let's just say *many, many* thoughts about my career. I don't think I'm cut out for psychology."

Sasha's eyes widened. "What do you mean? You're fantastic at it. You're always top of your class—"

"But I don't think I *like* it," Lyla blurted. "I only studied it, to begin with, because of Mom—"

Sasha took Lyla's hand.

"And *your* mom was so proud of me, following in my Mom's footsteps … and then … and then I was just *stuck*. And now that I'm close to finishing, I'm worried that I'll be trapped doing something that I don't like—something that I don't really want to do—for the rest of my life. It's like a joke that I've taken too far. Ten years too far …"

Sasha gently squeezed her friend's hand. "Oh, Lyla. You should have told me!"

Lyla shook her head. "I didn't want to talk about it. Talking about it makes it true … talking about it makes it real, you know? And it's nothing. Really, it's nothing. I'll get through this. I'm hoping that taking a semester off will give me a lot of free time to panic about my future … at least, enough to scare me back onto the academic path. And it had better work because frankly, I don't know what I'll do if it doesn't. If I leave my degree, I'm going to have to live with a crushing sense of failure for the rest of my life—and I'm not good at failure, you know that. Not to mention the horror of trying to figure out my next career path. And *agh* … I don't even know where to start! I don't know what I want to be when I grow up! The last time I had a concrete career ambition was when I was six, and I wanted to be a princess cowgirl, which isn't a viable career path in this troubled economy—believe me, I've checked. And honestly, the thought of starting all over again is just so *exhausting*. I don't know if I have the energy to start a new degree and—oh my God, you were right! I cannot stop talking. My mouth keeps going and going and going. What is this voodoo magic?"

Lyla dropped the empty cup onto the table and watched, transfixed, as it rolled onto its side. Both women turned to each other with wide eyes.

"It's a truth potion," Sasha said, her voice hushed.

"It's a truth potion," Lyla whispered. "Or … maybe it's not." She looked down at the cup and licked her lips. "Ask me what I think of Todd."

"O-kay," Sasha said slowly, surprised by the abrupt change in topic. "What do you think of Todd?"

"I think he's an interesting and complex guy. A real catch. You should have moved in with him—ah, *ha*!" Lyla crowed. "It's *not* a truth potion!"

Sasha stared at her friend warily, a crease appearing between her brows.

"So ... you don't think that Todd is an interesting, complex guy and that I should have moved in with him?"

"Oh *please*. Navel lint is more interesting and complex than Todd. And you already know that he was a terrible match for you."

Sasha sighed. "Yes. Yes, I do."

"He was so *bland*."

"Yes. Yes, he was." It was true—Todd was exceptionally bland; he was the human equivalent of carbonated water. "But you've told me this before."

"Many, many times before but it never hurts to say it again. I don't think this is a truth potion, Sasha."

"But you kept babbling—"

"I've been wanting to tell you about suspending my degree for ages; the potion just made me feel relaxed enough to do it. But I was still able to lie." Lyla stared at the teacup. "You could probably achieve the same level of truth-telling after a glass or two of wine."

Sasha sat back in her chair and frowned at the cup. "What does this mean? Do we need to test it more vigorously? What if I asked you something that you don't want to tell me?" She looked shrewdly at her friend. "Do you have any deep, dark secrets that you're keeping from me?"

"Loads!" Lyla mimed buttoning her lips together. "But they aren't coming out today."

Sasha exhaled in a rush, confused and relieved all at once. "So, if it isn't a truth potion, what is it?"

Lyla shrugged. "I don't know. Maybe it's just a truth *enhancer*. I told the truth about something I wanted to tell you."

"But Rosa said that a truth potion doesn't work that way. A truth potion makes you tell the truth no matter what. And I certainly didn't want to tell strangers about my sex life. Or the grocer about his terrible sweater."

"Maybe—secretly—you did. No, hear me out," Lyla said as Sasha opened her mouth to protest. "You're always trying to do and say the right thing, just in case a student is lurking around. You're always trying to set a good example. But ... maybe you secretly want to tell people what you really think. Maybe you want to be more like me."

Sasha mulled that over. "*Possibly*," she conceded. "But not at the cost of losing my job and my reputation."

"That's a good point." Lyla yawned widely. "This potion also seems to be some kind of relaxant. I feel very loose."

Sasha yawned, too. "Damn you." She thought back over her meeting with the Headmistress. "I felt relaxed, too. Well, up until the point where I became riddled with horror and anxiety about what was coming out of my mouth. Maybe the effect was stronger on me because I was tired." She closed her eyes, suddenly exhausted, the full weight of the day settling across her shoulders like a lead blanket. "I *am* tired, you know. I'm tired of moving and changing and leaving things behind."

"Then, why not settle down? Stop taking these lousy jobs that don't pay you what you're worth. You could get a permanent teaching position in New York and move in with me properly this time—not just leave your stuff in my spare room while you gallivant around. And we could live a truly decadent life filled with wondrous things! Like shiny appliances, and martinis, and carbs, and pretty men. *Pretty men*, Sasha—as far as the eye can see! We'd be living the dream … as I've said, many, many times before." Lyla sighed, not particularly hopeful. "Why not just *stop*, Sasha?"

Why not? Sasha thought. She searched for that voice at the back of her mind. For some reason, it was still oddly excited.

Just wait, it told her.

Sasha opened her eyes, a little disturbed by just how gleeful the voice sounded. "I'm just … restless, I suppose. Why else would I be gallivanting around, chasing teaching jobs? Or backpacking until I'm broke?" She rubbed her temples wearily. "Or maybe gallivanting is in my blood. Look at Mom and Dad."

"Yes, but they waited until retirement before they started their gallivanting."

Sasha lifted the teacup and set it upright in its saucer once more. "I guess I'm just doing my gallivanting early."

"Probably the optimal time to gallivant." Lyla picked up at the bottle of Truth Elixir and screwed on the lid. "So, to sum up: today, you drank tea that was probably laced with Truth Elixir—knowingly added by at least one member of staff at your place of work. Chaos ensued. What are we going to do now?"

Sasha squared her shoulders. "I'm going to confront the Headmistress."

Lyla's eyes widened. "Really?"

"*Really.*" It was the right thing to do.

"Good for you! Hang on, why not go to the police?"

"I don't think we have enough evidence. My drug test was negative, and I doubt the police will take drugging by *truth potion* seriously." Sasha could barely believe it herself. "I'll talk to the Headmistress first thing in the morning. If she confesses, we're going to the police. And then we're going home."

"And if she doesn't?"

Sasha lifted her chin. "We're still going home. Someone put something in my tea, whether we can prove it or not. I don't want to work in a place where I don't feel safe."

Lyla patted her hand. "Right answer. I'll come with you."

"No. It's better if I do it alone." Sasha squeezed Lyla's hand, noticing her friend's worried look. "I'll be fine."

Lyla exhaled. "Fine. But you call me as soon as—hang on ... you can't call me. You probably won't get a signal on your phone. *Agh*. We should have learned semaphore."

"I'll call you on Miss Adeline's landline from the school office."

"You call me the second you finish speaking to the Headmistress."

Sasha looked down at the copper-colored film clinging to the inside of the teacup and nodded. "Immediately after, I promise."

"Okay. While you do that, I'll pack our things. We'll leave as soon as you get back." Lyla looked around the kitchen. "Goodbye, Old Middleton. I knew that your old-world charm hid a strange, possibly nefarious interior, but I thought you'd make it harder for me to find."

"Bye, Old Middleton," Sasha echoed, her heart heavy.

She didn't want to go, she realized. Despite her restlessness, she liked Old Middleton. There was something about this place that felt special ... even more so than all the lovely places she had seen in her travels. To have to move on so soon from the charming village—and for such a terrible reason—was devastating.

And the thought of having to find another job ... and then another ... and then another ... was exhausting. It would be so much easier to stay.

But what choice did she have?

Mentally, she pushed aside her emotions and straightened her shoulders. "I guess I'd better finish writing my postcards tonight; I won't get a chance tomorrow."

But even as she was speaking, the little voice in her head chimed up.

Just wait, it said gleefully.

Just wait.

6

DREAMS OF HILLS AND HILL-MEN

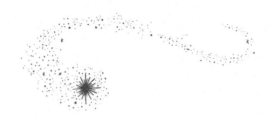

VERY EARLY WEDNESDAY MORNING, OCTOBER 24TH: HOURS PAST A PROPER, GENTEEL YOUNG WOMAN'S BEDTIME

DESPITE THE ADVENTURES OF THE DAY, OR PERHAPS BECAUSE OF THEM, Sasha could not sleep. For once, it was not the thought of the emptiness awaiting her that kept her awake, but rather a *feeling*. It was not a predictable feeling: it was not a feeling associated with tea-spiking or confrontations, terrible sweaters, or sex confessions. Rather, it was the strange, electric sense of excitement, of *anticipation*, that had been steadily building just beneath her skin since the night she had entered Old Middleton.

It was the tantalizing promise of something—an adventure, a puzzle, a mystery—just beyond her reach.

You'd better not be excited about the possibility of leaving this job, she told herself sternly, thinking about her upcoming confrontation with the Headmistress. *You'd better not be excited about adding another red dot to the map so soon.*

But that was not it.

This feeling was stronger, sharper, *shinier* than her customary restlessness. It almost made her feel giddy.

Sasha snorted at the very idea. She looked over at Lyla, who was sprawled face-down on her bed, snoring softly, and sighed. Falling asleep was never a problem for Lyla.

Resigned to a night of sleeplessness, Sasha turned over yet again, mindful of the creaking bedframe. But this time, her gaze fell upon the dream pillow. It was sitting on her nightstand in a puddle of moonlight, the golden stars on the surface glittering enticingly. She stretched out her fingers and grasped it, the fabric cool and slick against her fingers. Bringing it to her nose, she inhaled the spicy, floral scent.

Almost immediately, she yawned.

"Fast acting," she whispered. "I like that."

Sasha slipped it under her pillow, trying hard to ignore the fact that she was trying to cure her insomnia with a cushion filled with dried weeds and pizza spices.

What harm could it do? she thought as she yawned again and closed her eyes.

What harm indeed ...

ALMOST IMMEDIATELY, SASHA OPENED HER EYES AGAIN. BUT INSTEAD OF drifting in the emptiness of her typical dreamscape, she was on a hill that overlooked a vast, deserted plain—the same hillside she had seen in her previous dreams.

"I'm back!" she cried.

She spun around on her tiptoes, arms outstretched, grinning madly at the sky. But she stumbled to a stop at the sight of twin moons sitting side by side above the horizon—one tinged gold, the other silver—both fat and full in the darkness.

She stared in awe. "Things are a little bit different this time. Way to use your imagination, Sasha!"

A breeze tickled the ends of her hair and brushed against her cheek, leaving behind the scent of petrichor and brine.

"It even smells different." Sasha took a deep breath of the stormy air and smiled up at the moons. "That's *so* lovely. And so strange."

Sasha looked down at her feet; they were buried in familiar gold dust, the glittery grains butter-soft against her skin. "*So* strange," she whispered, wiggling her toes.

She bent down and scooped up a handful of dust, letting it pour through her fingers in a golden stream.

"I've seen pink sand in Bermuda, and black sand in Auckland, and pure white sand in Australia. But none of it compares to this ... *this* looks like stardust." She rubbed the fine grains between her fingers. "I really hope I remember this when I wake up."

Sasha jumped as thunder boomed somewhere behind her, the sound far too loud and far too close for comfort. She watched as sheet lightning set fire to the angry, green-tinted sky, illuminating the vast plains below. Roiling black clouds obscured the twin moons, plunging the hillside into darkness.

"Now would be a good time to dream up an umbrella," she said, looking around hopefully, but no umbrella appeared.

What *did* appear was a person.

They were standing below her at the base of the hill, looking up at the sky just as Sasha had done moments before.

Sasha was inordinately pleased. "I've dreamed up a friend! Go me!"

Lightning lit up the plain once more, revealing that the person was, in fact, a dark-haired man.

With a start, Sasha realized that the man appeared to have seen her, too. Without thinking too much about it, she waved at him.

The man did not wave back.

"Well ... that's just rude," she muttered.

Instead, he began to walk toward her.

"Oh. Okay." Sasha watched as the man strode quickly up the hillside. "This is new. What's the etiquette when it comes to meeting people in a dream? Am I supposed to wait for him? Or do I meet him halfway? And when we finally meet up, what do we do? Talk? What would we talk about? The weather?"

Thunder boomed ominously.

"Fine then," she said, addressing the sky. "I'll just be quiet and wait."

By the next lightning strike, the man was close enough for Sasha to see that he, too, was wearing pajamas: silky black pants and a matching robe that billowed dramatically around him.

"Trust dream people to have exotic pajamas." Sasha looked down at her worn, llama-covered pajamas and frowned. "*Hmm*, I'm not dressed up enough for this dream; I'm going to make a terrible first impression."

Then she remembered that this was a *dream*—her dream, in fact—and not a job interview, so she was entitled to wear whatever she wanted.

That resolved, Sasha looked up and found that the man had arrived at the top of the hill. The twin moons, demonstrating a flair for dramatic timing, broke free of the dark clouds and flooded the hillside with light, allowing Sasha to see the man clearly as they stood face to face for the first time.

In a turn of events that would have made Lyla proud, the first thing Sasha noticed was the man's chest—pale, lightly muscled, and bare except for a silver amulet—beneath his black silk robe. It was also heaving a little with the exertion of climbing the hillside.

"Oh!" Sasha said happily, staring at the man's impressive torso. "It's going to be one of *those* dreams. I've never had one of those before."

With a few quick strides, Sasha closed the distance between them and threw her arms around his neck. She gleefully noted the broad shoulders and hard muscle beneath her hands, and all the lovely, warm skin that pressed against her with each rise and fall of his chest. His hair, soft as feathers, fell over her hands as she clasped them behind his neck.

Way to use your imagination, Sasha! she congratulated herself. *Well done, you!*

"We may as well get started," she whispered into the man's ear, delighted that he was several inches taller than herself. "I have no idea how long this dream is going to last."

She leaned back, giddily succumbing to a delicious surge of hormones, and met the man's gaze—

Her heart gave a painful lurch.

It was not because he was handsome—though indeed he was, in a stereotypical dark-fairy-tale-prince kind of way. He had deep-set eyes fringed in long, dark lashes; moon-pale skin with fine features symmetrical enough to appear on a coin; glorious cheekbones, sharp and high; chin length, black hair that curled a little at the ends; and a particularly lovely, full lower lip.

No, Sasha's heart lurched because of the expression on his handsome face. He looked shocked—completely and utterly shocked. Which, all things considered, was not the most auspicious beginning to a dream of the adult variety.

"Great," she muttered, inexplicably hurt. "Trust me to have a complicated sex dream. I bet other people just fall asleep and the sex starts immediately. Not me. Apparently, I need a backstory, and a plot, and *angst*."

At that, the man's expression turned from shocked to incredulous, his dark brows rising further toward his hairline, and his lovely lower lip dropping dramatically toward his chin.

"Are you trying to engage me in some sort of *seduction fantasy?*" His voice, rich and low and satin-smooth—a voice that could invoke shivers and longings—was positively drenched in disbelief.

Sasha felt her disappointment turn to irritation. "Well, would it be that terrible if I *was* trying to engage you in a seduction fantasy?"

The man shook his head, clearly disappointed in her. "Yes. Yes, it would. Of all the dreams at your disposal, of all the wonders that you could experience, why would you want to engage in a common *seduction fantasy*? You truly need to dream bigger."

Sasha was deeply insulted. "Hey! This *is* dreaming big for me! This is my very first seduction fantasy!"

"But would you not prefer something more meaningful, more fantastic?" the man persisted. "Possibly something with a dragon—"

"Why would I want a *dragon* in my seduction fantasy? I mean, that's—that's just perverse." Sasha sniffed; imagine this deviant judging *her* taste in dreams. "Besides, you started it—striding up the hillside toward me like—like—like—"

"Like someone trying to get to their destination?"

"No!" she cried, frustrated. "You were striding toward me with intent."

The man raised an eyebrow. "Intent?"

"*Intent*," she repeated firmly.

"Of what kind?"

"*Sultry* intent."

The man gave a surprised bark of laughter. "Sultry intent? Surely not!"

"Surely *yes*." Sasha was getting angrier by the second. "You were striding along, all masculine and purposeful and ... and ... windswept in your seduction clothes—"

"We call them pajamas."

"—and full of *chestedness*." Sasha looked meaningfully at his naked chest. "*Heaving* chestedness."

The man, too, looked down at his naked chest. His lips twitched. "Forgive me for my heaving *chestedness* and sultry intent. I assure you, it was completely unintentional."

For some reason, that made Sasha even angrier. She swiftly removed her arms from around the man's neck. But before she could step away, he caught her around the waist, holding her firmly in place. The man's hands were large and strong and distractingly warm through the worn cotton of her pajama top—but she quickly brushed those traitorous thoughts aside and focused on maintaining her rage.

"All I'm saying," she continued righteously, "is that you shouldn't go striding around people's *seduction fantasies* full of chestedness and sultry intent if you don't intend to fulfill your end of the bargain."

The man blinked. "I do not typically engage in seduction fantasies. They are not part of my repertoire. I—" He stopped abruptly, his eyes growing wide as if something rather terrible had just occurred to him.

With a groan, he looked up at the sky. "Oh, come now," he said, addressing the clouds. "*Seduction fantasies*? Surely there are limits to what I must endure—"

"*Endure*?" Sasha interrupted, horrified. This was becoming more humiliating by the second. "You think that a seduction fantasy with me is something you would have to *endure*?"

The man froze. " 'Endure' was a particularly poor choice of word." His tone was cautious, careful—the tone of someone trying to make amends before they were confronted with something fatally pointy. "And I immediately regret my decision to use it. I never meant to imply—"

But Sasha was not listening. She was a mass of fury and thwarted lust. "Ha! Let me tell you, mister, you would be lucky to have a seduction fantasy with me! I am exceptionally gifted at—at—things. *Sexy* things. Like —" She made a vague hand gesture meant to denote all manner of sexy things.

The man stared at her hands, perplexed. "Castration?"

"What?! *No*! Why would you even say that?"

"You just made the universally accepted hand gesture for castration, which is somewhat perplexing—and disconcerting—given the context ..."

Sasha held up her hands. "That was *not* the universally accepted hand gesture for castration. I didn't even know that there was such a thing. And even if I did, why would I make the universally accepted hand gesture for castration during a seduction fantasy? There is nothing sexy about castrat —hang on, am I *boring* you?" she asked incredulously, as the man turned away to yawn.

"Apologies," he said, blinking. "I am wretchedly exhausted."

Sasha shook her head, her curls tossing angrily from side to side. "Unbelievable. You're 'wretchedly exhausted'? *How*? We haven't even gotten to the adult-type touching yet!"

"I have had a very trying day," the man said, with an extremely long sigh.

Sasha snorted. "Tell me about it."

She doubted that *his* trying day had included being drugged, fleeing from stores thanks to uncontrollable truth-telling and borderline-obscene hand gestures, invasive medical tests, polka bands, or a seduction fantasy that was completely seduction-free.

Truly, this was the final straw.

"I can't believe this," she said, addressing the clouds just as the man had done moments before. "My first seduction fantasy and my dream man acts all coy and uninterested and *exhausted* ... and really judgmental for a guy with a dragon fetish."

The man's eyes widened. "I do not have a dragon fet—"

"Not to mention," Sasha continued, ignoring the interruption, "he couldn't tell the difference between a sexy gesture and the universally accepted hand gesture for castration." She looked the man straight in the eye. "I'm sorry to say this, but you are terrible at sex charades."

The man blinked, clearly perplexed. "Sex charades? What are—?" He paused for a long moment, as if trying to think the matter through, then visibly collected himself. "This is not working."

"Agreed. This is a lousy seduction fantasy."

"My Lady," he said firmly. "This is not a seduction fantasy." He looked up at the sky and frowned. "At least, as far as I am aware ..."

He seemed uncertain, so Sasha decided she would try *one last time* to make this work. "Well ... can it become one?" she asked, her tone a little more hopeful than she would have liked. "I mean, I know that dreams aren't like real life, but if dream seduction is anything like real-life seduction ... well, it sure beats standing on a hill staring at gold dust, right?"

There was a long pause.

"You'd ... you'd actually prefer to stare at gold dust?" she asked.

The man opened his mouth to answer but closed it again.

"Really?" she asked in disbelief. "*Really?*"

He shrugged, his expression apologetic. "Staring at gold dust requires minimal effort, and right now I am—"

"Wretchedly exhausted," Sasha finished dryly. "Yes, you said that already."

"It would not be a stellar experience," he continued. "I would probably fall asleep during a vital moment—" The man stifled another yawn. "Or right at the very beginning ..."

Sasha's jaw clenched. "Ri-ght."

"Truly, you deserve better than a lackluster seduction fantasy."

"Yes. Yes, I do." Sasha gestured to everything around her. "And yet, here we are."

The man blinked in surprise and looked down at her. For the first time since this entire, humiliating experience began, Sasha had the feeling that he was finally *seeing* her rather than merely enduring her presence. A crease appeared between his brows as if he was trying to puzzle her out. He leaned forward just a little, bringing the scent of petrichor with him, close enough for her to feel the warmth of his breath ghost across her skin; close enough for the tips of his hair to brush against her cheek in the breeze. She suppressed the urge to shiver at the sensation and stood her ground, waiting to see what would happen next.

She felt the weight of his gaze like a touch as it alighted on her features, lingering on the arch of her brows, the crest of her cheekbones, the tip of her nose, the point of her chin. By the time his gaze slid to her mouth, dragging over her lower lip, Sasha realized that she was holding her breath, her heart thudding wildly against her ribcage. The intensity of his gaze, the intimacy of the moment … it should have been too much. She should have leaned back, moved aside, stepped away.

But she didn't.

Couldn't.

He stared at her lips for a long moment as if caught there, his gaze oddly bemused. She was about to ask him about that look when his hands, obscenely warm through the thin fabric of her t-shirt, tightened around her body, his palms flush against the sensitive hollows of her waist. She inhaled sharply as he traced the curve of her ribcage with the pads of his thumbs, leaving behind a trail of sparks.

"Would you, perhaps, settle for a kiss?" he asked, still staring at her mouth, his voice a little lower, a little rougher than it had been moments before.

Sasha exhaled shakily, and stared up at him, stunned. "A kiss?"

She was annoyed at herself for how breathless she sounded.

"A kiss," he repeated, his voice still dark with promise. "Possibly supplemented by some sort of—"

"Nuzzling?" she suggested hopefully.

He inclined his head, his lips twitching. "I would not be averse to nuzzling."

Sasha realized that she, too, would not be averse to nuzzling. For a lovely moment, she was especially pleased with the direction this dream was taking. That is until she realized what was truly going on …

"Hang on," she said, eyes narrowed, "are you trying to downgrade my seduction fantasy?"

"Somewhat," the man hedged.

"Ha! I knew it! *Unbelievable.*"

Still, for a split second, Sasha considered his offer. He was tall and beautiful, and his chest looked as though it had been sculpted from really good quality marble—like an expensive kitchen countertop—but she stopped that thought in its tracks. She was worth more than a bargain-basement seduction fantasy, dammit!

"You know what? Forget it—I'm not settling." Sasha paused. "Kaytie would be so proud of me. Besides," she continued, with as much disdain as she could muster, "you'd probably fall asleep mid-nuzzle."

At the mention of sleep, the man yawned again.

"*See?*" she said, full of righteous fury ... which she ruined by yawning.

"Damn you," she cursed, mid-yawn.

"Apologies," the man said, blinking sleepily. "As I said earlier, I am truly exhausted—it has been a beastly day. Speaking of which ..." His bleary gaze landed on her llama-print pajamas. "What do the beasts on your clothing signify?"

This was all quite enough for Sasha. "They signify my internal rage."

She pulled herself out of the man's embrace and, with a regal toss of her dark curls, turned away.

"Worst. Sex. Dream. Ever," she muttered to herself, as she began the trek down the hill. "Lyla is going to laugh her butt off at this."

"Wait!"

Sasha felt a tug on her wrist, then a strange, electric *jolt* pulsed through her body. Before she knew it, she was facing the man once again, his hand circling her wrist.

"Hey!" She tried to pull her hand from the man's grip, but he was terribly strong. He was also staring at her so intently that she was beginning to feel self-conscious. "No need to rip my arm off."

"Apologies," he said, his voice strained. He loosened his hold but did not let go.

"*Thank you*," she said dryly.

Sasha looked down at the man's long, pale fingers curled around her wrist. She could feel the heat of his skin against hers and, beneath that, an odd sort of electrical charge that made goosebumps scatter along her bare arms. Now that she was no longer in a lust-haze, she realized how strange it was that she could feel him at all.

"I thought you weren't supposed to feel things in dreams," she said to herself. "Which is strange because *that* feels pretty real." Frowning, she pushed her fingernails into her palm and winced. "So does that."

"You need to know—" the man began.

"Something's wrong," she interrupted.

Sasha stepped closer to the man, her heart beginning to beat wildly, and placed her free hand flat on his bare chest. The man looked down at her hand, seemingly amused despite himself.

Beneath her palm, Sasha felt warm skin and the faint thrum of a heart-beat. Experimentally, she moved her hand over the man's silver amulet—two crescent moons facing an eight-pointed star—and felt cold metal against her skin.

She snatched her hand away as if his chest was aflame. "What's going on? Why do you feel so *real?* How is it possible that I can feel things in this dream? Or—or is that typical when you're dreaming?"

"There is nothing typical about this dre—"

"You know what? Don't bother," she interrupted, realizing that she had just asked a figment of her imagination to explain dream realities. "The answer is probably something like misfiring synapses or a stunted R.E.M cycle or stress and knowing why I can feel things in dreams doesn't change anything." She shook her head.

"I can't believe this," she said, more to herself than the man. "I haven't dreamed of anything since I was five years old and now my first dream, which started off promisingly enough"—she took another look at the man's chest—"has deteriorated into some kind of esoteric discussion about dream realities. To say I'm annoyed is an understatement."

All in all, it was a rather impressive rant; it was a pity that the man was not really paying attention.

"A moment," he said, his expression thoughtful. "You said that your last dream occurred when you were five. What did you dream about?"

But Sasha was done with this entire situation.

"I'd like to wake up now," she yelled at the sky.

But nothing happened.

Then, lots more nothing happened.

And then some more nothing after that.

"Dash it," she muttered.

"Indulge me," the man said, tapping his fingers against her wrist to get her attention. "What was your last dream about? This may be very important."

"I don't remember," Sasha said, still looking up at the gathering storm clouds. "I was five."

"*Try.*"

Sasha turned to face him and immediately stilled at his expression. He was staring at her as if this was a matter of grave importance and not just a trivial question about a long-forgotten dream.

"Fine." Sasha closed her eyes with a sigh, humoring him.

But, to her surprise, the memory of that long ago dream started flooding back.

"I was walking up a hillside," she said in awe. She could see the hillside in her mind's eye, the slope rising and rising until it plateaued. "I remember looking down at my feet." She looked down in the vision and saw her five-year-old feet, small and bare. "The grass was silver, not green, and the ground ... the ground was covered in gold colored dust ..."

Her voice trailed off as an impossible thought became less impossible by the moment. She opened her eyes and looked around the hillside. Then, she saw it—tufts of long, silver grass, scattered around the hill in clumps, waving in the breeze.

"I've been here before, haven't I?" she asked the man, shocked to her core. "I don't—I don't understand ..."

The man was staring down at her with an expression that looked very much like pity. "And then what happened?" he asked. "After you climbed up the hillside?"

Sasha took a deep breath. "Nothing. I sat on the hill ... *this* hill ... waiting for what seemed like hours. And then—"

All of a sudden, she knew why she had blocked out the memory of this particular dream.

"These ... *monsters* ... started running across the plain," she whispered, the memory returning in a rush, the horror still sharp and fresh after all these years. "They were hideous—tall and thin and white, with long arms and thin, spidery fingers that reached out for me. Their eyes ... they were just black holes. I—I didn't want to look into them. And their teeth! They had *so many* teeth! Sharp and jagged, like broken knife blades. But the worst part was their screams ..." Sasha closed her eyes, remembering the sound, remembering the fear. "I've never heard a sound like that before. It wasn't a howl or a scream or a siren, but somehow all three rolled into one. I remember ... I remember covering my ears, but it didn't help—I could still hear them. The sound seemed to echo through my skull. It made me want to scream, and run, and hide ..."

"And then?" the man asked quietly.

"They called to me ..."

Look at usss, little girl. Look!

"But you did not listen," the man said.

It was not a question.

"I didn't listen," she agreed. "They started running toward the hill, running right for me ..."

"And then?"

Sasha could still see them swarming up the hill toward her—thousands of monsters, hands outstretched, mouths wide-open.

"I turned and ran and ran and ran."

She remembered running, her small feet sinking into gold dust, her footsteps falling in time with the beat of her frantic heart. She remembered stumbling, falling—the sudden shock of pain across her hands and knees as they scraped along a hidden rock; the sight of blood, thick and red, mingling with the dust. She remembered staggering to her feet, howling in pain and fear, and running, running, running—

Sasha gasped, as breathless as her five-year-old self. "Then ... I woke up."

The look in the man's eyes was almost heartbreaking. The pity there, the sadness. "I am sorry you experienced that." He squeezed her wrist gently. "I am profoundly sorry for your loss."

"What do you mean?" Sasha stared up at him. *What did he know?* "What did I lose?"

Sasha felt him release her wrist and panicked, assuming that he was about to leave. "No! Don't go!" she cried, grabbing his hand, her fingers brushing against his palm.

Suddenly, a bolt of electricity surged from where she had touched his skin, shooting up her arm, and leaving a strange buzz in its wake.

She quickly let him go, her hands tingling. "What—what was that?"

The man looked just as stunned as she felt. He stared at her as if she was something rare and dangerous.

"Who are you?" he asked, his voice hoarse.

Quick as the lightning overhead, the man grabbed her hands and turned them over, frantically staring at her palms and wrists.

"What is it?" she asked. "What are you doing?"

"Searching," he muttered.

As the man searched, Sasha stared down at his hands and saw lines and triangles and broken circles, all drawn in white ink and barely noticeable against the moonlit skin of his wrists and palms.

Tattoos, she realized.

Two of them looked familiar.

"What's going on?" she demanded. "*Tell* me."

The man looked up from her wrists and met her gaze, his brow furrowed. "I do not know."

The warm breeze that had been moving idly across the hillside suddenly roared to life, whipping through Sasha's hair and clothes. The man's robe blew wide open, his hair becoming a dark tangle around his face. He looked up at the sky; it was now thick with heavy, black clouds, and ready to unleash a flood.

"You must go," he said urgently. "You do not belong here, and you have already stayed too long."

Oddly enough, that *hurt.*

He's wrong, the little voice inside Sasha's head said soothingly. *He's got it all wrong.*

"I don't know about that," she said, remembering her five-year-old self standing on this exact hill. "I might belong here more than you think."

The man looked at her as if she were slightly mad and, for all she knew, she was. But it felt true. It felt as though something inside her was *finally* shifting into place.

"I hope for your sake that you are wrong," the man said. "Trust me when I say that this is not a place that you would want to belong. Please, for your own sake, *go*."

As if in agreement, the heavens opened, unleashing thick sheets of water onto the hill and the plain beyond. The warm rain soaked them both within seconds. But Sasha barely noticed. Over the noise of the rain, and the dull roar of the wind, she heard something that made the hair on her neck stand on end.

Something that made her heartbeat race.

Something that made her want to run far, far away.

Something horrifically familiar.

From the corner of her eye, illuminated by the lightning, she saw what appeared to be thousands of twisted, white shadows flooding the plain.

"The monsters!" she screamed into the howling wind. "They're back. How—?"

"*Run!*" the man shouted.

He turned and raised his hands toward the seething mass of creatures tearing toward them.

"But—but what about you?" she yelled above the wind. "Come with me!"

"I am fine. Run!"

"No!"

The man whipped around and stared at her in surprise. She should have been surprised, too; she had just asked a dream man to come back to reality with her. But something inside her insisted—no, *demanded* that he come.

"I'm not leaving without you," she yelled into the wind, and held out her hand to him.

The look in his eyes—the look in his eyes *killed* her. So many emotions were tangled in that pale gaze: there was still surprise... and also fear. But most of all, there was a terrible longing—as if she was offering him something infinitely precious, something that he desperately wanted.

Sasha's heart pounded in her chest. The sound of the wind, the storm, even the monsters seemed to mute, to fade away. Her whole world narrowed down to the longing in his gaze.

"Come with me," she repeated, her hand still outstretched.

The man leaned toward her ever so slightly, his hand rising to meet her own.

Sasha felt herself smiling through the rain. She reached out as far as she could, trying to close the distance between their fingertips.

Almost there, she thought. *Almost th*—

Howls—bloodthirsty and so, so close—tore across the plain, surrounding them in a wall of pure, horror-drenched sound that made Sasha's ears ring and her knees shake.

The moment between them shattered.

The man's gaze hardened. All the softness, all the longing fell away from his expression as he dropped his hand.

"Run!" he barked. "*Now!*"

There was such a strong command in that final word that Sasha flinched. She turned without question and, like her five-year-old self, ran.

She did not look back.

The Seduction Fantasy Goes Awry

7

THE CURSE OF THE DOUBLE-PENNY WELL WISH

WEDNESDAY, OCTOBER 24TH: MORNING.

SASHA SAT UP IN BED, BREATHING HEAVILY. SHE LOOKED AROUND: THERE WAS no hillside, no plain, and—thankfully—no monsters.

Unfortunately, there was also no beautiful, half-naked man, but that was nothing new.

The sun had just risen, filling her kitsch little room with the first pale rays of morning. She looked over at Lyla, who was still sleeping blissfully, and sank back against her pillows in relief.

A dream, a dream, just a dream, just a dream, her mind repeated, over and over again, as she stared up at the ceiling.

"Hang on," she whispered. *"Just a dream?"* Her eyes widened. "I had a dream! *I had a dream!"*

Not only had she dreamed, *but she had remembered it.*

Every. Single. Detail.

After all these years of dreamlessness, of blank emptiness, the relief—the *joy!*—Sasha felt was overwhelming. She bit her lip to keep back a sob.

"I can't believe it," she whispered, her body shaking. *"Finally,* after all these years—"

The sudden, shrill, off-key whine of the alarm clock had her sitting bolt upright again, clutching her heart.

This time she was not alone.

"Agh! That's it—I'm putting that clock out of its misery today," Lyla

grumbled. She slapped at the clock until the noise ceased with a final, petulant bleat.

"I had a real dream last night," Sasha said into the sudden silence. "And I *remembered* it!"

Sasha watched as Lyla's gaze turned from bleary to wide-eyed in seconds.

"*Yes*! Way to go, you!" Lyla reached over and sleepily high-fived Sasha. "I am *so* happy for you! Welcome to the club." She yawned. "Tell me all about it. Give me all the details; we need to savor this moment."

Sasha ran her hand through her hair, surprised that it was not wet. "I dreamed that I was standing on a hillside that was covered in gold dust, overlooking a plain."

"Wow. Geography. I'm so sorry—I was hoping you'd have a better first dream."

"And then a man came walking toward me."

Lyla suddenly looked more alert. "Okay, this sounds more like it! Continue."

"The man climbed the hill until he was standing in front of me."

Lyla grabbed one of her spare pillows and hugged it close to her chest. "Wait a minute; I'm trying to imagine the scene. What did he look like?"

Sasha closed her eyes briefly, recalling the dream. "At first, I couldn't see him very well; it was dark and beginning to storm. All I could see was that he was tall—quite a bit taller than me—"

"Huh. That's pretty rare; you're practically a giraffe."

Sasha ignored that. "And he was wearing black silk pajama pants and a black silk robe that was billowing out behind him in the wind."

Lyla looked gleeful. "He was *shirtless*! Your first proper dream and your dream man was *shirtless*. Well done!"

"Thanks! I was congratulating myself at that point, too. But when I tried to … *uh* … engage him in adult-type touching, he looked shocked and refused to play along."

Lyla frowned. "That doesn't seem fair."

"*I know*!" The memory of it still rankled. "At the very least, he should have been happy to see me, not playing hard to get."

"Trust you to have a complicated sex dream."

"That's what I was thinking!"

"Was he handsome?"

Would you, perhaps, settle for a kiss?

Sasha leaned back against her pillow and sighed. "Utterly gorgeous. And he had a voice to match."

Lyla snorted. "What a waste."

"Tell me about it." *Such a waste,* Sasha thought, remembering all those lovely muscles and warm skin. "He kept telling me that he was too 'wretchedly exhausted' to engage in a seduction fantasy and urged me to leave because I didn't belong."

"It's a sad day when even our dream men are troublesome."

"So true. But the strange thing was that it felt so *real.* All of it—the sand, the man, the storm …" Sasha could still feel the sensation of rain against her skin and the feather-like softness of the dream man's hair against her fingers. "And what's stranger still is that I've dreamed of that place before."

Sasha told Lyla about her five-year-old self's final dream. "The same monsters appeared in my dream last night, right at the very end. The dream man ordered me to run away while he stayed to fight them."

"That *is* weird," Lyla said, frowning. "It's almost as if you've come full circle, dream-wise."

The same thought had occurred to Sasha. "I wonder what it means?"

"Give me a couple of hours to do some research, and I'll get back to you." Lyla stretched her arms above her head, working the kinks out of her back. "I think you should focus on the positives." She dropped her arms. "You had your very first *remembered* dream in twenty-five years."

Sasha grinned. It seemed unbelievable. "True."

"And it wasn't all bad."

Sasha remembered the dream man's chest … and face … and voice. "Very true."

"And maybe tonight, the gorgeous Hill-Man will not only reappear in your dreams but will be more receptive to your advances."

Sasha laughed. "Hill-Man?"

"Hill-Man," Lyla said with a smirk. "Maybe he's just shy. Or a virgin—there can't be that many women on that hill."

"Hilarious. If I do dream again, I hope that Hill-Man's less inhibited and just-as-attractive brother will be waiting for me."

"When you're done with him, send him my way. At the very least, Hill-Man will provide something pleasant for you to think about while you confront the Headmistress this morning."

Sasha's eyes widened. "I'd forgotten all about that." She groaned and buried her face in her pillow.

Lyla reached over and patted Sasha's arm. "That's a very reasonable reaction. Do you want to take the pillow to the meeting?"

Sasha looked up, her face squashed and red. "It's tempting, but I'd better not. I'm going to adult my way through this."

"Adulting is *so* overrated. The pillow and I will be here if you need us."

"Good to have you both on stand-by." Sasha pulled the covers aside and swung her legs out of bed. "I'm off to have a shower. Then, we're going out to get breakfast because dreaming is hungry work." She took a deep breath and squared her shoulders. "After that, I'm going to get some answers from the Headmistress."

"Gotta love a plan. I'll get dressed."

Sasha nodded and, head held high, marched off to the bathroom, closing the door behind her.

～

From the next room, Lyla heard the sound of the old pipes groan and wheeze before the shower sputtered to life.

"Remember," she called out. "The water's always cold at first—"

Sure enough, she heard a gasp followed by a strangled, "*Gah!*" followed by a string of muffled curses.

Lyla shook her head. "And just like that, the shower claims its first victim of the day."

She stretched out her legs and wiggled her toes, limbering up for the day ahead. As she climbed out of bed, something shiny caught her eye.

Across the sheets of Sasha's bed, she saw what appeared to be gold dust glittering in the early morning light.

"Huh." Frowning, she padded across the room to get a closer look. Sure enough, there *was* glittery, golden dust sprinkled amongst the needlepoint blue birds flying across Sasha's sheets.

Turning, Lyla checked her bed.

Nothing.

Lyla looked around the room, trying to find the source of the glitter. Beneath Sasha's pillow, she glimpsed a flash of blue silk. She pulled the dream pillow free and held it up to the light—gold dust covered the surface, sparkling away in the morning sun.

"Are you leaking glitter?" she asked the pillow. "Miss Adeline has no patience for flibbertigibbets leaving glitter willy-nilly all over her genteel bed linen."

The pillow remained the picture of innocence.

Lyla was not fooled. She ran her thumb over the fabric, frowning as gold dust collected on her skin.

"*Hmm*, glittery sands, huh? I wonder if you inspired Sasha's dream?" She mentally shrugged—it seemed like a plausible enough explanation. She'd have to share her discovery with Sasha once she got out of the shower.

Lyla placed the dream pillow on the nightstand and began to brush the glitter off the bed. She looked down, expecting to see gold flecks sprinkled over the floor, but the glitter was nowhere to be seen.

"No use hiding," she told the glitter. "I'll only sweep you up later."

After a cursory glance under Sasha's bed, she shrugged and began to get dressed. By the time Sasha came out of the bathroom, Lyla had forgotten all about the gold dust; she was too busy mentally listing all the things she needed to pack and clean while Sasha was at her meeting.

Which, in retrospect, was a terrible oversight on her part.

LIKE MOST PEOPLE, SASHA DETESTED CONFRONTATIONS. SO, TO PREPARE, she and Lyla brainstormed over breakfast and then planned out her upcoming showdown with the sort of vigor and attention to detail more suited to organizing grand scale invasions of hostile countries. They made lists. They debated strategies. They considered possible outcomes and outlined plans of action for each.

Eventually, they decided to keep things simple: Sasha would march into the Headmistress's office and tell the older woman—politely but firmly— that they needed to have a chat.

At that point, however, Sasha and Lyla's strategies on how best to bring up the tea-spiking incident diverged dramatically.

"Headmistress, I'd like to discuss what happened during afternoon tea," was Sasha's preferred opening line.

"Did you drug me, witch?" was Lyla's.

"Are you kidding?" Sasha dropped her forkful of scrambled eggs in shock. "*That's* your opening line?"

Lyla, who thought the tactic was perfectly reasonable, continued to butter her toast unperturbed. "You need to use the element of surprise— don't give her time to prepare a lie. Just hit her with the accusation and observe her facial expressions. WHAM!" She stabbed the air with her butter knife for emphasis. "Given her interest in Old Middleton's history, she'll appreciate your reference to witch mythology."

"Ri-ght." Sasha picked up her fork and half-heartedly stabbed a few pieces of egg. "I think I'll stick to my own, more diplomatic approach."

"Suit yourself." Lyla resumed buttering. "Just remember to stay calm, firm, and professional before she admits to the spiking."

"Calm, firm, and professional. Got it."

"And then scornful, vengeful, unleash-the-fires-of-hell-and-scorch-the-earth angry once she admits to the spiking."

Sasha exhaled in a rush. "I can do that."

"Excellent! Go apocalyptic on her."

Sasha remembered Lyla's words as she looked up at the imposing façade of the Old Middleton Elementary School.

"Be calm, firm, and professional. Right." She took a deep breath and stepped through the massive, wrought-iron gates. "Here goes."

Be calm, firm, and professional, she told herself as she marched toward the entrance of the school building.

Be calm, firm, and professional, she repeated, as she climbed up the stairs and made her way through the ornate, stained glass doors.

Be calm, firm, and profes—

Sasha stopped in her tracks.

There, just inside the doorway, stood the Headmistress and Esther.

"Hello, Sasha," the Headmistress said, her smile brittle. "We've been waiting for you."

"Did you drug me, witch?" Sasha blurted.

The two older women exchanged a look.

"Yes," they said simultaneously.

Sasha stared at the women, stunned. "You ... you *did?*"

"It's all my fault," Esther said, wringing her hands. "I was distracted and—"

The Headmistress put a hand on Esther's frail shoulder. "Now, now, Esther. *I* am the Headmistress, and I take full responsibility for what happens in this school. Let's conduct this meeting behind closed doors, shall we?"

She glanced meaningfully at a passing group of students and quickly ushered the shell-shocked Sasha and distraught Esther into a nearby classroom.

"It seems," the Headmistress began, closing the door behind them, "that Esther brewed the wrong tea."

The mousy woman nodded, miserable. "I mixed them up. Instead of using the tea we use for company, I used the Headmistress's relaxation blend."

Sasha looked back and forth between the two women, still in shock. "Sorry, but I don't follow ..."

"I usually ask Esther to brew me a pot of relaxation tea after school," the Headmistress explained. "As you well know, children can be a little … *spirited* … and I'm not as young as I used to be. More often than not, I find myself with a devil of a migraine at the end of the day. The tea helps me unwind and keeps the migraines at bay."

"But it's strong," Esther continued. "Rosa's brews often are—especially if you're not used to them. Yesterday afternoon, I was distracted and put the relaxation tea into the pot rather than the other tea, just as I would most afternoons."

Sasha continued to stare at the two older women, trying to make sense of this miraculous new development. "So, let me get this straight: You gave me super strong relaxation tea instead of normal tea?"

The women nodded.

"By mistake?"

The women nodded again.

Sasha's eyes narrowed. "This super relaxation tea wouldn't happen to have primrose in it, would it?"

"I believe so," the Headmistress said. "Esther?"

"Quite a bit, I'm afraid. Rosa swears that it's a relaxant." Esther clutched her pearls, her dark eyes welling-up behind her glasses. "I am so, so sorry, Sasha!"

Sasha's heart began to pound—this was too good to be true. "So … I drank super strong relaxation tea? It wasn't—" She stopped, unable to believe this turn of events. "Yesterday was a nightmare. I was telling people terribly personal … *things*. I mean, the grocer … the baker … that poor nun —" She pressed her lips together, still mortified by the memory.

The Headmistress winced. "So we heard. We took the liberty of explaining what had happened to the grocer."

"And to the baker," Esther added. "We're still hunting down all of his customers, but we'll tell them, too. The grocer was very understanding. He suspected something was up; he thought it very odd that anyone would find his sweater objectionable."

"We also bought you a box of cakes and pastries," the Headmistress continued. "We thought you might have been—shall we say, *reticent?*—to enter the bakery this morning."

"They're on your desk," Esther said. "We bought you the good ones with lots of frosting."

Sasha's mind was reeling. This—this changed everything! There was no grand conspiracy between the Headmistress, Esther, and Rosa. There was no nefarious plot to drug her. Better yet, her workplace was not a front for psychotic, geriatric, drug kingpins, but just a place where overworked educators mistook tea labels.

She would not have to leave Old Middleton.

She would not have to leave Old Middleton!

Sasha was so happy, so relieved—she could have burst into song. This was the ultimate best-case scenario *ever*: an accidental tea-spiking with baked treats as compensation.

Mistaking Sasha's silence for something more sinister, the Headmistress cleared her throat uneasily. "Of course, if you'd like to press charges—"

"No," Sasha said, exhaling. "It was an accident."

"And it will *never happen again*," the Headmistress said pointedly to Esther.

"Never again," Esther swore.

"Good," Sasha said emphatically. "I'd hate for this to happen to the next substitute teacher."

The Headmistress stared meaningfully at Esther. "Quite."

"Quite," Esther repeated, her tone contrite.

The Headmistress placed her hand over Sasha's. "I know that it's too soon to ask for your forgiveness, but I *do* hope this incident hasn't soured your view of Old Middleton."

"We understand if you wish to leave," Esther said. She smiled hesitantly at Sasha. "But we'd like to convince you to stay."

"I would be delighted to stay," Sasha said slowly, trying to contain her joy.

The two ladies positively beamed.

"That's wonderful news," the Headmistress said, clapping her hands together.

"Absolutely wonderful!" Esther echoed.

At that moment, the first school bell rang.

"Well …" The Headmistress straightened her rose-colored, cashmere cardigan. "We'd better get to work. The children await!"

"And if there is anything you need," Esther said to Sasha, "anything at all, please let me know."

What Sasha needed was to tell Lyla about this development as soon as possible. "May I use the office phone?"

"Of course!"

The Headmistress smiled her twinkliest smile at Sasha. "We're so happy that you're staying, dear. You fit right in."

"You really do," Esther said, nodding. "Oh! I forgot—we also left you a small bag of relaxation tea near your treats."

"Marvelous stuff," the Headmistress said. "It's better than painkillers for migraines."

Sasha balked. "Ah, thanks but *no*."

"Take it anyway—you never know when it could come in handy."

"Especially in our profession," Esther added.

Sasha could not conceive of a situation where raging self-confession would be necessary or desirable. Nevertheless, she smiled politely. "Thanks. I'll just go and make that call."

～

"*RELAXATION TEA?*" LYLA'S VOICE CRACKLED INCREDULOUSLY FROM MISS Adeline's landline.

"Yes," Sasha whispered into the phone. She looked around the office, mindful of being overheard. So far, the space was empty. "Relaxation tea. Made by Rosa."

"A likely story. I bet they found out that you bought Truth Elixir and concocted this story to save their hides."

"No, you didn't see them—they were *really* upset. Esther was on the verge of tears."

"*Hmm.*" Lyla's tone was laced with skepticism.

"They bought me pastries and everything."

"Don't let them buy you. You're worth more than a donut."

Sasha rolled her eyes but stopped when she realized Lyla would not be able to see the eye-rolling in question. "I believe them."

"Of course, you do! You don't want terrible things to happen to you."

"And you *do?* Seriously? Look, this is the best possible outcome. Not the most exciting outcome, but the best by far."

"We didn't adequately prepare for this outcome."

Sasha couldn't help but grin. "Nó, we didn't. But it's definitely my favorite outcome."

"*Hmm.*"

"Come on, Lyla! You have to admit—it really is the best-case scenario."

Sasha could almost hear the gears turning in Lyla's clever brain. If this had been any other day, Sasha would have been happy to hear the sound; she loved watching her friend puzzle through tricky problems and situations. But Sasha had been through an Ordeal, and she wanted—no, *needed* —to put all of this behind her. She didn't have the energy to continue chasing conspiracy theories or elaborate drug plots. She needed her cynical friend to accept this happy piece of news with a minimum of fuss so that they could enjoy their remaining time in Old Middleton.

She held her breath and waited for Lyla's reply.

"I admit," Lyla said eventually, "that this *appears* to be good news. What do you want to do?"

Sasha exhaled in a rush. "I'd like to stay."

She quickly pulled the receiver away from her ear as Lyla screeched, causing Miss Adeline's ancient phone line to crackle and whine. "Ha! Of *course* you want to stay! You're *so* easy! All it takes is an old lady sob-story and a bag full of carbs, and all is forgiven."

Sasha cautiously placed the phone back against her ear. "Not *forgiven*. But I'm giving them the benefit of the doubt. Besides, I need this job, Lyla. I'm broke, and it pays almost twice as much as what I was getting in New York. If I want to find a job that pays even close to the same rate, I'd have to teach in Alaska."

"Not Alaska!" Lyla gasped. "It's so far and so cold, and so *far!*"

"Yes. Yes, it is."

Don't get any ideas! Sasha told that little voice in her head. *I'm not going to Alaska.*

But for once, the voice was strangely silent. Sasha hoped that it had fallen into a coma.

"It's Alaska or Old Middleton, Lyla," Sasha continued firmly. "The choice is yours."

There was another long pause on Lyla's end of the line.

"*Fine* then," Lyla said reluctantly. "But don't eat those pastries, you hear me? Heaven knows what's in them."

Sasha's shoulders sagged in relief. "The pastries aren't drugged. The drugging was an accident."

"Even so, why would you eat pastries given to you by a known food-spiker? Esther is clearly incompetent when it comes to food preparation. Why tempt fate by eating pastries that she carried around in a box? You know what they say: Fool you once, shame on them; fool you twice, etcetera etcetera ..."

"I don't want to go through my life not trusting people. I *like* people."

"Too bad—those days are over! Think about it: we're all too trusting. We try the free samples, we drink the Kool-Aid, we date bearded guys—"

"Hang on—bearded guys?" Sasha frowned. "What's wrong with bearded guys?"

"Nothing good comes from dating a bearded guy. If they're devious enough to hide their chins, they could be hiding anything ..."

Sasha decided to let that spectacularly misguided piece of wisdom remain unchallenged.

"The point is," Lyla continued, "from now on, you need to say, 'no thanks' to everything you're offered in Old Middleton, particularly from schoolteachers. That is, unless you enjoy performing sex charades in bakeries ..."

"Fine," Sasha said, more to appease Lyla than anything else. "I'll throw away the pastries, which will make me cry, but will keep me drug-free."

"But keep the tea. *Evidence.*"

Sasha shuddered. "Just as long as I never have to drink it."

"Sure, but I make no such promises for myself. So, I guess we're staying?"

"We're staying." Sasha could not keep the smile from her voice.

"Damn. Though, I tell you what—this place is *way* more interesting than I thought it would be. And Halloween is coming! Just imagine the trouble we'll get into ..."

~

SASHA FOUND OUT THE HARD WAY THAT GALLIVANTING AROUND WITH HILL-men in her dreams, even in a non-pelvic fashion, did not necessarily equate to a restful night's sleep.

The surge of adrenaline she had been riding since her meeting with the Headmistress and Esther had soon fizzled out, leaving her exhausted—the kind of exhausted that even three cups of coffee before midday could not fix. Her eyes were itchy, her limbs leaden, and her brain felt stuffed full of cotton candy. She could not concentrate on simple tasks, such as eating her apple at recess; or more complex tasks, such as teaching, which unfortu-nately was in her job description.

"Why couldn't I be a professional snack tester?" she grumbled wearily, as she headed back to class after recess.

To make matters worse, her body decided that any small pause in routine was a perfect opportunity for a nap. She caught herself almost nodding off while listening to Bryce tell a rambling story about his cat's weird smell. She felt her eyelids flutter shut during a staff meeting, and barely managed to open them again when the Headmistress asked her a question. She even started to fall asleep while sitting on a bench during playground duty, catching herself just before she fell sideways onto the ground.

"Are you drunk?" Mason Barnes asked, as Sasha scrambled back into a sitting position.

"I wish," Sasha said with a yawn.

But what was truly strange—even stranger than falling asleep on a bench surrounded by screaming children—was that every time Sasha slipped into sleep, even for a microsecond, she would dream.

At first, she was delighted; clearly, her twenty-five-year dream drought was over. No more nocturnal emptiness and boredom for her!

But very soon, this delight turned to dread.

Something was wrong.

Very, very wrong.

Each time she dreamed, Sasha found herself back on the hill, staring out over the plain, her feet sinking in gold dust.

Initially, she thought she was reliving the same dream over and over again. But then she noticed a crucial detail: in each new dream, the wailing, seething mass of monsters was closer and closer to her hill.

Closer and closer to *her*.

That's fine, she told herself firmly, as she bit into her sandwich.

Let them come closer, she thought defiantly, as she bent down to tie Joanna's shoelaces.

Nothing can harm me in a dream, she insisted, fighting to keep her eyelids open.

But when she closed her eyes for a moment during the children's naptime, she opened them to a vision of pure terror.

The monsters had arrived at the base of her hill.

From her vantage point above the plain, Sasha could clearly make out their twisted, white bodies and see their mouths—gaping black holes ringed with teeth like razor-shards—open in an endless scream. Their wails sounded *hungry*, making the hair on the back of her neck stand at attention. She watched, her heart pounding, as the monsters stretched out their arms toward her beseechingly, the claws on their long, spidery fingers as black as pitch and *so* sharp.

Don't make eye contact! the voice in the back of her head ordered urgently.

Sasha quickly looked away; she instinctively knew that looking those monsters in the eye would cost her something vital to her sanity. She prepared herself to run, to turn and escape. But, to her horror, she found that she could barely lift her feet. Her body felt heavy with exhaustion—her sleepless night, the stress of yet another move, the fear and uncertainty surrounding her drugging had all finally caught up with her. The glittery hill dust may as well have been quicksand for all she could move.

"Wake up!" she told herself urgently, trying to fight the exhaustion, trying to push her leaden limbs forward.

As if sensing her vulnerability, the monsters threw back their heads and howled in triumph. The sound tore through Sasha like a blade, leaving her raw and shaking. She threw her hands over her ears.

"Come on, wake up!" she gasped.

The monsters lowered their heads. As one, they began to surge up the hill, their spidery limbs making quick work of the climb.

"*Wake up!*" Sasha screamed at the sky, as the monsters crested the hill. "WAKE! UP!"

Suddenly, Sasha felt something on her arm: a sharp, insistent pain that came and went.

Came and went...

Came and went...

Came and—

Sasha's eyes flew open, and she flinched back in shock; three small faces were crowded inches from her own, staring at her in horrified fascination. A fourth small face—that of Mason Barnes—was staring at her upper arm, which he poked with steadfast determination.

Sasha grabbed Mason's hand mid-poke and placed it flat on her desk.

He smiled at her mischievously. "Oh, good. You're awake. My poking finger was getting tired." He held up his tiny index finger. "See? It's all red and bent."

"Were you sleeping?" Joanna asked.

Sasha shook her head, trying to clear it. "I was just resting my eyes."

Kaytie stared at her suspiciously. "Mrs. Landshome does that a lot."

"Especially after school," Mason added, "when she's been drinking the juice she keeps up her skirt."

"Did *you* drink skirt juice?" Bryce asked.

Sasha groaned. "No. No, I didn't. And let's never call it that again, okay?"

"Okay," Bryce said, sounding unconvinced.

Sasha took a deep breath and tried to slow her galloping heart rate. She looked down at the concerned faces of her small class and realized that she needed to pull herself together.

"Right." She gave them a shaky smile. "Ah ... what were we doing? Oh, yes. Have you all finished the counting exercise I gave you?"

"No!" they chorused gleefully.

"You're all terrible but honest." Sasha took another deep breath. *It's just a dream,* she told herself sternly. "Storytime comes after math, so if you don't finish your counting exercise, I won't be able to read you today's story, and it's a really exciting one."

The children looked torn except for Kaytie.

"What makes it so exciting?" she asked suspiciously. "I want to know more about it before I decide whether it's worth doing the counting exercise or not."

"Way to negotiate, Kaytie!" Sasha said brightly, smoothing down her navy skirt with shaking hands. "But you're going to have to do the counting exercise before the story no matter what."

Kaytie frowned. "I think I want to call my lawyer."

Sasha felt her eyes begin to shut of their own accord and panicked—there was no way she could face those monsters again while she was teaching, particularly when one of her students had legal representation.

"Right," she said, lurching off her seat. "New plan. We're going outside to play games."

"YAY!" the children cheered.

"Take that, math!" Mason yelled.

"Nice try, Mason—we'll do the counting exercise when we get back." Sasha grabbed the tee-ball set from the corner and a bottle of water from her handbag.

"Mason," she said, crouching down until she was at eye level with the small boy. "If I fall asleep again, at any point today, pour this bottle of water over my head."

Mason's eyes widened. He solemnly took the bottle of water, clutching it close to his chest as if it was something infinitely precious.

"This is the best day ever," he said in awe.

"Best day ever!" the rest of the children chanted as they gleefully ran out of the classroom, Sasha stumbling close behind.

∾

SASHA DRAGGED HERSELF INTO THE BOARDING HOUSE AND DROPPED HER BAG onto the floor with a muted *thump*. Fumbling, she pulled off her coat and tried, multiple times, to put it on the coatrack.

"I don't remember this being so hard," she muttered to herself as she missed the hook yet again. "Okay, one more time, here we go … yes! Good! *Agh*—no." The coat slipped off the shiny, copper hook and fell to the floor. Sasha stared blearily at the puddle of green wool at her feet and sighed, defeated. "Fine then. Be that way. Very rebellious of you. Lyla? Are you here?"

"In here," Lyla's voice called out, distracted.

Lyla, as usual, was reading in the rose drawing room. Her small frame was curled up on one of the terribly uncomfortable pink couches, her legs tucked neatly beneath her, her hazel eyes—narrowed behind her reading glasses—glued to the page.

Looking up at Sasha's approach, she raised an eyebrow at Sasha's soaked shirt, wet hair, and mascara-stained face. "Tough day at the office?"

Sasha snorted. "Like you wouldn't believe."

Briefly, Sasha explained about the naps, the monsters, and the surprise of waking up at the final school bell to Mason soaking her with the contents of her water bottle as the rest of the class cheered him on.

"He was thorough, wasn't he?" Lyla said admiringly. "Wait a minute." She ran upstairs and came back with a towel.

"Thanks," Sasha said gratefully, and began to wipe her face. "I thought playing ball games would keep me awake until it was time to go home. Nope. Two minutes into watching them do a counting exercise and I was unconscious."

"What do you expect? It was a *counting exercise*. That would be enough to send me into a coma." Lyla watched as Sasha dried her hair. "Why didn't you dry off before you left the school?"

"I was hoping the cold, wet feeling would keep me awake on the drive home. It did." Sasha wrapped the towel around her hair and collapsed onto the couch. "Honestly, I don't know what to do. If I stay still too long, I fall asleep. Nothing seems to keep me awake."

"Then why not go upstairs and have a nap?"

Sasha shuddered. "The monsters. I just—no."

"I can't believe I am going to advocate physical exertion, but why don't you go for a run? It might keep you awake, at least until dinner."

"You are an honest to goodness genius." Sasha reached across the couch and hugged Lyla. "Want to come?"

Lyla shuddered. "I'm a genius, remember? I know better than to exert myself physically like some common peasant. Be off with you." She waved Sasha regally toward the door.

Sasha changed into her running gear and made her way outside. She stood at the boarding house gate and planned her route. Then, closing her eyes, she prepared herself mentally for the journey ahead by visualizing the route as a golden path that stretched out before her. She breathed deeply and evenly, concentrating on the path until it was fixed in her mind.

When she was ready, Sasha opened her eyes and began to run. Despite the beauty of the brisk, fall afternoon, she tuned out all the sights and sounds around her, focusing solely on her golden path.

She ran and ran, leaving her monsters behind.

~

THIRTY MINUTES LATER, SASHA FOUND HERSELF WALKING—SWEATY, TIRED, but exhilarated—down Main Street. Lyla *was* a genius. She felt so much better after her run, much more like herself again. The monsters had faded away, and her focus had returned.

"I'm back, better than ever!" she said with a triumphant fist-pump. "Take *that,* inappropriately attired dream men and scary nap monsters. You can't keep me down!"

A small, gray cat watched Sasha from its perch on top of a mailbox. It *meowed* in solidarity.

"Thanks!" she grinned. "Right back at you."

All around her, the streetlamps were beginning to flicker to life. As she passed the shops that lined the street, Sasha noticed that many of them now had Halloween displays in their front windows. She smiled at the string of grinning paper witches hung across the bookstore window and the jack-o'-lanterns in front of the florist shop. Felicia was dressing one of her storefront mannequins in a frothy black tulle gown, complete with a black witch's hat. Sasha waved limply at the redhead and received a simpering smile in return.

She received a more enthusiastic greeting from Rosa, who was hanging cobwebs and swooping black bats around the cauldron, now filled with bubbling green liquid. Sasha waved back with a smile, but hurried past before Rosa could call her over. The last thing she wanted to do was talk about her dreams or Truth Elixirs.

She was about to turn toward the boarding house when she felt a sudden surge of exhilaration that had nothing to do with her run.

Turn around, the voice in the back of her mind said giddily. *Look!*

Despite her misgivings about letting a voice—especially a *gleeful* voice—in her head dictate her actions, Sasha turned.

Main Street was backlit by the remnants of a magnificent sunset, its lamplights twinkling against the shadowy buildings, and the pink and gold-streaked sky. At the end of the street, the ancient Middleton Gateway stood guarding the little village, its sandstone pillars glowing in the last rays of the sun and faintly glittering as if they were composed of gold dust ...

Sasha stilled. It had to be a trick of the light; there was no possible way that the gateway was made of the same gold dust from her dreams.

She rubbed the heels of her hands against her weary eyes and looked again. The stones were back to their customary beige.

I'm just tired, she told herself as she turned back toward the boarding house.

But the voice inside her head only laughed.

~

THURSDAY, OCTOBER 25TH

In a remarkably cruel twist of fate, Sasha's brisk run through the village failed to give her a peaceful night sleep. Instead, the added physical exertion only seemed to make her hillside dreams more intense.

She woke up the next morning as exhausted as if she actually *had* spent the night running from monsters. She had to drag herself to the shower, forgot to apply eyeliner to her left eye, and would have gone down to breakfast without putting on pants if it were not for Lyla.

"Are you sure you're not diseased, girl?" Miss Adeline asked suspiciously, as Sasha sat limply at the kitchen table, sucking down coffee like a dry sponge.

"I'm not ruling it out," Sasha said, refilling her coffee cup to the brim.

"You're too thin," Martha muttered, dropping a packed lunch in front of Sasha. "Terrible things happen to thin people."

Sasha looked down at her perfectly healthy physique. She opened her mouth to argue but decided against it; there was a look in Martha's eyes that said she was not above force-feeding if she felt the situation warranted it.

To make matters worse, Sasha kept misplacing things: one of her red pumps was missing, she could not find her hairbrush, and her toothbrush had disappeared from the bathroom.

It was disconcerting.

Despite her best efforts, Sasha's workday became an uneasy mix of normalcy and hillside visits. One moment she was listening to the howls of monsters; the next, she would find herself at the mercy of Mason's increasingly creative attempts to wake her up.

When Sasha finally stumbled into the drawing room after work, Lyla took one look at her pale face and shaking hands and insisted on another visit to the doctor.

It did not go well.

"A pox on the Old Middleton medical community!" Lyla yelled, shaking her fist at the medical center. She turned to Sasha. "I mean, *stress*? What kind of diagnosis is *stress*?"

"I might be stressed," Sasha said.

Lyla ignored her. "And the cure is *a good night's sleep*?"

"That would be great. If I could get one."

"*Exactly*. You told him that your sleep was full of terrifying dreams. And you also told him that you couldn't stop napping during the day——"

Sasha yawned. "Uh huh."

Lyla threw her hands up in disbelief. "Wasn't he listening? How could *more* sleep be the cure? You almost fell asleep in your soup last night. What kind of cure tries to drown you in your dinner?" Lyla shook her head, furious. "And what did he prescribe?"

"Over the counter sleeping pills."

"Over the counter sleeping pills *and no further tests*? That's it—I'm going back to check on his credentials. I'm not convinced that he has a medical degree. His first name is probably Doctor."

Sasha grabbed Lyla's arm before she could head back into the medical center and cause chaos. "It's obvious that there's nothing else they can do for me. The doctor's right—I'm probably just stressed. I'm in a new place, with a new job, and I had a long journey to get here. Not to mention the fact that I've just started dreaming again after twenty-five years. My brain is probably very confused right now. You watch, tomorrow will probably be much better."

~

Friday, October 26th

The next day was no better.

Desperate and fresh out of ideas, Sasha had taken the sleep medication recommended by the doctor. To her horror, her dreams became even more vivid—and even more difficult to escape. She awoke on Friday morning with a headache and a dry mouth, more exhausted than before.

When medicine failed, Lyla's next solution was research.

"I *will* find the answer," she muttered at the breakfast table, skimming through a book on sleep-disorders. "We will triumph—or die trying."

"We really need a new motto," Sasha said, stifling yet another yawn.

"Reading while you eat is rude and unhygienic," Miss Adeline said disapprovingly. She placed a serving of bacon on Lyla's plate more forcefully than was required and gestured at the book with the serving tongs. "Rude and unhygienic."

"But this is an emergency!" Lyla cried. "I'm trying to save Sasha's brain." She waved the book at Miss Adeline, the pages fluttering madly. "*This* could be her only hope! If we don't find a cure soon, terrible things could happen to her. She could fall into a coma, or suffer permanent brain damage, or fall asleep at the wheel and crash through all the stores and village landmarks on Main Street, recklessly mowing down screaming tourists beneath the wheels of her car until she is stopped, captured, and sentenced to prison for the rest of her life. Which would be terrible, because orange is *not* her color."

"That was so, so specific," Sasha said, shaking her head, and nearly toppling into her waffles.

Lyla shrugged. "I've given it some thought."

Miss Adeline stared at Lyla for a long moment, her tongs still aloft. "Carry on then," she said eventually, and went back to the stove.

Sasha listlessly pushed her scrambled eggs around on her plate and tried to get her mind to focus. Lyla was right; she needed a cure before she was fired ... or crashed her car through Main Street ... or was fired for crashing her car through Main Street. She wondered whether Rosa had a potion or charm to stop her dreams.

"What's the opposite of a dream pillow?" she asked Lyla. "Because that's what I need—something that will give me fewer dreams and more real-life."

"The opposite of dream pillow?" Lyla looked up from her book. "How about a 'reality rug'?' Or an 'actuality afghan'? Or a 'consciousness comforter'?"

"You are no help at all."

"Are you kidding? I'm nothing *but* helpful."

Sasha's eyes narrowed. "This all started after that Twilight Tour. *This* is what comes of a two-penny well-wish. We should never have thrown in the second penny." She shook her fork at Lyla. "We were messing with forces that we didn't understand!"

"Now you are just babbling incoherently. Have you been at the Truth Elixir?"

"No." Sasha placed her fork on her plate, her appetite gone. "But—now that you mention it, do you think my dreams are a side effect of the Truth Elixir?"

"No. I took it, too, remember? And I'm just fine—no monsters for me."

"What about the relaxation tea?"

Lyla snorted. "That wore off long ago. Do you think someone at school spiked your food?"

"No." Sasha yawned.

Lyla patted Sasha's hand fondly. "As if you'd know—you're usually unconscious."

Sasha's exhaustion was so obvious that her fellow teachers began to worry.

"Would you like me to take your class?" Shae asked, as Sasha sluggishly made her way down the hall. "It'll be no trouble."

Sasha was touched by her concern. "Thanks, but I'll be fine. Although I'm not much of an educator right now."

"Oh, please." Shae waved away Sasha's fears, her glittery nail polish catching the light. "It's *kindergarten*. The worst you can do is mess up storytime. Now, if you were teaching something with explosives, like Advanced Chemistry, I would have insisted on taking your class." Shae grinned. "I couldn't let you blow us all sky-high."

"I still might," Sasha said with a sigh.

"Here," Mrs. Landshome said, handing Sasha a steaming cup of coffee during recess. "Drink this. It'll fix all your ills."

"Thanks!" Sasha said. "Just what I—" She paused as the unmistakable smell of hard spirits wafted up from the cup, making her eyes water. "Mrs. Landshome, did you spike this coffee with alcohol?"

"No," the old woman said. "I spiked the alcohol with coffee. It's the better way to do it."

Oddly enough, the Headmistress's answer to Sasha's exhaustion was also a beverage.

"You do look *awfully* tired," the Headmistress said, tsking. "And even paler than usual. How about I get Rosa to mix you up a special tea?"

"Ah, no," Sasha said hastily. "No tea. Thanks. I'm already ninety-seven percent coffee." Although she seriously regretted declining Mrs. Landshome's spiked cup. "I'll rest this weekend, and I'll be fine by Monday. You'll see."

When Sasha returned home from work, Lyla frowned at her bedraggled appearance and shook her head.

"You look terrible. Mason's finger has probably been worn down to a stub by now."

Sasha snorted and pulled up the sleeve of her red sweater, revealing a sizable dark blue bruise.

Lyla stared at the bruise critically. "He needs to swap arms."

"That's mostly from yesterday." Sasha slumped onto the couch. "It wasn't too bad today; I only fell asleep three times, and I caught myself right away. For the most part."

"How did you manage that?"

"Coffee. So much coffee. If I have another cup, I'll have a heart attack." Sasha curled up on the couch beside Lyla, laying her head on her friend's shoulder. "This constant dreaming is a form of torture. It's like waterboarding but with dreams. *Dream*-boarding."

"Sleep deprivation is already a recognized form of torture. You don't need to make it worse."

"This *feels* worse. Any luck finding a cure for me?" Sasha gestured to the book in Lyla's lap.

"Nothing yet." Lyla glared at the pages as if willing the answer to appear. "Then again, there's still hope—I have one hundred and fifteen pages to go." She reached over and pulled a chunk of yellow crayon from Sasha's hair. "Art lesson today?"

Sasha grimaced. "Yes. We set up our easels, like real artists, and drew pictures of our favorite things. It was lovely—until I fell asleep and fell headfirst onto Joanna's artwork. Which was a tragedy, because it was fantastic."

Joanna's artwork was a bold, primary color depiction of a princess on a horse. Both the princess and the horse had resplendent locks, suspiciously like Joanna's own. Thanks to Sasha's impromptu nap, this brilliant depiction of interspecies-hair follicles was ruined beyond repair—as was the unfortunate easel.

"Those poor children," Sasha said, staring down at the crayon. The crayon stared back at her accusingly. "I'm the worst teacher in the history of educators—they're barely learning anything. If I stay still too long, I fall asleep, so we've just been playing games all day." She sat up and faced her friend, her shoulders slumped in defeat. "These are supposed to be their formative years, Lyla, and I'm wasting them!"

Lyla waved away Sasha's concerns. "Please. Knowing you, those children are playing educational games, which is the true tragedy here. Besides, it's kindergarten, not Harvard. A couple days of games won't impact their academic future."

"Yes, but they should at least know the alphabet by now. I haven't been able to stay awake past K for the past two days."

Lyla shrugged. "The rest of the alphabet is pretty overrated. On Monday, start from Z and work your way back until you meet up in the middle. It'll be fine."

Sasha groaned. "It won't be fine! It will *never* be fine!"

The moment was interrupted by the sound of a knock on the front door. It swung open to reveal the postman, Mr. Eldridge—a gentleman in his early sixties dressed in a pair of navy shorts and matching shirt, knee-high socks, and a wide-brimmed hat.

The two women watched as he straightened his hat and puffed out his thin chest.

"Miss Adeline?" he called.

"She's running errands," Lyla replied.

The man visibly deflated. "Oh. Well then, I'll just put the mail on the side table, as usual."

He shuffled across the room to the side table, then back to the door, his pale, white thighs almost glowing in the dim light of the foyer.

"Ladies." He tipped his hat to the women and left.

"Bye!" Sasha and Lyla called after him.

Lyla waited until she heard the door close behind him before shaking her head. "Mr. Eldridge is clearly a masochist. He also lacks the ability to read social situations; I'm surprised Martha hasn't gone after him with a feather duster. Did you know that the gossip around Old Middleton is that he delivers more than the mail to some of the village ladies, *if you know what I mean*? But I suspect that he started that rumor himself to add to his sexual allure."

"Good for him," Sasha said, and buried her face in a velvet throw pillow.

Lyla patted Sasha's head and surreptitiously pulled another piece of crayon free from her curls. "To get back to the matter at hand, you need to look on the bright side: even asleep, you're still a better teacher than Mrs. Landshome, with all her sarcasm and skirt-juice."

Sasha looked up from the cushion. "Can we please agree never to use that term again?"

"Nope. That term is gold. Would it help if I distracted you from the phrase by telling you that your skirt is on backwards?"

"What?" Sasha looked down at her lap and blanched. "Ugh! *No!* My skirt is on *backwards*. How—?"

"I guess not." Lyla placed the crayon pieces in her pocket. "Look, forget writing lesson plans for tonight. Why don't you go for a run?"

Sasha averted her eyes from the lining of her skirt. "I can't. Not after last night. That was a disaster." She winced at the memory. "It happened so fast. I just sat down on the grass to catch my breath and then—" She buried her face back in the cushion.

"It wasn't *that* bad," Lyla said, although it was. "And Violet apologized for turning the sprinklers on you … once she'd figured out who was sleeping on her prize lilies."

Sasha looked up from the cushion, her blue-eyes fierce. "No more running until this is fixed."

Lyla held up her hands in surrender. "Fine, fine. Then why not sketch? When we first got here, you said you wanted to sketch Main Street."

"I did! But then, I got busy—"

"—with teaching and tea-spiking and narcolepsy … Yes, I know. But you're free now." Lyla smiled when Sasha perked up. "Just try not to fall asleep face first onto your pencil."

"Excellent advice," Sasha said dryly, and went upstairs to get her supplies.

Armed with one of her larger sketchbooks and her best set of pencils, Sasha sat beside Lyla on one of the creaky, pink sofas, and turned to a blank page. As usual, there was an odd, bittersweet feeling that accompanied her itch to draw. By all accounts, Sasha should have been a professional artist, perhaps even one of particular renown. She had talent in abundance, an excellent technical education, and the ambition to make it far in the field. By now, she should have been living out her wildest dreams.

But she was, in a word, *cursed*. When it came to her art, Sasha was beset by a series of gradually escalating catastrophes.

First, there were the contests she had entered—only to find that her entries had mysteriously disappeared, or had been somehow ruined, or had never been unpacked.

Then, there were the buyers, who would be beguiled by her paintings only to disappear when it came time to purchase them—often literally, according to the police reports.

And finally, there was the owner of a prestigious gallery, who had begged Sasha to contribute two of her oil paintings to an upcoming show. It was to be her biggest opportunity yet, with the tantalizing promise of her own show in the future if all went well. That is, until the owner had called her in hysterics the night before the opening when his gallery had mysteriously fallen into a sinkhole.

Acts of God, twists of fate, karma, destiny, natural disasters—call them what you will, but they happened again and again. It was frustrating, and at times infuriating. Sasha *knew* she had the talent; all she required was an opportunity that did not literally disappear.

As the years went by, her dreams of becoming a world-renowned artist had dwindled to dust, buried under sensible things, such as rent payments, and grocery bills, and growing up.

But she continued to draw. It was still her happiest of happy places.

While Lyla read a new book on sleep patterns, Sasha adjusted the pink fringed lampshade on the side table to give her more light and began to sketch. She didn't have a subject in mind; she simply cleared her thoughts and touched pencil to paper.

But, to her dismay, a face began to take shape: a decidedly male face with dark, chin-length hair that framed a firm jaw and high cheekbones; deep-set eyes with a touch of imperiousness in their depths; and lips that tilted into a faintly superior smile. Despite that smile, there was something about his lower lip that made her want to ...

She dropped her pencil in disgust.

Hill-Man.

Typical, she thought. *Trust him to appear on my sketch pad where he's unwanted and distracting, rather than in my dreams, where he's wanted and distracting.*

It was a sore spot for Sasha that her dreams—which had started promisingly enough with half-naked men—had quickly degenerated into an infinite loop of weather and monsters. It was irrational, but she blamed Hill-Man for this development.

"Let's try this again," she muttered and turned the page.

She filled her mind with fall vistas and began to sketch. She visualized red and gold leaves and the clear starscapes of brisk October nights; pumpkin pie and the scent of spiced apple cider; and Halloween scenes of jack-o'-lanterns and grinning children dressed as ghouls and ghosts and beasties—

A cough startled her. Sasha jerked upright, realizing that she must have dozed off while sketching. Rubbing her eyes, she looked down at her sketchbook ... and found herself staring at a full-length sketch of Hill-Man, his robe billowing artfully to reveal a rather impressive chest.

"Dammit!" she muttered. Nevertheless, she carefully added a little more shading to his abs.

"Language," Lyla said absentmindedly, her eyes never leaving her book.

Sasha frowned down at Hill-Man, who regarded her with an enigmatic expression.

Then she shrugged. *If you can't beat them ...*

Quickly, she filled in the finer details: the dark shadows beneath his eyes; the blunt nails on his long, artistic fingers; the sharp curve of his hipbones that peeked above his low-slung pajama pants. She sketched the tattoos on the inside of his wrists as best as she could from memory, then the ones on his palms.

She was both surprised and a little mortified by the number of details that she remembered about him, including the ones that she could not sketch: the warmth of his chest under her palm; the feel of his hands, large and strong, easily spanning her waist; the scent of him—wood-smoke and petrichor, and something warm and peppery that made her mouth water.

There was a lot about him that made her mouth water, she thought glumly.

Idly, she added a little more detail to his chest. He had been wearing a silver amulet—a fanciful thing of moons and stars—but she could not quite remember the details. Truth be told, her attention had been focused on the chest beneath it. Had the star been in the center? Or had it—

"Wow."

Sasha jumped in her seat. "Lyla!" She clutched her heart. "Give me some warning next time you decide to creep up on me."

"How could I creep up on you? I'm sitting right next to you." Lyla took a closer look at Sasha's sketch. "From his fancy bedroom attire, I'm guessing that's Hill-Man."

"Yes," Sasha said glumly.

"It's a pity he was so virtuous." Lyla turned the page and whistled. "A real pity." She traced the air above the contours of his chest with the tip of her finger. "Though, he's bound to turn up on that hill again any day now."

Sasha shrugged half-heartedly. "I don't know about that … all I seem to do is run away from monsters. It's as though the dream is stuck in a loop."

Lyla thought about that for a long moment. "You know … maybe … maybe that's the problem. What if these monsters represent real life demons? You know, all your fears and anxieties? What if you're supposed to face them head on rather than run away? You have to admit—and I say this with love—that you do tend to run from situations—"

"—and from people and places," Sasha finished, frowning. *Always moving. Always looking for the next experience …*

"So, maybe this dream is symbolic," Lyla continued. "Maybe it isn't a coincidence that the first dream you've had in twenty-five years coincides with you taking the millionth substitute teaching job this year. Maybe it's time for you to face your demons so that you can transition to the next phase of your life."

"So … by that logic, I'm supposed to run *towards* these demons, not away from them?" The thought of it—of running toward those creatures—made Sasha faintly nauseous.

Lyla nodded. "Maybe then you won't be stuck on that hill anymore. Maybe Hill-Man will be waiting for you on the other side of the plain."

"Perhaps." Sasha glanced admiringly at her friend. "Look at you, using your fancy psychology degree to fix my brain."

"*Pfft*. They don't teach dream analysis in psych. I learned that from TV sitcoms and the psychic channel." Lyla tapped the sketchbook with the tip of her index finger. "You should probably hide this from Miss Adeline. If she finds out that you're drawing half-naked men, she'll probably give you a terrifying lecture on the sins of pornography and then evict you. Or have Martha do it."

"Ha! Right."

At that precise moment, the door of the kitchen creaked open.

"Quick!" Lyla hissed.

Together, they grabbed the sketchbook and, looking around the room for a suitable hiding place, jammed it under the low chaise just before the imposing figure of Miss Adeline entered the room.

The older woman looked at the flushed cheeks and bright eyes of her boarders suspiciously. "I just wanted to inform you that I'll be needing the drawing room tomorrow night." She straightened her shoulders proudly. "*I* will be hosting the Old Middleton Women's Historical Society Meeting this month."

"Yes, Miss Adeline," the women said in unison.

"May I attend?" Lyla asked politely, "I'd like to learn more about the town's history. I'll be very quiet and—"

"No," Miss Adeline said firmly.

"But—"

"*No*. Martha made cod for dinner. Go and wash up—it's rude to keep her waiting."

"Yes, Miss Adeline," the two women intoned, and dutifully went to do Miss Adeline's bidding.

~

Miss Adeline waited until her boarders had left the room before swooping down and throttling the crushed throw pillows until they were back to their original, puffy glory.

With a satisfied nod at her handiwork, she went back to the kitchen.

The sketchbook, with its hidden bounty of bare-chested hill-men, lay temporarily forgotten.

8

HERE THERE BE MONSTERS

FRIDAY, OCTOBER 26TH: NIGHT.

THAT NIGHT, FOR THE FIRST TIME SINCE SASHA BEGAN DREAMING, SHE could not fall asleep. In some ways, it was a relief: there was no hill made of gold dust, no screeching monsters, no tempestuous weather, no strange silver grass.

But, on the other hand, she was well and truly exhausted.

She *needed* to sleep.

Frustrated after over an hour of trying to toss and turn without making the bed creak, she carefully sat up and reached for the glass of water on her nightstand. But instead of finding the glass, her fingers brushed against something soft and cool. With a frown, she pulled the dream pillow out from where it was wedged between the placid shepherdess figurine and the cross-eyed china cat.

"Is this all your fault?" she whispered to the starry bundle. "I was blaming the extra penny, but did *you* start this whole mess?"

The pillow remained silent, obviously fearful of incriminating itself.

Sasha rubbed the slick fabric between her fingers. "Then again, when you were under my pillow, I dreamed of Hill-Man … which was much better than the monsters." She brought the pillow to her nose and inhaled.

Immediately, she yawned.

"Okay," she said, laughing quietly, "I'm giving you one more chance."

She settled back into bed and clutched the dream pillow to her chest. "Let me dream of Tahiti and Hill-Man—clothing optional."

She was asleep in seconds ... only to find herself on the hillside again.

"Dash it!" she cursed, sinking into gold dust. "What part of 'Tahiti' and 'clothing optional' did you not understand? *Hey?*"

Almost reluctantly, Sasha looked down the slope. Just like every other night, there was no Hill-Man.

"Typical," she muttered.

What was *not* typical was the dream pillow curled in her fist.

"Well, at least that's different," she said, rubbing the blue silk between her fingertips.

Before Sasha could ponder this new development, she heard it—the terrifying, high-pitched roar that quite literally haunted her dreams. Across the plain, the twisted forms of the monsters began to rise and make their way toward her hill.

"Oh, hell," she whispered.

The hair on the back of her neck stood up. Sasha could feel the adrenaline begin to pump through her body, preparing her to flee once more.

Abruptly, she remembered what Lyla had said. Maybe the way to get off this hill was not to run away from the demons but to run *toward* them.

Sasha looked out across the plain at the thousands of twisted, white bodies hurtling toward her. At this distance, they were terrifying—she shuddered to think what they would look like close up.

"Lyla, if you're wrong about this, I'll kill you. No, worse—I'll hide your reading glasses."

Sasha took a deep breath and closed her eyes. She blocked out the ear-piercing wails and focused all her attention on creating a golden path: a path that would cut straight across the plain, through the hordes of monsters, and safely to the other side. She held onto that vision and opened her eyes.

To her astonishment, there was now an actual golden path stretched out before her.

"O-kay," she said slowly, staring at the glowing vision. "That's—that's never happened during my real-life runs."

The monsters threw back their heads and screamed, incensed by the path of light.

Sasha watched the monsters shy away from her golden path as if it were made of flames and grinned. "Good! *Great!* That's an unexpected bonus."

Reluctantly, she returned to the task at hand.

"Right," she told herself. She jammed the dream pillow into the breast pocket of her pajama top and clenched her hands to stop them from shaking. "Let's do this. Face your demons, just like an adult." She released her hands and squared her shoulders. "You had better be right about this, Lyla."

She took another deep breath and began to run down the hill, the gold dust soft under her bare feet. As she reached the base of the hill, her path rose up to meet her, encasing her in glittering, golden light.

"Oh—oh ... *wow!*" she whispered, as the light seeped into her skin, saturating her with a feeling of such joy, such *hope*, that she started to laugh with the sheer wonder of it all. It made her feel as if anything was possible, even confronting a horde of monsters. Not even the sand beneath her feet slowed her down. In fact, in that tunnel of light, the ground felt almost buoyant.

She felt as though she was flying.

But Sasha's momentary hope faltered as lightning lit up the plain, illuminating thousands of white, corpse-like creatures running toward her, their bodies grotesquely deformed, their broken teeth bared, their dark talons reaching out for her.

They're only fifteen feet away, she thought, sheer panic flooding her synapses as the plain fell into darkness once more.

Don't look them in the eye! the voice in the back of her head warned urgently.

Sasha dipped her gaze, keeping it at the furthest point of her gold path, and kept running, closing the distance between herself and the monsters.

Twelve feet.

The ground shook beneath their running footsteps.

Nine feet.

Their screams were a wall of sound, tearing through her nerve endings like knife points.

Six feet.

Sasha mentally braced herself against the sound, against the unrelenting horror coming straight for her.

Five feet.

She almost faltered, fear and instinct wanting her to turn back, but caught herself and ran faster.

Four feet.

It's just a dream, she told herself, as thunder joined the monster's screams.

Three feet

You can do this, she reassured herself, buoyed by the light and warmth of her path.

Two feet.

She closed her eyes, then opened them again, determined.

They were here.

Sasha ran faster still.

And tore right through them.

Her golden path cut through the hordes of monsters like hot steel through butter. From the corner of her eye, she watched them scatter in her wake. She could hear them regroup behind her on either side, but her golden path kept them at bay.

They were *furious*.

Their screams changed in pitch from victorious to something frustrated and thwarted. Sasha could hear the metallic *gnash-gnash-gnash* of their razor-tipped teeth closing on thin air rather than her flesh. She could feel their hate, their anger, their *hunger* all directed toward her.

Out of nowhere, she found herself laughing maniacally.

"Suck it, you bastards!" she yelled. "I'm not five anymore!"

She laughed and laughed with an incredible, terrible glee that filled her arteries and fueled her muscles and lungs better than blood and oxygen. Her path began to burn brighter; it was so bright, so true in the growing darkness that she felt as though she could reach out and touch it.

At that moment, tearing across the plain, she felt invincible.

She ran.

She ran farther and faster than she had ever run before, her golden path allowing her to keep up a furious pace for what seemed like hours.

But there is only so long that one can perform an impossible task before it begins to feel impossible.

The end of the plain did not seem to be getting any closer. The horde of monsters ran behind her, clustered on either side of the path, their footsteps shaking the ground beneath Sasha's feet. A few of the faster, stronger ones sprinted by her side, easily keeping pace. They continually tested the edges of her golden path, falling back as if burned, their screams of rage almost shredding her sanity.

For the first time, Sasha wondered if she would make it.

For the first time, she wondered about the consequences of failing in a dream that felt so real.

Stop that, she told herself firmly. *You're going to make it.*

She cleared her mind, putting all her mental energy into the path, stretching it out toward the finish line at the end of the plain.

She lost all sense of how long she had been running. Time was measured by her footsteps, her ragged breaths, her rapid heartbeats, and yet the end of the plain was still nowhere in sight.

The burn in her thighs felt so *real*. The pull of oxygen into her lungs was getting harder and harder. The sand beneath her feet became less and less buoyant until it eventually became nothing more than a burden, dragging her down, slowing her steps. Her feet felt chaffed and bruised. With every step, every stride, she felt her a little more of her vitality drain away.

The path faded to a pale gold.

The monsters running beside her screamed in triumph.

"Look," one whispered near her ear.

"Yesss," hissed another. "Look into our eyesss. We have thingsss to show you, Lady. Many thingsss ..."

Sasha ignored them. A stitch stabbed at her side; she clamped her hand over the pain and stumbled onward.

The path before her flickered to a pale silver.

"No," she whispered fiercely, her mouth as dry as dust. "No ... I'm ... I'm going to make it."

Suddenly, Sasha felt something furnace-hot sear her right shoulder like a brand. She screamed and stumbled forward, desperate to escape that vicious heat. She staggered a few more steps before she felt the burning sensation once more, this time around her upper arm.

Without turning around, she knew that the monsters had her—that their bony, burning fingers circled her arm, black talons digging into her flesh.

Sasha gathered her remaining strength and tried to pull herself away.

"Let me go!" she screamed, breaking free.

But she screamed again as claws—white-hot and knife-sharp—sliced over her back, peeling back her skin from the flesh beneath in thin ribbons.

The pain was indescribable. It lit up every nerve ending and turned her vision black, almost sending her to her knees. She choked back a sob, wanting nothing more than to stop, to fall to the ground, to rest.

But she didn't. She raised her chin and pushed her exhausted body forward.

Desperate, Sasha looked up at her path—it was now ghostly white in the darkness.

"No, no, no," she moaned. "*No.*"

Again, Sasha felt a searing burn—this time at the back of her calf. She surged forward, away from the grasping claws, stumbling until she could right herself again. Her calf felt as though it was on fire. Her shoulder and arm felt wet, and she knew—she *knew*—that she was bleeding; she could feel the warm fluid ooze down her back, sticking her shirt to her skin.

The howls behind her turned triumphant—they were brays for blood and bone.

"Lady," a voice hissed, gloating. "Oursss! Look at usss! *Look!*"

Do not look at them! the voice in her mind screamed. *Do* not *look!*

Sasha did not look—she would not give them the satisfaction. Instead, she raised her gaze to focus on the end of her path ... and almost laughed again, this time in disbelief.

For there, just beyond the monsters, was a stout, gray stone wall, marking the boundary of the plain.

The end was literally in sight.

She was close, *so close,* but with a sick sense of horror, Sasha felt herself stumble, barely able to keep one foot in front of the other.

"No," she whispered weakly. She swallowed past the dust, past the horror, lodged in her throat. "*No.*"

A breeze came tearing down the plain from behind her, cooling the heat of her wounds and drying the sweat from her skin. With the breeze at her back, Sasha felt herself move forward again. She almost sobbed with relief, her pace lurching but constant.

"Thank you!" she called out to the breeze, even though it made no sense to thank the weather.

Nevertheless, she felt it push against her back even harder, propelling her forward as if it had understood.

Her path flickered back to pale silver.

The monsters *howled.*

"I'm—I'm almost there!" she rasped weakly to the creatures. "I'm almost there," she told herself.

She pushed her damp hair from her eyes and looked toward the wall, hoping that it would give her the courage to carry on. Now that she was closer, she could see that it was haphazardly built, the rough, gray stones stacked unevenly into a vaguely wall-like shape.

At least it's not too tall, she thought, relieved that she wouldn't have to scale a wall with those creatures at her back. She squinted into the distance, trying to gauge its height. *Maybe ... maybe a bit higher than mid-thigh. Easy to jump over—*

The thought almost stopped her in her tracks.

They'll jump over it, too! she thought, almost crying with the dreadful absurdity of it all. *Where's the barbed wire to keep them out? The spikes? The electricity?*

For a moment, she was furious at herself for dreaming up such a dangerously inadequate wall. But then a terrible thought struck her: Why did she ever think that the other side of the plain was safe from the monsters? What if this was just the beginning of her nightmare?

The thought almost brought her to her knees. Her path flickered back to white.

Stop that, she told herself firmly, willing the path to turn gold. *Just keep going—you're almost there!*

Suddenly, at the very end of her path, just over the wall, the gold dust began to rise, soaring skyward until it was a towering column skyscraper-high. It started to circle furiously, creating what appeared to be a small, golden tornado. From within this tempest, a dark figure rose from beneath the ground, gold dust swirling ferociously around his form.

Sasha dragged a hand across her eyes, sure that this was just an illusion, but no—the figure remained, rising upward in the golden whirlwind until his feet finally touched the ground.

The dust from the tornado tore across the plain. Sasha weakly lowered her head and shielded her face, feeling the dust brush roughly against her arms and clothing. When she dared to look up again, she saw the figure standing on the ground, the wind slowly dying around him, the gold dust settling around his feet.

With a sob, she recognized him—her Hill-Man was here! But this time, he wore black armor and a cloak made of shadows that roiled and seethed around him. He looked fierce and dangerous and more than a match for any of the monsters on the plain.

As he caught her eye, Sasha felt herself smiling at him, her relief overwhelming.

Surely ... surely, he would help her.

Please help me, she pleaded silently.

As if hearing her thoughts, Hill-Man held out his arms. "Come on!" he yelled above the sound of the wails.

Sasha scraped together the very last of her strength and staggered down the final steps of her path, launching herself over the wall. She threw herself into Hill-Man's arms, the grasping hands of the monsters finally falling away.

Hill-Man crushed her against his chest, her cheek landing hard against his breastplate. Sasha staggered, off-balance, and her legs collapsed beneath her. But before she could fall to the ground, she felt herself being lifted and carried bridal style. She swayed in Hill-Man's arms, feeling the urgency of his steps as he moved quickly away from the monsters.

Then, she felt him stop.

"Stay here," he ordered, lowering her carefully to the ground.

If she had the energy, she would have laughed at the idea.

As if I can move, she thought, trying to drag air into her lungs.

Weakly, she turned her head and watched as Hill-Man returned to the wall.

The monsters waited for him—thousands of them clustered at the edge of the plain—their hands outstretched over the wall, their teeth bared as they grasped and wailed.

"*WANT!*" they screeched.

Hill-Man knelt and touched his hands to the earth. Sasha felt the ground beneath her back begin to shake violently.

Oh, no, she thought, dread pooling in her gut. *What now?*

Just as she was wondering whether she had the energy to get up and run away from an earthquake, bright, white light burst along the wall, forming a shimmering shield between herself and the monsters and lighting up the area as bright as day.

The monsters fell back, covering their eyes.

Hill-Man stood in front of the wall of light, his arms outstretched at his sides.

"*Back!*" he commanded.

The monsters screamed defiantly.

Hill-Man stretched one hand toward the sky, fingers splayed. At his command, lightning split the heavens and touched the plain.

"Hear me now—*back!*"

The monsters reluctantly retreated. They wailed desolately, their arms outstretched, their hands grasping empty air.

It appeared that Hill-Man had the situation well in hand.

"*Good,*" Sasha wheezed to herself.

She closed her eyes and finally allowed herself to relax, to recover. As she tried to slow her heart rate, she was struck by the thought that no one had ever told her that dreams could be so vivid, so true-to-life, that surviving them was an actual point of concern.

Dreaming sucks, she thought, a touch hysterically. *No wonder people die in their sleep.*

Slowly, her breathing returned to normal. Sasha opened her eyes and instantly regretted it; Hill-Man was striding toward her, and he did not look pleased.

In a fluid movement, he knelt beside her and grabbed her shoulders.

"Do you know what you have you *done?*" he asked, shaking her slightly. "You have ruined your life!"

Sasha flinched away from his hands, her shoulder burning. "Stop manhandling me," she rasped. "I've been through an Ordeal."

Hill-Man released her immediately. "Of course, you have. Apologies." He ran a hand through his hair, clearly agitated. "The problem is that your *Ordeal*—as you so aptly termed it—is only just beginning and will probably end in a wretchedly melodramatic fashion for all involved, myself included. Which, admittedly, is nothing new ..."

Sasha did not like the sound of any of that, so she chose to ignore it.

"Tell me," he said, his tone urgent, "the Nightmares—did they bite you?"

Sasha shook her head weakly.

"Are you absolutely sure?"

Sasha opened her mouth to reply but stopped. She could have sworn that the monsters had clawed her back. But what if they had used their teeth?

Hill-Man noticed her hesitation. "May I have your permission to 'manhandle' you to check?"

Sasha half-heartedly raised her hand. "Sure."

"Brace yourself," he murmured.

Sasha felt herself being gently lifted, like a ragdoll, into a sitting position. She felt her sleeves being moved aside one-by-one, wincing as the fabric brushed against her wounds. She heard Hill-Man hiss between his teeth at one point and swear at another.

"No bites?" she whispered, as he released her.

"No bites." He exhaled sharply in relief. "Excellent. That is one less horrifying thing to happen to you this evening." His expression changed, becoming something that looked remarkably like pity. "Do you have any idea what you have just done?"

Sasha was so exhausted that she could barely keep her eyes open. "You told me to run from the monsters, so I ran."

"*Away* from them," he said in disbelief. "Not *toward.*"

"Semantics," she croaked. She tried to lick her dry lips, but there was no moisture in her mouth. "Water?"

"Of course."

Hill-Man took a deep breath and reached upward. To Sasha's surprise, his hand seemed to vanish. But when he pulled back his arm, his hand reappeared, holding what looked like a glass of water.

Sasha peered blearily at the glass. "Is that a mirage?"

"No, but it would not be the first in this place."

He placed the glass to her lips.

Sasha took a grateful sip, careful not to drink too much all at once. The water tasted delicious, cool and sweet and positively heavenly as it passed down her parched throat. She wiped a drop from her chin and took another small sip, and another, eventually taking the glass from him. "Thanks."

"You will not thank me soon." He shook his head. "Oh, the things that are in store for you …"

With water came bravery. "Sense," she gasped. "Speak *sense*. What's going on?"

Abruptly, he stood up and began to pace in front of her. Sasha could not summon the energy to track his progress from one side to the next, so she simply stared straight ahead and waited for him to came into view.

Finally, he stopped. With a graceful motion, he knelt beside Sasha once more, his shadowy cloak unfurling around them both.

"You bested the Wasteland without magic. In a *dream*." He stared at her as if she was some sort of anomaly. "You have done the impossible. And with the impossible—well, there comes certain gifts."

His lips twisted wryly on the final word in a way that made Sasha think that these gifts were not particularly *good*. She was so busy watching his twisty lips that it took her a moment to realize that he had started speaking again.

"What is of equal concern is that you appear to be able to come here at will. That cannot be allowed. *They* will not allow it. They will put a stop to it … or a stop to you—whichever they find easier."

Sasha instinctively did not like the sound of "they" or the part about someone putting a stop to her. She was quite strongly opposed to people putting a stop to her, especially since her trips to this dreamland were certainly not *at will*.

She made a gesture for him to continue, but Hill-Man was not looking at her—his attention was on the sky. Sasha also looked up; the lightning had abated, and the stars were beginning to emerge, delicate pinpricks of light spread across the sky in unfamiliar constellations.

"Listen to me."

Sasha turned her attention back to Hill-Man. He was staring at her with an intensity that she would have found alarming had she not just run for hours with a pack of bloodthirsty creatures at her heels. She had a new gold-standard for all things alarming.

"You are beginning to wake up," he said, his words quick, his tone urgent. "I will come for you, do you hear? Others may come for you, too, but do not leave with anyone else. Do not trust *anyone* else. Do you understand?"

No, I don't understand, Sasha thought desperately, but was too exhausted to argue. Instead, she tried to nod. "Yes. Waking up. Others coming. Wait for you. Right?"

Hill-Man looked inordinately relieved. He grabbed the amulet hanging around his neck and, with a sharp tug, snapped it free. He wrapped the heavy, silver chain around her wrist. "Keep this close and wait for me."

Sasha turned to look at her new jewelry, but Hill-Man reached up and took her face between his hands.

"I will come for you, Sasha Evangeline Pierce." He stared down at her fiercely, his green eyes so vibrant that, for a moment, Sasha was transfixed. "Wait for me."

Sasha stared at him, shocked. "How did you know my name?" She felt the familiar, fishhook pull behind her navel and gasped. "I'm leaving."

Hill-Man took her hands in his, his grip firm. "Wait for me—I will come for you."

"You already said that," she said inanely.

Sasha felt herself being lifted skyward, her hands wrenched from Hill-Man's as she flew toward the stars. Dazed, she watched Hill-Man grow smaller and smaller, until he was just a toy-like figure in a black cloak, standing on a field of gold dust.

"I will come for you!" he called after her.

At that moment, Sasha did not know whether that was a promise or a threat.

9

THE CONSEQUENCES OF JOGGING WITH MONSTERS

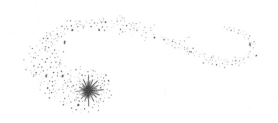

SATURDAY, OCTOBER 27TH

SASHA AWOKE TO FIND HERSELF BEING PULLED UPRIGHT OFF HER BED.

"Sasha!" Lyla cried, shaking her. "Wake up! Do you hear me? *Wake up!*"

Sasha's eyes fluttered open. "I'm awake," she croaked. "Stop shaking me. Why does everyone keep shaking me? It *hurts.*"

Before she knew it, Lyla had gathered her into a fierce hug.

"Don't do that again," Lyla mumbled frantically into Sasha's hair. "Don't you *ever* do that again!"

Sasha was shocked at Lyla's distress. "Hey, it's okay, Lyla. It's okay."

She clumsily patted her friend on the back, her limbs still heavy with sleep. When Lyla hugged her harder, she grimaced—something was digging into her chest. She pulled away from her distraught friend and reached into the pocket of her pajama top, her fingers closing around the silk cover of the dream pillow. With a tug, she dropped it onto the bed and watched, startled, as singed herbs and gold dust spilled from a charred hole in the center of the pillow, dirtying her bedcover.

"Miss Adeline is going to hate that," she muttered nonsensically. She turned her attention back to her distraught friend. "Really, Lyla." She tried to sound as soothing as possible. "Everything is fine."

Lyla's face was flushed, her eyes red-rimmed and wet with tears. "No, it damn well *isn't!*"

"Langu—"

"*Don't.* If there was ever a time to swear, it's now." Lyla wiped a hand over her eyes, angrily brushing away tears. "What happened to you? Are you okay?"

This was too much for Sasha. It was one thing to be running from monsters in a dream, but it was another thing entirely for logical, pragmatic Lyla to be sobbing over her as she slept. "What do you mean? I swear, between you and Hill-Man, if someone doesn't start telling me what's going on soon, I am going to start——"

"You were screaming and thrashing around as if you were having a seizure. And you were breathing *so* heavily. I couldn't—I couldn't wake you up no matter what I did." Lyla took a shuddering breath. "It seemed to go on forever ..."

"It's okay. *I'm* okay. It was just a dream." *Just a dream,* Sasha told herself firmly. "And frankly, if that's a dream, you guys can keep them. I'm out. I've had enough."

Lyla scanned Sasha's face, only relaxing when Sasha gave her a weak smile. "So ... it was really just a dream?" Her eyes narrowed. "How are you feeling? Does your heart feel as though it's about to explode? Does your brain feel like it's melting?"

Sasha shook her head. "Not at the moment. I'm okay."

Lyla's shoulders relaxed. "Are you *sure?*"

"Sure," Sasha lied. She felt as though she had just run a marathon with a pack of blood-thirsty demons.

Lyla rolled her eyes. "You're an awful liar." She wiped her eyes with the sleeve of her pajama top. "Okay, what kind of screwed-up dream makes you act like that?"

Sasha ran a shaking hand through her hair. "Well, it was one hell of a dream. And frankly, it's the last time I'm ever taking any advice from you because——"

"What's that on your wrist?" Lyla interrupted tersely.

"What are you talking——" Sasha looked down. "*Agh!*"

There, wrapped around her wrist, was a thick, silver chain that glittered away in the pale light of dawn. Tangled in the chain was a palm-sized, silver amulet of two crescent moons facing each other with an eight-pointed star suspended between them.

"You didn't go to bed wearing that!" Lyla screeched, her voice cracking. "And you weren't wearing it while I was shaking you awake—I would have seen it. I held your hands, Sasha! *I held your hands!*"

"AGHHHH!" Sasha yelled, staring down at her wrist.

"AGHHHH!" Lyla echoed.

The two women exchanged terrified looks.

"O-kay," Sasha said slowly. She stared down at the amulet. "No need to panic about this. I'm sure there is a logical—"

"FUCK LOGIC! This is some weird-ass supernatural—"

"How could you say that?" Sasha cried, her heart pounding. "*You're* the one who's always telling me to be logical!"

"Not this time." Lyla shook her head wildly, her eyes never leaving the amulet. "No *way*. There is *nothing* logical about—"

Sasha wrapped her hand over Lyla's mouth. "Not helpful, Lyla. NOT. HELPFUL!"

Lyla's hazel eyes widened. She nodded slowly.

Sasha carefully removed her hand. "Okay?"

Lyla inhaled shakily. "Okay." She looked down at Sasha's wrist. "Let's be logical about this illogical supernatural phenomenon. Does this bracelet have something to do with your dream?"

Sasha nodded.

"Okay. Tell me about your dream and don't leave anything out. Tell me every single detail."

The last thing Sasha wanted was to revisit that dream. But she took a deep breath and began.

"It started like all the others: I was on a hillside, with the demons on the plain below me. But this time, I did what you said to do—I ran *toward* the demons instead of away from them. But—but I don't think they were metaphorical demons. I think they were actual demons."

Lyla tentatively touched the amulet around Sasha's wrist. "I think so, too. Never listen to me again, okay?"

"Never again."

"You just ran?"

"I ran. I visualized a golden path that stretched all the way to the other side of the plain, and I ran along it. And you wouldn't believe it—I could actually *see* the golden path. It was *amazing*! The demons couldn't touch me on that path; it cut right through them." Sasha paused, remembering her fiendish glee at outrunning the monsters. "I ran for what felt like hours. As I got tired, the path became dimmer and dimmer, and the demons were able to get closer to me. They clawed at me a few times."

Lyla shuddered. "No wonder you screamed." Her eyes narrowed. "Where? Where did they claw you?"

"My back. My arm. One grabbed my calf."

"Turn around."

Sasha twisted a little so that her back was to Lyla. Lyla lifted Sasha's dark curls and pulled up the back of her damp t-shirt. She swore.

"What?" Sasha asked.

But she already knew.

"They got you alright. Here." Lyla lightly traced a long, curved line down Sasha's back. "There are three parallel lines. And another one, further away."

Sasha winced and flinched away from Lyla's touch. "Claw marks."

"*Claw marks?* What the actual fu—" Lyla stopped and bit her lip. "I know: *Not helpful, Lyla.*"

"Are they bleeding?" Sasha swallowed thickly, remembering the sensation of hot fluid dripping down her back.

"No, the blood has dried. We'll have to wash it off." Lyla gently brushed her fingers against Sasha's bicep. "And there's also something on the back of your upper arm. It looks like a burn."

Sasha twisted her forearm, so she could see where Lyla was pointing. An angry, red welt stretched between her shoulder and elbow. She made a strangled sound, somewhere between a laugh and a sob. "That's definitely a burn."

"Don't you worry—we're going to fix this. We're going to disinfect the hell out of those scratches and put a cold compress on your burn. I don't care if demons made them—they're no match for science and industrial strength disinfectant. We'll get you some antibiotics and a tetanus shot. We'll fix this. Where else did they get you?"

"Ah … my calf. They were trying to trip me up."

"Let's see it."

Sasha pulled aside the covers. Both women screamed as golden dust poured from the bed, falling in a thick, glittery stream onto the floor.

Lyla nudged the pile of gold dust with her bare toes. "It looks like most of the plain came home with you."

Sasha's heart felt as though it was going to come crashing out of her ribcage. "Okay. Okay. *Okay.* One thing at a time, okay?"

She carefully lifted her leg and placed it above the covers, turning it slightly. On the back of her calf was a vicious, red burn in the exact shape of a long-fingered hand.

Lyla gasped. "That's—that's *so* creepy. I'm—I can't …" She tore her eyes away from Sasha's leg. "We'll put a cold compress on it, too."

Sasha nodded mutely.

"What happened after the demons grabbed you?

Sasha stared at the handprint burned into her leg. She did not want to remember her dream—she wanted to forget it all. She wanted to jump into her car and drive back to New York … and then take a plane to Antarctica, where she'd hide in an ice cave until this entire situation blew over.

"Sasha? What happened next?"

Sasha shook her head and tried to gather her thoughts. "Hill-Man arrived."

"Hill-Man was there?" Lyla blinked. "Was he shirtless again?"

"No, he was wearing black armor. He was waiting on the other side of the plain; I ran right into his arms." Sasha touched her cheek gingerly. "Which is probably why this hurts so much. It turns out breastplates aren't soft and cuddly."

Lyla smiled weakly. "Huh, who knew? Then what?"

"The rest is hazy—I was recovering from the run. But I remember that he was upset. He said that I'd done something that I shouldn't have been able to do … and that I would be receiving gifts. But they didn't sound like good gifts. And then he told me—" Sasha closed her eyes; she could still hear the urgency in his voice. "He told me that he was coming for me … and that other people would be coming for me, too. But that I shouldn't trust them. That I should wait for him."

"That sounds ominous."

Sasha opened her eyes. "It was. Then he took something from around his neck—I guess it must have been this." She lifted the amulet, the metal glinting like star shine in the weak, morning light. "He wrapped it around my wrist and told me to keep it close. He knew my name, Lyla. My *full* name!"

"Hang on, he knew your middle name, too? The middle name you never use because it's too fancy? The middle name that your mother gave you when she was still high after the epidural?"

Sasha nodded. "And then I woke up."

The alarm clock chose that moment to screech into life. Both women jumped in shock.

Without missing a beat, Lyla picked up the clock and threw it out the open window.

"I think he really *is* coming for me," Sasha said quietly.

Lyla looked down at the dust-covered floor and nodded. "I think so, too."

"But … what is he going to *do* with me?

"I have no idea. But one thing's for sure—it sounds like a better option than *other people* coming for you. At least Hill-Man helped you during the dream." Lyla pointed her chin toward Sasha's new bracelet. "And maybe *that* is his way of trying to help you again."

Sasha mulled that over. "You're right. He was worried. Upset, but worried. And he tried to warn me. If he wanted to harm me, he could have thrown me to the monsters or something, right?"

"Right. But I still think you should be on your guard, even with him."

Both women were silent, contemplating the fantastic series of events that had utterly turned their perception of the world upside down.

Lyla stood up abruptly. "I don't know about you, but I could use a drink."

"It's seven in the morning, Lyla." Sasha looked down at the gold dust and winced. "Make mine a double."

Lyla carefully placed her arm around Sasha's shoulders, mindful of her wounds. "We're going to get to the bottom of this," she vowed fiercely. "We're going to do what we always do: break down the problem and conquer it piece by piece. No matter what, we'll work this out."

Sasha had felt never felt so grateful to have Lyla in her life. She buried her face against Lyla's side, her eyes wet. "Thank you, Lyla. If you weren't here ..."

Lyla gave Sasha a brisk kiss on the top of her head and released her. "But I am, for better or worse ... probably worse. First things first—I'm going to raid Miss Adeline's liquor cabinet. Then, I'm taking you to the doctor." She looked at the gold dust scattered across the floorboards and frowned. "And somewhere along the line, I'm going to clean this place up. Miss Adeline will have an aneurysm if she sees her genteel boarding house covered in gold dust."

Sasha wiped her eyes with the edge of the bedsheet. "Good plan. What do you want me to do?"

"Right now? Regain your strength. We'll get you some coffee and something to eat. I don't know how many calories a dream marathon burns up, but you look like hell, so I'm guessing *a lot*."

Sasha's stomach rumbled.

Lyla pointed to Sasha's midsection. "Your stomach has spoken. 'Eating' has now moved up on the to-do list just behind 'showering' and 'wound cleaning.' "

"Right. Good." Sasha looked down at the amulet. "And then what?"

"And then—after breakfast and the doctor—we'll come up with a battle plan. None of this 'pawn of destiny' crap. We're coming out fighting."

Sasha lifted her chin. "Damn straight."

It took two hours, but Lyla's plan had gone ... well, to plan. Fortified by Martha's cooking sherry—Miss Adeline had trust issues, Lyla discovered, and had hidden the keys to the liquor cabinet—a ridiculously large breakfast, a tetanus shot, and lots of lovely pain medication, Sasha was feeling more like herself.

"Does the Old Middleton Medical Center have a frequent user program?" Lyla asked, as they left the building. "Because if so, we need to get you a loyalty card."

Sasha walked gingerly ahead of Lyla toward the parking lot. "Please, don't even joke about it; I never want to come back here again."

"Got it. How do those bandages feel? It looked like the nurse put them on pretty tight."

Sasha flexed her back cautiously. "They're fine. I can't believe they believed your 'feral squirrel attack' story."

Lyla laughed. "Even the doctor didn't blink. It must happen all the time around here. We probably should have pushed our luck and told them that you were attacked by a runaway giraffe." She unlocked the car and opened the passenger door for Sasha. "Where am I driving us to next?"

"We need to figure out our next step." Sasha carefully eased herself into the passenger seat, mindful of her wounds. "Who's most likely to know what's going on here?"

"Rosa." Lyla said it without hesitation. She slid into the driver's seat and turned toward Sasha. "She's the one who sold you the dream pillow, and she seems to have a hand in all the hocus-pocus in this town. With any luck, she'll know what to do."

Sasha paused in the act of pulling on her seatbelt. "I don't relish the idea of speaking to Rosa. This whole thing seems crazy. Gold dust and monsters ... and jewelry that travels through a dream? I don't believe it happened, and I was *there*. What if Rosa calls the cops and has us committed?"

"Then we keep the engine running. If Rosa reaches for her phone, we jump into the car and drive to Mexico."

Sasha fastened her seatbelt with a decisive click. "That sounds like a solid plan."

"Glad you approve. In the best-case scenario, she'll tell us how to stop Hill-Man and the others from coming to get you."

Sasha's breath hitched. She was very much opposed to *anyone* coming to get her. There was so much riding on this plan. If Rosa couldn't or wouldn't help her ... well, Sasha was lost.

"How will they come for me anyway?" she asked, pushing aside that dreadful train of thought. "I was *dreaming*! How do you go from a dream to reality?"

Lyla gestured to Sasha's pocket. "Probably the same way that the gold dust and your new bit of jewelry came with you."

Sasha patted her pocket where the silver amulet rested, reassuring herself that it existed. "However that happened."

"What if ... what if you weren't in a dream per se ... but in *their* reality —in their plane of existence?" Lyla's eyes lit up. "Which makes sense! *That's* why you could feel pain and thirst and all those other physical sensations; it wasn't a dream at all! Which means that, to get to you, Hill-Man and the others would need to cross over from their plane into ours."

Sasha held up her hand. "Hang on ... are you talking about parallel dimensions?"

"Parallel *worlds*. They have their place of existence, and we have ours. And oh! It gets better." Lyla practically bounced in her seat with excitement. "If this is anything like those fantasy novels I've read, then each world may not even have the same time-zone ... so to speak. An hour here may be a year over there or vice versa."

"So...?"

"*So*, we may be worried about something that won't happen for years." Lyla grinned, clearly tickled with the idea. "Tough luck if Hill-Man comes for you when you're in your eighties and all saggy and senile."

Sasha smirked at the visual. "I can see it now. He'll burst into the nursing home in his black armor and fancy cloak, and I'll mistakenly think that he's after my chocolate pudding and smack him with my cane until he surrenders."

Lyla shook her head in mock sorrow. "Bitch-slapped by a feisty, dessert-loving geriatric. I almost feel sorry for him."

"And on that note, off we go to Rosa's. Hang on ..." Sasha's fingers closed around the amulet, the metal warm against her skin. "I need to get something from the boarding house first."

Lyla started the engine. "Let the adventure begin!"

ROSA SMILED IN GREETING WHEN SHE SAW THE DUO ENTER HER SHOP.

"What a surprise!" she said. She added another branch to a vase filled with red and gold flowers and turned to the two women. "How can I help you? More lust potions, Lyla?"

"Ha, I wish." Lyla exchanged looks with Sasha. "I still haven't found a willing victim for the last lot. This town is suspiciously short of attractive firemen."

"Given all the single women in town, it's probably a good thing," Rosa said. "Arson attempts would skyrocket."

"True, but it would be worth it."

Rosa laughed. "Aside from the firemen, what can I do for you?"

Sasha cleared her throat. *Here goes nothing,* she thought. "I'd like to know what was in the dream pillow you gave me."

"Oh! Well ... just the usual mix of herbs to give you a good night sleep. Did it work?"

"In a way," Sasha hedged. "What were they—the herbs? Specifically?"

Rosa looked slightly taken aback. "I'd have to consult my chart."

"We'll wait," Lyla said, her tone overly cheerful.

Rosa gave the women a puzzled look and pulled a worn, black leather ledger out from under the counter. She flicked through the pages then stopped, triumphant.

"Here, we are! Anise, bay leaf, hibiscus, jasmine, marjoram, willow, peppermint, peony, dandelion root, jasmine, lavender, poppy seeds, skullcap, spearmint, thyme, vervain, agrimony ..." She paused. "I think that's all."

Sasha leaned across the counter and tried to read Rosa's spiky handwriting upside down. "And what are those herbs supposed to do?"

"Well, they should have given you a good night sleep."

"What about my dreams?" Sasha persisted. "Would they have affected my dreams?"

Rosa looked back over the ingredients. And blinked. "Well ... some of the herbs may have made your dreams a little more vivid."

Sasha turned to Lyla. "Vivid."

"That's one word for it," Lyla said.

"The ingredients should also have lent you some protection while you slept," Rosa added.

"Protection?" Sasha pulled the dream pillow from her handbag and slapped it on the counter, its charred contents leaking through the gaping hole in the center. "Then I'm here to return this—clearly, it's defective."

Rosa stared at the burned pillow in shock. "What did you do to it?"

"I dreamed," Sasha said. She pulled out a plastic bag full of gold dust and placed it next to the pillow. "And *this* came back with me. Amongst other things."

Rosa's eyes widened. Gingerly, she touched the gold dust and then snatched her hand back as if burned. She looked up at Sasha with wide eyes. "Where did you get this?"

"I told you—it came back with me."

Lyla nodded. "It's true."

Rosa started at the two women for a long moment.

And then ran for the door.

Sasha and Lyla turned to each other, shocked.

"Is she running away?" Sasha whispered.

"Yes," Lyla whispered back. "Let's tackle her."

Before Sasha could answer—or Lyla could tackle—Rosa bolted the door and turned the door sign to read 'Closed.' She looked out the window as if making sure that she had not been seen, before pulling down the shades.

"We don't have much time," she said, walking briskly back toward the women. "I can't promise to help you much, but I'll do my best."

"We'll take what we can get," Sasha said, her heart pounding. She grabbed Rosa's hand. "I need to know what's going on. And in plain language, please. I don't want any ambiguity, any proverbs, or any weird mumbo jumbo. Plain language."

"I'll do my best," Rosa repeated, giving Sasha's hand a squeeze before releasing it. "Tell me exactly what happened after I gave you the pillow. You had a waking dream, right?"

Lyla laughed a little hysterically. "Boy, did she ever."

Sasha told her everything. By the end of it, Rosa was pale and shaking. Wordlessly, she reached down behind the counter and removed a crystal decanter filled with ruby-red liquid. She placed three matching sherry glasses beside it and filled each of them to the brim.

"Help yourselves," she said. She picked up a glass and, without any fanfare, gulped down the contents.

Lyla picked up a glass and looked at the older woman admiringly. "Rosa, you're my kind of woman." She took a tentative sip and made a pleased sound. "What is this?"

"Elderberry wine," Rosa said, pouring herself another drink, her hands unsteady. "I made it last year."

Lyla took another sip. "You are *definitely* my kind of woman. Go on," she said to Sasha. "Drink up."

Sasha picked up her glass but hesitated. "I don't know—I've already had two glasses of cooking sherry, a tetanus shot, and some painkillers."

"Drink it," Rosa said, well into her second glass. "Trust me—you'll need it."

"That sounds ominous enough to warrant alcohol," Sasha muttered and took a healthy sip.

The liquor pleasantly coated her mouth, sweet and full-bodied. Almost immediately, Sasha felt warmth flood her throat and chest, giving her a sense of ... well, not well-being exactly, but something tingly and pleasant. It was much better than the despair she had felt all morning. She took another long sip.

"Not bad, right?" Lyla asked, finishing off her glass.

"Not bad," Sasha agreed, placing her glass back on the counter. She wondered if she should ask for another glass ... or the entire decanter. She had a feeling she would need it.

Lyla placed her empty glass carefully on the counter beside Sasha's and smiled winsomely at the shopkeeper. "Now, you've liquored us up—what's this all about?"

Rosa glanced over at the gold dust. "It wasn't a dream. You crossed over."

"Crossed over to where, exactly?" Sasha asked.

Rosa opened her mouth to respond, but no sound came out. She closed her mouth and then tried again. Nothing.

"Dash it." Rosa exhaled shakily. "I *can't* tell you."

Sasha stared at the shopkeeper, disappointment warring with surprise. "Why—why not?" This was her only hope. If Rosa failed her ... "Please, why won't you help me?"

Lyla looked at Rosa shrewdly. "You said you *can't* tell us, not that you *won't* tell us. Why *can't* you tell us, Rosa? Who or what is stopping you?"

"You're a clever thing, aren't you?" Rosa said with a smile.

Lyla winked back. "I'm not just a hot body."

Sasha ignored Lyla's body positivity. "What's stopping you, Rosa?"

Rosa opened her mouth to reply and again, nothing came out.

"Is it a spell or a potion or something like that?" Lyla asked.

Rosa shook her head and looked around the shop. With a triumphant shout, she reached under the counter and pulled out a cloth shopping bag. Inside was a loaf of sourdough bread wrapped in brown paper. Using exaggerated gestures, Rosa pulled on her earlobe and then pointed to the bread.

Lyla frowned at the pantomime. "You can't tell us what's going on ... because your ear is crusty?"

Sasha stared at Lyla incredulously. "Really? *Really?*"

Lyla held up her hands in surrender. "You know how much I hate both mimes and games, and what Rosa did just then was a terrible combination of both. So 'crusty ear' was a pretty solid effort on my part."

Rosa huffed impatiently and made the gestures again, pulling on her earlobe and then pointing to the bread.

Suddenly, it clicked for Sasha. "Does the word sound like 'bread'?"

Rosa shook her head.

"Loaf?"

Rosa nodded frantically, her black braid swinging behind her.

Sasha mentally ran through all the rhymes for 'loaf.' Her eyes widened. "You took an oath?"

"You're a clever one, too." Rosa's shoulders sagged with relief. "Though, technically, it's not really an ..." She pointed to the loaf of bread.

"Oath," Sasha and Lyla supplied.

Rosa nodded. "It's more of a—dash it, I still can't say it. Well, any guesses?"

The women stared at Rosa blankly.

"I hate games," Lyla muttered.

"It's more of a ..." Rosa bent forward from her waist.

"Bow?" Sasha guessed. "Oh! A vow?"

Rosa stood up straight once again. "A very good guess." Her cheeks were flushed, as if she had been doing something far more strenuous than just bending forward.

"Good job, you!" Lyla said, patting Sasha on the back. "All those play-time sessions with your kindergarten class have paid off."

"Good job, *Rosa*," Sasha corrected. She looked at the older woman; Rosa's face was still flushed bright pink. "Are you okay?"

"Yes." Rosa rolled up the sleeves of her magenta caftan and fanned her cheeks. "That was tougher than it looked."

Sasha watched as the silk sleeves fell past the tattoo on Rosa's wrist. The white ink appeared to shimmer gold in the dim light of the shop.

And, just like that, the pieces started to fall into place.

"Does all of this have something to do with your tattoo?" Sasha asked the storekeeper.

Rosa looked shocked. She quickly pulled down her sleeve, but it was too late—Sasha had seen her tattoo. More importantly, she remembered where she had seen one just like it.

"Hill-Man has the same tattoo and several more."

"How many more?" Rosa asked.

Sasha frowned, trying to remember. "I think he had four altogether. He has them on his inner wrists and both palms."

"*Four?*" Rosa sat down weakly on a nearby stool. "Are you sure?"

Sasha nodded.

"*Four!*" Rosa buried her head in her hands. "How are we going to protect you from *four!*"

Sasha exchanged looks with Lyla.

"Protect Sasha from what?" Lyla asked tersely.

Rosa made a motion to speak, but no words came out of her mouth. She shook her head. "Sorry. I can't answer that."

"*Agh!*" Sasha wanted to pound her fists on the counter. "This is so frustrating."

"I know," Lyla said. "I'm ready to burn something down."

"This is no picnic for me either, ladies. I'm trying my best!" Rosa held out her hands apologetically. "Ask me more questions; we'll see what I can tell you."

Sasha tried to reign in her frustration; this was not Rosa's fault. "Right. Sorry. And thanks, by the way, for helping. I *do* appreciate it. Really, I do. I'm just … I'm just …" Her throat closed over the word.

"Terrified?" the older woman said quietly.

Sasha nodded mutely.

"Why do you have the same tattoo as Hill-Man?" Lyla blurted.

Rosa opened her mouth to answer and closed it, shrugging helplessly.

"O-kay." Lyla contemplated the shopkeeper. "Let's be logical. If you both have the same tattoo, then you're probably both in the same group or club, right?"

Rosa nodded.

"Now we're getting somewhere." Lyla watched Rosa closely. "Is this club magic related?"

Rosa's nod was so small that it was barely a nod. Tiny beads of perspiration began to collect along her hairline.

"I'll take that as a *yes*," Lyla said. "And since you seemed a little distressed when you found out that he has more tattoos, then that probably means he has more power or status in your group, right?"

Rosa gave another tiny nod and then grimaced. "*Careful.* That question was a little too close. It hurt to nod."

"How can you and a man in my dream be in the same group or club?" Sasha asked. "What kind of group is this?"

Rosa shook her head. Her entire face was as pink as her caftan.

"Is there someone else who has a tattoo that we can speak to about all this?" Lyla asked Rosa.

"Someone who can ... and will ... answer our questions?" Sasha added.

"Yes," Rosa said. She grabbed a pamphlet from the counter and began fanning her cheeks.

"Where can we find them?" Lyla asked.

"Oh, no." Sasha shook her head. Time was running out—she could *feel* it. "I'm done searching for answers. I think *they* should come to *us*. Rosa, please ask everyone in your secret magic tattoo club to come to join us for tea today at five at the boarding house. Given that I've 'crossed over,' I'm sure they'll want to see me just as much as I want to see them."

Rosa looked up at Sasha admiringly. "Look at you, taking charge of your destiny!"

"She's growing up so fast," Lyla said dryly.

Sasha gave her friend a stern look.

"Not to worry," Rosa said. "I'll contact them. We were meant to meet up tonight anyway at seven. We'll just make it earlier."

"Tonight, at seven?" Lyla turned to Sasha. "What else was tonight at seven?"

Their eyes widened.

"The Old Middleton Women's Historical Society is the magical tattoo club?" Lyla asked incredulously.

Sasha shook her head in disbelief. "No wonder Miss Adeline didn't want you at the meeting, Lyla!"

"It all becomes clear," Lyla said. "Well, whatever this club is of yours is, Rosa, I'm sure it's unimpeachably genteel."

"It would probably be best if you were both a little less ... *flippant* ... during the meeting." Rosa glanced back at the bag of gold dust, her lips twisting into a grimace. "This—this is a very serious matter."

"*Really?*" Even through the painkillers, Sasha could feel the white-hot burn on her calf; with each movement, the bandages chafed against the raw strips of flesh across her back. "What gave it away? Was it the fact that my nightmares literally came to life last night and tried to kill me? Or was it that a tattooed man in my dreams told me that he was coming to get me?" She shook her head, incensed, too many sleepless nights and far too much terror fueling her outburst.

"This isn't just a serious *matter*, Rosa—this is my *life*! And right now, I don't know what's going on. I don't know what's going to happen to me when I fall asleep, or what's going to happen while I'm awake. I'm *terrified*! So, if I appear to be flippant, even for a second, it's just a distraction to stop me from screaming."

Rosa watched her, silent, her dark eyes terribly solemn.

"We're taking this very seriously, Rosa," Sasha said quietly. "I *need* to know what's going on."

Rosa placed her hand gently on Sasha's arm, her smile almost unbearably sympathetic. "If things play out the way that I think they will, then you're headed for a complete and utter change in lifestyle. What you must remember is that whether this change is for better or worse will be your choice."

Sasha's heart sunk. "All of that sounds terrible."

"Not necessarily," Rosa hedged. "For what it's worth, anyone strong enough to cross the Waste—" She grimaced and stopped. With a frustrated sigh, she continued. "Let's just say that if you're strong enough to get through last night's ordeal, then I think you're more than ready for the challenge."

Sasha shook her head in disbelief. How could this be her life? Magic, monsters, tattooed men, other worlds …

You wanted adventure, the little voice in the back of her mind reminded her.

Yes, she answered testily, *but I was thinking of backpacking around Spain, not going to another world!*

It seemed that Spain would have to wait.

"I have a feeling that I'll have to be ready no matter what. Today at five, okay?"

"I'll make the arrangements with the others," Rosa said. "Though, be prepared—I'm not sure how much we can tell you. Not without breaking our …" She tapped the loaf of bread.

Suddenly, Lyla laughed. "Oh, we'll get our answers."

Sasha turned to her friend, curious. "What do you mean?"

"Don't you worry." Lyla placed her arm carefully over Sasha's shoulders, avoiding her bandages. "Leave it to me."

Rosa glanced uneasily at Lyla. "I can't promise anything—"

"I'll take what I can get," Sasha said.

"Very well. Then we will see you at five." Unexpectedly, the older woman grinned. "This should be *very* interesting."

10

THE WITCHES OF OLD MIDDLETON

Saturday, October 27th: Five o'clock (on the dot).

At precisely five o'clock, there was a brisk knock on the front door of the boarding house.

Sasha looked up from pouring tea into Ms. Adeline's second-best teacups, careful not to spill any onto the coffee table.

"Are you absolutely sure about this?" she asked Lyla, gesturing to the half-filled cups. "It doesn't feel right to me."

Lyla dumped the last of the cookies onto a gilt-edged plate. "We discussed this. We have no choice." She dusted the cookie crumbs off her hands. "Besides, 'it's better to beg forgiveness than ask permission.'"

"I've never liked that saying."

"Don't knock my motto. Now, keep pouring; this is no time to chicken out." Lyla stood up and headed for the doorway. "Let's hope the Historical Society takes the news better than Miss Adeline," she called over her shoulder.

When Sasha and Lyla returned to the boarding house from Stardust and Brimstone, an ashen-faced Miss Adeline was on the phone with Rosa. She hung up mid-conversation and silently handed Sasha the key to the china cabinet before walking off to the kitchen in a daze.

Sasha heard the front door open, followed by the murmur of voices. She tightened her grip on the teapot and kept pouring until all the cups were full, her palms slick with sweat thanks to nerves and more than a sliver of guilt.

"So, it begins," Lyla murmured as she re-entered the room.

Sasha placed the teapot gently on the coffee table and stood up.

"Ahh ... hello." Her eyes widened at the seven familiar faces. "*All* of you are members of the ... Historical Society?"

Rosa, the Headmistress, Esther, Daisy, Violet, Felicia DuPre, and old Mrs. Landshome stood in the entranceway of the drawing room. Miss Adeline and Martha moved amongst the group, collecting coats and scarves.

"There are quite a few others," Rosa said, handing her shawl to Miss Adeline. "But I thought it best to keep this between the higher-ranking members of the group."

Sasha nodded. "Well, you know best." She turned to the ladies and tried to smile. "Thank you all for coming. Please, help yourselves to tea and refreshments."

The women looked at each other and hesitated on the threshold.

"After all ..." Sasha turned to the Headmistress. "You said it yourself: you can say anything over a cup of tea."

The Headmistress shot her a shrewd glance, but led the way into the room, the rest of the women following in her wake. The tension was molasses-thick, but the familiar act of taking refreshments seemed to relax the group somewhat. Each woman placed a few dainties on her plate and took a seat on one of the dreadful pink couches. The soft clink of cups against saucers echoed loudly in the silence of the room.

Lyla glanced meaningfully at Sasha and then sat down beside her on the low chaise.

Sasha waited until the women were well into their refreshments before she spoke. "Rosa has probably told you all why you're here." She licked her dry lips. "Well, I assume she told you what happened to me last night."

"Somewhat," Felicia said pointedly, lounging in her armchair. "By the time she called me—last, as usual—the story was just a jumble of exclamations and high-pitched squeals." She took a dainty sip of her tea. "The whole conversation positively *reeked* of elderberry wine."

"Why, you spiteful fox!" Rosa fumed. "I was perfectly coherent! Just because *you* weren't able to grasp the nuances of what I was telling you—"

Martha slapped her hand down hard on the coffee table, making the remaining cups and plates jump.

"Put a sock in it, you two. You can argue *after* Sasha's story." She jutted her chin toward Sasha. "Go on."

"Right. Thanks, Martha." Sasha took a deep breath, readying herself. "So, you can understand why I need answers. Where do I go when I dream? What were those monsters on the plain? Who is the man on the hillside? Why does he have the same tattoos that you do? What do they mean? Please—I *need* to know."

Oddly enough, it was Esther who answered.

"You have to understand, my dear, that there are limits to what we can tell you," she said.

The Headmistress nodded. "There are our Vows to consider."

Felicia's smile was positively patronizing. "You can't expect us just to come out and tell you that Old Middleton lies on a Portal that links our world to another…" Her eyes widened in shock.

"Nor that we're witches who have sworn to guard the Portal from this side—oh no!" Daisy's fingertips fluttered to her lips.

"And," Violet chirped, "that the man you met is most likely the Shadow—"

Daisy quickly put her hand over her twin's mouth and shook her head.

The Headmistress peered into her cup and then back at Sasha. "Relaxation tea?"

Rosa smacked her lips together. "And Truth Elixir, if I'm not mistaken. Quite a bit, too."

"We may have dropped a little in there," Lyla said, unapologetically. "Oops."

Sasha bit her lip, her gut churning with guilt. "I'm really sorry. I didn't want to spike your tea. But after our talk with Rosa, we knew that you couldn't give us the answers we needed without it."

Almost simultaneously, each woman put her cup back on the coffee table.

"Dash it, Rosa," the Headmistress said, turning to the potion-maker. "I thought we told you to dilute those! Do you want another Fitchburg High?"

"Poor Fitchburg High," Daisy and Violet said, shaking their heads.

"I *did* dilute them," Rosa said stubbornly.

Felicia looked down at her cup. "This doesn't seem diluted to me, sugar."

"In Rosa's defense, we dumped the entire bottle of Truth Elixir into the teapot," Lyla said.

The Headmistress ignored Lyla and continued to stare at Rosa. "Well? Did you dilute the Truth Elixir?"

"Yes!" Rosa insisted. She stared at the teapot and winced. "Though, perhaps not as much as the other potions…"

The other women groaned.

Rosa folded her arms across her chest and raised her chin stubbornly. "The world could do with a little more truth if you ask me."

"But Fitchburg High, Rosa!" the Headmistress cried.

"Poor Fitchburg High," Lyla said, shaking her head solemnly.

The Headmistress looked at Lyla and Sasha for a long moment. "Indeed," she muttered. She turned to Esther. "They figured it out. I *told* you that you were too heavy-handed with the elixir. That tea is strong—you only need a pinch."

"Yes, yes—you were right." Esther turned to Sasha. "Well played."

Sasha's eyes widened. "Hang on—are you saying that you *did* spike my tea?"

The Headmistress blinked. "Well … yes. I thought you knew." She pointed to her cup. "I thought that's where you got the idea to put the Truth Elixir into the relaxation tea."

"It was," Lyla said. "It occurred to me in Rosa's shop that all I needed to do was replicate the circumstances of Sasha's afternoon tea experience. Tea plus elixir."

Sasha stared at Esther and the Headmistress, utterly aghast. "But … but I thought you gave me the wrong tea by *accident*. You apologized and gave me pastries … and Esther *cried* and—are you even sorry for what you did?"

"We're incredibly sorry!" Esther said. "We had no idea that you'd have such a strong reaction."

"*Very* sorry," the Headmistress said. "Do you really think that we wanted you running around the village, telling the baker"—she lowered her voice—"*sex things?*"

"That's not the point!" Sasha said, fuming. "I want you to be sorry for drugging me in the first place, not for the consequences! I want you to—"

Lyla put her hand on Sasha's, halting her tirade. "Focus. One catastrophe at a time. Let's get this bigger one sorted out before the tea wears off. *Then* you can go apocalyptic on them about the tea-spiking."

Sasha nodded reluctantly. "Fine." She turned to the Headmistress. "But after our discussion, I'd like to know why you decided to drug me in the first place. That was *not cool*. And I want the truth this time."

The Headmistress sighed. "I'm sure it'll all come out soon enough."

Esther looked speculatively at her cup. "This may benefit us. It appears that the Vow we made can be circumvented by the elixir—which is something we need to fix."

"As soon as possible," the Headmistress muttered.

"So ... we can speak freely?" Rosa asked.

The other women looked expectantly toward Esther. Sasha had assumed that the Headmistress was in charge, but the group appeared to be waiting for Esther's approval.

Esther nodded. "We can speak freely for now—at least until it wears off. We can consider the Vow lifted for this meeting."

The other women looked relieved.

"Well, that makes things easier," Miss Adeline said.

Sasha put aside her rage at being drugged and tried to focus on the matter at hand. "Right. Can I finally get some answers?"

"Ask away," Esther said. "Though, be prepared—after we are done, you will have to take an oath of secrecy."

Sasha and Lyla looked at each other. Lyla shrugged. "Sure. No one would believe us anyway."

Suddenly, the previous conversation finally hit Sasha. "Wait a minute— you're all *witches*? You mean, Mason Barnes was right all along?"

"*Mason Barnes*," the women groaned.

"Yes," Rosa said, "we're all witches."

"Though not like those terrible witches you see on television," Daisy tittered.

"All green skin and warts. Or twitching their noses." Violet tsked. "*Really.*"

Sasha gestured to Rosa's wrist. "Do you all have white tattoos?"

"Yes, but they're Marks, not tattoos," Esther clarified. "A tattoo is something that you choose to have drawn onto your skin. A Mark appears when you acquire power over an element."

Each of the women rolled up their sleeves, revealing a white Mark gleaming subtly against the skin of their wrists. But unlike Hill-Man, each woman had only one mark—except for Esther, who had one on each wrist.

"It is so inconveniently placed," Miss Adeline said, pulling aside her crochet glove. "And such a nuisance to hide."

Martha shrugged. "Unless you're using it. Can you imagine how complicated it would be to use it if it was on your foot?"

"Oh! So true, Martha dear," Daisy said, patting Martha on the knee.

Sasha raised her hand. "Sorry, this is getting confusing."

"The Marks relate to our mastery of a particular element," the Headmistress explained. "Once we acquire that power, the Mark appears."

Lyla craned her neck, trying to see the witches' exposed Marks. "Those look awfully familiar. I've seen them somewhere—Oh! Are those alchemy symbols?"

"Yes, that's right!" Rosa said, beaming. "And they're placed in the center of two fragmented circles to represent—"

"Strictly speaking, they don't need to know about that," Esther interrupted, sending Rosa a quelling look. "All they need to know is that some of us are Masters of Fire."

Esther gestured to Mrs. Landshome and Felicia, both of whom raised their wrists, showing an upright triangle within two, broken circles.

"Others, Water." Esther raised her left wrist, the Headmistress and Daisy copying her gesture; all had an upside-down triangle in the center of their circles.

"Earth." Rosa and Martha raised their wrists, showing an upside-down triangle bisected by a small, horizontal line.

"And Air." Esther raised her right wrist as did Miss Adeline, showing the same bisected triangle, only theirs was upright.

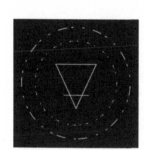

"Oh, I have one of those, too!" Violet said, flashing her wrist.

In the lamplight, the raised Marks glittered and shone—sometimes silver, sometimes gold.

"Awesome," Lyla whispered.

Esther looked at her Marks fondly. "They truly are. We use these Marks, and the power they represent, to guard a Portal—a Portal that opens each month on the first night of the full moon."

"Where does the Portal lead?" Sasha asked, as the witches lowered their hands.

"It goes from our world to what we call Otherworld." At Sasha's raised eyebrow, Esther chuckled. "Not a particularly imaginative name, is it?"

"Not really."

The Headmistress squared her shoulders defensively. "It is a perfectly fine name. What you fail to take into our account is that those who came before us—on whose shoulders we now stand—"

"Here we go," Mrs. Landshome groaned. "Watch her climb up onto her soapbox."

The Headmistress threw Mrs. Landshome a vehement look and ignored the interruption. "—were good people, the salt of the earth. They didn't align themselves with pretentiousness or false airs. They didn't feel the need to create grandiose titles or indulge in fancy place names."

"I like that," Lyla said. "There is nothing wrong with plain speaking."

The Headmistress sniffed, somewhat mollified. "Yes, well ... we should *all* remember that."

"Now," Esther continued, eyeing the Headmistress warily, "within Otherworld, the Portal comes out in a kingdom called Between."

"It was named Between because that kingdom sits in *between* our world and the Otherworld kingdoms beyond it," the Headmistress added, a touch defensively. She glared at Sasha and Lyla, eyebrow raised, as if daring them to comment.

"That's an appropriate name," Sasha said, smiling weakly.

The Headmistress nodded, her posturing relaxing. "I've always thought so."

Lyla looked at Sasha. "Are you getting all of this?"

Sasha opened her mouth to reply but was interrupted by Esther. "Adeline, get the map. That will help."

Miss Adeline stood and went over to the wall. With a ladylike grunt, she removed the painting of the unattractive child holding the unattractive dog and flipped it over. On the other side of the painting was a hand-drawn map. It was clearly very old; the parchment was brittle and the color of weak tea, the ink faded from the original black to a dull brown.

The other witches cleared a space on the coffee table, and Miss Adeline placed the map in front of Sasha and Lyla. Sasha noticed that someone practical—most likely Martha—had placed clear, plastic wrap over the entire surface.

Felicia tapped the plastic with one long, coral fingernail and grimaced. "Why is the map wrapped up like a sandwich?"

"To protect it from the elements, of course," Miss Adeline said. She brushed away Felicia's hand and, with a pointed look at the redhead, carefully smoothed out the indentation in the plastic caused by Felicia's fingernail.

"Very sensible, dear," Violet said.

"And ingenious!" Daisy added.

"I get that it needs to be protected," Felicia persisted, "but *cling wrap*? We're witches! Surely we can do better than *cling wrap*."

"I agree," the Headmistress said. "It's not the most dignified of coverings."

"It's doing its job," Martha said gruffly.

"Would you cover the Mona Lisa in cling wrap?" Felicia asked.

"Yes," Miss Adeline said firmly. "If it kept the dust off."

Sasha ignored the plastic wrap; she was more interested in what was underneath. The map showed two separate landmasses or continents.

"We're here," Esther said, pointing to the continent marked 'The Earther Realm.'

Sasha and Lyla leaned closer to the map.

"What is the Earther Realm?" Sasha asked. "Is it just the United States?"

"It's supposed to denote ... well, everything on Earth." Esther placed her finger on the continent to the right of the map. "And this is Otherworld. Now, see how there's a golden passageway that spans the chasm between the Earther Realm and Otherworld? That passageway represents the Portal between our worlds." She pointed to a spot on the map at the very edge of the Earther Realm. "Here is Old Middleton. Can you see how it's right next to the Portal?"

Lyla peered at the spot. "It is literally right on the Portal."

Esther nodded. "That's right. Old Middleton is on one side of the Portal and Between is on the other. It is our sister city, so to speak." She pointed to a small dot on the map directly opposite Old Middleton at the mouth of the Portal leading to Otherworld. "So, as you can see, Between is literally betwixt our world and the rest of the Otherworld."

"It functions as a guardian kingdom between the two realms," the Headmistress added.

Sasha tentatively traced the golden Portal with the tip of her finger, mindful of creasing the plastic. "So, how do you get to Between? Is the Portal a tunnel?"

Esther shook her head. "The Portal is an energetic link between our worlds. It opens to take a chosen Dreamer from our world to Between."

"What do you mean?" Sasha asked.

"As far as we can gather, the Portal allows one Dreamer—usually a child or teenager—to enter Between on the night of the full moon and live out their fondest dream."

"Does the Dreamer always come from Old Middleton?" Lyla asked.

Esther shook her head. "Dreamers can come from anywhere in the world; they travel on the astral plane via their dreams through the Portal."

Sasha stared at the map, trying to puzzle out how this information related to her own experiences. "So ... what you're saying is that I went through the Portal and into Between through my dreams, right?"

Esther nodded.

"But does that make me a Dreamer? You said Dreamers are typically children or teenagers—I obviously don't meet the age requirement."

Esther fiddled absentmindedly with her pearls, her expression pensive. "That's a puzzle—one of the many puzzles you've given us to solve. Though ..." She tilted her head, looking at Sasha intently. "You told Rosa that the hillside was familiar to you, that you had dreamed of it as a child. Perhaps you were *meant* to be a Dreamer, and something went wrong."

Sasha thought back to her first conversation with Hill-Man and the memory of her final childhood dream. "I'd been there before. Whether I was a Dreamer or not ..." She shrugged. "I don't know."

"You said that Dreamers 'live out their fondest dreams'?" Lyla asked. "What does that mean? If a Dreamer always wanted to be a princess in a magical kingdom, do they get to play at being a princess for the night? Or if they wanted to ride a dragon, do they spend the night riding dragons?"

"I certainly wasn't living out my fondest dreams," Sasha muttered.

You could have, that voice in the back of Sasha's mind said. *If Hill-Man had been more cooperative ...*

Sasha chose not to say that aloud.

Esther shrugged. "If that's what the Dreamer wishes. None of us have had the privilege of being Dreamers so we can't tell you from experience."

"But why?" Lyla asked. "What's the point of having one really good dream?"

"It's not *just* a dream," Esther said. "It's meant to be a life-changing experience. It could take the form of a quest or a journey or an adventure that feels longer than a night. As for the point of it, imagine if your fondest dream came true. Wouldn't that make you feel as though *all* your dreams were within your grasp? That kind of hope is a mighty powerful thing."

"I guess that would be pretty amazing," Lyla conceded. "Like living your own fairy tale."

"So how are Dreamers chosen?" Sasha asked.

"No one knows," the Headmistress said. "All we know is that Between chooses one lucky person per month."

"I don't think it's random," Rosa said. "Dreamers tend to be creative by nature. Past Dreamers have gone on to create wonderful plays, music, novels, art, and architecture. They've become inventors, great thinkers, strong believers. They've changed the world."

"And there's a benefit to Between, too," Esther continued. "The magic in Between is strong and abundant. The Dreamer shapes it and gives it a purpose. Without that purpose, the magic runs wild through Between, harming the land and its inhabitants."

"Hang on," Lyla said. "If this Portal can only open up once a month, then why did Sasha dream herself into Between several times this week? She was going back and forth every time she fell asleep."

The witches looked at each other uneasily.

"And that," Esther said with a sigh, "is another puzzle we need to solve."

"Technically it's impossible, dear," the Headmistress said to Sasha. "I've consulted the historical records extensively. There has never been a case where a Dreamer has repeatedly visited Between."

"Could someone have opened the Portal?" Sasha asked. "Perhaps one of you by accident? Or by mistake?"

The witches laughed.

"Oh, no—*we* can't open the Portal!" Esther said.

"We're just the Guardians. Our job is to make sure that nothing comes *out* of it," the Headmistress added.

Lyla's eyes widened. "Things can come out of the Portal? Like what?"

"Strange animals, fairy folk, the odd elf—that kind of thing," Mrs. Landshome said. "We just turn them around and jam them back in again."

"Besides," Esther said, "the Portal only opens from the Between side. And only one person can open the Portal."

Sasha had a bad feeling about this. "And who is that person?"

"Why, the Shadow King of Between," the Headmistress said. "*He* wields the Portal."

Sasha turned to Lyla. "I think they're talking about Hill-Man."

Lyla blinked. "Hill-Man is a *king*? Not a shirtless shepherd?"

"He's not a shepherd," Sasha said.

When it came to her dreams, there were many things that Sasha was uncertain about, but Hill-Man's sheep-herding tendencies were not one of them. In retrospect, there *was* something kingly about his manner; he was far too comfortable issuing commands. Sasha had the feeling that he was used to being obeyed—and not just by livestock.

Moreover, Sasha had terrible luck: accidentally mistaking a real-life king for a lust object in her first seduction fantasy was just the sort of thing that would happen to her.

"He's definitely not a shepherd," she repeated.

"Then why was he running around the countryside in his pajamas?" Lyla asked. "That doesn't sound very kingly to me."

Esther cleared her throat. "Hill-Man?"

Sasha turned her attention back to the witches. "Sorry, I didn't mean to be impolite. I was wondering whether the man I saw in my dreams—we called him 'Hill-Man'—was the King of Between."

"Was he short?" Martha asked. "Thin? Oddly shaped head, kind of like a parsnip?"

Sasha blinked. "Ah, no. Quite the opposite."

Martha shrugged. "Not the King, then. Probably just a passing citizen. Don't worry about him, girl."

Sasha sighed in relief. *Finally*, something was going her way. "Good. *Great.*"

Old Mrs. Landshome snorted. "I say we just get in touch with Ol' Parsnip Head, that weaselly magician king, and tell him to shut the Portal and get out of the girl's dreams."

Esther shot a worried glance at Sasha. "Given the events of Sasha's dream, that may not be possible—"

"Nonsense!" the feisty old woman interrupted, waving away Esther's concern. "That magician is no match for us—we know that from experience. We can get Sasha out of this mess in a trice." Mrs. Landshome cracked her knuckles and smiled—a terribly wicked smile. "I'll even volunteer to do it myself. Been a while since I've tussled with Ol' Parsnip Head."

"I second that," Martha said, smiling an equally wicked smile. "What's the bet that he's still scared stiff of you, Gussie?"

"I'll be insulted if he doesn't wet his breeches and run off screaming like a banshee at the sight of me."

Miss Adeline pursed her lips in distaste. "While I do not agree with the vulgarity, I do approve of the sentiment. Let's try to have this fixed-up before supper."

"Agreed," Martha said. "I've got a chicken in the oven, and I don't want it drying out."

Sasha's heart began to accelerate, this time fueled by hope. Maybe … maybe this had all been some big, supernatural misunderstanding. Maybe all she had to do was wait a little bit longer, and let these sassy seniors fix this entire mess by suppertime.

Rosa shook her head. "No. Sasha said the man in her dreams had four Marks *and* raised wards."

"*Four* Marks!?" the witches shrieked in unison.

Sasha's hope was sucker-punched right in the kidneys by reality. She sighed. Of course, it was too good to be true …

Esther clutched her pearls. "Why didn't you tell us that immediately,

Rosa? You said he was a wizard—you didn't say that he was a *four-Mark wizard!*"

"Yes, *Rosa*," Felicia hissed. "You left out the most important detail of the entire story!"

Rosa raised her hands helplessly. "There was so much to tell you all! And there are so many of you to tell! It's not surprising that I forgot a detail or two in the retelling—especially after four glasses of elderberry wine. And don't you judge me, Felicia," she said, pointing to the smug redhead. "I'd like to see how *you* would have reacted if you'd been in my position."

Esther's jaw clenched. "That's not just a detail or two, Rosa. Get the book, please, Adeline. There has obviously been a change in ruler, which isn't surprising in that place."

"It might not be a new king," Mrs. Landshome said, as Miss Adeline left the room. "Ol' Parsnip Head may have just got himself a wizard advisor."

Felicia snorted. "Why would a four-Mark wizard allow himself to be bossed around by a mere magician?"

"True enough, I suppose," Mrs. Landshome said grudgingly. Clearly, she had been looking forward to tussling with Ol' Parsnip Head. "Though, what four-Mark wizard would want to rule Between? No one wants to rule that dive."

Sasha turned to Lyla. "Are you getting any of this?"

Lyla shrugged. "I lost track after Ol' Parsnip Head came into the picture."

Miss Adeline came back, staggering under the weight of a large book. Martha quickly shuffled off to help her. Esther lifted the map off the table, and Miss Adeline and Martha lowered the book in its place.

Esther looked down at the book—encased in several layers of plastic wrap—and sighed. "Well, I guess it's safe."

"And dust-free," Miss Adeline said.

"Don't say a word," Martha warned Felicia, as Esther dutifully began peeling back the layers of plastic.

Felicia rolled her eyes. "You're both obsessed with that stuff. It's only a matter of time before you run out of magical objects to cover and turn the cling wrap on us."

Martha shrugged. "Well, if it would shut you up ..."

Esther peeled back the final layer of plastic wrap and smiled. "There we are!"

Lyla inhaled sharply. "Wow. That—that's an *old* book."

Esther trailed her fingertips over the cover. "It is indeed."

Even Sasha could see that the book was ancient. It smelt of old parchment and dust and time itself. The cover was made of hundreds of tiny, overlapping leather scales in a shade reminiscent of dried blood. On the cover, embossed in gold, were two crescent moons facing each other, an eight-pointed star suspended between them.

In the very center of the cover was a depression in the leather. Esther raised the cuff of her brown sweater and placed her Mark over the depression. The book emitted an audible click.

"Between. Show us the succession," she commanded, removing her wrist.

The book flew open to a spot toward the middle. An elaborate tree denoting the succession of Between's monarchs began to appear before their eyes, sketched in a spidery, black-inked font.

Esther traced her finger along the rapidly appearing branches. "Dash it —it appears Ol' Parsnip Head isn't the king anymore. Apparently—hmm, now this *is* odd—his whereabouts are unknown. 'Presumed dead or in hiding,' it says." She tsked. "We *really* need to stay up to date."

"This is unforgivable," the Headmistress moaned, wringing her hands. "We've become very lax. Those who came before us would be horrified by how poorly we're conducting our duties."

Mrs. Landshome rolled her eyes. "They're *dead*, Penelope. They wouldn't give a rat's ass about what we're doing."

"Language, Gussie!" Miss Adeline said sternly, much to Mrs. Landshome's delight.

During their bickering, the last name appeared on the tree.

"It seems that the new king is someone named *Lorn*," Esther said.

"Lorn who?" Felicia asked.

Esther tapped her finger against the branch, but nothing else appeared. "It doesn't say, which is also curious …"

"More like ominous," Mrs. Landshome said. "The fellow knows enough to keep his real name hidden."

Again, Esther placed her Mark on the book. "Lorn, Shadow King of Between."

As soon as she raised her wrist, the book's pages began to turn, stopping at a blank page. As before, the page started to fill with more of the spidery, black script.

"Ah, here it is," Esther said, satisfied. "Lorn, Shadow King of Between, Keeper of the Portal, Guardian of the Gateways to the Earther Realm, Wielder of Dreams …" She paused and swallowed hard. "*Sorcerer* of the Highest Order."

A terrible silence filled the room.

Sasha observed the ashen faces of the coven. The witches exchanged glances amongst themselves—uneasy, worried, even terrified glances—that did nothing to ease Sasha's concerns. Mrs. Landshome ignored the glances and reached up her skirt for her flask.

Rosa's shoulders slumped. "I was afraid of that."

"What is it?" Sasha asked. "What does that mean?"

Esther stared at the page, her fingers tangled in her pearls. "It means that getting you free from that place is going to be harder than we first thought."

Mrs. Landshome took a long drink from her flask and swallowed loudly. She wiped her wrist over her mouth and snorted. "We thought we'd just slap around a puny magician king until he let you go. But instead, we're going to have to deal with a sorcerer."

"I didn't think there were any sorcerers left!" Violet said, her hand over her mouth. "I thought they were all killed off during the Purge."

"Looks like there may still be a few running around Otherworld," Felicia said.

Daisy patted her twin's hand consolingly. "Violet dear, you know how our ancestors hid from the witch hunts."

Violet nodded, dejected. "You're quite right, Daisy."

Esther quickly scanned the page. "It says that he's been the King of Between for the last seven years. Originally from Between, he was the High King's Left Hand—"

"High King's Left Hand?" Lyla interrupted.

"The High King rules over all the kingdoms of Otherworld," the Headmistress explained. "The High King's Left Hand is his advisor in all magical affairs."

"Does the High King have a right hand, too?" Lyla asked the Headmistress.

"Yes. He's the High King's military advisor."

"Huh. Does the High King have someone looking after all his appendages?"

"*Really*, Lyla!" the Headmistress exclaimed, scandalized.

Lyla shrugged, unrepentant. "I was just checking. I'm in the market for a new career."

"If we could return to the matter at hand?" Esther asked, her tone stern. She turned back to the book. "It seems that Lorn became the Shadow King of Between after crossing the Wasteland under orders from the High King."

"Oh, no," Rosa groaned. "A *True King*, then. Not just someone they put into power."

Mrs. Landshome cackled, the whiskey starting to kick in. "Ha! No wonder Ol' Parsnip Head is hiding; he probably didn't want to challenge this Lorn fellow to keep his crown."

"What do you mean by 'true' king?" Lyla asked.

"Between isn't a hereditary monarchy," the Headmistress explained. "So, there are several ways to become the King or Queen of Between. First, you can be appointed to the throne by the High King. These sorts of monarchs tend to be more caretakers than functional rulers—Ol' Parsnip Head was an appointed king.

"Second, you can Challenge the current monarch for the throne. The battle is typically to the death." The Headmistress grimaced. "Which is both violent and somewhat disrespectful of authority.

"Third, you may be destined to become king or queen, in which case you are given a Golden Feather at the time of your birth by the Oracles of the Citadel of Prophecy—"

"Hang on," Lyla interrupted. "Golden feathers? The Citadel of Prophecy? *Destiny?* Can we just take a moment to absorb how *awesome* all of this is?" She shivered with delight. "My little fantasy-lovin' heart is all aquiver right now."

The Headmistress rolled her eyes. "May I go on?"

"Please," Lyla said gallantly.

"The destined kings and queens have more legitimacy than the caretakers, but do not have access to all the power of Between. To acquire that power, they must become a True King or Queen of Between. There's only one way to become a True King or Queen—you must defeat the Nightmares."

"The Nightmares are demons that invade our dreams when the Portal is open," Esther explained. "In Between, they roam the Wasteland, entering the minds of anyone unfortunate enough to wander into their territory, and infecting the dreams of those who are asleep. Sasha, I believe the Nightmares are the monsters that appeared in your dreams."

Nightmares. Sasha now had a name for the monsters in her dream—and an apt one at that. She could still hear the screams of the twisted white creatures as she ran across the plain. She could still feel their claws tearing into the flesh of her back, and the searing heat of a long-fingered hand branding her calf—

Look at usss, Lady!

"They also wait for the Dreamers," Esther continued, breaking Sasha's reverie. "If the Shadow King doesn't get to them first, the Nightmares take them, which is usually catastrophic—for both the Dreamer and Between."

Sasha remembered her five-year-old self running away from the monsters. She could still feel the terror, the bone-chilling fear—

Not helpful, Sasha, she told herself sternly. She clenched her hands together to stop them from shaking and squared her shoulders. "How do you defeat them?"

"You must cross the Wasteland—the vast plain upon which the Nightmares dwell," Esther said.

Lyla held up her hand. "Hang on—let me get this straight. To become a True ruler of Between, you have to defeat the Nightmares by crossing the Wasteland?"

The Headmistress nodded. "That's right. It's not as easy as it sounds; there are thousands of Nightmares. And if they catch you—well, the results would not be pretty."

"How 'not pretty?' " Lyla asked. "What are we talking about, here? Blood sucking? Dismemberment? Decapitation?"

"My, my—you are a bloodthirsty one, aren't you?" Felicia drawled.

Lyla raised an eyebrow. "Would you like to find out firsthand?"

"Ladies, *please*," Esther said sternly. She turned to Lyla. "To answer your question, the Nightmares swarm a victim and bite them, forcing them to relive their worst nightmares. They then feed upon the person's energy—their fears, their sadness, their lifeforce—until the person becomes nothing more than a husk."

"A *husk*?" Sasha repeated, horrified.

"A husk," Esther confirmed. "Then, infected with the essence of the demon, the victim becomes a Nightmare."

Sasha blanched. "I'm so glad that I found that out *after* I ran a marathon with them." She buried her face in her hands.

Lyla nudged Sasha with her elbow. "You crossed the Wasteland," she whispered to her friend. "Don't you realize what that means?"

But Sasha barely heard her—she was currently having a mild breakdown. "I could have been a husk," she whispered to herself as she rocked back and forth. "*A husk. A husk!*"

Felicia watched Sasha's rocking and raised an eyebrow. "She doesn't seem to be taking this very well, does she?"

"Hey!" Lyla cried. "Have some compassion—she was almost husked!"

"Sasha, dear," Esther said soothingly. "Would you like some tea?"

"No need," Martha said. She walked briskly over to Sasha's side and grabbed her by the shoulders.

"Snap out of it," she told Sasha, shaking her vigorously. "There's no time for this now! *Now*, you need to be strong. *Now*, you need to be brave. You can have a breakdown later."

"Riiiii-ghhhh-tttttttt," Sasha stuttered, flopping around like a ragdoll under Martha's hands.

Martha paused her shaking. "Better?"

Sasha exhaled slowly. "Weirdly enough—yes. Thanks."

Martha nodded, pleased, and walked back to her seat.

Sasha took a long, slow breath and leaned gingerly back against the couch. "Where were we?"

"Husk," Felicia said with a sly smile.

"Skip ahead," Lyla said firmly.

"We were talking about True Kings," the Headmistress said. "Lorn— the new Shadow King—is evidently a True King of Between. A True King always supersedes the claim of an appointed king. In this case, it looks like Ol' Parsnip Head ..." She paused, frowning. "We really shouldn't call him that. It's disrespectful; the man is—*was* a king. What was his real name?"

"Who *cares*," Mrs. Landshome groaned. "He's probably dead. You spend far too long worrying about dead people."

The Headmistress shook her finger at the old woman, a world of accusation in her outstretched digit. "At least *I* care about our history, Gussie, unlike *you*."

Mrs. Landshome stamped her foot. "I'm one hundred and four years old, dash it! It's hard to get more historic than that! With the way you keep going on and on about how much you love old things, you should be bending down and kissing my wrinkly, old—"

"Ladies!" Esther said tersely. "Can we keep to the topic at hand?"

Lyla raised her hand. "Can I just check that I've got all this?" She waited until Mrs. Landshome and the Headmistress stopped giving each other death stares. "The Shadow King—originally Ol' Parsnip Head—is now a guy named Lorn, who is the True King of Between because he crossed the Wasteland without getting husked by the Nightmares. And Ol' Parsnip Head ran away because he recognized that Lorn's claim to the throne was more legitimate than his own. Is that right?"

Esther nodded. "Exactly. Technically, Ol' Parsnip Head could have fought Lorn for the throne. But he showed great sense by slinking off into the sunset. A sorcerer who is a True King of Between—who has all that unlimited wild magic at his disposal—would be unbeatable."

"Hmm, *unbeatable*. Now, isn't *that* something!" Felicia practically purred.

She stroked her throat, her long, coral nails bright against her fading summer tan. "Just think of it—all that power! My, oh, my ..."

Lyla reached over and clutched Sasha's hand. "Sasha," she hissed under her breath.

But Sasha barely noticed; she was staring at the book, which was now busy sketching the features of a man—a man with sharp cheekbones and deep-set eyes, chin-length dark hair, and a wonderful lower lip.

A man dressed in black armor and a crown of what looked like mirror-shards.

A man who was wearing a silver amulet of two facing crescent moons and an eight-pointed star suspended between them.

A man who was looking at Sasha somewhat disapprovingly, even though he was just a sketch.

"That," she said quietly, "is the man in my dreams."

The witches all crowded around the table to get a better look.

Old Mrs. Landshome gave a low whistle. "Definitely an improvement on Ol' Parsnip Head."

"My, oh, my," Felicia whispered.

"Ha! You should see him with his shirt off!" Lyla crowed.

The witches all turned to Sasha.

"You saw him with his shirt off?" Felicia asked.

Sasha blinked, startled by the nine pairs of eyes staring at her intently. "Ah, yes."

Mrs. Landshome raised an eyebrow. "And?"

"And?" Sasha asked, confused.

"Spill, sugar. Was it a nice chest?" Felicia asked.

"Ah, yes," Sasha blurted, startled into an honest reply. "Yes, it was."

The witches sighed wistfully and turned back to the sketch.

"Pity it's just a picture of his head," Violet said.

"Esther, can you ask the book to show us his chest?" Daisy asked.

Esther shrugged. "I could give it a try."

Sasha stared at her incredulously. "You're *kidding*, right?"

"Ha, there's no need," Lyla said, reaching under the chaise.

Sasha's eyes widened. "No!" She lunged toward her friend, but Lyla pivoted away.

"Behold!" Lyla exclaimed, opening Sasha's sketchbook. "The Shadow King in all his glory."

The witches gathered around the sketchbook, cooing appreciatively. A few of them clapped.

Daisy patted Sasha's arm. "Lovely sketch, sweetie. I particularly like the shadowing over his abs."

Her twin looked at her in surprise. "Why, Daisy! I didn't realize you knew what abs were."

Daisy gave her a supremely cheeky smile. "I watch fitness infomercials while you're in the bathtub."

Lyla reached over and high-fived Daisy. "If you like ab-rich infomercials, then you'll love this picture." She quickly turned the page. "Sasha sketched a close-up of his chest and didn't even bother with his head. *See?*"

The witches crowded around for a closer look. Sasha buried her face in her hands.

After several moments, Felicia stepped back and primly smoothed out the creases in her skirt.

"If the Shadow King comes to take Sasha, then I am willing to make the supreme sacrifice and take her place." She placed her hand over her ample chest. "I believe it's my duty, as a member of this coven, to protect a citizen."

"Oh Felicia, you sly fox!" Violet waved her finger at the redhead. "It wouldn't be a *sacrifice* at all to be taken by this king."

"You can't call dibs on the Shadow King, Felicia," Martha said.

"Take a number, Felicia," Mrs. Landshome said bluntly.

"Well, I *never*," Felicia drawled. "I was just trying to be helpful."

"Besides ..." Esther looked over at Sasha. "I don't think Between would be amenable to a swap."

Sasha raised her head from her hands. "So, he *is* coming for me, isn't he?"

Esther nodded.

"What does he want with me?"

Lyla hit Sasha on the arm. "*That's* what I was trying to tell you when you were going through your husk crisis. You defeated the Nightmares, Sasha. That makes *you* the True ruler of Between." She turned to Esther. "I'm right, aren't I?"

"Yes," Esther said, smiling sadly. "That's probably the Shadow King's first concern. Technically, Sasha could fight him for sole rulership."

"No. *Hell no.*" Sasha shook her head vehemently. "There's *no way* I'm fighting a sorcerer. I mean, how could I? I'm not a witch; I don't have magic. I'd have no chance at all unless I brought a gun and even then—no. *No.*" She gasped out a disbelieving laugh. "I'm not killing another person over a fairy tale kingdom that I don't want to rule in the first place."

Felicia stared at Sasha, aghast. "You'd shoot that perfect chest?"

Lyla looked down at the sketch. "It would be a crime against humanity. And chests."

The other witches murmured their agreement.

Esther held up her hand for silence and turned to Sasha. "Without magic, there's no way you could win a fight against him."

"Could you defeat him?" Lyla asked Esther.

Esther shook her head. "Not alone. He's a sorcerer with all the magic of Between at his disposal. Even with help, the fight would most likely go his way, especially if we fought in Between." Her eyes narrowed. "It's odd that the High King allowed someone so powerful to become the Shadow King. Something about this seems strange ..."

Sasha threw her hands in the air, thoroughly demoralized. "This is getting worse and worse. What if I relinquish all claims to the throne?"

The Headmistress shook her head. "This isn't something that you can run away from."

"Why not?" Lyla asked. "Didn't Ol' Parsnip Head run away?"

Esther picked up her teacup, remembered that it was full of Truth Elixir, and put it back down. "He wasn't a True King, just a caretaker the High King put in power. Sasha, on the other hand, is an entirely different story. She's a *True Queen*; her ties to the throne—to Between— are much stronger than those of an ordinary ruler." She turned to Sasha. "I very much doubt that you'll be able to refuse a throne that you fought to win."

"Not only that, having a spare True ruler running around would threaten the Shadow King's leadership," the Headmistress added. "He wouldn't be able to rule effectively, knowing that Sasha could Challenge him for the throne at any time."

Lyla's eyes widened. "The 'others' Hill-Man spoke of—the people who may be coming to get Sasha—could they use her to take the crown away from him?"

Esther shrugged uneasily. "That's one reason they may want her. Another is that Sasha appears to be able to enter and exit the Portal whenever she dreams." She turned to Sasha. "I'm not sure how you're doing that. It may be that your presence here as a Dreamer opens the Portal when you dream. Regardless, the High King will want to put a stop to that as soon as possible. If people can enter Between or leave it at will, there could be dire consequences. Imagine if the Nightmares escaped into our world ..."

Sasha shuddered. "That can't be allowed to happen."

"But with you here—keeping the Portal open—it might happen,"

Felicia said. "Who's to say that the Nightmares won't follow you back the next time you dream of Between?"

"*Felicia*," Esther chastised. "Sasha has enough on her plate right now."

Felicia shrugged, unrepentant. "I'm just saying what we're all thinking."

"Care to guess what I'm thinking right now?" Lyla asked the redhead sweetly.

Felicia rolled her eyes. "It's a valid concern."

"She's right," Sasha said. The true horror of her situation was finally beginning to sink in. "I'm a liability. I have these *others* coming to get me by day, and Nightmares trying to hitch a ride with me by night. Not to mention the fact that Hill-Man—"

The Headmistress tsked. "You really should call him the Shadow King, dear."

"*The Shadow King* is coming to get me, too," Sasha corrected. "Is it possible that he wants to kill me so that I don't take his throne?"

"Did you get the impression that he wanted to kill you?" Esther asked.

Sasha thought back over her encounter with the Shadow King after her run with the monsters. His facial expressions had ranged from frustrated to concerned. Murderous intent had not been one of the featured emotions, thank goodness.

"Ah, no. Quite the opposite."

"Rosa mentioned that he gave you a token," Esther said.

"Well, he gave me this." Sasha pulled the silver amulet from her pocket and held it up by its broken chain for the women to see.

The witches stared at it in shock.

"May I see it?" the Headmistress asked, her tone awed.

"Sure." Sasha held the pendant out toward the Headmistress.

The Headmistress let her hand hover above the metal, careful not to touch it.

"What do you sense?" Daisy asked.

"Power," the Headmistress said breathlessly. "Lots and lots of power. There's a transportation charm—or perhaps a summoning charm. And protection charms, too—strong ones. There's something else, too … something to do with the Portal." She furrowed her brow, staring intently at the amulet. "Perhaps … perhaps it helps to open the Portal? Hmm … it won't tell me." She moved her hand away. "It's keeping secrets."

"Pretty much as I thought," Esther said. She turned to Sasha. "This is a rather solid sign that the Shadow King is offering you his protection. Clearly, he isn't worried about you Challenging him for his throne. After all, you won't be the King of Between—you'll be the Queen."

Esther's look was heavy with meaning, but Sasha's tired mind was unable—and somewhat unwilling—to interpret what she was trying to say.

Lyla figured it out in a flash. She elbowed Sasha. "He's going to try and marry you." She looked over at Esther. "Isn't he?"

Esther nodded.

"Lucky thing," Old Mrs. Landshome muttered and took a long drink from her flask.

Sasha stood up like a shot. "No. No way in hell."

Daisy looked up at her in surprise. "You don't want to marry that chest?"

Felicia raised her hand. "As I said, I would be more than willing—"

"Put a sock in it, Felicia," Mrs. Landshome snarked.

"Everyone put a sock in it!" Sasha fumed. "I am not marrying a man just because he has a nice chest."

"It's a *very* nice chest, dear," Violet said.

The others nodded.

Sasha felt as though something vital in the deep recesses of her brain was about to explode. "I don't know this man! I met him twice—*twice!*—in a dream, and now ... now I'm expected to *marry* him?! I have no intention of marrying anyone ... *especially* not a man who I've only met twice in a dream."

She shook her head in disbelief. "How did my life come to this? How did it get to the point where I have to marry or kill someone I've met *twice in a dream?* And sure, he may have a nice chest—"

"A *very* nice chest, dear," Violet corrected.

"Even better than the ones you see on infomercials," Daisy added.

"Yes, thanks for clarifying that," Sasha said testily. "But unfortunately, he doesn't have a personality to match. Each time we've met, he has been insulting, deliberately vague, aloof, and manhandle-y. Not to mention the fact that he yawned at me while I was trying to engage him in my first seduction fan—"

"But he did save you," Lyla interrupted.

Sasha stared at her friend in shock. "Et tu, Lyla?"

Lyla held up her hands in surrender. "Just stating the facts. I think you need to speak to him and figure a way out of this situation."

"I'm not sure if that's possible," Esther said. "Sasha keeps returning to Between. The Shadow King can't allow the Portal to remain open for an extended period of time. To close it permanently, he will have to take her back to Between."

Sasha's face drained of color. "Forever?"

Esther looked uneasy. "We'll see what we can do about that."

Sasha closed her eyes and sat heavily on the couch, all hope gone.

"Nope," Lyla said, shaking her head violently. "There's *no way* I'm going to let that happen." She turned to Sasha and grabbed her hands. "You're not going anywhere, you hear me? If Hill-Man tries to take you to Between, I'll get you the best immigration lawyers that my trust fund can buy. You just wait—once they get through with him, he won't even be able to walk you to the front door, let alone take you to another realm. Oh! And while we're at it, we'll get a restraining order against him. *That'll* blow his Otherworld pantaloons right off."

Sasha smiled weakly at her friend. "I'm not sure if U.S. law works on Otherworld kings."

"Hey, you're a U.S. citizen on U.S. soil. And in this great country, there are few things more terrifying than high-priced lawyers. And if—and this is a big *if*—the lawyers can't stop him, we'll try something else: bodyguards, exorcists, circus trainers. Whatever it takes. There's *no way* I'm letting you get carried off to another world like a character in some lousy fairy tale, even if this guy has a great chest."

"Oh, dear." Rosa pressed her hand to her lips. "Fairy."

"What is it?" Esther asked.

"The dream pillow—I must have added too much peony."

"Why are you putting peony in it in the first place?" Felicia sniped.

Rosa gave her a scathing look and ignored her.

"Peony?" Sasha asked.

"It assists communication between our world and Otherworld," Rosa explained.

Sasha stared at her. "I want my money back, Rosa."

Rosa winced. "It *did* protect you while you were dreaming—that's why it's burned."

"Fine then, keep the cash." Sasha sighed and straightened her spine. "Right, what's the plan?"

"First, we're going to summon this new Shadow King," Esther said. "Sooner rather than later."

Sasha watched as the witches turned to each other, chattering nervously.

"How soon?" Rosa asked.

Felicia cleared her throat delicately. "You *will* allow us time to freshen up, won't you Esther?"

Mrs. Landshome rolled her eyes. "The Shadow King is taken, Felicia."

"That's quite right, Felicia," Miss Adeline said. "He's Sasha's."

Sasha's eyes widened. "Hey, he's not mine!"

Martha ignored her. "All the primping in the world isn't going to change the fact that he belongs to Sasha. Deal with it."

Felicia shifted primly in her seat. "I have no idea what you mean, Martha. I just wanted to change out of my work clothes before starting any rituals."

"Seriously, for the record—I don't want him," Sasha said. "Felicia is more than welcome to him."

Felicia perked up. "Well, if she doesn't want him—"

"Zip it, Felicia!" Mrs. Landshome yelled, gesturing wildly with her flask. "He belongs to Sasha fair and square."

"And if she doesn't want him, I get him," Lyla said. "I'm her best friend."

Sasha stared at her alleged best friend. "*Really?* Are you drunk?"

Lyla shrugged. "He shouldn't go to waste."

"Well, that isn't fair at all!" Felicia said. "I don't think that—"

"Enough!" Esther roared.

All the women fell silent. Although Sasha had first wondered how mousy Esther had become the leader of the coven, one look at her now—eyes fierce, jaw clenched, power positively radiating from her thin frame—and it was no longer a question.

Esther took a deep, calming breath. "If you are all quite finished?" She waited until all of the women nodded "We have better things to do right now than fight over some man as if he was the last chicken leg at a picnic lunch. At the end of the day, he is just a man."

Daisy covered her mouth in shock. "But Esther—his chest!"

Esther raised her hand. "His chest notwithstanding. Now, to settle this once and for all. If Sasha chooses to reject the Shadow King's suit, then *he* will select his bride—and keep in mind that he may choose none of you."

Several of the women sighed. Sasha buried her face in her hands.

"We will summon the Shadow King at midnight," Esther continued. "Sasha, Adeline will take you to the Portal. Lyla, I'm afraid that you'll have to stay here."

"What?" Lyla cried. "No! I won't leave Sasha alone."

"I can't permit you to see our rituals," Esther said, a hint of steel creeping into her voice.

Sasha slung her arm around Lyla's tense shoulders. "Don't worry," she whispered into her friend's ear, "I'll tell you all about it."

"I want to hear every sordid detail," Lyla whispered back. She turned to Esther. "If you let anything happen to her—if you let him take her away —I promise I will—"

Esther held up her hand. "We won't let anything happen to Sasha—you have my word. We're on her side."

Lyla snorted. "Just remember that when the Shadow King and his magnificent chest shows up, okay?"

"You have my word," Esther repeated solemnly.

There was something about the way that Esther said the words. It felt like an oath, a *vow*—something that could be counted upon, something that could be trusted. Sasha could hear all that and more in Esther's voice.

Apparently, Lyla could, too. Reluctantly, she nodded.

Sasha squeezed Lyla's shoulder then stopped. "Hey, shouldn't you be comforting me?"

"Oh, yeah. Sorry about that." Lyla put her arm around Sasha's shoulder and hugged her, careful to avoid her bandages.

Sasha smiled sadly. "Better."

"We have a lot of work to do before the Summoning," Esther said to her coven. "Daisy and Violet—you're in charge of guarding the Portal. Alert us if you see any unusual activity and make sure that nothing comes through."

The twins nodded.

"Rosa, Adeline, and Martha—you're in charge of protecting Sasha. Draw the protection runes under her bed, and around all the entrances. Get her a more *appropriate* dream pillow and give her as many talismans as you can." She looked at the amulet still in Sasha's hands. "Although something tells me that she's already well looked after."

Esther turned to the Headmistress. "Penelope, I need you to go to the Archives. Find out why the Portal keeps opening, and how we can close it ourselves. We also need to know who else could be coming for Sasha—any information you can find. We need to know what we're up against."

The Headmistress nodded.

"Do you mind if I look in the Archives, too?" Lyla asked. "I'm a researcher. I'm also fantastic at finding useful information to wheedle out of situations; that seems like an appropriate skill in this situation."

"I'm sure Penelope will be happy to have some help," Esther said. "Especially since Poppy is still ill with the flu."

The Headmistress, however, did *not* look happy to have Lyla as an assistant. "Although I could use the help, is that really appropriate, Esther? Lyla isn't one of *us*. By tomorrow, Poppy may be well enough to return to work, and I'll have all the help I need."

"But—" Lyla began.

"Poppy can't even get out of bed," Esther interrupted. "Let Lyla help. She has Sasha's best interests at heart—that should motivate her to find answers.

"Trust me, I am plenty motivated," Lyla said, her expression grim.

The Headmistress pursed her lips, clearly unhappy. "Still … many of the books won't open without magic. And some of those texts shouldn't even be *seen* by someone outside of the coven."

"You can give Lyla the less sensitive texts," Esther suggested. "And you'll be there to oversee anything that she reads."

The Headmistress nodded reluctantly. "Very well—Lyla may assist me."

"Felicia and Gussie—gather the others," Esther ordered. "Activate the Sentinels and the runes on each of the buildings. We need to be ready for whatever happens."

Daisy leaned toward Esther, her expression eager. "Should we activate the Elders?"

"Not yet," Esther said. "They're our last resort to protect the village. We can't afford to squander their power frivolously."

Daisy's shoulders slumped. "Of course." She leaned back against the couch cushions and sighed. "But it would be *thrilling* to see them in action."

"Not to worry, dear," Violet said, patting her sister's hand. "Even without the Elders, I'm sure this will all be very exciting."

"You're quite right, Violet," Daisy said, perking up. "*Much* more exciting than usual."

"Finally, a little action around here!" Mrs. Landshome said gleefully. She tucked her flask back under her skirt. "Let's go, Felicia!"

Felicia rolled her eyes. "*I'll* go round up the others. You're barely sober enough to walk straight."

The old woman waved her off. "I once faced down a typhoon after a three-day drinking binge with Allied soldiers during World War II. I can certainly handle setting the runes after four slugs of scotch."

Martha looked at her admiringly. "The youth of today don't have your spirit, Gussie."

There was a devilish glint in Mrs. Landshome's pale blue eyes. "Ain't that the truth, Martha. Us older ones are made of sterner stuff. Mark my words: when the chips are down, we'll be the only ones standing."

Esther ignored them both—all her attention was on Sasha. "Then let's be off. Something tells me that we haven't got much time."

OF PORTALS AND WELL-DRESSED KINGS

"So …" Sasha began, as she watched Miss Adeline trace a pentagram in gold chalk on the floorboards where Sasha's bed usually stood. "Is this a good time to ask why I was drugged with Truth Elixir?"

Miss Adeline paused, her mouth pinched tight. "I have never approved of that practice. Far be it from me to challenge our coven leader, but there are more ethical ways of finding out if someone is a witch."

Sasha blinked. "They were trying to find out if I was a witch?" She thought back over her first meeting with the Headmistress, and suddenly all the odd questions—about her dreams, and her impressions of Old Middleton—made sense. "Well, that explains why she looked at my wrists. Which, by the way, was very creepy."

Martha picked up a piece of gold chalk and began sketching runes around the window with ruthless efficiency. "The elixir is quick, and usually, the girl is none the wiser."

"That's not the point!" Sasha fumed. "It doesn't matter how quick it is —or if the person realizes that they've been drugged or not! The practice itself is morally and socially unethical."

"Some would say that you lost the moral high ground when you potioned a whole coven," Martha said, pointing to Sasha with her gold chalk.

Sasha cringed. "I hated doing that. Lyla and I tried to find an alternative, but we couldn't think of anything. We had no other option."

"Neither did we," Martha said.

"Yes, you did! You didn't have to drug me. I live with you—couldn't you have just observed me? Or found a way to test me? Or just *asked* me?"

Miss Adeline and Martha exchanged a long look.

"Perhaps," Miss Adeline acknowledged.

"I still prefer the elixir," Martha said, returning to her runes.

"Unbelievable," Sasha muttered, and sat on the edge of her displaced bed.

"It's not always easy to identify a witch," Rosa explained. She was sitting on the floor, rummaging through a cardboard box filled with crystals, potion bottles, and other magical odds and ends. "Not all witches have Marks. Some don't even know they have powers—Poppy is an excellent example. The Truth Elixir opens their senses and allows the women to talk freely about their connection to magic—their dreams, their feelings, their instincts. From their conversation, Penelope can usually tell a hidden witch. She's very sensitive to dormant magic. You had her confused."

"I did?" Sasha asked. "What do you mean?"

"She thought there was *something* about you. A touch of magic hiding away in there." Rosa gestured to Sasha's chest. "But you ran out of the meeting before she could figure it out."

"I ran out of the meeting because I didn't want to get fired for talking to my boss about my sex life."

Martha snorted.

"That was unfortunate," Rosa said, biting back a smile. "But Martha's right—usually Esther isn't as heavy-handed with the elixir. No one has ever noticed that they were potioned before."

"No one has ever noticed?" Sasha's eyes widened. "Hang on, how many times have you done this?"

Miss Adeline paused her rune work. "In the history of Old Middleton or just lately?"

"Doesn't matter," Martha said. She moved over to the door and began sketching runes around the frame. "The answer is *plenty of times*. Sometimes we're right about a girl, sometimes we're wrong. It gets the job done."

Rosa looked up from the box and smiled sympathetically at Sasha. "Old Middleton is a magnet for people with *talents*. Given that it's so small and isolated, if a person comes here … especially a young woman … it's because they are drawn here. Well, usually. When we heard you were coming, we assumed you were one of us."

Something finally clicked into place for Sasha. "All the substitute teachers that I replaced—they were all witches, weren't they?"

Rosa nodded. "All of them."

"And the woman in the bakery? Ellie? She's a witch, too, right? She has a fire tattoo—I mean, Mark."

"Ellie was a find." Rosa pulled two potion bottles from the box and placed them carefully on the floor. "Fire elementals are so rare."

Sasha shook her head; she could barely keep up with all the revelations. "Mason Barnes was right—you're all witches."

She made a mental note to give the boy a sticker.

"Not all of us," Martha argued.

"Just most of us," Rosa said. She looked up from her rummaging, her hands full of rose quartz crystals. "We've had a lot of new members lately, haven't we?"

Miss Adeline brushed gold chalk dust from her fingers and stood up. "We have. That bothers me. Martha, can you remember a time when we had so many new members?"

"Yes," Martha said. "The war." She paused, her chalk poised above the doorframe. "Something's coming."

The women looked at each other, uneasy.

"Well," Sasha said, "that sounds pretty ominous."

Miss Adeline cleared her throat. "Nothing we can't handle."

Martha gave Sasha a wicked smile. "We've been through it all, dash it. They can bring it on."

"Here they are!" Rosa crowed triumphantly, pulling out two bracelets. "Hold out your hands please, Sasha."

Sasha did so, and Rosa slipped a bracelet on each of Sasha's wrists.

Sasha frowned down at the shiny, black and green crystals, and small, silver discs that now encircled her wrists. "These aren't drugged, are they?"

"*Pfft*, no—they're protection bracelets." Rosa pointed to the rough, black stones. "These crystals are black tourmaline. It's excellent for warding off all sorts of attack, particularly psychic attack. And these"—she pointed to the brilliant green crystals—"are peridot, which will help protect you from the Nightmares."

Sasha lifted her wrists to eye level, turning them so that the stones caught the light. "What about the silver discs?"

"They're engraved with protection runes. Oh! You'll also need this." Rosa reached into the box again and pulled out a dark green stone marked with pale green stripes. "This is malachite." She handed the stone to Sasha. "Keep it in your pocket—it's a powerful warning signal. If you're ever in danger, the stone will break."

"Wow!" Sasha ran her fingertips across the stone's smooth surface. It did not look like a cosmic alarm system, but she put it in her pocket, nevertheless. "Thanks!

"Don't mention it. I also brought along some potions and ointments to help heal those Nightmare wounds of yours—you don't want them to scar. Though, for the life of me, I can't find them in this infernal box. Tell me if you see a red jar in here …"

Rosa ducked her head and went back to rummaging through her box of mystical delights.

Sasha sat back and looked at the three women: Rosa, who was trying to find talismans and potions to keep Sasha safe; Miss Adeline, who was fussing over her pentagram and valiantly ignoring the gold chalk covering her perfectly pressed skirt; and Martha, fiercely drawing runes around the windows and doors, determined to protect Sasha at all costs. A surge of gratitude flooded her chest, leaving her almost breathless.

"Thank you—all of you—for helping me," she said quietly. "I can't imagine what I would have done without you. No one else would have believed me … they would have carted Lyla and I off to the nearest mental hospital. I'm—I'm just *really* thankful that you're all here and on my side."

"It's a pleasure, dear," Rosa said, beaming.

Martha snorted. "What were we supposed to do? Leave you to fix this mess by yourself? *Bah!*"

Miss Adeline shifted uneasily, clearly uncomfortable with too much sentiment. "You're a good girl—you have good posture, and your room is always tidy." She made a show of dusting the gold chalk from her skirt. "Now, shall I set the runes?"

Martha put down her piece of chalk. "Best to be thorough and do it together."

Sasha watched as the three women stood beside the pentagram and raised their hands, their palms facing the window. A low hum filled the room, charging the air with a prickly, electrical current that washed over Sasha, raising the hair on the back of her arms and neck. The ground beneath the pentagram began to undulate in waves that grew ever larger, spreading further and further across the room until they lapped at the edges of the door and the window frames. The runes began to pulse in the same rhythm, as if beating to a strange heartbeat. The gold chalk glowed and then became molten, the smell of burning wood filling the air.

The porcelain figurines scattered around the room shifted. To Sasha's amazement, the usually placid shepherdess on her nightstand lifted her crook, holding it menacingly like a baseball bat, ready to fight. The cross-eyed cat beside her bared its teeth, poised to pounce.

For one final moment, the runes and pentagram flared bright, bright gold. Then, they burned out in a shower of sparks that fell like shooting stars to the floor.

The porcelain figurines returned to their original positions.

The witches put down their hands.

"*Wow*," Sasha whispered. Cautiously, she stood up and walked over to the door. The gold runes—once made of chalk—now appeared to be carved into the doorframe. "That was *amazing*!"

The witches staggered a little and sat down on Sasha's bed.

"Are you okay?" Sasha asked, rushing over to the women. "Can I get you anything?"

Martha waved her off. "We're fine. It takes a bit out of you if you don't do it often." She looked at the runes with a satisfied smile. "I'd like to see anyone get past those wards."

Rosa nodded, pleased. "They are exceptionally powerful.

Miss Adeline glanced at her watch. "Ladies, we can't lollygag around—time is getting the better of us." She rose from the bed, followed by the other women.

"Better get this cleaned up," Martha muttered. She began to raise her hand.

"Mind the floors," Miss Adeline warned.

Martha rolled her eyes. "Addie, after fifty-eight years, I'm well aware of the floors."

Sasha was surprised to see Miss Adeline's lips twitch.

Martha made a flicking motion toward Sasha's bed. The bed rose several inches from the ground and floated smoothly across the room until it hovered over the golden pentagram. It remained suspended there for a moment before it lowered gently to the ground.

"Wow," Sasha said, her eyes wide. "That is amazing! And *so* useful if you ever need to move furni—Hang on." Her eyes narrowed. "On the night we came to Old Middleton, you dragged those suitcases, inch by inch—"

Martha waved away Sasha's remark. "If I had a mind to do so, I could have carried those bags up the stairs and into your room in a trice *without* magic."

"Martha is terribly strong," Miss Adeline said proudly.

"Then why all the dragging and scraping and muttering?" Sasha asked, remembering the commotion as Martha dragged the suitcases up the staircase.

Martha shrugged. "Part of the act. We're trying to keep a low profile."

"It's true," Rosa said. "The coven members have Vowed to conceal their powers. Can you imagine the ruckus if people found out that there were real witches in Old Middleton?"

Sasha thought back to the Twilight Tour—Travis and Lucas would be overjoyed to know that they had been right all along. "There would definitely be a ruckus."

"Now …" Rosa picked up several jars from beside her box. "Let's see to those Nightmare wounds of yours, and then we'd best be off. We don't want to be late."

Sasha's heart started to race. She *did* want to be late—so late that they would have to carry on without her.

"Right," she said instead. "I wouldn't want to miss it."

~

AFTER MARTHA AND ROSA HAD CLEANED HER WOUNDS WITH THE KIND OF zeal and vigor usually reserved for stripping paint from walls, Sasha found herself walking gingerly down Main Street toward the Village Hall, accompanied by a purposeful Miss Adeline.

The older woman led the way down the deserted street, avoiding the puddles of gold light beneath the lamp posts in favor of the shadows gathered around the empty storefronts. The sky was overcast, the stars tucked away behind roiling, black clouds. An icy wind sent leaves dancing around Sasha's boots, and swung the bucket of the old well as they passed.

In the eerie quiet of the street, Sasha felt as though she was being watched. She looked up; stone gargoyles leered down at her from their rooftop perches. The shadows thrown by the lamplight made it seem as though the gargoyles' wings were unfurling, their fingers reaching, their smiles tilting as she passed. Sasha quickly looked away toward the village clock, the damaged face ticking down the minutes until midnight.

Miss Adeline stopped in front of the pink Village Hall and unlatched the wrought iron gates. Looking furtively around the empty street, the two women passed through and slipped into the dark, unlocked building.

By flashlight, Miss Adeline led Sasha to the basement. Then, to a secret doorway which led to a secret staircase, which led to a secret passage that wound down, down, downward, and then—oddly enough—up, up, *upward* until they reached a long corridor.

At the end of the corridor was a solitary lamp … and Lyla sitting on a stone bench beneath it.

Miss Adeline beckoned Sasha toward the bench. "We'll summon you to the Portal Chamber when we're ready to begin. Lyla, you'll have to stay out here."

"Yes, Miss Adeline," the women intoned obediently.

Miss Adeline took a brass key from a chain around her neck and fitted it to the lock of a small door beside the bench. Crouching down, she entered the room and closed the door behind her.

Sasha turned to her friend. Her eyes widened. "What happened to you?!"

Dust covered Lyla's cream sweater and jeans. There were cobwebs in her hair and a long streak of dirt across her cheek.

Sasha pulled a particularly long cobweb from Lyla's hair, grimacing the entire time. "Since when is researching such dirty work?"

Lyla looked at the cobweb in Sasha's hands and flinched. "When the library is a secret chamber hidden beneath the Middleton Gateway and the books are alive and fight back." She laughed, a little hysterically, at Sasha's wide-eyed look. "You have *no idea* what I've just been through—I believe it qualifies as an Ordeal. Part of me thinks that the Headmistress did it on purpose … you know, making it as hard as possible so that I'd quit."

Sasha pulled another cobweb from Lyla's hair—this one with a small, dried-up spider clinging to the strand. "She obviously doesn't know you."

"*Obviously.* That poor, deluded woman—she has no idea how stubborn and vindictive I can be. How about you? What have you been doing while I've been literally fighting for knowledge?"

"I ate dinner and then watched the witches turn our bedroom into a magically fortified bunker. I definitely had the easier time."

Sasha fumbled through her bag and offered Lyla a packet of tissues.

"Thanks," Lyla said, with a relieved smile. She took a tissue and began cleaning the grime from her face. "You know, you look surprisingly calm for someone who's about to take part in an ancient pagan ritual designed to help you meet the man that you're supposed to kill or marry. Or marry then kill. Or kill then marry." She paused, the tissue poised above her cheek. "This is complicated, isn't it?"

"Or *none of the above*," Sasha said serenely. "Both options are equally off the table."

Lyla stared at her incredulously. "Seriously, you're taking this *far, far* too well."

Sasha plucked the soiled tissue from Lyla's grasp and handed her a fresh one. "I may have accidentally taken too many pain pills."

"Did you bring any for me?"

"Ah, no." Sasha looked down into her bag. "But I have gum."

"That'll have to do." Lyla held out her hand and sighed sufferingly. "I hope it's morphine flavored."

"Nope, mint." Sasha stuffed the dirty tissue into her bag and handed Lyla the pack of gum. "So, after fighting books—and I want to know all about that later—what did you find out?"

Lyla's eyes lit up. "Not a whole lot, but it's a start." She popped a piece of gum in her mouth and picked up a notebook from the bench beside her. "By the way, the Headmistress has trust issues. When we first got to the Archives, she wouldn't let me touch any of the books. It took a lot of flattery about her illustrious ancestors and two compliments about her hair to get her to hand them over."

"I'll remember that—just in case I need anything from her in the future."

Lyla flipped through the notebook, pausing on a page filled with notes. "Okay. We couldn't find any mention of how to close the Portal from this end. The Headmistress thinks it's impossible, but I'll go back tomorrow and keep hunting."

Sasha slumped. "That would have been too easy."

"Tell me about it. We also didn't find out much about the True Queens of Between. From all accounts, there haven't been many True Queens. In fact—and this is strange—there haven't been that many queens at all."

"That *is* strange." *And ominous,* Sasha thought. But decided to keep that to herself.

Lyla nodded slowly. "Just a bit. Or it could simply mean that the kings weren't inclined that way." She waved her hand dismissively. "But this is the good bit: True Kings and Queens are bequeathed certain *gifts* after they defeat the Nightmares."

Sasha's eyes widened. "That's what Hill-Man—I mean, *Lorn* said—"

"Don't!" Lyla interrupted, holding up her hand. "Don't humanize him. He's our enemy."

"He protected me from the Nightmares. *Twice!* He's not our en—"

"He *is,*" Lyla insisted. "He wants you in Between—*we* want you to stay here. That makes him our enemy. We need to defeat him, not befriend him. So don't you go 'Lorn-ing' him, okay? Keep it professional."

Sasha rolled her eyes. "Fine. As I was saying, *the Shadow King*—"

Lyla nodded approvingly.

"—told me that I was supposed to receive gifts after I ran with the Nightmares."

"You get two types of gifts," Lyla explained, "and I hope I've got this right because it was really difficult to figure out—the ink was barely visible on that old parchment." She peered at her notes. "First, you get to ask three 'boons' of the Shadow King. So basically, he has to grant you three favors."

"Really? That's great!" Sasha's eyes widened. "Do you think I could ask him to close the Portal and leave me alone?"

"Ha! Wouldn't that be a giant loophole? Go ahead—give it a shot."

Sasha nodded. "Will do. What are the other gifts?"

Lyla quickly scanned her notes. "*W-ell* ..." She peered at the page uncertainly. "It looks like Between itself gives you three gifts."

"Between gives me gifts? Hang on, how could a place give me gifts?"

Lyla shrugged. "I have no idea, but the Headmistress checked the source material, and that's what it said. Maybe someone gives you gifts on Between's behalf? Or maybe the gifts come from Between's treasury?" She raised her hands helplessly. "I'm so sorry—it's the best I could do under the circumstances, what with having to fight the books just to get them to open, and trying to decipher barely visible words, and—and having to read by candlelight like some moldy, medieval monk. Not to mention the *spiders*—"

Sasha pulled the almost hysterical Lyla into a hug. "Are you kidding? You did a fantastic job!"

Lyla slumped against Sasha's shoulder. "It's not enough! It would be easier if I could take the books from the Archives back with me so that I can study them overnight, but it's magically forbidden. I—I need more time."

"Well, I'm not sure if you'll get it." Sasha snorted. "I just realized that we started the drive up here a week ago today."

"We should have driven past."

"*Right* past."

"I'm going to remind you that I was against coming here in the first place, but I won't gloat—that isn't dignified. Oh! Just before we left the Archives, the Headmistress found a passage about Between's marriage laws. She said she'll go back down there tomorrow and read it. I'm going to go with her, whether she likes it or not."

Sasha hugged her tighter. "Thank you."

"You know, Hill-Man probably knows more about this situation than any book in the Archives, so use this meeting to your advantage. Gather as much information about Between, and this whole situation, as you can. Ask him how to close the Portal. Hell, go for broke and try to abdicate."

"Esther didn't seemed to think that was an option."

"Try anyway. Just ... don't go with him tonight, okay?" Lyla's voice was terribly small. "*Don't go.*"

Sasha shook her head vehemently. "I'm not going anywhere. I ran a marathon with a pack of monsters—Hill-Man doesn't scare me."

"Good. But just in case he tries something …" Lyla pulled away from Sasha. She reached into her pocket and pressed a plastic tube into Sasha's hand. "It's best to be prepared."

Sasha stared at the lurid, pink object sitting innocuously in the palm of her hand. "Did you get me pepper spray?"

"Yes. Yes, I did. And I chose the pink holster because it's deceptively innocent in appearance and will thereby lull Hill-Man into a false sense of security."

Sasha pulled her friend into another hug. "This is probably the most violent—and pink—gift that I have ever received. I love it."

"I was going to get you a stun gun, but they're illegal here without a license." Lyla sighed wistfully. "If only we were in Vegas …"

"Probably for the best," Sasha said, releasing her friend.

"According to the instruction sheet, this little canister can hit a target ten feet away, *and* it's good for fifteen bursts of up to two to three seconds. But if Hill-Man tries anything, forget about the bursts—just spray until it's empty."

"So, so violent," Sasha said, shaking her head. "*Thank you.*"

"Sasha?"

Sasha turned toward the voice. Esther was peering at them from the doorway. The coven leader was dressed for the occasion in a cowled, crimson velvet robe with her Marks embroidered above her heart in gold thread. Her customary pearls were gone, replaced by a gold pendant in the shape of a door.

"It's time," she said quietly.

Sasha reluctantly stood up.

"Right." She placed the pepper spray in her pocket, straightened her shoulders, and followed Esther. "Wish me luck."

"Don't go with him!" Lyla cried out.

Sasha looked over her shoulder and tried to give Lyla a reassuring smile. "I'm not going anywhere."

"A likely story," Lyla muttered. She turned to the older woman. "You promised you wouldn't let him take her away. I am holding you to that promise."

"She won't go with him. I won't allow it," Esther vowed.

"Good." Lyla sniffed and wiped her eyes with the edge of her balled-up tissue. "Then, go get him!" She gave Sasha a tremulous smile and a brave salute. "We'll figure a way out of this crazy situation *when you get back.*"

With a heavy heart, Sasha turned away from her friend and crouched down low enough to duck through the small door. When she emerged on the other side, her eyes widened in surprise. Before her was a large, circular room covered in sheets of beaten metal the color of old gold. Flaming torches surrounded the room, throwing shadows that flickered across the chamber in strange, beast-like shapes, and illuminating the protection runes etched into the walls. Beneath her feet, hundreds of tiny, gold tiles glittered in the dim light, making it seem as though she was walking on the same gold dust as the hillside of her dreams.

Looking up, Sasha stared at the vast, domed ceiling, where two crescent moons faced each other from opposite sides of the room, separated by constellations.

"Lovely, isn't it?" Esther said.

"It's breathtaking!" Sasha said, awed. "It's like the inside of a Fabergé egg! Well, except for that door over there."

She gestured to the far side of the room, where a curved door was set awkwardly against the golden wall. Rustic and solid, it was made from one of those dependable woods, like oak, its ungainly beams joined to the frame with clumsy, brass bolts. It was a door that would have looked quite at home in a tavern, or even quite splendid in an old barn. But here, in the golden finery of the opulent room, it looked comically out of place— almost as if it had been brought in by accident one day and was now trying to stay nice and quiet in the background so that no one noticed it.

"Well, that's the most breathtaking thing in the room."

Sasha's eyes widened. "That's the Portal, isn't it?"

Esther nodded. "That door is the *only* way for Dreamers to enter Between from our world. Come on. Let's join the others."

Sasha steeled herself and crossed to the center of the room, where the other women were chatting excitedly. Just like Esther, each of them wore a crimson velvet robe with their Mark stitched in gold over their hearts. They looked every inch the part of a coven of witches about to enact a powerful, ancient ceremony. Even old Mrs. Landshome looked less disreputable than usual, though perhaps not entirely sober.

Sasha looked down at her black leather boots, worn jeans, black turtle-neck sweater, and forest-green pea coat and realized that she was dressed more appropriately for a trip to the supermarket than a mystical ritual. Then again, it was a step up from her llama pajamas, which she had worn on all of her other magical adventures. She mentally shrugged. Given the day she'd had, it was remarkable that she had remembered to put on any clothing whatsoever.

"Well, isn't this thrilling!" Violet said, her cheeks flushed with excitement. "We haven't done this in a while."

Daisy straightened her robe. "No, we haven't! This is much more exciting than anything on television tonight." She patted Sasha's arm comfortingly. "Don't worry, dear, we'll sort this all out in a trice."

"Well, perhaps a little longer than a trice," the Headmistress said, fussing around the chamber. "He *is* a four-Mark sorcerer."

"He's a man first and foremost," Felicia said, her smile cat-like. "I'm sure we can use that to our advantage."

Unlike Sasha, Felicia had gone to considerable trouble over her appearance. She had arranged her hair in glossy curls and applied her makeup—pouty red lips and smoky eyes with extra lashes—with bold strokes. Even her robe was stylishly cut, showing off the contours of her figure and a generous amount of cleavage.

Martha put her hands on her hips and shook her head at the red-headed witch. "Well, I've got to admire you for putting it out there, Felicia."

"And it certainly is *out there* in that ensemble," old Mrs. Landshome said.

"I have no idea what you're talking about," Felicia drawled, and lifted her cleavage into place.

"Ladies." Esther crossed the room quickly, her heels clicking on the metallic tiles. "Please take your positions. We don't have much time."

The women hurried to take their places. Sasha looked down and noticed what appeared to be a massive compass etched into the floor. On this compass, however, the four points were denoted by the elemental Marks. The witches arranged themselves so they stood on the point that corresponded to their Mark: Rosa and Martha on Earth; Violet and Miss Adeline on Air; the Headmistress and Daisy on Water; and Mrs. Landshome and Felicia on Fire.

Esther took a small, navy blue velvet sack covered in stars from her robe and moved to the very center of the compass. She reached into the sack and withdrew a gold coin, which she placed at her feet.

"Sasha," she said, "I need you to stand at the back of the room."

Sasha stepped away from the compass and tried to suppress the impulse to flee the room entirely while the women had their backs turned.

The witches faced the oak door. Esther grasped the pendant around her neck—an exact replica of the Portal—and carefully opened it. As she did so, a beam of light streamed out from within the locket, reaching out to the Portal on the other side of the room.

The witches raised their palms, their Marks toward the Portal. Impossibly, a warm breeze began to stir in the still, windowless room, moving through Sasha's curls. There was a low moan, and the tiles beneath her feet began to tremble. The flames in the torches leaped and danced while faintly, in the distance, she could hear the trickle of water.

"Lorn, Shadow King of Between, we Summon thee," Esther intoned.

A mellow bell-tone filled the room. The voice in the back of Sasha's mind was almost giddy with joy.

Finally, it whispered.

Sasha felt the hairs on the nape of her neck stand up. Goosebumps raced up her arms.

The air began to hum.

"Lorn, Shadow King of Between, we Summon thee," Esther repeated, her voice strong.

The bell-tone became louder, resonating off the walls and ceiling. The room started to become unbearably warm, even as the wind blew harder, tugging on Sasha's hair and coat. Sasha pushed her hair back behind her ears and tried to keep her balance as the floor beneath her began to undulate.

"Lorn, Shadow King of Between, we Summon thee," Esther repeated a final time.

With an ominous creak, the wooden door opened. Light immediately flooded the dimly lit room, causing Sasha to shield her eyes. She looked down at the floor where the light pooled, turning the tiles pure gold.

When her eyes became accustomed to the light, Sasha slowly, carefully, looked up.

Standing in the Portal doorway was a dark silhouette framed by the bright, gold light. As Sasha watched, the silhouette moved forward until she could make out the figure of a man.

It took her only seconds to realize that this was not just *any* man.

Oh, no, she thought with a sinking heart, as Hill-Man himself stepped over the threshold into the golden room. *He came.*

Abruptly, the wind, light, heat, and sound came to a halt, leaving an eerie silence in their wake.

For a long, tense moment, everything was completely still.

"Damn," Mrs. Landshome whispered loudly. "He's wearing a shirt."

And just like that, the silence was broken.

The Shadow King raised an eyebrow. "Apologies," he said dryly. "I was unaware that there was a dress code."

Sasha, to her disgust, also noted that the Shadow King was wearing clothing—all of it fancy and unreasonably imposing. There was a long sleeved, black velvet tunic decorated with runes stitched in black, metallic thread; an elaborately patterned leather breastplate; form-fitting black leather trousers; and matching knee-high boots. He also wore a cloak composed entirely of shadows that shifted and seethed around his body, seemingly of its own volition. On his head lay a crown made of what looked like mirror shards, each as sharp as a blade.

Overall, he looked beautiful and majestic and terribly intimidating, and Sasha thought it incredibly unfair that he was dressed to impress. She felt herself becoming strangely irritated. Would it have been too much to ask for the witches to have Summoned him while he was wearing slippers and a ratty, old pair of pajamas?

Esther stepped forward. "Forgive my sister." She glared at Mrs. Land-shome. "My name is Esther, I am the coven leader."

The Shadow King bowed his head. "Lorn, Shadow King of Between. My apologies—I should have made efforts to introduce myself earlier. I had planned to do so once I got Between in hand." His lips twisted into a sardonic smile. "Regrettably, that has yet to occur."

Esther smiled politely. "No matter. Our coven welcomes you to Old Middleton."

Felicia crossed the room as quickly as her four-inch stiletto heels would allow and stood before the Shadow King. She smiled—a smile that dripped with honeyed charm—and slipped her hand into the crook of his arm.

"Yes. *Welcome,* Your Majesty!"

She curtsied a little, showing her cleavage off to its best advantage.

"And a generous welcome it is, too," the Shadow King said mildly. He gently pried Felicia's hand from his arm with a quick, "Many thanks," and turned toward Esther. "I assume you have Summoned me because of the recent ... incident?"

"*Incident?*" Sasha haltingly made her way across the floor toward the Shadow King. "More like a catastrophe."

The Shadow King started at the sight of her. "Sasha Evangeline Pierce. I was not aware that you were here."

Sasha shrugged. "Well, it's not by choice."

He ignored her comment. Oddly enough, he seemed inordinately relieved. "This is quite serendipitous! I was about to begin my search for you; I have been preparing Between for your arrival." He held out his hand to Sasha, palm up. "Are you ready to leave?"

"No," she said briskly, squaring her shoulders. "But I *am* ready to find out what all this is about." *Gather as much information about Between and this whole situation as you can,* Lyla had said.

"I will give you a full explanation as soon as we return to Between," he said smoothly.

Too smoothly.

"I would prefer one now if it is all the same to you." Sasha's earlier medication-induced calm was a distant memory, replaced by a mass of adrenaline and a prickly sense of fear. "I'm not going to Between until I know what this is about, and what's going to happen next."

The Shadow King stared at her, clearly trying to take her measure. Sasha stood very still and tried to project defiance and strength and I'm-staying-here-even-though-you-have-a-nice-chest vibes.

It must have worked. Abruptly, he dropped his outstretched hand and gave a weary sigh.

"I am sure that the coven has informed you about the importance of the Portal and why it needs to remain closed," he began. "Your presence here is keeping it open while you dream. To close it, you need to return to Between as soon as possible." He paused and looked at Esther. "You *did* inform her of all this, did you not?"

Before Esther could answer, Sasha cut in. "Yes. She did. What she didn't—couldn't—tell me is what will happen to me once I get to Between. Everyone here talks about Between like it's something out of a fairy tale. But there are *good* fairy tales, and there are *bad* fairy tales—ones where people get turned into poultry, or get eaten by giants, or are put into a coma for a hundred years. So you can't blame me for wanting to know if I'm stepping into a good fairy tale or a bad one before I follow you into that Portal. For all I know, Between could be the eighth ring of hell, full of terrible things like—like orgiastic rituals, and—and—nudist cannibals, and —and *macramé*," she finished lamely.

"Ha! *That* would be something to see," Mrs. Landshome cackled.

The Headmistress, however, was shocked. "Sasha! Is that any way to talk to the Shadow King? I mean, *really*, how could you mention"—she leaned forward and lowered her voice—"*orgies?*"

Martha rolled her eyes. "I bet it's not the first time he's heard the word, Penelope."

The Shadow King, Sasha noted, looked amused. "One hears a lot of deviant words while ruling Between." He raised his hand to stall the Head-mistress's tirade. "Her Majesty—"

Sasha started when she realized he was referring to her.

"—makes an excellent point. Even if it was framed rather graphically."

The Headmistress folded her arms, looking only slightly mollified.

Sasha nodded to the King, still a little shaken by the title. "Thank you."

The Shadow King inclined his head in return. "Let me assuage at least some of your fears. There are no ritualistic or Crown-sanctioned orgies. Those carried out by the deviant citizens of Between should probably be classified as 'hobbies' or 'pastimes.' I certainly have not ordered any to be performed."

"Pity," Mrs. Landshome sighed.

"Up until this morning," the Shadow King continued, "Between was free of cannibals, nudist or otherwise—"

"Hang on," Sasha interrupted. "*Was* free of cannibals?"

"*Was*, yes. We have just acquired one. According to public records, our new cannibal was intoxicated when he consumed the toe, which makes his cannibalism a misdemeanor at best and not a vocation. Then again, I suppose time will tell ..."

Sasha stared at the Shadow King, stunned.

"Macramé is lamentably common," he continued unperturbed. "To my knowledge, however, no one has used it for evil purposes ... yet. Given all the string and knots involved in the process, it is probably only a matter of time." He paused and placed his hand over a pouch at his hip, clearly remembering something. "I can make no such assurances about knitting." He peered at Sasha intently. "Better?"

Sasha blinked. "Ah ... sort of. Maybe? Hang on ... *a toe?*"

"A toe," the King confirmed.

Sasha shook her head. "The toe aside, I *still* don't know what's going on, and I really need answers."

The Shadow King held her gaze for a moment longer, as if weighing his options, and then nodded, clearly coming to some conclusion. He began to pace the chamber before her, his cloak billowing behind him in a non-existent breeze.

"Then let us begin at the beginning. From the moment you crossed the Wasteland, you became the True Queen of Between. To become a monarch of Between—a *True* monarch—you must cross the Wasteland and defeat the Nightmares *to prove your worth to the land*. Between, you see, has a fondness for grand gestures and impossible feats. It is wretchedly dramatic for a landmass."

"Hang on, Between is *sentient?*"

"Yes." The Shadow King flexed his shoulders with a grimace. "Very much so. Now, you crossed the Wasteland in a dream—a feat that is supposed to be impossible—"

"Why?" she interrupted.

"The Nightmares are infinitely stronger in a dream. No one should be able to do as you did—beat them in their own realm." He gave her a searching look then shook his head. "I, too, crossed the Wasteland; however, I was awake and did so with the aid of magic. Between recognized me as its True King ... and recognized *you* as its True Queen."

None of this was news to Sasha, but it was just as dreadful in the retelling. "What if I don't want to be the True Queen of Between?"

The Shadow King glanced over at coven, who were hanging onto their every word.

"Might we speak in private?" he asked, addressing the witches.

Esther nodded reluctantly. "Come, ladies—refreshment time. Sasha, *we will be close by.*"

There was a wealth of meaning in those final words: it was meant not only as reassurance for Sasha, but as a direct warning to the Shadow King not to try anything.

The Shadow King knew it, too. "Many thanks," he said wryly.

Sasha did not like the Shadow King's tone. It was not the tone of a man who was quaking in his knee-high boots after being warned by a coven leader. It was not even the tone of a man who was taking the warning of a coven leader seriously. No—it was the tone of a four-Mark sorcerer *humoring* a coven leader, and Sasha was not okay with that.

He could at least have the decency to pretend to be scared of Esther, she thought irritably.

The Shadow King's tone was not good for Sasha's nerves. For the first time since he had arrived, she seriously considered the possibility that she could be kidnapped and taken to Between against her will.

Sasha glanced at the coven and critically assessed what she knew of their abilities. Martha was probably more than a match for the Shadow King physically, assuming the battle came down to some sort of arm-wrestling match. Rosa's usefulness was probably inversely proportional to the amount of elderberry wine she had consumed. Mrs. Landshome probably had a trick or two up her sleeve, or—more likely—under her skirt, right beside her flask. Esther was clearly more formidable than she looked. And if Miss Adeline wielded magic with the same violence that she demonstrated when beating up throw pillows, then she would be a force to be reckoned with. The others were an unknown entity—particularly Felicia, whom Sasha thought was more likely to aid Sasha's kidnapping rather than stop it, especially if the Shadow King offered to remove his shirt.

There was obviously a lot of power in the coven but *still* ... Sasha wondered whether the coven would be a match for a four-Mark sorcerer. She placed her hand in her pocket and clutched her pepper spray.

I'll be a match for him, she told herself firmly.

She watched as Esther headed to the back of the room, the rest of the coven reluctantly following close behind. Together, they began removing cups and plates from two large, wicker picnic baskets. Despite their apparent activity, all of them—to Sasha's relief—kept an eye on the Shadow King.

The Shadow King noticed, too. His lips quirked as he beckoned Sasha closer with an imperious crook of his finger.

Sasha frowned at the imperious finger-crooking. She frowned harder when she realized that the Shadow King was standing several steps closer to the Portal than she was—all the better to drag her back to Between against her will.

She glanced nervously at the Portal and clutched her pepper spray harder. "Ah ... no, thanks. You can come to me."

The Shadow King noticed her glance. "I take it that you are concerned that I will whisk you away to Between against your will?"

Sasha shifted her weight, ready to run if need be. "It crossed my mind."

The King glanced down at her feet, as if he knew what she was planning. "I will not."

"Will not?" Sasha inclined her head toward the coven. "Or *cannot?*"

"Oh, I definitely *could* ... if I had a mind to do so."

Sasha's eyes widened. She shook her finger at the King as if he was a misbehaving kindergartener. "That is *not* reassuring!"

The Shadow King seemed amused by her finger shaking. "But I choose *not* to do so. There is a centuries-old treaty in place between the Middleton Coven and Between. It would be foolish and counterproductive to break it."

"Well, that's a relief." It was. It sounded rational, sensible—a solid reason not to kidnap someone.

"Moreover," the King continued, "I have no desire to make an enemy of you quite so soon in our acquaintance. I would rather that you come to despise me naturally over time."

To her surprise, Sasha found herself grinning. "So, despising you is inevitable?"

"Yes, according to most of the folk in Otherworld. We shall soon see if this extends to the Earther Realm. Now ..."

He beckoned her closer once more.

Sasha shook her head. "The weather is much better where I'm standing."

"Truly? My, my—the weather is fickle, is it not?" The Shadow King tilted his head, watching her shrewdly. "Perhaps a compromise? If we both step forward, we will meet in the middle."

Sasha glanced down at their feet. "That sounds reasonable, dash it. Okay, *fine*. On the count of three?"

The Shadow King inclined his head. "Three sounds reasonable."

"Right. One … two … *three*."

Reluctantly, Sasha stepped forward, meeting the Shadow King literally toe to toe, their leather boots almost touching.

"Let's speak plainly, so that there are no misunderstandings," she said, standing as straight as possible to minimize the King's height advantage.

"That sounds remarkably sensible," the Shadow King said approvingly.

The torchlight played across the sharp angles of his features, gilding him one moment and throwing him into shadow in the next. It made him appear changeable, *otherworldly*.

Sasha did not find that in any way reassuring.

"I don't want to be the Queen of Between," she blurted.

"Truly?" he said dryly. "I would never have guessed."

Sasha decided to ignore that comment. "I mean, it's a huge honor to be chosen," she amended, hoping that she hadn't insulted him.

The Shadow King folded his arms.

"But it's an honor that I'm going to have to decline. So …" She cleared her throat uneasily. "How do I go about abdicating? Do I need to fill out some paperwork? Or name a successor? Or—"

"You die," he said shortly.

Sasha's eyes widened. "I die? I *die*?! That's not how abdication works!"

"It is in Between. As we have already discussed, Between is sentient. By crossing the Wasteland, you Challenged Between for the right to rule. As with any Challenge, the outcome is binding. You proved yourself a worthy ruler, now you *must* take the throne. Between will accept no substitutions or excuses … except for death."

"But—but I didn't know that when I crossed! Otherwise, I wouldn't have done it."

"Between cares little about intentions—only actions. And your actions have won you a kingdom, Your Majesty." He gave her a mocking bow.

Sasha ran a shaking hand through her hair. "Rule or die, huh? That's not much of a choice."

The King grimaced. "I could not agree more." He leaned toward her, the shadows shifting so that he was now wholly in the light. "I, of all people, understand your reluctance to rule Between."

Sasha found that hard to believe. "Really?"

"*Really.*"

Sasha was surprised to hear the regret in the Shadow King's tone. His unexpected sympathy made her realize just how serious the situation must be.

She felt her stomach drop.

"Regardless, you *must* leave for Between," the Shadow King continued in that same regretful tone. "Otherwise, I cannot close the Portal. It would be catastrophic, for both our worlds, if the Portal remained open."

"Why does it open when I dream? The coven has no idea. If I knew what I was doing, I'd stop it in an instant."

The Shadow King looked up. "Can you see the Twin moons?" he asked, pointing to the motif carved into the ceiling. "They denote the moon of the Earther Realm and the moon of Otherworld. Each month, the twin moons move toward each other. When they both become full, they cross—we call it the Lunar Crossing—and the Portal opens, bringing forth a Dreamer from the Earther Realm into Between."

Sasha stared at the two crescent moons separated by stars and nodded. "I know this bit."

"When you were five years of age, Between chose you to be a Dreamer, which is why you recognized the hillside."

Sasha groaned. "Oh, no."

"Oh, *yes.* You have a gift. You are an artist, are you not?"

She wished. "No, I'm not. I'm a teacher. I just dabble—"

The Shadow King shook his head, suddenly angry. "You *are* an artist. You were *meant* to be an artist. But when your five-year-old self reached the Hill on the night of the full moons, there was no one to greet you. We checked the records—there was no King or Queen of Between to wield the wild magic, only a caretaker who failed you miserably." His anger leached away, his expression turning to one of genuine pity. "You were left alone ... and you paid a terrible price."

"My dreams," she whispered. "I didn't dream for years ..."

The Shadow King nodded, his motions heavy, slow. "Your dreams. Without dreams, you were powerless to manifest your gift. You were thwarted at every turn, were you not?"

"Yes," she said softly.

"That was the wild magic—it should have crafted your Dream, bringing it to life. But without a King or Queen to meet you, there was no one to help you shape the wild magic. Instead, the magic turned against your Dream, thwarting your progress rather than helping you achieve your desires."

"Oh—" Sasha choked on the word, unable to push past the misery that lodged, thick and tar-like, in her throat.

"And that left you with an emptiness inside—a vast chasm between what you wanted and what you could achieve. What you could *be*. Is that not true?"

Sasha could only nod.

"That emptiness has destroyed many others, eaten away at their very souls."

Sasha pressed her hand over her mouth. She suddenly felt the urge to scream. It was as if all those years of holding back, making do, carrying on —even though the situation felt so *wrong*—was finally catching up with her. She wanted to throw back her head and wail and wail and wail. Her shoulders shook, and she tried, with everything inside herself, to remain calm.

The Shadow King watched her struggle, his green-eyed gaze sympathetic. "I am sorry." His voice was *so* gentle. "I am truly sorry for your loss."

Sasha took a shaky breath ... and then another ... and then another.

"Right," she mumbled. "*Right.*"

Once she was certain that she would not scream, she removed her hand from her mouth. "I always thought there was a reason why I couldn't get anywhere. I guess it's comforting to know it wasn't my imagination." She inhaled sharply. Her chest felt as though it was caving in. "All those wasted years ..."

Suddenly, she felt something brush against her calves. She looked down and almost laughed hysterically. The Shadow King's cloak was butting against her legs like a cat.

"You may want to call off your cloak," she said.

The Shadow King stared down at the cloak, clearly perplexed. "I have no idea what it is doing. I believe ..." He tilted his head as if he was listening to something. "I believe it is trying to be comforting."

Sasha's eyes widened. "Really? Well, thank you," she said, addressing the cloak flowing around her boots.

The cloak patted her legs reassuringly and then expanded, the shadows rising upward until they surrounded both her and the King.

The Shadow King rolled his eyes. "Show-off," he said to the cloak. He looked down at Sasha. "It likes you and is shamelessly trying to get into your good graces."

Sasha felt the weight of the shadow cloak around her shoulders and, oddly enough, felt comforted. Safe and warm.

"Thanks, cloak."

She felt a responding pat on her shoulders.

"Marvelous," the Shadow King said dryly, addressing the cloak. "How little it takes to turn your loyalty. Let us hope that the rest of my clothing knows where its allegiance lies."

Miraculously, Sasha felt herself smile. "Is all your clothing sentient?"

"Thankfully not." The Shadow King mock-grimaced at his cloak. "Though, in Between, anything is possible. As you will find out."

At the mention of Between, Sasha's smile fell away. "Is that why I'm holding open the Portal? Because I am—I *was* a Dreamer?"

"Initially. From what I can gather, Between wanted to complete your Dream. So, once you were within range of the Portal, it kept bringing you back each time you slept. If Between had given me some indication of what it wanted … what it was trying to accomplish …" He shook his head, clearly frustrated. "Well, let us just say that things may have turned out differently."

Sasha felt all hope drain away to the dregs. She clutched the pepper spray like a good luck charm. "So … can't I just go back to Between on the full moon and finish this once and for all?"

"Not anymore. The moment you crossed the Wasteland—the moment you defeated the Nightmares—you were no longer a Dreamer but the *True Queen of Between*. The Portal will continue to open while you dream until you return and take your rightful place as ruler."

Sasha closed her eyes. "Damn you, Lyla! That's the last time I *ever* follow your advice."

"Lyla?"

Sasha opened her eyes. "My friend. She thought the Nightmares were metaphorical demons and suggested running toward them. You know—as a way of confronting my inner demons and all that."

The Shadow King looked horrified. "Under the circumstances, that was the absolute worst course of action you could have possibly taken."

"Thank you, that's comforting to know," she said dryly.

"Be sure to unleash the full extent of your wrath at this Lyla."

"I'll tell her you said that." Sasha impulsively reached out and grabbed the Shadow King's arm, the velvet of his doublet soft against her palm. "Please, isn't there any other way? Can't you close the Portal *somehow* with me on this side? I don't want to leave my home, my family, my friends … I just—isn't there *any* other way?"

The Shadow King looked down at Sasha's hand on his arm, her skin ghostly pale against the unremitting black of his clothing, and arched a royal brow.

Seeing his puzzled gaze, Sasha snatched her hand away, belatedly realizing that she had grabbed him each time they had met, which was probably not the way one was supposed to treat royalty.

Then she remembered that she was royalty now, too, so it was probably a moot point.

The Shadow King cleared his throat. "Unfortunately, I know from experience that if Between wants you to rule, then ruler you *shall* become. If you choose to resist, there will be dire consequences."

"Such as?" *Perhaps*, Sasha thought hopefully, *his definition of "dire" was entirely different from her own.*

The Shadow King stared at her, his gaze hard and unflinching. "You will visit the hill in your dreams for longer and longer periods until you will be unable to leave."

Sasha's eyes widened. "Are you saying that I'll be stuck in my dreams?"

"I am saying that you will fall into a coma—"

"A *coma?*"

"—from which you will never awaken." He looked around the chamber. "You may believe that a small price to pay to stay in Old Middleton."

Stuck in a coma in Old Middleton—it appeared that the Shadow King's definition of "dire" matched Sasha's own. "Thanks, but I'd rather be conscious while I'm here."

"Understandable. Nevertheless, should you fall into a coma, the Portal will remain open, and disaster will inevitably be unleashed upon both of our worlds."

Sasha stared at the Shadow King, horrified. "It just gets better and better, doesn't it?"

"There is very little good news," the Shadow King agreed. "Between is like a child—it *will* have what it wants, the consequences be damned. And right now, it wants you."

Dread pulsed through Sasha's veins. "I don't think I want to be the ruler of a sentient country. It seems incredibly pushy."

"You have no idea."

Sasha rubbed her eyes with the heels of her hands and tried to think of a way out of this situation. So far, the Shadow King was behaving reasonably; she wondered how far she could push him.

"Look, let me be clear," she said, dropping her hands and looking up at him. "I don't want to be in a coma. But I also don't want to be the True Queen of Between. And I certainly don't want to challenge you for sole rulership."

At that, the Shadow King looked amused. "Excellent. One less person who wants me dead."

Sasha blinked. "How many people want you—?" She stopped and shook her head. "Let's just stay on track, shall we?"

The Shadow King inclined his head and made an elegant *continue* gesture with the tips of his fingers.

"I may have this wrong, but if I don't challenge you then ..." She took a deep breath. "Then we rule together, right?"

"That is correct."

"And by together ...?"

"We marry," the Shadow King said simply.

We marry. Sasha's worst-case scenario stuffed into two very small words.

"Right," she said reluctantly. "*Marriage*. Please, don't take offense—"

"People always say that just before they are about to be particularly offensive."

Sasha opened her mouth to refute his statement but then changed her mind. "You're right. Please feel free to be offended."

The Shadow King smirked. "Many thanks."

"As I was trying to say ... I don't want to get married. I never planned on getting married. And I certainly don't want to be pressured into marrying someone I don't know by a sentient kingdom." It was, she thought, the fairy tale equivalent of a shotgun wedding.

"This has nothing to do with you personally," she continued hurriedly. "I'm sure that you would make someone a fantastic husband—"

"Truly, I would not," the Shadow King interrupted matter-of-factly.

"Well ... maybe a really well-dressed one?" she said, primarily for the cloak's benefit.

The cloak butted happily against her legs.

"I shall give your compliments to my tailor." The Shadow King looked down at his cloak, now curled around Sasha's calves, and rolled his eyes. "Your dubious praise of my sartorial choices aside, we are of the same mindset." He whisked the cloak away from Sasha's legs. "I have neither the desire nor the temperament to play husband. I am stretched to my limits with my duties as King, and I have no doubt that trying to engage in some form of marital arrangement would only add to those burdens."

Oddly enough, his comment stung. Sasha knew that it was utterly illogical—and somewhat hypocritical—to feel insulted by his words; after all, she had just confessed that *she* didn't wish to marry *him*. It was more the way that the Shadow King had phrased his remarks—that she would be *burdensome* to him—that made her fists clench.

"Wow. A burden, hey? I thought fairy tale kings were supposed to be charming and sweep women off their feet. You really shouldn't believe everything you read." Sasha shook her head ruefully. "To think, I actually bothered to say nice things about your fashion sense ..."

"Apologies." The Shadow King ran his hand tiredly over his eyes. "I acknowledge that my choice of words was not ideal. No offense was meant."

"Apology accepted," Sasha said, a little reluctantly.

The Shadow King noticed her reluctance. "Many thanks. Nevertheless, I have no desire to lead you astray; when it comes to charm, you are thinking of fairy tale *princes*, not fairy tale kings. Princes have nothing more to do than gallivant around kingdoms, wooing women, and drinking wine. Kings, on the other hand, are forced to spend their time in serious pursuits, like raising taxes, maintaining order, and kicking unruly citizens into swamps. It sours our temperament somewhat."

Sasha thought back over the fairy tales she had read as a child. "You're right. Most fairy tale kings were jerks."

The Shadow King gave her a mocking bow. "Fairy tale jerk, at your service."

"Well, I'm glad that we've established *that*." They were getting nowhere, Sasha realized with a sinking feeling, and time was running out. "Look, despite your poor word choice where your future wife is concerned"—she paused to glare at him—"you seem like a reasonable person—"

"What an odd assumption," the Shadow King interrupted. He appeared genuinely bewildered. "Whatever made you think that?"

Sasha blinked. "Uh ... sorry?"

The Shadow King considered her for a long moment, his gloved, index finger tapping his lower lip. "I wonder ... do you truly think that I am reasonable? Or are you simply trying to flatter me into submission?"

"Honestly? Both." Sasha made an impatient gesture. "You know what? Just work with me here." She held the King's amused gaze. "Is there *any* possible way that I—that *we* can get out of this arrangement?"

"Have you thought about the situation from my perspective?" the Shadow King asked. "I, too, crossed the Wasteland under duress. I, too, was forced to rule a kingdom that I wanted nothing to do with, and that I cannot escape. If I was unable to remove myself from the situation—to neither abdicate nor escape—how could I possibly assist you in doing so?"

Sasha was dumbfounded. "I didn't know that. I assumed that you crossed the Wasteland because you wanted to be the True King of Between."

The Shadow King threw back his head and laughed. "Oh, what a thought! To become the King of Between is akin to a punishment in my world."

"What kind of place *is* this Between?" Sasha's eyes widened. "Oh, hell —this is going to be a *bad* fairy tale, isn't it?"

"It has certainly been a dismal tale for me." His expression turned particularly bleak. "I do not know what you have been told but Between is not one of those beauteous fairy tale kingdoms found in storybooks used to lull good-tempered children to sleep. Rather, Between is the cautionary tale that parents tell hellishly disobedient offspring to frighten them into submission.

"It is a kingdom of wild magic, dangerous beasts, hourly disasters, and a population that consists primarily of petty thieves, assassins, spies, and one quasi-cannibal. Exile to Between is the number one punishment in Otherworld kingdoms and is ranked far worse than flogging, life imprisonment, and dismemberment by rabid wolves.

"And I will be blunt," he continued, relentless, "ruling the kingdom is little better than a punishment. For the past seven years, I have tried to create order out of the ever-changing, daily chaos that is Between, and I have failed miserably."

He said the final word—*miserably*—with such bone-deep weariness that it stopped Sasha in her tracks. She looked up at the Shadow King—looked past the handsome façade and *truly* looked at him. There were dark shadows beneath his eyes and a definite gauntness to his cheeks. His skin was far too pale, his cheekbones too sharp, and his broad shoulders were slightly slumped.

He was tired, she realized, and undernourished and maybe ... maybe a little hopeless.

Sasha's first instinct was always to help those who were in trouble, and at that moment, she truly wanted to help this tired, hopeless man.

But, she reminded herself ruthlessly, this tired, hopeless man was also trying to coerce her into co-ruling a lousy, fairy tale world. Forever.

He's the enemy, Lyla had said.

Don't volunteer for anything, she told herself firmly.

"That sounds exhausting," she said, meaning every word. "You look exhausted. Don't you have people to help you? Advisors, maybe? They could help you wrangle the petty thieves, and the assassins, and the spies into line."

The Shadow King snorted. "My advisors *are* the petty thieves, and the assassins, and the spies." His mouth twisted into a sardonic smile.

"According to Between, I do not need advisors: what I need is a *queen* to help me rule the kingdom."

Sasha clutched at that straw. "If that's true, wouldn't you like to choose your own queen? Someone that you care about?"

For a moment, the oddest expression crossed the Shadow King's face. It was something soft and wistful and yearning. All too soon, it was replaced by his customary sardonic smile.

"If being the King of Between is viewed as punishment by the people of Otherworld, then becoming the Queen of Between is the social equivalent of being exiled into the Hell Realm. There are no appropriate contenders for the position, which is probably why Between took it upon itself to intervene. Apparently, it wants a queen and believed this to be the only opportunity to get one."

Sasha balked. How bad *was* this kingdom? "If you want me to become the Queen of Between, then you should probably cut back on all the 'exiled into the Hell Realm' and 'ruling Between is a punishment' talk. You really aren't selling this situation at all."

"There is nothing to sell," the Shadow King said simply. "Between is not like other kingdoms. Ruling Between requires considerable cunning, moral flexibility, and the constitution of an ox. Between must have seen all three qualities in you to have chosen you for the role. You could, perhaps, take it as a compliment."

"Or not," Sasha said, horror-struck. "Cunning? Moral flexibility? *The constitution of an ox?*"

"They are perfectly good qual—"

"Just forget it," she interrupted, holding up her hand. "But thank you for being so honest."

"I see no reason to lie." The Shadow King shrugged—an elegant lift and fall of his shoulders. "You have the right to know what will befall you in Between."

Sasha's body tensed.

Befall.

That was an ominous word.

"And one way or another, you will come back with me—" the Shadow King continued.

Sasha clenched her fists. *Like hell I will,* she thought.

"—and it is best that you are fully informed about what is in store for you. I wish to prepare you … to give you a chance to adjust, which is something that I never received."

And just like that, Sasha unclenched her hands. "I *want* to be angry with you. I want to be furious with you." Her breath came out in a rush. "But it's not your fault. And you're in the same sinking ship as I am."

The Shadow King appeared taken aback by her response. "Thank you. We are, indeed, in the same sinking ship—or the same sinking kingdom, so to speak … which is a far more accurate description of Between than you could possibly imagine."

Sasha ignored the idea of a sinking kingdom and pressed on. "And you're quite sure we can't steer this sinking ship—I mean, kingdom—elsewhere? Tahiti, perhaps? Can't we both just run away?"

The King glanced up at the twin moons on the ceiling and sighed. "I have thought of little else for the last seven years. But no." He shook his head emphatically. "We cannot both just run away, especially me; I am quite literally tethered to Between."

Sasha felt herself deflate as even the dregs of hope left her body. If *he* had given up, then there really was no chance of escape.

"Right," she said, resolute. "To sum up: this situation is utterly dreadful. I am the True Queen of Between, and I need to return with you—or else there will be disaster and horror. And there is no way of getting out of ruling; if there were, you would have figured it out by now and run screaming from Between."

The Shadow King inclined his head. "An excellent and most succinct summary. I heartily endorse the running and screaming portion." He paused and looked at her in a way that was almost approving. Maybe even a little admiring. "I must congratulate you for taking this all so well. I was expecting hysterics or a physical attack."

Sasha shrugged. "I took too many painkillers before I got here. They've made me feel pretty mellow. I'm also still exhausted from that run."

"It *was* impressive. I have never seen the like."

"Thank you," she said.

Then frowned. She was suddenly aware of the fact that she was close enough to the Shadow King to count each of his eyelashes, and that her chest was a hairsbreadth away from being crushed against his breastplate each time she exhaled.

When had they moved so close to one another?

The Shadow King appeared to come to the same realization.

"Stop it," he said sternly to his cloak. "That is quite enough of that."

Sasha felt the cloak unfurl from around her legs and shoulders. Suddenly, the distance between herself and the King became much more socially appropriate.

"Please forgive my *cloak* for its forwardness." The Shadow King pinched the bridge of his nose between his thumb and forefinger. "I cannot believe that I just had to apologize on behalf of my clothing."

Sasha looked down at the cloak and shook her head. "Not cool, cloak. Not cool."

The cloak retreated sheepishly behind the Shadow King's legs.

Sasha was so focused on the cloak that she physically jumped at the sound of a throat being cleared at her side. She turned to find Felicia holding two glasses of pink lemonade. The witch had removed her robe and was now wearing a scandalously tight, pink angora sweater dress.

"Refreshments?" Felicia asked languidly. Without waiting for a response, she presented one of the glasses to the Shadow King. "Here you are, Your Majesty. You must be parched."

The Shadow King looked askance at the bright, pink liquid and took the glass a little gingerly. "Many thanks. It looks quite ... festive."

"I, too, am parched," Sasha said.

"I'm sure you are, sugar," Felicia said distractedly. "Aren't you going to try some?" she practically purred at the King. "It's raspberry lemonade, my own recipe. I assure you it's delicious!"

"And if not, I'm sure Rosa has an antidote," Sasha said.

Felicia shot her a dirty look. The Shadow King, however, appeared amused.

"One can only hope," he said and raised the glass to his lips.

From the corner of her eye, Sasha caught the calculating gleam in Felicia's eyes as the Shadow King brought the glass to his lips ... and her dismay when he then took it away again.

"Tell me," the Shadow King asked mildly, "what is in this?"

Felicia looked around shiftily. "Why, fresh lemons from my very own garden, sugar, water, raspberries—"

"Lust Potion?" the Shadow King asked.

Rosa stared at the red-headed witch, horrified. "*Felicia!* You tried to potion the Shadow King with one of *my* potions?"

She rushed to the Shadow King's side, followed by the rest of the coven.

"May I?" Rosa held out her hand for the glass and sniffed the contents. Her eyes narrowed. "Definitely Lust Potion."

"Well, let's hope it's only in the Shadow King's glass," Sasha said. "Otherwise, this is all going to get awkward very quickly."

The Shadow King shot her an amused look.

Felicia's eyes widened innocently, her hand fluttering to her throat.

"Why, how could Lust Potion have fallen into my lemonade? I must have mistaken it for the raspberry cordial."

"Raspberry cordial my eye!" old Mrs. Landshome yelled. "You can't just take it upon yourself to Lust Potion the Shadow King!"

"Yes! *Exactly!*" Sasha said, shaking her finger at Felicia righteously.

"We're a coven," Mrs. Landshome continued. "We should have Lust Potioned him *together*."

"What?! *No!*" Sasha cried.

The witches began to argue amongst themselves.

Sasha stared at the coven, utterly aghast. The Shadow King, however, simply took back his glass from Rosa and held it out to Sasha.

"May I offer you a refreshment?" His lips quirked. "I heard you were parched."

Sasha glared at the King. "Funny, but my mouth has suddenly moistened."

"Really, ladies!" Esther's voice rang out. "Have you all forgotten? Potions have no effect on sorcerers."

"Nor do aphrodisiacs, poisons, alcohol, or excessive flattery, more's the pity," the Shadow King added.

"Dash it," Felicia swore. "That's right." She glanced at the glass of lusty lemonade in the Shadow King's hand and sighed. "Well, so much for that …"

"Don't be too hard on yourself," Violet said to Felicia. "It's not like you meet sorcerers every day."

"You'll know for next time, dear," Daisy said, patting Felicia's hand encouragingly.

"I guess so," Felicia said, her tone sour and sulky. "Still, I don't know how I forgot that."

"You were distracted by his chest," old Mrs. Landshome said knowingly. "And maybe those leather pants," she added, directing a leer toward the Shadow King's legs.

"Hey!" Sasha cried, inexplicably insulted on the King's behalf. "There is a *person* in those leather pants." She clicked her fingers together. "Eyes back in your heads, all of you. Especially you, Mrs. Landshome—he's young enough to be your great-grandson!"

Sasha turned back to the Shadow King, who appeared entertained by the whole debacle. "Why are you taking this so well? They're all leering at you, and Felicia—Felicia just tried to potion you!" She stared pointedly at the witches. "Which is something this coven seems a little too comfortable doing."

The Shadow King shrugged. "It is not the first time someone has tried to potion me. In fact, I rather admire the audacity. If we were in Between, I would offer Felicia a ministerial position—such a blatant drugging attempt suggests the sort of ruthless initiative and moral ambivalence that would be an asset in Between's senior administrative positions."

"That's our Felicia," Mrs. Landshome said proudly.

"Moreover," the Shadow King continued, "the coven is not attracted to me, per se."

He took a sip of the lusty lemonade and made a pleased sound.

"You know," he said to Felicia, "it is really quite refreshing. The potion gives it a pleasant kick."

Felicia beamed. "Oh! Thank you, Your Majesty."

"Why—*why* are you drinking the lust juice?" Sasha asked. She grabbed the glass away from him. "And what are you talking about? Of course, they're attracted to you."

The Shadow King gave her a stern look and took back his glass. "It has no effect on me, remember?" Sasha rolled her eyes as he took another sip. "As for the coven, they are attracted to my magic, not to me. It exerts a pull on them ... 'like meeting like' and all that. Is that not correct?" he asked the witches.

Esther lifted her hands apologetically. "It's true." She closed her eyes and sighed helplessly. "His magic is powerfully alluring."

The other witches nodded sheepishly.

The King turned back to Sasha. "So, you see, I could have been a one-legged wildebeest, and the attraction would still be there. It has nothing to do with my appearance."

The coven looked at each other shiftily.

"No, nothing to do with your appearance," Esther said hastily.

"Nothing at all," the Headmistress reassured the Shadow King.

"Especially not your chest," Mrs. Landshome said. "Or your legs."

Felicia hastily placed her hand over the old woman's mouth and then drew it back in disgust when Mrs. Landshome licked it, chortling wickedly.

"Hang on," Sasha said to the Shadow King. "Why aren't you affected by this magical attraction?"

He finished his lemonade and handed his empty glass to Felicia. "In Between, I am surrounded by magic at all times; I am used to ignoring the pull."

Something appeared to occur to him. He turned to Esther. "Does this mean there are still no wizards in Old Middleton?" He frowned as Esther nodded. "*Hmm*, we are going to have to get to the bottom of that. I have a theory ..." He shook his head, exasperated. "But I have not had the time to work on the puzzle."

Esther's eyes lit up. "We would be grateful for any assistance that you can give us. It has been over a century and we are still no closer to solving the mystery."

"We will solve it," the Shadow King vowed. "This cannot continue."

"What cannot continue?" Sasha asked, puzzled by the turn in the conversation. "What about the wizards?"

The sound of a bell echoed around the chamber.

The Shadow King looked toward the Portal. "Our time is almost at an end; the Portal cannot remain open for long during a Summons." He turned to face Sasha. "It is time to say your farewells."

The witches surged forward and clustered protectively around Sasha.

"I can't allow you to take her," Esther said bravely. "I made a Vow."

"That's right!" Rosa said.

"She did!" Daisy and Violet said simultaneously.

The Shadow King sighed wearily. "Your concern for Her Majesty's safety is all well and good, but completely unnecessary. My intentions are honorable; I do not plan to devour her, nor do I have other wicked plans afoot."

"Pity," Mrs. Landshome said, staring appreciatively at his leather pants. "Sasha may have liked a bit of wickedness."

The Shadow King lips twitched at the old woman's audacity but said nothing. Instead, he addressed Esther. "This is her *Destiny* and the longer we prolong Her Majesty's entry into Between, the more trouble there will be. All manner of creatures will enter your realm. First, the mischievous ones will frolic through the Portal. Then, the destructive."

He turned his attention to Sasha. "And mark my words, there will come a time when neither the coven nor I will able to hold them back and both our worlds will suffer. This is just the beginning."

"Oh, dear," the Headmistress murmured, shaking her head.

"But she has friends and family," Violet said, wringing her hands. "She can't simply disappear—that would be terrible for them! They'll be so worried ..."

The Shadow King looked supremely unfazed. "People disappear all the time for all sorts of reasons. Most of them end up in Between. What is one more?"

Daisy looked up at the King, horrified. "That is a wicked thing to say, young man! Wouldn't *your* family be worried about you if you suddenly disappeared?"

The Shadow King's expression became still and blank. "No."

"That's—that's *dreadful*," Violet gasped, clutching her throat. "Everyone should have loved ones that worry about them."

"Oh, you poor, poor man!" Daisy whispered.

The twins rushed over to him.

"*Ahh*—no," the Shadow King said, as the twins embraced him. "This situation does not require physical contact. Really, *no*. Good gods," he swore, as the two tiny old women hugged him. "Fine. Hug me—though, let us get this over with as quickly as possible. Ah, marvelous—now there's *patting*."

"Ladies!" the Headmistress cried, stamping her foot. "Hugging His Majesty is not appropriate behavior!"

"Put a sock in it, Penelope," Mrs. Landshome said, clearly enjoying the spectacle.

The Shadow King's expression turned stoic; clearly, he had decided that the best course of action was to stand as still as possible and endure it.

Sasha would have been amused by the look of forbearance on his face —if she had been paying attention. Instead, she was trying desperately to think of a way out of the situation. She knew that she would have to go to Between eventually; the Shadow King had convinced her that remaining in Old Middleton would only lead to disaster. But she refused to go tonight: she had promised Lyla that she wouldn't leave with the Shadow King and she intended to keep that promise.

There had to be something she could do, something she could say, that would buy her a little more time. If only Lyla and the Headmistress had found something in the Archives ...

She blinked—the Archives!

"I wish to use one of my boons," she said, a lot more loudly than she realized. She winced as her voice echoed around the chamber.

Everyone turned to stare at her. Daisy and Violet released the Shadow King.

The Shadow King barely noticed that he had been liberated. He looked stunned. "Who told you about those?"

"Lyla."

"This Lyla of yours is somewhat troublesome," he muttered to himself.

"This Lyla of mine is fantastic," Sasha said loyally.

The Shadow King tipped his head back and looked at the ceiling as if seeking answers—or possibly just patience—from the constellations.

After a long moment, he looked back at Sasha. "Your Lyla is correct.

You are to receive three boons—assuming they are in my power to grant. What is the nature of your first boon?"

Sasha remembered her earlier conversation with Lyla. "Could you close the Portal and leave me alone?"

The King smirked. "A valiant attempt but no—that is not in my power to grant."

"Damn. Well, it was worth a shot."

"You must hurry," he urged, glancing at the Portal.

Sasha knew this was her one shot—she *had* to get this right.

"Then I request more time to prepare myself for this journey," she said, determined. "I want to learn more about Between. I want to learn more about what's in store for me there. I don't want to go into this unprepared. *I need more time.*"

The Shadow King's jaw clenched. "How much more time?"

Sasha's heartrate accelerated; he hadn't said no.

In for a penny, she thought.

But just as she was about to reply, the Shadow King held up his hand. "Before you answer, remember that every time you dream of Between, you are one step closer to falling into a perpetual dream state."

Sasha's heart sunk. *It's a risk I'll have to take,* she thought. *I need to give Lyla enough time to figure this out.*

She began to reply, but the King interrupted her yet again.

"And do keep in mind that every day you spend here threatens us all."

Sasha threw her hands up in frustration. "Dash it, would you just let me ask?"

"No, because I already know how this will all play out." The Shadow King began to pace the floor, his footsteps an impatient staccato on the tiled floor. "Even though you know it is impossible, you will ask for a large portion of time—a year, perhaps—because you know that I will challenge your request and you will want to start with a strong negotiation point." Sasha's eyes widened. "Then, you will ask me for a handful of months." Sasha lowered her gaze. "And in doing so, you will waste this boon because all I can give you is six days' grace before the High King figures out who you are and how to get to you."

"The High King?" the Headmistress whispered. "He knows about Sasha?"

"Oh, no!" Esther wailed. "The High King."

"Yes," the Shadow King said tersely. "*The High King.* He will do what he thinks he must in order to maintain the safety of Otherworld—and that means closing the Portal by any means possible." He stopped pacing and stood before Sasha. "I cannot guarantee Her Majesty's safety if the High King becomes involved."

The bell tolled once again in the chamber. The Portal began to glow.

"Your Majesty," the Shadow King said, his tone urgent, "make your request before it is too late."

Sasha glanced at the door. She needed to close the Portal permanently. If it were closed, the village would be safe from the Nightmares, she would be coma-free, and Lyla would have additional time to save her.

But, she thought with a sinking heart, *Between won't close the Portal until I'm in the kingdom—*

Her eyes widened—that was *it*! "Could I close the Portal by just visiting Between?"

The Shadow King's eyes narrowed. "Define 'visiting.' "

"I could come to Between for an hour," she said in a rush. She noted his incredulous expression. "Or two. Just enough time to appease Between and stop the Nightmares and comas. I could look around the city, maybe tour the castle—"

"Between wants a queen," the King interrupted. "Not a tourist. An hour or two will not appease it. Nor would a day or two," he said, with a knowing look, "so take that into consideration when making your next offer."

"O-kay … what if I stay for a week?" she countered. "It'll be a trial run, so to speak. But you have to give me a way to communicate with Lyla while I'm in Between."

Maybe that'll be enough time for Lyla to get me out of this mess, she thought.

It was a ridiculous hope, but it seemed that her heart refused to give up everyone she loved without a fight.

"And after the week is over?" the Shadow King asked.

He was still not saying no, Sasha realized. "Then, you'll give me a week to say goodbye to my family and friends, and then … then I'll come and live in Between."

That would give Lyla another week. Sasha hoped it would be enough.

"And when will this trial run begin?" the Shadow King asked.

Internally, she winced. "In six days."

The Shadow King's expression darkened. "Six days? The Portal cannot continue to open for that long. Creatures could cross over each time you dream—including the Nightmares."

The Nightmares. All at once, in terrible clarity, Sasha remembered their piercing wails, their jagged teeth, their nails tearing through her back. She could not—*would* not—be responsible for letting them into this world.

Sasha's resolve started to crumble. Unconsciously, she glanced at the witches, hoping for a sign, even a hint of what she should do.

As if she could read Sasha's mind, Esther nodded.

Do it, she seemed to say.

From behind Esther's back, Daisy surreptitiously gave Sasha a thumbs-up.

Heartened by their response, Sasha straightened her shoulders and turned back to the King. "*You* said that I would have six days at most, so I'm taking them all. This is my first boon. Give me six days to prepare. Then, I'll stay a week in Between as a trial run. After I say my goodbyes, I'll stay in Between ... well ... forever."

Forever. The word tasted like ashes in Sasha's mouth, but she raised her chin bravely.

"Why do you need an additional week to say your goodbyes?" the Shadow King asked. "Surely that could be accomplished in the initial six days?"

"I don't live in Old Middleton," she answered quickly. "I traveled here for a job. Most of my belongings are in another state; I'll need to bring them here ... somehow. My parents—" Sasha's heart ached at the thought of her parents. How could she possibly explain this to them? She quickly pushed the thought aside. "My parents are in another country. I need the extra time to contact them to say—to say my goodbyes."

The Shadow King shook his head, his crown glittering coldly in the torchlight. "You do not understand—the High King will resort to desperate measures to close the Portal."

"Six days," Sasha repeated, holding firm.

He clenched his jaw. "There needs to be a caveat: if there is any danger to Otherworld and its citizens or the lives of those in the Earther Realm, you will come earlier."

"*Immediate* danger," Sasha clarified. "The life-threatening kind. Apocalyptic."

The Shadow King sighed. "Very well. Immediate, life-threatening, apocalyptic danger. The ruination of our worlds."

That seemed reasonable. Sasha nodded. "Done."

"I can only do so much to keep you out of the High King's hands until then," the Shadow King warned.

At that moment, Sasha cared little about the High King or his hands; she was just so grateful to be staying in Old Middleton. "That's a risk I'm happy to take."

"That may be so, but are you also willing to risk falling into a coma? Six days will try Between's patience; it may decide that a dream queen is better than no queen at all."

For a second, Sasha faltered—but only for a second. "I'm sure you'll explain to Between that I'll be there soon enough, so there's no need for comas."

"You are quite infuriating," the King said, his tone speculative rather than annoyed. "I cannot help but wonder if other Earther women would have reacted so poorly to the prospect of becoming a queen."

Sasha shrugged. "It's hard to say. Some may have been even more obstinate."

She looked back at the coven and remembered their reaction to her sketches of the King.

"Then again, others probably would have gone with you if you'd taken off your shirt and asked nicely," she muttered under her breath.

The Shadow King's eyes widened. "I beg your pardon?"

Damn, he'd heard that.

"Nothing," she said hastily. "Nothing at all. I was just ... clearing my throat."

The Shadow King considered her for a long moment, his expression speculative. "Would removing my shirt hasten your return to Between?"

Yes, a voice at the back of her head said.

"No," Sasha answered.

The King lifted an eyebrow. "Not even if I removed it using sultry intent?"

"No," Sasha said firmly. "Not in the slightest. What a strange thing to ask."

Liar, the voice in her head whispered. *You're a lying liar that lies.*

The Shadow King made a displeased sound. "Of course not. That would be too simple. Do you still have my amulet?"

"Yes."

Sasha reached down under her sweater and pulled out the Shadow King's amulet. Rosa had fixed the chain and placed it around her neck.

The Shadow King gave the amulet the oddest look and then quickly looked away. When he turned back, there was an intensity to his gaze that was not there moments before.

"Very well," he said, his usually polished tones rough around the edges. "To Summon me, just touch the amulet and call my name."

"Got it," Sasha said, hoping that she'd never have to do it; the last thing she wanted to do was to spend more time with the haughty King than necessary. "Thanks," she added, though, just to be polite.

He turned to the coven and swept them a bow. "Prepare yourselves," he said ominously.

The witches looked at each other uneasily and then bowed in return.

The Shadow King turned to Sasha. "You have six days. Use them well."

He gave her a shallow bow and then, with a dramatic flourish of his cloak, turned and strode back through the Portal.

The gold light streaming through the doorway flickered and then died. A final bell-tone filled the chamber, and the Portal closed, becoming a normal, wooden door once more.

"Well," Sasha said into the silence. "That went ... that didn't go well, did it?" She turned to the coven. Each of the women looked exhausted and subdued.

"It would've gone better if the lemonade had worked," Felicia muttered.

"*Sure*, it would've," Rosa said scathingly. "Because having the Shadow King lusting over *you* would have solved all our problems."

"It didn't have to be *me*, though I certainly wouldn't have objected. My, my—he *is* a fine one, isn't he?" Felicia shivered in delight. "But, as I was saying, having him lust over any one of us would have done the trick." At Rosa's blank look, Felicia rolled her eyes. "Do I have to spell it out, sugar? Men are simple creatures, and a lustful man is an easily manipulated man —they're putty in your hands, willing to do anything and everything you want."

Sasha stared at the red-headed witch, utterly dumbfounded. "That is a terrible, outdated male stereotype! Your entire plan was unethical, manipulative—"

"Well, excuse me," Felicia interrupted testily. "I thought you were fine with the occasional beverage drugging."

Mrs. Landshome poked Sasha's arm. "She's got you there."

Sasha closed her mouth. That tea-spiking would haunt her forever.

"And besides," Felicia continued, "I was trying to help *you*. I thought this whole mess could've been fixed in a trice if the Shadow King started thinking with his pants."

"They were very nice pants," Violet said.

"Leathery," Daisy agreed, nodding.

"Not that it matters," Mrs. Landshome said, "because potioning our way into his pants isn't even an option. Damn sorcerers."

"Good," Sasha said. "Forget his pants." She turned to Esther. "This went badly, didn't it?"

Esther gave her a tremulous smile. "It could have been worse—you could have been taken back to Between tonight. You've bought us some time to figure out a plan."

The Headmistress nodded slowly. "I'll return to the Archives tomorrow and see what I can find. Though, in some ways ..." She stopped and bit her lip.

Mrs. Landshome gave her a withering look. "Spit it out, Penelope. You think Sasha should have gone with him, don't you?"

The Headmistress smiled apologetically at Sasha. "In all my time in the Archives, I've never read of a way to close the Portal from this side. If Sasha's presence here keeps it open ..." She held up her hands helplessly. "Well, we're just delaying the inevitable by asking for more time. And if the High King becomes involved, then the stakes will be much higher for you, Sasha. He won't ask you to go back—he will *take* you back whether you like it or not."

Daisy reached out and clasped Sasha's hand. "Even if we can't close the Portal from this side, surely we can figure out ways of making Sasha's stay in Between more bearable, can't we?"

"We certainly can," Esther said. "We have six days. We'll protect Sasha, keep an eye on the Portal, and see if there is another way out of this situation. Or, if nothing else, a way of making the best of it."

"That's all well and good," Felicia said, "but what about our Vow? We swore to protect this side of the Portal. Doesn't allowing the Portal to stay open while Sasha dreams violate that Vow?"

"We also Vowed to protect the inhabitants of Old Middleton, remember?" Miss Adeline said pointedly. "Sasha is an inhabitant. *That* Vow takes precedence."

Felicia huffed. "Fine. But now that seducing the Shadow King is off the table, I can't think of another way out of this situation. What I *do* know is that we're opening ourselves up to a world of trouble by going along with Sasha's crazy, six-day plan." She gave Sasha a rather pitying look. "If I were you, sugar, I'd spend the next six days looking for a wedding dress."

"I'll take that under advisement," Sasha said dryly. She turned to the rest of the witches. "Look, I don't want to cause trouble. I don't—I *really* don't. But if there is even the slimmest of chances that I can get out of this mess, then I have to try. I *have* to! If you can't help me—if helping me violates your Vow—then I understand. But *I* have to try."

"We'll help you," Esther promised. "*All* of us." She sent a hard glare toward both Felicia and the Headmistress. "We'll get you through this, one way or another. We'll get you through."

12

THE KING OF HER (TERRIBLE, FROZEN, BUT THANKFULLY WOLF-FREE) DREAMS

LATER THAT NIGHT...

"Do you think I did the right thing—asking for six days before my trial run?"

It was well past two in the morning. Sasha and Lyla sat in bed, both exhausted but too wired to sleep. The witches had made the women take a Vow of Secrecy—sealed with magic—before leaving the Village Hall, and then bundled them back home under cover of night.

As soon as they reached the safety of their bedroom, Sasha recounted the events of the Portal Chamber to Lyla in as much detail as she could remember.

"Of course, you did!" Lyla said incredulously. "Asking for six days before you leave everything behind to enter what sounds like a complete cesspool is *more* than reasonable." Her expression turned to one of extreme horror. "Hang on—that place is probably stuck in the Middle Ages! Have they invented plumbing yet? Or penicillin? Or zippers? Oh, hell ... it's probably riddled with all those weird old maladies, like scurvy, and ergot poisoning, and that one where you die from standing in a draft when you're not wearing a shawl."

"I'm sure they have plumbing," Sasha said, deciding to ignore the maladies entirely.

Lyla shook her head. "Nope. There is no way I'm letting you go to a medieval sewer-realm. Tomorrow, we're telling the witches that the trial run is cancelled—you're not going. They can send Felicia in your place."

Sasha looked at the runes on the windowsill and remembered what the witches had done to put them there. Every moment that she remained in this world put those same witches—and everyone in the village—in danger. Her heart sank. As much as she wanted to take Lyla's advice and call off the trial run, she knew that she had to go through with it.

She opened her mouth to announce her decision but hesitated. She had to tread carefully; Lyla would want to protect her, so she would have to appeal to her friend's logical side and calmly explain her reasons for going on the trial run. Otherwise, Lyla would strenuously object and there would be a Scene.

And Sasha was far too exhausted for a Scene.

"Lyla ..." she began.

"Oh, no." Lyla pointed to Sasha's face. "I *know* that expression—that's your noble, self-sacrificing expression." She stabbed the air with her finger accusingly. "It's the same expression your face makes when you decide to stay up all night marking exam papers so that your students can get their feedback as soon as possible. Or when you spend time on lesson plans rather than doing something fun."

Sasha tried to stop her face from making the incriminating expression. But it was too late: there was about to be a Scene.

"I can't believe you're really going to do this," Lyla said, her hand falling to her lap, her mouth twisting in anger. "You're going to leave everything behind: your family, your friends, your car, *me*—"

Sasha groaned. "Please, stop."

"—to take part in this ridiculous trial run!"

Sasha looked down at the little bluebirds embroidered on her sheets. They seemed so free and happy, flying around on all that white linen.

Bastards.

"Yes," she said simply. Looking up, she noticed Lyla's eyes begin to narrow. "It's only for seven days," she said in a rush. "You're used to me gallivanting around—"

"To places in *this* world. Places I can get to if you need help."

Sasha decided to ignore that excellent point. "Couldn't we pretend that I'm heading off to another teaching job in a remote location? Or better yet, a vacation?" There was a pleading note in her voice that she didn't like but was too exhausted to hide.

Lyla chose not to hear it. "You want a vacation? Fine, we'll go on a vacation. In fact, I vote that we spend the next six days putting as much distance between ourselves and Old Middleton as possible." She stood up and crossed the room to the pile of empty luggage in the corner, her stride determined. "I'll pack our bags immediately and we'll stage a daring escape. Take *that*, Hill-Man!"

"You're a fantastic friend for even suggesting it," Sasha said with a sigh, as Lyla began to unzip one of her suitcases, "but I can't run—"

"You sure can!" Lyla interrupted. "You've run away plenty of times. In fact, think of those times as practice for this very situation. And before you say it, we don't have to worry about money; I've got plenty in my trust fund, thanks to Mom and Dad." She looked up at the ceiling and blew a kiss toward the blush-pink light fixture. "Thanks, guys."

She turned back to Sasha, her hazel eyes bright with purpose. "We can go anywhere you want: Finland, Romania, the Swiss Alps—actually, scratch those. Let's go somewhere tropical with lots of lovely Wi-Fi and novelty cocktails. We may as well hide in style."

Sasha knew that Lyla meant well, but planning a tropical escape drenched in alcohol and plentiful internet access was only making it harder to do the right thing.

"Since when do *you* suggest running away from a situation?" she asked, trying a new approach. "You're always lecturing me about facing my fears and staying put." Her eyes narrowed. "This daring escape of yours wouldn't have anything to do with running away from your degree, would it?"

Lyla paused mid-zip and considered the question. "Honestly? Yes. But it's mostly about you." She held up her hand, halting Sasha's next words. "And you should lower your voice—we don't want to alert Martha and Miss Adeline to our plans."

"They're sleeping down the hall. How do you suggest we escape without alerting them?"

Lyla shrugged. "I haven't thought that far ahead. I guess we could tie our sheets together and escape through the window." She looked over at the window in question and frowned. "Then again, I don't fancy plummeting two stories to my doom ... and it would be to my doom, thanks to my poor knot-tying skills and our antique sheets. So, I guess we'll have to tiptoe out the front door. Which, admittedly, is a bit anticlimactic ..."

"Lyla," Sasha said firmly, as her friend headed toward the chest of drawers. "*Lyla*! Stop packing!"

"Shhhhh!" Lyla hissed.

"I will not *shhhhh*. Just *stop*. This is one situation that I can't run away from." *Oh, the irony!* Sasha thought bitterly. "The dreams, remember? No matter where I am, Between will keep dragging me back through my dreams until one day, I—I won't wake up."

Lyla paused midway through opening the top drawer, her hand clenched around the handle. "I will happily drag your unconscious body around the globe if it means keeping you from Hill-Man's clutches."

"Thanks," Sasha said, dryly. "That's generous of you ... and also really weird. But what you're also forgetting is that I hold the Portal open when I dream. And if the thought of dragging my comatose body around the world isn't enough to stop you from packing—"

Lyla defiantly dropped a pile of t-shirts into one of the open suitcases.

Sasha glared at her friend. "—then the thought of the Nightmares entering our realm *should*." She looked down at the bandage around her calf. "They can't be allowed to come here, Lyla."

For a moment, Lyla appeared to waver. Sasha held her breath as indecision crossed Lyla's features, her weight shifting from one foot to the other.

She's scared, Sasha realized, her heart clenching.

Then, Lyla rallied. She waved off Sasha's concern with a defiant flick of her wrist and headed toward the sock drawer. "There are enough witches in Old Middleton to make sure that the Nightmares stay on their side of the Portal. That's literally their job—they're the Guardians of the Portal, remember? Speaking of which, *your* job is to teach kids how to read and write and to warn them not to eat crayons. None of this hocus-pocus was in your job description."

"But what if the witches can't hold them back?" Without warning, Sasha's mind conjured a vision of the Nightmares tearing down Main Street, their razor-sharp talons extended, their vicious wails cutting through the air. She saw the helpless citizens of Old Middleton torn down one by one: the jolly baker, the grocer with the terrible sweater, little Mason Barnes—

Sasha shuddered, the motion pulling the skin beneath the bandage on her back. She winced in pain and forcibly pushed the vision aside. "I can't —I *won't* be responsible for unleashing the Nightmares upon Old Middleton! You—you didn't see them, Lyla. They'll rip everyone to pieces."

Lyla's jaw clenched. "Give the coven some credit." She pulled out several pairs of socks and piled them into her arms. "You don't owe the citizens of Old Middleton anything. If anything, they owe you."

"How do they owe me?" Sasha snorted. "I've caused them nothing but trouble."

"Are you *kidding*?" Lyla turned toward Sasha, her expression stunned. "Ever since you got here, you've been drugged, sleep-deprived, bullied by

Hill-Men, attacked by demons, poked by small children, practically kidnapped, and now forced into marriage by a sentient landmass! If it all weren't so unbelievable, I'd advise you to sue the village for grievous mental and bodily harm."

"Well, when you say it like *that* it sounds terrible." Sasha looked at her friend and sighed; Lyla was biting her lip, the pile of socks clutched to her chest.

"We're realists, remember?" she said gently. "If I stay, there are only Nightmares and comas in my future. That's no way to live, Lyla. I *have* to go on this trial run."

Lyla stared at Sasha for a long moment.

"Don't I?" Sasha asked quietly.

Lyla groaned and dropped the socks, most of them landing back into the drawer. "Yes," she said begrudgingly. She sat down on her bed, defeated, the springs creaking alarmingly. "But I had to try, right? I had to try and keep you here ... keep you *safe*."

"Right," Sasha said, exhaling in a rush, relieved that Lyla was finally on her side. "I'd expect nothing less."

Lyla swiped at her eyes with the cuff of her sweater. "And I want it noted for the record that I think this trial run is a terrible idea."

"Noted," Sasha said quietly.

Lyla looked over at the half-packed bags and the socks strewn around the floor. "And before you say it, this wasn't a Scene."

Despite everything, Sasha smiled. "It was a Scene and it was spectacular. But no more of them, okay?" She exhaled shakily. "We need to work together to get through this."

Lyla nodded slowly. "Got it." She swallowed hard and tried to smile. "So ... I hear that in six days, you'll be going on vacation to a zipper-less, disease-ridden fairy tale kingdom. How long will you be staying for?"

"Seven days," Sasha said, playing along.

"Well, be sure to bring lots of hand sanitizer."

Sasha snorted. "Probably not a bad idea."

"And bring me back a souvenir. Something small and non-virulent."

"I'll see if they have keychains." Sasha looked around the quaint little room, with its familiar porcelain figurines and floral wallpaper. "Look at this place—it's so normal, so *ordinary*. How could we have possibly known that it would all go terribly wrong?"

"Midwest America," Lyla said, as if that explained everything.

"I mean, they baked me a cake on my first day of school! How lovely is that?"

"Was it a nice cake?"

"Delicious," Sasha said, dejected. "Though, in fairness, I guess they drugged me the next day, which is *less* normal and ordinary."

"Yes. Yes, they did. And technically, they could do it again. Think about it—they've taken a Vow to guard the Portal. Who's to say they won't just hand you over to Hill-Man?"

Sasha remembered the witches surrounding her in the Portal room, a wall of scarlet standing defiant before a king. "They stood up to him tonight; they wouldn't let him take me. I think we can trust them."

Lyla huffed. "I don't think we can trust anyone but ourselves. I mean, how do we really know that the Nightmares will enter our realm if you stay?"

"The Shadow King told me. And frankly, I believe him; he certainly wasn't holding back any bad news."

Lyla laid back against her pillows, her expression speculative. "*The Shadow King.* I wonder what his motivations are in all of this ..."

Sasha brushed her fingers against the amulet around her neck. "I was surprised by how reasonable he was, all things considered. Blunt, terribly pessimistic, a little arrogant"—*exhausted, beautiful, far-too-tall*—"but reasonable and honest. Too honest, frankly."

"*Hmm*, was he?" Lyla's eyes narrowed. "How would we know? I mean, it's in his best interests to get a queen, right? He'd have someone to help him rule, and it sounds like he needs all the help he can get."

"He sees a queen as *burdensome*, remember?" That comment still stung.

Lyla rolled her eyes. "He's an idiot. You would be an incredible queen."

Sasha was taken aback. "You really think so?"

"Absolutely! As a professional child tamer, you've developed all the necessary skills to wrangle mythical beasts and deal with deviant peasants. Plus, your scolding skills are top-notch. You'd be an asset to that cesspool."

Sasha mulled that over. "I guess I do have a lot of experience bossing people around and being a good role model. And I like helping people."

"And you'd certainly make Hill-Man's life far more bearable."

"Well, I'd certainly try not to be burdensome."

"See? You'd be amazing! Best queen ever!"

Despite herself, Sasha was starting to warm to the idea of ruling a kingdom. "*Burdensome. As if.* He doesn't even know me. What is he basing his opinion on, anyway?"

Lyla shrugged. "Stereotypes? Urban legends? Country and western tunes? Who knows? Hang on, I think we got off the point. The point isn't whether or not you'd make spectacular queen—because of course you would. The point is that you don't *want* to be a queen, spectacular or otherwise. Right?"

"Ah … right."

Sasha knew that her voice lacked conviction. After all, Lyla had just convinced her that she would be the best Queen of Between ever.

Besides, there was also the all-too-real possibility that she wouldn't have a choice in the matter.

"I know this isn't what you want to hear," she began, "but becoming the Queen of Between is probably in my future whether I like it or not."

Lyla shook her head. "No. Unacceptable."

"The coven thinks I'm stuck in this situation," Sasha continued relentlessly. "So does the Shadow King. And he was—*is*—in the same position."

She could still hear the King's words in the Portal Chamber, his tone so terribly serious.

If I was unable to remove myself from the situation—to neither abdicate nor escape—how could I possibly assist you in doing so?

Sasha's stomach dropped at the memory. "If he hasn't been able to find a way out—"

"*Unacceptable,*" Lyla repeated. "It's one thing to go to Between on a trial run … which, I repeat, is a terrible idea. But it's another thing entirely to leave everyone behind—to leave *me* behind—to take part in an arranged marriage just so you can rule a fairy tale kingdom." She sat up, reached across the gap between their beds and took Sasha's hands. "I refuse to accept it."

"Lyla—"

"*No,*" Lyla said defiantly. "By my count, I have twenty days—six now, seven while you're gone, seven when you return—to find a way to keep you here. And I *will* keep you here—I promise!"

Sasha wanted to believe her. Lyla looked fierce and noble sitting on her rickety bed, and she knew from experience that when Lyla had a cause, she was the human equivalent of a wrecking ball: she would not let anything stand in her way. And right now, Sasha *needed* to believe that Lyla would find a way to keep her in Old Middleton.

But Sasha was also aware that her life was a long tale of thwarted plans and terrible luck. It was doubtful that would change now.

In fact, it was much more likely to get worse.

She squeezed Lyla's hands and released them. "I am so lucky to have you on my side. But, we need to face facts; no matter what you do, you might not be able to find a way to keep me here."

"Don't say that," Lyla said firmly. "That's quitter talk. There's *always* a way out of a situation."

"But in this case, there might *not* be." Lyla opened her mouth to retort, but Sasha held up her hand. "Please, I need you to work with me here, not argue with me. I'm not giving up hope; I want to find a way to stay with you in Old Middleton—that's my Plan A. But if I can't, I need a back-up plan ... a plan that will help me make the best of the situation. I need a Plan B, Lyla. And maybe a Plan C and D and so on, all the way to Z. I need *plans*!"

Lyla bit her lip, clearly thinking the matter through. "Okay," she said after a long pause. "Let's think about this logically. Aside from leaving your home, friends, family, acquaintances, job, car, me—"

"Why do you keep ranking yourself after my car?"

"—*forever*, which part of the situation is giving you the most horror? The thought of becoming the queen of a cesspool? Or the thought of being forced to marry the king of the cesspool?"

It took only a brief memory of the Shadow King—forbidding in his black armor and arrogant expression—for Sasha to decide. "The marriage part. *Definitely*."

"Good. That's the correct answer. As pretty as Hill-Man is, the last thing you want is to be under his control."

Sasha shook her head, her jaw clenched. "I wouldn't be under his control."

"Of course not! You have self-defense training and pepper spray. But he might *expect* you to be under his control; that might be the norm in Between marriages, especially royal ones—"

"I'm not going to let that happen," Sasha interrupted. And she meant it: if the Shadow King even attempted to take away her independence, he would soon find himself sitting on his very spikey crown.

"*We* won't let that happen," Lyla insisted. "You wanted plans? We're going to plan the hell out of this situation. In Plan A, we'll figure out a way to keep you in Old Middleton—and free of Between's grasp."

"Plan A is my favorite plan so far," Sasha said.

"It's definitely a winner. But if Plan A fails—*ugh*, that word makes me positively itchy." Lyla shuddered. "Let's rephrase that, shall we? *If Plan A is not entirely successful*, then there's Plan B—we'll find a way for you to become the Queen of Between without marrying Hill-Man. And to do that, I need to go back and read what the Headmistress found on Between's marriage laws."

Sasha traced the bluebird flying across her sheet with the tip of her finger. "Do you think that's even possible?"

"Why not? Co-ruling is just job-sharing. You don't have to be married to share a job."

Sasha had to admit that the idea had merit. She had endured several terrible jobs throughout adulthood, what was one more? If it were merely a job—not a forced marriage—then it would be bearable

"That would be great," she said, "but also too easy. Nothing comes easily to me; even the simplest things get all tricky and difficult."

So far, it appeared that marriage was going to be no different. Sasha had never really entertained the thought of marriage; she liked the freedom to gallivant whenever and wherever she pleased. But if she *were* to marry, then she'd like to choose her own partner: someone kind and caring, with a sense of humor. Someone who liked art and animals—particularly the fluffy kind or the abandoned kind—and food, and travel, and—

She halted that train of thought. There was no use thinking about what she wanted in a partner when what she *had* was an aloof sorcerer with a fondness for forbidding clothing, pessimism, and pointy headwear. After today's meeting, she was confident that any kind of marriage to the Shadow King and his sentient clothing would be fraught with sarcasm, stubbornness, and possibly bloodshed.

Plan A *had* to work.

Sasha leaned across the space between their beds, took Lyla by the shoulders, and looked her best friend straight in the eye. "You have twenty days to keep me unmarried and out of Between."

Lyla lifted her chin. "I'm on it."

~

AT SOME POINT DURING THEIR CHATTING AND SCHEMING, SASHA MUST HAVE fallen asleep because when she opened her eyes, she was standing on a hill. But it was not the hill of her previous dreams. This, more accurately, could be described as a mountain.

A very *cold* mountain.

A bracing wind whipped around her, stinging her face and bare skin. Her feet were ankle deep in snow and beginning to ache with a shockingly sharp, burning-cold pain, as were her fingertips. Even her gums felt cold.

"This is really awful," she said, addressing the sky through chattering teeth. "Why can't you put me on a b-beach? Aren't there any b-beaches in this place?"

"Unfortunately, not," a familiar, melodious voice answered from behind her. "Then again, you should be grateful that you were not deposited into one of our infamous swamps."

Sasha looked over her shoulder. The Shadow King was standing at the very edge of a cliff, looking every inch the part of the solitary, fairy tale king.

For reasons that were difficult to pinpoint, the Shadow King's appearance annoyed Sasha immensely. It was as if he *knew* that she was coming and had deliberately posed to his best advantage. His head was turned *just so* to give her the perfect view of his coin-worthy profile. His tall, lean frame, clothed in his customary black, stood in stark contrast to the white peaks surrounding him. Even his cloak was in on the act; it billowed dramatically behind him in the frigid wind, making him appear recklessly romantic. It was as if he was taunting her with all his fairy tale loveliness ... and that was utterly unacceptable.

"Are the swamps warm?" she asked testily, rubbing her upper arms. "If so, they *are* the better option right now."

The Shadow King took in her frosty appearance and frowned. With a quick movement, he unclasped his cloak.

"Forgive me—my chivalrous urges are somewhat rusty." With a few long strides he closed the distance between them and placed his cloak over her shoulders.

"Thanks," she said, surprised. "Is this cloak sentient, too?"

"No, this is just an ordinary cloak." He adjusted the onyx clasp around her throat. "Do not expend any effort trying to charm it."

Sasha smiled and drew the cloak around her more closely. "Thanks."

Even though it was just cloth and nothing more, the cloak was as soft as feathers and as warm as fresh-baked bread. Sasha found herself wondering whether it was the cloak's fabric or the King's body heat that was making it so delightfully cozy, but quickly realized that this was a dangerous train of thought, and so pushed it forcefully from her mind.

"But what about you?" she asked, distracting herself beautifully. "Won't you be col—hang on," she said in alarm as the King began to undo his knee-length tunic. "I'm not *that* cold."

The Shadow King raised an eyebrow and undid the final buttons. "Your feet may disagree."

Sasha looked down at her feet—or what she could see of them—buried beneath the snow and shivered. "They're okay."

The King snorted. "You are a dreadful liar." He laid his tunic across the snow beside her and held out a gloved hand. "Something you will need to rectify if you are going to rule a kingdom filled with liars."

"I'll take that under advisement," she said, placing her hand in his. As their fingers touched, she felt a strange *jolt* through the fabric of the King's glove—something warm and electric and *excited* just beneath the surface of her skin.

Frostbite, she told herself firmly and allowed him to help her step onto his coat.

"But, what about you?" she asked, releasing his hand. "Now you're freezing, and we're back to the original problem of one of us being cold and the other not."

"I assure you that I am quite warm, thank you. Besides, performing such chivalrous gestures reminds me of a time when I was a better person. I am positively aflame with nostalgia."

Sasha was unsure of the exact thermodynamic properties of nostalgia, but she had to admit that he did not seem at all concerned about the weather, possibly because he was still wearing a lot of clothing. She stared at his billowing black shirt, intricate black leather breastplate, and fitted leather pants.

"How many layers are you wearing?" she wondered aloud, staring at his torso. "It seems like a very complicated outfit."

The King's lips quirked. "Do you wish me to keep disrobing so that you may find out?"

For a moment, Sasha wondered if this was a trick question. "No ... a simple verbal response would be fine, thanks. Hang on—was my question inappropriate? Dash it—it was, wasn't it?"

The King tilted his head a little to the left, contemplating her question with more gravity than Sasha thought the matter deserved.

"Given that we are all but betrothed?" he said eventually. "No, I believe not."

If Sasha had her way, it would be the shortest betrothal in history. "And if we weren't 'all but betrothed?' "

"Then, I would have assumed that it was a strangely phrased invitation to engage in more intimate activities."

"Ha! No—definitely not my intention." Sasha shuddered, looking around at all the snow. "That would lead to frostbite in the most awkward places."

The Shadow King gave a surprised bark of laughter. "Truly, a dismal fate."

For a moment, the odd tension that was typically present between them dissipated, and Sasha took the opportunity to look around her. The vantage point gave her a heart-stopping view of the land below. She had to admit that the vista was breathtaking, the white mountain peaks harsh but beautiful against the purple and gold streaked sky. In the far distance, she could make out a walled city surrounded by a moat. Within the black, stone walls, tiny houses of all shapes and sizes were packed into spidery rows, smoke curling upward from their chimneys in wispy threads. In the center of the little city was an ungainly, black castle, its stone towers spiraling crookedly toward the sky. From this distance, the city looked like a toy model waiting for a child to come and play with it.

"Is that Between?" she asked, pointing to the walled city.

The Shadow King looked over to where Sasha pointed. His mouth twisted into a wry smile. "All of this is Between, as far as the eye can see —*that* is just the city. The lands around it are rather extensive and ever-changing."

Sasha huddled further into the King's cloak. "I can't tell you how happy I am to be in a Nightmare-free part of the kingdom. But why am I here, on this mountain?"

"If I were to lay a bet, it would be that Between is trying to show off, so to speak. This is one of the loveliest parts of the kingdom."

Despite the cold, Sasha could freely admit that it was a beautiful place; the landscape was harsh but pristine. "It really is lovely."

With a start, she realized that she liked it up here, high above the world. She felt as though she could finally breathe. A small tendril of hope gently unfurled within her chest.

I could get used to this, she thought. *It would take a while but ... I could get used to this.*

"And this is the only part of the land that is not lethal, diseased, or on fire," the King continued.

Sasha stared at him incredulously. "Couldn't you let me enjoy it for just a little bit longer before reminding me that it's a terrible place?"

The King shrugged. "You would not enjoy it for too much longer anyway; the mountain wolves will be out soon."

"Right," she said faintly. "Great."

"They have been known to devour people."

"Yes, yes, alright—that's quite enough from you," she said testily. "I hope you aren't in charge of tourism."

"Oh, no." *Now* he looked amused. "There are people appointed to do that thankless task. You will meet them in due course; they are infuriatingly optimistic. Then again, they need to be." The King looked down at the city, his expression resigned. "You truly see Between at its best from up here ... and by that, I mean at a great distance and far enough away to avoid most of the dangers."

"Great," she said with false cheer. "Maybe I can set up camp here during my trial run."

The King tapped his forefinger against his lips thoughtfully. "*Hmm* ... the idea has merit. I shall consider it."

Sasha groaned and rubbed her eyes with the heels of her hands. She felt exhausted, and the cold was starting to seep into the King's tunic. She wiggled her frozen toes.

Suddenly, something occurred to her. She removed her hands from her eyes and looked around. "How did you get up here? You don't look as though you've been mountain climbing."

"I flew up."

"O-kay, but how?"

Sasha scanned the area, trying to figure out this new puzzle. Perhaps he had a hot air balloon, or a glider, or a very small helicopter hidden behind a bush ...

"I keep forgetting that magic is new to you," the Shadow King said, his tone amused. "You will need to brace yourself for a rude awakening."

Sasha turned back to the King warily; he looked far too delighted by the idea of her future misfortune at the hands of magical awareness.

Just as she was about to reply, she felt the tug at her navel, signaling that it was time to return.

"I'm waking up," she said, relieved. Despite the King's clothing, she was almost numb. "It was—well, fun, I guess?"

She glanced around one last time but there was nothing to be seen, not even a rope tethered to the cliff.

When she looked back, the King still appeared delighted, which immediately put her on guard.

"Until next time," he said.

He gave her a shallow bow, took two long steps backward ...

... and fell straight off the edge of the cliff.

"No!" Sasha yelled, trying to run forward.

But she could not move; she was frozen in place by the tug at her midsection.

"Shadow King!" she screamed, trying to reach out to him. "*Lorn!*"

To her surprise, there was an answering screech. A bird the size of a robust cat flew up from the place where the Shadow King had fallen. It had the look of a raven, its long, black feathers shiny and sleek; in the fading light of sunset, they seemed to hold all the colors of a dark-hued rainbow: lush purple, rich garnet, and deep, emerald green.

"Bird," she said inexplicably, "did you just see a man dressed in black fall off the cliff?"

The bird tipped back its head and gave a gargled caw which sounded a lot like a laugh. With a flex of its powerful wings, the bird landed in front of her and—as much as a bird could—bowed.

Then, it all clicked.

"You're a sorcerer," Sasha said flatly. "And a bastard."

The tug on her naval became urgent. Sasha felt herself lift off the ground.

"How could you scare me like that?" she scolded in her best schoolteacher voice. "You should be ashamed of yourself. *Bad* bird!" She shook her finger at him for good measure. "*Bad* sorcerer."

The bad sorcerer's cawing laughter was the last thing she heard as she was hauled away across dreams.

13

DASTARDLY AND DANK

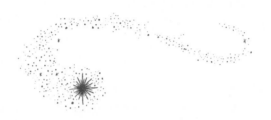

Sasha sat up abruptly, her bedcovers in disarray. The soles of her feet were prickling with cold, and her fingertips felt numb.

"Another dream?" Lyla asked sleepily.

"My almost-husband is a bird."

Lyla opened one eye and looked at Sasha blearily.

"Everyone's got faults," she mumbled and rolled onto her side, her back to Sasha.

Sasha thought that viewing the Shadow King's avian tendencies as a minor character flaw was greatly oversimplifying the issue. She would have liked to discuss the matter further, but Lyla had already gone back to sleep.

Sasha sighed and looked out the window; it was almost dawn. Was it even worth trying to go back to sleep, especially knowing that she could end up on a freezing mountain top or possibly submerged in a swamp?

Ultimately, her body decided for her. She yawned, still exhausted, and settled back against the pillows.

She was just about to close her eyes when she heard a dull thump coming from outside.

Quickly, she sat up and turned toward the window.

There, on the other side of the glass, was a small, pale blue creature perched on the windowsill. It was wearing a black leather tunic that stretched comically over its round belly and matching leather pants. Small horns jutted jauntily from the top of its head.

It simply sat there, staring at Sasha.

Sasha stared back.

(This went on for some time.)

Finally, Sasha decided that she needed back up.

"Lyla," she whispered. "There's a creature on our windowsill."

Lyla merely snuggled further under the covers.

"Lyla," Sasha whispered louder.

The creature wiped its hand inelegantly across his nose and then waved.

"Lyla, it's waving. *Lyla!*"

"Wave back," Lyla mumbled sleepily.

Sasha waved back.

The creature grinned—its teeth pointy and very, very sharp—and then stuck out its tongue.

Sasha's eyes narrowed. "Right."

She stuck out her tongue in return. It was juvenile, but apparently, that was the level they were playing on.

Delighted, the creature leaned against the window and wiped its tongue in a broad, wet stroke across the glass. The runes on the window frame flared to life.

"*Agh!*" the creature yelled and flew backward off the sill.

"No!" Sasha shrieked. She pulled off the covers and ran to the window, yanking it open.

The creature lay sprawled on its back on the grass below.

"Are you okay?" she yelled.

The creature gave her a thumbs up.

"Ah—good," she called down, relieved. "Are you in any pain?"

The creature gave her another thumbs up.

Sasha frowned. "Have you got any idea what that sign means?"

The creature raised its thumb once again.

"O-kay. I'm going to leave now. Let me know if you need anything."

As she closed the window, she noted that the creature's thumb was still up.

Suddenly, the bedroom door blew open. In the doorway was Martha—hair in curlers, floral nightdress billowing around her—wielding a cast-iron frypan and looking utterly formidable.

"What happened?" she cried, getting a firmer grip on the pan's handle. "I felt the wards flare."

Sasha pointed toward the window. Martha moved across the room far quicker than her age should have allowed and looked out.

"Huh," she grunted. "Imp."

Sasha peered over Martha's shoulder. All she could see was the creature's small, raised thumb. "Is it okay?"

"Ha, those things are pure magic; they could withstand a nuclear explosion. If it's on the ground, it's because it wants to be there."

"Oh. Good to know."

Lyla sat up, rubbing her eyes. "Are we being attacked?"

"Yes," Sasha said curtly. "You missed it. Remind me not to rely on you during the next creature-related crisis."

Lyla yawned luxuriantly. "You know that my brain doesn't open for business until midday." She looked blearily around the room. "What did I miss?"

Martha grunted again and closed the window. "Nothing this time. But if the imps are here, then there are bigger creatures right around the corner. Don't open this window, no matter what. You hear?"

She brandished her frypan at them warningly.

"Yes, Martha," the two women said quickly.

"Good." Martha took another look at the glowing wards and then nodded, satisfied. "I'm going downstairs to take your visitor back through the Portal." She handed Sasha the frypan. "You keep ahold of that until Addie comes home. She's on watch, but she'll be back in half an hour."

"Right," Sasha said, testing the weight of the pan.

Martha shuffled out of the door. "You girls just stay put."

Lyla curled back under her covers and closed her eyes.

"How can you sleep?" Sasha asked incredulously. "A mythical creature just tried to break into our room."

"I told you—I'm not really awake. Not till midday," Lyla mumbled. "In a few hours, this will all finally sink in, and I will freak out enough to please even you."

"You'd better," Sasha said, and practiced swinging the frypan.

～

THREE HOURS AND TWELVE MINUTES LATER, THE EVENTS OF THE EARLY morning finally hit Lyla.

"Oh, hell," she said, horrified. "A mythical creature tried to break into our room. *A mythical creature tried to break into our room!*"

Sasha smiled over her coffee cup. "It took you long enough."

"Well, it took a while for the caffeine to kick in." Lyla raised her cup to her lips once more, but then changed her mind and put it down again. "I don't want any more of this reality juice."

"Just let it all sink in for a bit," Sasha said, sipping her coffee. "I'm barely bothered by it now."

"Yes, but catastrophes make *you* perky. They make *me* anxious. Hell, the witches said this was all going to get worse, right?"

Sasha grimaced. "Right. A lot worse."

"So, what's going to be sitting on our windowsill tonight? Fairies? A dragon? Bigfoot?"

"I don't know." Sasha added another sugar to her coffee just to keep her hands occupied. "I'm hoping that the size of the creatures escalates gradually. That way, we won't get the dragon until day six."

Lyla looked down at her cup, wistfully. "I'm going to have to switch to Irish coffee. I don't think I'll be able to deal with a creature invasion sober."

"It might be a friendly dragon. The imp was pretty cool. Rude, but cool."

"That's a comfort." With a sigh, Lyla pulled back her chair. "Okay, enough wallowing—Plans A and B await. I'm going to hunt down the Headmistress and read through those marriage law documents. What about you?"

Sasha drank down the last of her coffee, wincing at the half-inch of sugar on the bottom, and stood up. "I'm going to try and track down information about the creatures. If we're going to get visitors, I want to be prepared."

Lyla positively beamed. "Oh! Good idea. I'm so proud of you for suggesting research. Usually, you suggest solutions that require physical exertion and sweating."

Sasha rolled her eyes. "I'm not illiterate. I usually don't have to bother with research because it's your favorite way of dealing with any situation, and you always tell me what you find."

"Well, maybe this research session will change your mind."

～

IT DID NOT.

If anything, it cemented Sasha's belief that she should stick to running away from all the obstacles she encountered in life rather than reading about them.

Within moments of telling Miss Adeline of her desire to learn more about the creatures of Otherworld, the older woman had filled Sasha's arms with crusty old books and countless crumbling parchment scrolls—all sealed away in cling wrap.

Sasha sat at the desk in Miss Adeline's study, surrounded by arcane knowledge and plastic wrap, and felt—for the first time since arriving in Old Middleton—*doomed*. The sheer amount of reading material set out before her looked insurmountable. She suddenly envisioned spending her entire six-day reprieve glued to her chair with a permanent headache.

Just as she was about to have a minor panic attack, a slender, blue-haired young woman arrived in the doorway, dragging a cart filled with books behind her.

Sasha groaned when she saw the cart. "No. No more books. I give up. Just put me in your cart and drag me to the Portal."

The other woman smiled at Sasha's distress. Sasha wondered if she was a sadist.

"You probably don't want to hear this," the mysterious, book-wielding woman said, "but there are more books in the car."

Definitely a sadist.

The sadistic woman grunted as she pulled the cart across the doorway, the wheels catching on the thick carpet. With a final tug—her biceps straining under the rolled cuffs of her red t-shirt—she yanked the cart into the room. She exhaled in triumph, blowing her pale-blue fringe out of her eyes.

"I'm Lottie Cheung, by the way. Librarian at the Old Middleton Library."

Sasha stared suspiciously at Lottie's expression. There was a mischievous glint in her dark, hooded, gaze; and a knowing slant to her wide, lip-glossed smile. Overall, she looked far too gleeful for Sasha's current mental state.

Lottie peered back through the doorway, tilting her head at an awkward angle so that she could see down the hall. Noting that the coast was clear, she flashed her wrist at Sasha.

"Wind witch," she said impishly.

Sasha tried to muster some enthusiasm and failed. "Sasha Pierce. Doomed True Queen of Between."

Lottie's eyes widened. "So, I heard. Wow. You know, I've only been here four months, and I've already met a coven, an imp, and now a queen. I am so glad I left San Diego; Old Middleton is much more exciting."

"Too exciting, if you ask me." Sasha eyed the stack of books that Lottie was unloading from the cart and groaned again. "Really, you can stop right now. There's no way I can read all of those books in six days. I just need something simple and straightforward that will tell me about the creatures of Between."

Lottie carefully set a stack of books at the edge of Sasha's desk and looked down at her cart. "I think I have the book for you."

She burrowed down to the bottom of the pile and pulled out a large book bound in navy leather.

"Yes!" she said, triumphantly. "This is what you want." She turned the book so that Sasha could see the cover. *All Things Dastardly and Dank: A Guide to the Beasties of Between (Both Human and Creature) by Codrumple Van Beestark—Adventurer, Beast-wrangler, Plumber.*

Sasha frowned. Plumber? "Are you *sure* this is the best book to read?"

Lottie nodded enthusiastically. "This is required reading at the Finishing School."

"Finishing School?"

Lottie looked around shiftily. "Ah ... let's just forget that I said that, shall we?"

Sasha's eyes narrowed. "Why do I need to forget—"

"*Dastardly and Dank* is *the* beginners guide to the fauna of Between," Lottie said quickly, "so it's the very best place to start." She gestured to the books stacked precariously on Sasha's desk. "All the other sources are more informative and probably more accurate. But given your time constraints, *DD* is the book for you. It's the kindergarten version, so to speak."

Sasha held out her hand for the book. "Well, that sounds like my level. Thanks."

Oddly enough, Lottie did not hand over the book; in fact, she moved it further away from Sasha's grasp. "*Umm* ... I heard you had some sketches of the Shadow King."

Sasha's mouth dropped open. "Are you kidding me? Are you seriously holding that book hostage for some half-nude pictures of the King?"

"They're *nudes?*" Lottie squealed.

She held the book even further away.

"Poor choice of words," Sasha groaned. Seeing Lottie's determined expression, she threw her hands up in surrender, the stones on her protection bracelets clattering away. "Fine. Sketchbook under the couch."

"Yes!" Lottie squealed.

She threw *Dastardly and Dank* onto the desk and raced off toward the drawing room.

"Sorry, Shadow King," Sasha muttered. She pulled the book toward her and, opening the cover, began to read.

Behold! Here be a document of the creatures and beasties—and some of the equally foul persons—that I, Codrumple Van Beestark, have encountered during my wanderings across the cursed, villainous, fetid puss-hole that they named Between—a place I would not recommend even to the lice that inhabit the crotch-hair of my worst enemy.

"Wow," she muttered, "no one likes this place, do they?"

Carefully, she turned the pages. The book contained sketches of all manner of fantastic creatures, some drawn in black ink, others in watercolors. Meticulously drawn red arrows pointed out their various features (stubby legs, angry fingers, poisonous horns). Each was accompanied by a short description of the beast's nature and habits.

Sasha flicked past all manner of alarming creatures until she found her blue visitor.

Imps. These odd beasties are renowned for their spying, their thieving of shiny objects, their lewd manners, and their general drunkenness.

"Huh. Lyla would love them."

She flicked forward a few pages, stopping at the sight of a little green creature solemnly giving her the middle finger. "Charming," she said, smiling at the creature's crooked nose and dull, red hair clumped haphazardly around its head.

Goblins. These pesky miscreants are renowned for their child-snatching, their bawdy off-key singing, their lewd manners, and their general drunkenness.

Sasha frowned, turning the page. "I think see a pattern here." The next page contained a fearsome beast, with the body of a strongman and the head of a bull. "I know this one ..."

Minotaurs. Terrible to behold and fearsomely dangerous, these creatures have a song that will send you to the brink of madness and beyond. Prone to existential crisis, particularly when drunk—

"Is *anyone* sober in this place?" she wondered, turning the page.

A thin, brown creature—its hair spiky and nose long—stared back at her with keen, beady eyes.

BROWNIES. Usually docile and hardworking, they nevertheless possess a powerfully deviant foot fetish, becoming so enraptured by a person's shoes that they'll try to steal them whilst still on their feet.

"Well, at least they're sober," she muttered, flicking ahead.

"Fairies!" she cried, delighted at the watercolor sketches of the pretty little creatures, with their rainbow-hued, gossamer wings.

FAIRIES. These little creatures have voices so sweet, they'll send your heart soaring when they burst into song. They appear at dusk, dancing across the sky like early stars, leaving glimmering paths of silver and gold in their wake.

"Oh, how enchanting!" she cried.

Though, they are also lusty, prone to inaccurate flattery and, when angered, have a bite that will sever a grown man's finger. Beware! For they have been known to attack genitals when drunkenly enraged. See the previous comment about severing—

Sasha stopped reading and winced. "And just like that, I am no longer enchanted." She turned to the front cover and shook her head. "Damn you, Codrumple! Why couldn't you let me have fairies, hey? *Hey?* You had to ruin those, too!"

"You could have told me which half of him was naked."

Sasha looked up from her book; Lottie was holding Sasha's sketchbook and looking disapprovingly at one of the sketches of the Shadow King.

"I'm not complaining, mind you," Lottie clarified hastily. "They're great. But if *I'd* commissioned these, the Shadow King's nudity wouldn't have been on the top half of his body."

Sasha carefully closed her book. "Running around pants-less would be incredibly irresponsible behavior for a king ... not to mention hazardous with all those Nightmares around. And drunk fairies," she added, glancing at *Dastardly and Dank.*

"That's true, I guess. But ... *still.*"

Sasha's eyes narrowed. "You *do* realize that the Shadow King is more than just a bunch of body parts, right?"

"Oh, of course!" Lottie's eyes lit up. "He's a four-Mark sorcerer! Do you know how rare that is? Having one Mark gives you amazing power ... when you learn how to harness it. But having four Marks *and* the magic of Between at your disposal?" She bit her lip. "The power he wields must be enormous!" She took another look at the sketch. "All that *and* a great chest."

Sasha was starting to become somewhat annoyed with the bawdy tendencies of the Old Middleton witches.

She stood up and grabbed the pile of books that Lottie had deposited onto her desk. "Thank you again for *Dastardly and Dank*; I really appreciate it. Here, I'll help you pack up the rest of these."

She quickly loaded up the cart and then held out the cart's handle to Lottie.

"Sure," Lottie said good-naturedly, taking the handle with a smile. "Let me know if there's anything else you need."

Sasha pointed to her sketchbook, still in Lottie's hand. "Ah ...?"

Lottie's grip on the sketchbook tightened. "You wouldn't think of selling some of these, would you?"

"Nope," Sasha said, retrieving her sketchbook with considerable difficulty.

"What about commissions?" Lottie persisted, looking longingly at the sketchbook. "I was thinking of something with the Shadow King sprawled on a fur rug. Something tasteful ... maybe with a strategically placed potted palm—"

"It was nice meeting you, Lottie," Sasha said firmly and ushered the witch out the door.

"Oh! Yes, lovely meeting you, too," Lottie said hurriedly, as Sasha shut the door firmly behind her.

Sasha dropped her sketchbook onto the desk and sat back down. "The Shadow King on a fur rug? A potted palm? What is wrong with these witches?"

Without any permission whatsoever, her imagination provided her with an incredibly detailed, and slightly saucy, image of the Shadow King on a fur rug, potted palm included. In fact, it was so detailed that Sasha's fingers itched to grab a pencil and start sketching.

"Traitor," she told her brain.

Looking for a distraction, Sasha quickly reached for *Dastardly and Dank* and flipped it open to a random page.

All thoughts of kings and rugs and potted plants quickly disappeared.

There, before her, was a familiar white figure. A Nightmare stared back at her, its eyes black and empty, its mouth gaping and filled with blade shards. The creature's long, white fingers were stretched toward her, its razor-sharp, black claws ready to strip the flesh from her body.

"Nightmares," she read in a whisper.

These loathsome demons are some of the most fearful creatures that roam Between—feasting, as they do, on the dreams of their victims. Their bites are venom-filled, causing their victims to fall into an everlasting sleep drenched in their worst fears and most painful memories—on which the demons feed. Once hope and heart fail, the victims rise to become the very likeness of the demon they were possessed by. They are then doomed to roam the Wasteland, preying upon the dreams of the Earther-folk during the Lunar Crossing, and the dreams of those in Otherworld all the times in between—

Sasha abruptly closed the book.

"That's enough of that," she said shakily.

She wondered whether finding out more about Between was really a good idea—or whether ignorance was, indeed, bliss.

"Sasha, it's lunchtime. Would you like a sandwich?"

She looked up; Martha stood in the doorway, holding a loaf of bread.

Yes, Sasha thought, *I would like a sandwich ... and a whole lot of alcohol, and a one-way ticket to somewhere Between can't find me.*

Martha frowned. "You look pale. I'll put a slab of beef in it to feed your blood. And maybe a pickle."

"Thanks," Sasha said instead, running a trembling hand through her hair. "I'll be right there."

~

MEANWHILE, LYLA SAT IN AN UNDERGROUND CHAMBER MADE OF SANDSTONE and bronze, lit only by candles that cast more shadows than they dispelled. She leaned back in her chair—a strange, wooden chair that had feet fashioned in the likeness of dragon claws, and winged creatures carved into the frame—and looked out the doorway, making sure that the Headmistress had gone to lunch.

Satisfied, she turned back to the bookshelves. Ordinarily, she would have been entranced by the display of ancient books, covered in the hides of mythical creatures she had only read about in fairy tales. But today, she had a mission. She cleared her throat.

"Okay," she said, addressing the books, "I know we've had our differences."

The sudden rustling of pages sounded very much like assent.

"But I'd like you to remember that I began our association with the very best of intentions. I told you that you were beautiful, remember? That you were the most wondrous books I had ever seen, and that I felt privileged to be here."

The books shifted a little, listening.

"And how did you respond? By being uncooperative and refusing to open—just because I wasn't a witch. Which is very narrow-minded, by the way. You might want to take a moment to think about that."

The books did not move.

"Or not. Some of you—not mentioning any names"—Lyla narrowed her eyes at a small, green book wrapped in a gold-leather cord—"*attacked me.*"

The rustling of pages sounded remarkably unrepentant.

"And yes, I may have overreacted—"

The books banged themselves against the bookcase.

"Yes, yes," she said testily. "I probably shouldn't have taken out the letter opener."

The green book with the gold cord moved forward on the shelf and rustled piteously, a tiny, letter-opener shaped nick on its cover. The nearby books hovered around it protectively, shielding the book from Lyla's view.

Lyla's eyes narrowed at the damaged book. "Don't you play innocent with me! I acted in self-defense. That's a *defensively produced* wound! *You* tried to set me on fire."

The damaged book stopped the pretense of piteous rustling and bounced on the spot, clearly laughing at her, its fellow books joining in.

Lyla decided to ignore that slight. "But let's move on from that unfortunate incident—I'm here to offer you a deal. I know that you don't want *me*, a non-witch, reading you. You've made that very clear. But I *have* to help my friend—that is non-negotiable, and time is running out. So, if you help me find what I am looking for—information that'll help my friend get out of this ridiculous situation—then I'll go back to loving you unreservedly from a distance and will never set foot in this library again."

The rustle of pages was measured this time, as if the books were considering her proposition.

"So, to sum up: you have two choices. You can choose the long-term gratification option, where you help me out for a couple of hours and then never see me again. Or you can choose the short-term gratification option, where you fight me for however long it takes for me to get the answers I'm looking for. And once I get them, I'll *still* come down here every single day to bother you because I am petty and vengeful. Do you hear that? Every. Single. Day."

The books clustered together, seeming to confer.

Lyla crossed her arms over her chest. "So, what's it going to be?"

As it turned out, magical books are all about short-term gratification.

They threw themselves against the bookcases, rustling their pages in the literary version of a battle cry.

Lyla picked up her notebook and turned it toward the books.

"Fine then." She calmly opened to a random page. Then, maintaining eye contact with the books, she slowly reached for the page ...

The sound of tearing paper was obscenely loud in the small room.

The books momentarily stopped their outcry and leaned away.

Lyla noticed and smiled sharply.

"Let's do this."

14

THE KING AND THE KINDERGARTEN TEACHER

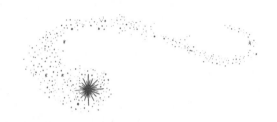

It was not until almost midnight that Lyla returned home, scorch marks on her jeans, her blonde braid disheveled and askew.

"*Ta-da!*" she cried, bursting into the bedroom. "All hail me!"

"Okay." Sasha paused, mid-way through unzipping her boots, and smiled at her friend. "And why are we hailing you?"

"When I left this morning, I had only questions. But now, I have returned with all the answers!" Lyla held her singed notebook above her head in triumph. "*All the answers!*"

Sasha stared up at the notebook in shock. "*All* the answers? You—you mean you found a way for me to stay in Old Middleton?"

"Well …" The notebook wavered. "*No.* The Headmistress is working on Plan A; the most powerful books won't let me read them. I was working on Plan B. So technically, I don't have *all* of the answers. But I have *some* of the answers." Lyla hoisted the notebook back to its position of glory. "*Some of the answers!* TA-DA!"

"No way!" Sasha beamed at her giddy friend. "You figured out a way that I can rule Between without marrying the Shadow King?"

"I did!" Lyla shouted joyously, throwing herself onto her bed, the bedframe creaking dangerously.

"YES!" Sasha cried, throwing her arms into the air, the charms on her protection bracelets jangling joyously with the motion. "Go you!"

"Yes, *go me*. I am the Empress of Research."

Lyla was still for a moment, catching her breath, and then scrambled back up into a sitting position. "Okay. Let's talk about marriage laws. And, may I say, Otherworld is a *very* practical place."

"How so?" Sasha asked, sitting on the edge of Lyla's bed, her half-zipped boot forgotten in her excitement.

Lyla flipped open her notebook and cleared her throat. "Otherworld—and this includes Between—recognizes two types of marriages. The first is called a *Joining*. It's basically a marriage of convenience. From what I could gather, the main reason for taking part in a Joining is to avoid paying taxes—couples pay less tax overall than single people. Oh, and they also get presents."

"Presents?"

"*Presents*. The crown gives all married couples some livestock—and sometimes a house—on the day of their wedding. It's a pretty good deal when you think about it."

Sasha shrugged. "I guess there are weirder reasons to get married."

"Getting married is weird in general; at least you might get a pig out of it in Between." Lyla turned to the next page. "Joinings are strictly business arrangements: there's no consummation." She looked up and grinned slyly at Sasha. "Though, there are ways of getting around that bit of the law. For example—"

Sasha held up her hand, halting Lyla's sure-to-be-lurid explanation. "We're getting off track. I don't need to know about that bit."

"Are you *kidding*? What if you—"

"Skip ahead," Sasha said firmly.

"But reading about how people got around that law was the best part of my day!"

Sasha threw a pillow at her.

"Okay, okay," Lyla laughed. "I'll skip ahead and spare you the sordid details."

She proceeded to turn page after page after page of her notebook.

Sasha raised an eyebrow.

"Don't judge me," Lyla said sternly. "Now, the second type of marriage is called a *Promising*."

"That sounds romantic-ish."

"I suppose. A Promising correspond to our understanding of matrimony: two people getting married because they care about each other."

Sasha shook her head. "Not appropriate in my case."

"Not at all," Lyla agreed. She quickly scanned her notes. "There was something about a third type of marriage—a Bonding—but they're rare. It's where you promise to link souls throughout eternity."

"That sounds terrible."

"Utterly dreadful. No chance of escape at all—you can't even get out of it by dying."

Sasha shuddered. "Let's never speak of it again."

"Agreed." Lyla's eyes lit up. "But don't you see, Sasha—*this* is Plan B! All we need to do is to make sure that you and Hill-Man get one of those Joining marriages and then you're set!"

The relief Sasha felt was staggering. "I—I can't believe it. I thought it would be harder than this. I thought—I thought I'd have to fight for it. I —" She stopped abruptly, a terrible feeling twisting her gut.

"No ..." She shook her head frantically. "This is all too good to be true. Nothing comes this easily for me. *Nothing.*" She reached over and grabbed Lyla's hand. "Are you sure? No—are you *positive?*"

Lyla nodded, practically bouncing on the bed. "The Headmistress double-checked all the references." She squeezed Sasha's hand. "I know that it feels too good to be true—it's like Joinings were made for you. But it's true." She grinned madly. "With a Joining, you can job-share royal duties with Hill-Man *and* keep your independence."

Sasha grinned back, just as madly, and allowed herself to feel the happiness of this miraculous discovery. "I'll be the Joined, Job-Sharing Queen of Between!"

"All of the power of a royal marriage with none of the pelvic contact. Isn't that wonderful?"

"Fantastic." Sasha valiantly ignored portions of her anatomy that disagreed with that statement. "Better than anything I could've hoped for or imagined."

Lyla closed her notebook. "With your permission, I hereby declare that Plan B is ready for action."

"Agreed!" Sasha exhaled in a rush. "Thank you, Lyla. *Thank you.* You are truly the reigning Empress of Research."

Lyla waved her hand regally. "Yes. Yes, I am. Though, I guess I should also give some of the credit to the Headmistress. She was really helpful today."

"But she's not here," Sasha pointed out. "So, feel free to take it all."

"Thanks! I shall." Lyla gave Sasha a brilliant smile. "Tomorrow, I'll flatter the Headmistress shamelessly until she lets me work on Plan A ... assuming the older books will let me read them without putting up a fight." She snorted. "Can you believe that some of them tried to set me on fire? *Again?* They're books, for goodness sakes, full of flammable pages. And yet, they chose to risk bursting into flame rather than letting

me get close to them. I mean, that's just suicidal, not to mention insulting
…"

Sasha squeezed Lyla's hand. "I owe you big time."

"Yes. Yes, you do. And you can start by letting me have the first shower." Lyla looked down at the cobwebs on her clothing and grimaced. "And most of the hot water."

"Deal!" Sasha said, laughing. "Have it all."

She released Lyla's hand and flopped down onto her bed, her arms outstretched as if to embrace the world. She still couldn't believe that Lyla and the Headmistress had figured out Plan B so quickly.

Maybe, she thought tentatively as she stared up at the ceiling, *maybe my luck is changing.*

She wondered if her patch of good luck would hold long enough for Lyla and the Headmistress to figure out Plan A.

That could be pushing it, she thought with a sigh. It was a much bigger task to remove Sasha from Between's clutches entirely without unleashing the Nightmares on Old Middleton.

If Plan A failed, and she was forced to live in Between permanently … Sasha's mind baulked at the thought of leaving everyone she loved behind forever, but she forced it back on track. If she *had* to leave, at least she could rule Between without having to truly marry the Shadow King. It would be job-sharing and no more.

And I still have two boons up my sleeve, she told herself.

For the first time since she crossed the Wasteland, she felt that things may not be as dark as she had previously feared. Not great … certainly not wonderful … but *all right.*

Well, she amended, *as alright as things can be when you're being forced to take up residence in a fairy tale kingdom filled with dastardly and dank beasts.*

"Five days left," she whispered.

"Five days left of freedom," Lyla echoed, as she hunted down her pajamas. "And not a male strip joint in this place."

Sasha laughed. "You've never been to a male strip joint."

"No, haven't … and I never will if I stay here. This village is the worst," Lyla said over her shoulder as she made her way to the bathroom.

Sasha snorted. "You'll get no arguments from me."

She closed her eyes and took a deep breath, her fingers reaching unconsciously for the amulet around her neck.

Five more days…

～

When Sasha opened her eyes, she was no longer in her room. To her immense relief, she was not on a mountain, or in a swamp, or submerged in a tar pit. Instead, she was seated on a high-backed, leather chair in what appeared to be a sitting room of some sort. Sasha looked to either side of her curiously, but the room was dim and full of shadows, the only light coming from three thick, white candles clustered on a tall candelabra by her left elbow, and the fireplace beside her.

That was a pleasant surprise after the frozen mountain top of her last dream. She stretched out her fingers toward the warmth and tried not to yawn. Hell, she was exhausted; there had been way too many dreams and not enough real sleep.

She was wondering whether it was possible to fall asleep in a dream when she noticed, with some surprise, that the Shadow King was sitting in a dim alcove directly opposite. He was reclining in a chair that matched her own, his long, leather-clad legs outstretched before him, black knee-high boots crossed neatly at the ankle. He was wearing another sinister black ensemble, the high-collared robes accentuating the pallor of his skin. As Sasha watched, the candlelight played across his fine features, the golden light transforming him into something otherworldly—a dark fairy tale carved from marble and clothed in shadows.

So, so lovely, Sasha thought to herself with a wistful sigh. *But pointy. And not for me.*

Cradled in the King's large hands was a small, silver book.

Sasha waited for him to notice her, but the contents of his book completely absorbed his attention. She was about to tease him about it when, suddenly, he spoke.

"Who is it that you smile for?" he whispered to the book. "Surely—surely it cannot be *me?*"

As Sasha watched, the Shadow King's fingertips hesitantly alighted on the page, his touch gentle, reverent. The gesture was so wistful, his expression so *yearning,* that her heart twisted hard in her chest.

And, just like that, Sasha's world tipped on its axis. For here was the Shadow King, stripped of his kingly mask—all that aloofness and cold authority gone—and so devastatingly vulnerable that Sasha was forced to rethink her first impressions of him completely.

What could he be reading, she thought, her breath catching, *to make him look that way?*

All at once, she knew that she had to leave. This moment felt too private, too intimate to watch. She needed to go, *now.*

But how? Sasha looked around the room for a possible escape but soon gave up; any move she made would attract his attention.

She was wondering whether falling asleep was the only alternative when suddenly, the King looked up ... and visibly started at the sight of her.

Sasha sat very, very still.

Caught.

"Hi," she said, a little breathlessly.

The King glanced down at his book and then back at her.

"Greetings," he answered warily.

He looked so, so flummoxed by her appearance that Sasha could not help but smile. Oddly enough, her smile only increased his bewilderment, which made her positively beam.

"Sorry to have interrupted you," she said, still smiling like mad.

"How long have you been here?" he asked in that same wary tone.

Sasha surreptitiously crossed her fingers. "I just got here." She cleared her throat. "Just now."

The King, Sasha noticed, looked exceptionally relieved.

"Good," he said. "Excellent." He closed his silver book and placed it carefully, cover-down, on the table beside him.

Sasha exhaled. *Dodged that bullet,* she thought, uncrossing her fingers.

The King turned his attention back to her. "Apologies." His lips quirked. "I appear to have missed the dress code yet again."

Puzzled at the King's expression, Sasha looked down and noticed what she was wearing: thick, black stockings, a long, cream-colored slip, and a single boot.

She groaned. "Lyla interrupted me while I was getting undressed for bed. I must have fallen asleep before I finished the job. Dash it." She stared at her bootless foot. "I didn't want to be unprepared tonight."

"Clearly your plan was a spectacular success. A moment, if you will."

The Shadow King stood up and disappeared into the next room.

Sasha looked at the silver book, its cover glittering like stars in the fire-light, and wondered whether it would be rude to take a peek at the title. But before she could decide whether or not to reach for it, the King returned, holding a black, silk robe that looked remarkably like the one he had worn on the hillside during their first meeting.

"Is that—?" she began.

"Behold, the seduction clothing," he said dryly, gesturing to the robe.

Sasha rolled her eyes. "Are you sure you can *endure* lending it to me?"

The Shadow King's lips quirked. "It would not be *burdensome.*"

Sasha grinned and, pulling off her remaining boot, stood up. She reached for the robe, but the King moved the garment out of reach.

"Allow me to assist you," he said.

In a courtly gesture, the Shadow King held out the robe and inclined his head.

"Ah ... thanks," Sasha said, taken aback.

She moved her curls to the side and turned her back to him.

A voice in the back of her mind—a voice that sounded suspiciously like Lyla—tsked.

You're turning your back on your enemy, it scolded. *No good ever comes from turning your back on your enemy. And dammit, move your hair back to where it was—he can see your jugular! Don't let him see your jugular!*

Sasha tried to ignore the Lyla-voice. She cleared her throat and placed her arm into one of the sleeves.

"This is your second chivalrous gesture toward me," she said. "Are you still aflame with nostalgia?"

"I am a veritable bonfire of nostalgia," he said.

Sasha could not help but smile as she dipped her arm into the second sleeve. "That sounds hazardous."

"It is. Then again, all things in Between are lamentably flammable."

Sasha felt the King shift his stance behind her.

"Perhaps," he said, his lovely voice low against the shell of her ear, "I should start carrying around spare cloaks and robes."

Sasha started as his words brushed along the sensitive skin of her throat, leaving a heated trail behind. She was suddenly very aware of just how close he was. If she tipped back her head, her curls would lie against the velvet of his tunic; if she stepped back a single step, she would be pressed against his broad chest, her body molded to his ...

But Sasha did none of these things. She stood, as still as she could, and allowed the King to slip the dark silk over her shoulders, the fabric falling in cool folds over her body like a caress.

She exhaled sharply, pushing aside that dangerous notion. "And I should start going to bed fully clothed. Thanks, by the way."

Sasha quickly turned away from the King and sank gratefully back down into the chair. To give the Shadow King credit, the man had a wonderful wardrobe. His robe was terribly luxuriant and smelt pleasantly of petrichor. It reminded her of the night they met.

With a mental sigh, Sasha knew what she had to do.

"This is awkward," she said in a rush, "but I would like to apologize for how I acted ... when we first met."

The King sat down opposite. "How so?"

Apparently, she would have to spell it out. "When I—ah—threw myself at you ... and then tried to engage you in adult-type touching ... and then yelled at you when you refused to engage in adult-type touching."

He lifted an eyebrow. "I take it that is not your usual seduction technique?"

Sasha found herself laughing. "Nooo. Though, in my defense, I thought you were a figment of my imagination. I would never have acted that way if I knew you were real."

The King languidly stretched out his long legs, crossing his boots at the ankle, left over right. "So, you are more forward with imaginary men than the ones you encounter in real life?"

He's amused, Sasha thought, observing him. *I'm sitting here mortified, and he's amused.*

"The ones in real life are usually more cooperative. Anyway, I just wanted to say sorry."

The King inclined his head regally. "There is no need to apologize. If anyone is owed an apology, it is you. You were a Dreamer. Your Dream should have been a thing of wonder and joy—not the debacle you experienced. I was ... confused by the situation. If I had known what was happening—if I had only been told ..." He shook his head, clearly frustrated. "Things would have been different."

Sasha knew better than to go down that path of *what-ifs*.

"Apology accepted." She looked around, trying to change the subject. "So ... where am I tonight?"

The King gave the room a cursory look. "My chambers. Possibly the least exciting location in Between."

I know a coven of witches who would disagree with that statement, Sasha thought ruefully.

Instead, she smiled. "What? No dragons hidden under your bed? No goblins in the closet? No lava pool in your *en suite*?"

"Not since Saturday."

At Sasha's horrified look, the Shadow King tipped back his head and laughed—possibly the first non-sardonic laugh he had uttered in her presence. It transformed him; he looked much more relaxed and far less diabolical.

"You're joking," she said flatly. "I hope you're joking. You'd *better* be joking."

The corner of his lips twitched. "Apologies. I could not resist."

He sounded completely unrepentant.

Sasha's eyes narrowed. "You know, the only reason I thought that a lava pool *en suite* was an actual possibility is because *you* told me that this place was terrible."

"It is. Clearly, I have done an exemplary job of putting my point across."

"Yes, mission accomplished. Don't strain your arm patting yourself on the back."

He settled back in his chair, still amused. Sasha followed his lead and also leaned back, slipping a little on the leather seat, thanks to her silky robe. She stretched out her legs, letting her stocking-clad feet settle in the plush, white rug.

They stared each other for a long moment—the king and the kindergarten teacher—the occasional crack and hiss of burning logs in the fireplace the only sound in the room. There was something charged about the silence—something tense and expectant. It made Sasha's skin tingle in a way that was not entirely unpleasant.

Oddly enough, it was the King who chose to break the silence.

"So ..." He steepled his elegant fingers together. "What scintillating topic of conversation shall we engage in tonight? Do you, perhaps, wish to know more about Between?"

Sasha's heart sank. A part of her knew that she should find out as much as possible about Between to prepare herself for the trial run. The rest of her, however, wanted to avoid the topic altogether. She was so, so tired of obstacles and bad news. Knowing her terrible luck, she would discover something dreadful—perhaps she would be forced to live out the rest of her days trapped in a tower, or under a sleeping spell.

Or in perpetual sobriety in an alcohol-free realm.

These were all horrific options and not worth exploring while she was exhausted.

Stick to bland conversation topics, she thought to herself with a sigh. *There's plenty of time to learn all the terrible truths when you're in Between.*

She was about to do just that when she looked up at the man lounging opposite—all broad shoulders and sardonic smiles and unconscious grace —and realized that she *did* want to know more about Between ... or at least one specific part of it.

"Actually," she said slowly, "I'd like to know more about you."

The King blinked. "You wish to know more about me? I am hardly Between's most interesting inhabitant."

"Really? You're a sorcerer; you open portals into other realms, you can turn into a bird, you wear clothing that has a mind of its own ..." *You stare longingly at silver books when no one is around.* "I'd say that was pretty interesting."

The King's initial surprise was replaced by a look of great forbearance. "Between has dragons. Hydras. A minotaur." He stared at her intensely over his steepled fingers. "My, my—are you truly unable to find a more exciting topic of conversation?"

"We come from different realms," she said, a little defensively. "It's not as if we can talk about politics, sports teams, or the weather."

The King bowed his head in assent. "Very well. Although I am sure to find the entire process excruciating, we may as well proceed. But I warn you—speak quickly. I am in an oddly hospitable mood, but I doubt it shall last."

Sasha's lips twitched. "You can keep your responses to two words or less."

"Ah, conversation at its finest."

"Okay then." Sasha sat up as straight as possible in her slippery robe. Something that felt like excitement made her grin at the taciturn King. "Let's start with all the bland, boring stuff first. What's your favorite color?"

"Green."

Before Sasha could ask the next question, the King held up his hand.

"Let me clarify. I like the green of the grass in the Summer Kingdom, not the green of the diseased swamps of Between, nor the green of pestilent boils."

Sasha blinked. "Ah, thanks. That was informative and way too visual. You could have just said 'the color of my eyes.' "

The King raised an eyebrow. "You have noticed the color of my eyes?"

There was a teasing edge to his tone.

Sasha decided to ignore it. "They *are* right in front of me. Next question —favorite food?"

"Anything edible."

"No." Sasha shook her head. "I refuse to accept that answer. I take food very seriously. Try again."

"I am holding fast to my answer. You will know why soon enough."

"Well, that sounds ominous. Let's move on." She smoothed the silk over her lap. "We've done color, food ... I think the next typical speed-dating question is star sign."

The King's brow furrowed. "Star sign?"

"Star sign. Astrology ... the twelve signs of the zodiac. Do you have those here? They correspond to the position of the sun at the time you were born. Hang on—I think it's the sun. Maybe it's the stars?" Sasha shrugged. "It's all just a bit of fun. I'm a Leo—the lion."

"Ah. We have something similar in Otherworld. We call them celestial signs. There are no Leos or lions. Instead, we have Viggo, the disgruntled goat; Arturo, the obnoxious boar; Mort, the vindictive seahorse; Petrel, the inebriated unicorn—"

"Wait, stop!" she said, laughing. "You're joking, right?"

The King ruefully shook his head. "I am afraid not. We have twelve truly terrible celestial signs. As you can probably guess, the astrologer who discovered them was from Between, hence the dreadful names."

"Which one are you?"

He gave an elegant lift of his shoulders, which was his kingly version of a shrug. "I do not know."

"Hang on—what do you mean? Is it difficult to figure out? Do you need a chart?"

"No. Only a birthdate."

Sasha became still. "Are you saying that you don't know your birthdate?"

There was a sudden wariness to the King's posture—a bracing of his shoulders, a tightness in his jaw. Sasha could almost see his kingly mask slip into place.

"I am saying exactly that," he said blandly. "And before you ask—yes, I can almost see the question hovering on the tip of your tongue—I am not trying to evade the question; I simply do not know the answer. I was not informed."

Sasha knew she should not pursue it; it was clearly a private matter. But, on the other hand, she was about to share a job with this man, and she wanted to know as much about him as possible.

She was also terribly, terribly curious.

I don't want to pry—" she began.

The King lifted an eyebrow.

"—much."

His eyebrow remained elevated.

"*More*," she finished. "But is this a common thing in Between? Are there lots of people who don't know their birthdate?"

The King tapped his lower lip with his index finger. Sasha had the distinct impression that he was trying to figure out precisely what to tell her —and what to leave out.

"No," he answered eventually. "Only orphans. Even so, the caretakers of the orphanage usually provide them with a date … typically the date that they were gifted to the orphanage."

Sasha frowned, trying to put the pieces of this king-shaped puzzle together. "So … are you saying that you're an orphan, but that you didn't grow up in an orphanage?"

"Yes."

Sasha had a dreadful feeling about all of this. "Were you adopted by a family?"

"No." His tone was curt, *final*. But there was something in his eyes— something wounded, something resigned—that was so at odds with the rest of his manner that it made Sasha press on.

"Did you grow up …" She paused, unsure about how to phrase what she wanted to ask. "Did you grow up somewhere that wasn't safe?"

The candles stuttered, leaving him in shadows. "Yes."

"Oh," she said gently, her heart twisting at the thought. What horrors had he gone through? She took a breath, readying herself to ask but stopped; there was something so haunted in the King's expression that the words just fell away.

He can tell me in his own time, she thought, her heart pounding at the realization that he had trusted her with something so personal.

Without thinking, she leaned closer. "Is that a secret?" she asked, not wanting to break his trust. "Should I keep it a secret?"

"Not at all." The candles flickered back to life, bathing the King in light once more. "It is common knowledge in Between. Everyone here is a terrible gossip."

Sasha threw her hands in the air, exasperated with him, but more exasperated with herself for thinking that he was starting to open up to her … that they were becoming friends. "Then why not just *say that*? Why make me work for it?"

"I said I was feeling hospitable." The King smirked. "Not gregarious."

"You're a terrible conversationalist," she said, shaking her head, "which is a shame because you're the only person that I have to talk to in this dream. Couldn't you try just a little harder?"

"Forgive me," he said, though Sasha thought he looked too amused to be repentant, "I get very little practice. I primarily give orders or yell at people for being incompetent. Idle chit-chat is not my specialty."

"You'll get no argument from me. From now on, I'll get all my information about you from Between's gossipiest gossips and take everything they say as fact."

"Oh, the things that you will learn!" He placed a hand over his heart and mock sighed. "Unfortunately, most of it will be true ..."

"Fine." She bit back a grin and tried to look stern. "I'll do it. Just remember that you agreed to this when someone tells me something outrageous and I believe it—like that you're secretly a troll." Sasha paused, her eyes widening. "You're not, are you? Secretly a troll?"

There was a devilish glint in his green eyes that Sasha did not trust one bit. "I guess you will just have to wait and find out."

Sasha sniffed. "I wouldn't be surprised if you were. Damn fairy tales."

The King leaned forward and rested his hands on his knees, his expression oddly intense. "The true question is: why do you wish to know more about me?"

He seemed genuinely puzzled.

"Really?" she asked, dumbfounded. "You think it's odd that I want to know more about you, the man that I'm going to be sharing a job with for the rest of my life?"

"A *job*?"

The Shadow King could not have looked more surprised if she had pulled a fish out of his robe and slapped him across the face with it.

"That's what this is, isn't it?" Sasha asked. "Job-sharing? We're going to be co-ruling a kingdom."

The King blinked. "My, my—what an amusing way to think of it. A job tends to have fixed hours—you work from sunrise until sundown. Ruling a kingdom has no such bounds; it begins when you open your eyes at some ridiculous hour each morning, and it *never ends*. Even sleep is no respite; most nights, you are rudely awakened because something is on fire or you are needed to break up a fight."

"Huh, sounds like parenthood. Still ..." Sasha lifted her chin. "I'm determined to think of it as a job. It makes it easier."

"You can leave a job," he said quietly.

For a long moment, they simply stared at one another, both painfully aware of the fact that they were now bound together for the rest of their lives by a sentient kingdom and a fateful trip across the Wasteland.

In her current state of exhaustion, this was far too much reality for Sasha. She looked away and watched the shadows dance across the walls. "You're avoiding the topic," she said, trying to steer the conversation to something safer. "I don't think it's *odd* that I want to know more about you. I think that it's *odder* that you don't want to know anything about me. Technically, I'm going to be your almost-wife."

Sasha's eyes widened—she had not meant to bring up the marriage laws.

Maybe he won't notice, she thought desperately, reluctantly meeting his gaze.

The King tilted his head. "Almost-wife?"

Damn, she thought. *He noticed.*

Sasha crossed her fingers for luck. "We're going to have a Joining ceremony, right? Which means that we'll be husband and wife in name only. I'll be your almost-wife, and you'll be my almost-husband."

Please, she thought, *don't contradict me. Don't mention Promisings or Bondings ... or some other terrible alternative that Lyla hasn't found yet.*

The King looked at her admiringly. "Well, well. Someone has been researching marriage laws." He bowed his head. "Well done."

"Oh, no. I can't take credit for that. It was Lyla."

At that, the King's eyes narrowed. "Hmm ... Lyla again." He drummed his long fingers on the armrest of his chair. "It appears that your Lyla is going to vex me at every turn."

"Well, she'll certainly try."

The King smiled darkly. "Almost-wife," he repeated, savoring the syllables. "You have a point. Perhaps I should try harder to get to know you, my almost-wife." He sighed, a patently false sigh. "Pity that it's so difficult to get a question in edgewise ..."

Sasha smiled sweetly. "You can ask all the questions you want in my next dream. It'll give you time to prepare a list."

The King smiled again, though this time there was an amused slant to his lips. Sasha thought that he was enjoying himself. What was more surprising, Sasha realized with a start, was that she was enjoying herself, too.

Well, somewhat.

"I have no birthdate," the King said, finally returning to the matter at hand. "Hence, no celestial sign."

Sasha was so relieved that he had changed the topic, she jumped at it, eagerly. "That's going to change. Everyone needs a birthdate, if only for the party and the cake. Oh! And the presents. And maybe a *piñata*, if you're lucky. You look like the type who'd enjoy a *piñata*."

"What, pray tell, is a *piñata*?"

"It's a hollow container, usually in the shape of an animal—most often a donkey for some reason. You fill it with candy and trinkets. The birthday person gets blindfolded and beats it with a stick until all the candy comes out."

The King stared at her for a long moment. "You believe that *I* look like the type of person who would enjoy beating novelty livestock with a stick until it yields its hidden bounty of treats?"

Sasha looked at the King's sinister apparel. "Honestly? Yes. But we're getting off the point—"

"There was a point to this discussion?"

"—that you need to celebrate your birthday," she finished sternly.

"Well, if I am to gain material possessions from the experience—including the innards of a donkey—then it might be pleasant to have a birthday party. After all, it shall be my first."

"You've *never* had a party?" Sasha was scandalized at the very idea. "That's it—pick a day, and we'll celebrate."

"Will you guarantee the presence of a *piñata?*"

"Maybe." Sasha grinned slyly. "You'll have to show up to find out."

"*Ahh* ... blackmail," he said approvingly.

"What?!" She laughed in surprise. "*No*—"

"I have no preference with respect to the day," the King interrupted, with an airy wave of his hand. "I shall leave you to your diabolical plans."

Sasha nodded, pleased. She was oddly excited about the idea of throwing the King a party.

His first party, she corrected with a pang.

The idea of living a childhood without a single celebration made her heart stutter. All children—all *people*—should have the chance to be celebrated. She decided, then and there, that she would make this party a wondrous experience to make up for all the lost ones before it.

She wondered if she would be able to locate a bouncing castle in Between ...

"Excellent," she said, positively gleeful at the idea of putting the Shadow King in a bouncing castle. "See? Answering all these questions wasn't so terrible, was it? You'll be getting a party because of them."

"No." The King tilted his head, his expression contemplative. "Not that terrible at all."

Sasha's smile stuttered at the King's expression. He was looking at her as if he was trying to see *within* her ... past her social self, past her barriers, and down, down to all her secrets and wishes and dreams. She would have felt exposed except ... *except* there was an odd tilt to his lips—a sort of reluctant, puzzled smile—that made Sasha think that he did not entirely disapprove of what he had found.

Before she could ask him about the look or his tilt-y smile, Sasha felt the hook behind her navel.

"Well, time to go," she said, a little breathlessly.

She stood up and removed the King's robe, placing it on the chair. She picked up her boot and clutched it to her chest, unsure of whether it would make the journey back.

"Farewell," the King said agreeably.

"Bye," she said, grinning despite herself. "Oh! There was an imp on my windowsill last night."

"Expect more this evening. They usually travel in small groups."

Sasha groaned as she felt herself lift off the ground. "Anything I can do to stop them?"

"The best thing to do with imps is to leave out a plate——" The King paused, smiling as Sasha drifted toward the ceiling.

"A plate of what?" she asked.

But before he could answer, she was gone.

SASHA AWOKE TO THE ODDEST SOUNDS: A THUMP, THEN A STRANGLED, "*Aaghh!*" which was followed by high pitched laughter.

This was repeated three times before Sasha opened her eyes ... just in time to see a line of imps on the windowsill testing the wards. In a surprisingly organized fashion, one imp would throw itself against the glass, only to screech, "*Aaghh!*" when the wards flared and launched the creature backward onto the lawn. Then, the rest of the group would burst into laughter, and the process would start all over again.

"Get down from there, you filthy beasts!" she heard Martha yell from the lawn below.

The imps merely turned and made a series of obscene gestures at the witch.

Suddenly, the ground lurched. Sasha's bed shifted beneath her as if she was on the high seas.

"*Aaghh!*" the imps cried, as they were all dislodged from the windowsill.

"Serve you bastards right!" Martha yelled, as the imps hit the lawn.

Unfortunately for Martha, another group of laughing imps took their place.

"Take that, witch-lady!" one of the creatures yelled.

From out of nowhere, Sasha heard the ominous rattle of thunder. Then, an absolute deluge of water hit the window, sending the imps flying.

"You get 'em, Daisy!" Martha yelled triumphantly.

Sasha sighed and settled back against her pillows; not even the raucous sounds of Martha verbally and physically bitch-slapping an army of imps could keep her eyelids from closing.

"A plate of what, Shadow King?" she mumbled as she fell asleep.

This time, Sasha awoke to find herself in a vast meadow of vibrant, green grass, dotted with cornflowers and yellow buttercups the size of her fingernail. The sky was a clear, brilliant blue overhead, with the occasional fluffy, white cloud drifting lazily past. A warm breeze gently ruffled her hair, carrying the scent of freesias and freshly cut grass.

It was so lovely, so non-lethal that she was instantly on guard.

After making sure no kings or beasts were hiding in the grass, Sasha shrugged and laid down amongst the flowers. It was only a matter of time before the summer heat against her skin made her muscles relax, and her eyelids droop. Lulled by the drone of cicadas, Sasha yawned widely and closed her eyes.

For the first time in over a week, she slept peacefully.

15

WHERE CHIVALRY DIES A TERRIBLE, TERRIBLE DEATH

MONDAY, OCTOBER 29TH

THE NEXT DAY STARTED PERFECTLY PLEASANTLY FOR SASHA. THIS, OF course, meant that it was destined to be an unparalleled disaster.

For the first time since she arrived in Old Middleton, Sasha felt truly rested. There had been pancakes for breakfast and an easy crossword in the paper.

Even better, the Headmistress had persuaded Sasha to take the day off. The entire school was taking a field trip to a local hotdog factory, and Shae had offered to include the kindergarteners with her first graders. Sasha was unsure of the educational value of hotdog manufacturing and was secretly disappointed that she would not be able to see Mason Barnes's talent for chaos in a non-educational setting. But, on the upside, she was thrilled to have another day to prepare for her rapidly approaching stay in Between.

By lunchtime, Daisy's rainstorm had finally stopped.

Sasha finished the last bite of her sandwich and peered out the window.

"Do you think it's safe to go for a run?" she asked a yawning Miss Adeline.

Miss Adeline looked up blearily from her coffee. Even though it was after midday, the older woman had just woken up after taking the night shift guarding the Portal. "I suppose it would be alright. Don't go too far. And be sure to wear your amulet and bracelets."

"Yes, Miss Adeline," Sasha said obediently.

"Rough night?" Lyla asked Miss Adeline.

Miss Adeline stifled another yawn. "There were a lot of visitors last night. It was difficult to persuade them all to return to Between."

Lyla paused, sandwich halfway to her mouth. "Did anything happen that'll make the evening news?"

Miss Adeline sniffed. "We are *professionals*. We had everything under control." Seeing Lyla's expectant expression, she relented. "We *may* have wrangled a pack of mountain wolves back into the Portal last night."

Lyla's eyes widened. "Miss Adeline, you are a complete badass."

"Language, Miss Lyla!" the older woman said sternly, but she smiled as she sipped her coffee.

Sasha buried her head in her hands. "I'm putting you all at risk."

"Nonsense," Martha tutted as she entered the kitchen with Daisy. "This is our job."

"And it's the most fun we've had in *years*," Daisy said. "Why, I'm just so excited to see what the day will have in store for me!" She sat down beside Sasha. "And to think, the most I had to look forward to before you arrived were my stories on the television."

"So, girls, what are your plans for this afternoon?" Martha asked, handing Daisy a sandwich and glass of iced tea.

Sasha grabbed an apple from the wooden bowl in the center of the table. "I'd like to go for a run. Then, I'll go back to reading *Dastardly and Dank*. Have any of you been to Between? It would be better to get a first-hand account."

Daisy shook her head. "No, dear. You're the first." She placed her hand on Sasha's arm and leaned toward her conspiratorially. "You'll have to tell us all the gossip."

The mention of gossip reminded Sasha of her dream last night. "You bet. I'll bring back all the sauciest scandals."

Daisy squeezed Sasha's arm affectionately. "You're a good girl."

"Do you really think you should be jogging?" Lyla asked Sasha. "There are imps and creatures about."

"The imps and creatures are bothersome, but they won't hurt her," Martha said. "And we've activated the Sentinels. But you should stay within the village borders. Under no circumstances should you go further than the forest."

"I only want a quick run," Sasha said. "I certainly won't be heading to the forest."

Lyla looked down at Sasha's feet. "Hang on—didn't you just run a marathon with a pack of Nightmares? Your feet must be pretty banged up."

"No. The only injuries I came back with were Nightmare-inflicted, and even those feel pretty good after Rosa's potions. In fact, I feel great today! Come on …" Sasha tugged on Lyla's arm. "Stop trying to dissuade me and join me instead. You could use the activity; you've been cooped up with all those vicious books for far too long."

Lyla tsked. "When will you learn that physical exertion isn't a civilized pursuit?"

Nevertheless, she followed Sasha upstairs to get changed.

THEY SET OFF AT A LEISURELY PACE, WHICH ALLOWED THEM TO DISCUSS Sasha's latest dream and the events of the past few days. The weather was so lovely, and there was so much to talk about, that they soon became distracted. Before they knew it, they had left the tiny village behind, swapping storefronts and houses for farmland and the occasional curious cow.

"Wow," Sasha exclaimed, looking over the dried remains of a cornfield, "this place is much smaller than I thought. We're already in farm country."

"I don't trust farms," Lyla said, breathing heavily. "Too many potential weapons disguised as tools."

"Trust you to make farming sound sinister." Sasha tilted her face up toward the sun. "Aren't you glad you came? Breathe in all that fresh air!"

Lyla groaned, clearly winded. "I could've breathed in the same air from an open window in the boarding house … and indoor air-breathing wouldn't have given me freckles. Damn my Irish peasant ancestors. *Agh.*" She reached up and touched her nose. "I can feel them forming."

Sasha glanced at Lyla's nose. "They're not forming."

"They are! And these new freckles will join all my existing freckles to create one mega-freckle." Lyla gasped out a breath. "Freckles and exercise. This is a terrible day …"

Sasha shook her head, her long ponytail swishing back and forth. "How can you hate exercise? It's so good for you!"

"Tell that to the heart attack I'm about to have."

Sasha noted Lyla's red face and pained expression with a frown. "Okay, let's turn back. We're not near the forest, but the last thing we want to do is to stay out too long and attract trouble or—"

Sasha paused. She could have sworn that she'd heard an odd cracking sound followed by a sudden weight in the pocket of her jacket.

Puzzled, she unzipped her pocket and reached inside. In the palm of her hand lay the piece of malachite Rosa had given her for protection, split right down the center.

"I think this is a bad sign," she said, staring at the broken protection stone.

"So is that," Lyla whispered, pointing ahead.

There, beside a rusted paddock gate, stood two honest-to-goodness medieval knights decked out in full armor—one in silver, the other in gold.

The two women slowed to a halt.

Lyla blinked. "Okay, that's not something you see every day."

The knight in silver lifted his visor, revealing a fringe of pure white hair and eyes of the palest blue Sasha had ever seen.

"My ladies," he said, bowing awkwardly.

Instinctively, the women bowed back.

"It appears that my companion and I are lost." He gestured to the gold knight, who turned toward Lyla, seemingly transfixed. "We were wondering if you could guide us to the Boarding House for Genteel Ladies of Unimpeachable Reputation."

The broken malachite scalded the palm of Sasha's hand. She quickly dropped it back into her pocket.

Run, she thought. *Run.*

"Why?" Lyla asked politely. "Are you looking to rent a room?" She surreptitiously tapped her foot against Sasha's in warning. "Because I'm not sure that you'd meet the entry requirements." She made of show of surveying the knights from head to toe. "While you might be ladies—I don't like to make assumptions—the armor doesn't really say *genteel* to me. Plus, I bet it's terrible on hardwood floors—and Miss Adeline is *very* fond of her hardwood floors. She might make you take it all off before you're allowed to step inside. Would you be okay with that?"

The white-haired knight stared at her in shock. "I would do no such thing!"

"Spoken like someone with an unimpeachable reputation," Lyla said approvingly. "*You* are worthy of the boarding house." She casually stepped closer to Sasha. "Though, I can't say the same about your friend over there." She gestured to the other knight. "They'd probably prefer a boarding house with looser morals."

The white-haired knight opened his mouth in disbelief. His companion, however, began to roar with laughter. Still laughing, he pulled off his helmet to reveal tawny, blonde hair that shone like a new penny in the bright, afternoon sunshine.

"Many thanks for your concern," the blond knight said, his deep voice filled with good cheer. "As luck would have it, we are neither ladies—"

"Certainly not," the white-haired knight spluttered indignantly.

"—nor are we looking to rent a room." The tawny knight looked at Lyla appreciatively. "Nevertheless, I would be more than happy to discuss the unimpeachability of my reputation with you at great length."

He gave her a short bow and a devastating smile.

His white-haired companion glared at him impatiently. "We are here for a reason," he said pointedly to the blond knight. "And it isn't to go wenching."

"Ah, *wenching*! Now, there is a pleasant word," the blond knight said agreeably. "And a far better pursuit than our current mission."

"We do the High King's work. There *is* no better pursuit."

There was a kind of zeal to the white-haired knight's tone that Sasha immediately disliked. It appeared that the blond knight agreed with her. The jovial light in his brown eyes died, and his glance became as hard as steel.

"Forgive me," the blond knight said, his tone syrup sweet. "How could I possibly think that wenching is a more noble pursuit than the kidnapping of an innocent woman on the orders of the High King?"

"Keep your voice down," the white-haired knight hissed, glancing at the two women.

The blond knight ignored him. If anything, he raised his voice. "How lucky I am to I have you, my noble companion, to steer me right in such matters! After all, elves are known for their chivalry and honor above all else."

Lyla tugged on Sasha's jacket. *That's an elf?* she mouthed, motioning her head toward the white-haired knight.

That's an elf! Sasha mouthed back, eyes wide with surprise.

The elven knight had the good sense to look uncomfortable. "We have our orders."

Sasha covertly tugged on Lyla's jacket. Slowly, the two women began to back away from the conversing knights.

Unfortunately, the elven knight noticed.

"Do not leave yet," he ordered imperiously. "We still require your assistance."

"The boarding house is up that way." Sasha deliberately pointed in the opposite direction, her heart beating so hard that she was worried that the elven knight would be able to hear it. "Keep walking through the forest for about three miles until you hit a freeway."

The men gave her a blank look.

"A particularly large and busy road," she clarified. "Then walk down that road for about an hour."

"Though, be warned," Lyla said solemnly. "Beasts roam that road. Large, metal beasts."

The blond knight seemed to be on the verge of laughter again.

The elven knight, however, was nodding gravely to himself. "That is much farther than we were led to believe."

"It would've been easier if you'd brought horses with you," Sasha added helpfully.

"True," the elven knight acknowledged. "Perhaps we could procure some along the way."

"I think we're fresh out of horses," Lyla said, making a show of looking around. "The guy down the road has cows. Would a cow help?"

The elven knight stared at her, bewildered. "How could a cow possibly help us?"

Lyla held up her hands in surrender. "Hey, we're just trying to be neighborly. Besides, why do you want to go to the boarding house?"

"We are here to find Sasha Perse," the elven knight said. "Do you happen to know her?"

"Short? About five-foot-two?" Lyla asked, holding her hand up to about that height.

"Red-headed girl with glasses?" Sasha asked.

The elven knight looked to his companion. "Do we know what she looks like?"

The blond knight looked back and forth between Sasha and Lyla. "I am sure we can trust their judgment. They appear to have met her."

The elven knight turned back to the women. "Then yes, that appears to be her. We were told that she has a companion."

"You mean her dog, Lyla?" Sasha asked innocently.

Lyla coughed.

The blond knight turned to her, a twinkle in his eye. "I hope you are not falling ill, my Lady."

Lyla glared at Sasha. "I'm fine. Just a small case of choking."

But the blond knight was not listening to her reply. Instead, he was staring at Sasha's throat with a pensive expression. He glanced at his companion—as if checking his reaction—then turned back to Sasha and gave her a broad, knowing smile.

Sasha found it unnerving.

"Now," she said, starting to retreat once again, "we'd like to continue our run."

Lyla followed her lead. "We'd ask you both to join us, but you aren't dressed for a jog, and you have important business to attend to at the boarding house."

"Of course, thank you for your assistance." The elven knight began to bow but stopped abruptly.

"Wait—what is that around your neck?" he asked Sasha.

With a sense of growing horror, Sasha realized that the elven knight had spotted the Shadow King's amulet.

Foiled by jewelry.

"Huh?" she asked, backing away more quickly.

The blond knight shook his head ruefully. "So close."

"Stop!" the elven knight ordered and drew his sword.

The blond knight sighed and also drew his sword. "Here we go."

The women turned and ran as fast as they could back toward the village.

"Damn it! We shouldn't have jogged so far!" Lyla gasped, clutching her side. "I'm already exhausted." She watched as Sasha easily outstripped her. "Go ahead and save yourself! Run and get help. Damn it," she wheezed, "why didn't I exercise more often?"

Sasha realized that Lyla had fallen behind and doubled back, shortening her strides until she matched Lyla's. She grabbed her friend's arm for good measure and dragged her along.

"I said save yourself!" Lyla yelled. "This is not saving yourself!"

"I'm not leaving you behind!" Sasha yelled back.

"We are having an Ordeal, Sasha!"

"*I know*! How much do you think that armor weighs?"

"I don't know. Lots? I've got no clue. It's the blond we have to worry about—his armor seemed lighter somehow. He was moving more easily than the elf."

Sasha chanced a look over her shoulder. "Damn it! They're way closer than they should be. We have to split up. Go to the coven and get help. I'll keep them distracted."

Lyla shook her head. "No. No way. We need to stay together."

"You just suggested splitting up!"

"I know! But I just remembered that splitting up always goes badly for people in movies."

"They're catching up, Lyla!" Sasha hissed, sparing another glance over her shoulder.

"I know! If we can take one of them down, we might have a chance."

"Take them down? Take them *down*? How can we take them down? They're *knights*! With *weapons*! We can't fight knights!"

"No! No—I didn't mean to fight them. I meant literally put one of them *down* ... onto the ground. *Gah*, I can't ... I can't breathe ..."

"What? You mean like *trip* them?"

"Yes!" Lyla gasped. "We can't ... can't outrun them. If we trip one, it might ... slow them down. We might have a chance."

Sasha glanced behind them—the knights were catching up. "Won't they just get back up again?"

Lyla tried to shake her head and promptly gave up. "They're like a tortoise. If we get them on their backs, then they're useless ... I think. We need to get blondie on his back."

Sasha thought the plan sounded ludicrous. Then again, she couldn't think of a better one. Running away wasn't working—the knights would surely catch up to them before they reached Main Street—and splitting up was not an option for Lyla.

Operation Tortoise Knight appeared to be their only hope.

"We are so screwed," Sasha groaned.

The sound of clanging metal was getting even closer. Sasha desperately scanned their surroundings, trying to find a weapon that could trip a knight. To her right was an abandoned feed barn. On the floor, near the barn doors, was a rusty, old chain, stretched between two posts.

"The chain, Lyla!"

She veered off and grabbed one end of the chain, removing it from the post.

Lyla grabbed the other end. "This is *a terrible* plan."

"I know!" Sasha wailed. "Can you think of anything else?"

"No." Lyla clutched her side. "My brain is frozen with fear."

"Who first?" Sasha hefted the chain into her arms.

"Blondie, remember?"

They turned and ran back toward the surprised knights.

"This is a terrible plan, Lyla!" Sasha yelled.

"I *know*!"

At the last possible moment, they separated and ran toward the blond knight, the chain outstretched between them.

"Ah, ha!" he cried happily, not at all dismayed by this turn of events.

Sasha had only a moment to wonder about that before the chain hit his armor-clad torso with a terrific crash. Sasha watched dumbfounded as the knight toppled backward—far more easily than she had anticipated—and landed on his back near a crumbling paddock gate. Even so, her arms *hurt* from the bone-jarring collision and she stumbled forward, desperately trying to stay upright and failing miserably.

She heard Lyla fall to the ground beside her.

Panting, Sasha turned and then screamed, pivoting just as the pommel of the elven knight's sword swiped through the air, landing a hairsbreadth away from her head. As she spun away, the elven knight reached out, grabbing the amulet around her throat.

The amulet glowed bright silver.

Crying out, the elven knight was launched violently into the air, landing heavily several feet away from Sasha, his sword stuck fast in the ground beside him.

The bracelets around her wrists felt hot against her skin. The amulet around her throat hummed.

Protection charms, she realized, looking down at her jewelry in awe.

With a pained grunt, the elven knight stood up and stumbled over to his sword. He pulled on the hilt and then pulled again, unable to dislodge it.

Something told Sasha that her jewelry would not be able to protect her from a stab wound. She quickly scrambled to her feet. As she did so, she heard a strange sound—the sound of a throat being cleared in an exaggerated fashion.

Against her better judgment, Sasha turned; the blond knight was staring up at her and pointing to his own discarded sword, which lay on the ground beside him.

He cleared his throat again in that same exaggerated way and gave her a meaningful look.

Take it, the look said.

Sasha glanced at the elven knight—who was still trying to retrieve his sword—then back at the blond knight.

I'd hurry if I were you, his new look said.

It had to be a trick, Sasha thought. But what choice did she have? She cautiously grabbed the hilt of the sword, expecting the blond knight to grab her at any moment.

But he didn't.

Instead, he lay docilely on the ground, *smiling* as she picked up his sword.

Sasha grunted a little at the unexpected weight.

"Ah, thanks?" she whispered uncertainly. "Lyla, make sure he doesn't get up."

Lyla sat up a little stiffly and then, with great purpose, straddled the blond knight's waist, and pinned his hands in place with her own—much to the blond knight's delight.

Sasha noted the blond knight's delight. She looked around and grabbed one of the rotted fence posts lying beside the old gate.

"Here," she said, handing it to Lyla. "If he moves, brain him."

Lyla swung the post a few times, and then placed the splintered edge against the knight's throat. "Got it!"

"How wonderfully blood-thirsty!" the knight said, still far too enchanted by the situation for Sasha's liking.

But she had bigger problems—the elven knight had finally liberated his sword.

He pulled up his visor. "Get up!" he yelled at his fallen companion.

The blonde knight shook his head sadly. "Alas, I cannot. I appear to be bested." He gestured to Lyla, still perched on his body.

"Damn straight," Lyla said shakily. "He's completely bested."

The elven knight stared at him in disgust. "You are *useless*." He turned to Sasha, his sword pointed at her heart.

"Surrender," he demanded.

"Stop trying to kill me," Sasha countered.

A vein on the elven knight's forehead started to throb viciously. "I have no wish to kill you. My intention is to take you back to the Summer Palace."

"Ha! In how many pieces?" Lyla asked.

"And what will await her there?" the blond knight asked. "Our orders were to bring her back, *by all means necessary*, without any knowledge of what might befall her in the Summer Kingdom."

The elven knight stilled for a moment. But then he lifted his chin and held out his hand to Sasha. "Give me the amulet and return with me to the Summer Palace; I will do all in my power to ensure that no harm comes to you."

"What do you want with the amulet?" the blond knight asked, his voice cold. "What were your orders, Adies?"

The elven knight glanced down at his companion, clearly agitated.

"What were your orders?" the blond knight demanded.

Adies was sweating, his jaw clenched. "I answer to the High King, not to you." He turned to Sasha. "Enough of this—it is obvious that you will not see reason."

With an abrupt motion, he closed his visor and swung his sword again.

Instinctively, Sasha raised her sword—and immediately wished she hadn't. If she had thought that hitting armor with a chain had jarred her body, it was nothing compared to locking swords. Her entire arm felt as though it was on fire. Her bracelets flared up, the runes turning to gold, as the protection charms fought to keep her safe. She tried to draw back her sword and watched in horror as the metal-on-metal action caused sparks to fly.

With a cry, she staggered back from the elven knight until their swords were no longer touching.

"What happened to *not killing me*?" she yelled at the knight.

The elven knight tightened his grip on his sword. "I am not trying to kill you."

"What was *that*, then? With the swords?"

"I intend to best you in battle, render you unconscious, and return you to the Summer Palace."

Sasha stared at him incredulously. "*Render me unconscious?* Head injuries can be fatal!"

The knight shrugged. "Then you had better best me in battle."

"I'm a kindergarten teacher, not a knight! This isn't fair! Can I get a head start or something?"

"Prepare yourself," the elven knight said ominously.

Sasha's sword fighting knowledge amounted to a few games of Robin Hood played with her young cousins at the age of eight; and one stage fight when she was cast as Captain Hook in a dismally bad, all-female summer camp production of *Peter Pan*. She knew that she was no match for a real knight, who was even now flipping his sword around in an unnecessarily showy manner.

She would be bested, Sasha realized with a sinking heart. She would be knocked out. She would develop a head injury that would mess up some vital piece of her brain, or the wound would get infected, or—

And then it hit her: She was going to die.

This is how it ends, she thought hysterically. *I'm either going to be skewered like a human shish kebab or killed with a blow to the head by a knight in twenty-first century Wisconsin.*

But just as she started to despair, she heard that little voice in the back of her head.

No, it said quite firmly. *That will not do. Fight. Win.*

Fight. Win.

The voice made it sound so easy. Fight. Win. But really, what was the alternative? Surrender? *Die?*

You're right, she thought, pushing down her hysteria and replacing it with anger. *It certainly will not do. To* hell *with that!*

Sasha held up her borrowed sword defiantly. *Fight. Win.* "What's the plan, Lyla?"

"Call the Shadow King, Sasha! *Call the King!*"

Sasha groaned—she was an idiot. Why hadn't she remembered that earlier?

Because you were too busy coming up with Operation Tortoise Knight, she thought in disgust.

Sasha quickly placed the fingers of her left hand on the amulet. "Shadow King!" she screamed.

For a moment, everyone paused expectantly.

Nothing happened.

Then, more nothing happened.

When nothing continued to happen, Sasha looked down at the amulet and shook it.

"Damn," she muttered. "Is this thing on?" She tapped the amulet. "Testing, testing—"

"*Enough,*" the elven knight cried, and began to circle Sasha, his sword coming closer and closer to all sorts of unprotected, stab-able parts of her body.

Hurry, Shadow King! she thought desperately, grabbing her sword with both hands. *Or Between will be minus one True Queen.*

Clearly, that same thought had occurred to the blond knight.

"You need to tell your friend to run and find one of those steel beasts you spoke of," he said to Lyla in a stage whisper. "Her protection charms will not last much longer."

Lyla looked down at him in shock, then up at her friend. "Sasha! Run! Get the car!"

The car!

Sasha took off running. The elven knight cursed and started after her, clattering all the way.

◈

"Run!" Lyla screamed as she watched Sasha sprint toward the village, the blond knight's sword clutched in her hand.

Never had she felt more helpless. She needed to do something, *anything!* She looked around; there were a few good-sized rocks within reach. Dropping her fence post, she grabbed two of the closest ones. Taking aim, she began pelting the elven knight's back as he took off after Sasha and *whooped* in triumph when one rock hit the back of his armor.

"That's an excellent shot!"

"Thanks!" she said automatically.

Then paused.

There was only one person who could have said that. She looked down at the blond knight and noticed, with some alarm, that he was holding a large rock in his hand.

Lyla snatched back her fence post.

"I have wood!" she yelled, brandishing the post menacingly. "And I am not afraid to use it. Don't even *think* of using that rock on me!"

Without breaking eye contact, the blond knight threw the rock high above them. Turning, Lyla watched as the rock soared through the air and then struck the elven knight on the back of the head. The elven knight staggered and grabbed his helmet.

"Ah … he will be feeling that for a while," the blond knight said in great satisfaction, watching as the knight lurched off toward Sasha.

Lyla's eyes narrowed. "What's your game, blondie?"

"*Blondie?*" he laughed. "How marvelous!" At Lyla's glare, his expression turned completely innocent. "Whatever do you mean?"

"You're not as vanquished as you appear to be."

The knight folded his hands behind his head, looking as relaxed and at ease as if he were at a picnic.

"Of course, I am! You and your friend bested me in battle fair and square, so I yielded to you both. Now, I have nothing better to do than lie here and enjoy the sights of the countryside." He gave Lyla a blatantly approving look.

Lyla tried to ignore him—really, she did; her best friend was in mortal danger, and she had no idea if they would make it out of this Ordeal alive. But while she was trying to ignore him, she could not help but notice that this odd knight had lovely eyes, and all sorts of burnished tones— bronze and copper and warm golds—threaded through his hair. And, unlike the elven knight, he wasn't trying to kill or kidnap them, which was refreshing.

Lyla tried to gather her wits. She glared down at the knight for good measure. "You've been doing more than just lying down there. Thanks to that rock of yours, your friend is going to be suffering from a mild concussion."

"Oh, he is not my friend. And hopefully, it will be more than mild."

Lyla leaned back and looked down at the knight suspiciously. "You're acting incredibly helpful for someone who has been sent to kidnap and kill my friend."

"No killing," he responded automatically. "As far as I am concerned, even the kidnapping is unnecessary."

"Did your friend get the memo on that? It certainly looked like he was trying to kill her with that damn sword of his!"

The knight shrugged as well as he could while lying on the floor with a petite woman straddling his midsection. "His orders are of no real consequence: his sword has been enchanted—without his knowledge—to ensure that it does no harm. Your friend is perfectly safe. In fact, he is in far greater danger than she is."

The relief Lyla felt almost made her swoon. "Are you sure?"

The knight nodded. "Absolutely. Moreover, I had one of my wizards weight his armor without his knowledge before we made the journey to your realm. It will feel progressively heavier as the day goes on."

Lyla threw her hands in the air in frustration. "Damn you! Why didn't you tell me that earlier? Do you have any idea how terrified I am? Or how terrified Sasha must be feeling right now? She's out there alone, and I can't even help her because I have to sit on you! *Agh!* I am *so sick* of all this fairy tale crap!"

She smacked her hand down hard on his breastplate.

"*Gah!*" she yelled in pain, snatching her hand away from his chest.

"Armor," the knight said, rapping on his breastplate with his fist.

"Thanks for confirming that," Lyla said dryly, flexing her hand. "So, if I leave you to help Sasha, will you stay vanquished?"

The knight sighed sadly. "Unfortunately, not. There are rules, you see. And appearances to maintain. It is a complicated business."

"Right. That would've been too easy. Though, does that mean that as long as I stay sitting on you, you'll stay vanquished and you won't try to attack Sasha?"

"Yes."

"Well ..." she muttered, "I guess that's something."

The knight tilted his head and smiled up at her, all dimples, and shiny white teeth, and twinkles in his tawny, brown eyes. "May I ask you a question?"

"Could I possibly stop you?" At his amused look, Lyla sighed. "Go ahead."

In stunned silence, Lyla watched as the knight gently traced the length of her leg, from ankle to knee, with the tip of his forefinger.

"What are these called?" he asked in wonder.

To her dismay, Lyla felt her entire body shimmer with arousal.

This is not an appropriate time or place, she told her body firmly.

"*Ah* ... legs," she said carefully.

The knight gave her a gently reproachful look, and again slowly traced the pathway from her ankle to the sensitive spot just behind her knee. "We have legs where I come from, but not these. What are they called?"

Lyla valiantly tried to emerge from her arousal haze—really, she did. She took a deep breath and tried not to squirm on his chest. "Ah, they are called yoga pants."

"Yoga pants," he said dreamily. "What wonderful things they are! Never have I seen the like."

"Women don't work out where you come from?"

"Work out?"

"You know, exercise for leisure." Seeing the knight's confusion, Lyla tried to elaborate. "It's where you spend a portion of time performing some kind of activity, like running, or push-ups, or swimming, or cycling, or picking up heavy objects, or dancing around in a rhythmic fashion."

"For what purpose?"

Lyla shrugged. "Health, well-being, a hot body, masochism—take your pick."

The knight tilted his head back and laughed. The motion made Lyla realize that he had a lovely throat, with strong lines that hinted at muscles and suntanned skin below. Lyla was stunned to realize that she was inappropriately attracted to this man's neck.

"Exercise in Otherworld is not usually for leisure," the knight said. "It is usually tied to one's position. Guards perform drills that include running and push-ups; sailors swim, particularly when sea creatures attack their vessels; blacksmiths lift heavy objects; dancers and minstrels dance around in a rhythmic fashion, and so on. Then again, some ride on horseback for leisure, though I suspect that means that the horse is exercising, not them."

"Huh. No workouts in Otherworld? That's one point in its favor."

"Your friend is going to stir things up quite a bit. I am not sure if Otherworld is ready for a queen in yoga pants."

"She's not going to be a queen," Lyla said firmly. "I'm going to find a way to get her out of this lousy fairy tale."

The knight's expression became unbearably kind. "She is holding the Portal open. She will need to return to Between, one way or another."

Lyla tsked. "Spoken like a quitter. I told you—*I'll get her out.*"

The knight inclined his head. "Your friend's destiny is in excellent hands. But, if that task should prove beyond even your formidable talents, then you have nothing to fear. In Otherworld, it is better to rule than be ruled, and your friend will be a queen."

Lyla sniffed disdainfully. "Of a diseased hellhole."

"Now, now," he chastised, "that is a rather harsh assessment of Between. Where did you hear such things?"

"From the King of Between."

The knight grinned. "Well, that does sound like something he would say. Admittedly, Between is a little … rough … around the edges, but certainly not irredeemable. Moreover, it is in desperate need. If your friend had a mind to do so, she could accomplish wondrous things as ruler and assist a great many people … including its King."

Lyla narrowed her eyes at the blond knight. "Is this part of your plan? Divide and conquer? Your buddy goes to kidnap my friend; meanwhile, you try reasoning with me so that if he fails, I'll convince Sasha to go back to the High King with you?"

The blond knight blinked in surprise and then smiled, a dazzling smile. "Even in this realm, women are completely mesmerizing. Here you are, perceiving elaborate 'divide and conquer' plots involving a two-pronged attack of both cunning and steel, whereas we simply planned to storm the boarding house, put a hood over your friend's head, and take her away." He sighed. "We men are simple creatures …"

"No argument here. But why should I believe a thing you say? You're the High King's knight—and he isn't exactly our buddy in this situation."

"Oh, I am not a knight."

Lyla looked down at him. "Your outfit suggests otherwise."

"Looks can be deceiving. If I wore the head of a cow, would I be a cow?"

"You'd be an idiot. And I doubt the cow would appreciate that scenario."

The knight tilted his head and smiled up at her again. Lyla felt inexplicably cross with him; regardless of his lovely neck and fantastic smile, this was a terrifying situation, and he was treating it all like a lark.

"You smile too much," she said testily. "That's completely untrustworthy."

His smile widened. "May I ask another question?"

Lyla rolled her eyes. "What is it this time?"

He reached up toward her sports top. "What is—?"

She slapped away his hand. "I thought knights were supposed to be chivalrous. Groping is *not* chivalrous."

"I am not a knight. Nor was I about to grope you. Though, I could see how some in my position would take advantage of their authority and grope away."

"What position would that be? Are you some kind of doctor?"

"Ha! Actually—" The knight stopped and listened.

Lyla could hear it too. It was the sound of a car engine—a car engine that appeared to be heading straight for them.

Lyla and the blond knight simultaneously turned toward the direction of the noise.

The blond knight grinned. "It seems that your feisty friend found a steel beast."

16

THE MAIL TRUCK OF DOOM

THE CAR. WHERE HAD SHE PARKED THE CAR? HELL, WHEN WAS THE LAST time she had used it?

Sasha tried to think, but her mind was a mess of adrenaline and fear. She was still too far away from the village, and the elven knight and his pointy sword were gaining on her with every breath she took.

And there was no sign of the Shadow King. She would be kidnapped, or stabbed, or knocked out long before she reached her car, or the King graced her with his presence.

Not helping, she scolded herself. She reached for her anger. *Stay focused!*

As she ran around the corner, Sasha saw the inexplicable sight of a mail truck parked on the side of the road. She looked around—Mr. Eldridge was nowhere to be seen. She slowed down enough to peer inside; the keys were sitting in the ignition.

With a *whoop*, Sasha jumped inside, put on her seatbelt, and started the ignition. With barely a pause, she tore down the road, then turned the truck until it was facing the way she had come.

Sasha kept the engine running and waited.

The elven knight rounded the corner, clearly winded but still surprisingly fast. With a start, he spotted her inside the truck.

"I'm giving you one chance," Sasha yelled. "Leave me alone and go back to where you came from, or I will hit you with this steel beast and crush you under the wheels like a bug."

The elven knight began to run toward her, his sword aloft.

"Are you *insane?*" she screeched. "Didn't you hear the bit about the bug?!"

The knight did not even pause.

"Right," she said, steeling her resolve.

It's you or him, she told herself.

She closed her eyes and floored the accelerator.

He'll swerve, she told herself. *He'll swerve.*

He didn't swerve.

The sound of metal hitting metal was awful. The collision itself was even worse—the impact seemed to echo through her very bones. Sasha hit the brake, her eyes still shut, dread at what she would see—at what she had *done*—pooling in the pit of her stomach.

Reluctantly, Sasha opened her eyes … and screamed.

"Are you *kidding?*"

The knight was holding onto the front of the truck like a medieval hood-ornament. Sasha hit the accelerator again and tore down the road, the knight holding fast. She swerved the truck from side to side in a series of gut-churning turns, desperately trying to dislodge the knight from the hood.

Grimly, he held on. Sasha could see his blue eyes through his visor narrowed in determination.

"Leave me alone and I'll stop the truck," she bargained.

The knight looked up at her, his gaze cold and laser sharp. "I have my orders."

"What happened to chivalry?" she asked, trying to get him to see reason. "Aren't knights supposed to help damsels in distress? Damsels like me?" She gasped out a half-hysterical laugh. "I'm currently in a *lot* of distress!"

"My orders are from the High King himself and—"

"The High King sounds like a jerk." Sasha turned the corner sharply, the knight tightening his grip on the hood. "You need to work for someone who doesn't ask you to kidnap nice ladies."

The knight blinked at her, dumbfounded, and looked away. "I have my orders," he muttered.

Moments later, they were back in the field. Sasha could see Lyla, still seated on the blond knight.

Nothing had changed, Sasha realized with a sinking heart. They were still in as much danger as they were before.

And in that moment, Sasha made a decision.

"Right." She gritted her teeth. "Enough of this."

She hit the brakes as hard as she could.

She caught a glimpse of the elven knight's horrified expression as he soared off the hood of the truck ... and landed with a sickening thud on the grass, right beside the blond knight.

Sasha waited for the elven knight to stand. She kept the engine running, her hands clenched around the steering wheel, her knuckles as white as bone.

But he remained in the grass, crumpled in an awkward heap.

"Get out of the mail truck, Sasha," she told herself, not taking her eyes off the knight. "He's going to get up any second now and you—you have to be ready."

But the knight did not move.

"Get out of the mail truck, Sasha." She stared at his still form. "You need to check his pulse."

But Sasha didn't want to check the knight's pulse while he was lying *so still* on the grass. She didn't want to contemplate what she would have to do if she felt his heartbeat beneath her fingers ... or how she would feel if she couldn't.

Then she saw Lyla, still sitting bravely on the blond knight. Her friend was right next to the elven knight; if he awoke, he could turn his attention on her defenseless friend.

Get up, Sasha, she told herself sternly, *Lyla needs you!*

Sasha squared her shoulders. Grimacing, she unclipped her seat belt, picked up her sword from the passenger seat, and gingerly climbed out of the truck. Her footsteps were heavy and slow as she warily made her way toward the prone knight, but her mind was racing.

This could be a trap, she thought, staring at his motionless body. She needed to check him, but she had to do it carefully—she would be vulnerable leaning over him, close enough to for him to grab.

"Right. Get up," she ordered the knight, hoping to call his bluff. "Let's finish this."

But the knight still did not move.

Dash it, she thought, staring at his breastplate, willing it to rise and fall, *I'm going to have to check his pulse.*

But if—*when*—she found a pulse, what then? If this was a movie, she would be cheering for the heroine to finish him off. But could she do that? Attack an unconscious man? And if so, how? A blow to the head? Her stomach clenched at the thought. Maybe ... maybe she could just tie him up, or—

"Sasha," Lyla said quietly, staring at the fallen knight. "I think—I think you ... stopped him. Permanently."

"*What?*" Sasha's stomach clenched even harder. "No ... I—I couldn't have. I—"

But now that she was beside the knight's twisted form, she could see that Lyla was right.

She had stopped him.

Permanently.

And all of a sudden, the full magnitude of what she had done hit Sasha like a wrecking ball.

"Oh ... oh, *no*," she said, shaking her head numbly. "I didn't want this. I just—I just wanted him to stop chasing me. I didn't want to stop him *permanently.*"

"You *did* hit him with a steel beast," the blond knight said.

Sasha pressed a hand over her midsection. "I thought he'd swerve. I thought—hang on ... what the *hell?*"

She watched in shock as the elven knight slowly began to hoist himself up. First, creaking to his knees; then rising shakily to his feet like a steel marionette.

"Is he a cyborg?" she whispered in disbelief as he bent unsteadily to retrieve his sword.

"No, an elf," the blond knight said, watching his companion stagger to his feet. "They're notoriously difficult to kill."

The elven knight shook his head, trying to clear the ringing in his ears. Seeing Sasha, he raised his sword.

"Prepare yourself," he commanded, a trifle breathlessly.

"Oh, give me a break!" Sasha groaned.

Nevertheless, she took a firmer grip on her sword, her heart racing.

The elven knight rose to his full height and began to lurch toward her ... straight into the path of the blond knight, who calmly reached out and locked his hand around the other man's ankle.

With a strangled shout, the elven knight tripped and fell to the ground with a spectacular crash.

This was all too much for Sasha. She ran up to the elven knight, turned over her sword, and whacked him solidly in the crotch with the pommel as hard as she could.

"You son of a bitch!" she screeched, hitting him again. "How *dare* you attack a defenseless woman!"

The knight arched up in pain, his visor snapping open.

Sasha hit him again. "Do you get your kicks from picking on unarmed women, you medieval bastard?"

The elf moaned again, his pale eyes leaking tears. "Stop! I beseech you, fair Lady!"

"Would you have stopped trying to kidnap me if I had beseeched you, you asshole?" she yelled.

"Probably not," the blond knight admitted. "Hit him again."

The elven knight looked at him in shock.

"She is right," the blond knight said, "you are an asshole. You attacked a defenseless woman and lost. *This* is your penance. Take it like the knight that you are."

The elven knight nodded slowly. He removed his helmet and placed it on the ground beside him. Then, he laid back on the ground and closed his eyes, his arms crossed over his chest.

"Very well," he said to Sasha, his tone stoic. "Do your worst. I am prepared to take my penance."

Sasha looked down at the knight—at his dented armor, at his bruised and tear-stained face, at the spectacular lump that was beginning to bloom on his forehead—and lowered her sword.

"I'm not going to hit you," she told him.

The elven knight's eyes flew open in surprise. "Why ever not?"

"It's no fun if you ask for it," Lyla said.

"It can be," the blond knight said, winking at Lyla.

Sasha ignored them both. "I *should* hit you," she said, shaking her finger at the elven knight. "If anyone deserves a crotch beating, it's *you*. What you did was wrong and shameful, and I want you to think about that while you're lying down there. Do you understand?"

"Ah … yes?" the elven knight said, thoroughly flummoxed.

"Hear that?" the blond knight asked his companion. "She is being compassionate and merciful on your sorry hide. However …" He looked up at the sky and grimaced. "I doubt that *he* will be so lenient."

Sasha looked up. Where there had been blue sky and fluffy, white clouds not two minutes ago, there was now a looming storm. Lightning, wild and dangerous, began to arc across the sky in silver streaks, dancing between the black cloud banks rolling across the horizon. A fierce, cold wind began to moan across the field, bending the dried cornstalks and the tall, sunburnt grass.

Lyla pushed her flyaway hair back from her face. "What the hell …?"

The elven knight's eyes widened. "No," he whispered.

"*Yes,*" the blond knight laughed. "I am afraid so."

Sasha watched in awe as the old paddock gate beside them began to glow gold. With an eardrum-piercing creak, it slowly swung open of its own accord. The wind tore through the open gate with a high-pitched whine, scattering gold dust across the field and filling the air with the scent of petrichor and rust.

In the eye of this gale stood the Shadow King.

He looked like wrath personified.

His black armor seemed to draw in the light and snuff it out; his shadow cloak seethed in anger, writhing wildly around him in the high breeze. An assortment of beasties that Sasha recognized from *Dastardly and Dank* flanked him on either side, as well as three of the most dangerous and disreputable-looking men Sasha had ever seen: one as small as a child, one as large as a giant, and the third just a touch taller than her own height, sporting a vicious, puckered scar along one side of his face.

Thunder boomed across the clearing, seemingly in greeting. The Shadow King looked up at the sky and nodded in return.

Even in the midst of her adrenaline-induced haze, Sasha had to admit that it was an impressive entrance.

The Shadow King immediately advanced upon the elven knight. "Adies." His voice was barely above a whisper and unsettlingly calm. "Whatever are you doing here?"

The elven knight stuck out his chin. "I am here to take this woman"— he gestured toward Sasha—"to the Summer Kingdom. She is holding open the Portal."

The Shadow King slowly began to circle the knight, his cloak flicking angrily at the prone man. "Truly?" The King's voice was glacier cold. "Then why did it appear as though you were trying to kill her?" The thread of menace underlying his words sent goosebumps down Sasha's arms.

Adies must have felt the same; his skin became even paler. "I was not trying to kill her!"

"It sure felt like it," Sasha retorted angrily.

The elven knight spared a glance at Sasha, reluctant to take his eyes of the irate King. "As I said before, I was trying to knock you out."

The Shadow King raised his hand to his ear. "I appear to have missed that. What did you say, Adies?"

"She was resisting," Adies said, his voice grudgingly louder, "so I intended to knock her out. She must return so that the Portal can close."

"And why is this matter any of your concern?" the Shadow King asked. "The Portal is mine to protect. *I* am the Guardian of the Earther Realm. Are you suggesting that I am unable to perform my duties?"

Even Adies, who was probably sporting multiple concussions, knew that he was on shaky ground. He immediately decided to delegate responsibility.

"We are here on the orders of High King Dresden." Adies looked to the blond knight to back him up, but the blond raised his hand.

"Do not involve me in this," the blond knight said. "I spent almost the entire time vanquished."

The Shadow King stopped circling and crossed his arms. "Well then, as you are now in the Earther Realm—which is my jurisdiction—you will follow my orders. You will return to Otherworld ... alone."

Adies shook his head. "I am sorry, Your Majesty, but I am afraid that I —that is, *we*—"

The blond knight waved him off. "*Vanquished*, remember?"

The elven knight glared at the blond. "I cannot leave without the woman. She must return with us. The High King wants her."

The Shadow King's expression darkened. "Really? And why does the High King want her?"

Adies shook his head again and winced, gingerly touching the bump on his forehead. "He did not say. He only said to take her by all means necessary."

"Oh, Adies." The Shadow King's tone was pitying. "Did you truly think that I would allow you to *take* the True Queen of Between?"

Adies frowned. "The True Queen of Between? But—but she is an Earther woman!"

"She bested the Wasteland," the Shadow King explained, as if to a child. "In a dream."

Adies turned to Sasha in shock. "You ...?"

Sasha lifted her chin. "Damn straight."

His concussions must have kicked in because Adies would not let the matter rest. "She has not been crowned yet," he said desperately. "Her life is still under the jurisdiction of the High King."

The Shadow King shook his head and sighed with patently false regret. "Adies, you know better than that. Between itself has already recognized her as its Queen."

The elven knight's shoulders slumped in defeat.

In a graceful move, the Shadow King crouched down beside the fallen knight. "Really, Adies," he whispered into the knight's ear, "did you think that you could raise your sword on a True Queen of Between and be allowed to keep your wretched life?"

The elven knight's eyes widened in horror. "Forgive me, Your Majesties

—I was not informed. I would *never* have—"

Abruptly, the Shadow King stood and raised his hand. Lightning arched across the field and came within feet of the knight.

Adies jerked back, horrified at the genuine prospect of being baked alive in his armor like a casserole in a pressure cooker.

The Shadow King reached down and, with no discernible effort, dragged the knight to his feet.

"Felzik," he ordered quietly.

The shortest of the three evil-looking men bowed to the King, and then led the others to Adies's side. Although he was small in stature, he was incredibly muscled—like a tiny, angry, bear.

He took Adies's arm and looked at the Shadow King in gleeful anticipation. "Your orders, Majesty?"

"Swamp him."

"No!" Adies cried, trying to free himself from Felzik's grasp. "You have no right! I am a knight of the High King's Fold! I have royal blood!"

"And now you're goin' for a swim in the swamp," Felzik said, tightening his grip on the knight. He turned to the King. "Which swamp, Majesty? Swamp of Perpetual Suffering, the Swamp of Eternal Angst, the Swamp of Festering Boils, the Swamp of Chronic Crotch Irritation, or that new one that came up last week that we haven't named yet?"

At the mention of each swamp, Adies became progressively paler.

The Shadow King shrugged negligently. "Your choice, Felzik."

Felzik smiled—a smile made up of sharp points and large gaps and lots of malice. "Then I suggest 'all of the above.' A tour of Between's Wetlands, so to speak."

"What?!" Adies yelled. "No! I demand to see the High King."

"All in good time," Felzik said placatingly.

The three evil-looking men bowed to Sasha.

Sasha stared back at them, puzzled. "Ah ... hi?"

The Shadow King cleared his throat. "You are the True Queen, remember?"

He mimed bowing his head.

"Oh," she said faintly.

Turning to the men, she bowed her head in return.

The three men gave her equally blood-chilling smiles and, with an efficiency that Sasha could not help but admire, dragged the struggling Adies back through the paddock gate. As soon as they passed the threshold, they promptly disappeared.

"Well," the blond knight said. "That was exciting." He turned to the Shadow King. "You certainly took your time."

The Shadow King rolled his eyes. "I could not come until I was Summoned. Then, the Portal would not allow us through … possibly because it was already open." He glared at the knight, "Besides, I foolishly believed that you had the situation under control. It seems that my faith in your abilities was grossly overrated."

"I had everything under control," the knight protested. "I played my part perfectly."

"Hang on, hang on." Sasha marched over to the blond knight. "You were on *our* side?"

Everyone nodded. Literally everyone.

"You knew about this?" Sasha asked Lyla.

Lyla held up her hands. "Hey, I only found out after you ran off to get the truck."

Sasha began to hyperventilate. She turned to the knight. "You were on *our* side, and yet you let me fight that—that—and I could have been *killed*. And then you let me hit him with the truck—and—and … *argh!*" She raised her sword, pommel up.

"Vacate the knight, Lyla," she bit out and stalked toward his crotch.

Lyla looked down at the knight in question. "Ah … Sasha—"

The blond knight's eyes widened. "Please stop, Your Majesty! I beseech you!" He held up his hands in surrender.

Sasha felt herself being pulled backward against a breastplate; a strong arm wrapped around her waist.

"Just let me hit him once," she pleaded with the Shadow King.

Thunder boomed in agreement.

She felt something graze her ear and, shocked, realized that it must be the King's lips.

"Although I have often shared your desire to castrate him," he whispered, his warm breath fanning across her wind-chilled skin, "he is, regrettably, correct."

Sasha threw the sword down in disgust.

Seeing that Sasha was no longer going to maim the knight, the Shadow King released her.

The knight, however, was taking no chances—he kept his hands up.

"It is true," he confessed to Sasha. "I gave Adies the enchanted sword that could not be used to harm you—just as Lorn and I had planned. And I had his armor weighed down, which was my own initiative. I was also ready to spring into action as soon as matters became dire. I had the situation well in hand."

The Shadow King looked over at Sasha—who was bent over, breathing heavily—and then raised an eyebrow at the sight of Lyla, who was still sitting across the knight's midsection.

"Clearly," he said dryly. He turned to Sasha. "So much so, that Her Majesty was forced to vanquish Adies with a vehicle."

Sasha stood upright. "You saw that?"

The Shadow King nodded.

"Did you also catch the bit where she tried to pulverize his crotch with my sword?" the blond knight added gleefully, lowering his hands.

The King winced. "I did. It was painful to watch, even from the other side of the Portal. Although it is Adies's fault for wearing elven armor."

"What do you mean?" Lyla asked, zipping her jacket against the rising wind.

"Elves are so chivalrous, that they believe no one would resort to attacking the groin of their opponent," the blond knight explained. "They view it as unseemly. Hence, their armor has a weak spot in that area."

"They need to take part in more tavern brawls in Between," the Shadow King said. He seemed to note Lyla's confused expression. "That is the first place Betweeners aim."

"I'll keep that in mind if I ever start a tavern brawl in Between," Lyla said.

"Don't get any ideas," Sasha muttered, pacing back and forth, still thrumming with adrenaline.

The King turned to the blond knight. "Then again, if you had been doing your job, Her Majesty would not have needed to resort to testicular violence."

"You wound me, my friend," the knight said, sighing sadly. "You and I both know that I could not do anything too obvious, otherwise I would lose the High King's trust. I was pursuing a long-term strategy. Besides, I did hamper Adies as much as I was able."

"It's true," Lyla confirmed, raising her voice over another round of thunder. "He managed to concuss that Adies fellow and trip him. He was helpful in a subtle, almost unhelpful way."

The blond knight smiled broadly at Lyla. "See? Lady Lyla defends me."

"I stand corrected," the King said. "You were only *mostly* useless, lying on the ground and acting like a glorified bench." He turned toward Lyla. "Hmm, so *this* is the notorious Lyla. I have heard much about you."

Lyla studied the Shadow King. "Aren't you going to say that it's a pleasure to meet me?"

"That is yet to be determined."

Lyla gave a surprised laugh. "Feeling is mutual, buddy."

"Do forgive my surly friend," the blond knight said to Lyla. He pushed his windblown fringe from his eyes and gave the King a reproachful look. "He was far more agreeable prior to his ascension to the throne—"

"We both know that's a lie," the King interrupted.

"—and I have high hopes that his manners will return once he is exposed to *fairer* company." The knight gestured graciously to Lyla and Sasha.

Lyla shrugged. "That's doubtful. We're not particularly nice."

"He'll probably get worse," Sasha added, still pacing restlessly. She felt as though the electricity in the air had somehow seeped into her nerve endings.

"That would be difficult," the King mused, "but I will attempt to meet your expectations." He gave Lyla a reluctant smile. "Very well. If you are prepared to tolerate my lamentable lack of civility, I will overlook your propensity to interfere in situations that are none of your concern."

Lyla appeared to think that over, then nodded. "Fine. And I will overlook your dismal manners and lack of charm—as long as you are willing to overlook all my schemes to ensure that Sasha never has to set foot in your diseased little kingdom."

The Shadow King tapped his lip with his forefinger thoughtfully. He then bowed his head. "Done."

Lyla mirrored his gesture. "Excellent."

The two exchanged eerily similar smiles.

As he watched the growing camaraderie between Lyla and the King, the blond knight's smile faded.

"A truce between you, then?" he suggested blandly.

"For now," the King said

"For *today*," Lyla corrected.

The knight's smile returned.

"Are you comfortable there, Ash?" the King asked the knight.

"Perfectly comfortable." He pointed to Lyla's legs. "Did you know that these are called 'yoga pants'? Are they not wonderful?"

"Positively miraculous," the King said dryly. He approached Sasha, who was still pacing. "And you—are you having fun?"

Sasha went to rub her eyes and stopped when she noticed that her hands were shaking. "No. Hitting a kidnapper with a chain, or a sword, or a truck is *not fun*." She looked up at the roiling clouds. "None of this has been fun at all."

"Not even a little?" Ash asked. "What about the bit where you tried to castrate him?"

"Ignore him," the Shadow King said dismissively. "He has perverse tastes."

"That bit *did* look like fun," Lyla added.

"So does she," Sasha said, then shivered.

The Shadow King noticed her shivering. "You are freezing. My apologies."

He raised his hand, pointing his palm toward the sky. Abruptly, the lightning ceased, and the wind started to drop. Before long, the sun began to break out of the clouds, the good weather restored.

Lyla looked up at the sky, wide-eyed. "Neat trick."

The King staggered backward a few steps before managing to right himself.

"Yes," he gasped. "Quite the *trick*."

"Be careful, my friend," Ash said, frowning. "You are not in Between."

"Thank you for the geography lesson," the Shadow King said, rolling his shoulders.

Ash crooked his finger, beckoning Lyla and Sasha closer.

"You should not use the word 'trick' when speaking to a sorcerer," he whispered conspiratorially. "Only magicians use tricks and sleight-of-hand. All magic folk hate being compared to street magicians; it is an insult of the highest order."

"Good to know," Sasha bit out, still peeved with the knight.

"An insult of the highest order, huh?" Lyla whispered back. "I'll keep that in mind." She looked over at the King, her smile devious.

The King, however, was oblivious to Lyla's devious smiles; he was too busy staring at the abandoned chain. He pinched the bridge of his nose and sighed.

"This"—he tapped the chain with the toe of his boot—"was a terrible plan. It would never have worked."

"We know," the women said simultaneously.

"We were in the midst of an Ordeal," Lyla explained. "Our brains were in shock."

"You were lucky that I was looking for an opportunity to be vanquished," Ash said.

The King waved his hand at the chain. It rose obediently off the ground and flew across the field, landing back in its original place.

"Speaking of which ..." The King held his hand out to Lyla. "If you would be so kind as to release Ash from your yoga pants."

Lyla, much to Ash's evident dismay, gave Lorn a bright smile. She took his hand and allowed him to help her to rise.

"Now me?" Ash asked, fluttering his eyelashes and holding out his hand.

The King simply raised an eyebrow.

"Chivalry truly is dead," Ash muttered. In a ridiculously easy motion, he flipped back onto his feet.

Sasha groaned. "It really was a terrible plan—he wasn't a tortoise at all."

The King glanced at Ash, as if checking his level of tortoise-ness. "I have no idea what you are talking about. Simply agree never to try it again."

"Never again," Sasha agreed.

"I was right!" Lyla said to Ash. "You weren't half as vanquished as you made out."

Ash smiled brightly in return ... until he caught Sasha's glare. "Let us make peace, Your Majesty," he said, offering his hand to Sasha.

Sasha stared at it for a long moment and then exhaled. "Fine. I guess you didn't try to kill me, which was nice of you."

She took his hand. With a well-practiced motion, Ash turned her hand over and touched his lips briefly to her fingertips, giving her a wink above her knuckles. To her surprise, Sasha found herself grinning back.

The Shadow King rolled his eyes. "If you have finished trying to beguile every woman in your vicinity, I do believe it is your time to leave, Ash."

Ash grimaced and released Sasha's hand. "As you anticipated, there is more afoot here than what appears on the surface. Adies was acting on orders very different from my own. He wanted your amulet."

"Indeed," the King said, his expression pensive. "In retrospect, I should have anticipated this development."

"We need to discuss this further."

The King nodded. "There are always plans within plans whenever the Summer Palace is involved."

Ash looked uncharacteristically solemn. "I must say, I am not relishing my visit to the High King. He is not going to be easy to fool. And when Adies returns from his tour of the Wetlands, he will reveal my part in this ..."

The King waved off his concerns. "Given what I have seen of others who have been given the 'tour,' Adies will not remember much about preceding events. He will simply be happy to be home."

"It could not happen to a nicer fellow." Ash grinned and turned to Lyla. "My Lady." He took her hand and brushed his lips across the top of her knuckles, his lips lingering on her skin. "It was an honor to act as your bench."

For a long moment, Lyla stilled, her gaze locked on the knight. Then she shrugged with admirable nonchalance. "You weren't particularly comfortable."

"You wound me," he said with false distress, a twinkle in his eye. "Nevertheless, my life has changed irrevocably—and entirely for the better—for meeting you and your glorious yoga pants." He bowed his head over her hand.

"Yes, yes—I am sure the pleasure was all yours," the Shadow King said impatiently. "Go through the gateway—it will not stay open much longer."

Ash reluctantly released Lyla's hand and gave the King a mocking bow before retrieving his sword.

"Farewell!" he called out, his sword aloft, and disappeared through the paddock gate.

Lyla sighed longingly.

Both Sasha and the King turned to her in surprise.

"What? He looks good from behind." Lyla turned to the King, eyebrow arched. "Don't you think?"

"Dreamy," the King said, deadpan.

Sasha looked at the dented mail truck, the crushed grass where Ash had been lying, and the open gateway.

"We need to talk," she said to the King. "About all of this."

The King also glanced at the mail truck. "I quite agree."

"So do I," Lyla said. She looked back toward the village. "I'm going to stall Mr. Eldridge. You two chat for as long as you like, but it's probably a bad idea to be standing next to a stolen vehicle."

She turned to the Shadow King, eyes fierce, hands on her hips. "I don't need to remind you that Sasha asked for this time in Old Middleton as part of her first boon—and that kidnapping her would be a violation of that boon, do I?"

The King inclined his head. "Many thanks for the reminder; I had forgotten completely. I would have kidnapped Her Majesty and dragged her back to Between, kicking and screaming, without your timely words. How lucky we are that you are here!"

Lyla's eyes narrowed. "Or I could forget about distracting Mr. Eldridge and try my hand at using the mail truck instead?"

The King shrugged. "Being hit by a mail truck would not be the worst part of my day so far. It may even prove to be refreshing."

"This is all very entertaining," Sasha interrupted. "But we *are* at a crime scene." She turned to Lyla and squeezed her arm. "I'll be fine. You go and distract Mr. Eldridge, and I'll meet you at the boarding house."

"Fine," Lyla said reluctantly. "Don't be too long."

Lyla directed a final suspicious glare at the Shadow King—who bowed mockingly in return—and headed back toward the village.

Sasha wished she could run off, too. But instead, she was standing in a field with a king, a stolen mail truck, and an inter-realm gateway disguised as a paddock gate.

Her high school guidance advisor had not prepared her for any of this.

"So," the King said, trailing his hand along the paddock gate, "I take it that today's adventure has changed your mind about staying in Old Middleton?"

He looked rather smug, Sasha thought. *Too* smug.

Given her day so far, Sasha was having none of it. "You told me that I had six days before the High King found me—"

"I was being uncharacteristically optimistic," the King interrupted.

"*Six days*, so why did I only get two? How did he find me so quickly? He knew all about me: my name, where I lived, the fact that I had a companion. *How did he know?*"

At that, the King was silent.

Sasha's eyes widened. "What did you do?"

The Shadow King's jaw clenched. "I was forced to announce our betrothal at the Gathering of the Summer Alliance Monarchs of the Lower Kingdoms. It was necessary to ensure your safety—"

"Well, *that* worked well!"

"You are alive, are you not? If I had not informed the High King of our betrothal and made it clear that you were under my protection, there is a good chance that the High King would have killed you outright. Moreover, others may have tried to kidnap you—even if just for sport."

"Kidnapping is a *sport* where you're from? Great! Otherworld needs to hurry up and invent baseball." Sasha ran a shaking hand through her hair. "So, this entire situation is basically all your fault."

"*All* my fault?"

"Yes!" she cried, finally at her limit. "All your fault!"

A vein at the King's temple began to throb. "I will gladly take my share of responsibility for the events of today, but am I really to be blamed for everything? For besting the Nightmares?" Sasha opened her mouth to argue. "For willfully choosing to keep the Portal open for all sorts of beasts and kidnappers to come wandering in—something that I expressly warned you about?" Sasha's mouth closed, and her expression turned shifty. "*Marvelous.* This is *all* my fault. You are needlessly blaming me for all your misfortunes. My, my—I feel married already."

"You're right," Sasha said, horror-struck. "We're arguing like a married couple, and it's only been ... what? Two days since I crossed the Wasteland?"

"Two days," the King affirmed. "And here I had hoped that it would take longer before we bickered in this manner. Perhaps a decade or two."

"Or never."

"Or never," he agreed.

"Let's just never do that again, okay?"

"Never, ever again."

There was a rare moment of accord between the two.

Surprisingly, it was the King who spoke first. "Your anger is completely justified."

Sasha stared at him, surprised.

"Although kidnappings and assassination attempts are regrettably common in Otherworld—and are mostly perpetrated by Betweeners—I doubt they have a place in your day to day life." He looked over at the mail truck and shook his head. "You were terrified during this ordeal, and I apologize for all you have endured."

"Thanks," she muttered, trying to hold onto her anger, "but Adies should be the one apologizing, not you."

"Unfortunately, Adies is otherwise occupied right now. At this moment, I doubt he is capable of saying much more than, 'No, please no!' Or, 'I beg you, not another swamp.'"

Sasha's lips twitched.

The King noticed the lip twitch. He looked around the field, his hand again trailing along the paddock door. "I understand why you wish to stay here as long as possible—please, believe me when I say that. And I apologize if my actions brought you to the High King's notice sooner than we had anticipated. I truly felt there was no other way to keep you safe."

Sasha's shoulders slumped. She was suddenly exhausted by the whole matter. "You did what you thought was right." Her eyes narrowed. "Even so, I want another boon; this one was a complete dud."

"I would be amenable to renegotiating the terms of this boon once you are in Between. Shall we depart?" He held out his hand to her.

"Nice try," she scoffed. "I still have four more days. Then again …" She turned toward the mail truck and pointed to the knight-sized dent in the front of the vehicle. "It's doubtful that I'll be going anywhere except jail."

The Shadow King said nothing. Instead, he approached the front of the mail truck, knelt on the grass—his shadow cloak billowing out around him—and placed his hands on the hood.

Before Sasha's disbelieving eyes, the damage began to reverse. With a high-pitched screech, the metal started to unbuckle, plumping out the dents and gouges. With a wave of the Shadow King's hand, fragments of paint and glass flew upward from the grass in a glittery trail and returned to their original places. Even the dirt on the hood disappeared.

The mail truck looked brand new. It even preened a little in the sun.

Sasha crossed over to the vehicle and ran her hand tentatively over the hood. "Wow. Now *that* is a useful skill! Can you fix the dent on my fender?"

She turned back to the King and noticed, with a start, that he had fallen back on his heels. His face was ashen, his hands shaking.

"Hey." She quickly crouched down onto the ground beside him. "Are you okay?"

He took an unsteady breath. "I keep forgetting that we are not in Between … and that I have already performed considerable magic today."

He grabbed hold of the hood of the truck, and unsteadily pulled himself to his feet.

Sasha ducked her head under his arm and helped to support his weight until he was completely upright.

"Thank you," he said quietly, pulling away from her.

Sasha pulled him right back. "Just let me help you. Let's sit on that log over there, okay?"

The King nodded, and together they walked the short distance to an old, fallen log.

Sasha made sure that he was settled before removing her arm from around his shoulders. They sat together in awkward silence, the King breathing heavily.

"So … performing magic is easier in Between?" Sasha asked, scrambling for something to say.

The King gave Sasha a half-smile as if he knew what she was trying to do. "I have become lazy. Between makes it very easy to do impossible things —sometimes many impossible things simultaneously. Performing magic in a place where there is less at hand feels … foreign and exhausting."

Sasha looked over at the truck. "I can't imagine what it would be like to perform magic." She smiled at the very idea of it—of her with magical powers. "It must be an incredible feeling to be able to control the weather." She looked up at the pale blue sky, the storm long gone. "Or to move objects with a wave of your hand ..." She waved her hand about in a fancy manner. "Or to perform spontaneous automotive repairs." She turned to the King, her smile giddy. "It's unbelievable and *wonderful*, the things you can do ..."

The King looked at her in surprise, but she could tell that he was pleased. "It *is* wonderful, but it requires discipline. If you do not develop self-control in the beginning, you will use up too much of your reserves and either die of magical depletion—a form of exhaustion—or implode."

Sasha blinked. "Are there many sorcerers?"

"No."

"Is that why? Exhaustion and imploding?"

"Those are two excellent reasons."

Sasha looked at the King's pale face in alarm. "You're not going to implode now, are you?"

Unconsciously, she leaned away from him.

He noticed and smirked. "No. You are not getting out of our betrothal that easily."

Sasha made a show of leaning toward him. "Don't be cheeky. You should keep in mind that I still have a mail truck and I won't hesitate to use it. Would you like something to eat?"

The King appeared to consider the idea. "It may help."

Sasha unzipped her pocket and reached inside. "Here," she said, handing him an energy bar.

The King peered at the silver packaging curiously. "Does the shininess enhance the flavor?"

"Oh, no! You're supposed to remove the wrapper."

She carefully unwrapped the bar and handed it back to the King.

The King gave her a sideways glance and gingerly bit off a small piece.

"What do you think?" she asked, smiling at his caution.

The King's face crumpled in disgust. "Agh, what is that horrific flavor? It tastes of dirt and swamp moss and *loathing*." He struggled to swallow the mouthful. "So much loathing ..."

Sasha frowned. "It's supposed to taste like a chocolate cookie."

The King stared at her in disbelief. "In which kingdom of Hell is that chocolate? I believe our swamps have a better flavor than this demonic morsel."

"Well, it's not supposed to be delicious," she said defensively. "It's supposed to be healthy and give you energy after exercise."

"All this is giving me is the desire to scrape my tongue with an axe."

"It's not that bad, you big baby."

Sasha took back the bar and bit off a healthy mouthful. "See?" she said, between chews. "Not that bad."

"Clearly, you have a cast iron constitution. Which, granted, will be an asset in Between and will probably serve as the cornerstone of your survival." The King watched her take another bite and shook his head in disbelief. "If I had not seen you eat it with my own eyes, I would have thought that this was an assassination attempt."

"Assassination via energy bar isn't all that sophisticated. I'm sure I could do better than that."

"I am sure you could. I was merely suggesting—" The King stopped abruptly and looked down at his hands in shock.

"What's wrong?" she asked, worried that she had inadvertently poisoned him with Earther Realm fitness food.

The King stared at the energy bar, clearly puzzled. "Nothing at all. Quite the opposite. May I have another bite?"

"Oh, so now you *want* the energy bar." Sasha handed it over nonetheless and watched as, grimacing, the King took another bite.

After a moment or so, he flexed his hands and laughed. "How extraordinary! They *do* give you energy. My magic is surging back."

"See?" she said with a smug grin. "Not so terrible."

"Still terrible, but the consequences make it bearable." The King handed her the remains of the bar.

"You can keep it," she said. "I have more."

He shuddered. "I will accept ... even though I am bound to regret it. Many thanks." He placed the bar inside a pouch on his hip and eased himself off the log. "I must see to Adies. Are you sure you are well?"

Sasha blinked. "I feel fine now."

And she did. In fact, she felt better than fine—she felt exhilarated.

That must have been a particularly potent energy bar, she thought.

The King stood before her and gave her an odd look. To Sasha, it appeared to be one of reluctant admiration.

Then again, she thought, *that's unlikely. He's probably just having problems digesting the energy bar.*

"For what it's worth," he began, "you handled the situation in a manner that was both brilliant and violent."

"Ah ... thanks?"

"And you may not want to hear it, but in a manner very befitting of Between."

"That's *terrifying*." Sasha laughed shakily, more from horror than humor. "This is the first time I've ever deliberately hit anything with a mail truck, and it isn't something that I ever want to do again."

"Well, there are no mail trucks in Between. The equivalent would be hitting someone with a cart or perhaps some oxen."

"I'll keep that in mind."

The King inclined his head. "I shall warn the oxen."

Sasha wanted to make light of the matter but found that she couldn't. "I don't want to hurt people," she said quietly. "When I saw him—Adies—lying there ..." She pressed a hand to her midsection, her gut clenching. "When I thought that I had stopped him *permanently* ..."

"He would have hurt you," the King answered, just as quietly. "There is no harm in defending oneself."

"Still ..." Sasha stopped, the memory of what had happened—what had almost happened—still far too raw. "I'm glad that he's in a swamp right now and not lying on the ground."

The King's cloak reached out and tentatively touched Sasha's calf, mindful of her injury.

"Thanks," she said fondly, reaching down to stroke the shadows.

The King rolled his eyes. "It is definitely time to leave."

"Right," she said, standing.

"Take care," he said and stepped toward her.

At that moment, Sasha had the distinct impression that the King was about to hug her. Which was ludicrous—the Shadow King was possibly the most un-huggable person Sasha had ever met. He was cold and aloof and covered in steel, and none of those were features of a good hugger.

But, given her day so far, Sasha decided that a hug was exactly what she needed—even if it was bound to be as enjoyable as hugging a sarcastic tin of tuna.

She leaned toward him.

Abruptly, the King caught himself and stepped back, muttering a gruff, "Farewell." He turned and began to stride back toward the gate.

"Were you going to hug me?" Sasha blurted out.

The Shadow King paused.

"Not at all," he said, over his shoulder. "Hugging is for peasants."

Sasha grinned, despite herself. "Would you like *me* to hug *you?*"

The King's shoulders stiffened. He turned toward her. "If I were to make a list of the most undesirable events that could befall me during my lifetime, 'hugging' would fall somewhere between 'being crushed to death between two trolls' and 'crotch rot.' "

"So that's a maybe?" Sasha asked, her grin growing.

The King gave her a look that could have frozen lava.

"A soft maybe?" she said, enjoying herself immensely.

"It would be a *no* hard enough to break diamonds."

"Huh, that sounds pretty hard." Sasha could not stop grinning "Well, it's your loss. I'm a fantastic hugger."

The King considered her for long a moment. "Your arms certainly appear strong enough to constrain an adult against their will for a prolonged period."

"Was that a compliment?" Sasha noted the smile curled around the edges of his mouth. "I'm taking it as a compliment."

Before Sasha could react, the King stepped toward her until they were only a handbreadth apart. He stared at her intently for a long moment, his eyes as green as the summer meadow in her dreams, before he slowly—ever so slowly—reached out and grasped the amulet around her neck, turning it over so that it was facing the right way. Sasha could feel the heat of his fingertips through the thin fabric of her jacket and was surprised when she felt a catch in her throat—a gasp of surprise and something more carnal— at the contact. The amulet glowed silver at his touch, the metal warm against her skin.

Sasha looked up at him in astonishment. His expression was pensive, as if she was a puzzle with too many angles and no corner pieces.

"It was a compliment," he confirmed, his fingertips lingering against the surface of the amulet.

"That's the correct response," Sasha said quietly.

For a moment, they simply stared at one another, something gentle— something unexpected—holding them in place.

That is, until the King visibly caught himself.

"Farewell," he said blandly. He released the amulet and strode back toward the gate.

"Bye," she called after him, somewhat flummoxed.

The Shadow King raised his hand in farewell. Sasha watched as the light from Between gathered around him like a halo and then disappeared as he closed the gateway behind him, leaving her alone in the field with a rusty, old paddock gate and a stolen mail truck.

With a sigh, she made her way back to the boarding house, pondering the mysteries of knights and gateways, kings and hugs.

~

To say that the witches were displeased that Sasha had almost been kidnapped on their watch would have been a spectacular understatement. They called an emergency meeting in Miss Adeline's rose drawing room that evening. After Lyla's lurid retelling of events—where she used various porcelain figurines to stage a reenactment of Sasha's adventures; a drunk shepherd statue played the role of the Shadow King—Martha silently put away the teacups and brought out the hard liquor.

The witches all gulped down their first cocktail and beckoned Martha for a second ... and then a third.

It was definitely a three-cocktail dilemma.

"Knights! In *Old Middleton*," Felicia gasped, pressing her hand dramatically to her chest. "Who would have thought?" She grinned slyly at Sasha and Lyla. "I bet it was quite a sight—those big, strapping men encased in armor."

Sasha stared at her incredulously. "Yes, it was ... in the split second before they tried to kidnap me."

"Meh, knights are overrated." Mrs. Landshome said. "It's like trying to fondle a tin can. I like my men accessible and ready for action."

"I'll drink to that," Lyla said, saluting the old woman with her gin and tonic.

"It was a good thing that the Shadow King came to your rescue, dear," the Headmistress said to Sasha.

Lyla almost snorted her sip of cocktail. "Sasha rescued herself. The Shadow King just swooped in at the end and took all the glory. Typical, really."

"Yes, dear! You were so brave," Violet said, patting Sasha on the hand.

"Not everyone would have the cold-blooded conviction to hit a knight with a mail truck," Daisy said admiringly. "Or crush his crotch with a sword ..."

"Repeatedly!" the twins finished in gleeful unison.

Sasha smiled gratefully at them. "Thanks. It could have all gone terribly wrong. I'm glad that the King appeared ... eventually ... and that his friend, Ash, had been there to help."

"Hmm, do any of you know who this Ash fellow is?" Lyla asked, a little too casually.

"Ash, Ash ... there is something about that name that rings a bell ..." the Headmistress muttered to herself.

Esther shook her head. "There are lots of knights in the High King's employ. Each kingdom sends its best and brightest to the High King as a tribute. This knight could be from anywhere in Otherworld."

"Dash it," Lyla muttered, and swallowed the rest of her drink.

"Did he have a nice chest too, dear?" Daisy asked.

Lyla frowned. "I couldn't tell—it was under all that steel. He did have a really nice neck."

"See?" Mrs. Landshome crowed. "What did I tell you? Knights—they're just a big tease."

Sasha patted her friend consolingly on the shoulder. "He seemed to be pretty friendly with the Shadow King. Why don't I find out more about this Ash fellow during my next dream?"

"You are the *best*," Lyla said, slinging her arm around Sasha's shoulders a little sloppily. She smiled broadly at the witches. "Actually, you're all *really* nice. I'm *so* glad to be here, on this chair, drinking with all you fine women."

"We're happy to be drinking with you, too, Lyla," Esther said with a smile.

Sasha rolled her eyes and took away Lyla's glass. "I think you need a sandwich."

Lyla sighed mournfully. "I need a lot of things. A sandwich, a blond knight with a nice neck ..."

Martha stood up. "I'd better get some snacks before we all get loose-lipped." She shuffled out of the room, Miss Adeline following close behind.

"Regardless of whom this helpful knight may be, we need to step up our plans," Esther said. "One of us needs to be around Sasha at all times. I also think that you should return to work tomorrow, Sasha. There are enough of us there to keep you safe."

"I'm more than happy to return to work," Sasha said, "just as long as the knights don't follow me. I don't want the children to be in any danger."

Esther's expression softened. "Don't you worry, we'll keep them out. Besides, I doubt the High King will be able to send anyone for a while."

"But how did they come here?" Sasha asked. "I thought the Portal was being guarded at all times."

"They didn't come through the Portal," Felicia said. "I was on guard and I would've noticed two gorgeous men encased in steel sauntering through." She raised her glass, letting the rim linger against her lips. "I would have been more than happy to detain them."

"Attagirl," Mrs. Landshome said, saluting her with her glass.

"Then how did they get in?" Sasha persisted. She turned to Esther. "I thought that the Portal was the only way to get to Otherworld from our world." She remembered the Shadow King entering Old Middleton through the Portal, his dark figure backlit by golden light. "Or vice-versa."

Esther shook her head. "The Portal was not meant for travel between our realms *per se*; it was created as a way to bring Dreamers to Between. For non-Dreamers, travel between our world and Otherworld requires a *gateway*."

"Do be careful." The Headmistress wrung her hands. "Given our Vows, there are limits to what you can tell her. And this time, there is no Truth Elixir to soften the consequences …"

Esther nodded, her expression pensive. "A timely warning, Penelope. We'll take this one word at a time."

She turned to Sasha and clasped her hands together over her lap. "Long, long ago," she began carefully, "when magic was far more prevalent in our world, travel between the realms was common … well, for those who had magic. Passages that linked our realm to Otherworld were scattered across every country and continent."

"Like subway stations," Mrs. Landshome piped up. She winked at Lyla. "I thought you New Yorkers would appreciate the reference."

Lyla grinned at the old woman. "Thanks for keeping this at my level."

"Each passage," Esther continued, "was marked by a gateway. Sometimes, the gateway took the form of a door."

"Like the oak door in the Portal Chamber?" Sasha asked.

"Yes, exactly! But, more often than not, it was an arch or a gate without a fence. After the—" Esther paused and grimaced. "Over time," she amended, "many of the gateways were destroyed—"

"Why?" Sasha interrupted. She found herself leaning closer to the coven leader, the mystery making her heart pound.

"And by who?" Lyla asked, swaying a little in her seat. "Who was busting up gateways?"

Esther tried to speak but stopped, her mouth twisting. Beads of perspiration appeared on her forehead. With a frustrated sigh, she took a napkin from the table. "I can't say." She dabbed at the moisture along her hairline, her face flushed. "All you need to know is that one by one, the gateways in our realm were either destroyed or became dormant. They no longer allowed us to enter Otherworld."

"But … you can open the Portal—" Lyla began.

"No, Lyla," the Headmistress said. "We are just the Guardians. Only the Shadow King can open the Portal. And only the Dreamer can enter it freely—we cannot."

Esther nodded. "We were taught that the Portal was one of the only active passages left in our realm. But after the events of the day…" She hesitated, her fingers straying to her pearls. "If the knights didn't come through the Portal, then it stands to reason that they entered the village through the Middleton Gateway."

"But the Middleton Gateway hasn't opened for over a century!" Rosa said. "Not since the wizards disap—"

"*Rosa*," Esther interrupted, warningly. She glanced over at Sasha and Lyla. "We do not need to delve into ancient history."

Rosa also glanced at Sasha and Lyla.

Sasha and Lyla glanced at each other.

(There was a lot of glancing.)

"Technically," the Headmistress said, interrupting the glance-off, "the Middleton Gateway hasn't opened from *this* side in over a century. There's nothing to say that it couldn't be opened from the Otherworld side."

"Opening it from the Otherworld side would have taken an enormous amount of power," Rosa said. "They would have to be fae … or have some sort of talisman to generate enough power to go through gateways."

"But *did* they come through the Middleton Gateway?" Felicia asked. "Think about it: if the knights came through the Gateway, then they could've walked up Main Street straight to the boarding house. Instead, the ladies found them in a field outside of the village."

"They were pretty lost," Sasha mused. "Maybe they just wandered off in the wrong direction?"

"And walked straight through the village without being seen?" Felicia asked. She shook her head, her red curls bouncing. "Something isn't right here."

The other witches exchanged uneasy glances.

"We're supposed to be guarding the passages from Otherworld," the Headmistress said tersely. "For years, we thought this meant the Portal, but it's clear that there must be another way into Old Middleton. Whether it's the Middleton Gateway or not, we need to find this other entrance. We aren't doing our job if two knights can just waltz past us."

Esther nodded. "Agreed. In the meantime, we'll have to appoint someone to guard the Gateway. Maybe it isn't as dormant as we thought."

"And we also need to know who opened a passage between Otherworld and Between for the High King. They must be enormously powerful!" Rosa said.

"Could it be the King's Left Hand?" Daisy asked.

Esther shrugged. "It's the most logical option. The Left Hand is the keeper of a wand that opens gateways. It could also have been the High Queen. She's fae and quite powerful, by all accounts."

"There are stories that fae royalty have the power to create passages," the Headmistress mused. "Small ones within their world and larger ones between realms." She turned to Esther. "It *could* be the High Queen."

The coven leader tugged on her pearls, clearly frustrated. "There are too many mysteries. We really need to get up to speed with what's happening in Otherworld. Technically, our duties only extend to guarding the Portal, but it's becoming increasingly clear that the events of Otherworld impact our realm in ways that we did not foresee." She glanced at Sasha. "Particularly now."

The Headmistress shifted in her seat, her shoulders rigid. "I have said for *years* that we need to spend more resources on acquiring texts for the Archives and look at the predicament we're in now! We don't have nearly enough information about gateways, or about crossing between the two realms—"

"Bah, *books.*" Mrs. Landshome snorted. "You can't find out what's going on *right now* in Otherworld by reading a moldy book that's older than me! What we need are scouts in the field, gathering information."

The Headmistress's eyes narrowed. "What you don't understand, Gussie—"

"Ladies," Esther interrupted, "this is a discussion for our next meeting. Right now, we have bigger things to worry about."

Sasha finished her drink and placed her glass carefully on the coffee table. She'd had three cocktails with only an energy bar to line her stomach, so she was feeling a pleasant buzz rather than the growing horror that the situation deserved.

"So," she enunciated, carefully, "is there a plan?"

Esther smiled apologetically. "Not as such. Just stay alert and take one day at a time."

"I'll drink to that," Mrs. Landshome said. "I propose a toast." She raised her glass, sloshing liquor over the rim. "To keeping everyone alive and un-kidnapped." She turned to Lyla and gave her a sly wink. "And to getting knights out of their armor."

"Here, here," Lyla said, refilling her glass.

Esther gave Mrs. Landshome an exasperated look but raised her glass nevertheless. "Alive and un-kidnapped."

Here, here, Sasha thought.

~

"Do you ever get the feeling that the witches aren't very good at their job?" Lyla asked tipsily as they prepared for bed.

Sasha paused mid-way through brushing her hair with her brand new hairbrush. She had never found the other one. "What do you mean?"

"I mean, they don't know how the knights came through the Middleton Gateway without being seen, or who activated it for them, or if they even came through it at all." Lyla pulled off her shoes and fell back against her pillows, eyelids already drooping. "And what *did* happen to Ol' Parsnip Head? That's a question for the ages ..."

"Maybe the witches have become a little complacent over the years," Sasha said, feeling a surge of loyalty toward the coven. "It doesn't sound as though a lot happens on this side of the Portal ... well, not until recently. And they all have day jobs. How much time can they devote to this whole witch business anyway?"

"*Maybe*," Lyla said, yawning. "But did you see the way that Esther shut down Rosa when she started talking about the Middleton Gateway? They're hiding something from us."

"They're probably hiding a lot from us. There's probably plenty of secret witch business that we'll never know." Sasha placed her brush back on her nightstand. "Though ... Rosa was talking about wizards, wasn't she? The Shadow King mentioned something about wizards on the night that the coven opened the Portal. You don't suppose—"

The sound of muted snores filled the room.

Sasha turned to Lyla and smiled; her friend was already asleep, still dressed in her clothing and sprawled haphazardly over her mattress. She covered Lyla with a blanket and sat down on her own bed.

As was becoming her habit of late, her fingers strayed to the amulet around her neck. The pendant's weight felt comforting in the palm of her hand—an anchor holding her steady, holding her *still* during these strange times. Brushing her fingers across the metal, she could feel a faint pulse coming from somewhere within the amulet itself. It was soothing, in a strange sort of way.

So soothing, in fact, that Sasha felt her eyelids begin to droop.

"Nope," she whispered, rousing herself. "Not yet. You've got things to do."

The witches may be content to take one day at a time, but Sasha had decided to take control.

17

THE PERILS OF MIRRORS AND MIST

THAT NIGHT, SASHA WAS PREPARED FOR WHATEVER BETWEEN MIGHT THROW her way. She went to bed dressed in her workout clothes, so that she was appropriately attired to run away from potential catastrophes; and her warmest coat, so as to ward off the chill of snowy mountain peaks. In her trusty, crossbody handbag, she packed a water bottle, just in case she found herself thirsty or on fire; and a flashlight, which would prove useful if she found herself somewhere dark, like a cave or a tunnel or the Shadow King's closet. One pocket was full of energy bars; the other was full of malachite and pepper spray.

She was *ready*.

When Sasha opened her eyes, she found herself at one end of a long, windowless corridor lit by a single torch in the distance. The passageway was made entirely of forbidding black stone, cold and slightly damp, the air tinged with the green scent of moss. Unlit torches lined the walls, festooned with dusty cobwebs; Sasha shuddered to think of the spiders lurking amongst the webs. At the far end, she could just make out a gold-colored door, the only bright spot in this place of darkness.

It was grim and creepy, and Sasha was instantly on guard. She held her breath, waiting for a creature to leap out of the darkness ... or the Shadow King to emerge from one of the dark alcoves. But as the minutes ticked by without a sign of either beasts or kings, Sasha allowed herself to exhale and conclude that the corridor was just a corridor, albeit a sinister one in need of a good clean.

Overall, she was almost disappointed by just how danger-free it all appeared.

"So, I'm in the castle, right?" she asked, addressing Between. "And I guess you want me to go through that door?"

The two torches closest to her burst into flames.

"I'll take that as a *yes*," she said, looking up at the flaming torches. "It's probably a *no*, and you're warning me to stay away, but there isn't anything else for me to do in this corridor, so I'm going."

Sasha braced herself for the unexpected and cautiously moved toward the door, the torches flaring as she approached. Strange shadows flitted across the walls, coaxed to life by the flames. From the corner of her eye, Sasha could see fantastic shapes—winged creatures and beasts with horns; serpents and figures with tails—but when she turned to face them, they disappeared, leaving only her own shadow behind.

It took a moment for her to realize that her shadow was wearing a crown.

"Curious," she said, staring at this shadow-version of herself.

She brushed her hand over the top of her head and found it crown-free as usual. Smiling at the strangeness of it all, she winked at her shadow and walked on.

Before long, Sasha stood before the golden door. Up close, it appeared to be made of beaten copper, its rich patina rainbow-hued in the flickering torchlight. She let her fingers slide across the surface of the metal, surprised that it felt warm to the touch, and reached up to grasp the doorknocker, fashioned in the shape of a sleeping dragon.

"Aren't you gorgeous?" she breathed, marveling at the details worked into the bronze: the tiny, folded wings, the curved nostrils on its little snout, and each exquisite scale.

The dragon's eyes suddenly flew open. Sasha snatched her hand back with a gasp. But the dragon simply surveyed her, its tongue flicking drowsily to taste the air.

Apparently satisfied, the little dragon bowed its head at Sasha and closed its eyes once again.

With a muffled creak, the door swung open, seemingly of its own volition.

"Not creepy at all," she told herself firmly.

Hesitantly, Sasha stepped through the doorway. The room reminded her strongly of the Portal room in Old Middleton. It was round—probably a tower room, she guessed—and domed. Scales made of copper or bronze covered the walls and rippled in the flickering torchlight. An immense

mirror dominated one side of the room; a model of a city—displayed like a
museum exhibit on a sizable wooden stage—covered the other.

Curious, Sasha crossed over to the model and smiled, delighted. As
far as cities went, the one depicted in the model looked as though it had
been designed by someone who was both extremely intoxicated and
dreadfully unqualified. It was, in short, a sprawling, poorly organized fire-
hazard. The streets were too narrow and mazelike, often leading to dead
ends or trapdoors; the thin, crooked houses were crushed against one
another like matches piled into a matchbox and looked as though a stiff
breeze would knock them, domino-like, to the ground; and every second
building appeared to be a tavern. The model, however, was masterfully
crafted: each tiny house was painstakingly depicted, from the tiny shingles
on each black-tiled roof, to the brass doorknockers on the front doors.
The fields surrounding the walled city were so detailed that Sasha could
see each blade of grass and the occasional dandelion bending in an
imperceptible wind. In the center of the city was a hunched, little castle
made of black stone, its twisted towers reaching crookedly toward the sky.
Far beyond the castle was a vast plain crowned by a hill, all covered in
glittery sand.

Sasha recognized this vista.

"It's a model of Between," she said in awe.

"Why, yes—yes, it is," a familiar male voice said from behind her.

Sasha turned, her stomach fluttering with a curious mix of anticipation
and dread. Sure enough, there was the Shadow King dressed in his
customary black, languidly reclining in a throne-like chair in front of the
mirror. Tonight, he was the very picture of regal indolence. In his hand was
a crystal decanter filled with wine the color of old blood; a goblet sat on a
table at his elbow, brimful of the ruby liquid. Beside it was a silver platter
holding a fat quarter of cheese, a crimson pear, and a golden apple. Sasha
thought that the scene looked like a painting by one of the Dutch Masters
('Sinisterly Dressed Man Sitting Beside Cheese Platter,' or something
equally fitting).

"So, you have finally come to see me, my lovely Queen!" he said,
smiling at her in pure delight.

Sasha stared back at him, bewildered. The Shadow King had never
appeared so happy to see her before.

Quite the opposite, in fact.

"I've come to see you several times." Sasha looked at his wine filled
goblet. "Are you drunk?"

The King laughed—a joyous, carefree sound—and placed the decanter back on the table. "No, but not from lack of trying. To your health, my lovely Queen." He picked up his goblet and saluted her before taking a sip.

Sasha stared at the goblet, then at the King, and frowned. "Yes. Let's drink to that. And then maybe you should stop drinking and have some of that cheese platter." She gestured to the untouched fruit and cheese. "I know you said that sorcerers can't get drunk, but I'm beginning to have my doubts ..."

"I assure you that I am not at all intoxicated. But I will happily devour the contents of the platter if it would please you."

"It would please me," Sasha said, still frowning at him dubiously.

The King watched her intently from over the rim of his goblet, his green gaze oddly bright. "Would you mind coming closer?" he almost purred. "It is awfully difficult to see you all the way over there."

Sasha's first instinct was to step back, not forward. There was something wrong, something *off* about the entire situation.

It's a trick, she thought, her fingers closing over the container of pepper spray in her pocket.

Sasha could not put her finger on it, but she was willing to bet her right kidney that this was not the Shadow King. His demeanor was far too light, too joyful. *This* Shadow King did not have a care in the world. There was not a hint of exhaustion or cynicism in his expression, nor an ounce of aloofness in his manner.

"Truly," this King said, sensing her hesitation, "the weather is *much* better beside me." He grinned conspiratorially, his words echoing their conversation when the coven Summoned the King to Old Middleton. "Come, let me show you."

Fairy tales were full of stories about doppelgängers and all the horrid things that could befall you if you trusted them.

"Thanks," Sasha said warily, "but I think I'll stay over here."

The King lowered his goblet and gave her that same glorious smile. "Oh, but you are cautious and clever! And courageous and bold and ever so lovely." He tilted his head, watching her carefully. "And you do not believe a word that I say, do you?"

"Not at all," she said bluntly.

If anything, he seemed pleased by her bluntness. "*Hmm*, why is that, my lovely Queen?"

My lovely Queen. How could such a pretty phrase feel so *wrong*? "It's a little out of character for you."

The King nodded, acknowledging her point. "For *him*, perhaps. But not for me. Though, give him time ..."

Sasha froze. He had admitted it—he *was not* the Shadow King.

But if he wasn't the King, then ... who was this creature?

Abruptly, Sasha became angry. "That's it—I'm out of here. It's bad enough that I'm engaged to a guy who turns into a bird, but *now* I find out that he has a creepy stunt-double hidden in a gold room. Nope. No way. What's next? A mad wife in the attic?" She shook her head decisively. "Nice to meet you. Have a nice life."

Sasha turned on her heel and stalked toward the door. She was wondering whether she could find that lovely green meadow again when the Not-King called out to her.

"Please wait! I rarely get visitors, and he has been keeping you all to himself."

There was something in his tone—something plaintive, something lonely and lost—that made Sasha stop in her tracks. Against her better judgment, she turned around.

Seeing that Sasha was not about to leave, the Not-King quickly stood up.

"Thank you," he said, clearly relieved. "As you can see, I am of absolutely no threat to you at all."

Sasha cautiously stepped back over the threshold. "What do you mean—oh!"

To her surprise, she realized that the King's double was not sitting in front of the mirror as it first appeared.

He was *inside* the mirror.

The Not-King rapped his knuckles against the mirror's surface, confirming Sasha's discovery. "I am trapped inside. There is no way for me to get out. Please ..." He lowered his voice, his expression solemn. "Do not be afraid of me. Not *you*. Never *you*."

Sasha slowly crossed the room, carefully judging the Not-King's reaction until she was standing directly in front of him.

"You're not Lorn—the Shadow King—are you?" she asked, wanting this imposter to confirm it.

"Not *exactly*."

Sasha clenched her fists. "I'm *so sick* of all the mysterious double-talk. Give me straight answers, Mirror Man, or I'm leaving."

The Not-King smiled down at her as if she had said something truly wonderful. "I am the Shadow King's Shadow. I am both a part of Lorn and not. For a better explanation, you will have to ask him yourself—some secrets are not mine to reveal."

Sasha filed that piece of information away for later examination. "How did you get in there?"

The Shadow made a showy gesture with his hands. "Magic."

"Damn magic," she muttered. "Can anyone else get in there with you?"

The delighted smile was gone, replaced by a sadness—a loneliness—that was almost palpable.

"No. I am alone, and so I shall always remain."

Sasha's feelings toward this alternate Shadow King softened. Being trapped inside a mirror was probably one of the dastardliest fates that she could imagine. The boredom alone would kill her.

"Can I get you out of there?" she asked impulsively, letting go of her pepper spray.

Sure ... let go of the pepper spray, she heard Lyla's voice mutter disapprovingly in the recesses of her mind. *And while you're at it, release the possibly dangerous doppelgänger from the mirror. What could possibly go wrong?*

But she pushed the Lyla-voice aside, and quickly scanned the mirror's frame, wondering if there was a catch or a lock. When none appeared, she hesitantly raised her hand to the mirror and let her fingertips touch the surface.

The Shadow smiled sadly. "No, but it is very kind of you to ask. Not to mention rather heroic. You will make a magnificent Queen."

Sasha was about to refute that when the Shadow reached out and placed his hand on the mirror, directly over hers.

"We are very lucky to have you," he said quietly.

Sasha looked down at their matched hands, separated only by the cool glass. When she looked up, the Shadow was staring at her intently. There was so much in his expression: such fierce joy and happiness and ... and an emotion she could not quite place.

Holding her gaze, the Shadow let his fingers trail upward to trace the curve of her cheek through the mirror. His gaze became ardent, his pupils dilated to the point where his eyes appeared almost black.

"Very lucky indeed," he whispered huskily.

Sasha's heart began to pound. She gave a startled laugh and stepped away from the mirror.

"You're *definitely* not the King. He doesn't look at me like—" She cleared her throat. "He finds the idea of a queen burdensome."

The Shadow slowly removed his fingers from the mirror and gave her that delighted smile once again.

"*I*," he said very deliberately, "am the Shadow King's Shadow. I am the side of Lorn that he rarely brings to light. That does not mean that it is not there. Rather, it is simply waiting to be uncovered. Do you understand, Sasha?"

Sasha weighed the Shadow's words. The conclusion was rather shocking.

"Yes," she said slowly. "I think I do."

"So clever; so utterly lovely," the Shadow said wistfully, looking at her in a way that was very flattering to Sasha's vanity.

Exceedingly flattering.

"Damn it," Sasha muttered. "The Shadow King *would* have to leave all his fun bits in a mirror." She held the Shadow's gaze, willing him to tell her the truth. "If *you* had been on the hillside the first time that the Shadow King and I met—"

"I would have made all your dreams come true," he said meaningfully, his voice dripping with innuendo.

Sasha nodded briskly. "That's good to know."

"Remember that, will you not?"

Sasha snorted, her heart rate finally returning to normal. "It's a hard image to forget."

The Shadow positively beamed. "Excellent! Because it is very, very important."

Sasha felt a tug at her navel. "Oh … it's time to go. It was strange … but rather nice to meet you."

"It was glorious to meet you." The Shadow's smile fell away. "But you must promise to keep our meeting a secret, my lovely Queen."

"A secret?" Sasha did not like the sound of this. "Why? And be quick, I haven't got much time."

"If people were to know of my existence, they could use me against Lorn."

"Are you dangerous?" She inhaled sharply. "Are you dangerous to me?"

"Never," the Shadow answered immediately. "I could never harm you. But I could be used to harm him." He pressed his hands against the mirror. "Please, *promise me*."

Sasha hesitated. The existence of the Shadow was important, significant—something that she needed to discuss with Lyla and the coven.

To keep it a secret …?

The tug behind her navel became more insistent.

"Only two people know of my existence, and you are one of them." The Shadow's tone was low and urgent. "The other, Maddox, would die for Lorn."

Still, Sasha hesitated.

"Between trusted you," the Shadow urged. "It brought you here because it trusted you to keep Lorn's secret."

And, just like that, Sasha caved.

"Fine," she said warily. "But only on the condition that I can break this secret if you ever try to harm me."

"I could never harm you," the Shadow said fiercely. "I would never harm you. *Please*."

Sasha felt herself become airborne. "I promise."

As she said the words, a strange warmth enveloped her. A bell-tone rang out across the golden room.

The Shadow looked inordinately relieved. "*Thank you*, my lovely Queen."

"You're welcome," Sasha answered, her mouth tingling oddly.

Without thinking, she grasped hold of the Shadow King's amulet. The Shadow saw this and smiled—a smile that held a world of secrets.

Sasha took one look at the Shadow's secretive smile and felt all her misgivings come flooding back. "I'd better not regret this. If I do, I swear I'll come and visit you with a can of black paint."

The Shadow threw back his head and laughed. "Meeting you was pure pleasure. Visit me again, my lovely Queen."

~

SASHA FLOATED UP AND AWAY FROM THE GOLD ROOM AND ITS ODDLY charming, mirror-version of the Shadow King, and emerged into the dark space between dreams and reality.

Just as she was preparing herself to wake up, she felt an abrupt jerk in her midsection and found herself being pulled sharply downward …

… until she landed, with a grunt, in a place that smelled of rotten eggs and diseased cucumbers.

"*Agh.*" Sasha tried valiantly not to gag. "*So* disgusting." She pressed her hand over her nose and mouth and looked around, trying not to gasp.

Mist … she was surrounded by mist. It churned around Sasha's knees, so thick that she could not see her feet, and drifted upwards in sheets, turning the entire world white.

But it was not the pure, pristine white of newly fallen snow—the sort of white that leaves you breathless with wondrous joy. No, this was gray-tinged and dismal—a dingy white that left you feeling the absence of color and life. A grimy white that seeped into your psyche and left you feeling colder and darker and *alone*.

Sasha quickly looked around, hoping to distract herself from such dreary thoughts, but what she could see of the landscape did little to elevate her mood. Twisted black trees emerged from the mist like broken fingers, stretching upward toward the non-existent sunlight. Dark boulders were scattered around, their edges jagged and slick with slime. And the *smell*— rotting vegetation and stagnant water and something sulfurous that was particularly unpleasant. Sasha could feel the smell sink into her pores, leaving a greasy film on her skin that made her want to scrub herself thoroughly with a washcloth.

Not surprisingly, she shuddered. "This isn't creepy at all."

She was answered by a frog-like croak near her feet, and the wet rustle of something moving amongst the grass further along. There was a small splash somewhere behind her, followed by a much bigger splash that made Sasha stand very, very still. Somewhere, an insect started to sing, echoed by a few hundred of its friends.

"Are these the swamps?" she asked Between, remembering her conversation with the King.

A bird screeched in response. Sasha looked up into the treetops and saw a flash of red fly away.

"I guess this is ... atmospheric," she said to Between, trying to be diplomatic. "Thanks for the tour."

Something howled in the distance, the mournful sound raising the hair on the back of Sasha's neck.

She swallowed hard. "I'm not a fan of howling," she told Between. "I'd like to wake up now. Thanks." But there was no fishhook feeling. No rising off the ground and drifting away toward awakening.

She was stuck here.

"Right." She pushed up the sleeves of her coat. "Let's think about this logically. In each dream, you've shown me something." *Or someone,* Sasha thought, recalling her meetings with the Shadow King and his mirror version. "So ... what do you want to show me? Why am I here?"

Sasha was not expecting an answer, but at that exact moment, the mist parted, revealing a crooked path slick with moisture and covered in moss.

"Oh. Okay. I guess I'm going down that path."

Sasha wrapped her hand around the pepper spray in her pocket and carefully made her way down the slippery path, thankful that she was wearing her sneakers and not her leather soled boots.

As she followed the twisty pathway across the wetlands, the mist ebbed and flowed around her, giving her glimpses of what lay beyond: bottle green stretches of water obscured by tangles of black grass; an ancient, stone footbridge covered in moss and black vines; something bone white and sharp that jutted out from a small patch of water; and finally, a small, wooden gate that stood, alone and fenceless, about thirty feet away in the middle of a clearing.

There was nothing fancy about the gate except for its color: someone had painted it a jaunty shade of buttercup yellow that looked so out of place in its eerie surrounds—so determinedly cheerful—that Sasha could not help but smile.

"Is that what you wanted me to see?" she asked Between. "Am I supposed to walk through it? There isn't a fence so—" She stopped, her eyes widening as she recalled what Esther had told her about standalone gates.

"This—this is a *gateway*, isn't it?" She peered at the cheery gate. "But why show it to me? Where does it go? Hang on—do you want me to walk through it?" She shook her head. "Sorry, but *no*. Tonight has been weird enough as it is, what with walking down shadowy corridors and talking to a man in a mirror. Is it okay if I just look at it?" She waited for a sign or direction, but there was only silence. "I'm going to take that as a *yes*."

She stepped off the path towards the gate and yelped as her right foot sunk rapidly into a pool of gritty mud.

"No! These shoes are brand new!"

Sasha sighed and lifted her leg ... or at least tried to—it would not budge. She pulled and tugged and dragged, but the mud stubbornly refused to release her; it was like trying to step out of a vat of superglue.

"Trust Between to have vicious mud," she muttered, wincing as thick, cold sludge filled her shoe. "Maybe—maybe if I had some leverage..."

She looked around, hoping to find a fallen branch or a thick stick or a robust twig within reach, but there was nothing.

"Great. I guess I'll just take off my shoe and hop to the gate."

She was about to do just that when five figures suddenly materialized from the mist. They each wore long robes—one in white, the others in gray —with their hoods pulled so low over their heads that Sasha could not see their faces. They appeared to float through the mist in single file, moving silently across the clearing toward the yellow gate.

The scene was so strange, so eerie that Sasha wondered if it was all a trick of the mist. If Lyla were here, she would have insisted that they were ghosts, doomed to haunt these terrible swamps for eternity. For a moment, the idea took hold, making Sasha shiver.

Not helpful, she told herself firmly. *Let's see if these ghosts have the upper arm strength to yank me out of this mud.*

She was about to call for help when she heard a familiar crack followed by a sudden weight pulling on the front of her jacket.

The malachite! she thought, reaching into her pocket.

Sure enough, the new piece of malachite Rosa had given her was now broken neatly in two, the raw edges rough against her fingertips.

Sasha had a terrible sense of *déjà vu*. This was precisely how her adventure with the knights had begun earlier today. But this ... this was worse: she was alone and outnumbered, and there was not a mail truck in sight.

It had all the hallmarks of an Ordeal.

To make matters even more dire, she was literally stuck: she could not run or hide or fight. She could not even duck down and untie her shoe without calling attention to herself. All she could do was hope that the mist kept her hidden until they passed.

Just hurry along, she silently urged the robed figures. *Nothing to see here ...*

Unfortunately, the robed figures seemed immune to telepathy. They glided through the mist, stopping at the gate. Sasha mentally groaned; if the figures turned around, they would see her standing there—one foot on the path, another in a malicious mud puddle.

This is definitely an Ordeal, she thought, bracing herself for discovery. She slowly pulled the pepper spray from her pocket and attempted to stand as still as possible.

The white-robed figure took the lead. He or she (*he,* Sasha thought to herself, noting the breadth of the shoulders beneath the robe) moved directly in front of the gate.

"This must be the one," the white-robed figure said, his voice oddly guttural. "It should be open. They all open when she dreams."

Sasha inhaled sharply. They were talking about her.

The white-robed figure tentatively opened the latch. For a moment, nothing happened. Sasha held her breath. Then, slowly, the gate trembled and swung open with a high-pitched whine, revealing not the clearing that surrounded it, but a dark, cobblestone street awash with lamplight.

And just like that, Sasha knew why Between had brought her here: she recognized that street—it was the end of Main Street, not far from the Middleton Gateway.

They're using a gateway to get to Old Middleton! she realized.

"Excellent!" The leader's voice was tinged with satisfaction. "Just as she said."

Sasha stared longingly at the familiar scene. At this time of night, Main Street was empty and quiet, the citizens of Old Middleton still in slumber. If she hadn't been trapped, she would have taken a chance and sprinted through the gate, robed figures be damned.

"Remember—it is the dark-haired woman you want," the leader told the others, startling Sasha from her thoughts. "Not her gold-haired friend."

Oh, no, she thought, her heart dropping to the pit of her stomach, *they're not using a gateway to get to Old Middleton—they're using a gateway to get to* me.

"Do you remember the location of the boarding house?" he asked.

"The source drew us a map," one of the gray-robed figures said.

The leader nodded. "Good. It is a house, not a fortified structure so you should be able to enter it with little difficulty."

Good luck with that, Sasha thought, with a sort of vicious satisfaction.

You're going to bounce off the wards like a tennis ball and then feel the wrath of Martha's frying pan.

"She will be asleep," the leader continued, "and will pose no problem."

Ha! Sasha clutched her pepper spray harder. *That's what you think ...*

"But you must hurry; she could awaken at any time and the gateway will close." He turned back toward Main Street. "Hmm ... it looks as though there may be a witness to contend with."

At first, Sasha did not understand what the leader meant. But as she scanned the scene, she realized that Main Street was not empty after all. On a bench perched on the street corner sat old Mrs. Landshome, sound asleep, her head tipped awkwardly to one side. The old woman was probably meant to be guarding the Middleton Gateway but had fallen asleep on her watch. She was snoring lustily, her little boots swinging in the air with the force of her snores, utterly oblivious to the fact that her realm was about to be invaded.

"Pity. I assume that you will be able to deal with the situation?" the leader asked.

"Of course," one of the gray-robed figures said flatly.

"We are not novices," the other said, his voice dripping with disdain.

Sasha's heart began to pound. *They were going after Mrs. Landshome!*

The same two gray-robed figures pulled back their hoods, revealing shaven scalps. Even from a distance, Sasha could see the strange tattoos drawn across their tanned skin: rows and rows of words and symbols written in a language that she did not recognize, coiled around the curves of their skulls like serpents.

I bet they're not tattoos, she thought, fear beginning to churn in her gut. *I bet they're magic markings. Dash it! This is getting worse and worse ...*

The two men began to chant, their words low and rasping and strangely repellent. The sound echoed across the clearing, building rapidly to a crescendo. Flames appeared in their hands—great, swirling balls of black and scarlet fire that seared away the mist, leaving behind plumes of black, acrid smoke. The fireballs grew and grew until, with a shout, the men threw them to the ground.

Before Sasha's eyes, the fireballs seethed and writhed, melding together to create a creature—something terrible made of flames and fangs that roared and spat, barely restrained.

"You know what to do," the white-robed figure told the men.

The two men stepped through the gate and onto Main Street. The creature made of flames bounded after them ... and headed straight for the sleeping witch.

"NO! Leave her alone!" Sasha screamed. "Run, Mrs. Landshome! RUN!"

Sasha tried to move toward the gate to stop them, to save Mrs. Landshome, but she found herself stumbling instead. She had forgotten that she was stuck fast.

She had also forgotten about her plan to stay silent and still.

The three remaining figures turned toward Sasha, clearly surprised.

"Leave her alone!" she repeated, trying desperately to pull herself free of the mud. She held up her container of pepper spray defiantly. "Or I'll burn off your faces with my burning spray!"

"This is unfortunate," the leader said with a sigh. "But we cannot have witnesses." He closed the gate and turned to the remaining gray-robed figures. "Take care of her."

Take care of her. The words sent a chill down Sasha's spine.

The two gray-robed men hesitated.

"This is why you are here," the white-robed man said quietly. "I do not need to remind you of the consequences of failing, do I?"

The men shook their heads.

"Then, *take care of her.*"

This time, the two gray-robed men did not hesitate. They turned and began to move swiftly toward Sasha.

As they moved, Sasha saw glimpses of armor beneath their robes.

"Get back!" she yelled. "I will fry your faces! Don't think I won't do it!"

The men seemed unimpressed by the threat of facial searing. They continued to approach.

Sasha desperately tried to yank her foot free from her shoe, but it was no use—she was stuck fast. She grabbed the amulet around her neck. "Shadow King!" she screamed.

But her heart sunk. The men were almost upon her; there was no possible way that the Shadow King would reach her in time.

She had to face this alone.

"Last chance," she sneered, releasing the amulet. She grasped the plastic container tighter with sweat-slick fingers. "Don't come another step closer or I'll melt your eyeballs!"

One of the figures reached for the sheath on his belt. Sasha saw the silver glint of a dagger and realized that this was *it.*

This was the end.

For the second time today, she was about to face death, and she was *so done* with all of this! She hadn't asked to become the True Queen of

Between—she didn't even want it. And yet, here she was, having to fight because of it. To die because of it.

Not now, the voice in the back of her head said firmly, just as it had done earlier in the day. *Not today. Fight. Win.*

Fight. Win.

And just like that, Sasha felt a terrible anger surge through her body, burning away her fear and igniting something vicious, something powerful within her very core.

Fight, she thought. *Win.*

She quickly shrugged off her handbag and wrapped the straps around her fist, prepared to smash it into her assailants' faces.

"COME ON THEN!" she roared, putting every ounce of rage she possessed into the words. "I WILL MELT OFF YOUR FACES! I WILL *END* YOU, ASSHOLES!"

Her voice cut through the mist like a lash. The sound of her fury shook the treetops until black leaves fell in sheets like a dark, vengeful rainfall. The earth trembled beneath her feet and split open, unleashing wide fissures that raced across the clearing. Wild winds gathered around her, tossing her hair and the black leaves skyward.

The men stopped abruptly.

"That's right," Sasha yelled, almost giddy with relief, with power. "Now, step *back!*"

The men raised their hands, and obediently stepped back. They were so close now that Sasha could see beyond their hoods to the terror in their eyes.

For a blissful second, she felt a wondrous sense of triumph … which was quickly replaced by a dreadful realization.

Their fear not directed at her.

Their fear was directed just *behind* her where the ground was still trembling, and the tempest was still raging.

"There's something really terrifying behind me, isn't there?" she asked the hooded men.

They nodded slowly.

"How terrifying?" she asked, bracing herself.

"*Truly* terrifying," the Shadow King said from behind her shoulder. "Then again, after all your talk of 'face melting,' I believe I am only the second-most terrifying person in this swamp."

"Oh, thank goodness!" Sasha gasped, her entire body sagging in relief. "I didn't think you'd make it in time."

"It was a close call," he said, his words clipped and cold.

Frowning at his tone, Sasha turned to face the King and started: he did, indeed, look genuinely terrifying. He stood like a statue in the eye of a storm—so still, so rigid that he seemed barely human. Shadows gathered around him like a dark mist, stripping the swamp of light. The high winds spun them around his form, joined by dark leaves and debris, until he was surrounded by a seething wall of pure darkness. His face was a mask of cold fury, his jaw rigid, his green gaze glacial and locked on the two robed men. His hands were clenched into fists by his sides, white sparks dancing across the surface of his knuckles.

He gave the impression of barely contained things: wrath and vengeance and horrific endings, wrapped in darkness and shadows.

Sasha decided to ignore it all. "I'm *so* happy to see you! I'm gonna hug you. A lot."

All at once, the tempest around the King abruptly stopped. The leaves and twigs dropped to the ground with a muffled thud; the shadows fled back into the mist as if scared away by Sasha's words.

All three men turned to Sasha in shock.

"What a truly dreadful thing to say," the Shadow King said, clearly shaken. "I would prefer to have my face melted."

Nevertheless, he stepped out from behind Sasha and stood at her side, his shadowy cloak snapping at her attackers.

"Kneel before the Queen of Between," he ordered quietly, his tone as sharp as a blade.

The robed men quickly fell to their knees, their faces bent so low that their foreheads touched the muddy ground.

"Yes! You'd better *kneel*," Sasha said, shaking her pepper spray container at the men. "How dare you attack a defenseless woman! You are in *so* much trouble now!"

"Would you like me to take care of this matter?" the Shadow King asked. "Or would you like to proceed with the face-melting?"

Sasha gasped as the fishhook tugged urgently at her midsection.

"You deal with them," she said, slinging her bag back over her shoulder and putting her pepper spray away. "Two wizards went through the gate; they're headed for Mrs. Landshome. I have to warn her!"

"Two wizards went through the gate?" the King asked sharply. "How do you know that they were wizards?"

"They created an animal out of fire. It was—gah, it was *awful.*"

"A fire beast," the King muttered to himself. His eyes narrowed. "Were the wizards' scalps covered in script?"

Sasha nodded frantically, feeling herself start to become weightless.

"Yes! And there was another man, too. In a white robe—he seemed to be their leader. He knew that the gateway would be open. He also knew that I open all the gateways when I dream."

The King appeared shocked. "How could he possibly know that?"

"I don't know. *I* didn't even know that. Oh! And he knew where I lived —he even had a map! The wizards said that a 'source' gave it to them."

Sasha began to rise but stopped abruptly, her foot still trapped in the mud. She felt the fishhook tug harder and harder to the point where it was almost painful, but she remained trapped.

"*Agh*! What is this mud made of?"

The King glanced over at Sasha's foot. "Enchanted quicksand."

Sasha's eyes widened. "*Enchanted quicksand?* I swear, this place ..." She felt a harder tug and winced.

"A little help? *Please*! I have rescue Mrs. Landshome!"

The King appeared to hesitate for a moment, then gestured at the mud. Sasha's foot broke free of her sock and shoe, leaving her right foot bare.

"Is Mrs. Landshome the red-headed witch who tried to drug me?" the King asked.

"No, Mrs. Landshome is the tiny witch who liked your leather pants. Oh, hurry up!" she said, addressing her midsection where the fishhook resided. "Mrs. Landshome is in danger! I need to save her!"

"Do be careful," the King warned. "You have been heroic enough for the one evening. Allow the coven to vanquish the wizards and share in the glory."

"We'll see." Sasha looked down at her sneaker, still trapped in the mud. "Damn. I liked those." *Finally*, she felt herself rise again. "And thanks! I owe you a hug."

"I think not," the King answered, staring at Sasha's red-polished toenails as she rose above him.

"Give them hell, Shadow King!" she called down as she hurtled toward the unsuspecting (and hopefully skirt juice-free) Mrs. Landshome.

～

SASHA'S EYES SNAPPED OPEN. SHE LURCHED UPRIGHT AND SWUNG HER LEGS over the bed, kicking off her left shoe and sock. She threw her sluggish body into a run, staggering out of the bedroom and down the circular staircase, clutching the rail with sleep-numb fingers.

"Mrs. Landshome's in trouble!" she cried out to Martha and Miss

Adeline as she jumped down the final set of stairs. She sprinted to the front door, shaking the porcelain figurines as she passed.

"Open, dammit!" she yelled at the wooden door as she fumbled with the lock.

The heavy door finally swung open, and she took off like a shot down the street, not bothering to close it behind her.

She had no idea how much time had passed between her dream and awakening. She had no idea if the two wizards had just entered Old Middleton or had long gone.

She might be too late.

"No," she told herself firmly. "I'm going to get there in time. I'm going to make it."

The concrete was hard and cold and unyielding beneath her feet, but she willed herself to run faster, her heartbeat wild behind her ribcage, the sound of her breathing too loud in the silent street.

She turned onto Main Street moments later and stopped dead in her tracks. At the end of the street, framed by the golden arch of the Middleton Gateway, she could see a wide circle of black and red flames.

"No," she mumbled, shaking her head in disbelief. "*No.*"

She was too late. Unbidden, her mind conjured a vision of Mrs. Landshome's small body sprawled on the pavement like a broken doll, her frail limbs twisted and broken, her pale blue eyes staring lifelessly at the stars—

Sasha forcibly pushed the vision away and sprinted toward the flames.

"Please!" she begged. "*Please* let her be okay!"

She flew past shops and lampposts, clocks and wells. As she neared the end of the road, there was a strange grinding sound, like stone rubbing against stone, coming from somewhere above her.

Sasha glanced up and immediately ducked; something swooped down upon her as it flew past, almost throwing her to the ground. She staggered forward, desperately trying to remain upright. Regaining her balance, she spared a glance over her shoulder: two dark shapes were flying above the village, each larger than any bird she had ever seen, their giant wings making that odd grinding sound with each stroke.

Sasha turned back toward the Gateway and continued running, her eyes on the flames. As she drew closer, the flames began to recede, revealing several figures standing at the center of the flame ring. With a sob of relief, Sasha realized that the figures were not the gray-robed men but Esther, the Headmistress, Rosa and—thankfully!—Mrs. Landshome. The witches appeared to be arguing amongst themselves, completely unaware of Sasha's approach.

"Those weren't kidnappers," she heard the Headmistress hiss at Mrs. Landshome. "Those were k—"

Sasha jumped over the dying flames and pulled Mrs. Landshome into a bone-crushing hug.

"I thought you were doomed," she gasped out.

"Ha! *Now* I'm feeling appreciated!" the old woman cackled, patting Sasha on the back. "See, Penelope? *That's* how you thank someone for stopping a kidnapping. You *hug* them—you don't lecture them to death."

"Sasha!" Esther exclaimed, shocked. "What are you doing here? It isn't safe for you to be here, especially now! Go back to the boarding house immediately!"

"I had to come," Sasha said, still breathing hard. She gently released Mrs. Landshome. "I saw—" She swallowed and tried to catch her breath. "I was in Between … in the swamps … and I saw two wizards coming to Old Middleton through a gate. They made a fire beast and were heading straight for Mrs. Landshome." She turned to the old woman. "Are you alright?"

"Never better," the old woman said, grinning.

Sasha looked around; aside from the witches, the street was empty. "What happened to the wizards and the fire beast?"

In the light of the flames, Mrs. Landshome's grin took on an evil glint. "Beaten."

"Everything is fine now," the Headmistress said, her smile brittle.

Sasha sincerely doubted that. The ground was on fire, stone creatures were flying around, and two men were missing. "But who were—"

"You said they came through a gate?" Esther interrupted. "What sort of gate?"

"A gate without a fence," Sasha said. "It was just … standing there in the middle of the swamp. It was a gateway."

"What I want to know is how dark wiz—" the Headmistress visibly stopped herself. "How *they*," she corrected, "managed to open a gateway to our realm. It shouldn't have been possible."

"They didn't open the gateway," Sasha said, her heart pounding. "*I* opened the gateway—I open *all* the gateways when I dream."

The witches looked stunned.

"You—you open *all* the gateways when you dream?" Esther asked. "Not just the Portal?"

"Oh, *no!*" the Headmistress murmured.

"It seems so," Sasha said, her gut twisting at the thought. "Their leader—a man in a white robe—told them. I don't know how he knew;

not even the Shadow King knew about it. The Shadow King is with the others."

"There were *others?*" the Headmistress Dean. She looked over at Esther, her hand fluttering to her throat.

Esther's shoulders slumped. "How many others?"

"Two," Sasha said. "But I don't think they were wizards. And they seemed terrified of the King."

"Well, they should be," Mrs. Landshome said. "They tried to get through a gateway on his watch. He's not going to be pleased."

The flames flickered out around them, leaving behind a circle of ash— the only evidence that something magical, something terrible had happened in the street.

It could have been so much worse, Sasha thought to herself, looking over at Mrs. Landshome. The old woman seemed unscathed. In fact, she appeared to be in excellent spirits. The relief Sasha felt at seeing the old woman safe was staggering. Slowly, she felt her fear begin to ebb away.

But the guilt … the guilt was growing stronger and stronger by the minute.

"So … what do we do now?" she asked, pushing aside her feelings; there were more pressing matters to deal with right now.

"There's nothing to do," the Headmistress bit out. "It's already been done. We were just cleaning up."

"May I help?" Sasha asked.

"No need," Rosa said kindly.

"You should not have come here, Sasha!" Esther said, shaking her head. "If something like this ever happens again, you need to tell Martha or Miss Adeline; it's far too risky for you to leave the boarding house. You could be kidnapped or—or worse."

"Esther is right," the Headmistress said. "You would have been no match for those wizards."

Sasha began to realize that she had charged from one deadly situation into another with barely a thought. "I—I just wanted to warn Mrs. Landshome."

Mrs. Landshome patted Sasha's hand. "You did a grand job. Don't listen to these fuss-buckets."

"We just want to keep you safe," Esther said, her expression so worried that it made Sasha feel even worse. "Now, Rosa—why don't you escort Sasha back to the boarding house?"

"Of course," Rosa said, crossing to Sasha's side. "It's been an exciting night, hasn't it?"

Sasha exhaled. "A little too exciting."

"And there's work tomorrow—we should be getting back to bed."

Sasha shook her head. "But, there's still so much I want to kn—"

"You look tired, dear," the Headmistress interrupted, her voice oddly compelling.

Sasha opened her mouth to argue but instead found herself yawning.

"Goodness! You're not wearing shoes!" Rosa said, looking down at Sasha's bare feet. "You must be freezing!" She took Sasha's arm and led her back up Main Street. "Come on, let's get you back to the boarding house, safe and sound."

Sasha looked over her shoulder at Esther. "But—"

"Everything is fine," Esther said reassuringly. "Stay in the boarding house—you'll be safe there."

Sasha reluctantly turned away from the flame ring and allowed Rosa to lead her back to the boarding house. With her adrenaline fading away, she could feel the chill in the air and beneath her feet.

As they passed the storefronts, Sasha heard that strange grinding sound coming from above her again. She looked up: two winged gargoyles stared down at her from the greengrocer, their expressions sharp, hungry. She could have sworn that their wings shifted as she passed.

"Do the gargoyles come alive?" she asked.

"Oh, yes," Rosa said, as if it was the most natural thing in the world.

Sasha decided to ponder that at another time—there was already too much to think about: mirror-men in gold rooms and kidnappers in misty swamps; fire beasts bounding toward Mrs. Landshome, and the mysterious disappearance of two shaven-headed wizards. Not to mention the coven having to deal with yet another catastrophe that Sasha had inadvertently unleashed on Old Middleton.

Those weren't kidnappers, the Headmistress had said before Sasha had entered the circle of flames. *Those were k—*

"Who were those men?" Sasha asked as they turned off Main Street toward the boarding house. "They were wizards, weren't they?"

"Yes, but not our kind."

Sasha recalled the dark script coiled around the wizards' skulls, the vicious language of their spell. "*Evil* wizards?"

Rosa made a humming sound beneath her breath. "In a manner of speaking," she hedged. "It's a little more complicated than that. Let's just say that they practice magic that's typically classified as Forbidden—nasty stuff, like raising the dead, and possession, and the creation of wraith beasts." The older woman shuddered and opened the boarding house gates. She beckoned for Sasha to enter before her. "Not anything that I'd like to try; that sort of magic leaves a mark."

"So … why were evil wizards after me?"

"We aren't sure. The Shadow King did warn that others would be after you. Perhaps the dark wizards want to use you to Challenge for the throne of Between."

Those weren't kidnappers …

Sasha exhaled sharply. "Do you think they wanted to kidnap me or kill me?"

"Oh, definitely kidnap." She said it so breezily that it was clear that Rosa was trying to sugar coat the experience.

Sasha was becoming rather tired of people concealing things from her —even if they thought it was for her own good. She was also getting more than annoyed with half-truths, of being told *just enough* to get along, of having to learn things as she went.

"I know that you and the rest of the coven are used to keeping secrets," she said slowly, with as much patience as she could muster after her recent adventures, "or covering them up to protect people. But this is my life, and I want to know what kind of danger I'm in. You can tell me the truth—no, you had *better* tell me the truth, because what I don't know could actually harm me."

It was too dark to see Rosa's expression, but Sasha could hear her sigh. "The truth is, we don't know what their intentions were toward you. But we stopped them, and that's what matters. And if the Shadow King knows about them—knows that they used a gateway to cross into our realm—then I guarantee that they won't be able to use that gate again."

Sasha didn't doubt that for a second. The Shadow King had been a mass of barely contained fury. Thinking back over her time in the swamp before his arrival made Sasha feel sick to her stomach; she didn't want to contemplate what would have happened if he hadn't arrived in time.

Sasha stopped at the front door of the boarding house—it was still wide open. "I was terrified for Mrs. Landshome. I thought that those men … that beast … would kill her."

Rosa laughed and led the way inside. "Not much can hurt Gussie." She switched on one of the hall lamps. "Those men never stood a chance."

"But that beast—"

"Was beaten, dear," Rosa said firmly.

Sasha rubbed her eyes with the heels of her hands. She was suddenly exhausted. All of this … it was just too much.

And the *guilt*.

"I'm a liability," she said. "It was bad enough when the imps appeared, but evil wizards? *That* affects all of Old Middleton. Someone could get hurt —what am I saying? Someone could get *killed*! And it will be my fault." Sasha dropped her hands and looked down at the older woman. "I should just leave now."

Rosa pulled a black leaf from Sasha's curls. "You were very brave tonight. You ran to the Middleton Gateway—on bare feet!—to rescue Gussie, with not a thought to your own safety. You knew what you were about to face—those wizards, that beast—and yet you came anyway. You didn't hide or run away, did you?"

Sasha shook her head numbly.

The older woman smiled. "We know what we're facing, and we're not running away from it either … and we are far more equipped to deal with it than you are." She pulled another leaf from Sasha's hair and smoothed back her wild curls. "You only have a few days left, Sasha. A few days left of normality before *everything* changes. You deserve this. Let us give them to you."

Sasha's stomach churned as another thought—a much more terrible thought—came to mind. "When I return from my trial run, the evil wizards … and the magical creatures … they'll return to Old Middleton with me, won't they?"

"We don't know." Lit by lamp light, Rosa looked so much older, her dark eyes serious and sad. "This has never happened before."

"But you suspect they will, right?" Hearing the words, Sasha knew the truth of them. Her shoulders slumped under the weight of the realization. "As long as I'm here—as long as I'm not in Between—Old Middleton won't be left alone."

"One thing at a time," Rosa said gently. She placed her hands on Sasha's shoulders. "There's no use catastrophizing. Focus on enjoying your last days here before your trial run."

"But the evil wizards—"

"Trust us to deal with them and whatever else Otherworld throws at us. Everything is fine."

Sasha raised an eyebrow. "Everything is fine?"

She reached into her pocket and pulled out the broken malachite, opening her palm for Rosa to see.

"Everything is fine," Rosa said firmly, taking the stones from Sasha's hand. "Now, off to bed with you before you catch a terrible cold."

~

SASHA LIMPED BACK TO HER ROOM WITH A HEAVY HEART AND FROZEN FEET.

Lyla stirred as she crossed the threshold. "Something happen?" she mumbled.

"Yes," Sasha said, as she sat down on the edge of her bed. "Two men and a fire beast tried to barbeque Mrs. Landshome."

"Oh." Lyla rolled over sleepily. "Barbeque. So delicious ..." She was snoring in moments.

Sasha envied her *so much*. Lyla was blissfully unaware of evil wizards and fire beasts and having to fight for your life in a swamp with only a handbag and a container of pepper spray—

She quickly stopped that thought in its tracks. "Not now," she told herself firmly.

She ran a hand through her hair and frowned when her fingers snagged on a black swamp leaf. She looked down at the evidence of her latest adventure sitting innocently between her fingers and exhaled shakily.

"There's plenty of time to think about that in the future. Just ... just not *now*."

She threw the leaf in the bin and busied herself finding a pair of warm socks. When she could stall no longer, she climbed back into bed. She sat back against her pillows, exhausted but worried about what her next dream would hold. The thought almost made her laugh. A few days ago, she had been desperate to dream. Now, she would be happy never to dream again.

"Three days left," she said, yawning. "And everything is fine."

∽

"EVERYTHING IS *NOT* FINE!" THE HEADMISTRESS SAID TERSELY AS SHE watched Sasha and Rosa head back up Main Street. "Dark wizards? *Fire beasts*? We can't keep this up!"

"We handled it," Esther said, staring at the ring of ash around them.

"Yes, *this time*," the Headmistress said. "But what's coming tomorrow? And the day after that? And the day after *that*?"

Mrs. Landshome groaned. "Enough, Penelope! Just drop it!"

There was a muffled shout from above their heads. Then, two men fell from the sky and landed with a crunchy thump on the ground beside the ancient witch.

Mrs. Landshome looked up at the two stone dragons hovering in the air high above them.

"I didn't mean for *you* to drop them!" she shouted to the gargoyles. "I wasn't even talking to you! Get back to your posts!"

The dragons dutifully turned around and headed back up Main Street, settling on Stardust and Brimstone.

Mrs. Landshome looked at the crumpled forms of the dark wizards and snorted. "Dash it—those Sentinels are so literal."

"They're enchanted stone, Gussie," Esther said, cautiously bending over the men. "What do you expect?"

"Are they alive?" the Headmistress asked, staring at the wizards uneasily.

Esther checked their pulses. "Yes."

"You should have been gentler with them," the Headmistress said to Mrs. Landshome. "We need to question them."

Mrs. Landshome snorted. "Sure. I'll be gentler with the next dark wizards that attack me with a fire beast."

"Well, we won't be getting much from them now." Esther stood up and wiped her hands on her skirt. "They're knocked out cold."

"Convenient," Mrs. Landshome muttered.

"Do you still think Sasha should be in Old Middleton?" the Headmistress asked.

"Yes," Esther said firmly. "I gave my word."

"Even after all *this*?" The Headmistress gestured to the unconscious wizards. "You gave her your word that you wouldn't allow the Shadow King to take her to Between. You didn't mention anything about dark wizards. What happened tonight could have endangered everyone in Old Middleton—"

"They were after the girl," Mrs. Landshome interrupted. "Not the village."

"But the village was still in danger," the Headmistress persisted. "Our job is to protect the Portal and the village." She pointed down at the dark wizard. "This is not our job."

"Have you been drinking Memory Muddle?" Mrs. Landshome cried. "This *is* our job! We're witches! We're *made* to fight dark wizards and fire beasts, and to guard the Portal and the citizens of this realm—*all* of them —with our lives. We've had it too easy—we've gotten too soft. Did you think that being a witch just involved potioning some poor girl's tea to check if she's one of us? Or going out and fixing the odd storm or flood or fire?" She kicked the nearest dark wizard in the shin. "*This* is what we were made for!" She kicked him again. "*This* is what your illustrious ancestors did! They fought the dark creatures. They protected the innocent. Hells bells, we lost our wizards to ward this place! Something is coming, Penelope! *This* is just the beginning."

The Headmistress pursed her lips but was silent.

"Gussie's right," Esther said. "Something is coming. Things are changing. And we need to step up to the challenge."

The Headmistress stared at the dark wizards for a long moment, and then made a show of straightening her coat. "We should call the Shadow King."

"Bah, we don't need him," Mrs. Landshome said. "We've been doing just fine without wizards since 1861."

"Still—" the Headmistress began.

"If we call him now," Mrs. Landshome interrupted, "he'll just flash those fancy pants of his and insist on taking that poor girl to Between where she'll be in even more danger—don't try to tell me that she won't! We can handle this on our own."

To illustrate the point, Mrs. Landshome gestured to the fairy lights festooned between the lamp posts. The strings of light obediently unwound themselves from the posts and drifted down, landing neatly at her feet.

Grabbing a length of the cord, Mrs. Landshome knelt on the cobblestones and began to tie up the wizards with the sort of brutal efficiency that suggested that this was not the first time that she had restrained an unconscious person with novelty lighting.

"Gussie's right," Esther said, kneeling to help Mrs. Landshome. "We are more than a match for whatever comes our way."

"Those lights belong to the village," the Headmistress said halfheartedly.

"We'll put them back," Esther said, knotting the cord.

"Your priorities are all backward, Penelope," Mrs. Landshome muttered.

With a begrudging sigh, the Headmistress also knelt and began to wind the cord around one of the wizard's feet.

"At the very least, we should inform the Shadow King that dark wizards have come to Old Middleton," she said.

"If he were doing his job, they wouldn't be here," Mrs. Landshome said, grunting as she pulled the cord tight.

"We'll write him a note," Esther said. She looked up at the sky; it would be dawn before long. "Now, let's get these two to the Portal before they—and Sasha—wake up."

18

THE EDUCATIONAL VALUE OF DRAGONS

"Ms. Pierce, there's a monster on the windowsill," Mason Barnes announced, quite matter-of-factly.

Unfortunately, Sasha did not hear Mason's important announcement; she was crouched down on the floor beside Joanna, who had managed to tie her shoelaces together in a knot that would have stumped seasoned sailors. But even as Sasha prodded and pulled at the knot, her mind was a million miles away, endlessly reliving the events of the previous night.

Let us sum up, she said to herself, as she liberated another quarter inch of the rainbow colored laces.

She had almost been kidnapped (again).

She had almost been killed (again).

The safety of Old Middleton had been compromised (again).

Mrs. Landshome had been attacked by a fire beast and two evil wizards (for the first time, as far as Sasha knew).

(The fact that the old woman had been invigorated by the experience was beside the point.)

Everyone is in danger because of me, Sasha thought with a heavy heart. *I could have stopped it, but I let it continue.*

She had chosen to stay in Old Middleton, putting the coven, the village, and Lyla at risk. The guilt of that choice was beginning to become unbearable. Worse still, she had broken a promise: she had sworn to the Shadow

King that she would go to Between if her presence in Old Middleton proved a danger to either realm—and the events of last night certainly qualified. The right thing to do would be to call the Shadow King and leave Old Middleton immediately. But the thought of actually doing it—of leaving everything and everyone she loved behind—was just unbearable.

Let's continue summing up, Sasha told herself firmly, pushing aside that thought as she undid another one of the smaller knots.

She had lost one of her shoes in enchanted quicksand—which was relatively insignificant in the grand scheme of things (even if they were her favorite pair).

And, finally—of far greater significance, and something that she really did not want to contemplate too carefully—she had discovered that part of her almost-husband was stuck in a mirror. The *fun* part of her almost-husband, if her meeting with the Shadow was any indication.

Sasha sighed and viciously stabbed one of the laces through a loosened knot. Her relationship with the Shadow King would be so much easier, and possibly a lot more pelvic, if his selves were reversed. The Shadow thought she was splendid; the real King would rather have his face melted off than hug her.

Sasha really did have terrible luck.

"Ms. Pierce, there is a monster on the windowsill," Mason repeated.

"One moment, Mason," Sasha said, still distracted, "I've almost got this."

With a relieved sigh, she undid the second to last knot.

"Yeah, one moment, Mason!" Joanna said, with an imperious tilt to her little chin.

"But Ms. Pierce, he is making a rude sign!" Bryce piped up, before jamming his finger up his nose.

"Two rude signs," Kaytie corrected.

"One with each hand," Mason added.

"He should be in time-out!" Bryce yelled indignantly.

"Bryce, take your finger out of your nose," Sasha said automatically. She gave another vicious tug to the laces. "There is nothing worth digging around for in there. Yes! I think we've got this, Jo—" She paused. "Hang on, did you say 'monster?' "

Sasha looked up at the window and dropped Joanna's laces in shock. There, sitting on the windowsill, was a squat, green skinned fellow about two feet high, clad in a pair of leather trousers, a canvas shirt, and a pointy little helmet.

"What is it, Ms. Pierce?" Joanna cried.

Sasha recognized him from *Dastardly and Dank*. He was a ... a ...

"A goblin!" she cried triumphantly. "It's a goblin."

The goblin gave her a toothy grin and then gleefully brandished his stubby middle fingers in her direction.

"He did it again!" Bryce yelled. "Time-out!"

"Time-out!" the children echoed gleefully.

Sasha narrowed her eyes. What did the book say about goblins? Drunken, lewd, and thieving, she remembered. What was the other thing ...?

She inhaled sharply. *Child-snatchers.*

The goblin grinned at her, a glint in his jaundiced eye, as if he knew what she was thinking ... and was going to do it anyway.

"Not in my classroom," she muttered fiercely.

Sasha stood up and ran toward the creature, hoping to grab him before he chose a child to snatch. But the goblin was too fast. He shot off the windowsill and started to run around the classroom, Sasha on his heels.

"Children, go and sit in the middle of the room where I can see you," she ordered, as she chased the goblin around the tables.

The children obediently sat down and cheered madly as Sasha and the little creature ran laps around the classroom. The goblin, however, was not going down without a fight. He knocked over desks and chairs, painting supplies and papers as he ran, laughing maniacally.

But his rampage of destruction was soon cut short. With a whoop of triumph, Sasha grabbed the creature by the ear.

"Hooray!" the children cheered.

"*Agh!*" the goblin cried, squirming viciously.

Sasha dragged her hair from her eyes and turned to her class. "Right," she said, exhaling heavily. "I'm going to take this goblin down to the Headmistress's office. I need you to sit quietly while I'm gone, okay?"

The children nodded solemnly.

"Very good." She tightened her hold on the squirming goblin. "I'll just be a moment."

Sasha opened the door and almost shut it again. Children were running down the hall, squealing in both fear and delight, chased by what appeared to be the entire contents of *Dastardly and Dank*. Goblins, imps, brownies, and other creatures that Sasha could not name came pouring out of each classroom.

"Wow," Mason said in awe, peeking out from around Sasha's legs. "Now *that's* chaos."

"Wicked!" Bryce gasped, as he and the other children clustered around Sasha's skirt.

"Get back to the middle of the room," Sasha ordered, closing the door.

The goblin took advantage of the distraction and twisted out of Sasha's hand.

"Hey!" she yelled and lunged toward him.

At that moment, a small, blue imp jumped down from the doorframe, landing on Joanna's head.

"My *hair*!" Joanna batted at her head frantically. "Anywhere but there!"

Sasha abandoned the goblin and rushed to help the distressed girl. "Get off!" she cried, swiping at the wriggling imp.

The imp gave her a thumbs-up and snuggled deeper amongst Joanna's lustrous locks.

"Right," Sasha said, determined.

She dove into Joanna's thick braid and quickly extracted the squirming imp.

"Leave my class alone!" she told the little beast.

With a grin, it bit her.

"*Agh!*" Sasha yelled in surprise and flung the imp across the room.

"Yay!" the children cheered.

Sasha looked down at the tiny set of teeth marks imprinted into the meat of her thumb. Thankfully, it hadn't broken the skin.

"Fine," she said grimly, grabbing a tee-ball bat from the sports equipment box. "No more playing nice. Kids—get behind me."

The children quickly assembled behind her, Mason peeking from behind her legs.

All around the classroom, Sasha could hear chittering and high-pitched laughter, as creatures scuttled behind furniture and toys. From the corner of her eye, she could see glimpses of them—a flash of fur, a hint of wings, or scales, or feathers—that would disappear when she turned to face them.

"Now, listen here," Sasha said, addressing the creatures in her classroom, "I don't want to hurt you. But I *will* resort to violence if you come near these children. Consider this your last chance. Leave *now*."

The grinning goblin foolishly chose that moment to jump in front of Sasha, gesticulating obscenely.

"Stop that!" she said sternly to the creature. "These are kindergarteners! They shouldn't know about that gesture for at least another year."

The goblin ignored Sasha; it appeared that he cared little for the proper educational development of minors. Instead, he lunged toward her.

With barely a pause, Sasha batted him across the room.

"Go, teacher!" Mason cheered, as the goblin soared into the toy chest.

Four imps emerged from a bookshelf and ran straight for the children; Sasha hit each of them out of the window in turn.

"Sorry!" she yelled as they soared through the air.

Mason tore away from the group to check on their landing.

"Are they okay?" Sasha asked, as she peered over his shoulder.

"Yep," Mason said. "One of them has his thumb up."

In the playground, Sasha could see a group of children fleeing from what appeared to be a small, dirty-white pony with a stubby horn in the center of its head. The pony belched and swayed unsteadily on its feet as it trotted placidly after the children.

"Ms. Pierce! Ms. Pierce! He's waking up!" Kaytie yelled, pointing to the toy chest.

Sasha turned her attention back to the goblin, who was groggily shaking his head amidst a pile of stuffed toys.

At that moment, the fire alarm went off.

"That's it," Sasha said, closing the window, "we're leaving. Everyone hold hands with a partner—we're going to the playground. Here ..." She handed out their nap-time pillows. "If anything comes at you, hit it."

"But we aren't supposed to hit," Kaytie said, reluctantly taking a pillow.

Sasha thought fast. "Just this once. Today is 'Hit a Monster Day.' "

"Oh, okay," Kaytie said. She gave a few vicious practice swings. "Let's do it!"

There was a crash behind them. Sasha and the children turned and watched in disbelief as a winged lion cub the size of a house cat batted a potted plant off the bench. With an imperious flick of its paw, it sent the next plant crashing down after it.

"What is that?" Mason asked, mesmerized.

"I don't know, but I don't think we want to stay around and find out," Sasha said, handing Bryce a pillow.

Once the little lion cub had murdered all of the plants, it turned its golden gaze to Fish Stick and Aluminum Foil, who were swimming around in circles, unaware of their imminent demise.

"Oh, no, you don't!" Sasha said, rushing over to the fish. Fumbling, she placed the cover onto the teeny tank with her free hand. "Bad kitty."

She shooed the little lion with her tee-ball bat, but the creature seemed supremely unimpressed. It merely stretched out its leathery wings and eyed her haughtily.

"Fine then," Sasha muttered, turning back to the children. "Does everyone have a partner?"

The children nodded.

"Right. To the playground and stay together. Let's go!"

"But what about Fish Stick and Aluminum Foil?" Mason asked. "You can't leave them here—they could get eaten!"

Sasha pushed her hair from her face. "Mason, please—I can't carry the tank and protect you—"

"But you *promised* that they were free citizens!" Mason cried, raising his tiny chin. "They need to be rescued, too."

"Yeah!" the children yelled.

Sasha was about to disagree, but Mason looked up at her pleadingly—a little scrap of defiance wearing denim overalls—and she sighed.

"*Fine.*" Sasha made sure that the cover on the fish tank was secure and then tucked the tank under her free arm. "*Now* we're going."

They waited for a break in the hall chaos and made a run for the front doors, the winged lion cub trotting behind them. Sasha batted away several beasties who grabbed onto Mason's trousers and shooed away a posse of imps who tried to drag Bryce away. She watched with a surge of pride as Joanna and Kaytie pillow-beat a goblin in tandem, only stepping in when their little arms got tired.

Sasha took a second to catch her breath, hoisting the fish tank more securely under her arm.

"Sorry," she said to Fish Stick and Aluminum Foil, as the fish valiantly tried to swim through the choppy seas of their rocking tank. "Come on, children! Run!"

The children ran. They were halfway to the playground doors when a fierce gust of wind tore down the hall.

Sasha herded the children to one side.

"Face the wall!" she yelled over the wind, shielding them with her body as best she could.

The children dutifully pressed their faces to the wall.

Out of the corner of her eye, Sasha saw several creatures—their leathery wings beating fruitlessly against the strong winds—being pushed back through the open doors.

When the winds finally died down, Sasha looked up and saw Esther at the end of the hall, her palms raised.

"Call him," Esther said briskly, lowering her hands. She nodded toward Sasha's amulet. "There aren't enough of us to deal with a situation this large; we need his help. I'll take the children outside."

"Right," Sasha said. She herded the children toward Esther. "Everyone follow Ms. Carter okay? I'll be back in a minute."

Sasha waited until the children were out the door before pressing her fingers to the amulet.

"Shadow King! We need you here!"

She ducked as the winged creatures Esther had momentarily distracted flew back through the doorway, swooping down toward her. Some looked like flying lizards, others like swallows, their beaks sharp and blood-red. All of them were screeching joyously.

"The sooner, the better!" she yelled at the amulet for good measure.

The amulet flared warm beneath Sasha's fingers, so she assumed the message had been received.

She looked down at the fish tank and grimaced. "What should I to do with—*yes!*" she cried, spying a utility closet. She opened the door and placed the fish tank inside. Aluminum Foil and Fish Stick glared at her from amongst the mops and buckets and bottles of disinfectant, supremely unimpressed by their new surroundings.

"I'll be back for you soon," Sasha promised the fish, as she closed the door. She then picked up her bat and ran for the doors.

When she arrived in the playground, it was to a scene of fairy tale chaos. Children and beasties were running in all directions, shouting and screeching like mobile fire alarms. One group of second graders had managed to grab a goblin and were taking turns to hug it, much to the goblin's disgust. A group of third graders was running after an imp, who was waving a stolen pair of trousers triumphantly above its small head. Joanna was pillow-beating two brownies who were trying to add her rainbow sneakers to their growing pile of stolen shoes—all liberated from the barefoot children running, free-range, around the playground.

Sasha looked at the scene in horror; she honestly did not know where to start. She quickly removed the goblin from the second graders and tied him to one of the fence posts with an abandoned skipping rope. She returned the stolen pants and defended Joanna's sneakers. She lost track of how many creatures she knocked over the fence.

But it seemed that for every creature-related problem Sasha solved, four others emerged. She noticed, with great relief, that the witches were doing a much better job of putting things to rights. She watched as the Headmistress rolled up her sleeves, her glowing Mark exposed, and directed a garden hose to unleash a torrent of water at a cluster of imps. Esther had managed to tether the winged creatures to a nearby tree, their plaintive cries echoing across the playground. Mrs. Landshome was gleefully barricading sprites within a ring of dancing flames; and Sasha was not even surprised to see Shae—who had been adamant during the

Twilight Tour that there were no witches in Old Middleton—suspend a small posse of bound goblins in the sky, where they spat and swore at all those below.

Mason Barnes had been right—all the teachers at the school were witches.

Sasha was about to go after the brownies with a shoe fetish when she heard a deep, masculine laugh coming from somewhere above her. She looked up at the Elder tree and frowned.

Reclining on a branch, as comfortably as if it was a chaise lounge, was the Shadow King.

For a split second, she registered how different he seemed when he laughed: it made him look younger, more carefree, more handso—

Sasha quickly tamped down that thought and focused on being suitably angry.

"This is no laughing matter," she scolded, shooing away an imp who was trying to peer up her skirt.

"Apologies," the King said, collecting himself. "But I could not help but relish the fact that these creatures were making a mess of someone else's realm for a change."

Sasha opened her mouth to retort but was distracted by the sound of a car alarm. Not just any car alarm—*her* car alarm. She turned toward the parking lot and realized, with growing horror, that the little horned pony she had seen earlier was methodically head-butting her car.

"Hey! Hey! Stop that!" she ordered.

Oddly enough, the pony stopped. It stood there unsteadily, staring at Sasha with blood-shot eyes, before belching hard enough to make itself stumble.

Sasha stared at the creature in disbelief. "Is that pony drunk?"

"Unicorn, not pony," the King corrected matter-of-factly.

"*That* is a unicorn?" The creature was mangy and stunted. Sasha could not imagine a creature more opposite a unicorn if she tried. "Are you sure?"

"Quite sure. I believe it came from the Goblin Kingdom, hence its less-than-majestic appearance. And yes, it is drunk. Though, I suppose it is a little early in the day to be intoxicated, even for him."

Sasha sighed and rubbed her eyes. "Would you please fix this?"

The King smiled, an almost affectionate smile, as a mob of barefoot children wielding safety scissors chased after the brownies who had stolen their shoes. "Yes. But it will happen again, and again, and again—as you well know."

Sasha did know. She dropped her hand from her eyes and looked up at him, defeated.

The King's smile fell away. "You made a promise to return to Between if the people of Old Middleton were in danger, Your Majesty."

He didn't have to remind her; Sasha had been thinking of that promise since the swamp.

"Before I—" Sasha cleared her throat, the words sticking to her throat like taffy. "Before I go, I need to ask one last time …" She looked up at the Shadow King, her expression bleak. "Is there *any* way—any way at all—that I could stay?"

It was a final plea.

The Shadow King shook his head slowly. "None that I know." Sasha could see the regret in his eyes, but his voice was sure.

She swallowed back the lump in her throat and nodded. "And—and after the trial run … when I return to Old Middleton …" She paused as a flock of winged creatures flew past her, their shrill cries as bleak as her heart. "Will the creatures follow me? Will the dark wizards follow me?"

"I will do all in my power to stop the dark wizards," the King promised. "But the Portal *will* open while you are in this realm. It opens to guide you back to Between … to where it believes you belong."

And that was that.

Sasha watched the chaos that she had inadvertently unleashed upon the elementary school and sighed. There was no point in delaying any further.

"Fine," she said wearily. "You win. I'll do it. Just call off your unicorn—that car cost me a fortune."

The Shadow King bowed his head in acquiescence.

"When will I leave?" she asked listlessly. "I need to collect my things."

The King carefully brushed gold dust from his hands. "Tomorrow evening."

Tomorrow evening? Sasha looked up at the King, her eyes wide with surprise. "But—but the Portal! The *creatures*—and the dark wizards and the fire beasts and—don't you want me to leave right now?"

"Do you wish to leave right now?" He raised a brow. "That *can* be arranged."

Sasha shook her head frantically. "No. Not at all. Forget I even asked. Tomorrow evening is fine. More than fine. *Great*, in fact."

"Sunset," the King said firmly.

"Sunset," Sasha repeated, relieved.

It was a reprieve. A small one, but a reprieve nonetheless and Sasha was infinitely grateful for it. She stared at the Shadow King—who now appeared as aloof and sinister as ever, his laughter long gone—and was suddenly curious as to why he was being so ... well, *kind* to her.

"I can be reasonable," he said unexpectedly. "On occasion."

Sasha started—could he read her mind? She made a mental note to ask the witches if telepathy was a sorcerer trick. "I know. I pointed out that you were reasonable when we were in the Portal Chamber, remember?"

The King arched an eyebrow. "I thought that was mostly empty flattery."

"Mostly," she admitted. "But not completely."

The King's lips twitched. "Your honesty is both refreshing and insulting."

Sasha was about to respond but was distracted by a tug on her skirt. It was Mason, the winged lion cub standing beside him.

"Ms. Pierce," Mason said, staring down at his companion, "he keeps following me around. What is he?" The little beast yawned widely and butted his head against the boy's palm.

Sasha turned to the King. "I've only read bits of *Dastardly and Dank.* What is he?"

The King looked critically at the leather-winged cub. "Truly? It is difficult to say. We have a lot of crossbreeds in Between, though this one appears to be a 'drion'—a dragon-lion crossbreed."

"Wicked! Can I keep him?" Mason asked.

"Yes," the Shadow King said.

Mason's eyes widened. "Wicked!" He cautiously petted the little beast's mane. "I'm going to call you 'Bunion.' "

"A truly noble name," the King said with a straight face.

Sasha stared at the King, horrified. "Are you nuts? You can't give a child a wild, mythical beast."

"Why ever not? It is the perfect time to acquire one. The beast is not yet full-grown nor is the boy. They will grow together."

"Never breed," she muttered to the King.

"Good gods, why would I do that?" he asked, clearly affronted. "I would rather raise drions."

Sasha chose to ignore that comment, mostly because she agreed. Instead, she pulled Mason away from the winged cub. "You can't keep it; it needs to go back to its home."

The little cub bared its teeth at Sasha and growled. Mason looked at the beast and then also growled at Sasha.

"It is probably for the best," the King said. "Drions have been known to grow as large as a wagon and feast on wild hill wolves. And, occasionally, on man-flesh."

Bunion had the good grace to look sheepish.

Mason was unperturbed. "Will he eat candy?" he asked, pulling a packet from his pocket.

The King shrugged. "I am not sure. Shall we find out?"

He gracefully dropped from the branch, landing in a low crouch.

"This isn't helpful," Sasha said sternly, as she watched Mason feed a piece of yellow candy to the happy drion. A moment later, the beast burped, setting fire to the grass around him.

The King was impressed. "Hmm. They are not usually capable of fiery destruction. Shall we give him another one?"

"Yes!" Mason said.

"No!" Sasha said. "The last thing we need is to make the beast more vicious." She took the candy away from Mason and, without thinking about it, smacked the King on the arm with the packet.

He looked down at his arm incredulously. "Which beast were you referring to?"

"No hitting, Ms. Pierce," Mason said automatically, patting the drion.

Sasha's jaw clenched. "I'm sorry, my hand slipped."

"Barely betrothed and already abused." The King sighed dramatically. "And to think, the coven thinks that *I* am the dangerous one."

"My hand can slip again," Sasha said meaningfully.

He gave her a dark smile. "My amulet, if you please?"

Sasha quickly removed the amulet and handed it to the King. He took it without a word and strode past her, his shadowy cloak billowing behind him.

When the Shadow King reached the ornate school gates, he stopped and stripped off his gloves, placing them on the ground. Crouching beside them, he carefully traced his hands over the wrought iron. Sasha watched in awe as every place his hands touched—every ornate curl of metal, every post—began to glow gold.

When the entire gate was golden, the King opened it with a flourish.

"Home," he said firmly to the creatures. "All of you."

The assorted beasties began to drift toward the gate—almost as if they had been sucked up by an industrial-strength vacuum cleaner. The creatures fought back, yelling and screeching and digging their heels into the dirt. But it did no good; they were dragged back to Between, first the winged creatures, followed by all the sprites, brownies, and imps. As soon as they crossed the threshold of the gate, they disappeared.

The unicorn trotted unsteadily up to Sasha, seemingly immune to the suction, and bumped its nose against her palm. Sasha grimaced; the little creature smelled of cabbage and sour beer. Nevertheless, she reached out and hesitantly stroked his muzzle.

"You, too," the King said sternly to the mangy beast.

The unicorn gave him a bleary glare and then meandered through the gate, neighing grumpily.

"And you," the King said, addressing Bunion.

The little drion stood protectively in front of Mason and pawed the ground defiantly.

"*Interesting*," the King said, staring at the little drion thoughtfully. "We will discuss this when we return to Between."

The last of the creatures—except for Bunion—made their way through the gates, one imp clutching a stuffed bear. Soon, the entire schoolyard was free of beasts—at least, of the non-human variety.

"YAY!" the children cheered, clapping wildly.

"That was wicked!" Mason yelled.

The King closed the gate firmly behind his creatures, and executed a low bow to the smiling, clapping children, the teachers cheering along with considerable relief.

"What else can you do?" Joanna asked, looking up at the King adoringly.

"Do?" he asked.

"What other tricks?" Mason explained. "Can you make a rabbit come out of a hat?"

"Or scarves?" Kaytie asked. "Can you pull scarves out of your hat?"

"Or a chicken?" another child requested. "Maybe a baby chicken?"

The King looked down at the children, puzzled. "What is this obsession with livestock and headwear?"

Mason shrugged. "That's usually what they do in magic shows."

"I saw the Amazing Hector pull four bunnies out of his hat when my Dad took me to Vegas," Bryce piped up.

"Just pull something out of something," Sasha suggested.

The King shrugged. "Very well." He scanned the crowd for a moment, and then reached down and removed Bryce's baseball cap. "This is a very small hat," he said, frowning at it. "I am not sure what we can fit in here."

He made a great show of placing his fingers inside the hat, followed by his hand, followed, quite impossibly, by his entire arm right up to his shoulder.

The children's eyes widened.

"Wow!" Mason yelled.

"This is trickier than it appears," the King said, rummaging around inside of the hat with a frown. "*Ah*, here we are." Slowly, he began to pull his arm back out of the hat. He struggled mightily doing so, like a fisherman reeling in a whale.

With mounting awe, the children watched as the Shadow King slowly pulled what appeared to be the top half of an enormous dragon out of Bryce's tiny baseball hat. Its head was as large as the King himself and covered in iridescent, blood-red scales. Its immense jaw was open, showing the children each of its sharp, white teeth.

The dragon turned within the King's grasp and trained its intelligent, gold gaze on the children. Throwing back its head, it roared, shooting flames thirty feet into the sky. Every car alarm in a three-mile radius simultaneously went off, and two nearby bushes burst into flames.

"You are being somewhat dramatic," the King scolded, frowning at the soot settling on his armor.

Abruptly, the dragon quietened, dark puffs of smoke rising from its nostrils, the smell of sulfur, ash, and Certain Death lingering in the air.

Sasha was frozen to the spot in pure terror, her face red hot thanks to her proximity to the dragon. The sheer power of the creature was so immense, its raw destructive potential so *petrifying*, that she felt her knees began to shake.

Of course, the children loved it.

"YAY!" they cried.

"Can I hug it?" Mason asked, stepping forward, his eyes maniacally bright.

That snapped Sasha out of her fear-induced stupor.

"Only if you want to get barbequed," she said, pulling Mason back to a safe distance from the fearsome beast.

Bunion growled his approval, and quickly placed himself between the dragon and the boy. Mason smiled at the little creature and gave him another piece of candy from his pocket.

"Let's say goodbye to the dragon now," Sasha said meaningfully to the Shadow King.

The dragon, clearly enjoying the adoration of the crowd, gave her a dirty look.

"It seems that the fun is over," the King said to the dragon. "Goodbye, my lovely one." He gave the dragon's snout an affectionate scratch. The dragon closed its eyes, reveling in the caress, small puffs of smoke rising from its nostrils. Then slowly, the King pressed the dragon back into the hat until each scale, and every fang had disappeared.

With a flourish, he flipped the hat over, showing the children that it was now dragon-free.

"Wow!" they cried. "*Hooray!*"

The King handed the hat back to a star-struck Bryce. He scooped up Bunion and held up his hand for silence. The children quickly stilled.

"For my last trick," the King announced dramatically, "I shall disappear. On the count of three. One——"

"Two!" the children yelled. "Three!"

With a click of his fingers, the Shadow King and Bunion sunk into the ground and disappeared without a trace. The children went wild, screaming and stomping and clapping madly.

The Headmistress ran to the spot where the Shadow King had exited and looked down at the ground, mystified. All that remained was the amulet, glittering amidst the scorched grass.

The children watched her expectantly.

Noticing their attention, the Headmistress picked up the amulet, patted her hair back into place, and pasted a broad smile on her face. "Ah ... and that concludes our super-secret magic puppet show! Can we all give a big round of applause for our magician?"

The children clapped enthusiastically. Esther discreetly put out the burning bushes.

The Headmistress held up her hands for silence. "Now ... let's have an early lunch!"

~

WHILE THE CHILDREN SPENT THEIR LUNCH HOUR TEARING AROUND THE playground, still in a state of boundless excitement over the impromptu magic puppet show, the atmosphere in the staffroom was rather more somber.

It was also about forty percent alcohol. Mrs. Landshome had liberally poured the contents of her flask into enough paper cups for everyone in the room.

No one had refused.

"Do you think the children believed that it was a super-secret magic puppet show?" Shae asked, brushing ash from her skirt.

Esther fiddled nervously with her pearls. "They seemed to believe it.

The Shadow King played along very well." She smiled tentatively in Sasha's direction.

Sasha chose to ignore her. She was also ignoring her sandwich in favor of Mrs. Landshome's whiskey, which was easing the shock of agreeing to live in a magical kingdom, effective tomorrow evening.

The Headmistress took a sip of her drink and sighed. "If they don't believe it, we could explain it using our go-to excuse."

"What's the go-to excuse?" Sasha asked.

"Gas leak," Esther said. "They're known to cause mass hallucinations."

"How many of these *gas leaks* can we expect in the future?" Mrs. Landshome asked.

Sasha swallowed a large mouthful of whiskey and winced. "This is the last one—I agreed to go to Between tomorrow at sunset."

The truth of that statement was starting to sink in. Sasha quickly took another fortifying sip, but not even the whiskey could dull the effects of what she had agreed to do.

"This is going to happen, isn't it?" she said, turning to Esther, a note of panic in her voice. "This is *really* going to happen. Of course, it is!" She threw her hands up in the air. "I've just agreed to it."

"Yes," Esther said sadly, "it appears so." She placed a comforting hand on Sasha's shoulder. "Go home. We'll take care of your class."

Sasha shook her head. "No. I'm okay. I—I want to stay busy."

Esther patted her hand. "Of course."

Something occurred to Sasha. "Hang on—what if someone was walking past the school during the super-secret magic puppet show?"

"Don't worry about them, dear," Esther said soothingly.

"It's nothing a cup of tea won't fix," the Headmistress added.

Sasha's eyes widened. "You're not going to potion them, are you?"

"Just try and get the dose right," Mrs. Landshome warned. "We don't want a repeat of the last time we used Memory Meddle."

Esther winced. "That *was* unfortunate. Rosa couldn't figure out why that poor woman turned that color. I still think it was a food allergy." Seeing Sasha's horrified expression, Esther waved her hand dismissively. "It all worked out in the end."

"No potioning people," Sasha told the witches firmly. She placed her hand around the Shadow King's amulet, now back in its customary place around her neck. "Don't make me pull rank."

Esther and the Headmistress shared a look and then smiled at Sasha.

"Of course, Your Majesty," the Headmistress said.

"If you insist, Your Majesty," the coven leader said.

"Watch us kiss your ass, Your Majesty," Mrs. Landshome added, refilling her cup.

Sasha decided to let the matter drop. After all, she had her own unique set of magic-induced problems to deal with right now.

❧

WHEN THE CHILDREN RETURNED TO THE CLASSROOM AFTER LUNCH, THEY were all still on an adrenaline high from the unexpected 'show.'

"Did you see the bit with the dragon?" Mason asked, as if Sasha hadn't been there. "That was the best magic trick *ever*! I bet not even the Amazing Hector can do that trick." He waved his hands around in a showy fashion. "I want to be a magician when I grow up. Ms. Pierce, can I be a magician when I grow up?"

"Sure, you can be whatever you want," Sasha mumbled listlessly, as she handed out pencils. "Until it's all ripped out from under you and you find yourself job-sharing with a guy who turns into a bird."

"That sounds like fun!" Bryce said. "Birds are wicked."

Kaytie was a little more perceptive than the other children. "What's wrong, Ms. Pierce? Didn't you like the show?"

The other children gasped as if even the thought of not enjoying the show was blasphemy of the highest order.

Sasha swallowed a lump in her throat the size of a plum and picked up a stack of construction paper. "I'm getting married."

"Oh!" Joanna said, clapping her hands. "My parents are married."

"Mine, too," Bryce said, as Sasha handed him a sheet of paper. "Well, sometimes. Mostly to other people."

"Who are you marrying?" Kaytie asked. "Is he a dentist? Dentists make me sad, and you look sad."

"Is he a zombie?" Mason asked, trying to balance a pencil on his nose. "No, wait—a zombie dentist?"

"Does he have bad breath?" Bryce asked.

"Or yellow teeth?" Joanna asked.

"Or feeds on the souls of the damned?" Mason asked.

Sasha blinked. "No, no, and—jeez, I hope not. I'm marrying the magician."

The children perked up.

"Oh! Wicked!" Mason yelled. "You're so lucky. He can do magic tricks for you all day long!"

Sasha snorted and continued to hand out the paper. "I'd settle for that disappearing trick."

"When are you getting married?" Bryce asked.

Sasha's stomach dropped. "I'm not sure, but it's going to be soon."

"Can we come?" Joanna asked. "I already have a dress to wear."

Sasha shook her head. "I'd love that, but it's going to be far away."

"Like the North Pole?" Mason asked.

"Or Canada?" Bryce suggested.

Sasha nodded, smiling despite herself. "Yes. Like the North Pole. Or Canada."

Joanna's big, blue eyes began to well with tears. "I'll miss you!" She ran up to Sasha and hugged her legs. Before Sasha knew it, a small horde of sobbing kindergarteners had engulfed her kneecaps.

"Oh, please don't," Sasha said, her own eyes welling up. She patted each of the children on the back. "There's no need to cry."

"Yes, there is!" Joanna sobbed.

"It'll be okay," Sasha said, sniffing. "Maybe. *Gah*, I hope so ..."

Bryce looked up at her, snot pouring inelegantly from his nose. "Can you visit us?"

"And do magic tricks for us?" Kaytie sniffed.

"And bring us presents?" Mason asked. "Like a polar bear? Or a Canadian?"

"I'd like a pony," Joanna sniffed. "You should bring us a pony."

"No—a salmon!" Mason cried, his eyes fiendishly bright. "So that Aluminum Foil and Fish Stick can have a new friend!"

The goldfish in question, restored to their rightful place on the bench, appeared less than enthused at the prospect of sharing their tiny tank with a robust river fish.

"We'll see," Sasha said, touched at their concern. "If it's possible to visit you, I'll do it."

"Don't forget the salmon," Mason whispered, patting Sasha consolingly on her leg.

19

THE CONTRACT

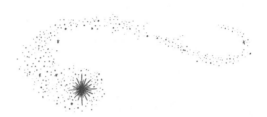

WHEN SASHA RETURNED TO THE BOARDING HOUSE LATER THAT DAY, SHE found Lyla behind Miss Adeline's desk, taking notes from Sasha's abandoned pile of reading material. She listened to Sasha's account of the events of the day, horrified and thrilled in turns.

"Dragons. And a drion. And Hill-Man in action." Lyla whistled. "How come nothing that exciting ever happened when we were at school?" Her eyes narrowed behind her reading glasses. "How are they explaining it? Gas leak?"

Sasha moved a pile of books from a nearby armchair and sat down in their place. "Super-secret magic puppet show. But gas leak was the backup excuse. How did you know?"

Lyla shrugged. "It's logical." She took off her reading glasses and stared at Sasha for a long moment. "We're avoiding the most important bit."

Sasha nodded. "Yes. Yes, we are."

"You're leaving early for your trial run."

It was not a question.

"Yes." Sasha ran a hand through her hair, her fingers coming away black with ash. "Tomorrow at sunset, I'm going to visit Between for a week. Then I'll return here and prepare to stay in Between permanently." She spared a semi-hopeful glance at her friend. "Unless you've found a way to keep me out of Between's clutches?"

Lyla looked crestfallen. "No, though I've tried." She pointed to her notebook filled with pages upon pages of notes. "Plan A is not going well."

She looked at up at her best friend, her expression resigned. "I don't want you to go on this trial run—"

"Lyla—"

"—but I'm not going to make a Scene about it. I'm also not giving up. While you're in Between, I'll research my brains out."

Sasha launched herself across the divide and hugged her friend. "Thank you, for everything. You are the very best best-friend ever." Frowning, she ran her finger across a burn mark on the sleeve of Lyla's sweater.

Lyla turned to look at the mark. "Yes. Yes, I am. I even have the scorch marks to prove it."

"You'll have to take me to the secret library one day." Sasha released her friend and settled back into her armchair. "I'll bring a fire extinguisher."

"*Ha*! Tomorrow, you'll have your own adventures to sort out. From the sounds of it, you'll need the extinguisher more than I will. Freaking *dragons*." Lyla shook her head in amazement. "To think I used to get excited about going to the pet store to look at hamsters. Come to think of it, I used to get excited going to libraries where the books just sat there passively and didn't try to kill me. Boy, was life dull back then ..."

For the first time since this entire catastrophe began, Sasha took a long, hard look at her best friend. Although Lyla had never been overly fashion-conscious, she always took pride in appearing cool, calm, and unruffled ("to get the upper hand in social interactions," she had once explained to Sasha). Ever since Sasha had defeated the Nightmares, *cool, calm, and unruffled* had been thrown out the window. Lyla looked utterly exhausted. She was paler than usual, her freckles standing out in sharp relief across the bridge of her nose. There were dark circles under her eyes, and a long scratch across her left temple. Her fingers were stained with ink and streaked with papercuts; her sweater and jeans were both singed in places; and her long, blonde braid was coming undone and spotted with soot.

Looking at her disheveled friend, Sasha was suddenly overwhelmed by how much she owed her. Lyla and the witches were putting themselves in danger to keep Sasha away from Between ... and she was repaying their kindness with dark wizards and fire beasts and dragons.

In that moment, Sasha made a Decision.

She reached over and closed Lyla's notebook. "It's time we stopped."

Lyla blinked owlishly up at her. "Stopped what?"

"I think it's time we accepted the situation and moved on to the next stage."

"What do you mean *accept the situation?*" Lyla asked faintly. "Do you mean forget Plan A? Do you mean *give up?*"

Sasha caught sight of *Dastardly and Dank* open on the desk. The Nightmares stared back at her, their mouths open, their hands outstretched toward her. She took it as a sign; Old Middleton—and Lyla—were not safe from their clutches until she became the Queen of Between.

She reached over and closed the book, trapping the Nightmares within the cover. "Yes." .

"Are you *nuts?* You're just going to run off and marry a medieval bird-man?

Sasha squared her shoulders. "Yes."

"And leave me behind in a cursed, man-free village in the Midwest with a bunch of witches *forever?*"

Sasha reached over and took Lyla's hand. "We accepted the fact that I have to go to Between on this trial run. Now, we must accept the fact that Plan A is a bust. Whether we like it or not—" She swallowed hard. "Scratch that—I don't like it. I don't like leaving you and my family and my friends one bit. But this trial run won't stop the creatures, or the evil wizards from entering Old Middleton; it'll just delay them." Her heart twisted, twisted viciously. But she kept going. "Becoming the Queen of Between and everything it involves—including marrying the Shadow King —is inevitable. Actually, let's just call it 'my new job.' That makes it far more palatable. My new job is inevitable. See? That sounds so much better."

Lyla shook her head, her eyes wide. "But—"

"You can't find a way around it," Sasha said firmly. "The witches can't find a way around it. Not even the Shadow King can find a way around ruling Between, and he *wants* to find a way around it. We need to accept it and make the best of it." She gave Lyla's hand a squeeze, pouring as much reassurance as possible into the gesture. "We need to make sure that we're still together as much as possible." Lyla looked as though she was ready to argue, but Sasha squeezed her hand once more. "We're realists, remember?"

Lyla crumpled. She looked down at their joined hands and took a trembling breath. For a moment, there was complete silence between them.

Then, Lyla straightened her shoulders and snapped her gaze back to Sasha. There was a core of steel in Sasha's clever friend, and right now she was a small, blonde bundle of determination.

"If you're going to take on this new *job* of yours, then you're going to do it on your own terms."

"What do you mean?" Sasha asked, relieved that Lyla was not arguing.

"What scares me most about this whole situation is that you'll be alone there ... which means that you're bound to run into trouble because we both know I'm the brains of this operation." Lyla conveniently ignored Sasha's eye-roll. "So, even though I don't agree with this whole acceptance scheme of yours, we should start figuring out how to keep you safe—and how to stay together as much as possible—while you relocate to Between to take up your new job."

"So, what do you suggest?"

Lyla released Sasha's hand and grabbed a pen. "We're going to write you a contract that ensures the conditions of your stay in Between."

"But why would the Shadow King abide by our contract? What's to stop him from signing it and then feeding me to a dragon?" Sasha's eyes widened. "Oh, hell ... he could do that, couldn't he?"

"No, he couldn't." Lyla turned to a fresh page in her notebook. "Not if you make abiding by the contract your second boon. I've been reading lots of fairy tales lately; magical folk are obsessed with bargains and contracts."

"You mean ... bargains like offering up your first-born child in exchange for a pile of gold?"

"Exactly! By the way, I don't know if swapping a first-born for a single pile of gold is a good exchange rate or not, so you probably shouldn't swap any children until we figure it out."

Sasha shrugged. "I'm not having children—teaching has turned me off breeding—so those kinds of contracts are going to work in my favor."

"You're right. Go right ahead then—but don't take their first offer. Make sure you haggle a bit; try to drive up the price. Back to the point—I don't know if sorcerers are bound to contracts like the fae, but it can't hurt to try, right? To have a little more security?"

Sasha remembered the dragon in all its fanged and fiery glory. "I'd like as much security as possible."

Lyla put on her reading glasses and cracked her knuckles. "Excellent! Let's make you as safe as possible. We know most of the traps that fairy tale characters run into, right? Let's make a contract that avoids them."

For the first time that day, Sasha truly smiled. "Like what? 'Please dispose of all poison apples and enchanted spinning wheels'?"

Lyla's eyes lit up. "Yes! We need to think of everything that has ever given grief to fairy tale characters and make sure you're covered."

"This idea is so crazy—and yet so fantastic—that it just might work."

"Damn straight. Now, where shall we begin?"

Two hours and thirty-seven minutes later, Lyla's hand was cramped, and Sasha's temples were throbbing. But there were four sheets of paper filled with Lyla's slanted handwriting sitting on the desk, and that made the women smile at each other giddily.

"I think we've got this," Lyla said, holding up the notebook in triumph. "Now, we just need to present it to Hill-Man."

Sasha yawned. "He's coming to pick me up tomorrow at sunset. We can ambush him with it then."

Lyla nodded. "I want to be the one who gives it to him. I don't want him wiggling out of this."

"Go get him. Make him beg for mercy." Sasha yawned again.

"No, stop doing that! No yawning!" Lyla stifled her own yawn. She threw down her notebook and pen. "This is your last night in Old Middleton and, so help me, we're going out for a wild night on the town."

"We're in *Old Middleton* and it's a Tuesday. The wildest thing we could do is go to an adult learning class at the Senior Center."

Lyla pushed her chair away from the desk. "Then hold onto your geri-atrics, Old Middleton—we're on our way!"

As it turned out, the only class offered on a Tuesday night was a weekly Build Your Own Birdfeeder class. Unfortunately, the class had been indefinitely postponed after a fight had broken out the previous week between two senior citizens over the last piece of sandpaper—a fight that had involved the entire class and only ended when four feisty seniors were taken to the hospital with stab wounds.

"It turned into a street-fight," the Senior Center operator said, shaking her head. "They made *shivs*. I guess it's our fault for offering a course with so many make-shift weapons. Next semester, we're sticking to chess."

Their plans thwarted, the women settled for pizza to go from Luigi's and the two bottles of elderberry wine that Rosa had left for them at the boarding house.

"Not exactly what I'd planned," Lyla said, serving each of them a slice of cheese pizza. "But, on the upside, I guess we won't get stabbed."

When the old grandfather clock chimed midnight, the women were still seated at the dining table, the remains of the pizza and the wine between them.

"I have to admit," Lyla said blearily, having consumed a goodly portion of the wine, "I'm having some problems with all of this fairy tale stuff." She drained the rest of her glass and reached for the bottle.

Sasha raised her head from the table. "*You're* having problems with all of this? *You?*"

Lyla waved her hand impatiently and refilled her glass. "Fine—probably not as many problems as you're having with all of this, given that you're the one about to live in a weird fairy tale land. But yes—*I* am having problems with this."

She began to refill Sasha's glass, but Sasha waved her away.

"Please, no more," Sasha groaned. "I am well on my way to becoming completely drunk."

"You *are* completely drunk." The wine bottle swayed dangerously between them, demonstrating that Lyla, too, was completely drunk. "Given your circumstances, that's probably an ideal state."

Sasha thought about that for a second and then gestured for Lyla to refill her glass.

Lyla laughed and began to pour. "That's what I thought."

Sasha lifted her overly full glass unsteadily to her lips. "You know ... that day when we first gathered the witches in the rose drawing room— after I ran across the Wasteland—I kept expecting them to say, *'Da daaah!* You're not *really* having waking dreams! It's all just a big, elaborate prank we play on newcomers brought on by drugged tea.' " She snorted at the idea and took a long sip of wine. "But it was all true. Magic ... magic is *real.*"

"Ha! And to think that my dad wouldn't let me read fairy tales when I was a kid because he thought they were full of nonsense."

Sasha laughed at the memory. "That's right! He'd get your nanny to read presidential biographies to you instead. You used to sneak over to my house to read *Cinderella.*"

"Yeah. Those presidential biographies were probably more fictional than the fairy tales." Lyla took another sip, sloshing a bit of wine onto the table. She frowned at the stain and wiped at it clumsily with the cuff of her sweater. "I wonder if Cinderella was just like you ... a woman going about her business—cleaning chimneys, talking to vermin—when suddenly, she's a story."

Sasha blinked rapidly. "Hang on—Cinderella could be true?" Her eyes widened. "Hang on, you mean *I'm* a fairy tale now, too?"

Lyla cleared her throat primly. "Once upon a time, a tall woman with fantastic hair ran across a field and won herself a kingdom ... and a matching king with a great chest. And they lived happily-ever-after in a non-pelvic, job-sharing situation ..."

Sasha decided to ignore the bit about the Shadow King's chest, and the bit about pelvises. Instead, she focused, as best she could in her intoxicated state, on the bit that mattered. "There's no way that I'm going to end up 'happily-ever-after.' I'm just an ordinary woman in a fairy tale kingdom, and *those* kinds of stories always go horribly wrong." She sighed mournfully. "I'm so going to get eaten by a dragon ..."

"What are the odds that your life was going to end well here, anyway?"

Sasha started to laugh, shocked. "Thanks a lot!"

"No, hear me out." Lyla carefully put her glass back on the table and leaned toward her friend. "Are you currently living 'happily-ever-after'? I'm not. At best, I'm living 'somewhat-pleased-ever-after' or 'moderately-jovially-ever-after.' "

Sasha acknowledged that her extremely intoxicated friend had a point. She was not *un*happy with her current life *per se*. But it was hardly the wondrous existence she had envisioned for herself when she was a young girl.

"Okay," Sasha acknowledged. "I concede that you have a point, but that isn't what I meant. What I meant was, in fairy tales, the heroes and heroines are already living in the fairy tale kingdom. Cinderella, Snow White, the other one ... what was her name? The one who kept sleeping."

Lyla peered at her blearily. "Ah ... Coma girl? Coma-rella?"

"Sleeping Beauty!" Sasha cried triumphantly. She raised an eyebrow at Lyla. "Coma-rella?"

Lyla shrugged and went back to drinking.

"My point is, they knew what to expect," Sasha continued. "They knew what they were getting themselves into. They knew all the crazy creatures in the land—they didn't need *Dastardly and Dank*. Some of them even had fairy godmothers, dammit! I don't know the crazy creatures. I don't have a fairy godmother. I'm *doomed*."

To Sasha's surprise, Lyla shook her head. "Nope. You know what? I actually think that you're better prepared than any of those girls." Lyla ignored Sasha's incredulous look. "Seriously, I've been thinking about this. First, most fairy tales are about barely literate peasant girls. I mean it— what kind of education did Cinderella get? It's not as if the friendly mice were teaching her physics. You have a college education, *and* you've been trained to deal with classrooms filled with uncontrollable children. Wrangling a dragon is going to be a breeze compared to teaching hyperactive kids how to read.

"Second, those fairy tale girls were usually unworldly teenagers. I remember reading somewhere that Snow White was only fourteen."

Sasha slammed her glass down on the table. "No way."

Lyla nodded sloppily. "Fourteen. I think most of the others were sixteen. They were young, sheltered little virgins roaming the forest, falling in love with the first guy they kissed. You, on the other hand, have just turned thirty and you've had more than your fair share of kisses. You've also traveled the world and have enough self-defense training to ward off any untoward advances from perverted princes roaming the forest."

"Perverted princes? Are you sure we've been reading the same stories?"

Lyla snorted inelegantly. "Oh please—most of those guys were definitely perverts. Take that prince in Snow White: he was riding around, kissing dead girls in forests. That's not romantic—that's necrophilia. Plus, she was fourteen, remember? He was a pedophilic necrophiliac. Come to think of it, the prince in Sleeping Beauty wasn't that much better. I mean, who kisses a woman in a coma? That's assault! Not cool, Prince Charming. Not cool ..."

"Wow, thank you for totally ruining those stories for me."

"You're old enough to know the truth. And don't get distracted—the point is that you're more prepared for this than you realize."

Sasha thought that over as best as she could in her wine-soaked state. "I guess that's pretty true. I'm better prepared than any of those girls. Could you imagine going through all of this at sixteen?"

"No. I could barely get through algebra at sixteen." Lyla took another sip of her wine. "Ha! Could you imagine dealing with Hill-Man at sixteen? You would have taken one look at all that manliness walking toward you and mistaken a fine appreciation of his chest for love."

Sasha laughed heartily. "So true! I would've been writing his name in my diary surrounded by little hearts."

"*Hill-Man and Sasha 4eva.*" Lyla laughed. "Do you remember when I thought I was in love with whatshishead—the first guy I kissed?"

"Steve Hines."

"That's right! Steve Hines. I thought he was the love of my life ... well, right up until he kissed Jennifer Bryce in woodshop right in front of me, that manwhore."

"Bastard," Sasha slurred, taking another drink.

"Bastard," Lyla agreed. "Sixteen. So many hormones, no idea what to do with them. Little did we know what was in store for us."

"I propose a toast." Sasha raised her glass. "To well over a decade of terrible dates and the power they gave us to separate love and lust."

Lyla raised her glass in return. "And may we always think with our head and not our heart or our pelvis."

Sasha *clinked* her glass against Lyla's. "I'll drink to that."

Lyla drained her glass and placed it back on the table with a satisfied sigh. "So, have we established that your interest in Hill-Man is definitely located in your pelvis?"

"Oh, definitely," Sasha said, the wine allowing her to be far more honest with herself than usual. "Which is why it's not going to play a part in any decision that I have to make, now or in the future."

"Good."

"But what I want to know is—what does a queen do? What does the Queen of England do?"

Lyla shrugged. "She queens. Waves at people. Christens ships with novelty-sized bottles of champagne. Rides around in a carriage. Wears a hat. You can do that. How hard can it be? Seriously, there isn't a degree for queen-ing so it can't be *that* challenging."

Sasha snorted. "Sounds too easy. There's probably more to it."

"Undoubtedly, but I guess you'll learn on the job."

Sasha shook her finger at her friend unsteadily. "I thought you had a problem with this whole situation—wasn't that how this conversation started? But you seem pretty positive about it."

"You rudely interrupted me when I was trying to explain my problem and made the conversation all about you."

Sasha stuck her tongue out at Lyla.

Lyla grinned. "My *problem* with this is that the existence of magic—and witches, and sorcerers, and books that write themselves, and winning a kingdom in a dream—is breaking my scientific brain. I keep looking for the trick: the trap doors, the sleight-of-hand, the invisible wires holding the whole thing up. And so far, there isn't a trick. It's real, and it's *killing* me. But I'll adjust—I'm pretty cognitively flexible." She refilled her glass again, slopping a little wine over the edge. "The one big, important thing we have in common is that neither one of us is an optimist. We're realists—just as you said before. We're just trying to survive whatever life throws our way."

"Here, here," Sasha said gloomily and took another sip.

Lyla put down the bottle. She reached over clasped Sasha's hand. It took a few attempts, but she got it eventually. "I'm going to do everything I can to try and find a way to get you out of this—" At Sasha's protest, Lyla quickly changed tactics. "Or find a way to make the best of this situation. But, in the meantime, if you *have* to be a queen, then the best thing you can do is to think of it as just another temp job with really weird looking coworkers."

Sasha thought back to the cavalcade of creatures she had seen today. "Right. Really, really, weird looking coworkers."

"Dressed in medieval clothing."

Sasha remembered the King's customary attire. "Dressed in medieval clothing ... that is sinister and occasionally sentient."

"Which is not weird at all. Perfectly fine, in fact." Lyla waved her hand airily. "Nothing to see here …"

An odd little thought pushed its way past all the elderberry wine and bounced around in the forefront of Sasha's mind, trying to be heard. "Hang on, what happens if I find someone else that I want to marry? Or want to touch in an adult-type fashion?"

"We'll get you a cross-realm divorce, and you can divide the kingdom down the middle. *WHAM!*" Lyla made a vicious chopping motion with her hand.

Sasha blinked. "Wow. So violent. But thanks! You're the best."

"I really am. Whatever happens, I'm not going to let you do this alone. We're in this together … just like we're drinking this wine together, but with more queen-ing and less drinking."

Sasha caught her friend in a sloppy side hug and sighed against her sweater. "Did we just drink two whole bottles of elderberry wine?"

"We did indeed. Victory is ours."

"We're going to regret that tomorrow ... along with all the other things I regret. Like coming to this place."

Lyla tried to pat Sasha's back but missed and patted the chair instead. "Coming here was a colossal error on your part, which I pointed out to you even before all this fairy tale stuff happened."

Sasha groaned.

"But," Lyla continued, "according to Rosa, everything happens for a reason. Maybe those Nightmares have been waiting for you to cross that Wasteland your entire life."

Sasha became very still. All those years without dreams. All her thwarted ambitions and failures. Maybe it all happened to bring her here—to this place, at this moment in time—to move her life forward to where it should have always been.

Or not.

"Destiny," Sasha said flatly. "I thought you didn't believe in destiny."

Lyla attempted to shrug but gave up. "I was sleeping in the bed next to yours the whole time we've been here and not once did I dream of Between. This whole thing seems like Destiny with a capital *D*. Besides, it's not like self-determinism has done much for me lately. I'm happy to give Destiny a try." Lyla tried, once again, to pat Sasha on the back and this time succeeded in hitting her somewhere in the vicinity of her kidneys. "And you...you *have* to give Destiny a chance. You can do this."

Sasha pulled away from Lyla and straightened her shoulders. "I can do this," she said, bravely. "I am not sixteen. I am not a criminally under-educated fairy tale peasant girl. I am trained to deal with chaos. I know self-defense. I will not fall in love with a forest-roaming pervert at first sight."

Lyla winked at her rather sloppily. "You've got it. You've *got* this."

"Damn straight," Sasha slurred. She looked down. "Now, if only I could feel my legs."

Lyla started to laugh.

"No, seriously—I can't feel my legs."

For some unfathomable reason, Sasha began to laugh, too. And then, somehow, they both found themselves rolling with laughter on Miss Adeline's third-best rug.

⁓

IF YOU HAD ASKED SASHA TO RECALL WHAT HAPPENED AFTER SHE FOUND herself on Miss Adeline's third-best rug, she would have sworn that she had closed her eyes for a mere second—just long enough to catch her breath between howls of laughter.

But this was not the case.

"Lyla, we need to get off the floor," she giggled, opening her eyes again. She blinked and tried to focus on the ceiling. "Huh. Were there always stars on the ceiling? Lyla? Seriously, who put the stars up there?" She carded her fingers through the thick shag rug beneath her.

"This rug is nice," she said, as she attempted to stroke it. "Isn't it nice? And luxuriant."

Sasha felt incredibly pleased with herself for remembering such a fancy word.

"And furry," she added. That was a less fancy word, but Sasha was still pleased, nonetheless.

The very small part of Sasha's brain that remained sober and functional quietly suggested that the rug she had fallen upon had not been as luxuriant or as furry as the rug she was currently sprawled over.

Sasha decided to ignore that part of her brain—what had it done for her lately? "I really need to get off the floor."

"That would be an excellent plan of action."

Sasha groaned. "Oh, no. Not *you*."

"At your service," the Shadow King's voice said dryly.

"That's doubtful," Sasha muttered.

She tried to turn her head toward the voice, but it felt too heavy—more like a large boulder on her neck than a human head. She decided to focus on the starry ceiling instead, which involved less effort on her part.

"Where are you lurking, you lurking lurker?" Sasha made a showy gesture with her hand. "Reveal yourself on the count of three. One, two—"

"Three," the King said, deadpan.

Sasha blinked, expecting to see the Shadow King in all his black-clad glory, but there was only the starry ceiling. "I still can't see you. Where are you?"

"If you would be so good as to turn your head to the right, all will be revealed."

"Fine, but you'd better be there," Sasha grumbled. "Turning is much harder than it looks."

She heroically turned her head to the right and, lo and behold, there was the Shadow King, sitting on a low footstool beside her.

"Oh," she said, pleasantly surprised by this turn of events. "There you are!"

The Shadow King, however, did not appear to be as pleasantly surprised by this turn of events. "Here I am," he said. "In my own chambers. Just like magic."

With considerable effort, Sasha wagged her finger at the King. "You know, you have a lovely voice. It's all low and warm and handsome—"

"Handsome?" the King repeated, clearly amused.

"—and it sounds the way that towels feel when they first come out of the dryer—"

"I sound like dry towels? Marvelous."

"But *then* you use your lovely, dry towel voice to say all sorts of pointy things. A voice like yours isn't meant to say pointy things. A voice like yours is meant to say round things. Like ... like ..."

"*Round?*"

"Yes," Sasha said emphatically, glad that he was finally getting with the program. "But even *rounder* words like *hors d'oeuvres*. Or *cinematography*. Or—or my name. My name is very round. Say my name."

His lips twitched. "Sasha."

Sasha frowned. "No, say it *rounder*."

"*Sasha*," the King said roundly.

"Yes! Just like that! That was lovely and round. Well done. Remind me to give you a sticker."

She stretched out her legs and sighed happily. "You have a round name, too, you know. *Lorn*. See? Very round. *Lo*—" She stopped abruptly and placed her fingers over her mouth. "I *can* call you that, can't I? *Lorn*? Or are you going to make me call you something fancy, like 'Shadow

King'?" She removed her hand. "Lyla wants me to call you 'Shadow King,' and I *can* do that but it's going to be really awkward, especially over breakfast."

The King raised an eyebrow. "Truly? How so?"

"Let me show you." She cleared her throat, and spoke in her roundest, poshest tones. "Pass the salt, *Shadow King*. Do these eggs taste weird to you, *Shadow King*? Here, lick this bacon, *Shadow King*." She grinned, triumphant. "*See?*"

The King looked up at the starry ceiling for a long moment, his lips folded tightly together, his shoulders shaking. "You spoke the truth," he said eventually, clearing his throat. "That was truly awkward and should be avoided at all costs."

"Told you." Sasha snorted. "*Some* people make you do that, you know—call them fancy things ... like *Headmistress*. You can't just call them *Penelope*. Can I call you Penelope?"

The King raised an eyebrow. "I would prefer Lorn to Penelope, if it is all the same to you."

"Deal! Lorn it is." Sasha waved her hand as regally as possible. "And you can call me—" She frowned at her hand. It felt odd, almost as if it wasn't doing exactly what she asked it to do.

"Should my wrist be bending like that?" She held out her hand and waved it in front of the King's face.

"I am not the right person to ask; my wrists often bend in odd ways." Nevertheless, the King peered at her wrist. "I believe yours is bending at an acceptable angle."

Sasha bent her wrist once more, just to make sure. "Good to know." She let her arm drop back to the rug. "Hang on ... what was I saying? Before the wrist," she clarified.

"You said, and I quote, 'You can call me—' and then you became distracted by your bendy appendage." He gestured toward the bendy appendage in question.

"That's right!" Sasha's smile was slushy. "You can call me..." Her slushy smile slid away, her forehead puckering as she tried to remember.

"Sasha?" he suggested roundly.

"Bingo!" she crowed. "Got it in one." Sasha let her fingers linger again in the lovely rug. "This rug is nice. It feels like a sheep."

"Many thanks. Tell me, are you intoxicated?"

"Yes!" Sasha cried gleefully. "I am. Elderberry wine packs quite a punch. I can't feel my legs." She tried to look down and failed. "Can you see them? Are they still down there?"

The King dutifully scrutinized the lower half of her body. "They appear to still be attached to your body."

"Phew. One less thing to worry about. I've had a tough day, Lorn."

"Really?" He leaned forward, closing the space between them a little more. "How so?"

"I agreed to get married today. Well, I'm pretending that it's job-sharing, but in reality, it's marriage."

"What a coincidence—so did I."

Sasha reached out sloppily toward Lorn and found his right boot. "My condolences," she said, patting his calf.

He looked down, amused. "Likewise."

Sasha tried to focus on his face and failed dismally. "Are *you* drunk? You're all blurry."

"No, but not for want of trying. Sorcerers cannot become intoxicated—I believe we discussed this on a previous occasion."

The thought of eternal sobriety struck Sasha as completely horrific. "Wow. That's terrible! Why not? Does your magic suck up all the alcohol?"

"In a manner of speaking. The actual explanation is beyond your current sobriety level."

"Oh, okay. You have firm calves." Sasha poked the King's calf vigorously with her index finger.

He blinked, shocked. "I beg your pardon?"

"You're welcome." Sasha sighed a great sigh. "I never thought I'd get married—I didn't *want* to get married. I move around too much. And I always date men who are pretty to look at but are so disappointing." She managed to move her head just enough to look him in the eye. "You're really pretty," she said accusingly.

"My apologies."

Sasha waved her hand magnanimously. "It's okay. It's not like you did it deliberately to spite me." Her eyes narrowed. "*Did* you do it to spite me?"

He shook his head. "Not this time."

"Good." Sasha decided that she liked elderberry wine; it made her feel warm and mellow, and utterly reckless. She decided to direct a little of that recklessness toward the King. "Who do you usually date?"

"I assume you are asking with whom I dally?"

"Sure," she said magnanimously. "Date ... dally ... datally ..."

His lips twitched. "I do not date."

"Why not? You look dateable."

"Many thanks. Unfortunately, there are not many opportunities for such things in Between."

"*Pfft*, you're a bird. You can fly to where there are more opportunities."

Lorn's mouth twisted into a sardonic smile. "The thought has never crossed my mind."

"Well … now that it has, you can try it out. Fly, my pretty. Fly …" Sasha used her hands to mime a bird flying off into the distance. The bird was clearly drunk and a danger to all in its vicinity.

Lorn watched the bird's drunken flightpath with a wry smile. "I thank you for your endorsement. However, my future dating potential will be severely limited once women realize that I am engaged to be married."

"I guess so," Sasha said agreeably. She let her hands fall back onto the rug. "Were you ever in love with someone?"

Even in her intoxicated state, Sasha recognized that the question was far too personal for him to answer. To her surprise, he responded.

"I thought so," he said, clasping his hands over his knees. "Very, very briefly, mind you. But it turned out to be a terrible case of mistaken identity."

"What do you mean?" Sasha put her hand over her mouth in horror. "Was she really something else? Like an imposter? Or a spy? Or a horse?"

Lorn bent his head for a moment, clearly trying to maintain his composure. He cleared his throat. "None of the above, thankfully."

"But—but what was the mistaken identity bit? Did she have different personalities—one nice and one evil? Oh, no—was she mean to you? Did she cheat and lie to you?"

"All the time," he said mildly. "But I had assumed that there was a true fondness for me hidden beneath all the cheating and lying. It turned out that I was mistaken. Ultimately, I believed her to be someone that she was not—the fault of which was entirely my own."

"Well—well—*screw her!*" Sasha said vehemently. "I can't stand cheating liars! There's just no excuse for it. Shall we set fire to her house?"

"In Between, we have outlawed arson unless you have a permit, and those are notoriously difficult to get. But I thank you for your support."

" 's no problem." Sasha clumsily patted his calf. "Don't worry. One day you'll meet a good woman, and she won't cheat and lie, and you'll live happily-ever-after."

"Excellent. I shall be sure to inform my wife of this fact."

"Oh. That's right—you're marrying me." She patted his calf again. "My condolen—hang on—*I'm* not a cheating liar."

"Well, that is a relief."

Sasha felt an impulse to be utterly truthful to ensure there were no more cases of mistaken identity. "But … it's only fair to warn you that I get bored easily. And then I usually leave. And according to my last two—three —maybe four boyfriends, I'm too sexually demanding. Which is such a double standard," she said testily, old grievances making her downright mad. "First, they're happy about it, and then it's, 'I have a headache, Sasha.' Or: 'We already did it three times today, Sasha.' Or: 'I think you broke me, Sasha.' The pretty ones break so quickly. No stamina." She looked up at him accusingly. "*You're* pretty."

Lorn buried his face in his hands. "*Sasha.*" His voice was choked with laughter. "I believe you shall regret this conversation once you awaken."

"I regret nothing!" Sasha chortled, waving her hands around sloppily. "It's the truth, the whole truth, and nothing but the truth." She reached out for the King's calf again, clutching it the same way that a toddler holds a stuffed bear. "I want to be honest with you. I want us to be friends. Can we be friends, Lorn?"

Lorn removed his hands from his face and looked down at her, latched around his boot.

"I believe we shall," he said, his tone stoic, "whether I like it or not."

"Good." Sasha yawned mightily until her jaw twinged. "I'm going to be moving to a new place soon. I'll need all the friends I can get."

"Have you ever been in love?" he asked, his tone curiously reluctant.

Sasha pondered the question for a long moment. "Not with my whole heart, no. But I'd like to be. Wouldn't you like to fall in love with your whole heart someday?" She frowned at his silence. "You can admit it, you know. I'm drunk—you can be truthful when you're drunk."

"But I am not drunk."

"I'm drunk enough for the both of us. We're almost married which makes us partners—if I'm drunk, you're drunk. Would it be easier to tell me if my eyes were closed? I'll close my eyes so that it won't feel weird." She closed her eyes. "Does that feel less weird now?"

"Remarkably so," Lorn said dryly.

Sasha waited. She waited so long that she almost forgot why she was waiting with her eyes closed.

"Very well," he said slowly. "I believe I should like that, too."

"It's a deal then," Sasha said, on the verge of sleep, still clutching his calf. "One day, we'll fall in love with our whole hearts."

"Whatever am I going to do with you, Sasha?" She heard Lorn whisper in his dry towel voice before the elderberry wine dragged her, unprotestingly, into sleep.

20

GATEWAYS AND GOODBYES

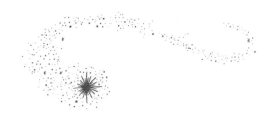

WEDNESDAY, OCTOBER 31ST: HALLOWEEN.

SASHA WOKE UP FEELING AS THOUGH A DRUNK LITTLE UNICORN WAS HEAD-butting the center of her forehead.

"*Agh*," she groaned, rubbing her temples.

"AGH!" she cried when she recalled, a moment later and in excruci-ating detail, her conversation with the Shadow King.

"Can't you just suffer in silence, like the rest of us?" Lyla moaned, rolling over on the rug and clutching her head.

Two hours, four cups of coffee, and a full breakfast later, both women sat listlessly at one of the bakery's outdoor tables, wearing sunglasses.

"The sun is so obnoxious," Lyla said, glaring up at the star in question. "And everyone is far too happy. Why are they so happy?"

"It's Halloween," Sasha mumbled, squinting at the passersby.

"Already? Time sure flies when you're in the midst of a fairy tale crisis. Speaking of which ..." Lyla looked over at Sasha. "Let's see if I have this straight ... Last night, you molested Hill-Man's leg, told him that he was pretty, and informed him that you broke your previous partners sexually—which isn't awkward at all."

Sasha winced at the memory.

"You also decided to be on a first-name basis, which I expressly forbid."

"I'm never drinking elderberry wine ever again," Sasha vowed. "It's the devil's juice."

"On the upside, you found out that he has no emotional entanglements, so that's a plus, right?"

"When did you become an optimist?" Sasha squinted at her friend. Even through her sunglasses, the world seemed obscenely bright. "I never thought I'd say this, but the sooner I'm in Between, the better. I've had enough of these dream meetings with the Ki—with Lorn."

"Right, because once you're in Between, you'll be meeting up with *Lorn* in reality—all day, every day—which will be *so* much better." Lyla tsked. "Clearly, you're still drunk."

"*Agh*," Sasha groaned and rested her head on the table.

Lyla patted Sasha on the back. "Yes, let all that angst out now. I want you on top of your game when we meet with Hill-Man at sunset to go through our contract."

"*Agh*."

"And we still need to figure out what to tell your parents and all your friends."

Sasha whimpered.

"Yes, yes," Lyla said consolingly. "Isn't this fun?"

TIME IS A FUNNY THING. THERE ARE DAYS WHEN IT DRAGS ITS BELLY, SLUG-like, toward its destination; and others when it slips, quick and slick, like oil through your fingers. As is usually the way when there is an unpleasant task ahead, time moved at breakneck speed on Sasha's last day in Old Middle-ton, hurtling her unwillingly toward her Destiny (with a capital D).

There were tasks aplenty to keep her occupied. She had decided to teach her class, telling the children that she would be gone for a few days. Joanna cried until her face resembled a small, soggy prune; Kaytie and Bryce drew goodbye cards that depicted Sasha as monstrously tall and oddly misshapen; and Mason attempted to glue her to a chair to stall her departure.

Sasha almost let him succeed.

Afterward, there was packing to do. While Sasha folded and sorted, she was continually interrupted by Lyla's paranoid packing tips, such as insisting that Sasha pack a suitcase full of bottled water and enough anti-septic to disinfect a small village; or her emotional outbursts, where she railed against Shadow Kings, the coven, and fairy tales in general.

"A pox on the entire fantasy genre!" she cried, shaking her fist at the sky.

Once that was finished, Sasha left an awkward voicemail message for her parents filled with half-truths and outright lies, crossing her fingers the entire time.

Before Sasha knew it, her small allotment of time was almost up. With a grunt, she dragged the last of her bags to the front door and triple-checked that she had everything she needed. Looking up, she caught sight of herself in the hall mirror and rolled her eyes at her expression: her cheeks were flushed, her blue eyes fever-bright, and her mouth ... well, there was something suspiciously smile-like tucked away in each corner.

She was excited, she realized, with a guilty heart. She had felt this way before every new job and each new travel adventure, and she felt it now—stronger than ever before—even though *this* adventure would tear her away from everything she knew and everyone she loved.

"What's the matter with you?" she asked herself aloud, mortified. "How could you be excited, you utter traitor?"

"Nothing wrong with a little excitement," Miss Adeline said. "As long as it doesn't lead to misbehavior."

Sasha turned and started at the inconceivable sight of the usually prim and proper Miss Adeline dressed as a stereotypical witch: black pointed hat, black dress, black lace-up boots, and all.

"You look fantastic!" Sasha said, smiling broadly.

Miss Adeline snorted and put a large bowl of orange colored candy—the hard, unpalatable kind—on the hall table. "This is our esteemed coven leader's idea of a joke."

"Could be worse," muttered a similarly dressed Martha, as she carried a silver tray filled with refreshments into the drawing room. "We could have been dressed as pumpkins."

Sasha rushed over to help her. "Let me—"

"Don't you fuss over me like I'm an old woman," Martha warned, "I could beat you at arm-wrestling any day of the week."

Miss Adeline nodded proudly. "That she could."

"No doubt about it," Sasha said, deftly stealing a cinnamon cookie from the tray.

Miss Adeline tsked. "Here, now—those are for later."

"I was just lightening the tray for Martha," Sasha said, grinning impishly. "Besides, there won't be a later for me. I've got to eat cookies while I can."

The thought was almost enough to put Sasha off her cookie.

Almost.

In an uncharacteristic display of sentiment, Miss Adeline placed her hand briefly on Sasha's. "I was only fifteen when I traveled across the country to Old Middleton, following my calling as it were. I was terrified. At the time, I thought it was the worst mistake of my life. In the end, it was the best thing that could have ever happened to me."

"Of course, it was—you met me," Martha said gruffly.

"That I did," Miss Adeline said, her features softening.

The two women exchanged warm smiles. Sasha looked down at her cookie.

"As for you," Martha said, placing the tray on the coffee table and turning toward Sasha, "this is going to be the making of you, mark my words. You're made of strong stuff—you can handle more than you imagine. Don't let anyone or anything get in your way."

"Right," Sasha said, trying not to get teary. "I'll crush everything in my path like a mail truck."

"That's the spirit," Martha said approvingly.

The front door opened, and Lyla and Rosa stepped inside, chatting away. Just like Miss Adeline and Martha, Rosa wore a witch's costume, her long, dark braid threaded with black sequined ribbon.

To Sasha's surprise, Lyla had dressed up for the occasion. She wore a smart, black shift dress and coat with matching black pumps, her blond hair twisted at the nape of her neck in a severe bun. She was also holding a shopping bag with the Stardust and Brimstone logo on the front.

Seeing Sasha's surprise at her attire, Lyla gave a little pirouette.

"This is my negotiation outfit," she said. "I want to appear business-like and formidable."

"Okay," Sasha said, "that explains the dress. What about the devil horns?"

A pair of red sequined horns were perched precariously on Lyla's head.

"Those are because I'm badass and like the color." Lyla reached up and made sure the horns were on straight. Satisfied, she opened her shopping bag. "I bought something for you, too."

With a flourish, she pulled out a tiara made of glittery, gold cardboard.

"Really?" Sasha asked incredulously. "*Really?*"

"You have to laugh about these things, or you'll cry." Lyla stood on her tiptoes and placed the crown on Sasha's head, carefully arranging Sasha's long, dark curls around the glittery piece of cardboard. "Plus, it looks amazing on you."

"I thought you were going to be at the shop tonight," Miss Adeline said to Rosa. "Isn't tonight your busiest night?"

Rosa waved away Miss Adeline's concerns. "As if I would miss saying goodbye to Sasha. Plus, I managed to finish the new bracelets." She reached into her handbag and pulled out a bundle wrapped in blue silk. "Lyla, help Sasha take off the bracelets she's wearing."

Together, Lyla and Sasha removed the protection bracelets, placing them on one of the side tables.

Rosa unwrapped the blue silk to reveal two silver cuffs. "There's nothing wrong with the old ones; it's just that the charms and stones dangle quite a bit. Now, these are far more streamlined." The cuffs were slender, silver bands, intricately engraved with Marks and protection runes. Rosa held them up proudly. "See? They won't get in the way."

"That's some fine workmanship, Rosa!" Martha said approvingly.

"Some of your best work," Miss Adeline said, admiring the engravings.

Sasha's eyes widened. "They are exquisite, Rosa! I can't believe you made them for me."

Rosa flushed happily. "I'm glad you like them. Here, hold out your hands." She eased the cuffs around each of Sasha's wrists.

"I like them," Lyla said, turning Sasha's hands back and forth so that the runes caught the light. "They make you look like a superhero."

"We'll set the runes as soon as the others arrive," Rosa said. She cocked her head. "Speaking of which ..."

Sasha could hear bickering even before the front door opened.

"Age before beauty," Felicia cooed to Mrs. Landshome, beckoning her through the door.

"I can't get past your cleavage," the tiny old woman said bluntly, looking up at Felicia's chest. "It's Halloween, not a beauty pageant, *Miss Atlanta Pineapple.*"

Felicia huffed and adjusted her form-fitting witch's outfit. "It's *Miss Georgia Peach.*"

"A fruit is a fruit," the old woman muttered, stumping into the drawing room.

Felicia rolled her eyes. "How someone hasn't dropped a house on you yet is beyond me."

The twins followed them inside, giggling into their black, lace gloves.

"I think Felicia looks fabulous," Daisy confessed gleefully. "Like one of those scandalous adulteresses on the daytime soap operas—the ones that usually come to a terrible end."

"That's always such a pity," Violet said, shaking her head. "I like their shamelessness."

Esther followed the twins and handed Martha a basket filled with gourds and candy.

"How are you doing?" she asked Sasha.

"I could be better," Sasha said.

Esther nodded, business-like. "We'll do all we can to make sure this goes as well as possible."

"We certainly will," the Headmistress piped up cheerily as she stepped through the door. She paused at the hall mirror and adjusted her pointy hat. "I do like these costumes, Esther, but I'm not sure if they set the right tone for the evening, what with the Shadow King coming and all. Perhaps we should have worn our robes?"

Esther took a glass of spiced cider from Martha and shook her head. "Those are only for ceremonial occasions. We can't wear them on the streets."

"Of course! You're quite right. It just seems a pity; tonight is the one night of the year when we could wear them out in public without causing a fuss." The Headmistress gave a final pat to her hair and joined the rest of the women in the drawing room.

Sasha looked around at them all and grinned. "You're not doing anything to dissuade Mason Barnes and the rest of the students that you're all witches."

The women groaned.

"I'd forgotten about Mason," the Headmistress said. "I wonder what he'll be dressed as tonight?"

"My money is on something vicious or contagious," Mrs. Landshome muttered as she reached for the cider.

Esther tapped the side of her glass for attention. "How long until sunset?"

"Probably another ten minutes," Daisy said, looking out the window.

Sasha's heartbeat began to accelerate. "Right," she muttered to herself. "Ten minutes."

Old Mrs. Landshome looked at her shrewdly. "Are you ready, girl?"

Sasha nodded once. "As I'll ever be. It's only a week. I can do a week." She refused to think about what would happen after the week.

"It's all going to work out, you know," Mrs. Landshome said, her pale blue eyes incredibly bright. "When it does, I want a full report on that chest, no details spared."

"*Gussie*," Esther said with a sigh, as the old woman cackled. She turned apologetically to Sasha. "Are you all packed?"

Sasha gestured to the bags sitting by the door. "Yes, and then some."

"Good. And do you have the contract ready?"

"Yes," Lyla said. "It's ready. Have you all read it through? Did we forget anything?"

"It's very thorough," Daisy said, with an encouraging smile.

"And clever," Violet said, beaming at Lyla.

"Not to mention unconventional," the Headmistress said, her lips pursed disagreeably. Noticing the other women's curious looks, she sniffed. "It's just not the way these things are usually done, that's all."

"That's the whole point," Miss Adeline said. "Most catastrophes can be prevented by exercising just a bit of common sense."

"True enough," Mrs. Landshome said. "It may be *conventional* to fall into a coma after pricking your finger on an enchanted spinning wheel, but it would be a hell of a lot *smarter* to avoid the damn spinning wheel altogether. Besides, the last thing Sasha needs is to fall into a magical coma." She grinned at Sasha *"Especially* when she has a husband who looks that good. Give him hell, girls!" She winked at Sasha and Lyla.

The Headmistress sat up, ramrod straight. "For the record, I don't want anything to happen to Sasha—"

Esther held up her hand for silence. "We know, Penelope. None of us do." She turned to Sasha, her expression mournful. "We thought we'd have more time to prepare you. We had planned to sit you down and teach you as much as we know about Between, but we were exhausted guarding the Portal and keeping the creatures out—not to mention all our other duties. We thought we'd have more time ..." She trailed off regretfully, fiddling with her pearls.

Sasha reached over and took Esther's hand. "I thought I'd have more time, too. You've all been incredibly kind and helpful; I don't know what I would have done without you." She gave the older woman's hand a squeeze and released it. "Frankly, I doubt anything could have prepared me for Between. I guess I'll just wing it."

"Wouldn't be the first time," Lyla said.

"Tick-tock, ladies," Felicia drawled. "I think sunset is upon us."

Rosa glanced over at the grandfather clock. "Quick! We have to set the runes on Sasha's bracelets."

Esther coaxed Sasha to hold out her hands. The witches crossed the room and surrounded Sasha, raising their palms toward the bracelets. Almost immediately, the air in the drawing room began to circle the coven, whipping around them, faster and faster. Sasha, standing at its center, felt the magic touch her exposed skin like hundreds of needlepoints of light. She inhaled sharply at the sensation—the impossible tang of a sea breeze filling her lungs—and bent her knees, trying to stay upright as the floor-boards beneath her boots lurched and groaned.

Looking down, she watched as her bracelets begin to glow gold, the runes etched onto the surface burning with bright, white light. The lamps in the drawing room flickered on and off, before plunging the room into darkness, her glowing bracelets providing the only light.

Sasha counted the seconds in the darkness with the beats of her racing heart.

The lamps blinked once … twice … and then came back on. The breeze gave one final circuit of the room and died, the warmth still lingering in the air. With one last groan, the floorboards settled beneath Sasha's feet.

The witches lowered their palms.

Sasha watched as the gold light around her wrists faded, and the bracelets slowly turned back to silver.

"*Fantastic,*" Lyla whispered, awed.

"There!" Esther said, clearly satisfied. "That went very well."

"Don't take them off," Rosa cautioned. "These are stronger than the ones you were wearing before, and they'll protect you from both magical creatures and physical attacks."

"Don't worry, I won't take them off," Sasha said, marveling at the miracles around her wrists.

"Good. Though …" Rosa bit her lip. "We'll need to replenish the enchantments periodically, depending on how often they're used. We'll have to figure out a way of doing that when you're in Between."

"The Shadow King could do it," the Headmistress suggested.

"But he's the one we're protecting her from!" Lyla cried. "That would defeat the purpose."

"The Shadow King is the least of her worries in Between," Felicia said, picking up a glass of cider.

"Thanks," Sasha said. "That's not alarming at all."

The grandfather clock began to chime six.

The witches all turned toward the clock and watched, silent.

With bated breath, Sasha waited until the final chime and then turned to Esther.

"It's time," the older woman said gravely.

Sasha took a deep breath. "Right." She touched the amulet. "Shadow King."

The witches drifted over to the drawing room windows. Martha pulled aside the curtains so that they had a clear view of the front gate. Sasha barely registered the children rushing past the boarding house dressed in costumes—beasts and ghosts and superheroes—all making their way toward Main Street to begin their Halloween festivities. Instead, her focus was on the boarding house's white, wrought-iron gate—a gate that was starting to glow gold.

With an ominous creak, the old gate swung open to reveal the Shadow King, who appeared seemingly out of thin air.

Sasha watched as Lorn looked up at the house, his lips quirking as he read the sign, then moved purposefully toward the door, his shadowy cloak flaring dramatically behind him.

"Are sorcerers like vampires?" Lyla asked curiously, as she watched him walk toward the door. "Do we have to invite him in? Because if so, let's just leave him out there."

The Headmistress looked at her aghast. "Where do you get these ideas? Why I never ..." she muttered, and quickly made her way to the door.

Sasha's heart was racing, her palms were sweaty, and her stomach was in knots. Even her teeth felt nervous. She took a deep breath and slowly let it out, just as the Headmistress led Lorn into the room.

He paused at the doorway, taking in the coven's Halloween attire.

"My apologies," he said with an amused smile. "I fear that I am, again, inappropriately attired."

"Just take it all off then," Mrs. Landshome said, well into her second mug of spiked cider.

Esther glared at the shameless old woman and gestured for the King to enter the drawing room. "Welcome, Your Majesty."

Lorn bowed his head. His gaze flicked over each of the witches and then settled on Sasha, eyebrow raised at her paper crown. "You appear to be dressed for the journey. Shall we depart?"

"Not so fast," Lyla said, stepping in front of Sasha.

Lorn took one look at Lyla's determined expression and sighed. "Lyla. Of course. I thought this was too easy." He gestured toward her devil horns. "Tell me—what fresh hell lies before me?"

Lyla smiled brightly at him. "As if I'd spoil the surprise. Come in and take a seat, Hill-Man." She turned and led the way to the kitchen.

Lorn turned to Sasha. "Hill-Man?"

"I found you on a hill," Sasha explained.

He waited.

"And I assumed you were a man," she finished lamely.

"Marvelous," he drawled. "A pseudonym that is both geographically accurate and anatomically assumptive."

With a bow directed at the coven, Lorn strode through the drawing room, a worried Esther, a taciturn Miss Adeline, and a reluctant Sasha following in his wake.

Lyla had gone to considerable lengths to ensure that the Shadow King was on the back-foot during the contract negotiations. She had chosen Miss Adeline's gloriously kitsch, mint-green kitchen as the meeting place, rationalizing that it would cause the most retinal discomfort to the otherworldly monarch. She had arranged the table so that he would sit all alone on one side, cowed by the wall of estrogen displayed before him. Finally, she had exchanged his kitchen chair for one that was quite bit smaller and slightly lower than the rest, which—she gleefully assured Sasha—would make him feel subservient.

Sasha thought that it would take more than a stunted chair to make a man as self-assured as the Shadow King feel subservient.

Sure enough, Lorn swept into the room, took one look at his micro chair, and immediately raised an eyebrow at Lyla.

"Do take a seat," she said with a serene smile, as she arranged herself opposite in her own vastly superior chair.

The King tsked. "And here I thought we would be meeting in good faith."

"Where did you get a strange idea like that?" Lyla asked, genuinely puzzled.

With an arch glance at his nemesis, Lorn laid his hands on the micro chair. The chair promptly began to transform, twisting and shaking until an imposing throne comprised of black obsidian and mirror shards dwarfed the table.

With a replica of Lyla's serene smile, the Shadow King took his seat.

"Not cool, Hill-Man," Lyla said, shaking her head. "Not cool. My only consolation is that your new chair looks uncomfortable."

"It is quite excruciating," he agreed.

"If you play nicely, I'll give you a cushion."

He tapped his gloved forefinger against his lower lip thoughtfully. "I will not lie—it is a tempting offer."

Lyla beamed. "Excellent."

Martha walked into the kitchen. She took one look at the throne, rolled her eyes, and walked out again.

With a disapproving tut at the ostentatious chair, Miss Adeline placed a dish of cinnamon cookies and four mugs of cider in the center of the table.

"Many thanks," Lorn said, taking a mug of cider and looking as out of place as a crowned and cloaked king could look in a 1950s-style kitchen. "You have a charming home," he added as an afterthought.

Sasha and Lyla were treated to the odd sight of Miss Adeline preening. "Why, thank you, Your Majesty," she said, more than a little delighted.

Martha entered the kitchen armed with two large throw pillows. "Lean forward," she said brusquely to the King.

"No!" Lyla cried, horrified. "That was my bargaining chip!"

Lorn leaned forward and sent Lyla a gloating smile—a smile that was almost knocked off his face when Martha jammed the pillows behind his back, practically throwing him off the chair.

"There," she said, grabbing his shoulder and pushing him roughly back into a sitting position. "All better."

She surveyed the visibly shaken king and sent Lyla a wink over his head.

Lyla beamed. "Thank you, Martha."

"Yes, many thanks," Lorn said dryly, straightening his crown.

Esther stared at Martha, horror-struck. "I think—I think that will be all, Martha," she said faintly. With a satisfied nod, Martha left the room.

"Mind that throne on my floor tiles," Miss Adeline said sternly to the King, as she closed the door behind her.

"A feisty pair," Lorn said.

"Like you wouldn't believe," Sasha said.

Esther cleared her throat. "Perhaps we should get started?"

Lyla nodded. "Yes. Let's."

"Agreed," the King said, having regained his composure. "Time is of the essence. I should probably begin by presenting you with this."

He removed a leather pouch from his belt. Untying the cord, he reached inside and pulled out a scroll tied with black ribbon—a scroll that was far too large to have been carried within it.

Lyla's eyes widened. Sasha was less impressed; after all, she had seen him pull a dragon from a baseball cap.

"What is it?" Sasha asked the King.

"The contract for our Joining. Tradition demands that I present it to your representative or advisor for checking. In this instance, I believe that to be the coven." He handed the scroll to Esther.

Esther took the scroll solemnly. "We will read it through."

"As will I," Lyla piped up, eyeing the scroll with suspicion.

"Really? What a surprise," Lorn said.

"Will *I* ever get a chance to see it?" Sasha asked dryly.

"There is a copy in Between, laid out in your chambers for your viewing pleasure," Lorn said.

"Great." Sasha stared at the scroll in Esther's hands, a dull weight settling in her stomach. "Is it worth asking you, straight out, if there are any nasty surprises in that thing?"

Lorn's mouth twisted wryly. "Why is it that everyone always expects the worst of me, even in this realm?"

"I'd say it was your outfit," Lyla said, gesturing to his all black ensemble. "And your chair."

Esther clutched her pearls. "If we may proceed?"

Lorn acknowledged Sasha with a tilt of his head. "There is nothing nefarious in that contract—beyond the act of marriage itself. It is a standard Joining contract befitting our station, guaranteed to ensure the safety and material comfort of us both. There are a few additions to safeguard Between; these, however, should not be cause for concern."

"I guess we'll be the judge of that," Lyla said. "How long do we have to look it over?"

"Until the eve of the wedding."

Again, the King reached into his pouch. This time, he pulled out what appeared to be a silver hand mirror. He slid it carefully across the table toward Lyla. "This is for you."

Lyla reached for the mirror then stopped, caution winning over curiosity. "What is it?"

Lorn noticed Lyla's hesitation and smiled darkly. "I am fulfilling the conditions of Sasha's first boon."

Lyla looked down at the mirror, puzzled.

Esther, however, gasped. She reached out and traced the intricate carvings along the silver frame. At her touch, the mirror began to glow.

"How extraordinary!" she exclaimed, awed. "This is quite the gift, Your Majesty."

The King bowed his head, clearly pleased.

"I know I'm pretty," Lyla said, deadpan. "But I'm finding it hard to figure out how my reflection is supposed to be part of Sasha's first boon."

Sasha peered at the mirror, perplexed. She tried to think back to when she had made the request in the Portal room. She had been frantic to stay in Old Middleton—had she been sufficiently crazed at the time to ask for a mirror?

Esther gave the mirror a final reverent touch. "It's a way for you and Sasha to communicate, Lyla."

"That's right!" Sasha said, finally remembering. "I asked for a way to keep in contact with Lyla while I was in Between." She turned to Lorn. "How does it work?"

"There are two mirrors," he explained. "One for each of you. You simply ask to see the person with whom you wish to speak." He picked up the mirror and held it before him. "Between," he said, and then turned the mirror so that the women could see their reflections.

The surface of the mirror glowed gold for a moment; then, a scene slowly came into focus. It appeared to be a sitting room of some sort, with two comfortable armchairs and a small table covered in parchment scrolls and books, many of which had spilled onto the floor. There was also a cheery fireplace and several candelabras scattered around, providing small pools of light. A fluffy, white rug covered the floor.

Sasha recognized that rug.

"Sasha's mirror is in my chambers," he said, confirming Sasha's suspicions. It also confirmed that he remembered their dream conversation; he had said her name. *Roundly.* "So that is what appears in the mirror."

Lyla's eyes narrowed as she took the mirror from the King.

"*Hmm*," she muttered, turning the mirror left and right, "what kind of secrets are you hiding in your chambers, Hill-Man?"

"None," he said. "I had all the torture implements and screaming peasants moved to the dungeons in anticipation of this meeting."

"Damn." Lyla handed the mirror back Lorn. "I guess it was nice of you to clean the place up for us."

He tapped the mirror's frame, and the scene disappeared. "Yes. Most accommodating of me."

Esther sighed wistfully, her attention still on the mirror. "It is truly an extraordinary piece of magic. And to have created *two* of them!" She shook her head, clearly dazzled. "The craftsmanship involved is remarkable."

Lorn dismissed her praise with an elegant wave of his hand. "I have an affinity with mirrors."

If only Esther knew, Sasha thought, remembering her encounter with the Shadow.

She looked over at the King and found him staring at her, his gaze intense. *He knows*, she realized with a start. *He knows that I met his Shadow.*

His gaze flickered briefly to Lyla and Esther, and then back to Sasha, his eyebrow raised. Sasha knew exactly what he was asking without uttering a word.

Do they know? Did you tell?

Sasha gave an imperceptible shake of her head. Lorn leaned back in his throne, surprised.

Sasha, too, was surprised—was a promise made in a dream genuinely binding? She hoped that trusting a man trapped in a mirror would not lead to her death or dismemberment.

The King gave Sasha a final puzzled look before turning his attention back to Lyla and Esther. "The enchantments on these mirrors are new and, as such, they are weak. The more you use the mirrors, the stronger the enchantments will grow. The stronger they grow, the longer you will be able to use them, and so forth." He held the mirror out to Lyla with a flourish.

"*Mirror, mirror on the wall ...*" Lyla reached across the table and took the mirror from the King's hands, her expression a curious mix of excitement and caution. "Thank you. *Now* I feel like we're in a proper fairy tale."

"Marvelous," Lorn said. "I am ever so glad to have met your expectations."

Lyla carefully placed the mirror on the table in front of her. "Well, I didn't say *that*. Shall we discuss our contract now?"

The King stilled. "*Your* contract?"

"Yes, our contract."

Lyla reached under the table into her shopping bag and pulled out a stack of paper. She handed Lorn several printed pages with a pleasant smile.

He took them warily and turned to Sasha, his eyebrow raised.

Sasha only smiled.

"Let us explain," Lyla began, handing copies to Esther and Sasha. "We know very little about Between or Otherworld. What we do know comes from the incredibly unfavorable information you've provided, a handful of facts that we've been able to gather from the coven, and the odd passage or two taken from the books that tried to set me on fire in the Gateway library.

"But there's one thing that we know for sure: terrible things typically happen to people in fairy tales. So, to ensure that Sasha goes on to live a long and prosperous life in your dreadful little kingdom, we have drawn up a contract to help her avoid the obvious causes of fairy tale mishap." Lyla put on her reading glasses and gave the King a charming smile. "It's important that we keep her away from all those terribly dangerous Nightmares and anything else that could harm her, don't you agree?"

"But of course," Lorn said mildly. He made a show of tapping his lip, pretending to be deep in thought. "Then again, the best way to have avoided this entire situation was to have advised one's friend to run *away* from the terribly dangerous Nightmares, not toward them." He smiled at Lyla—a smile completely devoid of humor. "Do you not agree?"

Lyla's eyes narrowed dangerously. "Esther, can I still be charged with regicide if I murder a fairy tale king?"

The King snorted. "If I had a gold coin for every death threat ..."

Esther began to speak, but Sasha beat her to it. "Children, please. One more quip and I'll put you both in time-out." She turned to Lorn. "My first boon was a complete and utter bust. You reassured me that I would be entitled to a new or modified boon, so this is it: I request that you agree to this contract, which aims to safeguard me while I am in Between."

Lorn made an impatient gesture with his hand. "The Joining contract is designed to guarantee your well-being—"

"But we aren't Joined yet, are we?" Sasha interrupted. "That leaves a whole week filled with potential catastrophes and possible death."

"You are the True Queen of Between," he stated firmly, "and as such, you will be afforded every protection that the kingdom has to offer. You will have a contingent of guards protecting you at all times, and my own safeguards—all of which will be at your disposal before and after our Joining."

"But what about the threats you take for granted?" Sasha persisted. "Things that your people know better than to eat, or drink, or touch? The guards can't protect me from those. They can't watch me every second of the day. This contract is designed to try and prevent accidental harm."

Unthinkingly, she reached across the table and placed her hand on his —and almost snatched it back. Even through Lorn's leather gloves, she could feel a strange electric charge, a spark at their touch.

He felt it, too, she realized, watching his pupils dilate.

Sasha swallowed and pressed on. "I'm walking into the unknown here, Lorn." His eyes widened at her use of his name. "I have no idea what's in store for me. I'd like some reassurance that I'm not going to accidentally put myself into a coma the moment I walk into Between just because I touched the wrong plant. Is that so unreasonable?"

He looked down at their joined hands. "It is not unreasonable."

Sasha sighed in relief and removed her hand, her skin still tingling in a strangely pleasant fashion.

"Excellent," Lyla said, turning to the second page of the contract, "Now, we have identified three broad categories of potential danger that Sasha may inadvertently encounter in Otherworld. The first is ..." She looked down at the contract. "*Accidental contact with magical items, particularly those that are evil or cursed.* These items may include, but are not restricted to: spinning wheels, music boxes, creepy-looking dolls, paintings—well, there's a list." She gestured to the Lorn's copy of the contract.

"What do you suggest I do with such magical items?" Lorn asked.

"Destroy them? Hide them? Bury them?"

"Label them." Lyla reached into her shopping bag and pulled out two containers filled with stickers. "We'd like you to put one of these stickers on all non-dangerous magical objects."

She placed a container of fluorescent pink stickers in front of Lorn, each labeled 'Safe Magical Object' in Sasha's clear handwriting.

"And we'd like you to put one of *these* stickers onto the deadly or lethal magical objects." Lyla placed a container of fluorescent yellow stickers labeled 'Dangerous Magical Object' next to the pink ones. "Ideally, we'd prefer it if you'd lock those objects away or keep them out of reach."

"Way, way out of reach," Sasha added.

"We've made plenty of labels so don't hold back," Lyla continued. "We'd also prefer it if you erred on the side of caution; if you aren't sure about an object, just label it as dangerous." She stopped and frowned at the labels. "Are you clear so far on the instructions?"

Lorn reached over to the 'Dangerous Magical Object' pile and peeled off the first sticker. With a small flourish, he attached it to his breastplate.

"Like that?" he inquired blandly, the fluorescent sticker looking particularly garish against his black armor.

"Congratulations," Lyla said, "you appear to have mastered the labeling system."

Sasha found herself smiling at the King.

Esther took a nervous sip of her cider and cleared her throat. "So, does His Majesty agree to label all magical objects?"

Lorn gestured to his chest. "Obviously."

"Excellent," Esther said with a brittle smile. "What's next, Lyla?"

Lyla looked down at the contract. "The second area of potential threat is *Other People*. We'd like you to identify anyone who may have evil intentions toward Sasha. Once they're identified, we need to devise strategies to ensure that their evil plans are thwarted. Now, according to most fairy tales, the number-one source of person-related threat is family members, mainly stepmothers or, in this case, stepmothers-in-law——"

Lorn held up his hand. "I have no stepmother. Or mother. Or father. Or stepfather. Or siblings. Or stepsiblings. Or pets. Or step-pets."

Sasha had already told Lyla that Lorn was an orphan, so this news did not surprise her. Still, Sasha thought that his orphan status was dreadfully bleak and terribly sad.

Lyla, however, thought it was a point in their favor. She nodded happily. "Well, that does narrow down the list of people who may wish to kidnap, kill, enchant, or cannibalize Sasha."

"Do you have to be so graphic?" Sasha asked peevishly.

Lyla waved away her concern. "We're being thorough." She drew a line through *family* on the contract. "Now, are there any women who may have wished to be the Queen of Between in Sasha's place?"

Lorn shook his head. "As I said in the past, the good women of Otherworld would rather chew glass than become the Queen of Between."

"What about the bad women of Otherworld?" Sasha asked.

He smirked. "They have far more ambitious plans in place." He paused a moment, his expression becoming pensive. "There *was* a recent betrothal offer from an unsuitable party—"

"Ah, ha!" Lyla crowed.

"—but when Sasha became the True Queen she voided their suit."

"Will they be a problem?" Lyla asked.

"Possibly," Lorn said. "We shall see."

"That's not particularly comforting," Sasha said sharply.

"Not at *all*," Lyla said, shaking her head.

"I have the situation under control," Lorn said firmly.

Lyla did not look convinced. "You'd better."

"I'm sure His Majesty will keep us updated about the situation," Esther said. She turned toward the King, her gaze steely. "After all, it is a matter of considerable importance."

The King inclined his head. "Of course." He gestured to the contract. "Shall we proceed?"

"Fine," Lyla said reluctantly. She quickly scribbled a note beside 'potential would-be queens,' then glanced at the next item. "How about former lovers?"

The King frowned. "What of them?"

"Are any of them disgruntled enough with you to try and do away with Sasha as a form of revenge?"

"Technically, many dallied with me because they were already disgruntled with their lives—it was typically their main motivation for doing so. It would be difficult to discern whether they were more or less disgruntled afterward."

"Huh." Lyla made a note of this on her contract. "Would any of these people have any reason to be angry with you? I mean, so much so that they would seek their revenge on Sasha?"

"It is doubtful," Lorn said with a shrug. "Though I can give the matter further consideration." He looked at Lyla with bemused irritation. "Shall I compile a list of my ex-paramours for your reading pleasure?"

"Why, yes," she said brightly. "That would be helpful."

"Would you like them ordered according to their level of distaste for me? Or by their access to weapons and assassins?"

Lyla smiled sweetly. "I was going to suggest alphabetical order, but either of those would do just fine. Now, what about mortal enemies?"

"I shall provide you with a list of those, as well."

Sasha balked. "How long is that list going to be?"

Lorn considered the question, tilting his head in an almost birdlike gesture. "Shorter than the list of paramours, longer than the list of family members."

"Great," Lyla said, making another note on her contract.

"It's *not* great," Sasha said, glaring at her friend. She turned to Lorn. "It's not great that people want to kill you."

He gave a negligent shrug. "I am accustomed to it."

"Good to know," Lyla said. "Though, let's not be quite so blasé about people trying to kill Sasha, okay?"

"Agreed," he said.

"Agreed," Sasha said faintly.

"Dearie me," Esther said, shaking her head. "Shall we continue?"

Lyla consulted her contract. "The final category of potential harm is: *Inadvertently consuming magical or poisonous food items*. What can be done to avoid this? We don't want a Snow White situation."

Lorn grimaced. "There are food items in Between that Sasha may find ... questionable." He turned to Sasha. "I will ensure that you are supervised during mealtimes and that my advisor, Maddox, is on hand should you have any questions."

"Thanks," Sasha said, her shoulders sagging in relief.

Lyla nodded, apparently satisfied. "Good. Finally, we want to make sure that Sasha will be staying somewhere safe and comfortable during her stay in Between."

"I *had* planned on keeping her in a paddock behind the castle," Lorn said, "but, if you insist..."

Sasha rolled her eyes. "How hard did I poke your leg last night?"

He smiled, clearly remembering their previous encounter. "You poked with strength and vigor."

"Good," she said flatly.

Esther cleared her throat. "Your Majesty? Her quarters?"

"Sasha will be staying in the Queen's Chambers, as befitting her station. The rooms are comfortably appointed and are currently being redecorated." He paused, as if remembering something problematic. "Hopefully, to Sasha's taste." He looked at Lyla with a fair degree of frustration. "Forgive me if this sounds repetitive, but there are no nefarious plans afoot on my part. Sasha is a queen and will be treated as such. Even in a squalid little kingdom like Between, there are standards on how royalty is treated. Fairly low ones," he conceded, "particularly in comparison to the Summer Palace, but still, there are *standards*."

Esther nodded, apparently satisfied. "Very good."

"You can't blame us for asking," Sasha said to Lorn. "This is a big step into the unknown for us. Until a couple of days ago, Lyla and I didn't even know that Between existed. We're not trying to insult you—we're just trying to make sure that there are no misunderstandings or false expectations. We don't know your customs or your traditions. We don't have a clue about what to expect. Even something that seems obvious to you, like where I'm staying, needs to be clarified. You can't understand what a relief it is to hear that I'll be staying somewhere safe and comfortable. So, thanks for that."

The King's irritation abruptly disappeared. "Of course," he said quietly. "My apologies. I promise to do all in my power to ensure that your transition to Otherworld goes smoothly."

Sasha felt a weight lift from her shoulders. "*Thank you.*"

His lips quirked. "Feel free to remind me of this promise whenever you are unhappy in your new surroundings—or if you see me behaving in a wretchedly dramatic fashion while affixing those stickers of yours to every object in the kingdom."

Sasha grinned. "Deal."

"So, to sum up," Lyla interrupted loudly, "you will provide Sasha with protection, and ensure her well-being against magical objects, people who may wish her ill, and questionable food items—thereby keeping her free from illness, disease, death, and magical maladies for the periods both before and after your Joining."

"I will," Lorn said firmly. "However, I am sure that those particularly fine, enchanted bracelets will do most of the work for me." He gestured toward Sasha's new bracelets.

Sasha looked down at her wrists and smiled. "Maybe so, but that doesn't mean you can slack off on the job."

"Do trust me when I say that it is not an option."

"Excellent," Lyla said with a cheery smile. She pushed a pen toward the King. "Sign."

With an arch glance at Lyla, the Shadow King quickly skimmed through the contract. Once he had finished, he picked up the pen and turned to the last page.

"What is the penalty should I renege on the contract? The standard disemboweling by hill wolves?"

Sasha stared at him aghast. "Disemboweling?" She turned to Esther. "*Disemboweling?*"

Esther looked slightly queasy.

In contrast, Lyla appeared utterly unfazed. "Worse," she said, holding Lorn's gaze. "You lose her. Between loses her. She comes back to us. *Forever.*"

"Which is a lot more palatable than having wolves chew on your lower intestine," Sasha quipped.

Oddly enough, Lorn did not appear particularly relieved about the safety of his digestive organs. Instead, he appeared troubled. "I can only sign for myself. I doubt Between will allow Sasha to leave—not without dire repercussions."

"Then you had better do everything you can to hold up your end of the contract," Lyla warned.

Despite the challenge in Lyla's tone, Lorn merely dipped his head in acknowledgment and began to sign the contract without a second's hesitation.

Lyla gave him a thoughtful look and then turned to Esther, who was smiling broadly.

"Esther, can you bind this contract as we discussed?"

Esther removed her black lace gloves, baring her Marks. "Of course."

Sasha turned to Lyla. "What do you mean *bind the contract?*"

Lorn finished his signature with a dramatic flick of his wrist. "She means to use magic so that my signature on this contract binds me to fulfill the conditions within. Should I renege, you will return immediately."

"Oh." Sasha mulled that over. "Hang on—if you renege, doesn't that mean I'll be dead, or in a coma, or cannibalized?"

"Probably," he conceded. "Let us hope it does not come to that, shall we?" He looked at the pen in his hand and rolled it between his thumb and forefinger. "I like this writing implement—it is exceedingly smooth."

"The contract?" Lyla prompted.

Lorn inclined his head and pushed the contract toward Esther. Reluctantly, he also handed back the pen.

Esther took a deep breath and pressed her hands onto the contract. The table surged forward then abruptly scuttled back into position. For a moment, the typed words glowed gold before returning to their original black.

Esther sat back and exhaled roughly. "There," she said, satisfied. "It is done."

The King grimaced. "It certainly is." He massaged each of his Marks in turn. "I will need a copy of the contract for Between's archives."

Lyla handed him one of the spares. "Pleasure doing business with you."

"Really?" He lifted one eyebrow. "The process was probably as pleasant as having swamp leeches applied to one's genitals."

"That's pretty much the experience I was going for," Lyla said.

"Mission accomplished," Sasha said, patting Lyla on the shoulder.

Esther looked older than when the negotiations had begun. "Thank you all," she said wearily. "That was almost civil."

Lorn stood up. "And on that note ..."

Sasha watched as the throne seemed to melt before her eyes, twisting and shifting until it returned to the shape of the small chair, the rose-print pillows falling onto the floor.

Lorn turned to Sasha. "May I have my amulet back?"

Sasha's hand flew to her throat. "Oh! Right."

Truth be told, she had forgotten she was wearing it. She pulled the chain over her neck and handed it to Lorn ... and was immediately sorry. She realized, with a start, that she felt oddly bereft without the weight of the amulet against her skin.

"Many thanks," he said, slipping the amulet around his neck.

As soon as the amulet hit his chest, he staggered back a step, his expression dumbfounded.

"Are you okay?" Esther asked, clearly concerned. Unthinkingly, she touched her Marks.

The Shadow King glanced at Sasha, his expression pensive. "It is of no consequence." He shook his head, as if to clear it, then directed his attention back to Sasha. "It is time to go."

"Right," she said with a tight smile, her heart racing.

"Right," Lyla echoed. "For the record, I disapprove of this entire enterprise."

"I would expect nothing less," Lorn said. He looked between Sasha and Lyla, his expression troubled. "I shall give you a moment to say your goodbyes."

He swept out of the room, his cloak billowing fretfully behind him. Esther smiled sadly at the two women and followed the King to the drawing room.

Sasha turned to her friend. "Does this count as an Ordeal?"

Lyla nodded. "It is most definitely an Ordeal—the most ordeal-y Ordeal of them all." She sniffed, her eyes beginning to well-up. "It's not too late to run off to Mexico, you know. We're small enough to escape through the kitchen window; I measured it earlier today."

Sasha gave her a sad smile and drew her into a hug. "We can't go to Mexico—mariachi bands make me sneeze."

"There are probably drugs for that." Lyla sniffed again and clutched her friend. "I am going to miss you *so much*! The only good part of all of this is that I got a magic mirror."

Sasha smiled tearfully. "Yes. There's that." She hugged Lyla as tight as she could, and then let her go, holding her at arm's length. "You'd better use it, okay? I'm going to miss you terribly! I don't know how I'm going to get through this without you."

Lyla's lower lip trembled. "Neither do I."

"Keep the mirror close by, okay? I'll call you and tell you all about my adventures."

"Is there a time difference between Old Middleton and Between? Will it be like calling Tokyo? Or Uzbekistan? Or Australia?"

Sasha shrugged. "Maybe. I guess we'll find out."

"Just ... stay alive, okay?" Tears slipped from beneath Lyla's reading glasses, her hazel eyes cloudy with sorrow. "And stand up for yourself— you're a queen now. Don't let anyone talk down to you."

"I won't," Sasha said hoarsely.

Lyla defiantly scrubbed away her tears with a napkin. Then, she reached up and straightened Sasha's paper crown. "And if you need help, scream into that mirror, and we'll find a way to bust you out of there. I'm positive Mrs. Landshome has a few tricks up her sleeve—or up her dress, right next to her flask."

"I bet she does." Sasha quickly dashed away her own tears, took a deep breath, and straightened her shoulders. "Right, let's do this."

Before she could change her mind about sneaking away to Mexico through the kitchen window, Sasha lifted her chin and marched back into the drawing room.

The Shadow King stood in the center of the room, flanked by an oddly subdued coven. As soon as Sasha entered, the witches surrounded her like a cloud of blackbirds, engulfing her in hugs and teary farewells.

"Take care and *do* wear a sweater," Daisy said, her blue eyes teary.

"Those castles can be so drafty," Violet cautioned, squeezing Sasha's arm.

"We packed you some cookies," Martha said, even more gruffly than usual, pressing a shiny, blue tin into Sasha's hands.

"Heaven knows what they'll have to eat in that place," Miss Adeline muttered, her lips pursed disapprovingly.

"Cookies? Bah, you'll need whiskey to get through this," Mrs. Landshome said, handing Sasha a small bottle of spirits. The old woman tugged on Sasha's sweater, forcing Sasha to crouch down until they were at eye level.

"He may be a sorcerer," she whispered, "but if he gives you any trouble, knee him in the gonads—it's hard to summon magic when you're crying on the floor like a baby."

"I am standing right here," Lorn said flatly.

"I *know*," Mrs. Landshome yelled.

"It's only seven days," the Headmistress said with false cheer, as she crushed Sasha in her embrace. "You'll be back before you know it."

"Just keep those bracelets on," Rosa whispered in her ear, "and you'll be just fine."

Even Felicia appeared to be somewhat distressed. She gave Sasha a stiff hug. "I'll try and wrangle up your wedding attire while you're away." Her tone was overly nonchalant, but her pale eyes were troubled. "We can't have you looking like a street urchin on the big day, can we?" She picked a stray piece of lint from Sasha's sweater and adjusted her collar to lay flat.

Finally, Esther hugged her tight. "Take care, Sasha. If you need us, use the mirror—we'll figure out a way to bring you back here." Sasha nodded, too overcome to speak.

Daisy turned to Lorn, her hands on her hips. "Now, young man, you had better treat her beautifully."

"Like a queen," Violet added.

The King looked up as if trying to gather strength from the ceiling fan. "Is it worth my while to reiterate that I am not the villain in this tale?"

"Even if you rode up on a white horse, dressed in shining armor, we would still be warning you," Daisy said.

"We just want to make things clear," Violet said.

"Has anyone asked Sasha what her plans are for me?" Lorn asked. "Has anyone asked whether her intentions toward me are honorable?"

"I should hope not," Mrs. Landshome said, pilfering another glass of cider.

The Shadow King gave the feisty, old lady a dark smile and turned his attention toward Sasha's luggage. "Is this all?"

Sasha nodded. "Oh! And this." She placed the tin of cookies that Martha had given her on top of the pile.

Lorn crossed the room and placed his hands on the bags. "Off you go then," he said to the luggage and gave the bags a small push.

The front door swung open of its own accord, and the luggage rolled out the door. Sasha had no idea if it would arrive in Between in one piece or even at all. In that respect, it was a lot like air travel. She found the familiarity comforting.

"We must be off," Lorn said, holding out his arm in a courtly gesture.

"Right," Sasha muttered. She gave Lyla a final quick hug and moved to the King's side.

"Right," she said faintly and placed her arm on his, forearms and hands touching.

Sasha realized, with a shock, that somewhere between the kitchen and the drawing room, Lorn had removed his gloves. It felt oddly intimate to be touching this way, skin to skin, but Sasha quickly quashed that thought. Instead, she focused on the strange jolt she had felt when their hands met. It had happened before—that same electric shock—but this time it felt familiar somehow. Comforting. His arm beneath hers felt strong and sure, and Sasha, shaky with grief and more than a little uncertain, allowed herself to feel anchored by that touch, to draw strength from it while she regained her own.

Before they passed through the doorway, Sasha turned back one last time. For the rest of her life, she would always remember the sight of the coven dressed in their witchy outfits, smiling at her encouragingly, Lyla standing amongst them with her devil horns slightly askew.

Then, Sasha straightened her shoulders and walked, arm in arm with the King, out the door and onto the street.

Outside, the Halloween celebrations were beginning in earnest. There was a sense of barely suppressed excitement, of almost tangible potential. Ghouls and superheroes, mermaids and wizards ambled joyously toward Main Street with their candy bags, lured by the scents of popcorn and fresh caramel.

"Where are we going?" Sasha asked, her heart beating triple-time.

"The Middleton Gateway," he said, gracefully leading them between groups of scampering, knee-high trick-or-treaters as if they were dancing along the street rather than walking.

Sasha glanced back at the boarding house gate. "But … didn't you come through there?"

"Only because I was Summoned by the amulet. To return to Between, we will need a gateway. I would rather use the one already available than create one."

They turned the corner, and there was Main Street, all aglow with fairy lights and jack-o'-lanterns. There was a cider stand in front of the cobbler's store, and an apple bobbing barrel set up outside the grocery store. The grocer—wearing a dreadfully fluffy, orange sweater—was refilling the barrel with lush, red apples to the cheers of the onlookers; while the baker, dressed as a rather portly vampire, was handing out cookies in the shape of black cats.

A small group of children waved at Sasha as she passed. One of them was Mason Barnes, whose costume consisted of a large box with black wheels. The box was painted a lurid shade of pink and covered in red, diseased-looking worms made of painted Styrofoam.

"Hello, Ms. Pierce," he said. "Hello, Magician."

"Hi Mason," Sasha said, as cheerfully as she could. "I like your costume. What are you supposed to be?"

"I'm chickenpox," Mason said, patting the box fondly. "But I'm also a fire truck because you can be anything you set your mind to."

"That's the spirit," Sasha said rather flatly.

"Are you going to Canada now?" Mason asked, staring up at Lorn.

Sasha tried to swallow the lump in her throat. "Yes, but I'll be back in a few days."

"Here." Mason handed her a candy bar. "They may not have these in Canada. They may have something that isn't as tasty, and you shouldn't compromise."

Sasha took the candy bar, feeling oddly touched. "Thank you, Mason."

The boy shrugged. "It's no problem. I've got lots of them." He reached into his bag and gave a pack of colored candies to the King. "Can you give these to Bunion? You can have some, too … the ones he doesn't want. Maybe the red ones—they taste like cough syrup."

"Very generous of you," Lorn said, taking the candies with a smirk. "I shall see to it."

The small boy nodded and turned back to Sasha. "You know, Ms. Pierce, I looked up Canada on the computer last night with my Dad, and it said that there are moose in Canada's zoos. You should probably look into liberating them."

"I'll get right on it," Sasha said.

"Good." Mason turned to the King, who was looking at the boy rather oddly. "Are you going to do any tricks tonight?"

Lorn kneeled so that he was at eye level with the tiny boy. "If you watch us very carefully, we shall disappear."

The boy considered that. "I guess that's a pretty good trick. Not an *awesome* trick, because there are no fireworks or screaming, but a *pretty good* trick. I'd rate it a five out of ten."

"I am glad it meets with your approval." Lorn stood up and offered his arm to Sasha. "Farewell, small man."

"Bye, Mason," Sasha said, as she allowed Lorn to lead her onward. "Be as good as you can be."

"I'll make no promises!" Mason called out.

"There is something about that boy," Lorn mused, as they left Mason behind.

"Yes," Sasha sighed, "I know."

The walk to the Middleton Gateway seemed impossibly short to Sasha. They seemed to fly past the trick-or-treaters and all the stalls. She tried to take it all in and memorize the scene: the smiling faces of the children as they collected their candy; the feel of the crisp, night breeze against her skin; the flurry of red and gold leaves around her boots; and the scents in the air—wood smoke and cinnamon, candy apples and caramel popcorn— that drifted across the street.

But before she knew it—before she was truly ready—they were standing before the sun-touched, sandstone arch of the Gateway. Lorn led her up the stairs of the dais until they were just before the archway.

"Ready?" he asked, as he placed his free hand on the pillar.

The sandstone turned the color of Between's gold dust at his touch.

Sasha felt a brush against her calves and knew, without looking down, that the cloak was trying to comfort her.

"No," she said, with a shaky laugh. "Not at all. This is not something they prepare you for in college."

The air began to fill with an odd humming sound.

Suddenly, a fierce exaltation began to well up behind Sasha's panic. She looked up at Lorn in shock.

He gave her a rueful smile. "Well, it is too late now."

With a long stride, the Shadow King led Sasha through the Gateway.

≈

As it was Halloween, no one paid attention to the man dressed in black armor—decorated with a fluorescent-yellow sticker—and the woman wearing a paper crown as they walked through one of the town's landmarks.

That is, of course, except Mason Barnes.

"Wicked," he said in awe, as he watched his teacher and her magician step through the Gateway arm in arm and leave behind only gold dust.

EPILOGUE

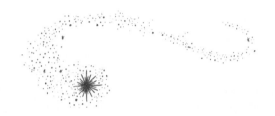

IN A DRAWING ROOM THE COLOR OF FADED ROSES, LYLA STOOD AT THE window surrounded by a black-clad coven of witches. She watched as her best friend since childhood walked out the door and into an uncertain future, led to her possible doom by a dark, fairy tale king in an impossible cloak.

With a heavy heart, Lyla followed Sasha's progress down the front path, through the boarding house gates, and then onto the street beyond. She craned her neck, trying to catch the last possible glimpse of her friend's dark curls before she disappeared, swallowed up by a crowd of children dressed as heroes and beasts. One by one, the witches moved away from the window until Lyla stood there alone, visualizing her friend's journey to Between.

To say that Lyla was displeased by this turn of events would have been an understatement.

She was devastated.

I failed her, she thought to herself, her heart twisting viciously. *And that is completely unacceptable.*

A throat cleared behind her, breaking her dismal train of thought.

"Well," the Headmistress said quietly, "that's that."

Only then did Lyla turn away from the window, severing her final connection to Sasha to face the witches. The coven stood like shadows, still and subdued in the dimly lit room.

As was her habit, Lyla pushed her heartache down, down, *down* until it was as small and as hard as a marble. She then hid it away in one of her lesser internal organs—probably her gallbladder—so that she could focus on the problem at hand.

"Oh, *no*," she said pleasantly. "This—this is just the beginning! We're going to work together to bring Sasha home."

The coven exchanged looks, none of which appeared optimistic. Worse still, most of them were distinctly pitying which left Lyla feeling itchy.

"I know you're upset," Esther said gently. "We all are, but I'm not sure what else we can do ... well, beyond making sure that Sasha is as happy and healthy as she can be in Between."

"No," Lyla said firmly. "We can do better than that. We *have* to do better than that. In a matter of moments, my best friend will be all alone in a strange world. She's soft-hearted and gullible and terrible at filling out government-issued forms, and they're going to eat her alive back there— maybe even literally. She needs our help!"

"I know this may be hard to hear, but perhaps ... perhaps you need to let go," the Headmistress suggested quietly. "This is her *Destiny*."

Lyla snorted. "If you think that I'm just going to stand by and let my best friend get carried off by King Chest-a-lot to become another doomed fairy tale heroine—oh! *OH*! Dash it—that's *it*! *That's it*!"

"What's *it*?" Daisy asked. She turned to Violet. "Did I miss something?"

"No," Violet said, peering at Lyla. "I think she's having an epiphany."

Lyla was, indeed, having an epiphany. The answer, she realized, was *right there*. It had been *right there* all along.

She groaned. "I'm an idiot."

"Well, you don't see us contradicting you," Felicia said, but the insult was half-hearted at best. It appeared that Felicia was more disturbed by Sasha's predicament than even Felicia had initially expected.

"What is it, dear?" Esther asked Lyla.

"Spit it out," Mrs. Landshome said, spiking her next glass of cider.

"Sasha is in a *fairy tale*," Lyla said to the coven. "Don't you see?"

"Not really, dear," Violet said.

"Are you drunk?" Martha asked Lyla bluntly.

"Maybe not drunk enough," Mrs. Landshome said, handing Lyla the glass of spiked cider.

"You may be onto something there," Lyla said and gulped down the drink. She swallowed the last sip of liquor and wiped her hand across her mouth. "I figured it out last night when I was drunk and forgot about it when I woke up sober."

"Sobriety is overrated," Mrs. Landshome said knowingly.

"Do tell us what you're prattling on about," Felicia said, her tone brittle. "The suspense is killing me."

"Sasha is in a fairy tale," Lyla explained, flushed with cider and discovery. This was *it*—she could feel it! "Fairy tales usually have a built-in failsafe: when the hero or heroine is in a terrible situation, all they have to do is perform the right task in the right timeframe to get free."

The witches turned to look at each other, brows furrowed.

Seeing their puzzled looks, Lyla plowed on. "Guess Rumpelstiltskin's name within three days and your first-born child is safe. Sew seven shirts out of nettles within seven years and your seven brothers are no longer swans. Sort out a warehouse full of grains before dawn and you're one step closer to getting your hot husband back. All of these are failsafes—they work to right the wrong ... to restore the status quo. Come on, ladies! Work with me here!"

"You know, that does make a strange sort of sense ..." Rosa mused.

"You shouldn't be encouraging this," the Headmistress warned Rosa. "This sort of false hope is destructive."

"No, you go ahead and encourage it, Rosa," Lyla said, relieved that someone was on her side. "Encourage away."

"But it *does* make sense, Penelope," Rosa insisted. "All of those fairy tales—there's a bit of truth in all of them. And for so many tales to have a failsafe ... a way to escape ... well, there has to be a grain of truth in that, too."

"I want to help Sasha," the Headmistress said, wringing her hands. "I truly do! And I know it seems like I'm overly harsh and pessimistic, but I don't want Lyla getting her hopes up on a fool's quest." She crossed the room until she was in front of Lyla and gently placed her hands on Lyla's shoulders.

"This is real life," she said, kindly but firmly, "not a story."

Lyla pulled away impatiently. "Is it though? Stick 'once upon a time' in front of Sasha's experiences in Old Middleton, and you have a pretty fantastic bedtime story."

"That's right!" Daisy exclaimed. "She even lost a shoe—just like Cinderella."

"Exactly right, Daisy," Violet said, nodding. "*Just* like Cinderella ... but without all the housework and talking rodents."

"And she even looks like Snow White," Daisy added. "All that dark hair and pale skin and red lips. Don't you think so, Violet dear?"

"She does!" Violet said. "Except a lot taller."

"She won a kingdom in a dream, Penelope!" Mrs. Landshome cried. "If that doesn't say 'fairy tale' I don't know what does."

"She also won a king," Felicia added.

"Lucky thing," Mrs. Landshome muttered. "I'd take that chest over ruling a landmass any day of the week."

"He's hardly a prize," Lyla said dryly, "but I like the fact that you're playing along. Trust me," she said to the Headmistress, "this is not the end of Sasha's story—it's just the beginning. I *know* it."

"But how do we figure out what this mystical, freedom-task is?" Felicia asked.

"The task she performed to rule Between was difficult enough," Violet said. "I shudder to think what she'll have to do to break free."

Lyla shook her finger at Violet. "Don't go down that path—that's failure talk. Let's focus on finding out what the task is first, and then we'll figure out a way to beat it."

"There are plenty of texts to consult," Miss Adeline said. "Surely, there has to be a clue in one of them."

"And what about the time limit?" Felicia asked.

"This is Between we're talking about, so it'll probably be measured in Lunar Crossings," Rosa said. "We might have to figure this out before one Crossing or twelve." She shrugged helplessly. "How can we possibly know?"

"Well, if it's the next Crossing, we're doomed before we start," Felicia said.

"You're just a big bag of sunshine, aren't you?" Lyla said to the redhead. She turned to Rosa. "It's not the next Crossing," she said, with more confidence than the statement deserved. "But I'm going to act like it is—the quicker we can get her out of that hell-hole, the better."

"No arguments here," Martha said.

Lyla turned to Esther. "I'll need help."

"We'll help," the coven leader assured her. "I'll assign some of the newer members to help you full-time; the rest of us will help whenever we can."

"Happy to do all we can, dear," Daisy said.

"*All* we can," Violet repeated.

"We'll get her out," Martha said firmly.

"She shouldn't be in that place to begin with," Miss Adeline said, lips pursed.

"You can count on me," Felicia said. At Lyla's surprised look, she pointed to Mrs. Landshome. "She tried to save this one's hide. We owe her for that."

"She's a good girl," Mrs. Landshome said approvingly.

The coven turned to the Headmistress.

"This happened on our watch," the Headmistress said, nodding slowly. "We should fix this."

Lyla squared her shoulders and straightened her devil horns. "Ladies, together we're going to perform an impossible task: We're going to beat a fairy tale."

"I'll get more liquor," Martha said, rushing out of the room.

"Keep it coming," Mrs. Landshome called after her, holding up her glass.

Behind the grate of the old fireplace, the logs burst into flame, sending the darkness fleeing to the corners of the room. It might have been a trick of the flickering light, but the witches suddenly appeared taller, quicker, *stronger*, their shadows dancing wildly across the drawing room walls.

Hang on, Sasha, Lyla said, willing her words to reach her friend. *We're coming to get you. Just hang on …*

PART II

THE WRETCHEDLY MELODRAMATIC TALE OF THE SHADOW KING

OR: What Lorn was doing while Sasha's life was being turned upside down

PROLOGUE

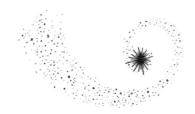

DURING HIS RELATIVELY SHORT, MOSTLY TERRIBLE LIFETIME, LORN HAD SEEN things—*extraordinary* things—that most in the Earther and Otherworld Realms had seen only in their dreams. He had soared above kingdoms on the back of a blood-red dragon and run with wraith wolves on the crests of snow covered peaks. He had walked through the fiery vistas of burning forests and swum with merfolk under the depths of cerulean seas.

Yet, if he had been pressed on the matter, Lorn would have confessed that one of the most extraordinary sights that he had ever beheld was that of a woman running across the Wasteland on a flickering golden path—her hair streaming behind her like a dark banner, determination etched into every inch of her form—as hordes of Nightmares howled in her wake.

He had charged to the Wasteland to rescue her, to whisk her away from that treacherous stretch of land and save her from the monsters of his kingdom. But when he arrived, Lorn quickly realized that he was superfluous: she was mere steps from rescuing herself.

No, *his* role was merely to witness the improbable instant that Sasha Evangeline Pierce crossed the boundary of the Wasteland and turned from a mortal woman of the Earther Realm into the True Queen of Between.

It was also his role to catch her as she staggered over the boundary wall, smiling up at him with such pure joy and relief that his dark heart twisted viciously behind his ribcage.

As Lorn carried her to safety, he looked down at the sweaty, exhausted woman in his arms and thought inanely to himself:

This is the new Queen of Between.
And then:
This is the True *Queen of Between.*
And then:
Good gods—this is my wife!
In retrospect, Lorn should have realized that this Dreamer was special.
If only he had heeded the signs …

1

THE SHADOW KING AWAKENS

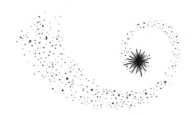

ONCE UPON A TIME, THERE WAS A SMALL KINGDOM FILLED WITH SUNSHINE
and joy. Its fields were abundant with fruit and grain, and its livestock
strong and hardy. Its people were good-natured and skilled in the ways of
music and art, and its king was respected across the length and breadth of
Otherworld. It was a place where people came from across the realm to
feast on fine food, partake of sublime art, and to bask in the light.

Next door to that kingdom was Between.

Between was a diseased little kingdom filled with wild magic and even
wilder weather—weather that had a yearly death toll in the triple digits,
thanks (in part) to a winter renowned for its lethal flaming snowstorms.

Its fields were generally barren, except for plants that were poisonous,
vicious, addictive, or—in one memorable instance—capable of wrestling
an adult male into a chokehold for four hours. Its livestock, which typically
fed on the poisonous, vicious, addictive plants, and drank from the wild
magic in the rivers and streams, was quite literally the stuff of nightmares
(albeit relatively tasty). Its lands were also filled with all manner of beasties,
magical and not, that ranged from herbivores to those that feasted, regrettably, on human flesh.

Between's people were comprised of those that other kingdoms
rejected. Thieves, assassins, spies, and the morally bankrupt all called
Between home, as did those who were in hiding, typically after a Plan or a
Scheme went terribly wrong. The fact that the majority of these poorly
conceived plans, or downright ridiculous schemes, were concocted after

drinking Between's especially potent brand of ale was one of the reasons why Otherworld's most reputable tourist guides listed Between's ale as the 'Fifth Most Dangerous Substance in Otherworld' (Betweeners argued that it should have made the top three).

The cultural offerings in Between were few and dubious at best. The only renowned arts were what Betweeners termed the 'practical arts:' thievery, assassination, and spying (colloquially referred to as 'procurement,' 'disposals,' and 'collection' by their respective practitioners). These were taught in an allegedly secret, Crown-run educational institution called the Academy of Practical Arts which was, quite literally, underground and situated next door to the Den—the largest practically legal gambling establishment in all of Otherworld.

As for the traditional arts, the only musical offerings in Between were the screams of its citizens as they fled from whatever catastrophes were taking place that week; or the drunken ballads composed by the rhythmically challenged, pitch imperfect house band of the Sleazy Weasel tavern. Both were equally hazardous to the eardrums of those unlucky enough to be in the vicinity. As for painting and poetry, these were mostly confined to the dirty limericks written on public restroom walls and the bawdy, stick figure drawings that accompanied them.

As notorious, cunning, and dangerous as its people were, their leader was even more so. Between's King was feared and reviled across the length and breadth of Otherworld, thanks to his extensive magical talents and his fondness for sinister-looking clothing. He was also the subject of several scandalous rumors—most of which were true—due to his antics in the Summer Court while serving as the High King's Left Hand.

Overall, Between was a place where people came to flee from their shady past or to create a shady future.

It was a refuge for the broken and the lost.

It was also a place where, during the Lunar Crossing, dreams quite literally came true—a feat that left Dreamers enchanted and the kingdom in chaos (more so than usual). Although wondrous in nature, each Crossing had little lasting effect on the King, other than exhaustion.

Until one day when the King awoke to a Lunar Crossing that changed his life.

～

Tuesday, October 23rd—appallingly early in the morning: When Lorn's life was terrible and contained 100% less Sasha

"Boss," a voice hissed. "Wake up, Boss."

Lorn—Shadow King of Between, Keeper of the Portal, Guardian of the Gateways to the Earther Realm, Wielder of Dreams, Sorcerer of the Highest Order—blearily opened one eyelid. Three blue imps the size of pleasantly plump squirrels were sitting on his cluttered bedside table, staring down at him from amongst empty potion bottles and crumpled pieces of parchment.

"Damn," he swore, surprised. "I survived."

"Yep!" the first imp said, grinning.

" 'Twas a pretty big explosion, though," the second imp, dressed in a refined gold waistcoat, said. "*Really* impressive!"

"Lots of people were screaming," the third imp said, as he scribbled away in a small notebook.

"Mostly you, though," the first imp added.

"Thank you, Izzy," Lorn said groggily. He tried to shift positions but promptly gave up; he felt as though a mountain had fallen on him ... which, technically, it had. "Refresh my memory: what happened after the mountain exploded?"

"You flew up in the air," Izzy said.

"Until you landed—*crash!*—on the ground," the imp with the small notebook said, gesturing wildly.

"Onto a bunch of rocks," the imp with the gold waistcoat said.

"With your face," Izzy added, with considerable relish.

Lorn winced. "That bit, I remember. But after that ... nothing."

"Then a bunch of rocks fell on you," Izzy said.

"*Big ones*," the imp with the small notebook said. "Here, I drew it for you." He flicked through several pages and then turned the notebook toward Lorn.

Lorn opened his other eye and squinted at the drawing. A stick figure dressed in a cloak and a pointy crown lay on the ground beneath several lumpy looking rocks, the smoking remains of a mountain behind him. A crowd of stick figure onlookers appeared to be either crying or cheering with joy at the sight of the crushed stick figure king—it was difficult to tell.

Lorn sighed. "Well, that explains why I feel so wretched."

"What do you think of the picture, Boss?" the imp with the small notebook asked, his expression heartbreakingly hopeful.

"A wonderful likeness. I shall treasure it always." Lorn gestured to the stick figure king's tongue, which was lolling out of its head. "Tell me, was my tongue actually on the ground? Or is this artistic license on your part?"

"It was on the ground," Izzy said, grinning. "With the rest of you."

"That explains so much." Lorn ran his tongue over his gums. "I was wondering why my mouth felt gritty."

"Can I put it on The Wall?" the imp with the small notebook asked, practically bouncing on the spot.

"Of course," Lorn said, resigned. "We must keep a record of my wretched existence for posterity."

"Hooray!" the imp with the small notebook cheered. He dashed through the open doorway to the sitting room and headed for what Lorn had titled 'The Wall of Perpetual Agony.' It was covered with drawings of a stick figure king experiencing all manner of excruciating catastrophes.

The imp added the latest picture to The Wall and gave Lorn a thumbs up.

"Looks good," the imp with the gold waistcoat said. "My favorite is still the one with the swamp monster."

Lorn knew which one he meant: it was a drawing of a massive, lizard-like beast gleefully slapping the stick figure king into the swamp with his tail.

"Nah," Izzy said, shaking his head. "The best drawings are the ones where the Boss is on fire."

"Or that one where he fell off the dragon," the imp with the notebook said. "Or—"

"Your concern about my well-being is truly touching," Lorn interrupted dryly. With a grunt, he painstakingly raised himself to a sitting position. "I thank the gods hourly for such compassionate companions."

"Hey, we care!" the imp with the small notebook cried indignantly, as he returned from the sitting room.

"Who do you think got you out from under the rocks?" Izzy asked.

Lorn grimaced at the taste in his mouth "Many thanks for that ... even if you did drag my tongue along the ground to do it." He reached for the glass of water on his bedside table and sipped it slowly. "Were there any other casualties?"

The imps shook their heads.

"And the mountain? Any more falling rocks or explosions?"

"Nah, all good, Boss," Izzy said.

Lorn settled back against the pillows, his shoulders sagging in relief. "Well, that is one piece of happy news. Do you have anything else to report?"

"Yep," Izzy said. "Mirror Man wants to know if you're alive."

His Shadow was worried about him, Lorn thought with a pang. Then again, his Shadow was always worried about him. "Tell him that I survived and will be up to see him as soon as I can."

"And Maddox sent this." Izzy handed Lorn a sheet of parchment. "Agenda for today."

Lorn looked over his agenda, prepared by his chief advisor, and balked. "There are forty-seven items on this agenda. *Forty-seven.* Some will take hours to complete. How am I expected to finish this in one day?"

Izzy shrugged. "Some of it was from yesterday."

Lorn reread the list. Sure enough, some of the items looked familiar.

"And don't forget the Lunar Crossing," the imp with the gold waistcoat said.

Lorn's eyes widened. "That is *tonight?*"

"Yep," Izzy said.

"Damn. I was hoping it happened while I was unconscious. How I am supposed to get all of this done *and* a Lunar Crossing?"

"Probably shouldn't get blown up again today," Izzy said.

"Or your list will be even longer tomorrow," the imp with the gold waistcoat added.

"Excellent advice. I shall——" Lorn stopped as a torturous growl filled the room. He stared down at his midsection in shock. "Was that my stomach?"

The imps leaned away from him warily.

"It sounds mad," the imp with the small notebook said.

"Maybe it will explode," Izzy said hopefully.

"Forty-seven items and not one of them is 'breakfast,' " Lorn muttered. He looked around the room; as usual, there was nothing edible to be found. "Do you happen to have something to eat in that vest of yours, Setzl?" he asked the imp with the gold waistcoat.

Setzl looked inside his extravagant waistcoat and pulled out a large onion. He sniffed it and grimaced. "It's been in there a while."

Lorn stared at the moldy onion and shuddered. "I know that we are experiencing a food shortage, but there should be limits to what is deemed edible. I shall refrain."

"*Finally*, you're talking sense," a voice grumbled from the doorway. "You must still have a concussion."

Lorn smiled as the owner of the voice—a wiry-framed, old dwarf in a white robe—charged into the room. "Well, you would be the expert on that. And good morning to you, too, Gahil."

Gahil, Between's foremost healer, waved away the greeting and stepped up to Lorn's bedside. "Bah. What's so good about it?"

"I am inclined to agree; I have a forty-seven-item agenda plus a Lunar Crossing."

Gahil snorted. "And I have a crotch-rot epidemic to deal with. I'll swap you." He looked over his shoulder at the two apprentice healers hovering in the doorway. "Do you intend to enter His Majesty's chamber sometime today? Or are you just going to throw me the potions I need from over there?"

The white-robed apprentices quickly came to Gahil's side, each staggering under the weight of a bag filled with potions and supplies. The bags clinked and jingled with each step, sounding cheerful and fragile all at the same time.

"Thank you for finally joining us," Gahil muttered, gesturing for the apprentices to open the bags. He removed a series of bottles, each filled with thick liquids in various ghastly shades, and set them on the bedside table.

Lorn looked at the bottles and shuddered, knowing from experience that the ghastliness of the color was a good indication of the ghastliness of the taste.

"Tell me," he said, frowning at the assorted potions, "who is the poor, damned soul who has to drink all those dreadful concoctions? Oh, wait—I have figured it out: it is me. *I* am that poor, damned soul ..."

The healer rolled his eyes. "What did you expect? Getting blown off a mountain has consequences." He went back to rummaging through his bags. "Granted, you haven't been this badly injured in a long while. It's usually just magical depletion or exhaustion or the odd broken bone. What happened this time?"

What happened this time? Lorn rubbed his eyes with the heels of his hands. It was true that the mountain in question was filled with volatile minerals, and combined with the lightning storm ... well, it was a recipe for disaster. But he had patched up that mountain several times this year without getting crushed.

Lorn knew what had happened, and frankly, it was embarrassing.

"Sleep deprivation," he confessed. "I had two hours of sleep the night before the incident, and two hours of sleep the night before that ... and possibly the night before that." He paused, registering the fact that he felt curiously refreshed. "In fact, last night was the most sleep that I have had in months."

"Should get knocked out more often, Boss," Izzy snickered.

"I shall take that under advisement," Lorn said. He turned to Gahil. "What was the damage this time?"

The old dwarf flicked his long, white beard over his shoulder and gestured for Lorn to lean toward him so that he could begin his check up. "Your armor took the brunt of it. *Again.* You should send a thank you note to your armorers for saving your life. *Again.*"

"They would probably prefer gold." Lorn winced as Gahil's cold hands skimmed over his face, probing each of his cheekbones. "Or a sack of fish —they are an odd bunch. They certainly earned the gold I paid them; the armor works marvelously well."

"It would work even better if you wore your helmet. You had a lump the size of a dragon egg on your forehead." Gahil ran his fingers over Lorn's head and grunted, pleased. "Gone now, along with all the bruising." He peered into Lorn's eyes. "You've got to stop hitting your head. This is your fourth concussion this year."

Lorn still felt groggy. "Fifth, but who is counting? I find it difficult to cast with the helmet; it limits my vision."

"Then get your armorers to make you a better visor. While you're at it, it's probably time to strengthen the enchantments on your armor; the rocks shouldn't have been able to hit you at all. You're lucky your fancy cloak shielded your head once you were on the ground. Follow my finger." Gahil held up his finger and moved it across Lorn's line of vision. "Good." He probed the bridge of Lorn's nose. "You broke your nose. *Again.* Which is also something that would be hard to do if you wore your helmet."

Lorn winced reflexively as Gahil's fingers pressed against the bridge of his nose. The bones had set, but it still felt tender. He winced again when Gahil pinched the tip.

"Impressive break, too," the healer said, flexing the tip of Lorn's nose. "And the swelling! It looked like you'd landed face-first on a pumpkin. Set it well, if I do say so myself. You can't even tell."

"Thwanks," Lorn said.

Gahil released Lorn's nose and gestured to Lorn's left hand. "Only the one wrist was broken, but you broke most of the bones of your left hand."

"Rock landed on it," Izzy said, staring at Lorn's hand in grim fascination.

"Flex it for me," Gahil ordered.

Lorn gingerly flexed his hand. He remembered the impact—the feeling of bones splintering, followed by wave upon wave of searing agony that radiated out from—

He abruptly cut off that train of thought and made a fist. "It feels fine."

Gahil nodded. "Good. The trick is to set it for only an hour or two, then let it heal by itself. Now, let's take a look at your right leg."

Lorn pulled aside the bedcovers. "What was wrong with my right leg?"

"You landed with your right leg twisted beneath you. Broke it in three places and dislocated your hip." Gahil began to probe the leg in question in various places over the top of Lorn's black, silk pajama pants.

Lorn winced and closed his eyes.

And, just like that, Lorn remembered the sickening thud as his body hit the ground and the heavy crack of bones snapping again and again and again. He remembered screaming, the sound forced out of him in choked waves that tasted of copper and bile—

His stomach lurched with the memory of the pain. He quickly opened his eyes and took a deep breath.

"You okay?" Gahil paused his examination. "You're looking a little green."

Lorn shook off the memory. "Fine."

"Well, if you're going to throw up, lean away from me." Gahil pulled up the legs of Lorn's pajama pants and grunted. Shadowy patches mottled the pale skin of Lorn's calves like old bruises, but instead of a riot of yellows, purples, and greens, these patches were the gray of faded ink. "How far up do these go?"

Lorn looked down at the dark patches and sighed. "Today? I am not sure."

At Gahil's gesture, Lorn lowered his pajama pants. The same faded marks crept up to mid-thigh.

"It could be worse," Lorn said, looking over the patches with a practiced eye. "They could be black and all over my body. I am clearly on the mend."

"It could be *better*," Gahil said pointedly. "You could have no patches whatsoever." He jabbed one of them with his stubby forefinger. "Forget getting crushed by a mountain—*this* is what'll kill you. Magical exhaustion." He poked the same spot again.

Lorn stared at him incredulously. "*Ouch.* I thought you were here to check my injuries, not to give me new ones."

"I'm trying to make an impression on you—magical exhaustion is no joke." The healer prodded the patch again for good measure. "You can't keep performing impossible magical feats and expect to live!"

Lorn pushed aside Gahil's finger and pulled his pajama pants back into place. "Tell that to Between. Impossible magical feats are part of my job description." He gestured toward his agenda. "And today, they are items one through thirteen."

"Midra's sack!" the healer cried, throwing his hands in the air in exasperation. "Do you *want* to die young?!"

"Do I have a choice?" Lorn asked, genuinely curious.

Gahil ran a hand over his bald head and sighed. "Well then, you'd better eat. Not that," he said to Setzl, slapping the onion away. "Put that back into whatever cursed place you found it. *Real* food. And rest; it's the only cure for magical exhaustion."

"Well, with a forty-seven-item agenda—" Lorn began.

"And a Lunar Crossing," Setzl added.

"—and a Lunar Crossing," Lorn amended, "the only way I shall rest today is if I am knocked unconscious again."

"Probably will be," Izzy said.

"Likely," the imp with the small notebook said.

"The odds are in my favor," Lorn said agreeably.

Gahil sighed, reached into his bag and pulled out a bottle filled with red liquid. "Then it's more Vigor Draught for you." He removed the cork and handed Lorn the vial. "And then take the replenishment potions I've laid out on the table."

Lorn eyed the row of potion bottles and grimaced. "Is there any way of making them taste better?"

Gahil blinked owlishly at Lorn as if the idea was utterly preposterous. "Why? The last thing you need is an incentive to hurt yourself more often."

"You make it sound as though I do this for fun." Lorn squinted at the Vigor Draught in his hand, the peppery smell of the viscous liquid making his eyes burn. "Have you had any luck making a pain potion that will work long-term on sorcerers?"

"We're working on it, but it's a difficult task. The only potions that seem to work effectively on you are the replenishment and recovery tonics. Your body sucks those right up. Speaking of which ..." Gahil gestured to the Vigor Draught.

Lorn dutifully drank down the red liquid, the taste of pepper and cinnamon sharp across his tongue. Immediately, he felt warmth flood his body, followed by a strange tingle that lingered across his gums. He flexed his hand and his magic sparked to life beneath his skin.

"That won't last long," Gahil warned. "It's just enough to get you on your feet."

"That is all I need," Lorn said

Gahil reached into his bag and pulled out two more bottles of Vigor Draught. "I'll leave these here for you—one for the afternoon, one for the Crossing." He placed the bottles on the bedside table.

Lorn swung his legs cautiously off the bed. "Many thanks, Gahil, as always."

"You want to thank me? Don't get injured today." Gahil shut his potion bags with a click. "I've got a crotch-rot epidemic to deal with."

"My condolences," Lorn said. "A moment—is it not the wrong time of year for a crotch-rot epidemic?"

"As long as there are crotches, any time of year is the right time for a crotch-rot epidemic." Gahil pulled his beard back from over his shoulder and patted it into place. "Drink those recovery and replenishment potions. All of them. Now."

"If I must," Lorn said with a grimace. He watched as the dwarf scurried out of the bedchamber, his apprentices struggling to keep up. "And I will attempt to stay uninjured," he called after him.

"Bah. I'll believe it when I see it," Gahil called out as he left Lorn's chambers.

"Not likely, Boss," the imp with the small notebook said.

"You'll probably get injured before you even leave the castle," Setzl said.

Izzy's eyes lit up. "Shall we bet on it?"

The thought of sustaining another injury so soon made Lorn's stomach twist. With skill borne of great practice, he quickly repressed his feelings and cleared his throat.

"I am tempted to place a bet myself," he said, his tone as flippant as he could muster. "Now, help me get dressed—I have forty-seven tasks ahead of me, and none of them should be attempted without pants."

~

BY THE TIME LORN HAD DRESSED IN HIS CUSTOMARY BLACK ATTIRE, HE WAS feeling more like his old self and less like the mountain-crushed version of the morning.

As he made his way through the dank, dimly lit castle, Lorn noted that everything seemed fairly normal. He passed the room filled with breezes and the other filled with storms. He greeted the guards carrying mops and the guards carrying buckets filled with fish. He spared a single, exasperated glance at the stream of golden dust falling through a new hole in the ceiling, and another at the two goats, who were clearly conspiring in a cobwebbed corner. He muttered a dry, "Good morning, Tractor," to the small, stunted unicorn, who was headbutting a low-hanging mirror; and barely even paused as the castle began one of its daily rotations, the view from the castle windows changing as he passed. He yawned his way through the Portrait Gallery, ignoring the paintings of the previous Kings of Between, each holding a Golden Feather and wearing an amulet that matched his own. He was particularly careful to overlook the empty space at the very end, closest to the door, where his portrait should have been.

Before Lorn knew it, he was inside the Less-Formal Meeting Chamber.

The Less-Formal Meeting Chamber was where Lorn conducted meetings with people he truly liked. Unlike the Formal Meeting Chamber, the lighting in the Less-Formal Meeting Chamber was more cheerful, the air less dank, and the chairs reserved for visitors more comfortable. Moreover, there was not a trapdoor beneath them that led straight to the swamps.

It was telling that Lorn always met with Maddox, his chief advisor, in the Less-Formal Meeting Chamber, no matter how terrible the meeting was likely to be.

Maddox was a refined older man whose age and true name were mysteries that many had pondered, but none had solved. He was as slender as a blade and just as sharp, and always impeccably dressed in head-to-toe gray. Rumor had it that he carried seven weapons hidden on his person, but the most dangerous of all was a thick notebook filled with priceless information. It contained secrets gathered from all of the kingdoms of Otherworld and lists of people that the Crown wished to reward or punish. It also contained the secrets, commands, and plans of the Shadow King himself, updated daily. Such a notebook would have been a treasure worth stealing; however, it was well known throughout the realm that Maddox had written every word in a code that he had personally devised and that no one in Otherworld had been able to decipher. In fact, the last person to try had become so frustrated that he threw the stolen piece of code down a well, quit his job as a spy for the Kingdom of Dox, and had taken up yak herding.

Lorn favored Maddox above all others for his unswerving loyalty, his unflappable nature, and his diverse skillset, which included an infallible memory, an in-depth knowledge of the customs and laws of all the kingdoms of Otherworld, and the ability to pick a lock in under ten seconds.

"I am pleased to see you up and about and not under a large pile of rocks," Maddox said, as Lorn entered the room.

"Many thanks." Lorn brushed gold dust off the seat of his armchair and sat down behind his desk. With a grimace, he also brushed away the thin film of gold dust that had settled on the surface. "It is always a novelty to hear that someone is pleased about my ongoing survival."

Maddox settled himself in the chair opposite. "The people of Between were also overjoyed to hear of your recovery."

Lorn raised an eyebrow. "Really? It was difficult to tell how they felt from Setzl's picture."

"That is understandable; it is difficult to convey joy and relief on a stick figure."

"And yet, he is able to convey various states of agony extremely well." Lorn brushed gold dust off the agenda that Maddox had set-out before him and sighed. "Speaking of agony ... forty-seven items, Maddox? *Forty-seven?*"

"And counting," Maddox said. "It does not include any of the unexpected catastrophes and natural disasters that will inevitably present themselves throughout the day."

"It also does not include the Lunar Crossing."

Maddox glanced at the agenda and shrugged. "I was concerned that a forty-eight-item agenda would break you."

"*Forty-eight items*, Maddox! *Forty-eight!*"

"It seems that I was correct. Just be grateful that here were no incidents of note at the Den last night."

The Den was a maze of gaming rooms situated beneath the city of Between. It was both a lucrative source of revenue for Between and an ongoing headache for Lorn, thanks to the outlandish catastrophes that occurred with painful regularity within its walls.

"Thank Midra for small mercies." Lorn swept a hand through his hair and groaned. "Do me a favor, Maddox: the next time I am trapped under a mountain, leave me there."

"I shall make a note of it. Do you have any questions about the agenda?"

"Aside from its obscene size? Yes. Agenda-item one." Lorn tapped the parchment with his finger. "It says that I am to meet Divinian Fanton at the independent township of Fisk '*immediately after waking.*' Do you happen to know why Divinian is luring me to a foreign town where its citizens actively despise magic folk?"

"If your trade and finance minister has requested your presence, then he no doubt requires your assistance to pull-off a Devious Scheme."

Lorn blinked. "Well, of course. But what *kind* of Devious Scheme? Fisk has refused every trade deal we have ever offered, no doubt because Between is a magic-filled land ruled by a sorcerer. Neither of those things have changed."

"True, but it appears that *their* circumstances have changed. The

Collection department has informed us that Fisk has a water problem—specifically, all their water has mysteriously dried up. I am sure our illustrious trade minister has found a way to twist their dire predicament to our advantage. His Devious Scheme no doubt involves some form of showmanship on your part because he has requested that you wear—and I quote—'some really fancy robes and that pointy crown of his.' He also requested your presence *immediately*, so it would be best if you left. Immediately."

"Very well," Lorn said, standing. "Before I leave for what is sure to be a horrific day, I will ask you the eternal question: Have you found a way to free me from Between?"

Maddox pursed his lips. "Unfortunately, I must answer as always: *not yet*. As you can imagine, breaking a magical contract with a sentient kingdom is somewhat challenging. But I am currently pursuing a few promising leads …"

"That is all I ask. Well, that and—"

Maddox wordlessly pulled two oatcakes from one of his many pockets and handed them to his King.

"—breakfast. *Thank you.*" Lorn took a bite of one of the cakes and headed for the door. "Let us hope that the good citizens of Fisk are too busy eating breakfast to form an angry mob to greet me."

"Ah, optimism." Maddox shook his head. "The second leading cause of death in Between."

"A lingering effect of the concussion; it should wear off in an hour or two."

Lorn inclined his head at his advisor and went off to find something suitably fancy to wear to tackle agenda-item one.

AN INTRICATE MATTER

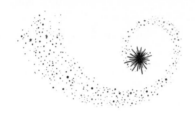

When Lorn arrived at the independent township of Fisk—a fertile pocket of land that sat off the border of Aurora, Between's geographical neighbor—Trade and Finance Minister Divinian Fanton was slumped against the gates, waiting for him.

That is, Lorn *suspected* that it was his trade and finance minister. The man in question was wearing an outrageously large, yellow felt hat pulled so low over his face that only his sparse goatee was visible from beneath the brim. Two garish, yellow ostrich feathers were jammed into the hat's magenta band and hung limply over the side. From their rhythmic fluttering, Lorn surmised that his minister was asleep on his feet and snoring quietly.

"Please, no need to awaken on my account," Lorn said dryly, as he approached the gates.

The figure started and pulled back the ridiculous hat, revealing a man who was clearly in the early stages of an impressive hangover. His complexion was sallow and greasy; his left eye was glassy and red-rimmed, and the magenta eyepatch covering his right eye was slightly askew. Even his mustache appeared hungover, the meager hairs sticking up in multiple directions.

Divinian Fanton squinted up at Lorn, the expression on his long, thin face pained.

"Mornin', Boss. I was just resting my eyes in preparation for what lies ahead."

Lorn swept his gaze over Divinian's attire. "I would be terrified to rest my eyes while wearing that outfit; it seems designed to induce nightmares."

Divinian looked down at the sour yellow and magenta ensemble clinging to his emaciated frame. "Now, now—you just don't understand what you're seeing. And that's alright, allow me to educate you." Divinian gestured theatrically to his attire. "This is the very latest fashion, direct from Vetch."

"It is eye-wateringly bright."

"*Exactly*. The good people of Vetch recognize that not all of us have the physical presence and regal demeanor necessary to pull off a dramatic, monochromatic look." Divinian glanced meaningfully at Lorn's all-black, ceremonial attire. "It's all about bold colors to counter the coming winter. They call this color palate 'paradise sunset.' " He made a showy turn so that Lorn could admire him from every angle.

Lorn blinked. " 'Diseased mustard' would have been more appropriate. That shade of yellow is positively virulent."

Divinian scratched at the scraggly, black hairs peeking out from his low cut, yellow silk shirt. "Some of us require exceptionally bold, somewhat virulent colors to bring out our complexions."

"Your complexion could not be any further out in that ensemble. And yet, despite the terrifying clash of colors, you wear it with aplomb." Lorn inclined his head. "Well done."

"Many thanks, that's kind of you to say. And thank you, by the way, for looking appropriately fancy yourself." Divinian gestured to Lorn's ceremonial attire. "It's important that you make a particularly regal impression on the good people of Fisk."

"About that." Lorn stepped closer to his minister and lowered his voice. "Explain to me why you have requested that I—a sorcerer—accompany you to a town that despises magic folk, especially on a day when I have a forty-seven-item agenda?"

"Ah." The minister suddenly looked more alert. "Our friends here in Fisk have themselves a problem." He gestured for Lorn to accompany him to the ceremonial greeting basin. "Their wells have dried up under *mysterious circumstances*. More importantly, so have the water supplies to their fields. Even the basin here is practically dry." He gestured to the stone bowl, which was only a quarter full.

"*Hmm*, that is quite a puzzle." Lorn could see the townsfolk starting to gather in the street, their expressions ranging from wary to hostile. "Did we have anything to do with these 'mysterious circumstances?' "

Divinian grinned, which made him look even more disreputable. "Not this time. This is a *genuinely* mysterious circumstance."

Lorn looked around, searching for an obvious cause of the problem. "Presumably they tried to fix it themselves?"

"Yep. Brought in plumbers, farmers, priests. Dug some things up, buried some other things, tried drilling and tilling. Pretty much tried every-thing ... except for magic."

Lorn glanced back at the crowd. Many of the people were pointing at him and whispering, their expressions now more hostile than wary.

"Wonderful," Lorn muttered. "It looks as though I am to be greeted by an angry mob. My, my—that brings back memories of childhood ..."

Divinian squinted at the gathering crowd. "Nah. Apparently—how should I phrase this delicately?—the people of Fisk were silent supporters of the Purge. They weren't the ones burning magic folk, but they weren't exactly offering them shelter either. So, it's unlikely they'll burn you at the stake. It's more likely they'll stand there and silently judge you until another mob comes along and burns you at the stake."

"Marvelous," Lorn said dryly. "That is a great comfort to me."

"Well, unless they're fans of dehydration, they'd better be on their best behavior—their last well is at the dregs."

"So, I am here to restore their water supply?"

Divinian tapped the tip of his nose. "Got it in one, Boss."

Lorn glanced shrewdly at his minister. "Something tells me that this is not a publicity stunt designed to change their minds about magic folk."

Divinian looked affronted. "Of course not! We're not running a charity for Purge-friendly townships. In exchange for fixing this little problem, we'll be getting a goodly share of those lovely corn crops up yonder ... once they're full of corn, that is." He gestured to the fields beyond the town's walls. "And assuming this goes well, then it could be the start of a fruitful trade partnership with the very fertile township of Fisk. And once Fisk trades with us, then maybe some of those other towns prejudiced against Between—"

"And against me."

Divinian inclined his head. "And good sorcerers such as yourself, will also be more willing to trade with us."

Food. Something that Between desperately needed ... and probably the only reason that Lorn would willingly subject himself to an angry, magic folk-hating mob. The wild magic that ran rampant through Between made farming a game of chance. Farmers who sowed potatoes might wake up one day to find a sinkhole in the middle of their fields, or a pond, or poisonous weeds, or stunted radishes, or—very occasionally —potatoes.

The only crops that thrived in Between were those that had some sort of magical or medicinal property, particularly anything poisonous or virulent. This was wonderful for Between's thriving potions and poisons trade but detrimental to feeding its citizens. No matter how many times Lorn spoke to the land or tried to stabilize the earth, the magic continued to disrupt the fields, transforming or destroying all in its path. As a result, Between was forced to buy, barter, or steal most of its food—with a preference for the latter—as many magic folk-hating towns refused to trade with them.

The people of Between were no longer starving, thanks to the work of Lorn, his ministers, and the Procurement department, but it was always a close call.

A very, very close call.

"Very well," Lorn said, resigned. "I shall temper my instinct to burn the place down and flee, laughing maniacally." He looked at the vast expanse of fertile land. "How much corn are we set to acquire?"

"Well, I've conducted some preliminary negotiations with the mayor. But I've always been a firm believer that the reward should match the effort, so if this turns out to be a trickier task than I anticipated ..." Divinian's voice trailed off meaningfully.

"I am almost certain that it will be a far trickier task than you anticipated," Lorn said solemnly. "At least another acre of corn trickier."

Divinian grinned. "Say no more. Ah, here comes the mayor." He lowered his voice to a whisper as four guards marched toward them, a rabbity-looking man with red-rimmed eyes and a weak chin, his fingernails chewed to the quick, trailed hesitantly behind.

The rabbity man paused midstep when he saw Lorn, his pale eyes comically wide. But he quickly caught himself, and rushed to keep pace with his guards, wiping the sweat from his forehead with a fancy handkerchief.

"He's a weak fuss-bucket," Divinian continued, as the mayor nervously smoothed down the folds of his blue ceremonial robes, "easily led by a few flattering words but even more motivated by a pinch of fear. Let me do the sweetening—you just stand there in all your regal glory and look powerful and slightly menacing."

Lorn stared darkly at his minister.

Divinian winked. "That'll do a treat. Feel free to throw your lovely cloak around in a showy fashion when the occasion demands it."

Lorn's stare became even darker. "I will do no such thing. I am a sorcerer, not a street magician."

The Cloak of Shadows, however, flapped happily in the breeze, ready to show off.

Divinian noticed. "Your cloak wants to be thrown around in a showy fashion."

Lorn looked back at his cloak. "Do not encourage it."

As the mayor approached, Lorn and Divinian stripped off their gloves and dipped their hands into the ceremonial basin. They then raised them, palms forward, in the traditional Otherworld greeting.

Lorn hated the greeting: it was designed to reveal the Marks of magic folk like himself, and it never failed to make him feel *other*. He watched as, predictably, the mayor's breath caught at the sight of the Marks on each of Lorn's wrists and palms, his expression the typical mix of fear and awe.

Lorn mentally rolled his eyes.

Really, what was he expecting? he thought, exasperated. *Dragon tattoos?*

"Greetings from the Kingdom of Between," Divinian intoned cheerfully. "Peace and prosperity to all in Fisk."

"Safe passage to you … both," the mayor replied in the ritual manner, still eyeing the Marks on Lorn's hands.

Despite his evident unease, the mayor remembered his role as host. He took a towel from the shelf beneath the basin and handed it to Lorn, bowing his head.

Lorn ignored the mayor's shaking hands and accepted the towel. "Many thanks."

The mayor quickly stepped away from Lorn and shared a nervous glance with his guards.

Lorn took note of the glance but said nothing. Although he was officially in a foreign land and at the mercy of the mayor's good graces, Lorn was not at all afraid of the mayor, who was visibly sweating at the evidence of Lorn's power; or of the mayor's guards, whose hands were clenched white around their spears, their eyes wide behind their visors.

But the crowd …

Lorn knew from terrible, painful experience that the crowd was a living, dangerous thing. Even now, after all these years, his body *still* remembered, *still* reacted to large groups. He found himself unconsciously scanning the gathered townsfolk for small turning points: hostile expressions shifting into something mean and vicious, hands clenched into fists or reaching for weapons, low murmurs becoming dark, vicious chants …

Thankfully, he found none of them in this mob.

Yet.

Nevertheless, Lorn felt his magic itch beneath his skin, ready to react as soon as the first rock was thrown, or fists were raised against him.

You are no longer a child, he told himself firmly, trying to regain control of his emotions and his magic. *There is no danger here, not anymore. If anything, you are the dangerous one now—it is the crowd that should be afraid.*

Oddly enough, the thought of unleashing destruction upon the crowd calmed Lorn somewhat. His magic receded, and he was able to turn his attention back to the mayor.

"Mayor Kleg," Divinian said, all easy charm. "Let me introduce His Majesty, The Shadow King of Between, Keeper of the Portal, Guardian of the Gateways to the Earther Realm, Sorcerer of the Highest Order, and a *very* busy man." He turned to Lorn with a jaunty bow. "Your Majesty, Mayor Kleg of the independent township of Fisk."

The mayor took a long look at the Shadow King—dark and pointy and sinister in his ceremonial garb and Cloak of Shadows—and swallowed hard.

"Your Majesty," he said, executing a shaky bow. "Your reputation as the Left Hand of the High King precedes you. As do … *other* things."

"Mayor Kleg," Lorn said, his tone as bland as porridge. "It is a pleasure to be in Fisk."

The mayor's eyes darted between Lorn and the growing crowd. "It—it is a pleasure to have *you* here. In Fisk."

Such a terrible liar, Lorn thought to himself with a sigh as he handed the towel to Divinian. *Kleg would never last a day in Between.*

The crowd muttered darkly, evidently sharing the mayor's true sentiments.

"Happy to see that you're looking well, Mayor Kleg," Divinian said, ignoring the growing tension as he dried his hands.

The mayor eyed Divinian's 'paradise sunset' attire with polite horror. "As are you, Minister Fanton. You're looking well and bright … and *bright.*"

"Kind of you to say, especially when I know I'm not looking my best." Divinian handed the mayor the towel and smiled weakly. "Just between the two of us, I'm a touch under the weather. Probably something I ate."

"Or drank," Lorn suggested.

"Most likely," Divinian said agreeably. "Never know what's in the water these days. Speaking of which …" He turned to the growing crowd. "The good citizens of Fisk are looking a little parched. Let's fix that, shall we? As I said, His Majesty is a very, very busy man. We can't keep him long."

The mayor seemed to collect himself. "Of course, of course. Let me show you the wells." He returned the towel to its place beneath the basin, and turned on his heel, beckoning for Lorn and Divinian to follow him through the crowd to the town square.

The townsfolk obligingly parted for the men. Lorn ignored his instinctual fear of turning his back to a hostile group of magic folk-haters and followed the mayor. From the corner of his eye, he could see parents pulling their children out of his path and hiding them behind their backs. The children peeked out from behind their parents' legs, their wide eyes curious and excited.

As if I were a beast in a fairy tale with a taste for child-flesh, he thought with a sigh.

As the mayor approached the well, Lorn felt the crowd close behind him like a locked gate. He felt their eyes boring into the back of his head; felt his back tense, exposed.

Vulnerable.

His cloak must have sensed his distress; it stretched out behind him and snapped at the people nearest to Lorn, making them step back. Lorn smiled darkly and let his fingertips tangle in the Cloak's shadows in a subtle caress.

"Here is our primary well," the mayor said, stopping beside a large, stone structure. "And as you can see, it is practically dry."

Lorn peered inside. It was, indeed, practically dry. He pressed his hand against the sun-warmed tiles just inside the mouth of the well and opened his senses. For a moment, all he could feel was rock and, beneath it, the earth itself. But then it appeared: a trace of water sliding silver-bright and cool against his mind. The more he probed, the more it seemed that there was still water under Fisk, but it had been trapped and rerouted.

Why had the water been rerouted?

Lorn frowned and knelt beside the well, laying his hands flat on the ground. He closed his eyes, and the elements spoke to him in a series of impressions and sensations. First, he felt the earth, rich and dark, and the water passing through it along well-worn passageways, nourishing the soil and moving onward, onward. But then ... a disturbance. Something substantial had been burrowing beneath Fisk, tunneling its way underground, crashing through rocks and soil, and blocking the water's path. He felt the earth's distress, felt the tremendous *pressure* building up, desperate for release.

Lorn could see the blockages in his mind's eye—could chart their path across Fisk—even though he could not tell what had caused them in the first place.

"*Interesting,*" he murmured to himself.

It would not be too difficult to fix, he realized with relief. A little time consuming perhaps, and more taxing than it would have been in Between where he had so much magic at his disposal. Still, it was doable.

Lorn opened his eyes and looked up at the worried faces of the crowd.

"Well?" the mayor asked, wiping sweat from his brow.

Conscious of the eyes upon him, Lorn gave a dramatic sigh. "Oh dear," he said, for good measure.

Divinian picked up on the cue immediately. "Not dire news is it, Your Majesty?"

"Exceedingly dire," Lorn said, standing.

The mayor stared up at Lorn. "Exceedingly dire?"

Lorn brushed the dirt from his hands. "*Exceedingly* dire."

Divinian shook his head sorrowfully. "That is the worst possible kind of dire. I'm sorry, Mayor Kleg, I thought this would be an easy fix but"—he spread out his hands in a helpless gesture—"it appears you have an exceedingly dire situation here."

The crowd murmured amongst themselves, clearly distressed.

The mayor wrung his hands. "We knew it was bad but ..." He looked back at his citizens and took a deep breath. "Can you fix it?" he asked Lorn.

Lorn tapped his lower lip with his forefinger. "It will be immensely difficult."

"*Immensely* difficult?!" Divinian exclaimed.

"Not to mention incredibly strenuous," Lorn added.

"Surely not *incredibly* strenuous?" Divinian asked, clutching his throat.

"And far more intricate than I had anticipated," Lorn said with another great sigh.

"Intricate!" Divinian cried. He glanced at the townsfolk as if to check their reactions; they were wide-eyed, hanging on his every word.

Seemingly satisfied, he turned back to the mayor. "Did you hear that, Mayor Kleg? *Intricate!*"

"Not *intricate!*" the mayor moaned. He twisted his handkerchief in his hands, the very picture of distress. "Can anything be done?"

"I believe so," Lorn said. "Though performing such an intricate task surely deserves an additional acre of corn."

"And twelve bushels of onions," Divinian added. "After all, it *is* intricate."

The mayor nodded. "Of course, of course! Please—do what you must."

"Then step aside, Mayor Kleg," Lorn announced dramatically. With a mental roll of his eyes, he whipped his cloak behind him in a suitably showy fashion. "I shall bring you water."

The Cloak of Shadows billowed happily.

The crowd *oohed.*

The mayor stared up at Lorn in awe. "*Thank you*, Your Majesty!"

Divinian sent Lorn a wink over the mayor's head. "Okay everyone, give His Majesty some room. Step back, step back—he needs space and silence. Didn't you hear? The problem is *intricate!*"

The crowd dutifully retreated to the edges of the square. Lorn walked purposefully to the first blockage point, the Cloak of Shadows gleefully streaming behind him. The mayor and Divinian followed at his heels, the crowd trailing behind them at a discreet distance, hopeful and excited.

At each blockage point, Lorn stopped and knelt, pressing his palms to the ground. He closed his eyes and, with a small application of power, coaxed away the rocks and soil, working with the elements to restore the water's underground path. He worked slowly, careful not to cause a sink-hole or another collapse, gently restoring order beneath the town.

He had been working for about an hour, the crowd silently tracking his progress across the length of Fisk and cheering when the first two wells began to fill, when he felt the final blockage. It was *the* blockage—the primary source of the lost water supply to the surrounding fields. The pressure was so immense that he staggered back on his heels.

"Problem?" Divinian asked.

Lorn tilted his head, considering. "Possibly."

He pressed his palms to the black earth and tried to ascertain the exact point of the blockage. Looking up, he noted that it was right beside a sturdy brick building with a bright blue door that stood, all by itself, at the very edge of town.

He gestured toward the distant building. "Mayor Kleg, it may be prudent to evacuate that building."

"That is the tavern," the mayor said. "It should be empty at this time of the morning."

Divinian perked up. "A tavern, you say? Allow me to do the evacuation honors."

"Very heroic of you," Lorn said.

"Happy to do my part," Divinian said.

He strutted off, disappearing behind the tavern's broad, blue door.

Five minutes later, a small crowd staggered out of the building—most still clutching their tankards—followed by Divinian, who was wiping foam from his mustache.

The mayor stared at the drunken group weaving their way over to the crowd, then turned nervously back to Lorn. "It appears that some of our citizens have taken it upon themselves to extend our water supply by drinking ... other substances."

"Truly noble of them," Lorn said.

"Everyday heroes," Divinian said, brushing specks of ale off his doublet.

The mayor eyed the merry drunkards dubiously. "Ah ... quite."

Lorn flexed his hands, feeling his magic gather and spark. "I have found the final blockage, but it is considerably larger than the others. I require everyone to stay behind me and remain silent; what I am attempting requires great delicacy and concentration."

"You heard His Majesty," Divinian said, addressing the crowd. "Silence! You too, fellas," he called out to the drunks. "Try and sip quietly."

The crowd nodded eagerly.

Lorn closed his eyes. Pressing his palms to the ground, he sent tendrils of power burrowing into the earth toward the blockage. He gently coaxed the debris away, painstakingly scraping back soil and rock. He grimaced under the strain of sustaining such delicate, intricate spell-work.

I should have asked for two extra acres of corn, he thought wryly to himself.

Of course, it was when Lorn was at the most perilous point of the entire operation that the disturbance occurred.

"What's that charlatan doing here?" a raised voice slurred from the tavern door.

Everyone except Lorn turned toward the voice—a voice that belonged to a brutish man holding a tankard of ale in one hand and wiping the sleep from his eyes with the other. He tottered out from the darkness of the tavern, sloshing ale as he went.

"Huh," Divinian whispered. "Must have missed one while I was 'rescuing' that tankard of ale. "Oi!" he called out to the straggler. "Mornin', sunshine. Come and join us back here; His Majesty is about to do something impressive and magical and needs everyone to vacate the spot where you're standing and stay quiet."

The straggler ignored Divinian; his gaze was fixed on Lorn. "I said"— he raised his voice even further—"what's that *charlatan* doing here?"

Lorn opened his eyes and spared a glance at the brutish man, noting his florid face and the cruel tilt to his smile—a smile that grew as he realized that he was now the center of attention.

"You know, you're not the first one to call me a charlatan," Divinian called out, smoothly, stepping between Lorn and the brute. "People see my stunning looks and enviable figure and think to themselves: 'Surely that fine-looking fellow couldn't possibly be blessed with both brains *and* beauty! Surely, he got his fancy ministerial position based on his looks alone!' " The minister smiled smarmily at the drunkard, showing a fine set of yellowish teeth, and paused to adjust a ruffle on one of his shirt cuffs, allowing the crowd to laugh at his expense.

Eventually, Divinian held up his hands for silence. "But let me reassure you, good people of Fisk, that this is not the case. In fact, I'd like to take the opportunity to put those scurrilous rumors to rest right now: I am highly qualified for my position and got it fair and square. Well," he mused, scratching his scraggly goatee, "not *exactly* fair. I may have misled some of my competitors about the date of the interview, and misinformed others about the location ... and dropped a few others down a sinkhole. But it was *mostly* square."

The drunkard blinked blearily at Divinian, utterly bewildered. "What you goin' on about?"

"What am *I* going on about?" Divinian pressed his hand to his chest, clearly affronted. "That's where you've got it wrong, old hat. The question is: what are *you* going on about?"

With great difficulty, the brute seemed to collect himself. "I wasn't talking about *you*. I was talking about *him*." He waved his tankard at Lorn. "That one. *The charlatan*."

Lorn tensed. He knew what was coming.

Divinian did, too, but pretended not to. "Well, I'll have you know that His Majesty is also qualified—overqualified, in fact—to fix this scrape you're in, what with him being a terrifyingly powerful sorcerer who has complete mastery of the elements and all that. He also has a rather fetching cloak."

The Cloak of Shadows managed to preen.

The drunkard snorted. "I don't know about his cloak, but he shouldn't be wearing that crown."

As one, the crowd turned to Lorn and stared at the Crown of Blades on his head.

"There's a field of Nightmares that would disagree with you, old hat," Divinian said, his tone deceptively mild. "His Majesty *earned* his pointy crown. Can't say that about many of the other kings in Otherworld, can you? Not that there's anything wrong with a hereditary monarchy, mind you. Seems to have worked well for the elves."

"Damn elves," someone in the crowd muttered.

"But for my money," Divinian continued, "I'd rather have a king who proved that he was a worthy ruler ... not just one who was lucky enough to be born in the right house."

The crowd murmured their agreement. After all, why should some people slip from the womb and find themselves tucked, all safe and sound, into a golden crib with a silver spoon thrust into their chubby little fist ... while others have to make do with an old beer keg bed and a wooden fork?

"Or one who married into the right bed," Divinian continued. "Not that there's anything wrong with that. I, for one, intend to marry well, and if my beloved just so happens to be the ruler of a prosperous kingdom, well ... who am I to complain?"

"Rightly so!" one townsman called out.

The rest of the crowd laughed.

But the drunkard was not to be dissuaded by logic.

"Worthy leader? *Bah*! Where's your Golden Feather, *Lorn*?" he jeered. "All the *real* kings have one—presented, all official-like, by the Citadel, don't they? *Destined* to become king, weren't they? But not *you*!"

Lorn inwardly groaned; that damn Golden Feather was the bane of his existence. Without it, he was cursed with all the responsibilities of ruling a kingdom without any of the perceived legitimacy. The fact that Between would only yield its power to a True King who defeated the Nightmares— regardless of Golden Feathers—was too subtle for most, including this drunk, to grasp.

The corn had better be worth it, Lorn thought to himself. *It had better be the most succulent corn ever to grow in Otherworld.*

Lorn could feel the mayor shuffling nervously beside him.

"You have to forgive Derrek, Your Majesty," the mayor whispered. "He has just returned from sea after a terrible incident." The mayor shook his head sadly. "He was on a fishing vessel when a monstrous sea serpent came out of nowhere and smashed the ship into pieces. Derrek was the sole survivor—the only one that the sea serpent did not devour."

Lorn spared another glance at Derrek. "Well, that is understandable— Derrek does not look particularly digestible."

The mayor blinked. "Ah ... quite."

The indigestible Derrek also did not appreciate being ignored.

"Oi! *Lorn*!" he yelled. "Do you know why you don't have a Golden Feather? *Hey*? It's 'cause the Citadel knows the bastards of magical creatures have no right ruling a kingdom."

The crowd gasped.

Not this again, Lorn thought, gritting his teeth.

He spared a glance at the crowd behind him and sighed. It was just as he thought: they were not shocked by Derrek's words—just his audacity to speak them aloud. It was more than likely that the entire population of Fisk believed that magic folk were the illicit offspring of humans and magical creatures.

If only I could go back in time and strangle the fool who started that ridiculous rumor, he thought with a grimace.

The mayor cleared his throat, clearly uncomfortable, but said nothing.

The crowd's reaction only seemed to spur Derrek on.

"Can't have some creature's bastard ruling Otherworld, can we?" he sneered. "Can't have a half-hydra as High King, can we?"

Some of the crowd laughed uneasily.

Derrek grinned, all teeth and malice. "All of your lot should go back to Faire where you belong. What say you, *Lorn?*"

Although Lorn would have loved to have responded to Derrek—possibly with a good smiting—he had more pressing concerns. Beneath his palms, he could feel the blockage beginning to give, the earth shifting in a manner that would either liberate the trapped water ... or drown the entire village.

He could not spare Derrek a moment of this time.

Divinian, however, could.

"Derrek," he said, his tone utterly chilling. "There comes a time when every drunken sod goes too far and gets punched in the face. And how do I know that, you ask? It's because *I* am often that drunken sod. So, heed my words and spare your face: the magic folk are people, not creatures ... and feathers are only useful to birds, not kings. And unless you—and your fellows Fiskers—have developed a taste for brushing your teeth with the juice from a pickle jar, and bathing with only a moist napkin, I'd be very quiet and let the *incredibly powerful King* coax the water back into your wells ... before he decides that he's had enough of your guff and goes home."

This time, the crowd's dark murmurs focused on Derrek.

"I've had enough of bathing with a moist napkin, Derrek," a woman said pointedly.

"Hear that?" the man standing beside her said. "My wife is a fine woman and deserves more than a moist napkin."

"I like water!" an old woman cried.

"Shut it, Derrek!" an even older woman yelled. "Or you'll *wish* that serpent had eaten you!"

Derrek, however, was not to be dissuaded.

"You fools!" he yelled. He staggered out from the tavern doorway and onto the street. "Since when has this town started trusting magical folk?" He spat on the ground. "You think he's *helping* us? What's to say he didn't get rid of the water to begin with, hey? What's to say he isn't poisoning it right now? *Look at him!*" He jabbed a meaty finger at Lorn. "Tell me that he isn't a dark wizard! Tell me that we shouldn't throw him over the Dark, Dark Mountains to rot with the rest of the dark lot!"

"Right," Divinian muttered. He pulled up his sleeves. "Punch in the face it is."

Lorn could feel the last fragments of the soil barrier yielding. "A moment," he said quietly to his minister.

Divinian paused.

Derrek did not. "Oi! Abomination! What have you to say for yourself, hey? *Hey?*"

"Would you mind stepping to your left?" Lorn asked Derrek pleasantly.

Derrek blinked, stunned. "Pardon?"

"About two steps ... to the left."

With a mean glint in his eyes, Derrek shuffled two steps to the right. "I don't take orders from *creatures*."

"Pity," Lorn said, and twisted his palm against the ground.

Suddenly, the earth beneath Derrek's feet burst open, and a small geyser erupted, throwing a jet of water—and Derrek—high into the sky.

Divinian grinned. "Behold!" he announced to the crowd over the gush of water and Derrek's outraged cries. "The Shadow King has restored water to your township. And he also gave you a bonus water feature. I think that deserves a round of applause."

The people of Fisk stared up at Derrek in shock as he thrashed around on top of the geyser like a portly, belligerent salmon trying to fight his way upstream.

There was a smattering of applause from the children.

"Thank you, people of Fisk," Lorn said dryly. "Truly, I am overwhelmed by your gratitude."

"How long will he be up there for?" the mayor asked, staring up at Derrek in horrified fascination.

Lorn eyed Derrek's flailing form critically. "It depends on his athleticism, so my estimation is 'not long.' It might be wise to put something below him to break his fall, such as a wheelbarrow full of pointy rocks."

The mayor could not seem to tear his eyes off Derrek. "Of course, a wheelbarrow ..."

"Don't forget the pointy rocks," Divinian said. "The pointier, the better."

Lorn watched the crowd over the mayor's head. Many were still staring up at Derrek in shock. But others ... others were staring at Lorn, their eyes guarded, their stance fearful.

Lorn sighed at the predictability of it all. With a particularly lovely gesture of his hand and a flick of his fingers, he transformed the way that the light hit the water *just so*, turning the geyser every color of the rainbow. The droplets shimmered and glittered as they tumbled through the air, almost as if jewels of every color were falling from the sky.

The children's eyes turned saucer-wide. The littlest ones escaped from their parents' grasps and ran toward the fountain, hands outstretched to catch the colorful droplets.

"That's very nice, that is," Divinian said, nodding to the geyser. "Cheerful." He elbowed the stunned mayor. "Pity it can't stay like that, hey? Would make quite the tourist attraction, wouldn't it? No other town has a rainbow geyser. Bet everyone would like to see that."

The mayor's expression turned from stunned to speculative in an instant. "Tourist attraction, you say?"

"Absolutely!" Divinian said. "It's got everything that you want in a tourist attraction: spectacle, size, color, liquid ... it's a winner!"

"That is, assuming you remove Derrek," Lorn said. "He does rather ruin the aesthetics of the piece, what with the screaming and flailing around."

"His Majesty is right," Divinian said. "Tourists usually aren't fond of attractions that scream." He sighed dramatically. "Pity your geyser is only temporary."

"Yes," Mayor Kleg said slowly, staring up at the rainbow geyser "About that—how ... how *temporary* does it have to be?"

Divinian grinned. "Maybe you and I should have a chat about making your temporary geyser into a perpetual spouter. That is, after you thank His Majesty for his excellent work."

The mayor turned to Lorn, all obsequiousness and smiles now. "Of course! Thank you, your Majesty. *Thank you.*" He bowed low. "The people of Fisk are deeply grateful."

Lorn turned to the people in question and found that they were staring up at the geyser again—this time with considerably more wonder than horror, even though Derrek was still flopping around on the top, screaming mightily.

"I shall take your word for it," Lorn said.

He spared a moment to stare at the beauty of Fisk's newest water feature ... and frowned at the smiling children running beneath it, gleefully unaware of the fact that they could be crushed at any moment by a large, magic folk-despising drunk.

With great reluctance, Lorn levitated Derrek off the top of the geyser and back onto the ground, perhaps a little more roughly than Derrek's internal organs would have preferred.

"You've gone soft," Divinian whispered to Lorn, as Derrek bounced across the ground, managing to hit all the rough sections of the road even when they weren't directly in his path. "The old you would have left him up there for a couple of hours. You weren't worried that he was going to fall off, were you?"

"No, I was rather hoping he would," Lorn whispered back. "I was more worried that the children would break his fall."

Divinian shook his head. "You really have gone soft. Though, I suppose it's prudent; people don't like it when their kids get crushed. It might make them mobby."

"Exactly. Nevertheless—"

Lorn stopped abruptly. A strange sort of lethargy fell over him, making his limbs feel heavy and sluggish—a feeling that he recognized all too well as a symptom of magical exhaustion. He critically evaluated the feeling; it was relatively mild as far as magical exhaustion was concerned. It would probably pass with another oatcake and a small rest.

He wondered idly how many new dark patches this pretty fountain had cost him.

"Minister Fanton," he said loudly. "I shall leave matters here in your capable hands."

The finance minister stared at Lorn for a long moment, and then looked down at Lorn's hands. Lorn followed his gaze and noticed that his hands were trembling. He quickly folded them into fists.

Divinian gave Lorn a small nod and bowed floridly. "Of course, Your Majesty." He then turned to Mayor Kleg and flung his arm over the older man's bowed shoulders.

"Very busy man, His Majesty," he said to the mayor. "He has a forty-seven-item agenda, can you imagine? You were very fortunate to secure even a moment of his incredibly valuable time."

"Of course, of course!" the mayor stuttered. "A very busy man."

"Now," Divinian said as he steered the mayor back toward the town, "let's discuss tourist attractions, shall we? And crops—all those lovely crops that are now getting a much-needed drink, thanks to His Majesty's excellent work …" He sent Lorn a wink over the top of the mayor's head and turned away.

Lorn could feel the Mark between his shoulder blades—the Mark that tethered him to Between—begin to pull at his skin like a too-small scab on a wound.

Between wanted him home.

"I am coming," Lorn said to Between, flexing his shoulders to relieve the pull of his tether. "Try to keep the chaos to a minimum until I get there."

Lorn turned his back on the independent township of Fisk and its hostile citizens, happy for once to be returning to his kingdom.

3

FOUR DARK WIZARDS AND A RADISH

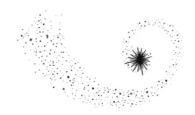

THE FEELING DID NOT LAST.

When Lorn arrived in Between, he was greeted at the city gates by a large crowd and the sound of a horn.

A mournful horn.

Lorn groaned. "No. Not today. I do not have time for this today."

"Yeah … sorry about that, Majesty," Jakobsen, the head of the castle guards said. "We tried to delay them but—"

"—we did a terrible job," Lennox, the deputy head of the castle guards finished, adjusting her helmet.

"Fine," Lorn said with a sigh. "Let us get this over and done with so that I can get onto agenda-item two."

He strode into the city, trailed by his guards and the curious citizens of Between, and followed the sound of the horn to the ceremonial greeting basin. A group of men in gray and purple robes waited beside it. One man, flanked by two guards and slightly red-faced with exertion, continued to sound the horn. Three others stood close by, hidden beneath their cowled robes. The final man—his dark hair disheveled and his eyes wild—sat on the ground, eating what appeared to be an exceptionally large radish.

"Ambassador Zoth," Lorn said, raising his voice to be heard over the noise, "exemplary horn-blowing as usual. But is there any way that we could postpone this spectacle to a later date? I have a forty-seven-item agenda, and I have only just finished agenda-item one."

Ambassador Zoth, the official emissary of the desert kingdom of

Zadria, cut off his horn solo mid-note and handed the instrument to one of his guards with a stifled yawn. The ambassador looked sour and rumpled, which was precisely how someone from a nocturnal kingdom should look before midday. His olive complexion was ashy, and there were pillow marks on the left side of his face.

Lorn knew exactly how he felt.

"Apologies, Your Majesty," the ambassador said, straightening his tunic, "but this must be done now." He cleared his throat. "Four wizards from the Kingdom of Zadria wish to Challenge for the throne of Between."

"Usual terms, I suppose?" Lorn asked.

"To the death," Ambassador Zoth verified, nodding.

Lorn sighed. "Well, I suppose that is one way to avoid the rest of my agenda. And the Challengers?"

The three men in cowled robes pulled back their hoods. To Lorn's surprise, they appeared to be identical triplets.

Almost identical, he corrected.

Like most of the Challengers Lorn had encountered from Zadria, the triplets bore the markings of Death Cultists. Each had a disfigurement from the Cult's initiation ceremonies: one triplet bore a terrible scar where his right eye should have been, the socket blackened as though it had been scorched; another had lost most of his ears—all that remained were jagged-edged flaps of flesh that gleamed white with scars. The final triplet was missing his top row of teeth; black metal grinned back at Lorn in the semblance of a smile, each false tooth filed to a sharp point.

Ah, the joys of joining a cult that demands a flesh sacrifice to enter, Lorn thought wryly.

But there were benefits to joining this particular cult. Spells in the dead language of the Elder Gods had been painstakingly burned into their olive skin in wisp-thin, black lettering. It dipped around the contours of their faces and curled around their shaven scalps until not a patch of bare skin remained. It was old magic, rarely used and if not Forbidden or entirely Dark, then certainly Gray enough to be frowned upon by most reasonable folk. Not that the Death Cultists cared about such things; all they cared about was power, and the power in those words would magnify any spell they cast.

"We Challenge," the triplets intoned.

As one, they looked up at the Crown of Blades on Lorn's head, their expressions identical in their greed. Lorn wondered if they would still want the crown if they knew how uncomfortable it was to wear.

"You said there were four Challengers?" Lorn asked Ambassador Zoth.

"Ah ... yes." The ambassador nudged the radish-eating wizard with his foot. "High Priest Zamiel? Do you challenge?"

"*Aghhh!*" the radish-eating wizard yelled, spitting radish pieces all over the ambassador's boots.

"That would be a 'yes,' " the ambassador said.

Lorn looked down at the wizard and frowned. "Are we sure that High Priest Zamiel is ... *well enough* to Challenge?"

"Yes, of course," Ambassador Zoth said, surreptitiously shaking bits of radish from his boot. "High Priest Zamiel is at the height of his powers."

"I am the Radish King!" High Priest Zamiel cried, arms outstretched toward the sky.

A few feeble purple sparks erupted from his fingertips.

The ambassador pinched the bridge of his nose.

Lorn watched as the Radish King picked his radish off the ground and began chewing on it once more. "Although I am sure that the Radish King will be a formidable opponent, I believe I shall waive the right to attack during his Challenge."

The ambassador raised an eyebrow. "You mean ... you will merely defend yourself and no more?"

"That is correct."

The ambassador stared at Lorn for a long moment, his hooked nose twitching. "That is a noble sentiment, but potentially lethal."

Lorn shrugged. "Well, the Challenge *is* 'to the death.' Now—"

"Majesty!"

One of the castle guards shouldered his way through the crowd until he reached Lorn's side, clearly winded.

"Were you referring to the Radish King or to me?" Lorn asked.

The guard blinked. "Who?"

"*I* am the Radish King!" High Priest Zamiel cried.

The guard looked back and forth between the two kings. "Ah ... I think I'll direct this problem to the Shadow King, if that's okay with you, Your Radish Majesty."

The Radish King shrugged and went back to his root vegetable.

The guard turned to Lorn. "You have to come quickly, Majesty! A sink-hole has appeared right at the edge of the pumpkin farms down Wimple Way. If it grows, we'll lose the entire crop ... and we can't afford to lose the entire crop."

Lorn groaned. "No, we cannot. You have no idea what I just went through to earn a bit of corn." He handed the guard his agenda. "Here, add it to the list."

"Your Majesty!" another guard yelled, sprinting up from behind Lorn. "Come quickly to the Castle! A lake has sprung up in the old—"

"Add it to the list," Lorn interrupted, gesturing to the agenda.

"Got it," the guard said, pulling a pencil from his doublet.

Lorn turned to the Zadrian wizards. "Are you *absolutely* sure that you wish to Challenge for the throne?"

"Yeah ... I wouldn't," the second guard said as he wrote his task on the parchment. "This is a forty-nine-item agenda."

"*And* there's Lunar Crossing tonight," Jakobsen added.

Perhaps I should lose, Lorn thought longingly.

Then he remembered that the Challenge was 'to the death.'

"Damn," he muttered.

The Death Cult triplets exchanged looks and then simultaneously pulled back the sleeves of their robes, revealing intricate tattoos—a tribute to their fallen god. Black ink skulls leered at Lorn with sharp-toothed grins from the front of their forearms, whereas gray ink skulls screamed silently from the back.

Lorn ignored the tattoos and looked at their wrists. Each wizard had only one Mark, but the power spells branded onto their scalps would enhance the potential of those Marks exponentially.

"The Challenge stands," the ambassador said. "The first Challenger is High Priest Rahven, Master of Wind." He gestured to the wizard with the scarred eye-socket, who nodded in response. "Should he be defeated, High Priest Vitzh, Master of Fire, will be the next Challenger."

The wizard with the missing ears raised his chin defiantly.

"Should *he* be defeated, High Priest Xar, Master of Earth, will be the next Challenger."

The metal-toothed wizard grinned his ghastly grin.

The ambassador looked down at the Radish King. "And so on..."

"Very well." Lorn stripped off his gloves. "Jakobsen, prepare the crowd. Lennox, please inform Maddox that there may be a change in leadership."

Lennox looked at the wizards and sniffed. "Unlikely, but I'll do it anyway." She raced off toward the castle to find Maddox.

"Right you lot, you know the drill," Jakobsen called out to the onlookers, herding the crowd back behind the perimeter of the city square. The crowd quickly complied.

Once everyone was clear of the square, Lorn knelt and touched the ground. Iron barricades rose from the cobblestones, waist-high, and enclosed the square. They shimmered with golden light, warded to protect the onlookers from the magic of the Challenge.

"Good luck, Majesty!" Mistress Baker called out to Lorn from over the barricade. "Nice to see you up and about."

"Many thanks, Mistress Baker," Lorn said.

"Aim for the one-eyed wizard's blind spot," a one-eyed man yelled from the crowd.

"Excellent advice, Master Librarian," Lorn said.

Ambassador Zoth gestured for silence and turned to Lorn. "Let us review the rules of the Challenge."

The crowd groaned.

"Why?" Master Baker called out. "You put the King through at least one of these Challenges every month. Odds are that he knows the rules by now."

"He's got a lot of incentive to get it right," Mistress Blacksmith said, "given that the Challenge is 'to the death' and all."

"Yeah!" the crowd called out.

Ambassador Zoth held up his hand. "Please. I know this is tedious." He looked down at the Radish King. "You have no idea how tedious," he muttered. He cleared his throat. "Nevertheless, this is an ancient ritual, and it should be honored as such."

The crowd grudgingly muttered their agreement.

Seeing that the crowd was now subdued, the ambassador continued. "The Challenge will conform to the rules set out by Magnus the Great."

" 'May he be drinking with the gods,' " the crowd intoned.

The ambassador nodded in approval. "As such, this will be a test of prowess with elemental magic *only*. All four elements and their associated forms may be used. No other branches of magic are allowed, particularly those that have been declared Dark or Forbidden." He stole a glance at the Death Cultists. "*Particularly* Necromancy—the raising of the dead is strictly banned and will lead to automatic disqualification."

The Death Cultists looked particularly perturbed by that news.

"After all," the ambassador continued, grimacing in distaste, "no one wants a repeat of the zombie infestation of the village of Little Biscuit."

"I should say not!" Mistress Baker said, disgusted. "There were all those discarded limbs littering up the streets, trying to trip people up. It was disgraceful!"

"Not to mention unhygienic," Master Baker added. "They couldn't get the smell of festering flesh out of the village for months."

The crowd muttered their agreement.

The Death Cultists rolled their eyes.

The ambassador raised his hand for silence. "There will also be no physical transformations—animal or otherwise—during the Challenge. All casting should be directed at one's opponent, not at buildings, structures, livestock, vehicles or onlookers."

"Here, here!" the crowd chanted.

"Try not to kill us by accident, Majesty," Master Librarian called out.

"I shall do my best," Lorn replied.

"A period of preparation will be allowed before each Challenge," the Ambassador continued. "Given that there is more than one Challenger, His Majesty—"

"Radish King!" High Priest Zamiel yelled.

Ambassador Zoth sighed. "The current King of Between," he clarified, "will determine the length of each preparation period. I will announce the start of each Challenge. Understood?"

The triplets nodded curtly.

"Your Majesty?" the Ambassador asked Lorn.

"All too well," Lorn said.

"Then take your places," the Ambassador instructed, "and begin your preparations."

The triplets moved to the opposite side of the city square and turned to face Lorn. The Zadrian guards picked up the Radish King from beneath his armpits and carried him across the square, depositing him on the ground beside the trio of wizards.

Lorn closed his eyes and felt for the presence of Between in his mind.

Well? he asked Between. *Do you fancy any of these as your new ruler? The Radish King, perhaps?*

Lorn felt the ground rumble beneath his feet.

I shall take that as a 'no.' What of the triplets? You could have three rulers for the price of one.

Again, the ground rumbled, stronger than before.

"Majesty!"

Lorn opened his eyes.

Another of the castle guards vaulted over the barrier and came running to his side. The guard skidded to a halt, suddenly aware of the fact that he was standing between Lorn and several Death Cultists.

"Wow," he said cautiously, "this looks like a really bad time, but—"

"Add it to the agenda," Lorn said.

The guard shook his head. "Nah, Majesty—you have to come *now*; the sinkhole has reached the first pumpkin field."

Lorn's stomach dropped. They could not afford to lose that field.

"Very well." Lorn turned to the Challengers. "Change of plans: I shall have to fight you all simultaneously."

The crowd gasped.

"Ah ... Majesty," Jakobsen called out, as the castle guard quickly vacated the square. "Just to be clear ... 'simultaneously' in this context means 'all four wizards at once.' Are you *sure* that's what you meant?"

The crowd held its breath.

"A brilliant elucidation of the obvious, Jakobsen," Lorn said. "Yes, that is what I meant by 'simultaneously.' All four wizards at once."

Jakobsen still looked skeptical. "Yeah ... I still don't think you get it. You'll be defending yourself from four wizards *and* attacking at the same time. *Simultaneously.*"

Lorn sighed. "Yes. That is the plan."

The triplets turned to Ambassador Zoth, their expressions eager, *hungry*.

The ambassador shrugged. "The idea is suicidal, but who am I to judge?"

The crowd gasped again.

"But Majesty ... you sure you should be doing that?" Master Baker called out. "You were under a mountain yesterday." The crowd murmured their assent.

"Thank you for the timely reminder of yesterday's brush with death, Master Baker," Lorn said, "but unfortunately, there is no other option."

"Here, now—don't make him doubt himself," Mistress Baker said, elbowing her husband. "He needs our support." She turned to Lorn. "You just go ahead and kill those wizards, Majesty. Kill them good."

"Crush them all, King!" a tiny girl cried, her hair braided in a coronet, her small fists waving menacingly. "CRUSH THEM ALL!"

"CRUSH THEM ALL!" the crowd chanted.

"Thank you, Lorette," Lorn said to the tiny girl. "Very motivating."

"Any last words?" the ambassador asked Lorn solicitously.

"My condolences to whoever wins," Lorn said.

The ambassador blinked. "Not particularly memorable, but we will note it for the records. Now, begin your preparations." With that, the ambassador quickly rushed to join the crowd behind the warded barrier, his guards following close behind.

Lorn faced the Challengers across the length of the City Square.

The Death Cult triplets smiled identical vicious smiles at Lorn and closed their eyes. They began to chant, their words filling the courtyard with a low, guttural drone. The black script that covered their skulls began to pulse, began to *writhe*, called to life by the wizards' words.

Lorn felt the power of those words pour over his skin like tar, heavy and slow and poison-thick. And yet, even as the sluggish, greasy feel of the triplets' magic repelled him, he could feel the temptation in its dark depths.

All this power could be yours, it whispered to Lorn—a promise that tasted of blood and ash. *Just ask. Just ask …*

Enough of that, Lorn scolded, ruthlessly pushing the magic aside. *I have quite enough to deal with at the moment.*

Lorn pulled back the cuffs of his coat and readied himself for a fight that he had to win. He was a seven-Mark sorcerer and Master of all four elements, but he was still recovering from his time spent under a mountain, and the events of this morning had already left him somewhat magically depleted.

He needed to win and win quickly, which left him only one option: he would have to call on the power of Between. It would almost assure him of victory, but there was always a price to pay for using such ancient magic. The backlash once it left his body would physically *hurt,* and there was no time in his forty-nine-item agenda for a prolonged recovery.

Still, did he truly have a choice?

The decision was abruptly taken out of his hands.

Before Lorn could call for it, before he even had to ask, Lorn felt the immense power of Between surge through the tether Mark between his shoulder blades. He gasped aloud as the ancient magic flooded his body, burning through his blood star-bright, and drenching every synapse, every cell with raw power, almost too much for his skin to contain.

At that moment, Lorn felt, with aching clarity, his connection to Between. He could feel the life force of Between in the weight of the soil, the movement of each body of water, the burrowing roots of each plant, the heartbeat of each creature that walked on its surface. The ground beneath Lorn's feet rumbled, ready to do his bidding; sheet lightning flickered across the darkening sky in anticipation of his command.

Lorn knew that this would cost him later—no human could hold such power without physical repercussions—but for now … for now it was *exhilarating*! Between wanted him to fight. Between wanted him to *win.* And he was nothing if not Between's servant.

White-hot sparks flickered over his fingertips. The Cloak of Shadows billowed behind him, ready.

"Let us begin," Lorn said, bracing himself to contain the power that flowed like quicksilver through his veins. "Ambassador, if you would be so kind as to declare—"

The high-pitched screech of a horn suddenly filled the city square.

Lorn and the Challengers shared a bemused look and turned to the ambassador, who was now playing a sequence of frenzied high notes on his horn reminiscent of the battle cry of a deranged chicken.

"May we dispense with the horn until the end of the Challenge, Ambassador Zoth?" Lorn asked, raising his voice to be heard over the noise. "I would like to die with my eardrums intact."

"Here, here!" the crowd chanted.

"Radish King!" the Radish King yelled in agreement.

"Many thanks for your support," Lorn said to the vegetable monarch.

The ambassador removed the horn from his lips, slightly winded. "The horns are a Zadrian Challenge tradition."

"They'll be Zadrian headwear if you keep it up," Mistress Blacksmith warned, flexing her impressive bicep.

"You make a compelling argument, madam," the ambassador said, staring appreciatively at the display of muscle. "No more horns."

"If only we could make that a permanent rule ..." Master Baker muttered.

The ambassador pointedly ignored Master Baker. "Very well. Let the Challenge begin!"

"Go, Majesty!" the crowd cheered.

"My good fellows," Lorn addressed the Death Cultists. "I have pumpkins to save ... or you do, if you win. So, if we could dispense with the traditional taunts and posturing that precede the Challenge, and move straight to the killing, I would be most appreciative."

Unfortunately for Lorn, Death Cultists were notoriously fond of both taunts and posturing. They ignored Lorn's request completely.

High Priest Rahven made a series of swooping hand gestures, swaying his body back and forth like a willow tree caught in a storm. Wind raced across the city square at his command and billowed dramatically through his cloak. "Lorn," he rasped, as the wind lifted him several feet off the ground. "Your reign is at an end!"

Lorn sighed.

High Priest Vitzh raised his hands to eye level and clapped them together. Flames, red-gold and black, burst to life across his palms. He flexed his hands, and the flames flowed like lava onto the ground, surrounding him in a ring of fire. "Soon, your blood will stain the stones!" he intoned, the fires raging higher as if in agreement.

Lorn raised his hand to the sky.

High Priest Xar stamped his boot on the ground. The earth trembled and began to undulate. "Pray to your god now, sorcerer!" he sneered as the cobblestones began to quake. "For your time has—*AARGH!*"

Lightning fell from the sky. An eye-searing white light engulfed the city square accompanied by a *BOOM* loud enough to rattle every window in the city.

Everyone—the crowd and Challengers alike—turned away from the square, eyes squeezed shut, hands clutched protectively over their ears, the sharp reek of ozone filling their nostrils.

When it was safe to turn back, and their vision had cleared, they found a smoking crater where High Priest Xar had been standing.

For a moment, there was complete silence.

Then, the crowd roared.

"GO, MAJESTY!" they cheered.

High Priest Vitzh and High Priest Rahven stared at the crater in shock. The Radish King peered at it with interest, then went back to chewing his radish.

Ambassador Zoth cleared his throat and averted his eyes from the greasy film at the base of the crater. "It is with great sorrow that I announce that High Priest Xar is now—"

"A smear," Jakobsen provided helpfully.

"I was going to say, 'no more,' " the ambassador chastised. He turned to Lorn. "Do you require a rest period?"

Lorn lowered his hands and brushed the gold dust from his palms. "Let us continue—time is fleeting."

The ambassador cast a speculative look at the remaining Zadrian wizards, his hooked nose twitching. "Then let the Challenge begin … again."

This time, there were no taunts.

The brothers shared a look and began to work together: High Priest Vitzh quickly conjured his red and black flames while High Priest Rahven bound the fire with gusts of wind, shaping it to his will.

As Lorn watched, the flames first danced, then began to rise above the rickety buildings that surrounded the city square, writhing and twisting until they were barn-high. High Priest Rahven held up the Wind Mark on his left wrist, and the tower of flames morphed into a terrifying fire beast, all wings and fangs and flames. The heat that radiated off of it was so intense that Lorn could feel his breastplate begin to warm through his tunic. It was a brilliant display of power and control of the elements, meant to intimidate and awe.

The citizens of Between, however, were not impressed.

"Showy," Master Baker said disapprovingly.

The rest of the crowd muttered their agreement.

As if sensing the crowd's disapproval, the gargantuan fire beast roared and turned its attention to Lorn, spewing ash and flames down onto the sorcerer in a burning arc.

"NOOOOOO!" the crowd shrieked.

In a heartbeat, the Cloak of Shadows flew up and shielded Lorn from the hellfire raining down upon him.

"Many thanks," Lorn murmured. He took a quick breath and stepped out from under the cloak, the flames retreating at the sight of his upraised Fire Mark. Reaching out, Lorn felt for the wind fueling the beast and grasped its tail, winding it around his left wrist like a cord.

High Priest Rahven's eyes widened as he realized that he was losing control of his spell. He dug in his heels and gestured frantically, but it was too late—Lorn pulled the last threads of the bespelled wind free and calmly spooled it around his wrist.

Without wind, the fire beast lost its structure; it thrashed and roared and began to unravel, tumbling down toward the square in a cascade of flames. The wards around the perimeter flared bright gold as the flames spilled uncontrollably, heading straight for the gathered citizens. Reflexively, they shrieked and ducked, their hands over their heads.

Quick as a snake, Lorn flicked his wrist and unleashed the bound winds, sending them roaring across the square. At his command, the winds surrounded the flames and drew them upward, spinning them clockwise, faster and faster toward the sky.

High Priest Vitzh screamed in frustration as he lost control of his flames, the dark script on his scalp sputtering to a standstill. "Do something!" he hissed to his brother.

High Priest Rahven raised his Wind Mark at the fiery tornado, but the winds refused to obey. Frustrated, he turned to Lorn and cast, sending a gale toward the King thick with Dark Magic.

Lorn raised his right hand and flicked the winds aside as if they were a speck of lint. They crashed into the wards and dissipated into gray mist. He then looked up at the fiery tornado, closed his left hand into a fist, and pulled it downward sharply.

The tunnel of flame obediently stopped its ascent and hurtled back toward the square.

High Priest Vitzh raised his right palm, his Fire Mark exposed, determined to regain control of the tornado of flame. He stepped beneath it, chanting frantically.

He really should have known better.

There was a terrible scream as the fiery tornado enclosed High Priest Vitzh within its walls of flame and ash.

Then, a sizzling sound.

Then … silence.

Lorn raised his Fire Mark, and the flames died away, leaving behind a pile of wet ashes. A final plume of greasy, black smoke rose toward the sky, writhing angrily in the breeze.

"YAY!" the crowd roared.

The ambassador grimaced at the pile of ash. "It appears that High Priest Vitzh is now—"

"Crispy," Jakobsen supplied helpfully.

"—*defeated*," the ambassador said pointedly. He turned to Lorn. "Do you wish to take a break? Or would you prefer for the carnage to continue?"

"Let us continue with the carnage," Lorn said, flexing his hands.

High Priest Rahven stared at Lorn with utter loathing.

"Ready?" Lorn asked the Death Cultist.

High Priest Rahven spat at Lorn.

"I shall take that as a *yes*," Lorn said.

The Radish King threw away the remains of his radish and stood up. "Radish King!" he declared, purple sparks sputtering from his fingertips.

"Then let us end this," Lorn said, raising his hands. "I have gourds to save."

~

"WHAT PART OF 'STAY UNINJURED' DID YOU NOT UNDERSTAND?!" GAHIL yelled as he marched into Lorn's Less-Formal Meeting Chambers, followed by his scurrying apprentices.

"It is nothing," Lorn said, jaw clenched. "Jakobsen should not have called you. He has been wretchedly melodramatic about the whole matter."

Gahil ignored him. "*I told you* I have a crotch-rot epidemic! I am neck-deep in diseased genitals—"

Lorn tsked. "*Such* a visual."

"—and you decide that this is a fine time to take on four wizards—"

"Technically, it was three-and-half wizards at best."

"Bah!" Gahil threw his beard over his shoulder. "I don't care if it's three-and-a-half wizards or twelve-and-a-quarter wizards! I don't have time to patch you up after a wizard pissing contest!"

Lorn snorted. "If only. Far less chance of injury in that type of contest."

"Dehydration," Jakobsen suggested helpfully.

"I stand corrected," Lorn said.

Gahil looked at Lorn's drawn expression and raised an eyebrow. "Shall I guess what hurts?"

Lorn took a shaky breath. "Please, be my guest."

Both men looked down at the desk where Lorn's left hand rested, his wrist twisted at a particularly gruesome angle and puffed up like a flesh-covered balloon.

"Midra's sack, I just fixed that!" Gahil yelled. "Though ... *huh*." Medical curiosity swiftly replaced his anger. "I've never seen a wrist twisted quite that far around before. Didn't know it was even possible." He brought his face close to the injury. "Still don't quite believe it. Well done."

"Many thanks," Lorn bit out.

Gahil gently probed Lorn's fingers. "Is this your only injury?"

Lorn nodded tightly.

"You fought four wizards, and *this* is your only injury?"

"Technically, I fought three wizards," Lorn said through gritted teeth, as Gahil began to examine the back of his hand. "The Radish King fought a tree."

"And what a battle it was," Jakobsen said solemnly, his lips twitching. "One for the ages."

Gahil stared at the two of them. "Why is he called the Radish Ki—you know what? I don't care." He went back to examining Lorn's wrist. "So, who won the mighty battle? The radish or the tree?"

"It was a draw," Jakobsen said. "The Radish King managed to split the tree in two, but the tree fell on him on the way down." He shook his head. "Both will be missed."

"It was a very elegant tree," Lorn said.

Gahil carefully lifted Lorn's hand from the desk. "So, which one of the wizards did this nasty piece of work on your wrist?"

"The Radish King," Lorn said, through gritted teeth.

Gahil stared at Lorn, shocked. "*The Radish King* landed a blow?"

"Well, technically, it was the tree," Jakobsen explained. "His Majesty here was fighting the last wizard when the Radish King sent a spell toward the tree. One of the branches shot off in a shower of purple sparks and hit the King's wrist front-on while he was casting."

Gahil probed Lorn's wrist. "Hit him front-on, you say? That doesn't explain why it's twisted at this strange angle."

"You're right about that," Jakobsen said. "Majesty did the rest of the damage himself."

"He did what?!" Gahil exclaimed.

"*Agh!*" Lorn cried out. "*Careful,* Gahil! Are you trying to twist it all the way around?"

"I should twist it right off!" Gahil snarled. "What does he mean *you* did the rest of the damage?"

"Here, let me tell the story, Majesty," Jakobsen said. "You save your breath for screaming in agony."

"Many thanks," Lorn bit out.

Jakobsen cleared his throat theatrically. "After the Challenge—which was spectacular, by the way! His Majesty *annihilated* the first wizard. The fellow was boasting about what he would do to the King when *BAM!*—lightning bolt crushed him. And then the second one tried to burn the King alive with a fire beast when *BAM!*—the King dropped a fire tornado on him. There was nothing left of him but ash and a meaty smell. And the last one—*that* was a doozy! You should have seen how fast the King was casting. I mean, his hands were a blur! He shot these balls of pure wind—*whoosh! whoosh! whoosh!*—and they circled the wizard, crushing him tighter and tighter, and lifting him higher and higher until he was a speck in the sky. And then—"

"Let me guess?" Gahil interrupted. "Bam?"

"Yes, but you need to say it with more vigor. It was more like *BAM!*" Jakobsen clapped his hands together sharply. "The wizard hurtled back to the ground and landed all crushed, like a crumpled ball of parchment, in the crater with the first wizard. Thrilling stuff! Though, it's going to be hard to scrape them all up to take back to Zadria—"

"I have a crotch-rot epidemic," Gahil interrupted. "Can we speed this up?"

Jakobsen shrugged. "Okay, but I can't for the life of me see why you'd want to hurry back to that." Seeing Gahil's expression, he quickly moved on. "After the battle, His Majesty bandaged up his wrist and went to fix the sinkhole that was swallowing up the pumpkin patches. One of his spells ricocheted off a knot of pixies hidden under one of the pumpkins—you can't use magic on magical creatures, you know—"

"Really?" Gahil asked dryly.

"Yep! And the spell hit him right in the wrist. I swear, I could hear his wrist *twisting.*" Jakobsen shuddered. "Ghastly sound."

Lorn swallowed hard. "Thank you for reminding me." He turned to Gahil. "The pixies were not pleased to be hit with a spell."

"Yeah, well I bet they'd have been even less pleased if they fell down a sinkhole," Gahil said.

"That's what I told them!" Jakobsen said. "Prickly lot, they were. Anyway, Majesty saved all the pumpkins. There'll be pumpkin cakes and pumpkin pies all month thanks to him, so you can't be *too* angry with him." He looked slyly at the healer. "You're fond of a nice slice of pumpkin pie, aren't you, Healer Gahil?"

"Don't sass me, Flynn Jakobsen," Gahil groused, "or I'll forget to warm up my hands before your next annual check-up."

Jakobsen mock shivered. "Got it."

"So ... what we've got here is a magical injury. Thought so." Gahil beckoned for the apprentices to open his bags. "Now, let's get this wrist untwisted and splinted. If you keep it immobilized for the rest of the day, you might even be able to use it by tonight."

"Lucky it is not my dominant hand," Lorn said. "Oh, wait—it is."

"Tough." Gahil pulled a thick roll of bandages out from the bag and began to set them out on the desk. "While I'm here, let's see how those patches are going, shall we?"

He beckoned for one of his apprentices to check.

The apprentice removed Lorn's boot and began the effortful task of peeling back his leather pants. He paused when he reached the thick, white band of scars around Lorn's ankle. The apprentice looked up at Lorn, a question in his eyes.

"Shackles are heavy," was all Lorn said.

Gahil looked up from the bandages and stared at the old scars. For a brief second, the old healer looked immensely sad. But then he caught himself and cleared his throat.

"Do you intend to roll up those pants sometime *today*?" he asked the apprentice. "Or are you waiting for them to become sentient, so they can do it themselves?"

The apprentice quickly went back to his task, pulling back Lorn's pants to his knee. Ink-black patches the size of plums had joined the faded-gray marks of this morning, startlingly dark against the pallor of Lorn's skin. Jakobsen peered over the apprentice's shoulder. "Looks like that fungus in the Thieves' Forest, doesn't it?"

"Your medical opinion is duly noted, Jakobsen," Gahil said. He reached into his bag and handed Lorn a potion bottle, his expression sour. "This is what comes from dueling three-and-a-half wizards and doing Midra knows what else this morning. Lethargy?"

Lorn nodded tightly.

The dwarf's eyes narrowed. "Headache?"

"Like the Minotaur stuck his spear into my left eyeball and left it there."

"Sounds like a nice case of magical exhaustion. You didn't rest long enough after the last bout." Gahil looked down at the dark patches. "How far up do they go?"

Lorn took a shaky breath. "Honestly? I have no wish to know. There is still too much to do."

"How's that agenda going?"

"I am about to start item two."

Gahil snorted. He carefully picked up Lorn's ruined wrist. "This isn't going to tickle. In fact, it'll be a good test for that famously high pain threshold of yours." He gestured for his apprentices to stand behind him. "Given that this is a magical injury, I'm going to need your help to untwist it. But control your magic, you hear me? I don't want you to blast me through the wall."

"Give me some credit—I have not done that since I was a child."

"It took me a week to recover," Gahil muttered.

"Apologies for the thousandth time." Lorn winced. He looked down at the bottle in his hand. "Is there any chance that you have invented an effective pain potion since this morning?"

"No, you're stuck with the usual one; it'll work for a couple of minutes." Gahil watched as Lorn dutifully swallowed the potion, grimacing at the taste. "And I have this nice piece of leather for you to bite down on."

One of the apprentices handed Lorn a thick, leather strap.

"Ah, we meet again, old friend," Lorn said wryly to the leather strap.

"Once you've helped me untwist this wrist, try to pass out," Gahil advised.

"Oh, to be that lucky ..." Lorn said with a wistful sigh and placed the leather strap between his teeth.

4

AN ALMOST TYPICAL CROSSING

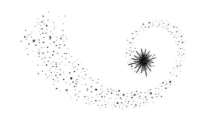

THE ONLY DOWNSIDE TO PASSING OUT, LORN THOUGHT WRYLY, WAS WAKING back up again.

"You could have done at least *some* of these tasks while I was unconscious," he griped to Maddox, gesturing to his agenda. "For instance, agenda-item fifteen: *signing bills, agreements, proclamations, and announcements*. We both know that you sign my name as well as I do."

"Even better," Maddox agreed. He pushed the stack of documents in question toward Lorn. "But many of these are magically binding; they have to be signed by the ruler of the kingdom."

"And to think, that could have been the Radish King." Lorn dutifully picked up a quill and began awkwardly signing the documents with his right hand, his left still bandaged and out of commission.

Maddox opened the box containing the royal seal and prepared it for Lorn's use. "I, for one, am pleased that you emerged victorious. The paperwork necessary to change rulers is staggering …"

Lorn rolled his eyes. "I am pleased to have spared you from such administrative burdens."

"See that you continue to do so. The citizens of Between are also quite pleased that you won; there have been raucous celebrations at the Sleazy Weasel all afternoon. The house band has already commemorated your exploits in a new song."

Lorn looked up from his paperwork. "Is it terrible?"

"It contains a sixteen minute, improvised yodeling solo."

"I shall take that as a resounding *yes*." Lorn shuddered and went back to signing.

"They also wrote a song to commemorate one of your fallen Challengers entitled, 'Oh Radish King, We Hardly Knew You.' The lyrics include: *his purple sparks/struck my heart*, and *branches are just death sticks waiting to fall*. Truly stirring stuff."

"The elves will love it." Lorn picked up the royal seal and carefully stamped a series of proclamations.

"Any feat that is immortalized by yodeling and death sticks is one for the ages. I am sorry to have missed it. Unfortunately, I was busy evacuating the lower portion of the castle after a lake sprung up in one of the old dungeons."

Lorn paused, the seal hovering above the parchment. "Agenda-item forty-nine: *the lake in the castle*. I had forgotten all about that. What did you do about it?"

Maddox shrugged. "What we usually do—closed the door and put a 'Do Not Enter' sign on it."

"And did that work?"

"For now. The lake appears to have stopped growing. Technically, it is more of a pond than a lake."

"I shall attend to it after item—" Lorn paused and listened. "Are those the Zadrian mourning horns?"

Sure enough, the sound of mournful horns drifted across the city from the Zadrian embassy, located in the Ambassadors' Quarter—which, after a recent sinkhole incident, had been renamed 'The Ambassadors' Eighth.' Several dogs began to howl along, accompanied by the lowing of a chorus of cows, followed by the bellowing solo of a creature that sounded even larger than a cow and not nearly as melodious.

"Right on time," Maddox said, standing. He crossed the room and closed the windows, muting the sounds from the city below. "There will be horns and wailing aplenty in the desert kingdom tonight."

Lorn grimaced. "Be sure to send the King of Zadria the usual box of condolence turnips." He placed the seal back in its box and ran a hand through his hair, suddenly very weary. "There has been a Challenge from a Zadrian wizard every month for the past four months ... and today there were four wizards, which reeks of desperation on their part. Are we any closer to finding out whether it is the Zadrian King or the Death Cultists who want the throne of Between?"

"The Collection department is on it ... although the fact that you have battled Death Cultists each time strongly suggests the latter." Maddox returned to his seat, brushing gold dust off the cushion before sitting down. "Odds are that they want the Portal, not the throne."

"If all they wanted was the throne, then I would be tempted to lose—let someone else try to keep this place from falling into a sinkhole or bursting into flames each day. But allow the Portal to fall into the hands of the Death Cultists?" Lorn shook his head. "That can never come to pass. Their reasons for wanting the Portal are likely nefarious at best and apocalyptic at worst. We must do all that we can to stop that from happening."

"But of course," Maddox said. "A magic cult that tinkers in Forbidden magic, and currently resides in a godless kingdom should probably not have access to a gateway to other realms."

"Probably not. Though …" Lorn looked down at the splint around his wrist. "Should I fail one of these Challenges—"

"Highly unlikely," Maddox said briskly, cutting him off. "After all, you just fought off four wizards and inspired a sixteen-minute yodeling solo. Your only injury came from a tree—a tree that is of no further threat to you because it is now dead. Which, come to think of it, is probably for the best—it was starting to amass a body count. Moreover—"

"Maddox," Lorn interrupted quietly. "*Should I fail …*"

Maddox stared at Lorn for a long moment. "The new king would have a very short reign."

Lorn's eyes narrowed. "How short?"

"Stabbed-in-the-kidneys-as-soon-as-he-raises-his-hands-in-victory *short*."

Lorn exhaled in a rush. "Excellent—an appropriately bloodthirsty response. But, just in case the kidney-stabbing fails, I would like a contingency plan in place. Several, in fact. Have the Disposals department devise a list of regicide plans for my successor immediately. It may seem petty but inform them that I would like my successor to suffer *a lot*—after all, they killed me."

"That is extremely understandable."

"Moreover, I would like for the Collection department to begin a search for my successor."

Maddox blinked. "Pardon, but I thought I was going to stab him in the kidneys?"

Lorn shook his head, thinking of Derrek, thinking of all the whispers that followed him whenever he was at the Summer Palace. "No, my *true* successor. I have no Golden Feather—" Lorn held up his hand to halt Maddox's arguments. "I have no Golden Feather, which means that the Destined King of Between is out there somewhere ... probably hiding, clever bastard. I would rather that we find him now so that he can be crowned, preferably as soon as you stab my murderer in the kidneys."

Maddox nodded reluctantly. "It is probably wise to be prepared."

Bells—some high and sweet, others deep and resonant—began to chime. Lorn looked over his shoulder to the wall behind him, where time-pieces of all shapes and sizes covered the shelves.

"You had best hurry," Maddox said, closing away the royal seal in its box. "You are due to preside over the Court of Pettiest Complaints." He gestured to Lorn's agenda. "Item three. The citizens have been lining up for hours, ready to tell you their woes."

"Wonderful. The basis of more forty-seven-item agendas." Lorn stared at the timepieces longingly. "One day, I shall master Time, just as I mastered all the other elements, and your agendas will no longer defeat me."

"Of course, you will," Maddox said, his tone placating. "But for now, you are listening to the petty complaints of your people."

Lorn pushed the stack of signed documents toward Maddox and stretched his cramped hand. "Remind me to institute a court session where the citizens of Between are forced to listen to *my* petty complaints."

"Listening to your petty complaints constitutes fifty-percent of my job description. If you institute that court session, I will notify my union."

Lorn mock shuddered. "I would rather duel Death Cultists." He looked down at agenda item three and sighed. "I am not in the best frame of mind for this task."

"Of the entire agenda, this is one of the least taxing items; you need only sit on your throne for an hour and nod when required."

Lorn snorted. "Please—we both know that is a terrible lie. The session always degenerates into a full-scale brawl, or a fire, or a brawl surrounded by fire. We have only just repaired the damage to the throne room doors from the previous session."

"Would you like me to take your place?"

Lorn considered the offer. As tempting as it was, he shook his head. "The citizens want to be heard by their King. They requested it ... as you no doubt remember."

Lorn recalled the incident in stark clarity. It was in the early days of his reign when the entire kingdom was in chaos—even more so than now. The people were starving, vicious beasts and dark creatures terrorized the city, and wild magic was running unchecked across the land. The citizens of Between were angry and close to revolt, thanks to a string of ineffective kings who had failed to keep them safe and fed. They had demanded a forum to air their grievances, and so the Court of Pettiest Complaints was born.

"It does me no true harm to listen to them," Lorn conceded. "Ignore them, however, and one day they may decide that *I* am their pettiest complaint and deal with me accordingly."

"Well, avoiding assassination is an excellent incentive for performing an agenda item. Still, missing one session will not incite a riot; the citizens of Between are exceptionally fond of you."

"All the more reason to attend the court session and keep it that way."

Maddox pulled a small stack of oatcakes from one of his hidden pockets and passed them to Lorn. "You can listen while you eat."

"Listening to complaints while eating is bound to be terrible for my digestion." Nevertheless, Lorn took the cakes gratefully and went off to listen to the petty complaints of his people.

~

As it happened, the Court of Pettiest Complaints went better than Lorn had expected. There were only three brawls and two relatively small fires, which elevated the session to one of the most successful in the history of Between.

Some complaints had merit and required immediate assistance from the Crown. This included the farmer who had awoken to find a dragon sitting on the crushed remains of his barn, and a shepherd whose entire flock had all mysteriously turned turquoise during the last Lunar Crossing. Other complaints had less merit and were unable to be solved by anyone. This included a cobbler who claimed that his teeth were itchy, and four other citizens who (quite rightly) alleged that Between smelled too much like rotten cabbage. There was the usual string of creature-based problems ("A vicious mountain wolf ate my chickens!" was followed almost immediately by, "Vicious chickens ate my pet mountain wolf!" which Lorn assumed was a chicken-organized revenge killing); and the expected objections to policies ("Taxes should be based on height—short people use less resources!") and departmental paperwork ("The essay portion of the arson permit takes too long to fill out—it's taking all the fun out of recreational burning!").

Finally, there were the complaints from drunken citizens who had mistakenly joined the Court of Pettiest Complaints queue thinking that it was the entry line to a tavern. "This is the weirdest lavatory I've ever been in," and "This tavern needs more boiled peanuts!" were two of the most common grievances aired by this group.

All of the complaints were cataloged by the official scribes, who sat below the throne's dais. Soon, every nag, protest, objection, criticism, and whine would be compiled, assessed, delegated wherever possible, and then returned to Lorn in the form of endless agendas.

Lorn frowned down at the scribes and flirted with the idea of setting their lists on fire. But as tempting as it was, he quickly dismissed that thought. Given that this was Between, the fire would inevitably rage out of control and would then have to be dealt with as agenda-item fifty.

When the last protester left the throne room, and the troll guards finally closed the newly repaired throne room doors, Lorn removed his crown with a relieved sigh and tried to stretch the kinks out of his back.

"You look like you need a break," Jakobsen said, offering Lorn a small parcel of dried apples. "Pity you can't take one."

Lorn took the apples from his head guard with a dark look. "If you were not bearing food, I would swamp you."

Nevertheless, Jakobsen was right; Lorn was exhausted. His wrist felt as though it was on fire, and he had developed a pain behind his right eye to match the earlier pain behind his left eye.

"Well, at least the pain is evenly distributed now," he told Maddox, who had come to the throne room to check on Lorn's progress.

All Lorn wanted was to slink back to bed and sleep the rest of the day away. But there was still much to do. He straightened his shoulders and attempted to charge through his remaining tasks. There were ambassadors to meet with, ministers to scheme with, a pond to remove from the castle, and a dragon to coax off a barn.

There was also a small, drunken unicorn to extricate from the castle wall.

"Tractor," Lorn said in exasperation, looking down to where the feral little creature was stuck, horn-first, in the stone wall. "Must you head-butt everything at eye-level?"

"Yep," one of the castle guards said, pointing to the row of holes that dotted the corridor, all at horn-height.

"It's a calling," another guard said, patting the mangy beast fondly.

Tractor huffed in agreement.

Before Lorn knew it, the first set of bells began to peal, warning that the Lunar Crossing would take place in two hours.

Almost immediately, the citizens of Between started their well-practiced

Crossing routines, performing the tasks necessary to ride out whatever the Dreamer had in store for the kingdom.

Lorn strode briskly through the city, carefully dodging livestock and carts, people hurrying home with their children in tow, and revelers running to the taverns.

"Dark times are coming! You are all doomed!" one jaundiced looking man in a floppy, purple hat called out from his perch atop an apple crate. "All of you, DOOMED. *You're* doomed!" he yelled to a passing castle guard.

"Ah … thanks?" the guard yelled back over his shoulder.

"And *you're* doomed!" the man cried, pointing to a nearby cow. The cow glared at him.

"And you—*you* are *especially* doomed," the man shouted, pointing to Lorn.

"Could not have said it better myself, Frank," Lorn said agreeably and tossed the man a coin.

Lorn made his way to the city square, where a canvas booth labeled Lunar Crossing Information Center had been hastily erected an hour before. In accordance with most of the buildings in Between, the Information Center was both structurally unsound and highly flammable. Within the booth, Maddox stood behind the splintery plank that served as a counter, directing a handful of castle guards and fielding questions from a line of concerned citizens.

As Lorn approached the booth, a man holding a black chicken wrapped in a sumptuous, teal-silk shawl stepped up to the front of the line.

"It's Endora, you see," the man said to Maddox, gesturing with his chin to the chicken. "She has a sensitive disposition."

Endora clucked pitifully.

"And the Lunar Crossing stresses her enormously."

Endora clucked in agreement.

"Understandable," Maddox murmured with a straight face.

The man patted Endora. "So … where would be the best place to put her during this time, keeping in mind she doesn't like drafts, loud noises, other animals—particularly yaks—any rhythmic movement that could be construed as folk dancing, the smell of cooked fat, the color magenta, or any musical or theatrical performance that requires audience participation?"

Lorn looked down at Endora. "This is clearly a chicken of exquisite taste and refinement."

"That she is," the man said proudly. Endora preened.

"And thus," Lorn continued, "she should be housed in the Aurorean Embassy, in the royal suite typically occupied by Prince Ashlyn."

The man's eyes bugged. "Why, *thank you*, Majesty!"

Endora clucked approvingly.

Maddox handed Lorn a luxurious square of black cardstock that was embossed with the royal insignia—two facing crescent moons with a very pointy star suspended between them. Lorn scribbled a note on the back and handed it to the man. "Give this to the guards at the Aurorean Embassy—they will give you entrance."

The man took the card and grinned. "Thank you, Majesty! A good Crossing to you!" He and the pampered Endora rushed away.

"You have made one chicken very happy," Maddox said.

"I am in the business of making dreams come true," Lorn said.

"And what of Prince Ashlyn, whose chambers are about to be sullied by poultry?"

Lorn shrugged. "Well, I can only do so much. Is everything going well?"

Maddox nodded. "We are a well-oiled cart. The Guardians are beginning to assemble at each of the gateways; the imps are checking the wards around the Wasteland; the castle guards are currently assisting the citizens; and the Arrows are at their stations around the countryside, ready to report any disasters." The Arrows were the fastest runners and the best riders in Between and acted as lookouts, relays, and messengers for the Crown. "The guards will also do a final patrol to ensure that everyone is indoors at the final bells."

"Excellent work as always, Maddox. Is there anything else I should know before I check the gateways and the wards?"

"A Zadrian betrothal party has entered Between."

"My best wishes to the happy couple; they will get the usual box of congratulatory carrots. Is there any reason why this is something of note?"

"They have come to petition for your hand in marriage."

Lorn blinked. "For *my* hand?"

"Well, it is certainly not for mine."

The idea was so baffling to Lorn that he wondered whether his concussion had returned. "A moment," he said, holding up his hand. "This morning, the Zadrians tried to kill me … and this evening they are trying to *marry* me?"

"It is remarkable what a difference a couple of hours can make." Maddox handed a key to one of the passing guards and ticked off an item on his notebook. "It appears that the Zadrians are trying a new approach to gain the throne. Truly, their persistence is to be admired ..."

Lorn was still having problems processing this new development. "So ... at first ... they tried to kill me with magic ... and now they intend to kill me with matrimony?" He paused. "They do intend to kill me during this marriage, do they not?"

"Oh, yes," Maddox said. "The potential bride in question is a serial widow—six marriages, four dead husbands."

Lorn frowned. "And the other two?"

"Both husbands petitioned for divorce after she ... well, let us just say that there was disfigurement involved. And genitals."

Lorn shuddered. "Enough said. I think I will decline the honor of this betrothal. Although the woman in question seems appropriately blood-thirsty to rule Between, the Disposals department would object to a queen who dispatches husbands without submitting the proper paperwork. Also, I would object to being killed. Where is this betrothal party? The Formal Meeting Chamber?"

"I was able to divert them to the Wetlands; I thought it would be a wonderful opportunity for the Zadrians to get a better look at the land they wish to rule. They are currently touring the Swamp of Perpetual Suffering."

Lorn grinned. "You are a wonder, Maddox! Many thanks. Feel free to compensate yourself handsomely from the Small Treasury using the key in your left breast pocket that we both pretend you do not possess."

Maddox touched the pocket in question where a suspiciously key-shaped object lay. "I have no idea what you are talking about." He spared Lorn a sly look. "How is the agenda going?"

Lorn quickly turned on his heel. "Apologies," he called over his shoulder, "but I have no time to make idle chit-chat. I am exceptionally busy. I am a *king*, you know..."

"I shall just add the unfinished items to tomorrow's agenda!" Maddox called after him.

Lorn made his way through Between, checking the kingdom's magical fortifications. Although the city was exempt from the transformations that occurred during the Lunar Crossing, Lorn knew that if something could go wrong in Between, it would.

It never hurt to triple check.

And then check once more.

Lorn examined the wards on the city gates and the colossal, black stone walls surrounding the city. As he adjusted the wards near the gates, he

heard cheering coming from somewhere above him. He looked up. High
overhead, the castle guards were stationed at their posts, surveying the city
below. A few of the more adventurous citizens stood in the viewing galleries
along the walls, waiting for the show to begin. They spotted Lorn and
waved.

"Merry Crossing, Majesty!" they called.

"Merry Crossing," Lorn called back. "Try not to fall off the wall."

They cheered raucously.

Lorn briefly wondered if they were drunk—it was a fairly safe bet—
then continued on his way. He passed through the city gates and followed
the cobblestone road until he reached the Between Gateway—a soaring
sandstone structure composed of a lofty arch supported by immense,
carved pillars. It stood alone, on a stone platform before the walled city.
The gateway network served as the most common form of transport across
Otherworld. Each kingdom in the Summer Alliance under the High King
and Queen's rule had a gateway outside their city walls, allowing its citizens
to travel across Otherworld at set times during the day and night. The
travel schedule was organized and operated by High Queen Orelia, the fae-
born monarch Joined to High King Dresden. She was the only one who
had both the power—as a fae of royal blood—and the permission to wield
the gateways of Otherworld.

As Lorn arrived, the Between Gateway flashed gold.

"Stand back!" one of the Gateway watchmen—a burly troll armed with
an axe—boomed. "Gateway opening!"

A small crowd carrying baskets and packs tramped out of the Gateway,
appearing as if from thin air. They quickly made their way past the
watchmen and headed for the city gates.

"Hurry along now," the other watchman called out to the stragglers.
"The Crossing is almost here."

Once the last person had exited, the watchmen placed a large, wooden
sign in front of the gateway that read 'closed.'

"No more trips today!" they announced. "Gateway's closing early for
the Crossing!"

Lorn strode up to the Gateway and placed his hand flat upon the warm
sandstone. He opened his senses and felt the ancient magic laying dormant
beneath his palm.

"Did the High Queen shut it down?" the first watchman asked.

"She did indeed," Lorn said, removing his hand from the pillar. "There
will be no more travel tonight."

"Good. The last thing we need is a bunch of elves wandering in during the Crossing and getting turned into yaks or something. We'd never hear the end of it."

"We would be assaulted by terrible poetry for months," Lorn agreed.

"Damn elves," the second watchman muttered. He turned to Lorn. "Are you off to check the other gateways?"

Lorn nodded. "And I had best get on with it—it is getting late. Once the Minotaur arrives to guard the Gateway, you are both free to leave."

"Excellent," the first watchman said, rubbing his hands together. "The Weasel has a keg of ale with my name on it."

The second watchman rolled his eyes. "*Literally*. He won't let anyone else drink from it."

They bowed to Lorn and began to pack up for the night.

Lorn turned away from the Between Gateway and continued his inspection. Although the sandstone arch was the most prominent gateway in Between, there were many others scattered around the kingdom. These other gateways were not majestic structures like the Between Gateway; rather, they looked like ordinary garden gates, or farm gates, or fence gates. The only way to tell them apart from ordinary gates was that gateways always stood alone without fences, solitary and out of place in the middle of swamps and farms and fields and even caves. Once the Crossing began, the Portal would open all of the gateways in Between, turning them into passages to other realms.

As Lorn arrived at each gateway, he was greeted by its Guardian, each easily recognizable by a prominently worn garment—cloak or scarf, shirt or vest—in bright scarlet. The Gateway Guardians were the best and bravest fighters in Between, sworn to protect the kingdom by ensuring that no one —human or creature—entered or emerged from the gateways during the Crossing.

"Are you ready for tonight?" Lorn asked the griffin, who guarded a rickety, metal gateway beside a tar pit.

The griffin flexed its mighty wings, opened its beak, and screeched in a manner designed to peel eardrums.

Lorn removed his hands from over his ears. "I pity anyone foolish enough to cross you this evening. You are truly *glorious*."

The griffin puffed out its feathery chest and snorted as if to say, "*Of course I am.*" But it rubbed its immense head against Lorn's shoulder as the King passed, clearly pleased.

As with every Crossing, Lorn left his favorite gateway until last. The underground chamber was as warm as fresh toast, and filled with soft, golden light, thanks to the crystal orbs scattered around the room. It was also filled with a dragon, her garnet-colored scales iridescent in the shifting light. She rested on a nest of scarlet silk, her immense body curled between Lorn and the Faire Gateway, an exquisite crystal door carved with flowers and vines.

"Kyra," Lorn said with a smile. "How are you this evening, my lovely one?"

Kyra lifted her head and stared at Lorn with sleepy golden eyes. She made a pleased sound in greeting, somewhere between a hum and a purr.

Lorn crossed the chamber to her side and raised his hand. "May I?"

She lowered her head in assent and Lorn gently scratched her muzzle. He grinned as the dragon's eyes fluttered shut in pleasure, a ring of smoke rising from her nostrils.

"How are we this Crossing, hmm? Joyous? Restless? Bored?"

Kyra whined at the latter.

"Ah … bored. We shall have to see what we can do to alleviate that in the future."

Kyra snorted and pressed her muzzle against his hand in the universal gesture for more-delightful-scratching-please.

Lorn dutifully scratched a little harder and stared past Kyra's coiled body to the Gateway. As always, something within Lorn thrilled at the sight of that enchanting door. His magic sparked beneath his skin, recognizing the power not only imbued in every crystal petal and creeping vine, but in the realm beyond, with its powerful fae-run kingdoms and lands filled with magical creatures under their protection

Kyra turned her immense head toward the door and snorted again; she had good reason to be bored. Unlike the bustling gateways that stood before the Otherworld kingdoms, traffic through the Faire Gateway was sparse at best. After the Most Terrible War, the surviving fae rulers had sealed the entrances to their realm, no longer wishing to be dragged into the infighting between the citizens of Otherworld and their gods. When they were finally coaxed into reopening the Faire Gateway, travel was highly regulated. Aside from High Queen Orelia, who was the living link between the two realms, the only Otherworlders allowed to enter Faire were the magic folk, and even they were only permitted as far as the Twilight Market—a vast labyrinth of spindly little shops and voluminous canvas tents that appeared, as if by magic, from sunset to sunrise at the entrance to Faire—and not a step further without a royal invitation.

As for the citizens of Faire, they typically only entered Otherworld during the solstice festivals, drawn to the ancient magic unleashed across the land during that time. Many also toured Otherworld as part of their coming-of-age rituals. Although such tours were promoted by Faire as way of increasing understanding between the realms, Otherworld's rulers grumbled that it was more likely that the Faire kingdoms wanted to avoid the damage that fae adolescents—new to liquor, debauchery, and full-strength magical powers—could do to their own realm.

At the thought of such tours, Lorn mentally groaned; the last thing he needed tonight was a group of overly attractive, magically gifted, notoriously tricky fae roaming his kingdom in search of dubious adventures ... of which Between had many. It had taken three long days to clean up after the last tour; even so, strings of smoked sausages, and what looked suspiciously like undergarments, could still be found dangling from the rafters in various taverns across the city.

(And the less said about the incident with the butter churn the better.)

"Let us hope that it is a quiet night," he said to his companion.

Kyra gave Lorn a look of disgust, and lowered her head back to her nest, dejected.

Lorn's lips twitched. "I take that back. Let us hope that there are many trespassers for you to terrify and possibly set alight."

At that, Kyra perked up and looked hopefully toward the crystal gateway.

By the time Lorn arrived at the Wasteland, the second set of bells were beginning to peal across the countryside, warning citizens that there was only an hour to go before the Crossing.

The imps were waiting for him.

"Took your time, Boss," Setzl said.

"We thought you were leaving all the work to us," the imp with the small notebook said.

"I can always return to the castle," Lorn said.

"Nah," Izzy said with a grin. "We'll let you help."

Lorn rolled his eyes. "Many thanks."

Together, Lorn and the imps checked the wards on the boundary wall surrounding the Wasteland, shoring up gaps and fortifying weak areas where the spellwork had worn bare.

"Looks good, Boss," Izzy said, dusting off his hands. "Should hold the Nightmares."

Lorn nodded, pleased. "Let us hope so. The wards seem strong, but you never know how the Dream will affect the boundaries."

"We'll keep them strong," Setzl assured him, adjusting his waistcoat.

From the corner of his eye, Lorn could see a small group of Nightmares gravitating toward them, drawn to their magic. The Nightmares stopped when they reached the boundary, careful not to touch the wards that stretched along the walls.

"King," one particularly tall Nightmare hissed. Lorn recognized him as their leader. "*Our* Dreamer tonight."

Lorn grinned, careful not to make eye contact with the monster. "Not tonight."

The leader threw back his head and wailed. The rest of the pack joined in, their mouths open to the rising moons. The sound of their wails was a terrible thing; it clawed at Lorn's eardrums, his nerves, his sanity, threatening to strip each away. He clamped his hands over his ears, but it did little to relieve the sound.

"Ouch," the imp with the small notebook said, staring accusingly at the Nightmares.

"Wailing will not make it so," Lorn told the Nightmares, pitching his voice so that it was audible over the noise. "Save your strength for feasting on all of those Earther dreams later this evening."

The wailing stopped abruptly. "Yesss," the leader said. "Delicious Earthersss!"

"So much pain!" one Nightmare wailed.

"So much angst!" another cried.

Lorn removed his hands from his ears, his shoulders sagging in relief. "Yes. You have all those lovely dreams to feast upon, both here and in the Earther Realm—leave the Dreamer for me."

"We will beat you to the Hill, King. To the Dreamer." The leader flexed his claws toward Lorn, yearning. "We will have you, too."

"You will try," Lorn said agreeably, and turned back to the wards.

The final bells rang out across Between, warning that the Crossing would take place in thirty minutes. The Nightmares wailed with excitement, drifting off to join their brethren deep in the heart of the Wasteland.

"Better be careful, Boss," Izzy said.

The imp with the small notebook nodded. "Otherwise ..." He flipped open his book and held up a drawing.

Lorn peered at it and grimaced. The stick figure king was lying on the ground, surrounded by a crowd of stick figure Nightmares with pointy fingernails and sharp fangs. They appeared to be chewing on the king's limbs with considerable relish.

"How wretchedly morbid." Lorn flipped the notebook shut. "I thought we agreed that you would only draw the *real* catastrophes that befall me— not *imagined* ones."

The imp with the small notebook shrugged. "Just practicing for when it happens."

"Probably will happen, Boss," Izzy said.

"Likely," Setzl said, nodding.

Lorn rolled his eyes. "Your faith in me is truly astonishing. Remind me to swamp you all." He brushed the gold dust from his hands and stood up. "If you need me, I shall be in the Portal Chamber until the Crossing."

"Got it, Boss!" Izzy said.

With barely a thought, Lorn sunk beneath the ground. He felt Between open a passage for him within the cool earth, hurtling him across the countryside until he emerged inside the city walls, steps from the castle.

The guards at the door barely blinked as their King rose from the ground.

"Hi, Majesty," they said, bowing.

"Everything ready?" Lorn asked as he strode toward the guards, the cobblestones falling back into place behind him.

"Looks like it," one of the guards replied. "They're about to close the gates."

Sure enough, the city's immense, black-iron gates were beginning to creak shut. The drawbridge, however, remained down, just in case the city needed to be evacuated.

As Lorn took one final glance at the Gateway, he saw Between's most fearsome Guardian—the Minotaur, wearing his ceremonial scarlet robe and wielding an extremely sharp spear—greeting the troll watchmen and taking his position before the Between Gateway.

The final series of warning bells rang out across the city, but aside from the patrolling guards, the streets were empty. The citizens of Between all had a healthy sense of self-preservation and were now secure and snug behind their locked doors, or inside the many taverns or the Den's gaming halls, waiting out the Crossing.

Lorn climbed the castle steps and entered the dim foyer, the lanterns doing little to dispel the perpetual gloom. The guards bowed to Lorn as they rushed past, hurrying to perform their Crossing duties. In the center of the foyer, a hunched old woman, dressed in what appeared to be a pile of rags, dragged a filthy mop around in a lazy circle.

Lorn paused beside the woman. He stared down at the wet spot beneath her mop, then at the floor surrounding it and sighed. "Agatha," he said patiently, "when we discussed extending your duties to mopping the foyer, I did stress that I wanted the foyer cleaned, did I not?"

"What?" Agatha grunted, not even bothering to look up.

"*Cleaned*," Lorn repeated, still in that patient manner.

"It's clean," Agatha muttered, her voice the hoarse rasp of sandpaper dragging across a dry wooden beam.

"I beg to disagree." Lorn pointed to the floor. "If you look carefully, you will notice that the part of the floor beneath your mop is dirtier than the part around it."

"Mop's fault," Agatha grumbled, shaking her head, her matted, white hair trailing along the dirty flagstones. "Mop is *bad*."

Lorn looked at the mop. Aside from the fact that it was filthy, it seemed relatively new. "Or, could it be—and this is just a guess—that the water you are using is unspeakably foul?"

They both stared down into Agatha's water bucket. Within the depths of the oily water, a fish swam around in graceless circles, trying to avoid the floating chunks of turnip.

Agatha shrugged. "Same water as always." She squinted up at Lorn, her filmy, yellow eyes barely visible amongst the dry folds of her leathery skin. "*Mop*," she said pointedly, "is *bad*."

Lorn pinched the bridge of his nose. "Very well. Carry on, Agatha."

He left Agatha and her fish to finish dirtying the floors and moved briskly over to one of the three alcoves carved into the far castle wall. He stopped in front of the alcove marked *Procurement* and rang the bell on the counter.

A procurement attendant dressed in orange robes with a small, metal fox pinned proudly over his heart appeared behind the counter. He bowed his head. "Something we can do for you, Majesty?"

"Agatha needs a new mop. And while you are at it, swap her bucket for one filled with clean, fish-less water."

The attendant stole a quick look at Agatha, who was still mopping the same dirty flagstone. "Getting the mop and bucket is easy, Majesty—it's the swapping that will be a problem." He dipped his head toward Lorn's conspiratorially. "I don't want to get on Agatha's bad side."

"Your fear is quite reasonable—all Agatha's sides are bad. Nevertheless, this needs to be done and soon, lest the entire foyer starts to reek of fish."

The attendant took another glance at Agatha and winced. "Well ... I could see how that would be a bad thing. But what if she notices that I've swapped out her bucket?"

Lorn stared at him incredulously. "You are a thief. You were trained at the Academy of Practical Arts to make entire caravans disappear. A bucket is well within your skill set."

"Right." The attendant rolled his shoulders. "I've got this. Nice pep talk, Majesty. Inspirational even."

"I assure you that it was entirely unintentional. I merely wanted a mop and bucket."

A delicate chime filled the foyer. The sound was so captivating, so ethereal that everyone stopped what they were doing and looked up.

Floating overhead was an exquisite, fae-charmed clock crafted to look like Between's squat, black castle. It was an exact replica, from the scorch marks on the iron doors to the slippery, black tiles on its crooked stone towers. As it chimed, the twin moons that floated above the castle—the gold Otherworld moon on the left side of the clock and the silver Earther Realm moon on the right—moved closer to one another until they almost touched.

Lorn checked the time and then looked at the three doors beneath the clock face. At that precise moment, a small, black-armored figurine wearing a pointy crown and a shadowy cloak—a replica Shadow King—emerged from the left door and moved until it was beside the center door. The center door was a miniature version of the Portal; when the Crossing finally arrived, the center door would glow gold. The right door remained closed, as always.

Lorn bowed his head at his counterpart and continued across the foyer. He nimbly avoided the uneven flagstones in the center of the walkway and dodged the stream of gold dust falling from the ceiling. He stepped behind the pillar with the strange scorch marks, and made his way to a small, hidden door.

The doorknocker—a bronze owl—blinked up at him curiously.

"Portal Chamber, if you please," Lorn ordered.

The owl nodded, and the door swung open.

"Many thanks," Lorn said, ducking beneath the door frame and emerging, quite conveniently, in the Portal Chamber, high in the center tower of the castle.

Lorn moved quickly into the beautiful room, its beaten bronze walls aglow in the lantern-light. He looked to his right, where a scale model of his kingdom was set out on a platform against one of the curved walls. Lorn instinctively checked for any overt signs of chaos—plumes of smoke, rising flames, sinkholes, rampaging creatures. But the streets appeared bare and chaos-free.

"What were your *exact* words to the imps when they told you that I was concerned about your well-being?" a voice—*his* voice—asked from behind him. "Oh, yes. 'Tell him that I will be there as soon as I can.' Your exact words. *As soon as I can.* Which, apparently, is twelve hours later."

Lorn winced and turned toward the immense, wall-length mirror behind him. His reflection stared back at him, which was not a particularly unusual occurrence when looking at a mirror. What *was* unusual was that his reflection was not standing as Lorn was, but rather sat comfortably in a throne-like chair, ankles crossed neatly right over left, his expression far frostier than the one Lorn was currently wearing.

"Apologies," Lorn said to his Shadow. "As it turns out, this *is* as soon as I could come."

As always, eye contact allowed the Shadow to see Lorn's memories. The Shadow raised an eyebrow as he watched the kaleidoscope of images that comprised of Lorn's day: rainbow water geysers and wizard duels, petty complaints and barn dragons, twisted wrists and pumpkin patches, and lots of Vigor Draught and agony …

"Admittedly, you do seem to have been busy," the Shadow said eventually, glancing at Lorn's wrist. "That geyser was a pretty piece of whimsy. Such lovely magic … no doubt wasted on the dullards of Fisk." He sniffed disdainfully. "And to think, that was not even the highlight of your day!" The Shadow's expression turned gleeful. "Challenging *four* wizards at once? My, my—you are growing into your power so fast! I could not be prouder of you if I had spawned you myself."

Lorn flinched as if struck. Clenching his jaw, he slowly crossed the room until he stood before his Shadow, his footsteps on the metal tiles echoing across the chamber. "Yes." His tone was as hollow as a drum. "I have become quite the weapon." He nodded toward the open window, where the sounds of the Zadrian mourning horns drifted into the golden chamber with the breeze. "*That* is my doing."

The Shadow waved his hand dismissively. "If the situation had been reversed, do you think your Challengers would have spent even a moment mourning your death? No, they would be too busy celebrating their victory … however it is that Death Cultists celebrate. Perhaps by acquiring more skull tattoos or ritually sucking out the soul of some poor, unsuspecting peasant." He shrugged languidly. "Something festive and destructive. Besides, *this*"—the Shadow gestured toward the window—"is not *all* your doing. If those four wizards wanted to live, they should not have Challenged a seven-Mark sorcerer to a death duel."

"Four-Mark," Lorn corrected. "I doubt all of my other Marks are common knowledge."

"Regardless, your reputation is well-known throughout Otherworld.

Those wizards knew of your exploits as the Left Hand of the High King. They knew what you were capable of."

Lorn remembered the exhilarating surge of power as he and Between had become one ... and the immense control it had taken to use only a fraction of it.

"Not even I know what I am capable of." Lorn rubbed his eyes, tired of it all. Tired of himself. With heavy steps, he crossed to his customary armchair opposite the mirror and sat down. He leaned his head back against the plush, velvet cushion with a sigh. "The people of Fisk are right to fear me."

The Shadow watched Lorn for a long, searching moment. "Your magic saved that terrible little township. And despite all those new patches that you acquired by helping them, I doubt even one of them is grateful."

"I do not need their gratitude—I need their crops."

"What a lovely piece of self-delusion. Everyone needs gratitude, particularly after helping their enemies, and there was barely a scrap of it in that terrible place." The Shadow snorted. "The audacity of them asking for your help when they would have left you to rot in your hour of need. You should have taken all of their crops!"

"Divinian probably has by now."

"I should hope so!" The Shadow leaned forward in his chair, his expression fierce. "A Purge-friendly town does not deserve the help of the most powerful sorcerer in Otherworld. They barely deserve the help of the Radish King, that glorious vegetable monarch. Such a pity we did not get a chance to know him better." The Shadow sighed sorrowfully. "Trees—leafy killers."

A terrible thought had been teasing at the edges of Lorn's mind all day. "Do you think that I will share his destiny?"

"Whose destiny?" the Shadow asked, adjusting his cuff.

"The Radish King's."

The Shadow paused. "I doubt it. Spitting root vegetables at people in a city square and getting crushed by a tree is a pretty specific destiny."

"Madness," Lorn said quietly. "So many of my predecessors went mad. It almost seems like a requirement to rule Between."

The Shadow made a dismissive gesture and sniffed. "*Please.* You shall die of malnutrition first. What did you eat today? A handful of oatcakes and some dried apples? Are you a man or a horse?" The Shadow smiled slyly at Lorn. "Then again, there were those incredibly flattering comparisons made by some of your previous paramours ..."

When Lorn did not answer, the Shadow sighed.

"You will not go mad," he said solemnly. "I will not allow it."

Lorn opened his mouth to argue but then changed his mind; he needed reassurance, not another dire fate. He bowed his head. "Very well. I am more likely to die of magical exhaustion before I go mad anyway."

"That is a possibility." The Shadow smiled, his tone deliberately light. "Besides, is madness such a terrible destiny? Madmen have such tremendous personality and flair! And remember, of the four Challengers today, the Radish King was the only one to land a blow, *and* he won the heart of the crowd. Madness won the day." The Shadow gestured to Lorn's wrist. "How it is healing?"

Lorn glanced down at his wrist. It looked like a real wrist again, rather than a grotesque, bloated mass of twisted flesh. He had endured the agonizing pull and twist of healing ligaments and tendons all day but now … now it just felt strangely itchy.

He tentatively flexed his fingers. "Well, it is still there."

"Excellent." The Shadow surveyed his true form critically. "You still look a little peaky. Perhaps a Vigor Draught or two would do the trick."

Lorn did not even bother to argue. He reached into the bottomless pouch at his hip and summoned the red potion into his palm. He stared at the bottle and wondered, not for the first time, whether it would be enough to help him accomplish all the feats expected of him during the Crossing.

He quickly crushed that thought and drank down the potion with a grimace. Prickly warmth immediately flooded his body. He closed his eyes and leaned into the sudden surge of well-being as his magic flickered and sparked beneath the surface of his skin.

"The Portal has awoken," the Shadow announced.

Lorn opened his eyes. At the far side of the room, the Portal—an otherwise plain, wooden door—began to glow gold. Through the open window, Lorn could see that the two lush, full moons now touched in the night sky.

The Shadow stood up from his chair. "Do you have the tribute?"

Lorn crossed the room to a bronze chest etched with moons and stars. He opened the heavy lid and pulled out a scarlet velvet pouch. The contents gave a metallic *clink* as he carried it across the room and placed it in the center of an intricate compass carved into the floor. Unlike an ordinary compass, the cardinal points were marked with the elements—Earth, Wind, Fire, and Water.

"Very good," the Shadow said, barely able to contain his excitement. "Now, the mirror!"

Lorn turned to where the Dreamer's Mirror—enchanted to reveal the innermost dreams of each Dreamer—stood mounted on a stand beside the

Portal. As Lorn watched, his reflection became obscured by swirling, white mist. The mist slowly dissipated to reveal a series of images: a bowl of pastel-colored candies; a ginger cat, sleepily curled into a ball; a plush, white toy owl, its glass eyes the color of honey; wooden blocks in primary colors; and a kite crafted in the shape of a peacock with a long, blue-ribbon tail.

Finally, the mirror revealed a small boy with slippery black hair, golden-brown skin, and serious brown eyes.

"He is just a babe!" the Shadow gasped, utterly delighted. "You know how I love the Dreams of the little ones!"

"You love the Dreams of the older ones, too," Lorn said.

"Yes, but the young ones have so much unbridled imagination! It is such a pity that their Dreams tend to be so short; the little ones tire so quickly."

Lorn touched the surface of the mirror and opened his senses, attempting to get a glimpse of the kind of Dream that this young Dreamer would desire. For Dreamers who were adventurers at heart, Lorn would help Between to spin dreams fit to burst with magic and wild creatures, danger and excitement, and *happily ever afters*. For Dreamers who sought knowledge, Lorn and Between would craft journeys through hidden libraries filled with stories gathered from three realms. For Dreamers who sought beauty, Lorn revealed Between's underground caverns, whose gem-encrusted chambers glittered like the night sky; or lifted the Dreamers amongst the mountain peaks, where they could gaze down in wonder at the fantastical world laid out before them.

But this Dreamer ... this Dreamer yearned to fly. And just like that, Lorn's exhaustion was burned away by a surge of excitement, of antic-ipation.

"Ah," Lorn said, smiling, "this one is a little bird."

"A Dreamer after your own heart. This has the potential to be glorious!"

In the back of his mind, Lorn could feel Between trembling with excitement.

Are you ready to be enchanting? Lorn asked Between.

He was answered by a quick flutter of magic across his Tether Mark, like a meteor shower falling between his shoulder blades.

A bell pealed, echoing throughout the chamber. Lorn's dark armor unfurled over his body; the Cloak of Shadows appeared at his shoulders. He straightened his spine, bared his Marks and began the series of hand gestures that would safely open the Portal.

The Shadow rubbed his hands together gleefully. "Showtime!"

With a final flick of Lorn's wrists, the Portal opened. Light streamed into the room, turning the copper walls to molten gold.

The bell pealed once more, triumphant.

"Showtime," Lorn agreed and walked through the Portal, ready to greet the Dreamer.

5

WHEN DREAMS COME TRUE

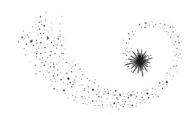

"Boss," Izzy hissed. "Wake up, Boss."

Lorn blearily opened one eyelid and saw three small, blue imps sitting on his cluttered bedside table, staring down at him from amongst empty potion bottles and crumpled pieces of parchment.

He had a sudden, terrible sense of déjà vu.

"Did we not do this already?" he slurred. With great difficulty, he dredged up the memory of the previous morning. "Yes. Yes, we did."

Lorn closed his eye and tried to go back to sleep. After all, he had done quite enough for the time being. He had opened the Portal and turned his kingdom upside down to accommodate the delightful whims of the Dreamer—literally, in this case. The four-year-old Dreamer thought that gravity was something that should be negotiable and had spent his time in Between flying around the kingdom, gleefully changing the natural order of things as he went.

Once the Dreamer had returned to the Earther Realm, there was still no time for Lorn to rest; there had been the clean up to oversee, which had been just as strenuous. Although the Dreamer had been overjoyed to see wolves and foxes sitting in the trees, and fish scampering amongst the long, silver grass, the creatures themselves had been less than amused. It had taken two hours to coax the animals back to their homes, and a further half hour listening to them whine and moan for being misused in such a manner. The wolves had been impossible to console: the pack leader had made an obscene gesture to Lorn with his tail and then proudly led his pack away, growling about pride and revenge and possible disemboweling as they went.

It was all somewhat disconcerting.

As a result, Lorn was exhausted—mind, body, and soul—and hoped to stay in bed until next week if possible.

Clearly, Between had other plans.

"Boss," Izzy hissed once again, this time louder. "Up, *up!*"

Lorn rolled onto his side, away from the intrusion. "I will defenestrate anyone who disturbs me right now."

"Ooh, big words, Boss," Izzy snickered.

"*Fancy,*" Setzl said approvingly.

"Spell it," the imp with the small notebook said, clutching his stubby pencil.

Lorn sighed, deeply and sufferingly. "Why are you disturbing me?"

Izzy shook his little head. "Not us, Boss. The Portal."

Lorn rolled back toward the imps. "What do you mean? The Portal is done for this month. As am I—I truly have nothing left to give. Allow me to wallow in exhaustion."

Setzl shrugged. "Tell that to the Portal."

"Impossible."

But Lorn's tone was less than confident. Just because something had never happened before did not mean that it *could not* happen—particularly in Between.

The little imps shook their heads in unison.

"Not sleep time yet, Boss," Izzy said. "Portal has other ideas."

With another long, suffering sigh, Lorn staggered out of bed. He dragged the heels of his hands over his eyelids and reached blindly for his robe.

"You had better be right," he muttered as he shrugged into his robe, "or I will toss you through the Portal."

The imps gave identical sharp-toothed smiles.

"Gotta catch us first, Boss," Izzy said.

By the time Lorn entered the Portal Chamber, he was only slightly more awake.

"My, my! Are we not looking fetching?" his Shadow declared, glancing over Lorn's bare feet, black silk sleeping pants, and matching robe. "I hope you did not venture through the castle dressed like that." He flicked a non-existent piece of lint from his own impeccable, ceremonial attire. "After all, you are a king—there are standards to maintain."

"I am so wretchedly exhausted that it is a miracle that I am not naked." Lorn stifled a yawn and turned his attention to the far end of the room where the Portal—which should have appeared as a simple wooden door now that the Dreamer had left the kingdom—was glowing brightly. "What is wrong with the Portal?"

His Shadow gave an elegant shrug. "It has been glowing for the past ten minutes or so. Glowing and then flashing away. It is a pretty spectacle but odd nonetheless."

Lorn peered at the Portal, a crease appearing between his brows. "The fact that it is glowing or flashing so soon after a Dreamer is a concern."

"I have never seen it flash that color before, nor in that rhythm."

The Shadow was correct. The light from the Portal shone as golden as ever, but now there was a thread of silver that flickered across the surface. Moreover, it was pulsing rhythmically, almost like—

"A heartbeat," Lorn and his Shadow said simultaneously.

Automatically, Lorn raised his hand to his chest.

"Not ours," his Shadow confirmed. "This one is fluttering like a bird, impossibly fast. *Someone* is excited."

"But who?" Lorn turned to the imps, who dutifully checked their chests, albeit on the wrong side. Setzl checked his watch.

"Nothing, Boss," he confirmed.

Lorn and his Shadow exchanged a look.

"Perhaps it is still connected to the Dreamer?" the Shadow mused.

Lorn shook his head. "No, it does not feel like the Dreamer. The energy is completely different. Almost … almost as if …" He took a few steps toward the Portal.

"Careful," his Shadow warned.

Suddenly, a blast of silver light burst forth from the Portal and engulfed Lorn.

"Lorn!" the Shadow called out, shielding his eyes from the light.

When the Shadow managed to turn back, the light—and Lorn—had disappeared, leaving behind an odd bell tone that echoed through the chamber. Gold dust pooled on the floor where Lorn had stood mere seconds before.

The Shadow shook his head disapprovingly. "And … he is gone." He turned to the imps. "I told him to be careful, did I not?"

The imps nodded. "Was good advice," Izzy said.

"*Thank you,*" the Shadow said. "He never listens to me. I am not just here for my looks, dammit!" He stared at the Portal for a long moment. When Lorn did not reappear, he groaned in frustration. "We need to find him. Best be careful when you venture near the Hill—the Nightmares might be roaming."

"Right, Mirror Man!" the imps said. With a shark *crack*, they were gone.

The Shadow adjusted his tunic and turned toward the model of Between. "What have you stumbled into this time, Lorn?" he murmured, scanning the landscape for Lorn's figurine. Unable to find it, the Shadow settled back into his chair and resigned himself to wait for Lorn's return.

～

To LORN'S UTTER SURPRISE, HE FOUND HIMSELF DEPOSITED AT THE FOOT OF the Dreamer's Hill, his bare feet sinking into the soft, golden dust.

He called on his magic, bracing himself for whatever he would find … or whatever would find him. But there was no sinkhole or fire or flood or magical creature waiting for him. Better yet, there were no Nightmares; they had swarmed the Hill only hours before, so it was a miracle they were not there to greet him, teeth bared.

The land appeared empty.

Why have you brought me here? Lorn asked Between.

There was no response.

"Why have you brought me here?" he repeated, this time aloud. "What do you want me to do?"

Lorn was answered by the *boom* of thunder somewhere overhead. He looked up; the twin moons sat behind thick banks of black clouds, the sky itself tinted an unhealthy shade of green. The wind was picking up, tinged with the scent of ozone.

A terrible storm was coming.

Lorn looked away from the sky and scanned the Hill. "There must be a reason why I am here."

And then, he found it.

Someone was standing on top of the Hill, looking down at him.

Lorn stared back, horrified. "Midra's sack—what is that idiot doing? Surely they have enough sense to get down from there immediately."

The person waved at him cheerfully.

"Apparently not," Lorn said dryly and began to climb the Hill, ignoring his exhausted body's protests.

The person continued to wave.

"Ah, yes … *wave*," Lorn muttered to himself as he stepped over a clump of silver grass. "Hand gestures will be an excellent defense against the Nightmares."

A flash of lightning lit up the hillside. Lorn glanced up at the person and noted that they had not moved; in fact, they appeared to be placidly watching his climb.

Lorn shook his head. "Have they no sense of self-preservation? Good gods, there are *signs* around the Hill warning them of the dangers. Did they not see them? Do I have to build a moat around this place? Do I—*agh*." He stumbled on a loose patch of ground and swore as he regained his balance.

"Do not fall to your death," he told himself sternly as he continued the climb. "Think of the indignity of surviving rampaging dragons and exploding mountains only to be defeated by *dirt*."

Lorn spared a glance at the top of the Hill—the person was still there, waiting for him.

"They had better be drunk," he muttered as he climbed the final steps, breathing far more heavily than he should have after the climb. "If they are not, I shall fling them into a swamp myself."

At that moment, the twin moons broke free of the cloud bank, allowing Lorn to see the person at last. He paused in surprise.

It was a woman, pale-skinned and tall, her long, dark hair flying behind her in the rising winds. She was dressed in strange, shapeless garments that were covered in drawings of beasts.

Probably the latest fashion from Vetch, he thought wryly.

She was also barefoot, like himself, which seemed rather odd under the circumstances.

But what was strangest of all was that she was staring at his chest with the kind of ravenous glance that wolves usually give to a particularly succulent slab of beef. It was both alarming and somewhat flattering—but mostly alarming.

Just as Lorn was about to ask what her intentions were toward his chest, she ran up to him and threw her arms around his neck in a lush embrace.

Lorn froze. He had very little experience with hugging. He could count the number of hugs he had received during his childhood on four fingers. And as an adult ... Well, no one dared to hug a sorcerer—at least, not unless they were intoxicated, wearing enchanted armor, involved in a bet, or a combination of all three. This woman, however, seemed completely unaware of the fact that she was doing something rare and possibly dangerous to her health.

"We may as well get started," she whispered, her voice husky and full of delicious promise.

She stepped even closer, molding the warm curves of her body against the hard planes of his own. "I have no idea how long this dream is going to last."

She must be incredibly *drunk,* Lorn thought.

He surreptitiously sniffed her hair, expecting the sour smell of ale or spirits, but instead found the scent of flowers and warm spice.

Or perhaps, he considered, taking another breath of that summery scent, *it is a case of mistaken identity?*

The woman leaned back and stared deeply into his eyes. She did not look intoxicated. Nor did she start screaming at the sight of him, so she was not expecting someone else. Instead, she smiled up at him—a smile that promised all sorts of sensual delights.

There is not an ounce of fear in her eyes, Lorn thought to himself in wonder. *Or scorn, or distaste … or recognition.*

Lorn was trying to wrap his head around this impossible situation when the woman's expression changed. Her lovely smile slipped away, replaced by a frown and a sigh.

"Great," she muttered, disappointment and annoyance wiping away all trace of sultry promise. "Trust me to have a complicated sex dream. I bet other people just fall asleep and the sex starts immediately. Not me. Apparently, I need a backstory, and a plot, and *angst.*"

And just like that, all of the puzzling elements of this encounter—the woman's appearance on the Hill, her strange garments, her fearlessness in the embrace of a sorcerer—began to make sense.

She is an Earther, Lorn realized, staring down at her in surprise. *But how could she have found her way to Between?*

Irrespective of how she got to Between, it was clear that she thought she was dreaming … and a very specific, very *pelvic,* sort of dream at that.

"Are you trying to engage me in some sort of *seduction fantasy?*" Lorn blurted, trying to get his tired mind to grapple with this new development.

The woman blinked, clearly startled by the question. But her surprise quickly turned to irritation. "Well, would it be that terrible if I *was* trying to engage you in a seduction fantasy?"

Of all the people in Otherworld to ask that question, Lorn was possibly the very worst. He was, quite literally, the King of Dreams. He had *standards* when it came to dreams—very, very high standards. It was a point of pride for Lorn that the Dreams he crafted made the hearts of Dreamers sing, their imaginations spark, their souls *soar.* To craft a Dream that centered solely around the gratification of one's genitals—without including a quest, or an adventure, or even a moral—offended Lorn's higher sensibilities.

"Yes," Lorn answered. "Yes, it would. Of all the dreams at your disposal, of all the wonders that you could experience, why would you want to engage in a common *seduction fantasy*? You truly need to dream bigger."

As it turned out, this was the wrong thing to say.

"Hey!" she cried, her tone sharp. "This *is* dreaming big for me! This is my very first seduction fantasy!"

"But would you not prefer something more meaningful, more fantastic?" Lorn persisted. "Possibly something with a dragon—"

The woman stared at him incredulously. "Why would I want a *dragon* in my seduction fantasy? I mean, that's—that's just perverse. Besides, you started it—striding up the hillside toward me like—like—like—"

Lorn frowned. "Like someone trying to get to their destination?"

"No! You were striding toward me with *intent*."

"Intent?"

"*Intent*," she repeated with great emphasis.

"Of what kind?" Lorn asked, genuinely puzzled. As far as he knew, his only intent was to stop her from being devoured by Nightmares.

The woman's eyes narrowed. "*Sultry* intent."

The idea of anyone finding his clumsy climb up the Hill *sultry* made Lorn laugh in disbelief. "Sultry intent? Surely not!"

"Surely *yes*." The woman's tone was adamant. "You were striding along, all masculine and purposeful and … and … windswept in your seduction clothes—"

"We call them pajamas," Lorn interjected, not quite sure why he felt the need to make that distinction.

The woman chose to ignore it. "—and full of *chestedness. Heaving* chestedness." She stared at his chest once again, this time almost accusingly.

Despite Lorn's immense exhaustion—or possibly because of it—he was starting to find the absurd nature of the conversation almost refreshing.

"Forgive me," he said, "for my heaving *chestedness* and sultry intent. I assure you, it was completely unintentional."

His words only seemed to make the woman angrier. She removed her arms from around his neck and began to pull away. Without thinking, Lorn quickly reached out and held her fast around her waist. *For her safety*, he told himself, his fingers tangling in the soft fabric of her beast-covered shirt.

(He manfully ignored the warm skin beneath.)

The woman seemed surprised by Lorn's actions—almost as surprised as he was—but she continued her rant with a single-minded focus that he could not help but admire.

"All I'm saying," she continued, full of righteous indignation, "is that you shouldn't go striding around people's *seduction fantasies* full of chestedness and sultry intent if you don't intend to fulfill your end of the bargain."

"I do not typically engage in seduction fantasies. They are not part of my repertoire. I—" Lorn stopped abruptly, struck by a terrible thought: Had Between decided that seduction fantasies *were* part of his repertoire? Until now, Dreamers had been children, young teenagers at most, and seduction fantasies were utterly inappropriate. But if adult Earthers were venturing into Between ... was *this* the future of Dreams?

"Oh, come now," Lorn said, addressing Between. "*Seduction fantasies?* Surely there are limits to what I must endure—"

The woman flinched in his arms. "*Endure?*" She stared up at him, the hurt in her expression visible in the bright light of the twin moons. But then she shook her head sharply, the hurt replaced by something fiery and righteous. "You think that a seduction fantasy with me is something you would have to *endure?*"

Lorn knew at once that he had made a terrible, terrible mistake.

" 'Endure' was a particularly poor choice of word," he said apologetically, "and I immediately regret my decision to use it. I never meant to imply—"

But the woman was justifiably furious. She unleashed a torrent of words and gestures including one that looked troublingly like the universally accepted hand gesture for castration.

When he pointed this out, she was far from appreciative.

"That was *not* the universally accepted hand gesture for castration," she cried, staring at him as if he were a dullard. "I didn't even know that there was such a thing. And even if I did, *why* would I make the universally accepted hand gesture for castration during a seduction fantasy?"

But Lorn was only half listening; he was trying to get his sluggish brain to figure out what to do next. *What do you want me to do?* he pleaded to Between. *I have already crafted a Dream for the True Dreamer tonight. Do you wish me to craft a Dream for this Earther, too?*

But Between was silent, which was odd. Moreover, his Tether Mark was utterly unresponsive. Lorn wondered if sentient realms ever fell asleep.

Sleep, he thought yearningly and yawned.

The woman broke off her rant and stared at him in disbelief. "Hang on, am I *boring* you?"

"Apologies," Lorn said. "I am wretchedly exhausted."

"Unbelievable. You're 'wretchedly exhausted'? *How?* We haven't even gotten to the adult-type touching yet!"

"I have had a very trying day," Lorn said honestly.

The woman snorted. "Tell me about it." She looked up at the sky. "I can't believe this," she yelled to the clouds. "My first seduction fantasy and my dream man acts all coy and uninterested and *exhausted* … and really judgmental for a guy with a dragon fetish."

Lorn was shocked at the very idea. "I do not have a dragon fet—" he began.

You do like dragons, an inner voice piped up. *And you did dally with the Dragon Queen …*

That is not the same thing at all, he told himself sternly.

"Not to mention," the woman continued, interrupting his internal dragon fetish debate, "he couldn't tell the difference between a sexy gesture and the universally accepted hand gesture for castration." She looked Lorn straight in the eye, as righteous as a priestess. "I'm sorry to say this, but you are terrible at sex charades."

"*Sex charades?*" Lorn's tired mind balked. Sex charades—what did she mean? Did she expect this seduction fantasy to involve some sort of degenerate sexual pantomime?

"What are—?" he began but paused as his exhausted imagination dutifully tried to conjure up something that an Earther would find degenerate enough to qualify as a sex charade. For some reason, all Lorn managed to visualize was a stage where two dwarves wearing leather underwear stood awkwardly next to a goat. As Lorn watched, one of the dwarves began to gyrate half-heartedly but stopped when his beard got caught on his studded belt.

Everyone waited while he tried to untangle himself.

Eventually, the goat wandered off.

"This is not working," Lorn told himself sternly.

"Agreed. This is a lousy seduction fantasy."

Lorn realized he had said that *aloud.* Could this situation get any worse?

"My Lady," he began. "This is not a seduction fantasy. At least, as far as I am aware …"

"Well … can it become one?" the woman interrupted. "I mean, I know that dreams aren't like real life, but if dream seduction is anything like real-life seduction …" She gave him a wry half-smile. "Well, it sure beats standing on a hill staring at gold dust, right?"

If this conversation had occurred at any other time, Lorn might have agreed. But right now, he barely had the energy to stare at gold dust, let alone perform carnal acrobatics with someone who expected sex charades.

When Lorn did not immediately answer, the woman's smile dropped away. "You'd … you'd actually prefer to stare at gold dust?"

Lorn opened his mouth to answer but closed it again when he realized there was no diplomatic way to say 'yes.'

The woman stared at him incredulously. "Really? *Really?*"

Lorn shrugged ruefully. "Staring at gold dust requires minimal effort, and right now, I am—"

"Wretchedly exhausted," the woman finished for him. "Yes, you said that already."

"It would not be a stellar experience," Lorn continued, too tired to be anything but honest. "I would probably fall asleep during a vital moment —" He stifled another yawn. "Or right at the very beginning …"

"Ri-ght."

"Truly, you deserve better than a lackluster seduction fantasy."

"Yes. Yes, I do." The woman huffed and gestured half-heartedly around her. "And yet, here we are."

Perversely, now that Lorn had told the woman that a seduction fantasy was not a possibility, he finally allowed himself to *see* her. And he blinked, for even in the moonlight, there was so much to see. There was something fierce in the tilt of her chin, and something joyous and free in the depths of her wide-set eyes. There was bravery in the stance of her broad shoulders, and a certain wildness in her mass of long, unruly curls. And the combination of all these fierce, joyous, brave, wild features was *enchanting*.

Would it truly be a hardship to give this woman a taste of her Dream? a voice in his mind—a voice that sounded suspiciously like his Shadow—asked.

Lorn stared at the smile hidden beneath her full lower lip, his hands shifting against her waist. With a start, he felt his heartbeat quicken as his palms pressed against the warm curves of her body; he felt his breath hitch at the thought of even warmer skin beneath.

No, he thought to himself in wonder, *it would be no hardship at all.*

"Would you, perhaps, settle for a kiss?" Lorn blurted. Then he blinked, completely shocked by what he had just said.

The woman seemed just as surprised. "A kiss?"

To Lorn's further astonishment, he continued speaking. "A kiss. Possibly supplemented by some sort of—"

"Nuzzling?" she suggested, her tone interested, possibly even hopeful.

Lorn considered that. "I would not be averse to nuzzling."

But just as Lorn was beginning to warm to the idea of nuzzling—and whatever that would entail—the woman's dark brows curved downward into a frown, taking her smile with it.

"Hang on," she said, "are you trying to downgrade my seduction fantasy?"

"Somewhat," he admitted.

"Ha! I knew it! *Unbelievable.*" She shook her head, her long curls whipping around her angrily. "You know what? Forget it—I'm not settling." She paused. "Kaytie would be so proud of me. Besides," she continued before Lorn could ask who this Kaytie was, "you'd probably fall asleep mid-nuzzle."

At the mention of sleep, Lorn yawned again.

"*See?*" she said accusingly. Then yawned herself. "Damn you," she cursed, covering her mouth.

"Apologies." Lorn rubbed his eyes, desperately trying to stay awake. This was an unparalleled disaster. "As I said earlier, I am truly exhausted—it has been a beastly day. Speaking of which …" His tired eyes focused on the strange drawings on her clothing. "What do the beasts on your clothing signify?"

The woman's eyes narrowed. "They signify my internal rage." She lifted her fierce chin, tossed her wild curls and began to walk down the Hill.

Toward the Nightmares' lair.

"Wait!" Lorn called out, grabbing her wrist. The moment Lorn touched her skin, a strange current surged from their point of contact and charged through his body. It felt like magic, but like none Lorn had ever felt before. It tasted of lightning and stardust, and the power of it shook him to the core.

As he tried to recover from the sensation, Lorn realized that the woman was attempting to pull her hand from his grasp. He looked down at her slender wrist and realized he was clutching her like a lifeline. "Apologies," he said hoarsely and gentled his grip.

She looked at him through narrowed eyes. "*Thank you.*"

Lorn was wondering whether he was the only one to have felt that disconcerting jolt when the woman stared down at her wrist and frowned.

"I thought you weren't supposed to feel things in dreams," she said, seemingly to herself. "Which is strange because *that* feels pretty real."

As Lorn watched, she pressed her fingernails into her palm and winced. "So does that," she muttered.

"You need to know—" Lorn began, ready to tell her that it felt real because it *was* real.

"Something's wrong," she interrupted sharply.

Before Lorn could explain, the woman closed the distance between them and placed her hand flat on his chest, then slowly dragged it over his skin to his amulet.

Lorn held very still, bemused by her brazenness. He was just about to comment on it when she snatched her hand back as if she had been burned.

"What's going on?" she asked, her eyes wide. "Why do you feel so *real?* How is it possible that I can feel things in this dream? Or—or is that typical when you're dreaming?"

"There is nothing typical about this Dre—"

The woman held up her hand, cutting him off. "You know what? Don't bother. The answer is probably something like misfiring synapses or a stunted R.E.M. cycle or stress and knowing why I can feel things in dreams doesn't change anything."

She will not listen to me, Lorn realized with a sigh. *She believes I am a figment of her imagination.*

Sure enough, the woman continued to ignore Lorn.

"I can't believe this," she said to herself. "I haven't dreamed of anything since I was five years old and now my first dream, which started off promisingly enough"—she glanced meaningfully at his chest—"has deteriorated into some kind of esoteric discussion about dream realities. To say I'm annoyed is an understatement."

Lorn stilled. "A moment—you said that your last dream occurred when you were five. What did you dream about?"

But the woman was not listening to him.

"I'd like to wake up now," she yelled up at the storm clouds.

Lorn, too, looked up, wondering if the woman could transport herself back to her realm.

Moments passed.

The woman stayed in place.

"Dash it," she swore.

"Indulge me," Lorn said firmly. Her last dream had been when she was a child, and now she found herself in Between. She *had* to be here for a reason. "What was your last dream about? This may be very important."

"I don't remember. I was five."

"*Try,*" he urged.

"Fine." The woman reluctantly closed her eyes, her dark lashes fluttering closed like delicate wings. At first, she was clearly humoring him, but then her expression changed to one of wonder. "I was walking up a hillside..." she began, slowly but surely recalling her long-forgotten Dream.

And as she spoke, everything Lorn had ever known about Dreamers, the Portal, even his role as the King of Dreams, was neatly turned upside down.

She was a Dreamer—a Dreamer whose initial Dream had been thwarted. And she had *returned.*

All Lorn could think about as she relived her first trip to Between—her wait on the Hill, her encounter with the Nightmares—was the tragedy of it all. She was Destined to change the world through her gift, but without her Dream that was impossible. A Dream was an endless source of creativity for the Dreamer; a touch of wild magic that resided in the Dreamer's soul, fueling their thoughts, their ambitions, their creations, and paving the way for their gift to be shared with their world.

But if a Dream was thwarted, then there was no channel for the wild magic. Instead, it turned on the Dreamer, destroying what it should have been creating.

When she finished her terrible tale, Lorn squeezed her wrist gently. "I am profoundly sorry for your loss."

The woman looked up at him, her eyes wide and bewildered. "What do you mean? What did I lose?"

How could he even begin to explain it to her? Lorn released her wrist, trying to put her experience into words. But the Dreamer reached for him, catching his hand, her fingers brushing the Mark on his palm.

"No! Don't go!" she cried.

Suddenly, that same jolt of power surged from where she touched his skin, shooting up his arm.

The Dreamer quickly let him go, shocked.

She felt it too, Lorn realized.

"What ... what was that?" she asked shakily.

It had to be magic, Lorn thought. "Who are you?" he asked instead.

Lorn grabbed her hands and turned them over, looking for Marks, tattoos, anything that could explain the sensation and the feeling that accompanied it—something that tasted like recognition entwined with the oddest sense of yearning ...

"What is it?" she asked. "What are you doing?"

"Searching," he said.

But Lorn found nothing. No Marks, no spark of magic beneath her skin. She was not a witch or sorceress and yet, the way that his magic reacted to her was nothing short of—

"What's going on?" she asked. She straightened her shoulders, bracing herself. "*Tell* me."

"I do not know," Lorn answered honestly.

He would have said more, but the winds chose that minute to tear across the plains, blowing Lorn's robe wide open, and flinging the Dreamer's curls toward the sky. It appeared that the storm was almost upon them.

But that was not what worried Lorn. Beneath the whine of the winds, he heard a call—a call that spoke of a terrible hunger.

A call that said prey had been spotted.

"You must go," Lorn said urgently, mentally preparing himself for the fight ahead. "You do not belong here, and you have already stayed too long."

"I don't know about that." The Dreamer surveyed the Hill as if she owned it, her chin tilted upward defiantly. "I might belong here more than you think."

She looked so certain, so *sure* that Lorn was momentarily stunned.

"I hope for your sake that you are wrong," he said instead. "Trust me when I say that this is not a place that you would want to belong. Please, for your own sake, *go.*"

But it was too late. The rain broke free of the clouds in thick sheets of warm water, drenching them thoroughly in seconds. The storm had finally arrived.

And so had the Nightmares.

They poured onto the plain, the sound of their running footfalls loud enough to rival the thunder. They should have been sated for the night, glutted on Earther dreams, but it seemed that the opportunity to feast on a Dreamer and a sorcerer was tempting enough to bring them out in their thousands.

Lorn turned his body to shield the Dreamer from the sight, but it was too late.

"The monsters!" she cried above the storm. "They're back. How—?"

"*Run!*" Lorn yelled.

He turned his back on the Dreamer, and pulled up his sleeves, raising his Marks toward the hordes of monsters tearing toward them.

"But—but what about you?" he heard the Dreamer yell from behind him. "Come with me!"

Lorn almost laughed at the thought. Oh, to escape!

"I am fine," he answered. "Run!"

"No!"

Lorn looked back at the Dreamer, shocked. Why was she still here? They were about to be swarmed by Nightmares and—

"I'm not leaving without you," she cried, and stretched out her hand to him.

Lorn stared back at her, his pulse hammering in his ears, unable to believe his eyes. She stood there, drenched and clearly terrified, her hair plastered to her face, her eyes huge and as dark as bruises. But her hand was outstretched toward him, open, beckoning.

She was trying to help him, he realized. Trying to save him.

Lorn's heart gave the oddest twist.

"Come with me," she begged.

Her hand did not waver.

Everything else—the rain, the rising winds, the Nightmares—fell away. It was as if Lorn had finally mastered Time and held the Dreamer and himself entwined in this second together.

Oh, how he wanted to take her hand!

At that moment, as if she could read his thoughts—as if she was trying to sway his choice—the Dreamer smiled at him. It was a smile of such unabashed hope, of pure joy that his heart twisted anew.

The howls—victorious and so, so close—shattered the moment.

"Run. *Now!*" he ordered, throwing every ounce of his authority into the words.

The Dreamer flinched as if he had slapped her. He immediately wanted to apologize, to explain, to reassure her, but there was no time.

They had run out of time.

With a heavy heart, Lorn turned his back on the Dreamer and faced the monsters, hoping that he could buy her time enough to return to her realm; hoping that he could save her just as she had offered to save him.

The Nightmares swarmed up the Hill to meet them in a white wave, their long, spidery limbs making short work of the climb.

As always, the leader was at the head of the pack. He sniffed the air. "Dreamer?" he asked, his voice a greedy whine.

"Gone," Lorn said, hoping it was true. He could not even spare a glance over his shoulder to check. He raised his hands, Marks bared, toward the monsters. "Go back—there is nothing for you here."

The leader sniffed the air again, scenting Lorn's magic. He hissed in rapture. "There isss you, King." He raised his arms toward Lorn, reaching for him, his talons extended. "*Oursss.*"

Lorn slashed the air with his right hand. Sheets of lightning split the sky at his command, illuminating the Hill as bright as daylight. The Nightmares fell back, shielding their eyes, their wails mingling with the simultaneous *boom* of thunder, so close that the earth shook beneath Lorn's feet.

"Not tonight," Lorn swore. He took advantage of the Nightmares' momentary distraction and cast again, surrounding himself with a wall of flames. "It is Wednesday. I refuse to die on such a ridiculous day."

He clenched his shaking hands. Taking a deep breath, he lifted them above his head and opened them to the sky. The wall of enchanted flames leaped higher and higher, rushing upward to meet the twin moons.

The Nightmares surged forward, testing the fiery boundary for weaknesses.

The boundary held, but for how long? Lorn was shaking with exhaustion.

His wall of flame flickered …

Once.

Twice.

"King," the leader hissed, sensing victory. "We will fight you. We will win. *Oursss.*"

Lorn held up his hands, ready to cast again, his legs trembling with fatigue but planted firmly on the ground.

"So be it," he said grimly.

The Nightmares howled and surged forward, the metallic *gnash* of teeth a sharp staccato against the soft rain. And just as they were about to reach the flickering flame wall, Lorn's vision turned to silver and gold.

For the Shadow, the wait felt like an eternity. He sat for a while, his foot tapping impatiently. Then, he got up and paced. He scanned the model of Between for Lorn's figurine and frowned when he found it on the Hill.

"That is odd."

The Shadow's frown deepened when he saw that it was surrounded by Nightmares.

"And that is dreadful," he said, pressing his hands against the mirror.

And just as he was beginning to seriously worry, the Portal pulsed again with that odd silver light and shot open.

The Shadow sighed and shut his eyes against the bright glare. "Must you be so dramatic?" he demanded.

The Portal ignored him and flared again before closing, that odd bell note echoing once more within the chamber.

The Shadow opened his eyes and blinked at the sight of a drenched

Lorn standing at the entrance of the Portal, his hands outstretched as if he was in the middle of casting.

"What happened to you?" the Shadow asked, horrified at the state of the Lorn's attire.

Lorn turned toward him, his gaze wild.

The Shadow's eyes widened as he watched Lorn's memories of an Earther dressed in beast-covered garments, waiting for Lorn on the Hill … and everything that had transpired between them.

∼

STILL IN SHOCK, HIS HEART POUNDING WILDLY IN HIS CHEST, LORN WATCHED a dizzying array of expressions cross the Shadow's face and braced himself for the inevitable rant.

Sure enough…

"You sodding idiot!" the Shadow cried, staring at Lorn incredulously. "You had that beauty throw herself at you, and you refused her advances? How could you?"

With great effort, Lorn lowered his hands and staggered to his armchair. Numbly, he sat down. "Is that *all* you can say?"

"What more is there to say? There was a bewitching woman on the Hill, whose only request was one that you could have easily fulfilled with the judicious application of your pelvis and you refused her." The Shadow shook his head in dismay. "Granted, it has been a while; there is probably an inch of dust gathered on your genitals from disuse—"

"Such a visual …" Lorn muttered, trying to slow his heart rate.

"—but surely you still remember the basic mechanics of the act. Midra knows how rare it is for someone to approach you so brazenly in the first place! They are all too terrified that you will turn them into a toad or some such thing. Or too concerned that their reputations will suffer if they are seen dallying with one of the magic folk in public."

"Now is not the time for this discussion," Lorn said tersely. "We have more important—"

But the Shadow was on a roll. "And before you say it, I know that you have become some sort of monk as penance for your previous life of debauchery—"

"Not this *again*," Lorn interrupted. "You are, quite literally, a part of me —you are privy to all my deepest thoughts and feelings. You, of all people, should know that is not the truth of the matter! Why do you insist on deliberately misrepresenting my motives?"

"Exactly! I *am* a part of you—the best part, if we are being specific—"

Lorn rolled his eyes.

"—and I *know* that you need companionship, and you refuse to seek it out!"

"I am surrounded by companions every second of the day!"

"*True* companionship, not just imps and servants. A partner would be ideal, though at this point, I would settle for a bedfellow. And tonight, in answer to all my prayers, the Portal dropped this delicious Dreamer into your lap. You were supposed to fulfill her Dream, Lorn. Her glorious, tawdry Dream!"

Lorn sat back against the armchair, his chest still heaving. "I did not know that she was a Dreamer. At first, I thought she was a drunken reveler or some sort of inter-realm trespasser—"

The Shadow snorted. "What does it matter? When a beautiful woman graciously offers you a debaucherous adventure—and seems entirely unconcerned about your status as one of the magic folk—then the proper response is: 'Thank you, my lady. Allow me a moment to remove my breeches.'"

"Oh, good gods," Lorn muttered. "Please, stop." He dragged his wet hair out of his eyes with a shaking hand. "If you could get your mind out of the gutter—"

"Possibly my favorite location."

"—for one moment, you will see the true problem here. She is a Dreamer, yes—one who has returned. *Returned.*"

The Shadow's gaze turned inward, clearly sifting back through Lorn's memories.

"Apologies," he said eventually. "I missed that the first time. I was some-what distracted."

"Clearly." Lorn looked over at the Dreamer's Mirror. It was blank, reflecting only the room. "Have you ever heard of a Dreamer returning?"

"Never." The Shadow tapped his forefinger against his lips in thought. "So, she is a Dreamer whose initial journey to Between did not yield a Dream—most likely because a caretaker king was in power, those fools."

"Until tonight, I believed that Dreamers were allowed a single night in Between. So how did she return?"

"Perhaps she was geographically close to the other Dreamer, and the Portal pulled her through. Or perhaps she found a gateway in her own realm and wandered through when the Portal opened for the first Dreamer ..."

"And that is another mystery—the Portal opened twice tonight. *Twice.*

How? I thought that *I* was the only one who could wield the Portal. Who opened it the second time?"

"Well, it certainly was not *me*."

Lorn tried to think through the matter logically, but soon gave up. He was exhausted, drenched, and severely disturbed by the events of the evening. "Regardless of how she entered Between, one thing is certain—if she returned to Between to fulfill her Dream, then I failed her. The thwarting of a single Dream is usually catastrophic for the Dreamer. The thwarting of two?" Lorn shook his head—the thought could not be borne. "What is to become of her?"

The Shadow was silent. The Vault of Dreams was filled with volumes describing the lives of Dreamers whose Dreams had not been fulfilled. They were not happy tales.

Lorn could still see the Dreamer in his mind's eye, her dark curls plastered to her face with the rain, her hand outstretched toward him, trying to rescue him. "There was something about her. Something …" He brushed his fingers over the Mark on his palm, remembering his reaction to her touch. "Something familiar. Something …"

Wondrous.

"Well, the returning Dreamer is a problem for another day," the Shadow said. "You need to go to bed." He gestured toward Lorn's midsection. "Immediately."

Lorn glanced down. Ink-black patches were blooming across his abdomen like dark flowers. "Well, that is inconvenient."

"*Dire* is a better word. To bed with you!"

Lorn was tempted—*oh, so tempted!*—to flee back to the warmth of his bed. But instead, he slumped further into his chair. "I should stay, just in case the Portal opens once again, and the Dreamer returns."

"*Please.*" The Shadow sniffed. "As if you could fulfill a seduction fantasy right now—you can barely move. Not to mention the fact that you are currently as sexually alluring as a dead fish."

With great effort, Lorn rolled his eyes. "So, so complimentary. But still—"

"Go to bed," the Shadow said firmly. "You are so exhausted that you are wet. Wet! You, Master of Water, *wet*. If the other magic folk hear of this, you will never live down the shame…"

The Shadow was making light of it, but Lorn could see the concern in his eyes. They both knew that Lorn was too exhausted to dry himself with magic.

"I shall send for you if the Portal opens," the Shadow continued.

"Tonight's mysteries will not be solved in moments. The only thing you are accomplishing by staying here right now is the ruination of that lovely armchair."

Lorn looked down at the poor, drenched chair and sighed. "Fine."

Just as he was about to rise, there was a series of *cracks* as the three imps reappeared.

"Yo, Mirror Man. Can't find the King," Izzy said.

"Nowhere," Setzl said.

"Or anywhere," the imp with the small notebook added.

Lorn cleared his throat. The imps turned and stared at their drenched monarch in surprise.

"Found him," Izzy said.

"Many thanks," the Shadow said dryly. "Job well done."

Izzy smirked at Lorn's wet clothing. "Go swimming, hey Boss?"

"In a manner of speaking," Lorn said. "And on that note, I am off to bed."

He rose weakly to his feet, bracing himself on the chair until his legs felt strong enough to hold him up. He turned to his Shadow and hesitated.

"Are you leaving?" his Shadow asked. "Or do you intend to sleep standing up?"

Lorn ignored him. "You have more sway over Between than I do—"

"*That* is debatable."

"You do," Lorn insisted. "Between is, quite literally, a part of you. So, I would ask that … if you could request …" He ran a hand through his hair, jaw clenched.

"No more seduction fantasies?" his Shadow suggested gently.

Lorn exhaled in a rush. "I know that it is my duty, to both Between and the Dreamer, but—"

The Shadow cut him off. "Say no more. I—" Abruptly the Shadow stopped and tilted his head as if listening.

"What is Between saying?" Lorn asked.

The Shadow listened for a moment longer and then turned to the King. "All will be well."

Lorn blinked. "It will? In Between? Since when?"

The Shadow merely smiled—a smile that held a secret. "As well as it can be in Between."

"That is not at all reassuring," Lorn muttered, and slowly left the room.

∾

THE SHADOW WATCHED HIS TRUE FORM CLOSE THE DOOR BEHIND HIM AND sighed sadly. "Make sure that he is not disturbed until late morning," he told the imps. "Do what you must."

"Biting?" Izzy asked hopefully.

"Of course! I would think less of you if you did not bite. Now, make sure he gets to his room—the last thing Lorn needs is to fall out a window along the way or something equally melodramatic."

Izzy gave him a smart salute. "Got it, Mirror Man."

The imps left the room with their customary *crack.*

The Shadow arranged himself in his chair, smoothing the creases from his velvet tunic until it fell around him in neat folds.

"Could you at least try to reign in the chaos tomorrow?" he asked Between. "He needs a reprieve."

He was answered by the sound of stone moving against stone.

"True," the Shadow conceded. "The Challengers were not your doing, nor the cretins in Fisk, nor—well, just try to treat him kindly." He picked up a decanter from a nearby side table and poured himself a glass of wine. "Strictly between us, a seduction fantasy would probably do him a world of good; Midra knows that he is wound tighter than a goblin's purse strings. But I believe he has had quite enough of being a disposable object of desire to last the rest of his lifetime." He lifted the glass to his lips and paused. "Please do not taint his time with the Dreamers—he loves it so."

The sound of stone moving against stone was even louder this time.

The Shadow smiled. "Well ... if it is just the *once*. Though, let us be honest—any plan hatched in Between, especially one that is unduly complicated and designed to bring Lorn even a crumb of happiness, is probably doomed to fail. Nevertheless ..." He lifted his glass in salute. "If it involves the liberation of Lorn's libido, then I endorse it wholeheartedly."

6

TO CATCH A DREAMER

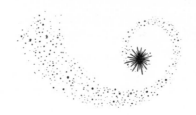

THE NEXT MORNING, LORN AWOKE TO THE SOUNDS OF SCREAMING, followed by cursing, followed by someone complaining—quite loudly—that they had been bitten.

So, an ordinary day in Between.

He also awoke to a fantastic collection of faded patches over his body and the sour taste of regret.

"Bollocks," he groaned, remembering his time with the second Dreamer in a series of mortifying flashes.

He had failed her.

If only he had known that she was a Dreamer from the very beginning!

If only Between had spoken to him!

If only she had not wanted a seduction fantasy!

If only ... if only ... if only—

Lorn stopped himself; that was the path to madness. He rubbed the sleep from his eyes and turned to the mirror on the far wall.

"You cannot wallow in angst," he told his reflection firmly. "Own your mistakes, try not to repeat them, and if the opportunity arises, make amends. You have a kingdom of deviants to rule and other Dreamers to protect. There is nothing more that can be done for her now."

Come with me.

Lorn stilled, caught in the memory of the Dreamer, her rain-slick hand stretched toward him, offering salvation ...

He shook his head, trying to clear the image. "I shall never see her again."

And with that rather gloomy pronouncement, Lorn swung his legs out of bed and went to make himself presentable enough to meet the catastrophes that lay ahead of him.

~

AS IT TURNED OUT, LORN WAS WRONG; HE DID SEE THE DREAMER AGAIN—and again ... and again ... and again ... and again—all in one day.

She appeared for the first time while Lorn was in a meeting with the ambassador from the Kingdom of Trundel.

"Boss," Izzy said, appearing on his desk.

"Not now, Izzy," Lorn said. "I am in a meeting."

"Dreamer's here," Izzy said, ignoring him. "On the Hill."

Lorn blinked. "A Dreamer? How? The Crossing is done for this month."

The dwarven ambassador leaned toward Izzy and sniffed. "Have you been at the ale, imp?"

Izzy glared at him, indignant. "Not *yet*. Better hurry, Boss," he said, turning to Lorn. "She comes and goes real quick."

Lorn's heart began to pound. "She? The second Dreamer from last night?"

Izzy nodded. "Better hurry."

"Apologies," Lorn said to the ambassador, pushing back his chair. "I must deal with this situation."

"Need an axe?" the ambassador asked, gesturing to the weapon at his hip.

"Let us hope not," Lorn said and quickly sunk beneath the ground.

When Lorn arrived at the Hill, he caught a brief glimpse of long, dark curls and a gown of blue just as the Dreamer faded out of sight, leaving behind the scent of summer flowers.

"Bollocks," Lorn swore.

"Told you," Izzy said. "She's quick."

Lorn stared at the imp. "A moment—you said, 'she's quick.' Has she been back more than once today?"

"Yep. Couple of times."

The relief Lorn felt was staggering. "Let me know the second she returns."

"Got it, Boss Man."

Lorn straightened his shoulders. He would put this right. He would explain the situation to the Dreamer, fashion some form of (seduction-free) Dream for her and be done with this matter by the end of the day.

"And then everything will return to normal," he told himself as he returned to the ambassador.

Which, Lorn later realized, was a ludicrously hopeful thought. And there was no place for ludicrously hopeful thoughts in Between.

By nightfall, Lorn was at his wit's end. It quickly became apparent that the Dreamer was able to come and go from Between at will. She would alight on the Hill for mere moments, butterfly-light, and then—despite Lorn's best efforts to reach her—fly back to her realm.

"Boss, she's here," Izzy announced during Lorn's meeting with Maddox.

"Wonderful!" Lorn answered, departing immediately … only to find the Dreamer gone once he reached the Hill.

"Lady Dreamer's back," Setzl announced while Lorn fixed a sinkhole.

"Not the best time," Lorn grimaced as he battled against gravity and a considerable amount of suction to pull the earth back up to where it was supposed to be.

Nevertheless, Lorn made the journey to the Hill, only to watch the Dreamer disappear.

"Dreamer! Now!" the imp with the small notebook said excitedly, just as Lorn lowered himself into his bath.

"We need to talk about boundaries," Lorn muttered as he reluctantly reached for his towel.

And so it went, on … and on … and on … for the next day or so. It was *maddening*.

"This is obviously not working," Lorn said, as he arrived just in time to watch the Dreamer disappear once again. "We need a better plan."

"We could lay some traps," Izzy said.

"An interesting idea, but inappropriate," Lorn said. "This is a Dreamer, not a swamp rat."

The imp with the small notebook shrugged. "So? We get bigger traps."

"The point is not the size of the traps, but rather the fact that trapping people is impolite." Lorn looked out across the Wasteland. The Nightmares were roaming, restless and excited, far too close to the Hill for comfort.

They were waiting for their opportunity to pounce on the Dreamer … and Lorn. "We need to catch her before the Nightmares get to her first."

"Big traps—" Izzy began.

"No traps," Lorn interrupted firmly.

"This could go on for days, Boss," Setzl warned.

"Weeks," the imp with the small notebook said.

"Years," Izzy said.

Lorn paused. "Perhaps a very comfortable trap. Something with an armchair and a footstool—"

"A cozy throw rug," the imp with the small notebook suggested.

"Pastries," Setzl said. "Maybe a bucket of ale."

"And a big, steel trap," Izzy added. "With lots of sharp bits to hold her in place."

"And just like that, the idea has lost its appeal." Lorn turned to Izzy. "Well done."

Izzy shrugged. " 'Twas nothing."

There was another reason that Lorn needed to catch this particular Dreamer as quickly as possible, he soon discovered.

"What do you mean the Portal keeps opening?" Lorn asked his Shadow.

The Shadow glanced warily at the Portal. "It appears to open each time the Dreamer falls asleep and dreams of Between." The Shadow gestured to the floor, where an odd collection of objects had gathered: one red, leather, high-heeled shoe; a hairbrush, complete with several strands of dark, curly hair tangled amongst the bristles; an orange toothbrush, and a pink velvet pillow. "These objects have been collecting over the past few days. Quite the assortment of treasures."

Lorn frowned down at the untidy pile. "There is always a swap. If these items are here, what of ours has traveled over to the Earther Realm?"

"Imps, probably a few brownies. Perhaps some kind of reptile …"

Lorn groaned. "We need to close the Portal permanently."

"Yes, we do. It is not, however, in our power to do so. She is the one who opens the Portal, and only she can close it."

Lorn groaned once again and began to pace impatiently before the mirror, his footsteps quick and clipped across the copper tiles. "Unless I camp out on the Hill—which, given my agenda, is not an option—we cannot catch her. And yet, we must complete her Dream as soon as possible lest we begin exchanging Nightmares between our realms."

The Shadow stared at the red shoe and shook his head. "Who would have thought that refusing to play out a seduction fantasy would quite literally jeopardize two realms?" He sighed wistfully. "Life is *so* odd ..."

Lorn snorted. "Given how exhausted I was, it would not have been much of a seduction fantasy—the realms may still have been doomed. At the very least, the Dreamer would have returned to Between demanding compensation for the lackluster experience."

"I, for one, hope that she returns so that you can fulfill her Dream and save us all with your magical talents ... amongst other things." The Shadow looked meaningfully at Lorn's crotch.

Lorn clicked his fingers to get the Shadow's attention. "Please maintain eye contact. If you were not, quite literally, a part of me—"

"Your fondest dreams, your darkest desires ..." the Shadow singsonged.

"—then I would find your continued assertions that I should have been intimate with a stranger for the good of the realm *distasteful*."

The Shadow leaned toward Lorn, his expression serious. "I only want the best for you, Lorn. I want you to have a companion. Appealing to your royal responsibilities is the only tactic that I have not yet tried. Did it work?"

"Not at all. If we could get back to the matter at hand?"

"But of course!" the Shadow said magnanimously. He sat back in his armchair and made a show of getting comfortable. "Please, continue."

"Many thanks," Lorn said dryly. "The other option is to find the Dreamer in the Earther Realm."

There was a sharp *crack*, and Izzy appeared at Lorn's side.

"She's here, Boss," Izzy announced.

There was another sharp *crack*, and Setzl appeared beside Izzy.

"Now ... she's gone," he announced dramatically.

"Of course," Lorn said. "It is barely even surprising anymore."

There was another *crack*, and the imp with the small notebook appeared on the back of the Lorn's chair.

"Thieves' Forest is on fire," he reported. "Again."

Lorn turned to the model of Between. Sure enough, the Thieves' Forest was beginning to smolder.

"A little earlier than usual," the Shadow noted.

"It usually catches fire later in the month," Lorn agreed. He watched as a series of furtive figures ran out from amongst trees. "I had best do something about that."

"Should," the imp with the small notebook said, "before the screaming starts. Oh, and the Minotaur is in the Weasel."

Lorn raised an eyebrow. "The Minotaur?" He scanned the model of

Between for the crooked little building that represented the Sleazy Weasel tavern. Sure enough, the figurine of the fearsome Minotaur was inside. "So he is. What is he doing there?"

The imp consulted his notebook, where he had drawn a lumpy shape with horns holding a cup. "Getting drunk—"

Lorn sighed. "I guess that makes a modicum of sense. It *is* a tavern."

"—and wrestling things—"

"Oh, dear."

"—and singing."

Lorn pinched the bridge of his nose.

"Are you sure you cannot send someone else to deal with him?" the Shadow asked.

Lorn shook his head. "The Minotaur does not realize his own strength when he is intoxicated; sending the castle guards to deal with him would be a quick way to fill Gahil's infirmary. Besides, he is a magical creature and hence my responsibility."

"He only listens to the Boss," Izzy said to the Shadow.

"Barely," Lorn said. "Regardless, I had better stop him from singing before the sound sends everyone mad." He quickly stood up and made his way to the large window on the opposite side of the room.

"Boss, what about the lady Dreamer?" Izzy asked.

Lorn paused. He was at a loss. He owed the Dreamer a Dream, but he could not fulfill his side of the bargain unless she stayed still. The idea of the armchair trap was becoming more and more appealing.

"We carry on as before." Lorn looked over his shoulder at his Shadow. "Pay a visit to the Vault of Dreams from your side of the mirror and see if you can find out who she is. If we can ascertain her identity, then perhaps we can locate her in the Earther Realm and sort this out once and for all."

"Ah ... a Plan," the Shadow said. "I approve. I shall do so immediately."

"Excellent. Time is fleeting."

With a few quick strides, Lorn leaped gracefully onto the broad, stone window ledge and then stepped off into the empty sky.

A few heartbeats later, a large, black bird soared high into Between's green tinged sky and flew off to wrangle forest fires and wrestle the intoxicated Minotaur into submission.

∾

SEVERAL HOURS LATER, LORN—HIS CLOTHING COVERED IN SOOT, ALE, AND Minotaur hair—returned from his tasks and wended his way through the city. His stomach growled, reminding him that he needed to eat. But even more urgently, he needed a drink—something strong enough to dull the memory of what he had just endured.

He strolled through the twisted streets and tangled alleyways, nodding to the pickpockets in the shadows and greeting the drunks in the gutter by name. He skirted the Night Market with its maze of crimson tents selling everything from perfumes to rare animals until he came to an open court-yard close to the city walls. A small crowd sat at trestle tables, eating dinner beneath multi-colored lanterns.

Lorn made his way to one of the food tents—the Crusty Spoon—where the shopkeeper greeted him with an apologetic smile.

"Not much left, Majesty," the shopkeep said, mopping his forehead with a white towel, careful not to let the fabric catch on his horns. "We're waiting on the next slab of meat." He gestured to a pit behind him where a roast was cooking over hot coals. "Shouldn't be too long."

Lorn's stomach growled at the smell of grilled meat. "Not to worry." He handed the storekeeper a gold coin. "Just give me a plate of whatever you have left and a mug of that illegally brewed ale that you persist on selling without a permit."

"I have no idea what you are talking about, Majesty," the shopkeep said with a straight face and handed him a plate of carved meats and a mug of permit-free ale.

Lorn took his plate to an empty bench and sat down to eat. After the first blissful mouthfuls, he looked up at the tables around him and realized that he was the only one dining alone. Couples and families filled the other benches, eating together and talking about their day.

Perhaps I should have asked the Minotaur to dinner, he thought to himself.

As he ate, Lorn could not help but overhear the conversation from the table closest to him.

"And then the other customer," a man's voice said, "some fancy fellow from the Upper Kingdoms says, 'It's nice and all, but I was hoping for one a little taller.' "

Lorn stole a glance at the next table and saw the man's companion nodding—the feather in his cap bobbing along—wholly absorbed in the story.

"So, what did you say?" the companion asked.

"Well, I told the customer, 'With all due respect sir, it's a pig—they don't come any taller.' "

"Well, of course not!" his companion said, clearly outraged on his behalf. "A pig is a pig!"

"Exactly! But this customer?" The man snorted. "He said, 'Well, can't you make him taller?' And I said, 'Sure thing, sir. Would you like me to have him fitted for stilts or heeled boots?' "

His companion threw back his head and laughed. "You always know what to say. You're such a clever one; it's one of the reasons that I Promised myself to you."

"Nah." The man was clearly chuffed. "The cleverest thing I ever did was to Promise myself back, beloved."

This is all very heartwarming, Lorn thought irritably, *but which did the customer choose—the stilts or the boots?*

He waited for the conversation to resume, but there was only silence. Lorn chanced another glance at the couple from the corner of his eye. At first, he noticed that they were holding hands, their red thread bracelets—the symbol of their Promising ceremony—touching below their entwined fingers. But then he saw their expressions; they were staring at each other with so much genuine adoration that Lorn quickly looked back down at his plate, oddly unsettled.

You have a spy network, he consoled himself. *Tomorrow, you can ask the Collection department to find out if there is a pig wandering around Otherworld in heeled boots.*

That should have reassured him, but the unsettled feeling remained ... and it grew when he glanced around the clearing at the other diners, their red string bracelets peeking out from beneath their cuffs and coats.

Lorn quickly looked back at his plate. "Clearly, I am suffering from indigestion," he muttered to himself. And with that fine piece of delusion, he hurriedly finished his dinner.

∾

By the time Lorn returned to the Portal Chamber later that evening, his 'indigestion' was long forgotten, buried beneath several more agenda items and the odd impossible task.

His Shadow raised an eyebrow at his entrance and gestured to Lorn's attire. "Rough day?"

Lorn collapsed into his customary armchair and looked down at his clothing. He rolled his eyes and dusted off the soot and debris that he had collected in his travels. "I have no wish to speak of it."

The Shadow ignored his wishes. "The fire should have posed no difficulty for you ..."

"Putting out the fire was relatively straightforward." Lorn pulled a twig from his collar. "Dealing with the Minotaur was not." Reluctantly, Lorn glanced at his Shadow and allowed his memories to pass between them.

The Shadow's lips quirked, and then he roared with laughter.

"Well," Lorn said, watching his Shadow double over, wheezing, "at least one of us is amused."

The Shadow gasped, trying to catch his breath. "I cannot believe that you sang with him!"

Lorn grimaced at the memory. "It was the only way to get him to stop."

"And there was *hugging*."

"I would like it noted for the record that I did not participate in that hug."

The Shadow smirked. "I have long urged you to engage in more phys- ical displays of affection; I suppose this is a start. You took him outside the city walls?"

Lorn nodded and began to brush off his tunic. "With two barrels of ale to keep him company. The journey would have been considerably quicker if I could have used magic on him."

"It has always struck me as fundamentally unfair that magical creatures are impervious to magic and yet magic folk are not."

"Yet another example of how life is horrifically unfair." Lorn gave up on grooming and settled back in his chair. "He was lonely, you know. Lonely and miserable and feeling terribly sorry for himself."

The Shadow arched an eyebrow at Lorn. "Was he?"

Lorn glared at his Shadow. "Yes. *He* was."

"*Hmm*, well—if that is the cause for such behavior, it will not be long before *you* are the one drunkenly singing at the Weasel, causing madness and mayhem to all around you."

Lorn snorted. "Maeve would have me gagged and tied to a chair if I attempted it. She was very displeased that the Minotaur had driven off her customers. When I arrived, she was about to brain him with a meat cleaver."

The Shadow shuddered. "Maeve must never be displeased." His eyes narrowed. "You changed the subject."

"Yes, I did. And allow me to change it once again—what have you found out about the Dreamer?"

At the mention of the Dreamer, the Shadow's expression went from a frown to a smirk so fast that Lorn was instantly on his guard.

"I paid an enlightening visit to the Vault of Dreams," the Shadow began.

"And?"

"I found our Dreamer's volume."

Lorn waited for the Shadow to elaborate, but he merely sat there, smirking disconcertingly. "And? Do tell—I can feel myself aging in the interim."

"Just heightening your anticipation." The Shadow ignored Lorn's glare. "As it turns out, a caretaker was on the throne at the time of her Dream— just as we had suspected. The imbecile simply opened the Portal and left the Dreamers to fend for themselves."

Lorn's jaw clenched. Dreamers were children! What kind of person left children at the mercy of monsters?

"I wonder how this caretaker would fare on the Hill—alone—with the Nightmares roaming?" Lorn looked idly toward the model of Between, where the Nightmares clustered on the Wasteland. "Shall we find out?"

The Shadow smiled—a dark, sharp smile that did not reach his eyes. "Why, yes! And what a fitting way to celebrate the Dreamer's return." He gestured to the table beside Lorn, where a slim book bound in silver leather sat, waiting. "I took the liberty of asking Maddox to pick up her volume for you."

Lorn felt his magic react to the sight of the book; felt it skip through his blood, warm as embers, ready to ignite.

"What is that?" he asked quietly, refusing to touch it. "It cannot be the Dreamer's volume."

"I assure you it is."

Lorn's heart began to pound. "Impossible. The book is silver."

"Yes, I noticed that. Odd, really. Lovelier than the customary black."

Lorn gritted his teeth, holding his magic in check. "Why is it *silver*?"

"That I do not know. But we should find out who she is." The Shadow looked fondly at the book. "She, of the silver tome."

Something in Lorn, the part of him that kept him wary, the part that held him safe, shied away from that pretty, silver book. All at once, he knew ... *he knew* ... that this was the beginning of something irrevocable. Laying his hand on this book would be the act that separated his life neatly into two portions—the one he had lived before this moment and the one after— and he was not sure if this would be the making of him or the destruction of everything he was.

Stay away, Shadow King, that protective part of him whispered. *Keep the little you have and live to fight another day.*

His Shadow broke the silence. "Do it," he said, his tone sure. He met Lorn's tormented gaze, seeming to read his concerns in a heartbeat. To

Lorn's surprise, his Shadow smiled ruefully. "As if the first half of your life was all that wondrous anyway. What do you have to lose?"

Lorn could not refute that. Before he could change his mind, he quickly placed his left hand flat on the silver book, the Mark on his palm touching the cool, leather cover.

"Show me," he commanded. "Show me the Dreamer."

When he raised his hand, the book became suffused with bright, silver light. With an audible click it shot open.

Startled, Lorn stepped back as the pages of the book flipped gleefully. Unlike other Dreamer volumes that filled with words at Lorn's command, this one began to fill with pictures—delicate sketches in black ink accented with watercolors. The illustrations quickly filled the pages, eager to tell him the story of the Dreamer within.

They began with a tiny girl holding a stuffed unicorn and a toy sword, a paper crown perched lopsidedly on her dark pigtails. As Lorn watched, the girl frolicked across the pages, waging great imaginary battles, her sword held aloft. She read books to her stuffed toys, laughed with her red-headed friend, sketched fantasy landscapes with her crayons on any surface that she could find, and crafted glorious dreams by night, her nocturnal adventures so vivid, so bright, that they were almost tangible in the darkness above her bed.

Lorn was charmed by what he saw. He found himself smiling at the Dreamer's antics, touched by her wide-eyed joy at everything her small world presented before her.

So, when it came time to watch this child with her glorious dreams and her big heart stand on the Hill and wait for a Dream that never happened —to watch her bright-eyes grow wide in terror as the Nightmares tore across the Wasteland and chased her down—he was filled with a terrible rage at the caretaker king who had let this happen.

And that rage burned brighter as he watched the little girl's dreams simply ... disappear. The little girl put down her unicorn and her sword, her imagination stunted by her inability to dream. She stared listlessly at the blank pages in front of her, her crayon slipping from her fingers. When she slept, her dreamscapes faded away to darkness, never again tinting the skies above her bed.

With growing sorrow, Lorn watched the consequences of all those lost dreams: doctor visits, sleepless nights, tears, *fear* ...

Lorn had seen enough. He moved to close the book, but the sketches continued, faster now, as if they desperately wanted him to see the rest of the story. The little girl grew into a teenager, at first confused by her new shape and then bemused as she grew so much taller than her peers. She attended high school, then college, gathering friends as one might gather spring flowers. She flirted—shyly at first, then with considerably more sass —with a parade of besotted young men, learning about love and desire, and how to tell the two apart.

But most of all, she tried to become the artist that she was always meant to be. Lorn watched her paint, watched her sketch, saw her skill and her passion for art grow even though she was thwarted in every attempt to share her gift with the world.

He saw her fail again, and again, and again.

And, inexplicably, he saw her rally herself and rise—again, and again, and again.

Despite the loss of her dreams and the thwarting of her ambitions, the Dreamer remained unbowed. Her heart was still large, her spirit unbroken, her view of the world matured but untainted. Lorn saw her teach, saw her travel, saw her—in a series of brushstrokes—become the woman he had met on the Hill, whose very presence he had initially questioned and dismissed as an aberration.

Finally, the book sketched a familiar face, one with blue eyes bright with wonder; a generous mouth curved into a wide smile; a fierce chin that tilted defiantly; and long, dark curls that fell in a wild mass around her pale face.

"Who are you?" Lorn whispered to the book.

With a series of flourishes, the book sketched her name.

"*Sasha Evangeline Pierce*," the Shadow read aloud. "A lovely arrangement of syllables, is it not? A delightful mix of the strange and the ordinary."

Lorn started at the sound of the Shadow's voice; he had been so absorbed in the story unfolding before him that he had forgotten where he was entirely. He reached for the now-still book and carefully turned back the pages, reversing the Dreamer's story until she was a child once more, holding her sword and unicorn aloft. He stared at the little girl on the Hill, her tiny toes buried in the golden sand, and his heart gave an odd twist.

It was an unsettling reaction and undoubtedly the product of a Dark magic spell.

"Is this book cursed?" Lorn asked.

The Shadow tilted his head, clearly puzzled. "Whatever do you mean?"

Lorn placed his hand over his heart and grimaced. "I have the oddest feeling …"

The Shadow snorted. "Your lack of self-awareness is truly astonishing! How ever did you function before I came along?" He held up his hand. "That was a rhetorical question—we both know that you were a wreck without me. The book is not cursed. You are merely reacting to the fact that your Dreamer is an absolute delight."

"Highly unlikely. If it is not cursed, then I am having a coronary. Either way ..." Lorn gingerly closed the book, just in case.

Thankfully, his heart rate calmed and resumed its typical activity.

Definitely cursed, he thought to himself.

"Regardless of curses, there is something afoot." Lorn turned to the Shadow. "Why is the book silver?"

The Shadow gave an elegant half-shrug. "I am unsure."

Lorn's eyes narrowed. "You said 'unsure,' not that you did not know. You have a theory."

The Shadow opened his mouth to speak but then paused.

"Sasha Evangeline Pierce is special," he said eventually.

"Well, obviously. She returned to Between, and she holds open the Portal whenever she dreams. The question is—why?" Frustrated, Lorn began to pace across the chamber. "There are many Dreamers just like this one, who waited on the Hill for naught. So why her? Why now? Why *silver?*"

The Shadow was about to answer when the Portal began to flash weakly, its gold light stained with silver.

"There appears to be something wrong with the Portal," the Shadow said.

Lorn paused his pacing. "Is it her again?"

The Shadow frowned as the Portal continued to flash, the light becoming weaker by the moment. "It must be. But why—?"

He was interrupted by three *cracks*. The imps quickly turned to Lorn.

"Boss, the Dreamer is here," Izzy said.

"On the Hill, I presume?" Lorn asked.

The Shadow sniffed. "Where else would she be?"

The imps shook their heads. "Not anymore," Izzy said.

"She's running," Setzl said.

"Fast," the imp with small notebook added.

"Where could she possibly be running?" the Shadow asked.

"Across the Wasteland," Setzl said.

Lorn and his Shadow shared identical looks of horror. "She must be running from the Nightmares," Lorn said.

"No. Toward them," Izzy said, his tone faintly admiring.

Lorn's eyes widened. "*What?*! How long has she been running?"

"Long time," Izzy said.

"Why did you not call us sooner?" the Shadow yelled.

"We only just found out!" the imp with the small notebook yelled back, clearly insulted.

"We were fixing wards on the city wall," Izzy explained. "The breeze tried to help her, but couldn't, so it came and got us."

"She's getting tired, Boss," the imp with the small notebook said. "Nightmares are closing in."

Setzl peered uneasily at the Portal. "Better hurry, Boss."

Lorn barely heard the imps. He had already crossed to the Portal, determined to rescue the Dreamer, his heart pounding with each step. He raised his hands and quickly made the sequence of gestures to open the gateway.

But the Portal would not open.

"Come on!" he muttered, gesturing once again.

But the Portal remained closed, the silver light flickering feebly across its surface.

"Lorn!" the Shadow called out. "The Portal will not let you through— she is holding it open. It will not listen to you."

"Then, take me to her!" Lorn ordered the Portal. "Take me to the Dreamer as you did before."

He braced himself, ready to be engulfed in the Portal's light, ready to be transported to the Hill.

But he remained in place.

"Lorn, look ... the Dreamer's Mirror! *Look!*"

Lorn turned toward the Dreamer's Mirror. The surface rippled then cleared, revealing not a Dream, but the improbable sight of Sasha Evangeline Pierce tearing across the Wasteland on a pathway of palest gold, hordes of Nightmares following in her wake.

Lorn felt his stomach drop as a Nightmare lashed out, its black nails scraping the delicate skin across Sasha's back. He watched as she faltered and almost fell, but stumbled forward, desperately trying to stay upright.

Lorn had seen enough. He felt his dark armor unfurl across his body; the Cloak of Shadows appeared across his shoulders.

"Help her," his Shadow said tersely.

Lorn did not bother to answer. In a heartbeat, he sunk beneath the ground of the Portal Chamber, transporting himself as fast as he could to the Wasteland.

7

THE TRUE QUEEN OF BETWEEN

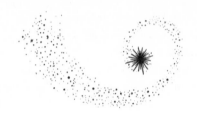

LORN TORE ACROSS BETWEEN, FASTER THAN HE HAD EVER TRAVELED before. In his mind's eye, he saw two Sashas—the woman running for her life on the Wasteland, and the small child in the silver book—both being chased by the monsters of his kingdom.

Please Midra, let me get there in time, he prayed, hoping that Between's unreliable patron god would be sober enough to hear his prayer.

When he emerged at the far side of the Wasteland, it was as if time slowed to a crawl. He was prepared for the worst, his heart pounding at the thought of what he would find. But Sasha was still running—stumbling, he amended—so exhausted that she could barely put one bare foot in front of the other. It was sheer willpower that kept her moving along her path, battling her way through the monsters that clustered around her as she made her way to the boundary wall, straight toward him.

She will not have to battle a moment longer, he told himself.

Lorn began to step forward, ready to cast, ready to come to her rescue. But to his shock, he could not move—Between held him back through his tether Mark, anchoring him to the ground.

What are you doing!? he asked Between, desperately straining against Between's hold. *I have to save her!*

Lorn gathered his strength and tried again to step forward. But just as before, Between trapped him to the spot like a butterfly pinned to a board.

"Enough!" he roared, trying to shake free of Between's hold. "They will take her! They will *destroy* her! Let me go—let me save her!"

He held his breath, waiting to be freed. But the pressure on his back did not ease.

The shock of it, the *horror* of it, twisted in Lorn's gut. "She is a Dreamer!" he cried, trying to reason with Between. "Surely, you would not allow harm to come to a Dreamer!"

The pressure on his tether Mark intensified to the point where it felt as though a wheelbarrow filled with lead had been emptied between his shoulder blades. Lorn felt his knees begin to buckle.

"*Please,*" he pleaded as he watched Sasha shield her face from the rising dust. "Please, let me save her ..."

And suddenly, Lorn understood—he was not here to save her. Sasha Evangeline Pierce had chosen to Challenge Between by crossing the Wasteland, and the rules of such a Challenge were clear—no one was permitted to interfere. *That* was why the Portal would not take him to her. Lorn was not to play the role of rescuer; his role was merely to act as a witness to her triumph ... or to her failure.

Please, let it be her triumph, Lorn begged any deity that was listening.

He watched, helpless, as Sasha staggered forward, his heart pounding in time with her footsteps. She was so close to the warded boundary wall and the freedom that lay beyond it, but from where Lorn was standing, he could see that she was on the verge of collapse. Her skin and clothes were drenched in sweat, her limbs trembling, her face a red mask of exhaustion and pain.

She had nothing left to give to this Challenge.

The Nightmares sensed it, too. They howled in victory and began to close in, talons extended, teeth bared.

She is not going to make it, Lorn thought, watching in mute horror as the Nightmares reached for her again and again, Sasha using her remaining strength to fight them off, to pull away.

Lorn's magic sparked beneath his skin, wanting to surge forth, wanting to save her. But Lorn knew that it was useless to fight the immense power of Between. He closed his eyes, unable to watch, but then opened them again, gritting his teeth. A caretaker king had failed Sasha as a child, and he had failed her as an adult. His punishment would be to watch as the monsters of his kingdom ran her down and destroyed her.

Perhaps once she failed, once the Nightmares captured her, Between would allow him to intervene...

But just as Lorn was preparing himself to watch the unthinkable unfold, Sasha looked up at him and smiled—a smile of such joy, such radiance, such *hope* that Lorn was momentarily dazzled.

And, just like that, Lorn's resignation dissolved.

"No," he told himself, told Between. "Not now. Not like this. I will not allow it." Lorn pulled back his sleeves and bared his Marks, preparing himself for the fight ahead. He held out his arms to her.

"*Come on!*" he called, his voice sharp with desperation.

Sasha's chin rose, and she lurched forward, faster than she had been moving before.

Lorn willed her on as she came closer ...

Closer ...

Close enough to feel the heat of her golden path ...

Close enough to see the sweat beading on her upper lip ...

Closer enough to hear her gasps for breath ...

So close that they were mere steps apart.

Then, for the second time in their short acquaintance, she threw herself at Lorn, the Nightmares' talons grazing the fabric of her shirt as she lurched over the boundary wall to safety.

Finally free to act, Lorn seized the moment; he gathered Sasha swiftly into his arms and lifted her away from the boundary, away from the grasping hands of the Nightmares.

The creatures howled. "Oursss!" they screamed, their cries angry and thwarted.

Lorn ignored them. His focus was entirely on the woman in his arms. The relief he felt, the gratitude that she was safe and whole, was so powerful that it almost brought him to his knees.

Thank you, he said to the deity who had answered his prayer. He tightened his hold on her; nothing would hurt her now.

As he carried Sasha further away from the Wasteland, he looked down at her; her eyes were closed, her hair plastered to her face with sweat. She was too exhausted to do anything but struggle for breath.

In that instant, he thought inanely to himself:

This is the new Queen of Between.

And then:

This is the True *Queen of Between.*

And then:

Good gods—this is my wife!

The thought was so unexpected, so shocking that he stumbled for a moment and almost dropped her.

My wife, he thought numbly as he settled her on the ground and turned back to confront the Nightmares.

My wife, he thought in growing alarm as he raised the wards on the boundary wall, ignoring the anguished cries of the monsters as they shielded their eyes from searing light.

My wife, he repeated yet again as he strode back to her side, wondering if there was any way around this new development.

Bollocks, he swore when he realized that there probably was not.

Lorn looked down at Sasha—crumpled on the gold dust like a discarded ragdoll—and was struck by such a strong feeling of sympathy for the poor woman that he gasped aloud.

She was doomed. *Doomed.*

Lorn knelt beside her and took hold of her shoulders. "Do you know what you have you *done?* You have ruined your life!"

Sasha flinched away from his touch. "Stop manhandling me!" she whimpered, her voice as dry as sand. "I've been through an Ordeal."

"Of course, you have." Lorn released her gently, feeling like an utter bastard. "Apologies. The problem is that your *Ordeal*—as you so aptly termed it—is only just beginning and will probably end in a wretchedly melodramatic fashion for all involved, myself included. Which, admittedly, is nothing new …" He trailed off, noticing the raised, red marks on her arm. His blood chilled. "Tell me, the Nightmares—did they bite you?"

Sasha made a feeble attempt to shake her head.

"Are you absolutely sure?"

She opened her mouth to answer but hesitated. He saw the uncertainty in her expression, the hint of fear.

Lorn's heart dropped. "May I have your permission to 'manhandle' you to check?"

"Sure," she rasped.

"Brace yourself," he advised, more to himself than to her.

Lorn carefully lifted Sasha into a sitting position, murmuring an apology when she winced. He gently lifted the torn fabric of her sleeves, hissing when he saw the burns—angry, red welts, painfully stark against her pale skin. He shifted her forward and swore: the back of her shirt was torn to ribbons, as was the skin beneath. Tracks of blood, still wet and syrup-thick, marked the path of the Nightmare's claws along her flesh.

Well done, Between, he thought angrily. *What a stellar way to welcome your queen.*

He clenched his jaw. The claw marks were terrible, but a bite … a bite would be catastrophic—he needed to press on. He quickly continued his search, the exhausted Dreamer limp and still in his arms. But aside from a scattering of claw marks and burns, Lorn's search yielded nothing.

Thank Midra, he thought, almost sagging in relief. If she had been infected ... well, he did not even wish to contemplate it.

"No bites?" Sasha whispered.

"No bites. Excellent," he said, trying to be reassuring but probably failing dismally. "That is one less horrifying thing to happen to you this evening."

Then again, he thought to himself, *she was now bound to a sentient kingdom—she may have preferred to live out the rest of her life as a Nightmare.*

"Do you have any idea what you have just done?" he asked.

Sasha squinted up at him. "You told me to run from the monsters, so I ran."

"*Away* from them," Lorn said, horrified by how she had misinterpreted his words. "Not *toward.*"

"Semantics." She attempted to lick her dry lips and failed. "Water?"

"Of course."

Given their time constraints—Lorn never knew when she would simply disappear—he made a split-second decision to do something utterly Forbidden. He reached up and created a rent—a portal from the Wasteland to the glass of water on his bedside table. Using his amulet, he poured his power into the small space and visualized his chambers.

Thankfully, it worked. Lorn reached inside the rent, grabbed the glass from his bedside table, and drew it out of his chambers, closing the rent behind him.

"Is that a mirage?" Sasha asked, staring warily at the glass.

"No, but it would not be the first in this place."

Lorn knelt beside her and held the glass to her lips. Although she was obviously thirsty, she drank cautiously, a few sparing sips at a time. Lorn admired her restraint.

"Thanks," she said, taking the glass from him.

"You will not thank me soon." Lorn shook his head in disbelief. "Oh, the things that are in store for you ..."

"Sense," she mumbled. "Speak *sense.* What's going on?"

Her gaze was so open. *Too* open. Lorn could read everything in those deep blue eyes—frustration and fear and ... and *gratitude,* which he found both baffling and dreadful.

Unable to bear that look a moment longer, Lorn stood up and began to pace. How could he explain that life as she knew it was over? That everything she knew, everyone she loved, would soon be left behind?

Between, he thought, *what have you done?*

Lorn stopped and knelt beside her once more. "You bested the Wasteland without magic. In a *dream*. You have done the impossible. And with the impossible—well, there comes certain gifts."

Lorn wondered briefly what gifts Between would give Sasha for crossing the Wasteland. Each gift that he had received was equally a blessing and a curse.

Oh, how he pitied her!

"What is of equal concern," Lorn continued, his stomach dropping at the thought, "is that you appear to be able to come here at will." The moment that the High King and Queen found out that Sasha was holding open the Portal, she would be in extreme danger—they would not allow such a threat to Otherworld. "That cannot be allowed. *They* will not allow it. They will put a stop to it … or a stop to you—whichever they find easier."

Lorn was about to say more but felt the ground tremble beneath him. He looked up; the stars were beginning to emerge. Any moment now it would be morning in the Earther Realm, the time that Dreams typically ended.

Lorn quickly turned back to Sasha. "Listen to me—you are beginning to wake up. I will come for you, do you hear?" Suddenly he remembered the Death Cultists and their latest betrothal tactic. It was unlikely that news of a new Queen of Between would be well received in Zadria. "Others may come for you, too, but do not leave with anyone else. Do not trust *anyone* else. Do you understand?"

Sasha nodded weakly. "Yes. Waking up. Others coming. Wait for you. Right?"

Lorn grabbed the silver amulet hanging around his neck, its weight reassuring in his palm. Two crescent moons facing an eight-pointed star, the amulet was many things: a symbol of Lorn's position, a conduit of his power, a means of opening and creating Portals, a protective talisman, and a Summoning tool.

It was the latter two that he needed most right now.

With a sharp tug, Lorn snapped it free from around his neck.

"Keep this close and wait for me." He wrapped the heavy, silver chain around her wrist. Then, very gently, he took the Dreamer's—no, the *Queen's* face between his hands. "I will come for you, Sasha Evangeline Pierce." He used her full name, hoping that it would give him the power to imprint this memory on her consciousness. "Wait for me."

Sasha's eyes widened. "How did you know my name?"

Suddenly, her body jerked; it was the Summons to the Earther Realm.

"I'm leaving," she said, startled.

Lorn grabbed her hands, enclosing them tightly within his own. "Wait for me." He could hear the desperation in his tone. He held her gaze, trying to make her realize just how important this was, trying to ensure that she would remember this moment when she awoke. "I will come for you."

"You already said that," she said faintly and began to rise from the ground.

Lorn held onto her as tight as he could until her hands were wrenched from his.

"I will come for you!" he called after her, willing her to remember his words.

As Lorn watched the new Queen of Between float skywards toward her realm, his amulet wrapped around her wrist, a terrible sense of foreboding overcame him. "This is sure to end badly," he muttered.

Lorn turned back toward the Wasteland. The Nightmares were still clustered around the glowing boundary wall, staring up at the sky where Sasha had disappeared moments before, chittering in disappointment.

"I would like it noted for the record that I hold you all responsible for this wretchedly melodramatic state of affairs," Lorn told the creatures. "Did you *have* to chase her? Could you not have just left her alone?"

"*No!*" the leader hissed. "Chase, devour ... it is what we do." The rest of the Nightmares howled their agreement.

"That is fair," Lorn said with a sigh. "I suppose you were only doing your job. Nevertheless, look at the mess we are in now. You were defeated, which means that every intoxicated imbecile across Otherworld will flock to Between to try and copy her feat—"

"Good," the leader interrupted. "More deliciousss dreamsss for usss."

The Nightmares howled with excitement.

Lorn ignored them. "We now have a queen—a queen who is able to travel back and forth from this realm, which is bound to get us into a world of trouble with the High King. Not to mention the Death Cultists, who may try to use her in their Schemes ... or try to dispose of her altogether."

The Nightmares chittered darkly.

"And most problematic of all, I ... I now have a *wife*."

"Condolencesss, King," the leader said slyly. The Nightmares began to make dry, wheezy noises that sounded suspiciously like snickers.

"Oh, be gone with you," Lorn grumbled, waving the Nightmares away. "You have done quite enough damage for today."

As the Nightmares slunk back to their lairs, still snickering, Lorn picked up the fallen water glass. It was empty, its surface covered in gold dust.

"This is sure to end badly," he repeated with a sigh. And with that dreary pronouncement, Lorn slipped beneath the ground and made his way back to the Shadow to break the news.

When Lorn returned from the Wasteland, the Shadow was in a frantic state.

"Where is she?" he cried, his eyes wild. He stormed to the front of the mirror and pressed his hands against the surface as if trying to push his way out. "Is she alive? Is she harmed? Why did you not bring her here? Do not tell me that you left her on the Hill alone!"

Lorn began to speak but then gave up and turned toward his Shadow. He watched as the Shadow lurched back in surprise, his expression rapidly shifting from worry to incredulity as he experienced Lorn's memories of the event.

Before the Shadow could speak, the little silver book on the table began to shake. With a sudden jerk, it flew open and began sketching Sasha's triumphant run across the Wasteland and her encounter with Lorn.

With bold strokes, the book began to write.

Lorn glanced at the words and sighed. "And so it begins..."

The Shadow craned his neck to see the message. "Sasha Evangeline Pierce," he read, "*True Queen of Between.* Well," he said faintly. "That was unexpected."

Lorn remembered looking down at the exhausted woman in his arms. "Yes. Yes, it was."

The Shadow sat down heavily on his chair. "What an odd day." He stilled, his hands hovering above his armrests. "Do you know what this means? You have a companion!" His eyes widened. "Better yet—you are to be married! Married!"

Married.

Lorn realized that he was holding his breath. He exhaled in a rush. "So I am. Congratulations to me."

The Shadow's smile was positively giddy. "I am overjoyed! This is everything that I have ever wanted for you. Oh, happiest of days! This calls for a toast."

"It certainly calls for alcohol," Lorn agreed. He walked over to a tall cabinet by one of the windows—a lovely thing fashioned from bronze and inlaid with mother-of-pearl. "Now"—he placed the empty water glass on one of the shelves—"let us see if I can find something in here that will allow me to get roaring drunk ..."

The Shadow snorted. "If only. Whatever you choose will only give you a headache."

Lorn felt the Shadow's gaze as he rummaged through the bottles and potions.

"Truly, this is a cause for celebration," the Shadow said, "for *rejoicing*—not inebriation and unconsciousness!"

"Is it?"

Lorn removed a decanter of amber liquid and its dainty, matching glass from the cabinet and carried them back to his armchair. With a wave of his hand, a small table scuttled across the room and settled next to his chair, ready to hold the glassware. Lorn poured the liquor into the tiny glass and frowned at the thimble-full of liquid.

"Cheers," he said, and drank straight from the decanter instead.

"Manners," the Shadow tsked. "That particular liqueur is rare and almost priceless; it is meant to be sipped and savored, hence the tiny glass. Just because events have taken a turn toward the unexpected is no reason for you to become a savage."

Lorn swallowed a rather large gulp of spirits and cleared his throat. "I have been through an *Ordeal*. I require far more alcohol than that tiny glass is able to hold."

"I shall get the imps to fetch you a bucket."

"Many thanks."

Lorn took another long drink, barely tasting the floral sweetness of the rare drink. The events of the evening were finally starting to sink in, but they still seemed utterly unbelievable ... which was saying something when one ruled a land where unbelievable things happened on an hourly basis.

"There is a now a Queen of Between," Lorn announced. He thought that saying the words aloud would make the event seem less unbelievable. It did not, so he tried saying it in a slightly different way.

"There is now a True Queen of Between."

That was no better, so he tried again.

"I now have a queen."

The Shadow studied his true form, his expression puzzled. "Are you well? You appear to be stuck in some form of repetitive verbal loop."

"I am quite well—many thanks for asking. I am, however, finding it difficult to comprehend the fact that Between has acquired a queen. Even the idea of it is utterly preposterous." Lorn stared accusingly at his decanter. "And this is doing nothing to make it less so. Dammit, I chose the wrong bottle ..."

"Why is the thought of having a queen so preposterous? You are, after all, a king. Kings marry. Those kings with the inclination to do so marry women who become queens. Surely, this is not news to you."

"Thank you for explaining the complex concept of heterosexual royal marriages." Lorn saluted the Shadow with his decanter and took another long sip.

The Shadow rolled his eyes. "Did you truly think that you could gallivant around as a bachelor for the rest of your reign?"

"I thought I would do just that … until Maddox found a way to break us free of Between, or I died a terrible—and most likely ridiculous —death."

Lorn took a moment to ponder what form of terribly ridiculous (or ridiculously terrible) death would likely befall him. Perhaps he would be stomped to death by stampeding chickens. Or crushed beneath flaming rocks. Or he would fall out of bed into a sinkhole. He sighed—so many possibilities! He made a mental note to check the Den to see whether they had a betting pool on this very subject.

"Escape or death," Lorn continued. "*That* was what my future was supposed to hold. Now, thanks to an Earther and a pack of Nightmares, all my best laid plans are in ruins. Honestly, is *nothing* sacred in this place?"

The Shadow shook his head. "There must be some elf in your ancestry; there is no other reason for such melodrama. Do you hear yourself? Escape or death?" He snorted. "How could you be happy with so little in life?"

Lorn shrugged. He was starting to feel rather languid. *I must be in a state of shock*, he thought happily to himself.

"Do not misinterpret," he said to the Shadow. "I am not exactly joyous about my prospects. I have merely come to a state of acceptance. As you well know, I was not always so placid about my dreadful Destiny."

The Shadow considered Lorn's words for a long moment. "This is true. At first, you were angry about your Destiny … then whiny about your Destiny … then Scheming about your Destiny …and now elf-ish about your Destiny."

"I prefer the term *resigned*—it contains fewer elves."

"You were not always planning to escape or die—you entertained the prospect of marriage right before your coronation. You even proposed! Do you not remember?"

Lorn did, indeed, remember. He also remembered the woman in question with the same sort of nostalgia that one feels when recalling a particularly difficult tooth extraction. Nina was a small woman, but every inch of her was filled with nefarious schemes and wily ways that she hid beneath silk gowns and dimpled smiles and long, milk-white hair. It was impossible to know what she *truly* thought or felt at any given moment; she seemed to delight in contradictions. She spent most of her time plotting ways to increase her wealth, while flinging pouches filled with gold to the beggars lining the Summer Kingdom's streets. She could plot the downfall of her enemies with chilling detachment but would sob as if her heart were broken during plays about tragic love. When the rest of the Summer Palace courtiers had shunned him, she had been his champion, training him in the ways of the court and defending him to all those who spoke against him. And yet, she had used him more than anyone else in the palace. She was exciting and brilliant and dangerous—a threat whispered in a voice as sweet as spring honey—and she *reveled* in it.

"I quickly lost my taste for marriage after Nina rejected my proposal," he said, brushing the memories aside. "If she—ambitious creature that she is—did not wish to become the Queen of Between, then it was a foregone conclusion that no one else would."

"Ah, *Nina.*" The Shadow laughed. "She would have cleared out the Large Treasury, cheated on you with most of the castle guard, and fled the kingdom before the sun had set on your wedding day."

"Most likely," Lorn said agreeably. "In fairness, she probably would have given away most of the stolen funds before crossing the city gates." He shrugged. "I thought her ruthlessness would be an asset to Between."

"That brand of ruthlessness is an asset in a bar fight, not in a queen. Between is better off without her—as are you."

"You will find no argument here." Lorn examined his feelings for Nina and was not surprised to find that he now felt nothing but a curious sort of detachment about the whole affair. Even the old sense of betrayal—the type that you feel when someone that you're rather fond of laughs uproariously in your face during your marriage proposal—was missing.

The Shadow interrupted his thoughts. "Nina aside, we both know that there have been other times during your reign when you have contemplated the idea of taking a queen."

Lorn stilled—he knew what the Shadow was about to say next. He tried to deflect. "I admit, there have been one or two occasions when I considered the *possibility* of a queen—preferably someone willing to do her fair share of the work ruling this cesspool, and who would not spend her free time plotting my gruesome death."

The Shadow raised an eyebrow. "Ah, such lies. I was referring to those times when you entertained the possibility of a very different type of queen. A queen that—"

Lorn held up his hand, halting the Shadow's words. "Those times—those times I was not in control. I was not *myself.*"

The Shadow was silent because he knew that this was true. For it was only when Lorn was lying alone in his chambers, broken after performing one of the impossible tasks that Between regularly asked of him, and so ravaged by pain that he was unable to control his thoughts, that he would allow himself to imagine a different kind of queen: a vibrant, bold woman who would bring beauty and culture and color to his drab and dreary kingdom. This dream queen would be an equal, an ally, a *friend*—a solace in his time of need.

And sometimes ... sometimes Lorn would allow himself the exquisite torture of imagining a true relationship with this dream queen. One filled with a love that was tender and true and strong enough to overcome all the obstacles in their day to day lives—

Lorn firmly pushed those thoughts away. "Those were idle fancies ... or more likely hallucinations brought on by Gahil's ghastly potions. I do believe that he makes them taste disgusting on purpose."

The Shadow inclined his head. To Lorn's relief, he did not pursue the subject further.

"Still," the Shadow said instead, "look at how your romantic prospects have changed in just a week. First, there was the Zadrian betrothal party—"

"I had forgotten about them," Lorn interrupted. "I wonder if they are still touring the Wetlands."

He turned toward the model of Between. Sure enough, a group of figurines dressed in gray and purple was wandering, clearly lost, around the Swamp of Eternal Angst.

"Forget them," the Shadow said dismissively. "The betrothal party is of no consequence. You are now all but married to a Dreamer!"

Lorn grimaced. "It is rather telling that my only matrimonial prospects to date have been a renowned husband-killer who planned to dispose of me on my wedding night, and a woman from a completely different realm, who believes me to be a figment of her tawdry imagination."

The Shadow blinked. "Well, when you say it like that, it is not as flattering as I had initially thought. Still, of the two matrimonial options, clearly the right choice has been made."

" 'The right *choice* has been made,' you say?" Lorn placed the decanter on the table and picked up his abandoned glass, spinning the delicate stem between thumb and forefinger. The amber liquor caught the light, highlighting the golden flecks suspended within. "An odd word to use—*choice*—given that neither Sasha nor I had any choice in the matter."

"You are a king," the Shadow said firmly. "Your choices are never your own. Look at High Queen Orelia—do you truly think she wished to be Joined to a succession of dismal High Kings? Good gods, any sane woman would have fled back to Faire to avoid such a cheerless fate." He snorted. "But it was her duty; she was chosen by the fae royal houses to rule Otherworld, just like every high queen before her. Her sacrifice is the price of peace between the two realms."

He stared at Lorn, all seriousness now. "You, too, must do what is needed for the good of your kingdom and the people within it. That is the way it *must* be."

"Of course, it is!" Lorn clenched his jaw. He had done nothing but sacrifice for Between—the dark patches scattered over his body were a living reminder. "Ever since I was crowned, *all* I have done has been for the good of the kingdom and the people within it!"

The Shadow bowed his head. "In that respect—and in so many others—you have been an exemplary King of Between. It is Sasha's Destiny to become the Queen of Between—that is why her book is silver. She, too, does not get a say in the matter ... as wretched as that may be."

Lorn looked down at the sketch of the new Queen of Between. He stared at her fierce little chin and her wild, dark hair, and remembered the look of determination on her face when she had torn across the Wasteland, followed by a horde of demons. "And that is where you are wrong. I am sure she will have plenty to say on the matter when she gets here." Lorn also remembered her lying crumpled on the ground, gasping for air, her body marked by the Nightmares. "That poor, poor, deeply cursed woman."

"I doubt that Sasha is cursed *per se*. Well, not any longer—her dreams have clearly returned." The Shadow tapped his lip in thought. "I do believe she will be an asset to Between. She just bested the Nightmares in their own domain which is unheard of. *And* she lived deprived of dreams without becoming wholly disillusioned or raving mad. She is brave, resilient and best of all—"

"I actively fear what you are about to say next."

"—she wants to *pounce* on you."

Lorn rolled his eyes. "Marvelous. An important quality in a queen."

"I rank it high on the list."

"You forget two things: first, this will be a Joining—there will be no pouncing."

The Shadow grimaced. "True. Damn Joinings; all the horrors of a matrimony with none of the benefits."

"Not true! I believe that Sasha and I are entitled to a box of congratulatory carrots and the pig of our choice. And to think, I was under the impression that there was no reason to celebrate this union ..."

The Shadow shook his head. 'There is truly no hope for you."

Lorn ignored him. "Second, you have forgotten that she is also in considerable danger. Do you think the Zadrian betrothal party will be happy to hear that I am married?"

"Oh dear," the Shadow said, turning to the model.

"Yes, *oh dear*. They may choose to restore my bachelor status by doing away with Sasha. Or, they may hatch a plot to use her in some way, especially if they manage to defeat me during one of their monthly Challenges. To make matters worse—"

"Are they not sufficiently dire for your liking?" the Shadow asked dryly.

"—Sasha is somehow able to open the Portal while she dreams. *That* will earn her the notice of both the High King and Queen."

"Which is why you must announce the new Queen of Between at the High King's Gathering of the Summer Alliance Monarchs of the Lower Kingdoms tomorrow."

Lorn dropped his glass onto the table in shock. "A moment—you wish me to *announce* her presence to the High King ... the very man who is duty-bound to put a stop to her Portal-opening antics? I may as well draw a target on her back and send the High King a map to her house."

The Shadow tsked as the amber liquor rapidly spilled from Lorn's glass onto the table beneath it. "*Do* fix the spill. That table is an antique and I happen to be very fond of it."

Lorn looked down at the puddle. "I may be wrong, but I believe that spilled liqueur is the least of our concerns right now."

The Shadow sat up rigidly in his seat. "You may be happy to live in chaos and filth, but I find it bothersome, especially since I am forced to look at it *every single second of the day* without the power to fix it." He banged his fist against his glass prison. "It is enough to drive one insane."

Lorn opened his mouth to argue, but the Shadow's expression made him pause. "Apologies," he said quietly. "Of course."

Lorn raised his hand over the spill; the liquid lifted off the surface of the table until it was suspended in mid-air. Before the Shadow's eyes, the droplets hardened into amber colored crystals which glittered in the copper hued light of the chamber.

"Very pretty," the Shadow said approvingly as he watched the stones fall into Lorn's palm. "You should have those set in silver for Sasha."

"An excellent idea," Lorn said, placing the stones on the table. "That way, she will have something appropriately regal to wear during her extensive tour of the High King's dungeons." He spread the stones across the table. "I had best get these to the jeweler with all haste."

The Shadow relaxed and settled back into his chair. "The High King would never incarcerate a king or queen."

"It has happened before."

"And look what happened! The High King in question was deposed in a rather messy fashion. Dresden is far too sensible to jeopardize his rule. After all, Midra knows what he did to get it ..."

"The walls have ears," Lorn said automatically.

"Not these walls." The Shadow smiled fondly at the copper walls of the Portal Chamber. "As I was saying, the best way to ensure Sasha's safety is to announce your betrothal in the presence of the other Lower Kingdom monarchs. The High King *will* find out about Sasha one way or another; do it on your terms and his actions will be held accountable by the other monarchs."

Lorn considered the plan. "The idea has merit," he said eventually. "But it will all come to naught if he finds out that Sasha is holding open the Portal. He is sworn to protect Otherworld."

"The High King does not need to know that Sasha is holding open the Portal. After all, it is only while she dreams."

"For now," Lorn said darkly. "The longer she is away, the harder Between will try to bring her back. I fear that there will come a time when the Portal will open even while she is awake."

The Shadow waved away his fears. "She will not be holding the Portal open for much longer; you will be bringing her to Between very shortly."

"A stellar plan—assuming that I knew where to find her. I have no idea where to begin my search, and it is not as if I can traipse through the Earther Realm like a tourist."

"Well, not in that outfit." The Shadow looked askance at Lorn's armor and Cloak of Shadows. "It is lucky for us all that you have a coven at your disposal *who can*." The Shadow gestured toward the Portal. "Ask the assistance of the Middleton Coven. Surely they will be able to find her."

Lorn blinked. "Why did I not think of that?"

"Well, you have been rather busy, what with all the melodrama and decanter swilling."

Lorn ignored that comment. "Many thanks. You have been of great assistance."

The Shadow gave an ironic half-bow. "I live to serve."

Lorn filled his glass once again, his mood lifted. "I will send them a message tonight." He paused, the decanter suspended above his glass. "Even so, it will take time to find her. She is out there … alone. Unprotected." He looked up, just in time to see the Shadow hide a smile behind the rim of his goblet. He was about to ask why his counterpart was smiling when the Shadow spoke.

"I am sure that the coven will be able to locate her quite quickly—and quicker yet if you ask Sasha for her location when she next appears in Between."

Lorn blinked. "That would work."

The Shadow inclined his head. "It would indeed. So, relax! It will be but days until she is here; she should be safe enough in the meantime. *And you gave her your amulet.*"

"True." Lorn's shoulders sagged in relief. "It will afford her some protection. If only I could have instructed her on how to Summon me before she was snatched back to her own realm." He glanced at the silver book and hesitated. "What if she does not want to come to Between?"

The Shadow blinked. *"Not want to come?* The people of the Earther Realm are fed tales of Otherworld from childhood. What Earther would refuse the opportunity to rule a fairy tale kingdom? For an Earther, this would be something out of their very dreams!"

At that moment, a massive, blue and orange winged beast flew past the window, screeching at a pitch that shook the glass windows in their frames.

Lorn winced. "More like one of their nightmares."

The Shadow dismissed the creature and Lorn's comment with an airy wave of his hand. "There is no need to bore her with the reality of the situation. Sell her the fantasy! *Lure* her here! I am sure that you can use your considerable charms to coax her into coming—that is, assuming that you can remember where you placed them. And if that fails, use your crotch."

Lorn shook his head, resigned. "And now you are back to being wretchedly unhelpful."

"Sasha belongs here," the Shadow said quietly. "It is her Destiny. One way or another, she will rule Between, just as it was your Destiny to rule Between."

Lorn snorted. "As you well know, I did not receive a Golden Feather; it may be my Destiny—*our* Destiny—to escape this place yet." He stood up and walked over to the mirror until he stood directly in front of his Shadow.

"I will free you from here," Lorn vowed, placing his hand on the glass. "And then we will roam Otherworld, just as we planned."

The Shadow smiled sadly at his true form and raised his goblet in salute. "I will leave you to your pretty delusions."

But Lorn was not going to be dissuaded tonight. If Sasha had taught him anything, it was that the rules he had thought immutable before could be bent, *broken.*

"I *will* free you from here," Lorn repeated. "One way or another."

"You will try," the Shadow said with that same sad smile. He put down his goblet and contemplated his true form. "If you are truly that desperate to leave Between, you could always bargain with the Fates to change your Destiny ..."

Even the thought made Lorn's gut churn. In Otherworld, if you found yourself in a bad situation, the Fates were always happy to help you out of it—for a price. Unfortunately, that price was usually very high and terribly unpleasant.

"Do not even jest," Lorn said sharply. "The last thing I need is to attract *their* attention. My life may be wretched, but I refuse to be used as a tool for their dubious ends."

"Good to know," the Shadow murmured.

Lorn ran his fingers along the ornate frame of the mirror. "In the meantime, I shall endeavor to enchant a few more mirrors so that you can roam a little more around the castle. None of the popular rooms, of course —that would lead to too many questions. But there are still plenty of interesting rooms that no one enters."

"Ah ... now *that* is an offer that I am happy to accept!"

Lorn turned on his heel, his cloak billowing around him, and crossed the room until he stood before the model of Between. He surveyed his dominion, with its shabby little city and ungainly castle, and shook his head.

"In a matter of days, we will be bringing a queen into this terrifying, disease-ridden little kingdom." Lorn frowned as a fight broke out in front of the cobbler's shop. "We had best try to clean it up a little. Perhaps we can get rid of some of the rogue elements and create a decent first impression."

The words had just left his mouth when a sinkhole appeared on the outskirts of the city walls. With a sigh, Lorn watched as a wagon, two barrels of ale, and the depressed Minotaur got sucked into its depths.

"The Minotaur is having a terrible evening," Lorn said.

"It is all relative, really," the Shadow observed. "Somewhere in the Earther Realm, a woman has just turned her life upside down." He paused. "And yours, too."

Lorn dropped his forehead against the wall in defeat.

"Yes," the Shadow said soothingly, "that is probably the best response."

WHEN ONE RULES A LAND COMPOSED OF CHAOS AND WILD MAGIC, ONE learns to become adaptable. By the time Lorn had returned to his chambers, the shock of the night's events had worn off, and he was fueled with purpose.

He had charged to the Wasteland to rescue the Dreamer from the demons of his kingdom but had found that he was not needed—she had rescued herself.

But now ... *now* she needed him.

Sasha Evangeline Pierce was currently sitting in her own realm, utterly unaware of the danger she posed to Otherworld ... or of the danger Otherworld posed to her. It was Lorn's duty to somehow protect both Sasha and his realm from one another.

Lorn strode across his sitting room and sat down at his desk. He pushed aside the maps of faraway places and cleared away the books about obscure magic that he never found time to read. He laid out a fresh piece of parchment, picked up his second favorite quill, and cracked his knuckles, determined.

At the Academy of Practical Arts, the instructors impressed upon their students that success in any endeavor began with a Plan. Embarking on an endeavor in the Practical Arts without a Plan was a sure path to failure, lots of screaming, and possibly the loss of a limb or two. As a student, Lorn had taken that advice to heart; now, as a king, he still created a Plan for his most ambitious endeavors.

"This situation clearly qualifies," he muttered to himself.

He dipped his quill into his inkwell and began sketching out what he decided to call The Queen Plan—one of the simplest plans that he had ever devised.

The Queen Plan consisted of two steps:

Step one: Locate Sasha in the Earther Realm.
Step two: Bring her to Between.

At that point, Lorn hesitated. He knew, with the conviction of the damned, that there would come a time in the not-too-distant future when his reign would end abruptly. He *wanted* to believe that this abrupt end would come about as a result of finding a way to escape from Between. But it was much more probable that it would come about thanks to a lucky cast by a Challenger, a natural (or unnatural) disaster, or by magical exhaustion.

"Escape or death," he said, remembering his talk with the Shadow.

For the first time in a long time, the thought of either fate gave Lorn pause. Sasha would one day have to rule this terrifying place alone—at least until his successor was found.

Lorn's quill hovered over the parchment. "It is best that she not become too reliant on me," he murmured and wrote down a final step.

Step three: Ignore her as much as possible.

"Nor should I become too familiar with her," he mused.

To that end, he went back and scratched a line through her name, replacing it with her title. From now on, she would simply be 'the Queen' to him and no more.

"Better," he told himself. "A little distance between us can only be a good thing."

Lorn read over the deceptively simple plan and frowned at how deceptively simple it was.

"The problem," he told himself, "is how to achieve these three steps."

Lorn puzzled over that for a long moment, then went back and added a few notes.

Step one: Locate ~~Sasha~~ the Queen in the Earther Realm *(delegate this task to the Middleton Coven)*.

Step two: Bring her to Between *(ignore the Shadow's suggestions to use charm or any form of pelvic persuasion. Instead, use reason and logic—inform the Queen of the dangers should she remain in her realm. Try to avoid getting everyone imprisoned by the High King while doing it)*.

Step three: Ignore her as much as possible *(do not address or think of her by name; place her lodgings in the tower furthest from my own; be conveniently occupied during meals and at other times when she may expect interaction; literally disappear whenever she is walking toward me, etc.)*.

Lorn reread the list.

"It is a start," he told himself.

As he placed The Queen Plan in his drawer, his fingers brushed against a folded piece of parchment neatly tied with a scrap of frayed, red cloth.

Hesitantly, Lorn withdrew the parchment. He stared at the bundle for a long moment and then untied the binding, the faded fabric coarse against his fingertips. He painstakingly opened the brittle parchment, careful not to tear the fragile, well-folded seams.

It was Lorn's oldest possession: a map of Otherworld, hopelessly outdated and stained with dirt, charcoal, and rust colored smudges. He had stolen it from his captors—his small, nimble fingers easily snatching it from a sagging back pocket—and hidden it inside his tunic. Each night, while his captors slept, Lorn would pore over the map by a stub of candlelight, shielding the light with his thin frame.

Lorn smiled wryly at the Xs scattered around the map, highlighting all the places that his younger self had dreamed of visiting. That is, until he found the X sitting in the middle of Between.

"Well, you got here," he told himself quietly. "And now you cannot leave."

There were words printed carefully on the bottom corner of the map in charcoal, the writing childish and hesitant, smudged and slanted.

When I am free

Beside the words was a rust colored mark the size of his palm.

Tentatively, Lorn reached out and brushed the pads of his fingers over the stain. His magic recognized the old blood and sparked to life.

Almost immediately, Lorn could *feel* the memory—the crush of the crowd surrounding him at all sides ... the sour smell of sweat and ale ... the chants ... the jeers ...

"*Abomination!*"

"*Beast spawn!*"

"*Creature! Creature! Creature!*"

Then, the sharp *crack* of bones and the copper-tang of blood filling his mouth ...

And the fear ... Midra, the *fear*—

"That is enough of that," Lorn told himself firmly, and carefully folded the map back up again, the loose threads of the fragile tie coming away in his hand.

When he was done, Lorn held the package in his palm and marveled. How could something so heavy with memories feel so light? He wondered, not for the first time, why he kept it. He did not need a physical reminder of those dark days. Why not throw it in the fireplace and be done with the past once and for all?

Lorn searched within himself for an answer and felt nothing but a curious reluctance to part with the little map. With a heavy sigh, he placed it back in the drawer.

"Some questions are too large for simple answers," he told himself. "And this question will not be answered today."

Before he closed the drawer, Lorn paused, arrested by the sight of his old map sitting beside The Queen Plan—his past and his future summed up by two pieces of paper in a wooden box.

"You," he told himself, "are not allowed to drink from the decanter ever again. It makes you far too fanciful."

Lorn was about to leave his desk when he caught a glimpse of tomorrow's agenda, laid out on top of a teetering pile of books. Unable to stop himself, he took a glance and rolled his eyes.

"Thirty-nine items," he muttered. "Imagine how many more items will be added once the Queen arrives. Maddox will be positively gleeful."

Lorn paused, horrified by the thought of these future agendas. The Queen would require guidance, protection, training in the ways of Otherworld, instruction on how to rule … the list made his right eye throb.

Step three of The Queen Plan was doomed.

Unless I delegate her care to Maddox, Lorn thought with a brilliant flash of inspiration. *Then I will barely see her. Excellent plan. Well done, me.*

And with step three of The Queen Plan restored, Lorn prepared himself for bed.

Yet, when he finally drifted off to sleep that night, it was not to thoughts of The Queen Plan or of old maps, matrimonial assassination attempts or even the dire consequences of announcing his betrothal to the High King on the morrow.

Instead, what he saw was the expression on Sasha Evangeline Pierce's face when he appeared at the edge of the Wasteland at the end of her run. She had looked up at him with such relief, such pure *joy* that his heart had stuttered in his chest.

No one has ever looked so joyous to see me, Lorn thought to himself as he slipped off into sleep.

Make her joyous to see you, a voice cajoled deep in the recesses of his mind.

Such were the very small crumbs of affection that the Shadow King had received in his life that his heart clutched at that vision of a smile and gave him his sweetest slumber in years.

8

THE ADMINISTRATIVE AFTERMATH

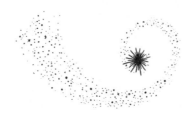

Dawn—an utterly reprehensible time of day—found Lorn meeting with Maddox before leaving for the High King's Gathering of the Summer Alliance Monarchs of the Lower Kingdoms.

"Do we have any idea what this meeting will be about?" Lorn asked as he quickly skimmed the documents that Maddox had laid out for him to sign.

"Yes. We were able to liberate a copy of the agenda from one of the High King's scribes." Maddox placed the agenda in question before Lorn. "Unless there are last minute amendments or new matters arising, it appears that it will be the usual fare of petty grievances and even pettier tax announcements—this time, to fund that ridiculous new trade road."

Lorn glanced over the agenda; it appeared that Maddox was correct. "Marvelous. Several hours of my life that I will never get back."

"Also, the Zadrian ambassador has made an appointment to meet with you. He wishes to raise the issue of a betrothal party sent for your hand—"

"Which has mysteriously become lost somewhere in the Wetlands."

"—*of which we know nothing about*," Maddox reprimanded.

Lorn inclined his head. "Very well. Should he question me about their whereabouts, I shall feign ignorance beautifully. Given the events of last evening, the *alleged* Zadrian betrothal party is now too late." Lorn gazed shrewdly at his chief advisor. "I am surprised that you have not mentioned the new Queen of Between."

Maddox sent Lorn a reproachful look. "I had hoped that you would tell me yourself."

Lorn snorted. "You can stop the act. We both know that you would rather ferret out a secret than hear it directly from me."

"I do not need to ferret out secrets—not anymore. As you well know, the Collection department provides me with a daily report summarizing the findings of all their spies, including the ones posted around the Wasteland. To say that their report was more interesting than usual would be a profound understatement."

"I am sure that it was. It is not every day that a Dreamer takes on the Nightmares and wins."

"True. Their reports are usually filled with stories about people who take on the Nightmares and lose." Maddox shuddered. "So, as you see, my secret ferreting days are no more."

"Do you miss ferreting?"

Maddox sat back in his chair. "It is a younger person's game," he said eventually. "I shall allow the youth to have their fun. I am content to watch from the sidelines."

"It is probably for the best that you retired." Lorn picked up his quill and began to sign the stack of documents. "Our new spies would have nothing to do."

"You flatter me, but there will always be secrets to uncover. Then again, the existence of Her Majesty is not one of them. Her feat has already been immortalized in a song performed at the Weasel late last night."

Lorn blinked. "News travels fast."

"The spies were not the only ones who witnessed Her Majesty's run; there were also a few shepherds passing the boundary wall with a fondness for gossip and ale."

"*Hmm.* Well, I guess that could not be helped. What is the song like?"

"The chorus is catchy enough, and the lute solo is rather stirring. The lyrics, however, leave a lot to be desired. Apparently 'queen' is a problematic rhyme. Comparing her beauty to a 'sprouting bean' was the highlight of the song."

Lorn grimaced and signed the last document with a flourish. "Remind me to avoid the Weasel until they come up with a new tune."

"That is most wise." Maddox gathered up the documents and carefully enclosed them in a leather folder. "When will Her Majesty arrive?"

"Ah, a question for the ages. Unfortunately, I still have to locate her in the Earther Realm."

"No small feat." Maddox's eyes lit up. "I shall put it on your agenda."

"Yes, I am sure that you will," Lorn said curtly.

Maddox ignored Lorn's tone. "To think—we are about to have our first Earther Queen of Between."

"Who would have thought that a magicless Earther woman would cross the Wasteland and win the throne?"

"It *is* odd that it was not someone from Otherworld. Or Faire."

"Either of those would have been a better option." Lorn gestured out the window to the city below. "All of this will be foreign to her. She will require so much training, so much guidance … Just the thought of it is enough to give me a headache of epic proportions."

"Perhaps you should look on the bright side? A swamp beast could have crossed the Wasteland in a dream. Or a Death Cultist. Or even the Minotaur whom you hugged last evening."

Lorn pinched the bridge of his nose. "For the record, *I* was not the one who initiated that hug."

Maddox's lips twitched. "If you say so, Your Majesty. And before you ask, your singing partner is fine; we winched his drunken hide out of the sinkhole, just as you requested. Apparently, he did not even notice that he had fallen in."

"A glorious side effect of Between's ale, no doubt," Lorn said dryly. "If you could perhaps—"

"Look into finding a suitable companion for the sodden fellow? I have already sent out scouts."

"Many thanks. I—"

There was a sudden *crack*, followed by the sound of stone grating upon stone. Both men looked up as a stream of gold dust fell merrily from a brand-new hole in the ceiling.

"Will you get that?" Maddox asked blandly. "Or should I just get a bucket?"

Lorn waved his hand and sealed the breach in the ceiling. With another wave of his hand, the gold dust that had fallen onto the floor rose in a spiral and flew obediently out the open window.

"Nicely done," Maddox murmured. "What about the rest of it?"

Lorn looked up at the hole-free ceiling, and then down at the now clean floor. "Whatever do you mean?"

Maddox pointed to the gold dust that had fallen around the objects on Lorn's desk. Then, to Lorn's horror, he continued pointing … to the dust settled amongst the curtain folds and pooled on the rugs, to the specks of it scattered across the tops of all the furniture, and to the mounds of gold dust piled precariously on top of the rafters.

Lorn grimaced at the mess. "It is not as if we can get rid of it entirely; it is magical residue. More of it will come with each spell … or Crossing … or magical act. Trying to clean it away is an exercise in futility. Do you think the Queen will notice it?"

"Yes. And the cobwebs, too." Maddox gestured toward the cobwebs festooned between the rafters and nestled amongst the curtains and tapestries. "But only after she notices the stains on the flagstones." He nodded at a mid-sized orange stain on the floor beside Lorn's desk.

Lorn looked at the floor and frowned. "I cannot remember how that got there. Was it during the explosion last May?"

"August," Maddox corrected. "The flood was in May. Moreover, I believe that there is a creature nested somewhere in the walls of this room. The spies stationed behind the secret panels have complained about the smell."

"We named him Terrance," a voice called out from behind one of the secret wall panels in question.

"Spies are neither to be seen *nor* to be heard," Lorn told the wall sternly.

"Sorry, Majesty," the voice said, contrite. "Won't happen again."

A strange, animal-like whine came from behind a different secret wall panel.

"That goes for you too, Terrance," Lorn said dryly.

"We'll keep an eye on him," the voice behind the wall said.

"As I was saying," Maddox continued as if the previous interruption had not happened, "Terrance will need to be removed from the wall on hygiene grounds alone. And there is—"

"*Please.*" Lorn held up his hands in surrender. "Enough. It is obvious that we need to clean this place up as quickly as possible."

His usually unflappable advisor looked uneasy. "I believe that is beyond even my considerable talents. With the castle constantly shifting, we are in a neverending state of chaos. Whatever we clean becomes filthy within moments; whatever we fix breaks within days—"

"Yes. I am well aware." Lorn sighed. "But regardless, we should try to look our best. In honor of the Queen, let us give the castle a thorough cleaning."

Maddox stared at him blankly.

"Possibly just the main rooms?" Lorn amended.

Maddox's expression became, if possible, *blanker.*

"Or perhaps we could ask Agatha to clean all the staircases rather than just the one at the entrance?" Lorn suggested. "That is, assuming that we can keep the fish out of her bucket ..."

Maddox winced, which was somehow even worse than his blank look. "Agatha, as you well know, is a member of a union. Extending her workload will involve negotiations—"

"Do it. And perhaps we could hire some more staff?"

"New staff has been hard to come by; people still remember what happened to the old staff. The only reason Agatha remains is that she is practically invincible."

This time, Lorn winced. "But what happened to the old staff was an accident, a once-in-a-lifetime event—"

"That has happened twice this year alone. Both times on a Wednesday."

"Damn Wednesdays," Lorn muttered. He threw his hands in the air in surrender, knowing a lost cause when he saw it. "At the very least, we will need to assign the Queen chambers befitting her station." He paused, remembering step three of The Queen Plan. "As far away from mine as possible."

To Lorn's relief, Maddox nodded, albeit slowly. "I believe that is well within possibility. Perhaps you could speak to the castle and ask it to keep Her Majesty's chambers in the same position—at least until she becomes accustomed to the eccentricities of the castle?"

Lorn nodded. "Prepare the room, and I shall do my best to talk some sense into this place. Whilst I am at it, I suppose I should do something about that stain." Lorn gestured to one of many rugs scattered around the room. Obediently, the carpet slid across the floor ... revealing an even larger orange stain beneath it. Lorn pinched the bridge of his nose between thumb and forefinger and moved the carpet back. "The lesser of two evils ..."

"My personal motto," Maddox said. "I shall order more rugs."

"Large ones, if you please."

Maddox opened his ever-present notebook, took out a pencil, and began a new list. "In accordance with the standard royal Joining contract, we are to provide Her Majesty with all the trappings of her position: clothing, jewels, gowns for the coronation—"

"Let us wait on those until she comes to Between; she can select what she wishes based on her preferences."

Maddox's lips quirked. "I believe the wording in the Joining vows states that you, personally, are responsible for her clothing and personal effects."

Lorn gestured to his customary black attire. "Do you really think that *I* should be the one to purchase her wardrobe? Good gods, what has the poor woman done to deserve *that?*"

"True, Between does not need two sinister looking monarchs. I will consult our legal advisors and see if you are permitted to delegate the task."

"Many thanks. Tell them that I would prefer to give Her Majesty a sack of gold and have her purchase whatever she wants."

Maddox made a note in his book. "A sack of gold—truly the path to marital bliss. Speaking of the Joining contract, I will have our scribes draw one up. Is Her Majesty aware of the … happy news of her Joining?"

Lorn snorted—*happy*. "Not as yet. And frankly, I am not looking forward to telling her. I doubt that any woman, regardless of where she resides, would take kindly to being informed that she has been betrothed to a stranger by a sentient kingdom."

"Perhaps the news will be sweetened once she hears that she is entitled to three boons for besting the Nightmares in their domain. I wonder what she will ask for?"

"Most likely to go home."

Wisely, Maddox let that drop. "Will you contact the Middleton Coven to assist you in your search for Her Majesty?"

"As soon as I return. With any luck, the Portal will remain closed now that the Dreamer has become the Queen." Lorn grimaced. "I would like to give Her Majesty a few more hours before confronting her with the terrifying reality of her new position."

"That is very generous of you. Then again, it also allows you to stretch out the remaining moments of your bachelorhood."

"A happy side effect of my generosity."

"You will also need to go to the Summoning Chamber to acquire Her Majesty's gifts."

Lorn had been dreading that task.

"Yes," he said with little enthusiasm.

Maddox arched one eyebrow but said nothing. "And you will need to appoint guards to protect Her Majesty once she enters Between."

That was an easier task.

"I was thinking of the Elite. Felzik gets positively itchy if he has nothing meaningful to do."

Maddox nodded and quickly jotted down a few notes. "An excellent suggestion. I believe the Elite is still surveying the southern border. I shall send a message to them immediately." He paused. "Should I inform them that Her Majesty will require rudimentary defense training?"

That poor, doomed woman, Lorn thought. "More than rudimentary, if she is to survive the daily catastrophes in this place. Please ask Felzik to meet with me to discuss what will be required."

"Very well." Maddox jotted another note in his book and then hesitated, his pencil poised above the parchment. "The Zadrians will be displeased about your upcoming marriage. They may choose to remedy the situation by *removing* the impediment to your bachelorhood."

Lorn nodded slowly. "It had crossed my mind. We must keep Her Majesty out of their clutches."

"But of course. Then again, the Death Cultists may choose not to kill her—they may instead try to recruit her to their cause, thereby taking the throne by stealth."

"True, though I doubt Her Majesty would be amenable to joining a cult that enjoys necromancy and sacrificial rituals. Then again, she may have morbid taste in hobbies." Lorn shrugged. "I suppose we shall soon find out."

Maddox inclined his head, but his brow remained furrowed. "Even without the Death Cultists, Her Majesty may still pose a threat to your throne; she may choose to Challenge you for sole rulership of Between."

Lorn barked out a surprised laugh. "I do not know which part of your statement is more preposterous: the idea of a magicless Earther Challenging me for sole rulership, or the idea that she would *want* to rule this terrible place by herself."

But Maddox's brow remained furrowed. "Technically, it could happen. And the consequences would be rather ... terrible for Her Majesty."

Lorn immediately sobered. His last Challenge still weighed heavily on his mind. He was beyond grateful that the Radish King had chosen to duel a tree. If he had not, Lorn would have had no choice but to fight him. The outcome would have been dreadful for the Radish King and devastating to Lorn's conscience. To fight a magicless Earther would be far worse.

Unwillingly, Lorn remembered the Queen reaching out to save him during their first encounter and *smiling* at him during their second.

Far worse? Lorn thought with a sinking heart. *The consequences would be unbearable.*

"Then she must not be allowed to Challenge," Lorn said firmly. "Maddox, if Her Majesty even so much as *looks* as though she is about to utter the word 'Challenge,' you have standing orders to lock her in her chambers until she sees the error of her ways. Do it politely, of course,

with the utmost respect for her position and personhood, etcetera, etcetera
..."

"Kidnapping and incarceration," Maddox recited, writing the words in
his notebook. "Not the ways I had anticipated serving my Queen, but I
have noted them for the record."

"Excellent." Lorn looked around the room. "Is there anything else that
requires my attention before I leave?"

Maddox handed Lorn a thick envelope. "The Kings of Vetch have
invited you to the Kingdom of Vetch Seven-Day Winter Solstice Bacchanal
Extravaganza. And yes, that is the official name."

"And what a fancy name it is for an orgy." Lorn opened the envelope.
"Why not call it that and save money on the printing? Printers charge by
the letter, you know, and their costs are exorbitant."

"I shall keep that in mind when drafting your Joining invitations. Would
'Man Joins Woman' suffice?"

"Cheap and to the point. I approve."

The invitation from Vetch was neither cheap nor to the point. It was a
gorgeous confection of white silk cardstock, glittery white stones, and
extravagant silver lettering. As Lorn removed it from the envelope, a shower
of white glitter fell to the table, and the lush scent of exotic oils filled the
chamber.

Lorn tsked. "So wretchedly melodramatic." He sniffed. "And redolent
with aphrodisiacs. My, my—how tawdry."

Wordlessly, Maddox stood up and opened the shutters. "Shall I accept
on your behalf?"

Lorn tossed the invitation out of the nearest window. "As usual, it is a
resounding *no* from me. This is one of the few times that I am grateful to be
tethered to a kingdom."

"Technically, your tether allows you to be away from Between for three
days."

"And as much as I long to be free of this place, I am still declining this
invitation. Which says something, does it not?"

Maddox returned to his seat and frowned disapprovingly at the white
glitter scattered over the table. "It seems that an invitation from Vetch
appears every month."

"The Kings of Vetch are trying to lure me to their kingdom."

"Any guesses as to why? A trap, perhaps?"

"If their trap is anything like their fashions, then it is bound to be both
garish and capable of causing extreme retinal discomfort." Lorn stood and
brushed glitter from his tunic. "Well, if that is all, I will be off. Before I

leave, I shall ask the eternal question: Have you found a way to free me from Between?"

"Unfortunately, not. But I am trying."

"That is all I ask. Well, wish me luck—I am about to inform the High King that we have acquired an Earther Queen."

Maddox blinked. "Before you have located her? And knowing full well that the High King will undoubtedly order you to bring her back as soon as possible?"

"Yes and yes."

"*Hmm* … an interesting strategy. I shall ready the city's defenses just in case it all goes terribly wrong."

"Oh, it will," Lorn said and left the chamber.

9

THE JOLLY MONARCHS OF THE LOWER KINGDOMS

It was a long-standing decree that the monarchs of the Summer Alliance—the thirteen kingdoms of Otherworld that united after the Most Terrible War—were to meet with the High King to discuss matters of importance to their kingdoms and to Otherworld itself. The monarchs of the Upper Kingdoms of Vetch, Dox, Siddle, Nook, and Vale met with him twice per year. The monarchs of the Lower Kingdoms of Between, Dragaz, Neeth, Trundel, Vahlora, Aurora, and The Ranges, however, were expected to meet with him quarterly.

This was not because the Lower Kingdoms were of greater importance —far from it. Rather, they earned the High King's attention because they were the most troublesome. If there were a plague or war or terrible disaster that threatened the safety of the realm, then the High King would be able to guess—with unnerving accuracy—that the problem had most likely originated in the Lower Kingdoms (and probably in Between).

Some of the Lower Kingdoms were troublesome because they were magical by nature. Between, of course, was a cesspool filled with gateways to other realms and wild magic. Dragaz, the Dragonian Kingdom, was inhabited, as the name suggested, by hordes of dragons which were magical, temperamental, and capable of raining fiery death on all those unfortunate enough to be standing below them. And Neeth, the Wraith Kingdom, was populated by Nightmares, demons, and other creatures of mist and magic that had a terrible habit of breaking free of the wards around their lands in order to go on adventures—adventures that typically led to chaos, and screaming, and madness.

The other Lower Kingdoms were primarily vexing because of their people. The citizens of Trundel, the Dwarven Kingdom, tended to be drunken, lusty, belligerent, and armed with axes, which made them wonderful companions in a bar-fight and terrible guests at afternoon teas. Whereas the citizens of Vahlora, the Elven Kingdom, tended to be elitist, thanks to their ancient ties to the formidable fae kingdoms, and utterly dull to be around, thanks to their adherence to strict codes of honor and etiquette. These character flaws could have been overlooked if they did not write poetry—*terrible* poetry—that they willfully foisted upon all within earshot. Their poetry was so dreadful that 'poetry recitation' was recognized as the leading cause of death for elves outside of Vahlora.

To the High King's great relief, two Lower Kingdoms were not troublesome at all. Aurora, 'The Golden Kingdom,' was filled with peaceful, good-natured folk who excelled at art, music, animal husbandry, and food preparation. They were universally loved, except by the elves, who refused to acknowledge that Aurorean poetry was far better than their own. Even Aurora's closest neighbors, the nefarious Betweeners, thought the Auroreans were "a good sort," and tried not to rob them more than strictly necessary.

The Ranges was another non-bothersome kingdom, mostly because it was surrounded by mountain ranges and ice lakes and thus isolated from the chaos around it. It was also tiny and cold, which meant that its small population tended to indulge in solitary activities, like ice fishing and cross-stitch, and did most of their heavy drinking at home.

Unfortunately, Aurora and The Ranges were not enough of a positive influence to subdue the chaos inflicted by the other Lower Kingdoms. The High King's predecessors had found that frequent meetings tamed the flamboyance of some of the catastrophes—if not their frequency—and the current High King had no intention of making his reign infinitely more difficult by changing this ritual.

Hence, High King Dresden enforced the quarterly meetings for the good of Otherworld.

So it was that Lorn found himself at Southern Keep, the traditional meeting place of the Lower Kingdom monarchs. Southern Keep was an austere, gray stone tower tucked away in the southernmost part of the Summer Kingdom, the seat of the High King and Queen. It was close enough to a gateway to ensure that the monarchs could travel quickly between the meeting and their kingdoms, and far away enough from anything of value to ensure that any damage done by the monarchs during the meeting would not be too expensive.

Each monarch was allowed to bring four guards or attendants to the meeting. Lorn chose, as always, to bring the imps. Izzy, Setzl, and the imp with the small notebook trailed in the wake of Lorn's Cloak of Shadows, looking around their surroundings with a practiced eye.

"I believe we are the first to arrive," Lorn said.

"Good. More time for sneaking," Izzy said, rubbing his hands together.

"Well, that is the idea." Lorn stared up at the tower and grimaced. "I would rather chew glass than attend this meeting."

"We've tried that," Izzy said.

"Glass chewing," Setzl clarified.

"*So* crunchy," the imp with the small notebook said, shaking his head at the memory.

Lorn looked incredulously down at the imps. "Why, in Midra's name, did you do that?"

"We were drunk," the imp with the small notebook said.

"I would hate to think that you would try that sober." Lorn walked up to the entrance of the tower and paused. "And as much as I would like to question you further, we will have to pursue this conversation about your drunken mastication habits another time."

"Wise," Izzy said. "It'll take a while."

"I am sure," Lorn said. "I take it that you are sufficiently sober this morning to do your jobs?"

Izzy snorted. "We're *professionals*."

"Gotta be sober to eavesdrop and sneak," the imp with the small notebook said.

Setzl sighed happily. "My favorite things!"

"See you upstairs, Boss," Izzy said.

With a *crack*, the three imps disappeared.

For a moment, Lorn was tempted to follow them. With a click of his fingers, he could have transported himself straight into the meeting chamber; with a simple thought—and the right kind of flick of his wrist—he could have flown to the tower window, swift as a bird.

But he did not.

Lorn knew firsthand that *this* High King did not take well to displays of magic.

Or to magic folk in general.

Or to him in particular, Lorn thought wryly, as he began the long climb up the broad, winding staircase.

Lorn shook off that thought and the feeling it inspired—something prickly and itchy, composed of rejection and bewilderment and the sour taste of something very close to betrayal—and strode quickly up the remaining steps until he stood at the entranceway.

A throat cleared to his left.

"His Majesty, King Lorn, of Between," the crier announced to the room—a room that was empty except for a handful of servants and guards, all dressed in the white and gold livery of the Summer Palace.

"Yes," Lorn said dryly to the bowing servants and guards. "It is me. In all my glory. Stellar work as always, Reginald." He looked around the austere, gray stone room. "I see that the High King still does not trust us with extraneous bits of furniture."

Reginald, the High King's official crier, also looked around the room. "That is correct, Your Majesty. After the ... ah ... *incident* ... that took place last meeting, there are only the essentials."

He gestured to the semi-circular table in the center of the room, and the seven ornate thrones placed around the table's curved edge. The most ostentatious throne—the seat of the High King—had been set against the straight side of the table, flanked by two smaller chairs reserved for the High King's Right and Left Hands. There were also a handful of plain, wooden chairs and tables lined up for the scribes and other servants. But aside from those, not a single ornament—not a portrait or trinket, cushion or curtain—livened up the room.

"Probably wise," Lorn said.

He nodded to the crier and strode past the servants—most of whom flinched as he approached. Lorn recognized two of them as spies from the Academy of Practical Arts; he passed them without pause and took his place on the replica Shadow Throne of Between—a throne carved from polished black obsidian and decorated with mirror shards.

"Will I ever escape this damn uncomfortable chair?" he muttered, trying in vain to find the least torturous position.

One of the servants respectfully handed him the agenda for today's meeting. With a sigh, Lorn unrolled the parchment and quickly scanned the contents, checking to see if it was the same agenda that Maddox had presented him with earlier.

"You *do* know that it is terrible form to get here early, do you not?" a deep, male voice called out from the doorway. "One might assume that you are trying to kiss the High King's rotund buttocks."

"His Royal Highness, Crown Prince Ashlyn, of Aurora," the crier announced.

Lorn looked up as Ash—clad in ceremonial bronze armor, his red velvet cloak set at a jaunty angle across his broad shoulders—clasped the crier's shoulder in welcome. He then crossed the room and sat down beside Lorn on the gold throne designated for the ruler of Aurora.

"Your assessment of the High King's buttocks is both disturbing and revelatory," Lorn said. He watched, bemused, as Ash arranged his cloak so that it draped in the most flattering way possible. "You *do* realize that you look like a Crutzelfest ornament in that ensemble, do you not?"

Ash laughed. "Crutzelfest is a joyous time of year—I am happy for the comparison. Far better than looking like an undertaker." He gestured toward Lorn's sinister attire.

"If it is any consolation, you both look equally idiotic."

"His Majesty, King Trevelyan, of the Ranges," the crier announced.

The King of the Ranges gave both men an appraising look as he walked haltingly toward his throne, his tall frame leaning heavily on a silver cane. A giant, tawny-coated hound, her features almost foxlike, stalked by his side, her bearing just as regal as her owner's.

Lorn gave an exaggerated sigh. "Not all of us possess your innate majesty and poise, Trevelyan."

Ash clutched his chest in feigned distress. "You wound us, Trev."

Trevelyan waved away Ash's comment. "I do not mean to wound, merely to educate you younger folk with the wisdom that I have gained as the ruler of a kingdom that exports textiles. I am particularly well versed in sartorial trends ... whether I wish to be or not."

"Your kingdom also exports fish," Lorn said, as the older man approached the throne beside Ash's. "Are you as well versed in fish?"

"The things I know about fish would make you shudder; let us never speak of the subject again." Trevelyan spared a glance down at his ornate, silver armor. "Now, silver is classic. Regal. *Understated*. An excellent choice for a king."

"True," Lorn acknowledged. "You do look exceptionally regal."

"And understated," Ash said. "Even the touch of blue is in keeping with your regal, understated, look."

He gestured to Trevelyan's shoulder length, white hair—a sign of his elf ancestry—which was streaked with cobalt blue and held back in a queue at the nape of his neck.

Lorn nodded solemnly. "Indeed. You are a sartorial inspiration to us all."

"Teach us your ways," Ash said.

Leaning on the table for support, Trevelyan pointed his cane at the two men. "Enough flattery. Any moment now, Ash will comment on the rotundness of my buttocks." He placed his cane back on the floor and gave a cursory look around the room. "Is it just me, or is there even less furniture than the last time? I could have sworn there was a bookcase at the last meeting."

"It appears that we are being punished," Lorn said.

"We should probably enjoy our thrones while we still have them," Ash said.

With a grimace, Trevelyan lowered himself slowly onto the polished, gray throne of the Ranges. His attendants rushed to help him, but he waved them away.

"Impossible." Trevelyan gestured for his hound to sit at the ground by his side. The hound obeyed, placing her large head on his knee. "There are times when I curse my predecessors for creating a solid marble throne. You would need a spine of gelatin to find this ungodly rock comfortable."

Lorn gestured to his throne. "Try sitting on rock and mirror shards."

"Gold is not much cozier," Ash said, banging on the armrest of the Aurorean throne with his gauntlet.

Trevelyan inclined his head in acknowledgment. "I do so hope that whoever crafted them is rotting merrily away in the Hell Realm."

"Now *that* is something to drink to," Ash said.

The servants sprang into action, quickly filling up goblets and placing them before each monarch.

Trevelyan raised an eyebrow at Lorn. "*Shall* we drink?"

The emphasis was deliberate. Lorn raised his cup to his lips and opened his senses, searching the wine for potions and poisons. After a moment— after he was *sure*—he raised his goblet in a toast.

"Cheers," he said and took a sip. The two other men quickly followed suit.

Ash smacked his lips together appreciatively. "*Ahh*, it is the good stuff!"

"Damn," Trev said.

"Agreed," Lorn said. "This is bound to be a dreadful meeting."

"Perhaps not," Ash said, ever optimistic. "The High King may simply be bestowing his largess upon us in gratitude for keeping the Lower Kingdoms in such fine form."

"Speak for your own kingdom," Lorn said. "No, it is more likely that the High King is trying to distract us from how terrible this meeting is going to be."

Ash rolled his eyes. "What a dreary pronouncement! How can you be so sure that this meeting is bound for disaster?"

Suddenly, the sound of trumpets blared from the base of the tower.

"I rest my case," Lorn said, and took a long drink from his goblet.

Trev groaned. "I had forgotten that *he* would be here." He glanced at the empty throne at the opposite end of the table—a breathtaking construction of pure white crystal—and grimaced. "During this meeting, he will inevitably do or say something offensive, and I will be forced to walk over to him and cuff him around his ears, just as I did when he was a child—"

"Simpler times," Ash said.

"A golden age," Lorn agreed.

"Indeed," Trev said. "But now that he is the official representative of the elven Crown, I doubt that the High King would approve of such behavior."

Lorn shrugged. "Well, perhaps not in public ..."

"Trev is right," Ash said. "After the last ... ah ... *incident* ... the High King has become less tolerant of such lapses in protocol. Trev will be issued with a formal complaint and a summons to the Summer Palace—"

"Followed by some form of tedious punishment that I would prefer to avoid, and an insincere apology that I have no wish to give," Trev finished. "So, I am relying on you both to reign me in; if I look as though I am about to yield to temptation, stop me."

"You can count on us," Ash said.

The sound of horns grew louder.

"I make no promises," Lorn said, and took another drink.

"Perhaps we are too hard on him," Ash said.

The other men groaned.

Ash held up a hand. "Come, now; hear me out. He is only young, not even eighteen. Much of what we find so detestable about him may simply be the brashness of youth. His father is tolerant and wise—"

"Unlike most of the people that he rules," Trev said.

"Here, here," Lorn said.

Ash inclined his head in agreement. "And kind—as is his mother. I am sure that, in time, he will display similar wisdom and kindness. It is in his blood."

"Get off my cloak, you moronic troll, or I will have you *flogged*," a strident male voice yelled from the staircase.

"Perhaps he is adopted," Lorn said.

At that moment, two elven horn players—looking somewhat winded from their climb up the stairs—appeared in the entranceway. Taking a deep breath, they began to play a tune that was both boldly triumphant and terribly off key.

As the song reached a crescendo, the two horn players stepped aside to reveal a tall, slender man clothed in pure white armor and a plush, white velvet cloak. A white crystal crown completed his ensemble. The young elven man surveyed the room haughtily, his eyes the flawless ice blue of glacial lakes, his skin the pale perfection of newly fallen snow. As he turned his head, his white hair settled across his shoulders like cornsilk.

Overall, he looked like an extremely attractive icicle.

"His Royal Highness, Crown Prince Varran, of Vahlora," the crier announced.

"*And?*" the crown prince demanded, his lovely features twisting into a sneer.

The crier looked puzzled. "*And*, Your Highness?"

"Here we go," Trev said under his breath.

"What of my other titles?" the prince asked, tapping one white, leather boot impatiently against the stone floor.

"Ah, the brashness of youth," Lorn said, with a knowing look at Ash.

Ash shrugged apologetically and took a long sip of his wine.

"I am sorry, Your Highness," the crier said, bowing, "but the High King requested that I only announce primary titles—to ensure equality, you understand." He leaned toward the prince conspiratorially. "If I may say, Your Highness, not all are as well-endowed with titles as yourself."

The prince nodded, somewhat appeased. "True. Still, I shall speak to the High King about this breach in protocol."

"Marvelous," Lorn said. "We will spend the entirety of the next meeting in the entranceway, waiting to be announced."

The elf prince turned toward Lorn, his sneer becoming even more pronounced. "*Sorcerer*," he bit out.

"Hello, Varran," Lorn said pleasantly.

The elf's sneer faltered in the face of Lorn's agreeableness but returned with gusto when he saw Trevelyan. He raised his chin and cleared his throat.

"*Gentlemen*," he said, beginning what was obviously a rehearsed speech, "I would wish you good day." He raised his chin even higher. "However, it would be—"

"You have something on your armor," Trev announced.

Varran looked shocked at the interruption.

"On your left shoulder," Ash supplied helpfully.

"There is also a little something above your codpiece," Lorn added, gesturing vaguely toward the prince's crotch.

Trev tsked and turned to Ash and Lorn. "One of the unfortunate consequences of wearing all white. It is impressive, but *so* difficult to keep clean."

Varran looked down at his armor and blanched. Quickly, he turned and gestured to his attendants to assist him. There was much whispering and rubbing until finally, the elf prince turned back to face the three men, considerably more flustered than he had been before.

He flicked a long strand of platinum hair from his face, straightened his shoulders, and took a breath. "Gentlemen, I would wish——"

"You are welcome," Trev interrupted once again.

"It was our pleasure," Ash added.

"Really, do not even mention it," Lorn said with a magnanimous wave of his hand.

The prince's face turned a rather unflattering shade of red. "My thanks," he bit out. He lifted his chin again. "As I was saying, I would wish you good day. However——"

"Get out of the way, boy—you're blocking the entrance," barked a voice from the stairwell.

The crier cleared his throat. "His Majesty, King Medas, of Trundel."

Varran started and looked over his shoulder.

Sure enough, behind him was the dwarven king. For the leader of a people who were renowned for their gaudy ways, Medas was surprisingly nondescript in appearance. Unlike his burly attendants, he was lean and clean-shaven, his dark hair cut close to his scalp beneath his red-gold crown, his leather and bronze armor practical rather than ostentatious. Like most of his people, Medas was short in stature, but he made up for it by wielding a very large ceremonial axe, which he now brandished threateningly at the elven prince's kneecaps.

Wisely, the two horn players quickly vacated the doorway, as did Varran, albeit more grudgingly.

"*Thank you*," Medas said. "Let's remember that we can't go around blocking entranceways. That's how people typically get stabbed with axes."

"Might I suggest *chopped* by axes?" Trev asked.

Medas shrugged and circled the table to his throne—a bejeweled monstrosity made of red gold.

"That would do, too," he said, seating himself. "As long as someone gets injured for entrance-blocking, I'm happy. It is a *safety* issue, people."

Ash smiled. "How go the mines, Medas?"

The dwarven king squinted down at the agenda, which a servant had placed before him, and grimaced. "I would rather be trapped in one than be at this meeting." One of his attendants handed him a pair of glasses, which he put on with a sigh. "No offense to you all."

"We all feel the same way," Trev said.

"I *had* contemplated setting fire to the tower," Lorn said.

"Well, at least there is a contingency plan." Medas scanned the room. "Still no furnishings?"

"Note the lack of curtain rods," Trev said.

Medas smirked. "Pity. But not surprising." His eyes narrowed as a servant poured wine into his goblet. He looked over to Lorn—who gave him a subtle nod—before taking a sip. "Damn, it's the good stuff."

"Our thoughts exactly," Trev said.

Medas looked meaningfully toward Varran, who was petulantly unrolling his agenda, clearly upset that his prepared speech had been interrupted.

"It's insufficient compensation," he muttered, taking a long drink.

"What isss?" a sibilant female voice hissed from the entrance.

For a moment, it was difficult to see where the voice had come from; four ghostly figures gowned in gray, cowled robes blocked the entrance. They appeared to be levitating, the hems of their robes drifting back and forth along the stone floor in a non-existent breeze.

The crier swallowed heavily, his eyes wide. "Her Majesty, Lyssandra, of Neeth," he announced, his tone hushed.

The gray figures moved silently aside, revealing the wraith queen, who surveyed the room unblinkingly. She was tall and unnaturally slender, her long limbs reminiscent of a praying mantis. Her skin was talc white, her lips stained crimson, as were the talons on each of her overly long fingers. Her hair—midnight-black with thick, red streaks—was elaborately teased so that it seemed to tower above her, the strands interwoven with tiny bones and thin, snow-white feathers that matched those on her white gown.

It was her eyes, however, that were her most arresting feature. Fringed with sooty black lashes, they were as black as pitch, both pupil and iris, their depths as fathomless as the dark oceans of Xenitha that bordered her kingdom—oceans that hid terrible monsters and dragged sailors to their doom.

"Good wine in exchange for terrible company," Lorn answered. He smiled broadly at Lyssandra. "Your presence shall improve the situation immeasurably, Your Majesty."

"Immeasurably!" Ash agreed magnanimously, as he stood and executed a flawless bow.

"As always," Trev concurred.

Lyssandra shot them a skeptical look as she floated across the room, her blood-red cloak trailing behind her like a fresh kill.

"Flatterersss," she hissed, though she sounded pleased.

Her eyes narrowed at Varran, who was so wrapped up in tearing the bottom of his agenda that he had missed her entrance. Within a flash, she appeared behind Varran's right shoulder, her lips beside his ear. "Kneel, pretty princeling or I will drain you dry," she said menacingly, baring her long, white fangs.

The prince jumped in shock and promptly fell off his throne, landing at the queen's feet.

"Better," she said, satisfied, and took her seat beside the elven prince on a dark throne made of crystal and mist.

Varran remained on the floor, breathing heavily in shock.

"For—forgive me, Your Majesty," he stammered, his lips against the ground. "I did not see you arrive."

Lyssandra touched the heel of her boot against the elf's paler-than-usual cheek. "Inattention can be deadly, pretty princeling." She languidly dragged her heel across his jawline before placing her foot back on the ground. "Keep your eyesss open."

Cautiously, Varran stood up and gave her a florid, albeit shaky, bow. "Thank you for the instruction, Your Majesty."

"It's been an educational experience all 'round today, hasn't it, Varran?" Medas said.

Varran ignored him, and sat unsteadily back on his throne, favoring the side furthest away from Lyssandra.

"Commander Alia, of the Dragonian Forces," the crier announced as a wiry woman climbed nimbly up the final steps of the staircase and stepped into the entranceway.

"Thank you, Reginald," Alia said. She surveyed the room with a smile. "Your Majesties, Your Highnesses."

She gracefully pulled aside the heavy fabric of her cloak and bowed. As she stood, her cloak fell away from her bare arms, revealing scars that ran from the crest of her shoulder down to her wrist, stark and shiny-white against her olive skin. Intricate gold bracelets curled around each of her muscular arms just below the bicep, highlighting rather than covering the old wounds. The gold matched the breastplate on her green, dragonhide armor, the iridescent scales catching the light as she entered the room.

"Welcome, Alia!" Ash said. "What an unexpected pleasure to see you!"

Trev frowned. "Is Dragma not coming?"

"She is having *words* with one of her attendants," Alia said with an exasperated sigh. "I thought I should come up ahead and warn you that the Supreme Ruler of the Dragonian Kingdom is, for want of a more apt term, *in season.*"

"Hells," Medas swore.

Alia inclined her head in agreement, her long, black braids swinging with the movement. "As we all know, this makes Her Majesty somewhat more ... tempestuous ... than usual in all respects."

"It's like throwing mead on a bonfire," Medas said.

" 'In all respects?' Whatever does that mean?" Varran asked.

"She's angry and horny as hell," Medas clarified.

Varran stared at him in shock, unable to form a reply.

"Perhaps we should moderate our talk of carnal matters in present company," Trev said to Medas, noting Varran's expression.

"It *is* rather early in the day," Lorn said.

Medas patted Varran kindly on the back. "I'll hold off on the truly ribald stuff until noon."

The prince shrugged him off. "Your vulgarity knows no bounds." He turned to Trev with a sneer. "There is no need to patronize me; I am *well* acquainted with carnal matters." He glanced at the empty Dragonian throne, his cheeks beginning to flush. "Just ... not those pertaining to the Dragon Queen."

"Best not get her attention, pretty princeling," Lyssandra warned. "She will sap you dry." She dragged her black tongue across the tips of her razor-sharp teeth and then sharply sucked in a breath, making Varran jump.

"Surely you jest," Varran said shakily.

"Oh, no," Lorn smirked. "That is an accurate description. Think of it as a glorious entry into manhood ... followed by exhaustion, dehydration and probable death."

The prince blanched even further.

"You seemed to have survived the experience," Trev said to Lorn.

Lorn shrugged. "I am a little more resilient than most."

Varran stared at Lorn with wide eyes and a touch of admiration.

"So," Alia continued, "unless you *want* to test your sexual endurance—or to be beaten to a pulp with your own forearm—I would suggest not arousing or antagonizing her respectively."

"Barzel's fiery ass, Alia—are you *warning* them? Whose side are you on, anyway?"

"Her Majesty, Queen Dragma, of Dragaz," the crier announced and quickly moved away from the door.

The woman in the entrance was as tall as Lorn, as muscular as Ash, and looked as though she could easily snap Varran in half with her bare hands. She marched into the room as if it was a battle arena, her golden eyes flashing, tiny flames licking the ends of her long, red hair.

The princes stood and bowed as the dragon queen passed, her green and gold dragonhide cloak rustling like dry leaves as it dragged across the flagstones. Lorn collected the end of the cloak and held it as Dragma settled on the bone and dragonscale throne, the air around her crackling with white hot energy. Once the queen was seated, Lorn placed it neatly on the floor beside her boots.

"Such manners," she purred as Lorn took her hand and placed a careful kiss across her knuckles before returning to his throne to her right. She smoothed down the folds of her dragonhide tunic. "Perhaps it *is* best that Alia warned you; it would have been a shame to have accidentally killed one of you."

"But of course," Trev agreed. "It ensures that we are all on our best behavior." He beckoned one of the servants, who quickly filled Dragma's goblet.

Ash took a chair from the far side of the room and placed it at the dragon queen's right hand. He bowed floridly at Alia and gestured for her to sit.

"I agree," Alia said, arranging herself on the chair. "The service is definitely better when you warn them that their lives are at stake. Thank you, Prince Ashlyn."

"I serve to live," Ash said with a wink and went back to his throne.

"How are you faring?" Medas asked Dragma, eying her with concern.

"I feel itchy," she grumbled. She skimmed her long, black nails across the iridescent skin of her throat. "And hungry. And stabby."

"Have a drink," Trev said soothingly. "It is the good stuff."

Dragma groaned. "Not the good stuff!" Nevertheless, she took the goblet and drank deeply. Once she had drained it dry, she slammed the goblet on the table, wiping her mouth across her forearm.

"Better?" Lyssandra asked, looking at Dragma admiringly.

The dragon queen shrugged. "Maybe after ten more of those."

Trev again beckoned the servant. "Keep Her Majesty's cup full."

The wide-eyed man took one look at the talons drumming restlessly against the wooden table and quickly refilled Dragma's goblet.

"So," she barked, "where is he? If he's not here soon, I vote we start without him."

"Your loyalty is without peer, Dragma," the High King said dryly.

"All rise for His Royal Majesty, High King Dresden, of the Summer Alliance," the Crier announced

Looking at the man standing in the doorway, one could have been forgiven for thinking that Reginald—excellent crier that he was—had accidentally announced the wrong person. This man did not look like a High King, the supreme ruler of twelve kingdoms—thirteen, counting his own. Rather, this man looked like a retired soldier wearing a borrowed crown. Beneath his gold armor, the man's physique was muscular and spare from decades of fights and drills; his complexion sun-browned from years spent outdoors rather than languishing within castle walls. His nose was slightly crooked from a badly set break, and there was a scar above his left eye—both of which gave him a somewhat disreputable appearance. There was also a certain vigilance in his stance that spoke of years spent waiting for terrible things to make their presence known. Even now, his hand hovered over his sword, ready.

The High King glanced around the room, noting the assembled monarchs and the sparse furnishings, and sighed. Before he had ascended the throne, Dresden had a reputation for being a powerful, vital figure, who could be counted on to win unwinnable battles. But since becoming High King he seemed faded, as if the burden of his fifth decade and keeping the kingdoms under his rule in check had sucked something vital and joyous from him. All in all, he looked like a man who had purchased an apple pie only to find that someone had forgotten to add the apples.

The assembled monarchs quickly stood and bowed deeply to the High King. He gave them a half-hearted nod and walked briskly to the diamond throne of the Summer Kingdom. Behind him marched his White Guard—six elven knights in white armor—as well as four scribes, a flock of attendants, and a man in a white, cowled cloak.

The servants scrambled to seat the High King's entourage, placing a chair near the High King for the cowled figure, and setting up tables for the scribes. Another servant filled the High King's cup with wine and, bracing his shoulders, gulped down several healthy swallows.

Lorn rolled his eyes. *Tasters,* he thought disdainfully, as the attendant refilled the High King's cup. *We are truly going back to the Dark Times.*

It struck Lorn as barbaric that the High King would rather squander a servant's life to poison than hire one of the more skilled magic folk to do the same task without risking anything more than indigestion. He looked over at the seat reserved for the High King's Left Hand—the seat that Lorn had occupied until seven years ago—and noted that it was still empty.

What was more surprising was that the seat reserved for the High King's Right Hand was also empty.

Lorn was not the only one who noticed.

"Will the Right Hand be joining us this for the meeting?" Trev asked the High King.

"The Right Hand has resigned from his position," the High King answered. "Any guesses as to *why* he resigned, Medas?"

Medas shrugged. "A lack of work-life balance? Intestinal discomfort? A desire to devote more time to his lute lessons?"

"More likely he resigned due to your barbaric assault on his person during the last meeting," Varran said righteously, shaking his head in disgust.

"He is the general of the Summer Alliance's combined armies," Medas said. "He should be used to being barbarically assaulted. It's practically in the job description."

"The Right Hand disagrees," the High King said. "It seems that castration via curtain rod—"

"*Attempted* castration via curtain rod," Medas corrected. "I was not successful, thanks to a lack of back-up." He looked reproachfully at the other monarchs.

"We thought you had the situation well in hand," Lorn said.

"You were doing very well," Lyssandra agreed.

The others nodded.

"I stand corrected," the High King said with a brittle smile. "It seems that '*attempted* castration via curtain rod' was not in his job description, for he resigned his post. Officially, the Right Hand stepped down yesterday, in part because he never wanted to attend another meeting of the Lower Kingdoms ever again."

"We know how he feels," Lorn muttered.

Dragma snorted.

Medas waved off the High King's comment. "You should be thanking me. If he was unable to stop me from *attempting* to castrate him with a drapery fixture, and had to be rescued by your guards, the servants, and Reginald, then he isn't much of a general, is he?"

"Not much," Lyssandra agreed.

"Pathetic, really," Dragma said.

"You *are* rather formidable, though," Ash said to Medas. "I doubt many could take you down single-handedly."

"I had a cold that week," Medas said. "I was not even at my best."

"Let us speak frankly," Trev said. "Gerald was not a particularly stellar Right Hand. He was adequate ... at best."

"Now, now—let us be fair," Ash said. "*Anyone* who filled the position of Right Hand was likely to be unfavorably compared to his predecessor." He inclined his head toward the High King. "Your term as Right Hand set the bar extremely high, Your Majesty. Your feats are the stuff of legend."

The High King shifted in his seat, uncomfortable with the praise. "Hardly."

"Come on, enough with the false modesty," Dragma said, waving her goblet impatiently. "None of us thinks that you're a great High King—"

The High King raised an eyebrow.

"—but *everyone* agrees that you were an excellent Right Hand. The Battle of the Sticks alone would have put you in the history books."

"Winning an unwinnable battle against hordes of darklings with only a handful of men will do that," Trev said.

"Impressive," Lyssandra said.

"Truly a battle to rival the Age of Gods!" Varran said, his eyes aglow with wonder and admiration.

"I did not win that battle alone," High King Dresden said gruffly.

"And yet the battle was won," Lorn said. "Gerald, on the other hand, was defeated by a curtain rod."

"*That's* what I was talking about!" Medas said, crashing his fist down onto the table, then jabbing a finger toward to the High King. "*You* won the Battle of the Sticks. Gerald couldn't even march across my kingdom without accidentally setting fire to two of my villages. He's lucky that I only *attempted* to castrate him." He shook his head. "To think, we lost the curtain rods because of him ..."

"I miss the curtain rods," Trev said with a sigh.

"Pity," the High King said, "because they will not be returning until you all learn some restraint."

"We are never getting the curtain rods back," Dragma said.

"A moment of silence for the curtain rods," Lorn said.

High King Dresden rolled his eyes. "Regardless of what you thought of

Gerald's performance as Right Hand, he is gone. I shall announce a tournament for the position next week. To ensure that there is not a repeat of this situation, Medas and his curtain rod will wrestle the finalists to ensure that the winner is capable of holding his own against ornamental furnishings."

"Happy to do my part for Otherworld," Medas said, bowing his head.

"Your loyalty has been noted," High King Dresden said and turned to his agenda.

"I cannot help but notice that there is still no Left Hand," Trev said. "It has been ... what?—seven years since Lorn left the post?"

"That is correct," the High King said, not bothering to look up.

"Well, it must be difficult to find someone as qualified for the position as Lorn," Ash said, ever loyal to his friend. "I doubt there is a more powerful sorcerer in Otherworld."

"I certainly haven't met one," Dragma said.

"Well, that is what comes from conducting a Purge of magical folk," Lorn said, arranging his agenda neatly before him. "It leads to a lamentable lack of applicants for magical roles in government."

"I assume that High Queen Orelia is still wielding the Wand of Infinity and performing the majority of magical duties?" Trev asked.

High King Dresden made a sound that could be interpreted vaguely as agreement and kept looking at his agenda.

Trev turned to Lorn. He raised an eyebrow but said nothing.

Lorn, too, was silent. Although he had plenty to say about the High King's lack of desire for a magical envoy—not to mention the Purges that had left them without suitable candidates—it appeared that the High King was not in the mood for a discussion.

"So, we've got no Right or Left Hand," Dragma said.

"Handlesss," Lyssandra said. "Poor High King."

"We shall rise above it," the High King said. He finally looked up from his agenda. "In the meantime, all matters that you would have raised with either the Right or Left Hand can now be directed to my newly appointed secretary, Fallon." High King Dresden gestured toward the man in the cowled cloak sitting behind his left shoulder.

Fallon stood up, pulled back his hood, and bowed.

"It is an honor to meet you all," he said, a trace of a guttural accent coloring his words.

Lorn studied the new secretary. He noted his shaved head and weathered complexion, stocky physique, and calloused hands and frowned—this was not a scholar. In fact, he looked more like a dockworker. Lorn made a mental note to ask the Collection department for a profile on this fellow as soon as possible; hopefully, one filled with sordid secrets ripe for a spot of bribery.

Dragma was also studying the new secretary, though her motives more carnal in nature.

"Expendable?" she asked the High King hopefully, as the secretary took his seat once more.

"No," High King Dresden said curtly, "so look elsewhere. Let us begin, shall we?" He took a sip of wine from his goblet and cleared his throat. "Although it seems remarkable that I have to repeat the rules of the meeting when we meet so frequently, I shall do so. Yet again. First, ensure that all weapons have been removed from your persons." He leveled a pointed look at Medas who was still holding his axe.

Reluctantly, the dwarven king threw his axe onto the table. He then turned to the other monarchs. "Come on—I know I'm not the only one."

Before long, there was a sizable arsenal on the table.

The High King shook his head. "Every time," he muttered. He turned toward Trev and looked meaningfully at his cane.

Trev merely raised an eyebrow.

"We all know that is not just a cane, Trev," High King Dresden said pointedly.

"I have never tried to hide the fact that I carry a sword in my cane," Trev said smoothly. "The fact remains, however, that relinquishing it removes my mobility. What if something were to occur during this meeting —fire, flood, other acts of gods—and I needed to escape?"

"Then I am sure that either Lorn or Lyssandra would be pleased to levitate you," the High King said. "Or perhaps Ashlyn would agree to carry you from the room."

Ash grinned at Trev. "I shall throw you over my shoulder like a fine side of beef."

"Such an unflattering comparison," Trev muttered, reluctantly placing his cane onto the table.

"He did say a *fine* side of beef," Lorn said.

The High King leveled a no nonsense look at Lorn and the two queens. "I trust you three will keep your powers leashed for the duration of this meeting."

"That depends on the duration of the meeting," Dragma growled. "So best make it snappy."

"Faster is better," Lyssandra agreed. "Lessss time to slip up."

Lorn inclined his head. "I will endeavor to contain myself."

"See that you all do so," the High King said. He took a deep, cleansing breath. "This is the final Gathering of the Summer Alliance Monarchs of the Lower Kingdoms for this year and, as such"—he gave a warning glance toward Varran—"I expect it to be brief." He turned Lyssandra. "And with minimal bloodshed."

Lyssandra tilted her head in mocking acknowledgment.

The High King turned toward Medas and Lorn. "With an absence of provocative commentary." He directed his final glare at Dragma. "And with as little molestation as possible."

The dragon queen merely raised a shoulder. "I make no promises."

"Which is probably the best that we can expect under the circumstances." The High King sighed wearily. "Let us begin. I welcome you all to the meeting."

He raised both of his hands, palms forward, wrists exposed in the traditional Otherworld greeting. In this company, Lorn was not the only one who bore Marks. Like all elves, Trev and Varran had the Mark of Destiny on the inner wrist of their left hand—a delicate arrow, as ruby-red as ripe apples, coiled into a circle the size of a thumbprint. Should Destiny herself ever need them, the mark would transform; the shaft of the arrow would uncurl like a vine until it pointed them toward their Destined task.

Lorn's gaze flicked over the unblemished skin of the other monarchs but paused at the Mark on Fallon's wrist.

Not a Mark, he amended, looking closer at the mess of puckered, white flesh. *More of a burn or a brand.* He made a mental note to ask the Collection department to find out more about this mark.

"I call upon all our respective gods to look favorably upon this meeting and grant us the strength and wisdom to ensure the safekeeping of Otherworld," the High King continued.

Lorn strongly suspected that Midra, the patron god of Between, would be too drunk to hear the High King's plea but still, it was a nice touch.

"Today, the Kingdom of Vahlora will be represented by Prince Varran. And, as has been the case for the past two years, the Kingdom of Aurora will be represented by Prince Ashlyn." The High King turned to his secretary. "Let us begin."

Fallon cleared his throat and picked up his agenda. "The first item is to discuss matters arising from the previous meeting. The first pertains to the new trade road that had been proposed by the Right Hand."

There was a collective groan.

"Enough with this new trade road!" Dragma said. She slapped her hand on the table hard enough to make the goblets jump. "It is a terrible idea! It takes away valuable lands from each of us and is no better than the trade roads we've already got."

"I am with Dragma on this," Medas said. "In fact, I thought we made it clear at the last meeting that we all *strongly disapproved* of it."

The dwarven king was right—the monarchs *had* made it clear that they all strongly disapproved of the new road. They had expressed their *strong disapproval* in several ways: Trev and Ash had used diplomacy, suggesting other possible routes that could accomplish the same aim; Lorn had used subtlety, implying that the land confiscated from Between would become mysteriously diseased should this plan of action come to pass; Dragma had expressed her disapproval vocally by threatening to move dragons—vicious, territorial, dragons—to the disputed lands; whereas Medas had expressed his disapproval physically by attempting to castrate the Right Hand with a curtain rod.

High King Dresden raised his hand for silence. "The new trade road is non-negotiable. The current trade roads were created well over forty years ago—they are outdated and overwhelmed and cannot be widened any further. We are getting a new road; the only negotiable aspect is the route."

The monarchs grumbled but said nothing.

Fallon gamely continued. "As you can see, the proposed route has been changed to reflect the objections raised in the previous meeting."

The servants gave each of the monarchs a copy of the amended route map.

"Somewhat better," Ash mused.

"Not as terrible," Dragma mumbled.

"Excellent!" Varran said.

Trev turned to the prince. "*Not* excellent. The new road is now cutting off the water supply to the southern quadrant of your kingdom."

Varran took another look at the map. "Oh." He pasted a sneer on his face. "I demand that this egregious error be fixed immediately!"

"Much better," Trev said approvingly.

"I'm with the boy," Medas said. "The proposed route cuts off the main road out of one of our central mines. This will need to be changed, or I'll bring my own curtain rod to the next meeting."

"Given our desire for a quick meeting—" High King Dresden began.

"Hell, yes," Dragma muttered with feeling.

The High King ignored her. "I would ask you to make any corrections to the maps and send them to the Summer Kingdom within a fortnight." He motioned for Fallon to continue.

"To fund the new trade road," the secretary began, "a road tax will be raised."

All the monarchs groaned. The servants quickly handed them another sheet of parchment.

"The document you have just received describes the tax in detail," Fallon continued. "You may ask questions or raise any objections to the tax—"

"Which will be ignored," Medas muttered darkly.

The High King chose to ignore that comment.

"—at the next meeting."

"I hope that the proposal for this new tax makes allowances for the poorer kingdoms, such as Between," Lorn said piously.

Ash started to laugh but abruptly turned it into a cough.

"Are you quite well, Your Highness?" Fallon asked Ash.

"Dust," Ash said, clearing his throat. "Please, go on."

"The tax will be scaled appropriately," the High King said, eying Ash suspiciously.

"That is all I ask on behalf of my people," Lorn said, placing his hand over his heart.

Ash coughed again and quickly took a sip of his wine.

"Thus ends matters arising from the previous meeting," Fallon announced. "We shall now discuss new items. On page four of the agenda"—Fallon waited while the monarchs turned to the correct page—"you will find a list of the Summer Alliance subjects sentenced to exile in Between."

All eyes turned to Lorn.

"Between looks forward to welcoming its new citizens," Lorn said.

The High King nodded his approval.

"On page five of the agenda," Fallon continued, "you will find the list of Summer Alliance subjects sentenced to exile over the Dark, Dark Mountains."

Even after all these years, Lorn still shuddered at the mention of the Dark, Dark Mountains—the physical boundary that separated Otherworld from the wild Dark Land beyond. He, of all people, knew the evil that dwelled in those mountains. Exile to the Dark Land meant certain death ... or worse.

Lorn quickly skimmed the short list of names and offenses and stopped himself from making a pleased sound. There was *talent* on this list.

"Between would also be happy to welcome those on this list," he announced.

High King Dresden raised an eyebrow. "Even the cannibal?"

Lorn quickly re-read the charges. "To be fair, it says here that he only consumed a toe, and that he was drunk at the time. That would be just a misdemeanor in Between."

The High King grimaced in distaste. "You are welcome to him and the rest. But I have no wish to see their names on this list again; if they reoffend, you are to deal with them."

"I shall fling them over the Dark, Dark Mountains personally," Lorn said.

The High King stared at him for a moment, as if trying to determine whether Lorn was joking or not. In the end, he merely sighed. "See that you do. Next item, Fallon?"

Fallon consulted the agenda. "The next item on the agenda is: *New complaints raised since the last meeting.* The King of Aurora wishes to raise the matter of three caravans of merchandise lost on the Great Trade Road bordering his territory and that of Between."

Everyone turned their attention once again to Lorn. "The road has several potholes," he said mildly. "It is most likely that they fell into one."

"The caravans were lost without a trace," Ash said.

Lorn gave an elegant half-shrug. "The potholes are rather deep."

Ash snorted. "Two of those caravans were filled with Aurora's finest malt whiskey."

"The potholes are also evidently thirsty," Lorn said.

The High King turned to Lorn. "If the ne'er-do-wells of the Kingdom of Between—"

"They prefer to be called *citizens*, Your Majesty," Lorn interjected.

The High King gave him a stern look. "—could keep their hands off the Aurorean caravans, then we may proceed to strike this item off the agenda."

Lorn bowed his head. "We shall do our best to ensure that the matter does not arise again."

Ash sighed. "We are never getting those caravans back, are we?"

"Not a chance," Lorn said, striking the item off his agenda.

Fallon tried not to smile. "One of the Faire kingdoms have alerted us that a group of fae males has gone missing. They were engaged in the final ritual in their passage to adulthood—their tour of Otherworld—when they disappeared somewhere around Dragaz."

Alia stared meaningfully at the dragon queen. "Your Majesty?" she prompted. "The fae men?"

Dragma stopped drumming her talons on the table and frowned thoughtfully. "Tall, beautiful, strapping group of men?"

"Presumably," Dresden drawled.

"Were virgins?"

"Note the past tense," Ash said with a laugh.

Dragma smiled indulgently, as if recalling a fond memory. "Yes. They are currently being detained."

"Detained?" the High King asked.

Alia gave her queen a look of fond exasperation. "At Her Majesty's pleasure, so to speak."

"Should I inform the Faire kingdom that they need to send a rescue party?" the High King asked.

"They are there quite willingly," Dragma said. "And are free to leave at any time." She shrugged languidly. "They just do not wish to leave."

"Try not to break any of them," the High King said.

"So far, they appear to be rather resilient," the Dragma said, clearly impressed.

"Ah, to be young again," Trev sighed.

Dragma sent him a lascivious glance. "You're only fifty, Trev. There's plenty of life in you yet."

"Very pretty," Lyssandra agreed.

"Ladies, you make me blush," Trev said, placing his hands over his cheeks.

"King Trevelyan's enduring allure is to be recorded for posterity," the High King noted wryly, looking over at the scribes, who dutifully recorded this in the proceedings.

Fallon bit back a smile and continued. "The High Priest of the Church of Unified Gods—"

All of the monarchs groaned.

"Why do we let that cult continue?" Dragma growled. "Otherworld has many gods and goddesses—"

"Something for everyone," Alia interjected.

Dragma slapped her hand on the table. "*Exactly*. And we are free to worship one or all or none of them. Why should they be pressured into joining a single church? And why should we be pressured into worshiping there?"

"Agreed," Medas said. "If I have to listen to another petition from those unification crackpots asking me to persuade Kamus to join their church, I will visit their High Priest with my axe."

"Note that they did not ask Kamus himself to join," Trev said. "Which shows an enormous amount of self-preservation on their part."

"Kamus *is* renowned for smiting," Medas mused. "Probably why he's so beloved by us dwarves."

His burly attendants raised their axes. "Hail Kamus!" they cried.

"If we could continue without the chorus?" High King Dreden asked, looking pointedly at the dwarven guards. The guards merely grinned back.

Fallon rustled his agenda to get the monarchs' attention. "The High Priest of the Church of Unified Gods is conducting an audit on the various weapons and gifts bestowed upon us by the gods and goddesses—"

"All the better to appropriate them," Trev murmured. The rest of the monarchs muttered their agreement.

"—and asks for your cooperation to find their whereabouts. So far, they have discovered that several God Weapons thought to have been housed within the vaults of the Summer Palace are missing."

Everyone looked at Lorn.

"It was not Between," Lorn said.

Everyone still looked at Lorn.

"This time," he added.

"I doubt they were stolen," the High King said. "We know from history that the God Weapons come and go as needed: they find their way to those who are destined to wield them—as did mine." He touched the pommel of his sword, the God Weapon Solstice.

"Out of interest, which weapons were ... hmm, let us say *liberated* from the Summer Palace vaults?" Trev asked.

Fallon consulted his notes. "Of the missing weapons, the most note-worthy are the ones that were previously wielded by High Kings: Hargaz the Infallible Dagger, Stellora the Celestial Sword, Barzel's Blue Breath Jar, the Wand of Shadows, and the Light Giver."

Medas whistled. "Quite an illustrious list."

The High King turned to Lorn. "If you could use your resources to find the whereabouts of these weapons—"

"He means spies," Medas interrupted.

"Spies? I have no idea what you are talking about," Lorn said with a straight face.

"—then I would be most grateful," the High King finished pointedly.

"And should Lorn give this information to you or to the High Priest?" Trev asked the High King.

"To me. I, of course, would be happy to pass on the information. Let us move onto the next item on the agenda: *All new matters arising*. Do any of you wish to raise any new matters?"

Varran sat up straight in his seat, his shoulders back, his chin in the air. "Yes. I wish to raise a new matter, a matter that should have been raised long ago ..."

"Here we go," Medas muttered.

"My people are proud people ..." Varran began.

Trev beckoned for a servant to fill his goblet, motioning for him to keep the wine flowing.

"The elven folk are renowned across Otherworld for their heroism, their chivalry, their decency—"

"Their oddly similar hairstyles," Medas interrupted.

The High King sighed. "*Medas.*"

Medas looked around at the assembled monarchs. "Come on, you know it's true; all elves look identical from behind—it's all that long, white hair. Show of hands if you have ever accidentally approached an elven man thinking that he was an elven woman or vice versa."

All but the High King and his secretary raised their hands.

"So, so pretty ..." Lyssandra sighed, reaching out to touch a lock of Varran's hair.

Varran moved out of her reach as surreptitiously as possible and turned to the High King.

"You let *him*," he said, pointing disdainfully at Medas, "disparage the elven race in my presence?"

Medas held up his hands in mock innocence. "I was doing nothing of the sort. If anything, I was praising the immense, albeit interchangeable attractiveness of all members of the elven race. My fondness for elven women is a matter of public record."

"*You* should not even think of approaching our womenfolk!" Varran seethed, stabbing his finger at Medas.

"Or menfolk," Lorn added. "Given that they are visually interchangeable."

Varran's face turned the color of a ripe plum. "*Neither* of you should
think of tainting the honor of elvish women ... or men ... with your
advances. The purity—"

"If this is going to be a lecture on how the purity of the elven race
needs to be preserved, I petition for the return of my sword," Trev said.
"And I say that as the half-elf bastard that I am."

"Enough," the High King said wearily. "Varran, get to the point, or you
will lose the floor."

Varran took a deep breath, clearly trying to calm himself. "As I was saying,
we elves are a proud people with a long, glorious history. We were chosen to be
the very instruments of Destiny herself!" He lifted his wrist, proudly showing
off his Destiny Mark. "I have prepared this poem to put forth my petition."

With a flourish, he removed the tie from a fat roll of parchment. In
mounting horror, the monarchs watched as Varran began to unroll the
parchment ... and unroll the parchment ... and unroll the parchment until it
fell off the table and stretched out across the floor.

The prince cleared his throat. "*Listen well to this tale of the elven plight/for
their treatment is a serious blight/upon the—*"

"Agh, *poetry!*" Dragma crashed her fist down on the table. "Get to the
point, pretty boy, or we'll soon find out whether or not you're flammable."
She snapped her fingers, and tiny flames danced over her fingertips. With a
negligent flick of her hand, the flames raced gleefully across the table
toward the poem.

Varran shrieked and pulled the parchment away from imminent
combustion.

"Stop enslaving my people!" he said quickly, gathering up his poem and
putting it protectively behind his back. "We were once the rulers of Otherworld, and yet today, elves are *servants* in all of your kingdoms. They wash
your dishes, do your laundry, and scrub your filthy floors on their hands
and knees. It is *disgusting*, the indignities that they endure!"

"You do realize that we pay *your people* for their services, do you not?"
Trev asked.

"A pittance," Varran said with a sneer. "They deserve more. They
deserve *better*. I demand that all elves indentured in your kingdoms be set
free immediately and allowed to travel back to their homeland to embrace
their heritage and their Destiny."

The High King steepled his fingers together, his expression thoughtful.

"There are at least a hundred elven workers in the Summer kingdom alone. What do you plan to do with the sudden influx of elves into your kingdom?"

Varran raised his chin. "I will help them to discover their Destiny."

"Personally?"

A crease appeared between the prince's brows. "Well, no."

"Probably wise," Lorn remarked. "Starting a Destiny discovery service for hordes of unemployed elves would be both time consuming and exhausting."

"Not to mention tedious," Trev said. "Just think of all the poems that such a noble endeavor would require." He turned to his nephew. "Think *smaller.*"

The prince glanced at Trev, uncertain, but quickly rallied. He threw back his shoulders. "Very well—I demand that you set free the elven workers who are working in your castles *immediately.*"

"More manageable," Trev said approvingly.

"Still tedious," Medas muttered.

"This is obviously a matter of great importance to Prince Varran," Ash said kindly. "So, consider it done: Aurora will release all elven workers from their castle duties. Those working in the kingdom in other roles may return to Vahlora—if they so desire—with our assistance and great thanks."

Varran smiled gratefully at Ash. "Thank you." He turned to the rest of monarchs, his confidence growing. "Will you follow Prince Ashlyn's noble lead and release my people from servitude in your castles?"

"There are no elves working in Between's castle," Lorn said.

"I find that hard to believe," Varran scoffed.

"You would if you saw the castle," Ash said with a grin. "That place is a sty. No self-respecting elf would set foot in it."

"Thank you, Ash," Lorn said mildly. "Prince Ashlyn is correct—the castle *is* a sty. It is full of incompetent guards, trolls, imps, goats, wild magic, Tractor the unicorn, and Agatha, who sweeps the entrance staircase twice a week and recently tried to mop the foyer with a fish. There is not an elf to be seen ... unless they wandered in by accident and are currently trying to find their way out of the basement as we speak."

"If that is the case, you would not object to a castle inspection, would you?" Varran asked, his tone arch. "I would like to see this elf-free castle for myself."

"But of course!" Lorn spread his hands out in a gesture of welcome. "I would suggest any day but Wednesday. Statistically, most accidental injuries occur on Wednesdays."

"What of purposeful injuries?" Dragma asked.

"Those typically occur on Friday nights; the end of the week bar brawls artificially inflate the numbers." Lorn turned to the prince. "Irrespective of the day you visit, you should plan on wearing something non-flammable." He looked critically at Varran's all white ensemble. "And perhaps something that will hide blood and gore."

Varran stared at him in horror.

"What of your castle, Lyssandra?" Trev asked. "Is it overrun with elves?"

"Elvesss," the wraith queen said with a wistful sigh. "I have not seen a live elf in my castle in yearsss." She stared at Varran's hair, transfixed. "So, so pretty…"

Varran's face completely drained of color.

"To get back to the matter at hand—what if we do not comply?" Medas asked.

Varran gratefully turned away from Lyssandra's hungry gaze. "If you do not release my people within the next thirty days, I shall command them to stop their duties immediately and picket your castle."

Medas blinked. "Actually, that sounds like fun. Trundel refuses your request. Do your worst."

The High King rubbed his temples. One of his servants quietly refilled his goblet.

"Varran," he said, after taking a long drink, "did you have your father's permission to put forward this petition?"

Varran lifted his chin. "I am sure my father would be—"

"That is a *no*," Trev interrupted. "My brother is incapacitated, not an imbecile."

"Your *half*-brother," Varran corrected vehemently.

The High King raised his hand for silence. "Enough. Varran, this is a noble sentiment but problematic. Have your father sign an official request, and we will revisit the topic next meeting … may the gods help us." He turned to the remaining monarchs. "I am reluctant to ask, but are there any other further matters?"

"Yes," Lorn announced, girding his loins. "Between has recently acquired a queen, for want of a better word."

The monarchs turned to Lorn in surprise. The High King, however, looked strangely relieved. Lorn was about to contemplate that further when Ash clapped him heartily on the back.

"Congratulations!" Ash said, smiling broadly. "This is wonderful news!"

"Perhaps it is, perhaps it is not," Trev said, watching Lorn recover from

Ash's enthusiastic pat. "Matrimony can be a thing of joy and solace. Or, in my experience, something that you awaken from unexpectedly during the night when your spouse tries to kill you with a dagger." He frowned at the memory. "Or tries to poison you during your evening meal." He frowned again. "Or tries to sabotage a bridge that you were due to commemorate later that day ..."

"How many times do we have to tell you, Trev—your love life is cursed," Medas said wearily. "For your own safety, go and see a curse-breaker before your next marriage."

"Nonsense," Trev said, bristling. "I have just chosen poorly ... again and again, and again. Lorn—learn from my mistakes." He gestured to his ruined leg. "Get a magically bound, no-harm matrimonial contract drawn up before you welcome your new queen into Between."

"Wise words," Lorn said. "I shall try not to follow your matrimonial example."

Dragma mock sighed. "This is a dark day for the women of Otherworld."

"It truly is," Alia said, shaking her head forlornly, her lips twitching with a suppressed grin. "The Kings of Vetch will also be beside themselves."

"Devastated," Ash said, not bothering to suppress his grin.

Lorn rolled his eyes. "They will live."

"Hang on." Dragma glared at Lorn. "You aren't marrying that devious piece of fluff, are you? The one that you used to collude with at the Summer Palace? The one whose gown I set fire to during the Solstice ball ... mostly by accident?"

Ash laughed. "I had forgotten about that incident."

Alia snorted. "Odds are that *she* hasn't and is probably plotting her revenge." She turned to Dragma, exasperated. "You need to keep an eye on the people you set fire to."

Dragma waved her hand dismissively. "If I had to spend time each day worrying about all the people that I set fire to, then I'd never get anything else done." She turned back to Lorn. "Well? You didn't answer my question."

Lorn shook his head. "No. It is not Nina."

The monarchs let out a collective sigh of relief.

"No offense," Medas said to Lorn, "but if you took Nina as your queen, I would probably have to invade your kingdom as a purely defensive measure. That woman would want a gold mine or two and wouldn't be afraid to crush my kingdom to get it."

"That is an accurate assessment of her character," Lorn said. "Nina even mentioned it on occasion."

Varran frowned. "Nina? One of the ladies-in-waiting to High Queen Orelia? I believe she is my second cousin."

"I'd invade Between for that reason alone," Medas said, ignoring the Varran's glare.

"If we could get back to the matter at hand?" High King Dresden asked. Once there was silence, he turned to Lorn. "So, you have accepted the Zadrian betrothal offer. This is an excellent development."

Lorn's first thought was that the High King knew about the Zadrian betrothal party. His second was that the High King looked far too pleased. Clearly, the High King was *Scheming*.

"How so?" Lorn asked, hoping to get a clearer picture of the Scheming in question.

The High King leaned back on his throne, his pose triumphant, *sure*. "The Zadrians have wished to join the Summer Alliance for quite some time. But because of old grudges, some have been less than enthusiastic about accepting their inclusion."

"You mean, that old grudge we all developed when the Zadrians and their god Zarel tried to take over Otherworld?" Medas asked.

"And opened the Hell Realm, unleashing the darklings?" Dragma asked. "*And* allied with the dark fae?"

"And created the wraithsss, whom they imprisoned to do their terrible bidding?" Lyssandra asked.

"Which plunged Otherworld into the Most Terrible War that decimated our people, destroyed the land, led the fae and the vast majority of magical creatures to retreat to Faire and seal the gateways to their realm, and prompted the Elder Gods to leave us?" Trev asked.

"Which in turn led to the formation of the Summer Alliance, who swore to ensure that none of this would ever happen again?" Medas finished.

The High King's jaw clenched. "Ancient history. The Zadrians were defeated—we killed their god. The dark creatures were banished over the Dark, Dark Mountains into the Dark Land or imprisoned once more in the Hell Realm. The wraiths were freed and given their own lands and their own queen. The magical creatures that stayed behind were free to roam over Otherworld and settle wherever they wished. The Faire Gateway was unsealed, and peace with the fae kingdoms maintained through a succession of high queens. Time marched on."

He leaned forward over the table, his fists clenched, his expression fierce. "A unified Otherworld is a strong Otherworld. Zadria is the last kingdom before the Dark, Dark Mountains. Should a time come when we need to fight those dark forces once again, I would rather have the Zadrians as my ally than my enemy."

"Some would argue that the Zadrians *are* one of the dark forces that we should be fighting," Trev said.

"Not at all," Dresden said dismissively. "The Zadrians are remorseful. Repentant."

"All the skulls and the chanting and the dabbling in Death Cults suggest otherwise," Medas muttered.

"The actions of a small minority," the High King stressed. "And all the more reason to bring them into the fold, so to speak. Having them unite with a Summer Alliance kingdom will keep their excesses in check."

Lorn lifted an eyebrow. "You believe that uniting with *Between* will keep their excesses in check? When was the last time you visited?"

"I have faith in you," the High King said blandly. He leaned back into his throne. "If you can curb the excesses of Betweeners, you can curb the excesses of the Zadrians."

"I did not curb the excesses of the Betweeners," Lorn said. "I just gave them outlets."

"This was not a bridal suit for the hand of Melfarcia, was it?" Trev asked. "The one they call the Black Widow of Zadorea?"

"Her title is the *Countess* of Zadorea," the High King corrected. "Be sure to use it."

"Melfarcia?" Medas balked. "The woman they've labeled the 'Biting Bride' for her tendency to marry men with strategically valuable land holdings and then remove their—"

"Medas," the High King interrupted, a warning in his tone.

"—manhood with her teeth during—"

"*Enough*, Medas!" High King Dresden barked.

Medas raised his hands in surrender. "I was merely trying to ascertain the identity of the new Queen of Between."

"She keepsss the piecesss as trophiesss," Lyssandra added with a touch of admiration.

Dragma shook her head, bemused. "What a waste of man-flesh."

Varran looked as though he was about to be sick. "Can someone actually ... bite ... *through* ...?"

"Rumor has it that she had her teeth filed especially for the task," Medas said.

"Wise," Lyssandra said. She ran her tongue languidly over her own sharp fangs. "Makesss the job easier."

"You can't fault her commitment," Alia said.

"That is disgraceful!" Varran gasped. "Why has something not been done?"

"Like what?" Dragma asked. "Have her teeth filed back?"

Trev turned to Lorn. "As one cursed groom to another, I offer you my sincere condolences. I shall have my finest silversmith fashion you a bite-proof codpiece as a wedding gift. Suitably engraved, of course."

"With what?" Medas asked. "*Behold! Beneath this shield lies the Royal Genitals of the Shadow King—leave them how you found them?*"

"A useful gift," Lyssandra said approvingly. "Better than glassware."

"If we could return to the matter at hand?" the High King asked, his tone one of great suffering. He turned to Lorn. "I understand that Melfarcia may not have been your first choice in a queen—"

"Not if you want to maintain the length of your coc—" Medas began.

"—but her holdings are quite vast," the High King continued loudly, directing a fierce glare toward Medas, "as is her influence within the Zadrian kingdom. This betrothal will profit you both. It has my approval."

Lorn had a terrible feeling that this situation was about to take a turn for the worst. The High King looked smug. *Terribly* smug—the sort of smug one typically displays when a Scheme had gone to plan. The fact that Between had thwarted this Scheme was not going to go down well.

"Then I am sorry to disappoint you," Lorn said smoothly, "but I have not accepted Melfarcia's betrothal suit. Between itself has selected the new queen."

The High King's face turned ashen. "Who is she?"

"She resides—"

"What is her name?" the High King interrupted, his tone desperate. "What is her family name? Who are her people?"

"Her name is Sasha," Lorn answered, careful to hide his growing unease.

"Her *full* name," the High King demanded.

Lorn's heart began to pound. It was unheard of to ask for someone's full name. To possess someone's full name was the first step toward gaining power over that person through means both fair and foul. Everyone in Otherworld knew this … and knew better than to hand over such precious information.

The High King's questions raised alarm bells in all the monarchs—all, that is, except Varran, who seemed oblivious to the sudden tension in the room. Trev cleared his throat, the caution behind the sound clear as a bell. Medas caught Lorn's eye and shook his head ever so slightly. Beneath the oak table, Ash nudged Lorn's ankle in warning.

"What does it matter?" Dragma huffed. "As long as it isn't Nina. In fact, I'm calling this new queen Not-Nina."

"Sasha," Lyssandra hissed, "Such a pretty name. Very soft. Very round."

Lorn was grateful that the queens were trying to deflect attention away from the matter at hand, but he knew the distraction would not last.

"Her name is Sasha Perse," he said blandly, deliberately changing the pronunciation of the Queen's surname and withholding her middle name entirely.

"Sasha Perse," the High King muttered. "Write it down," he ordered his scribes, who shared a bewildered look and did as ordered. The High King's expression changed immediately. He became almost jolly. "So, where is she from?"

Lorn straightened his agenda, trying to hide his growing unease. "She is from the Earther Realm."

"The *Earther* Realm!" Varran cried, outraged. "But they are savages!"

"They would say the same about us," Lorn said.

"How, by the glorious nutsack of Kamus, did you manage to become betrothed to an Earther?" Medas asked.

"She was a Dreamer," Lorn said.

"You are marrying a *child?*" Varran asked incredulously. His lip curled in disgust. "Your depravity knows no bounds!"

"It pains me to say this, but I'm with the boy on this one," Medas said.

Lorn rolled his eyes. "She *was* a Dreamer, twenty-five years ago. She recently returned and bested the Wasteland in a dream."

Ash whistled. "A True Queen."

Lyssandra leaned toward Lorn, her dark eyes wide. "Bested my children? In their domain?" She drummed her blood-red nails on the table. "Curiousss. I must meet her."

During the exchange, the High King's pallor had returned. "How can this be?" he asked hoarsely.

Lorn gave an elegant shrug. "Who am I to speculate on the great mystery that is Between? Apparently, it wanted a queen, and it went out and found one."

To everyone's surprise, the normally level-headed High King pounded his fist on the table. "What did you do?" he spat vehemently.

Lorn felt his magic begin to gather beneath his skin, ready to protect him, ready to attack. And beneath the magic, Lorn could feel the familiar sense of betrayal begin to rear its head. As the High King's Left Hand, Lorn had risked his life daily for this man—that should have at least earned Lorn the High King's respect, if not his regard. But right now, the High King was staring at Lorn as though he was a stranger.

He looked furious.

He looked thwarted.

He looked terrified, Lorn realized, utterly shocked. And it was that realization that led Lorn to command his magic to heel.

Things here were not as they seemed.

Lorn took a deep, cleansing breath. "I sat back and watched."

The High King's eyes narrowed. "Why do I find that so hard to believe?"

"Probably because you are naturally suspicious," Dragma said drolly.

"Silence!" the High King barked.

Dragma bared her teeth at his tone. Reflexively, her talons gripped the table, gouging the wood; flames began to dance across the backs of her hands. The temperature in the room began to rise, as larger flames began to lick the ends of the dragon queen's hair.

Medas pushed his goblet of wine toward Dragma. She took it quickly and gulped down the contents, but the flames continued to grow.

Alia reached out and gently caressed the inside of the queen's wrist. "Please," she whispered soothingly, placing her lips against Dragma's ear. "You must be calm." At Alia's touch, the flames extinguished. Dragma took a shuddering breath, and slowly settled back into her throne, Alia's hand entwined with her own.

The High King barely registered that he had been moments away from being flambéed. His dark gaze was fixed on Lorn. "What is your role in all of this?"

"I was an innocent bystander," Lorn said calmly. "Irrespective of my role in all of this—which I assure you is reluctant at best—Sasha is the True Queen of Between with all the dubious honors that the title bestows upon her." He maintained eye contact with the High King. "Including my protection."

There was a wealth of meaning in those three words.

The High King's jaw tightened, but he retreated into his throne. As much as Dresden obviously disliked Lorn, he had seen Lorn's power first-hand. He would have to be an idiot to challenge Lorn without the support of a Left Hand.

The High King was many things, but an idiot was not one of them.

In a rather reckless manner, quite unlike his usual strategic self, Lorn decided to press the issue. "Will this True Queen also get your approval?"

The High King looked down at Lorn's armor, then back at Lorn, his expression speculative. "We will see," he said, his tone neutral.

It was a dubious thing to say. There was almost a threat lurking beneath the words, and the other monarchs took note; all, that is, except Varran, who had lost the thread of the conversation some time ago and was now sketching a picture of a horse on his agenda. The silence that followed the High King's words was dark and charged with suspicion. The monarchs of Otherworld were sacrosanct; the fact that the High King had practically threatened the Queen of Between did not sit well with any of them.

"So," Ash said jovially into this strained silence "There is going to be a wedding!"

"A Joining, I would think, given the circumstance," Trev corrected.

Lorn nodded, playing along. "That is correct."

"And when will thisss joyousss event occur?" Lyssandra asked.

"Shortly," Lorn said. "As soon as the Queen enters Between."

"She is not yet in Between?" the High King asked sharply.

Lorn's magic prickled under his skin. "She only just crossed the Wasteland. I thought it prudent to allow her to prepare for her time in Between."

Lyssandra nodded approvingly. "I'm sure she needsss to put her affairsss in order."

The High King stared at Lorn, his dark gaze intense. "How long will she be in the Earther Realm?"

"Not long," Lorn said, hoping that the High King would not be able to tell that this was a Very Large Lie. "As Lyssandra said, the new Queen of Between needs to get her affairs in order before she leaves her realm for ours."

The High King's eyes narrowed. "If her presence in the Earther Realm should threaten Otherworld in any way—"

"It will not," Lorn said quickly, telling another Very Large Lie. "I will bring her back personally."

The High King steepled his fingers together but remained silent. It appeared that he was Scheming again.

To Lorn's absolute shock, the High King's secretary was beaming.

"May I extend my congratulations to you both," Fallon said. "I hope yours is a joyous union."

Lorn blinked in surprise. "That is exceptionally optimistic of you, Fallon, and completely unrealistic in the circumstances. But I shall take your good wishes nonetheless."

The secretary merely continued to smile. "Stranger things have happened."

The High King turned to his secretary and stared at him, clearly puzzled. Catching the High King's gaze, Fallon's smile abruptly disappeared. He quickly looked back down at his agenda.

"Does anyone wish to raise any other matters?" he asked.

The monarchs all shook their heads.

"Then I will draw this meeting to a close," the High King intoned. "May the gods and goddesses smile upon you and your kingdoms."

~

AS THE MONARCHS WERE PREPARING TO LEAVE SOUTHERN KEEP, THE HIGH King crossed to Lorn's side and paused.

"Leave us," he ordered his entourage and the other monarchs.

The other monarchs exchanged concerned looks—all except Varran, who was trying to remove a wine stain from his tunic with his handkerchief.

"Very well—I shall lead the way," Trev said, limping toward the stairway.

"Not *you*—you will slow us all down!" Varran hissed, pocketing his handkerchief. "It will take us forever to get down the stairs!"

"That's the point, boy," Medas muttered as he pushed Varran toward the door, nodding to Lorn as he went.

"It isss?" Lyssandra asked. "Do we want to go slow?" Alia stood on her tiptoes and whispered in the wraith queen's ear. "Oh, yess." Lyssandra nodded. "We shall all go slow. And remain in earshot."

Dragma shook her head. "We need to work on your subtlety, Lyssandra."

Ash passed Lorn and clasped him briefly on the shoulder. "I shall see you soon. Most likely on the staircase."

He bowed his head to the High King and followed the other monarchs to the entrance.

The High King rolled his eyes and waited until the room was empty. "You seem to be missing something," he said quietly, gesturing to Lorn's chest.

For a moment, Lorn wondered if had forgotten to put on a shirt. Then, he realized. *Bollocks*, he thought. *My amulet.*

He looked down at his chest as nonchalantly as possible. "So I am. The chain broke."

The High King lifted an eyebrow. "I hope you have not misplaced it. In the wrong hands, it could open all the gateways in Between."

"Then it is a lucky thing that I know exactly where it is." *I tell so many lies,* Lorn thought with a sigh.

The High King stared at him for a long moment. "Lucky indeed."

He turned on his heel and walked briskly toward the door.

Lorn exhaled sharply. "This is becoming a wretchedly melodramatic state of affairs ..." he muttered to himself and followed the High King from the room.

10

A SMALL SPOT OF TREASON

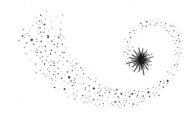

THE *TRUE* GATHERING OF THE SUMMER ALLIANCE MONARCHS OF THE Lower Kingdoms took place one hour and seven minutes after the departure of the High King and his entourage.

Rather than being held in an austere stone tower, it took place in a nearby woodcutter's cottage that had been warded by the Shadow King himself. In contrast to the bare stone and sparse furnishings of Southern Keep, the cottage had a roaring fire, comfortable armchairs, delectable pastries, spiced mead, curtain rods ... and the notable absence of the elven prince.

"*Please* tell me that your brother will be well enough to join us for our next meeting," Medas said to Trev as he settled into his customary armchair, "thereby sparing us from Varran's attempts at policy creation and poetry."

"Or both simultaneously, in this case," Lorn said.

Dragma snorted and took a pastry from the nearest tray. "Damn elves and their poetry—we need a realm-wide ban on both." She waved the pastry in Trev's direction. "Your brother is an exception."

Trev carefully lowered himself into his chair. "Half-brother, as Varran so astutely pointed out." He watched with a smile as his hound seated herself on the rug beside his chair.

"I have never understood such mortal termsss," Lyssandra said. "Which half of him isss your brother and which half isss not?"

"An excellent point," Ash said, picking up a tray holding mugs of spiced

mead. "I believe Tristen would say that he is entirely Trev's brother, regardless of conventions." He offered a mug of mead to Trev. "How is he
faring?"

"He is making progress," Trev said, taking it with a nod of thanks. "His
leg has healed. Now, it is simply a matter of ensuring that the infection does
not return. If all goes well, he will be at the next meeting."

"Excellent." Medas accepted a mug and raised it to Ash in thanks.
"What was Varran up to with his 'free the elves' speech, anyway?"

"It appears that Varran has taken up with disreputable company," Trev
said.

"Charlatans? Gamblers? Thieves?" Dragma asked.

"Betweeners?" Lorn suggested.

Trev snorted. "If only. No, it is a group of nobles who are campaigning
for the elven race to rule Otherworld once more."

"Back to the Dark Times, then," Dragma grumbled.

Lorn shook his head. "Lots of chivalry and no sanitation … and the
curious notion that all magic folk are their servants. We will have to keep an
eye on them—I have no desire to be a slave under elven rule."

"Who does?" Medas asked. "I'll be paying them a visit with my axe
before I let that happen."

Lorn tsked. "Why go to all the trouble of dragging your axe to Vahlora
when there are experts who will happily do the job for you?"

Trev placed a meaty bone on the floor for his hound and eyed Lorn
speculatively. "It is hardly surprising that you would advocate the use of
assassins—"

"Ah, ah," Lorn interrupted, holding up his hand. "They prefer non-
Betweeners to use the terms disposal expert or disposal practitioner."

"Forgive me," Trev said. "*Disposal expert*, given that they just so happen
to be based in Between."

"As is the academy that trains them," Ash added. "And the union that
controls them."

"Which are both run by the Crown," Trev continued, "thereby making
you the head of all the assassins—pardon me, *disposal experts*—in Otherworld." He bowed his head to Lorn. "Is that not so?"

"I deny such allegations," Lorn said, brushing pastry crumbs from his
lap. "They are scurrilous rumors designed to discredit my integrity."

"Are any of your disposal expertsss based in Vahlora?" Lyssandra
asked.

"Four of them," Lorn said.

Lyssandra nodded, pleased. "Marvelousss."

"What I don't understand is why Varran wants to 'free' the elves when they aren't enslaved in the first place," Alia said, taking a mug of mead from Ash's tray. "They're *employed*. They can leave at any time."

"I guess 'free the elves' sounds nobler than 'fire the elves,' " Lorn said.

"I think that is a mistake on his part," Ash said, placing his tray back on the table and taking a mug for himself. "Surely, 'fire' is an easier word to rhyme. Allow me to demonstrate." He cleared his throat theatrically. "A poem ... in the elven style:

All the Elves you must fire,
and do not dare rehire
my people;
for they should not perspire
as if in the depths of Hellfire
in their paid employment in the mire—"

"Shall we draw lots on who gets to stab him first?" Lorn asked the group. "Or should I just go ahead and do the deed?"

"I vote that we stab him in reverse height order," Medas said, patting his axe.

"I did warn you that it was in the elven style." Ash mock sighed. "My talents are wasted on in this room."

"I liked it," Lyssandra said.

Ash beamed at her. "*Thank you*, Lyssandra!"

"She's just being polite," Dragma said. "She would've stabbed you as soon as your back was turned."

"Probably," Lyssandra conceded.

"The true horror is that Ash's terrible efforts are better than any poem ever written by an elf," Trev said.

"See?" Ash said. "At least Trev appreciates my art." He gave a florid bow to the enthusiastic applause of Alia and the queens, then collapsed into his seat. "Now, *this* is a chair!" He groaned happily. "Plush, padded, supportive—"

"Not made of metal," Medas added, patting his armrest fondly.

Lorn sipped his mead. "Did you know that in the Earther Realm, they have chairs that massage your muscles?"

"Sounds rather deviant to me," Ash said, taking a meat pastry from a platter. "Which means that I heartily approve."

Trev's eyes widened. "How would one go about procuring such a marvelous chair?"

Medas snorted. "I have people to massage me, and I have chairs to sit on. Combining the two would be confusing—who knows where it might lead? Speaking of where things lead, did you read the fine print on the new trade road tax?"

Dragma groaned. "No, but odds are that we'll bear the brunt of it."

Lorn nodded. "We will. My sources inform me that we will be paying at least a third more than our Upper Kingdom neighbors."

"Not Between," Ash said, laughing. "I cannot believe that you have convinced the High King that your kingdom is poverty-stricken when its wealth rivals the Upper Kingdoms."

"He will not stay convinced if you keep 'coughing' each time that I mention it to him," Lorn said pointedly.

"Apologies. I shall do better next time. But have you considered what will happen if the High King discovers that you have been lying to him— and his tax collectors—about Between's true wealth?"

"They will not find out," Lorn said. "And even if they heard a rumor— or a cough—that made them suspect otherwise, they would find it impossible to prove."

"I would like to speak to your accountants," Dragma said with a grin.

"I am sure that could be arranged," Lorn said.

"Are you engaging in tax evasion simply for the sport of it or is there a specific reason?" Trev asked.

"Petty vengeance, mostly," Lorn said. "As far as Dresden is concerned, Between is a blight on Otherworld and beneath his notice. To give him credit, he does regulate our gateway traffic and maintains the trade roads, but that is where his generosity toward us ends. Despite being part of the Summer Alliance, he has provided no practical assistance to Between whatsoever during the entirety of my reign. There are no Summer Kingdom soldiers to assist us during the Crossings or to help manage our daily catastrophes; there is not even a Summer Kingdom ambassador residing in the city. Our pleas for help during the worst of the food shortages went unheard—we would have starved had it not been for the generosity of the people in this room. And yet, he sends his outcasts to Between without thought or compensation and demands taxes equal to those of the prosperous Upper Kingdoms. The way I see it, Between pays enough. We *all* pay enough; even with this new tax, we will bear the brunt of it."

Lyssandra bared her fangs. "He is becoming tediousss."

"I hear you." Dragma snorted. "I miss the old High King. He didn't exploit us quite so much."

"Bernard was fair," Lorn said. "He was a good man."

"Who died rather oddly," Trev said lightly. The monarchs exchanged meaningful looks and simultaneously sipped their mead.

"I had high hopes for Dresden," Ash said. "He is a strategist, a warrior, and clearly has Otherworld's best interests at heart."

"Well, the upper half's," Medas grumbled. "And just because he's good in battle doesn't mean that he's suited for the crown. Can't Orelia keep him in line?"

"She is far too occupied keeping Faire and the gateways in check," Lorn said. "Particularly since there is still no Left Hand."

"Which is ridiculous," Medas said. "I know that Dresden seems to have a problem with magic folk, Kamus knows why—sorry Lorn, Lyssandra, Dragma."

"No offense taken," Lorn said.

"It is hisss losss," Lyssandra said.

"Screw him," Dragma said, drinking her mead.

"But not appointing a magical champion is ridiculous," Medas continued. "The folk in Faire use magic. The occupants of the Dark Land use magic. The Hell Realm is filled with magic. How are we to face them in battle without a magical presence to augment our defenses?"

"True," Lorn said. "But even without the threat of war, the Left Hand should be keeping an eye on the lands, taming natural disasters, and maintaining harmony with the magical creatures around us. They are supposed to be working to ensure the prosperity of Otherworld."

"The sword and the wand; the Right Hand and the Left." Trev tapped his mug against his lower lip thoughtfully. "There needs to be both for us to prosper. But for whatever reason, Dresden has decided to put all his faith in the sword."

"In retrospect, we should have seen this coming," Ash conceded. "He was a soldier and the Right Hand for two of his brothers." He turned to Lorn. "You were a wonderful Left Hand. The greatest since Magnus."

"Here, here!" the other monarchs cheered.

"Your attempts to gain my favor with inaccurate flattery are much appreciated," Lorn said.

"Inaccurate? How so?" Ash asked.

"I truly doubt my skills are equal to those of Magnus," Lorn said. "Though, I will probably meet a similarly terrible end."

Medas grimaced. "Falling into the Hell Realm. Not the way I'd like to go."

"I thought Magnus died during the Purge of magic folk?" Alia said.

Trev shook his head. "No. He died before the Purge. I remember the day well. He was fighting the beasts that had emerged from the Hell Realm—"

"How did they come up from the Hell Realm?" Alia interrupted. "The Elder Gods sealed the Hell Realm after the Most Terrible War so that the dark creatures and hell beasts could no longer roam Otherworld. It should've been impossible for them to break free of the seal."

Trev shrugged. "No one knows the particulars. All that *is* known is that a gigantic fissure appeared between the Barrier and the Dark, Dark Mountains and the beasts came pouring out. Magnus had been performing a survey of the land on the orders of High King Brom and rushed to battle the beasts. Just as Magnus appeared to be triumphant, the beasts pulled him down into their realm. The fissure closed, sealing his doom. The Purge happened immediately afterward."

Dragma snorted. "How convenient."

"Very," Lorn agreed. "Magnus would never have allowed the Purge."

"The Purge made no sense," Alia said. "Why would High King Brom want to kill off his most powerful allies against the Dark Land?"

"Propaganda," Trev said. "At the time, there was a widespread rumor that magic folk intended to overthrow the Summer Alliance monarchs and rule Otherworld. No one wanted a repeat of the Most Terrible War, so people were quick to punish the magic folk."

"Well, the magic folk would have done a better job of ruling; High King Brom wasn't the most stable of leaders," Dragma said.

"That is an understatement—he was utterly crazed," Trev said. "Magnus and Orelia had to keep him in line."

"Well, if Brom planned the Purge as a means of ridding himself of possible threats to the throne, it backfired spectacularly," Medas said. "He was dead within a week and replaced by his brother Bernard, thanks to Between's disposal experts."

"*Allegedly,*" Lorn stressed. "There was no proof—" He waited for the other monarchs to stop laughing in disbelief. "There was no proof that we would admit to."

Medas rolled his eyes. "Well, in comparison to Brom, Dresden is not such a terrible High King."

"I feel for Orelia," Dragma said. "Her husbands have been a dismal lot. The first was a magic folk-killing lunatic, the second liked books more than people, and the third is Dresden. She should have found herself a couple of strapping knights, set fire to the Summer Palace and run off with them back to Faire."

Alia rolled her eyes. "That's the advice you give to everyone. Besides, all her marriages have been Joinings. With the right contract, she could have all the strapping knights she wanted without burning down the palace."

Dragma shrugged. "Where is the fun in that?"

"Arson has its charms," Lorn agreed. "I believe Orelia would probably be amenable to a touch of palace-burning."

"You would know," Trev said. "You are closer to her than any of us."

"And she's not easy to get close to," Alia agreed.

Lorn tilted his head, considering Trev's comment. During his time at the Summer Palace, Lorn had spent many amiable hours in the company of High Queen Orelia. Like most of the fae, she was unearthly beautiful, with her sleek, midnight-black hair and silver-flecked eyes. Many thought her cold and unfeeling, exquisite but untouchable, like a gilded statue. Not Lorn. He knew that she had a dry sense of humor and a love of bawdy songs and sunrises and gingerbread, and she shared all of these joys with him and more during their many morning walks and throne room discussions.

"I would not say that we are close," he said eventually. "Certainly not friends. Though, I did have the privilege of her confidence. It has always pained me that she seemed so miserable in all of her marriages; after all she gave up—her home in Faire and all those she loved—she deserved so much more than three dismal Joinings."

"Well, if something happens to Dresden, Orelia will be joined to his dear brother *Eunice*." Medas grimaced. "If I were her, I would start gathering my kindling and strapping knights, just in case."

"That's assuming they can sober him up long enough to crown him," Trev said. "The last time I saw him he was passed out on the throne room floor of the Summer Palace with a tankard of ale in each hand."

Dragma shrugged. "That's just a typical Thursday night for me."

"Yes, but he was supposed to be conducting a Court of Complaints on behalf of his brother at the time."

"He has the right idea," Medas said. "Rampant drunkenness is usually the best way of getting through a Court of Complaints."

"How I envy him," Lorn said with a sigh. "Speaking of throne rooms …" He leaned toward Trev. "Your late second wife's cousin is conspiring to assassinate you and take your throne."

"What, again?" Trev asked mildly.

Lorn took a small mirror from his bottomless pouch and tapped the frame. The mirror grew until it was the size of a serving platter. With a flick of his wrist, Lorn slid the mirror to the center of the table.

Curious, the other monarchs leaned forward.

"The Ranges—Treasury," Lorn said to the mirror.

On the other side of the mirror, a small imp waved in greeting but stopped abruptly. Frowning, he rubbed a dirty spot on the mirror's surface with his tunic.

"Many thanks," Lorn said. "Show us what Cedric was up to last night."

The imp gave him a thumbs up and quickly disappeared.

Within the depths of the mirror, a room began to appear. Guards stood around the walls dressed in midnight blue livery. In the center of the room stood a dais holding two blue velvet cushions. One cushion was empty, on the other sat a delicate crown made of silver flowers covered in sapphires.

"You have spies in my treasury?" Trev asked.

"You are welcome," Lorn said.

Within the reflection, a man appeared. His features were bland and rather forgettable, but there was something obscenely hungry about his gaze ... a gaze that was currently focused on the dainty, floral crown.

"Soon," the bland man crooned, reverently lifting the floral crown from its cushion. "Soon, you—and this entire kingdom—will be mine." He raised the crown to eye level. "So it has been promised, and so it shall be."

"Isn't that the queen's crown?" Dragma asked as the bland man placed the delicate crown firmly onto his rather large head.

"Yes," Trev said. He gestured to the silver crown set with a single, fig-sized sapphire on his head. "The king's crown is otherwise occupied." He eyed his cousin-by-marriage with a fair degree of distaste. "I must say, the queen's crown looked far more fetching on my dear, late, unlamented wives than on Cedric."

"This makes ... what? Three times that he's tried to murder you?" Dragma asked as they watched Cedric laugh maniacally.

"Four," Trev corrected. "But who is counting?"

Trev's hound looked up from her bone and growled, her fox-like ears standing to attention.

"My thoughts exactly, Chulla," Trev said to his hound. He turned to Lorn. "So, how does he plan to do away with me this time?"

"Poison, purchased from a vendor in Between," Lorn said. "I believe he was trying to be clever; he asked the vendor for 'something to incapacitate vermin' while winking outrageously. The vendor thought that Cedric's eye was spasming, so he took him at his word and sold him an elixir to intoxicate swamp rats. At the most, you would have been deliciously drunk for about two days."

"Well, that sounds like more fun than the beheading he had planned for me the last time."

The monarchs watched as Cedric tried to remove the crown, only to discover it was stuck fast. He tugged at it—at first gently, then with escalating desperation. Eventually, he sighed and called over a guard, who hauled on the crown with very little success.

"Oh, dear," Lyssandra said, as the guards returned with a tub of butter and began to grease the crown and Cedric's head.

Trev grimaced. "I shall have to get it cleaned." He tsked at the scene. "It is all a little unseemly, is it not?"

"Kind of makes you wish for the days when people would just physically fight you for the throne," Medas said.

Lorn snorted. "Speak for yourself. I constantly have to fight for the Shadow Throne of Between. I would happily give it away ... if only the battles were not to the death."

"Well, that *is* incentive to win," Dragma said.

They watched with equal parts amusement and disbelief as the guards eventually liberated Cedric's large head from the tiny crown, leaving behind a ring of bruises and dairy spread.

"Odds are that Cedric takes to wearing a hat for the next week or so," Alia said with a grin.

The vision faded away. Lorn touched the surface once again and the mirror shrunk down to the size of his palm. "Thus ends today's entertainment." He put it back in his pouch.

"Well." Trev leaned back in his chair and idly passed his cane from hand to hand. "What shall we do about dear cousin Cedric?"

"Kill him," Dragma said bluntly. "Dead men can't poison you."

Chulla looked up from her bone and howled approvingly.

Alia laughed, delighted. "See? Even Chulla agrees with the plan."

Trev gave Chulla a loving pat. "That is because my darling is uncommonly intelligent." Chulla barked in agreement and went back to her bone.

"I would be happy to do away with Cedric," Trev continued. "But ... he *is* family."

"Perhapsss one of my children should pay him a visit," Lyssandra suggested with a sharp smile.

"A pleasant possibility," Trev said. "What did you have in mind? I want to avoid outright death, but I would not be opposed to a fair degree of suffering."

The wraith queen idly dragged her blood-red nails across the armrest of her chair. "Recurring nightmaresss, perhapsss. And waking hallucinationsss. Childhood fearsss alwaysss work best. So, so enduring ..."

Trev's smile turned dastardly. "Sounds marvelous."

"You really should get him out of your kingdom," Lorn said. "I know that you are opposed to killing him but given that Cedric has tried to assassinate you several times without going through the proper channels, I am sure that the *alleged* Union of Most Excellent Assassins would take care of him for you, free of charge. They detest it when someone tries to undercut them." Lorn paused. "Or so I have heard ..."

Trev rolled his eyes. "Really, there is no need to keep up the pretense."

Lorn merely smirked and toasted Trev with his mead.

Medas twirled his signet ring thoughtfully around his index finger, the sizable ruby catching the light. "The region of Gaoul in the outer provinces of my kingdom is lovely this time of year."

Trev raised an eyebrow. "It is under nine feet of ice and filled with feral beasts."

"As I said, lovely this time of year. Surely, you could use an ambassador in the region to assist you in some matter of grave, and most likely lethal, importance."

Ash clapped Medas on the back, which almost toppled the smaller man from his seat. "Ah, ha! *Masterful.* Why not give Cedric a knighthood or an empty title of some sort—men like Cedric love collecting useless titles—and then send him on his way to Gaoul accompanied by some of the finest mind beasts that Lyssandra can conjure? As a parting gift for the journey, so to speak." Ash bowed his head toward Lyssandra, who gave him a darkly approving look.

"And if that doesn't work, set Lorn's 'alleged' assassins onto him," Dragma added. "Or send him to me; I doubt he'd last a week in my court."

"I give him three days," Alia said blandly, reaching for another pastry. "Four, if he hides in a broom closet."

Trev grinned. "My friends, you are truly diabolical! I heartily approve of your plan. I believe a toast is in order." He raised his glass. "To my dear, soon-to-be-late Cousin Cedric."

"Ah, Cedric. We barely knew you," Lorn said.

"Just enough to dislike you immensely," Dragma said.

"Truly, a pustulent boil amongst men," Medas added.

The monarchs exchanged mock solemn glances and drank.

"Speaking of diabolical plans," Trev said, turning to Lorn, "I could not help but notice that when you mentioned the new Queen of Between, the High King went—what is that phrase the young ones are using nowadays?"

"Unicorn-shit crazy," Medas supplied.

"Exactly," Trev said.

"Yesss," Lyssandra hissed. "He is Scheming."

At the mention of the Queen, Lorn's mood sobered. "He is indeed. There are two matters that I find puzzling about this entire situation. The first is why he was actively trying to marry me off to the Zadrians. It is no secret that they want the throne of Between; I have survived enough Challenges from their wizards and magicians in the past seven years for that to be obvious."

"Do you think that this Zadrian betrothal alliance is merely another scheme to take the throne?" Ash asked.

Lorn nodded. "It certainly seems that way."

"With Melfarcia as the bride in question, I doubt they were thinking of an alliance; they knew she'd cut the marriage short ... along with your manhood," Medas said.

"I thought the same," Lorn confessed. "Albeit without that rather vivid mental image."

Dragma snorted. "Fools. They were pitting a sharp set of teeth against a sorcerer."

Lorn smiled fondly at her. "Your faith in me is a glorious thing, Dragma. However, a Between Joining has a protection clause built in for each party—we are not allowed to harm one another. Her teeth would have fallen out the moment she tried."

"Ah, Between—an imminently sensible place," Trev said approvingly. His smile faded. "Then again, that means you could not have harmed her either, even if her plans were nefarious. Is that correct?"

Lorn gave an elegant half-shrug. "There are self-defense clauses in place. And Maddox has standing orders to step in should that appear to be the case."

Ash shuddered. "Good to hear. But what is even better is that you do not have to concern yourself with the Zadrian alliance anymore."

Lorn nodded. "True, but it appears that our High King *is* concerned about this alliance—enough to give his approval to their betrothal suit. The question is, why? What would he gain from it?"

"You heard what he said during the meeting—he wants to unify Otherworld, and strengthen our fortifications against the Dark Land," Ash said. "He believes the Zadrians will be strategic allies ... assuming that they are as repentant as he says."

Medas snorted. "And if you believe that, I have a mine at the bottom of an ocean that I would like to sell you."

Lyssandra tilted her head, puzzled. "That mine is inconveniently placed. It would be a poor investment."

"There is no mine," Medas said with a smile. "I was being sarcastic."

"Ah." Lyssandra tapped her talons against her armrest. "Sarcasm. So much to learn ..."

"You're doing great," Dragma said, saluting her with her mead.

"But why risk giving the Zadrians—a kingdom with a bloodthirsty history and ties to some rather disturbing cults—direct access to both the Portal and the Nightmares?" Ash asked.

Lyssandra reared up in her seat, her teeth bared. "My children must never fall into their handsss! I will not have them sent to the Hell Realm and be enslaved or unleashed upon Otherworld and used as a weapon. Not now, not when they are finally free." She quickly turned to Lorn, her chest heaving in anger. "*This must not come to passss.*"

Lorn held up his hands in a gesture of peace. "I will not let this happen. I have done all in my power to ensure that the Zadrians will not take Between. I will protect your children and the Portal for the rest of my reign. I promise you this, Lyssandra."

Hearing the truth in his words, the wraith queen slowly began to settle. In a rare show of emotion, she reached out and lightly touched Lorn's hand, her icy fingers barely brushing his fingertips for the briefest moment. "I know thisss, Shadow King."

Lorn smiled and inclined his head to thank her for the privilege of her trust.

"So, we need to determine what Dresden *truly* stands to gain from your alliance with the Zadrians," Trev said. "Or what he stands to lose now that you have broken the suit permanently."

"Exactly," Lorn said. "That is the first puzzle. The second puzzle is why Dresden looked utterly terrified when he found out that there was a True Queen of Between."

Dragma *hummed* beneath her breath. "He turned as white as a corpse. Rather unbecoming on him."

"And demanded her name," Alia added.

"Not acceptable," Lyssandra said.

"I am assuming that you did not take leave of your senses and give him the true name of your queen?" Trev asked.

Lorn tsked. "So little faith. Of course not. The name I gave him is close enough that, should he find out the truth, it will seem as though he misheard."

"Your queen is in trouble," Medas said bluntly. "Take her out of the Earther Realm, marry her immediately, put her in armor, and keep her by your side until she can wield an axe for herself."

"Sound advice," Alia agreed.

Lorn nodded, a lead weight in his chest. "I believe I shall follow it to the letter."

"It goes without saying that we will all assist your queen however we can," Dragma said. "I will gift her with dragonhide for her Joining gift."

Lorn's eyes widened. "That is a magnificent gift, Dragma. I cannot thank you enough."

Dragma waved away his gratitude. "She will need all the help she can get." She hmphed. "Are you sure we can't just kill Dresden? It would solve most of our problems. I *am* in season right now—it would make an excellent defense in any court of law."

Alia laughed. "Dragma, you bring this up after every meeting."

"Mostly in jest," Dragma said with a shrug. "But if he raises a hand to the new Queen of Between then I suggest we vote on it."

"If he raises a hand to the new Queen he will find himself missing a hand," Lorn said tersely.

The other monarchs turned to him in surprise.

"What is the matter?" Lorn asked, genuinely curious.

"Well, well, well," Dragma crooned with a leer.

"Ah, ha!" Ash crowed. "*Now* we start to hear the truth of the matter."

"That's quite the bloodthirsty response for just a Joining, don't you think, Trev?" Medas asked coyly.

"Quite," Trev agreed. "One does not usually bring certain death down upon one's kingdom by harming the High King unless one truly *likes* one's betrothed."

"Isss she asss pretty asss her name?" Lyssandra asked.

"Go on," Alia urged. "Show us!"

"Show us! Show us!" the monarchs goaded.

Lorn rolled his eyes. "You are acting like children in a playground. Soon, you will be making up rhymes about the new Queen and myself sitting in a tree ..."

Nevertheless, Lorn pulled out the enchanted mirror once again. With a tap, the mirror expanded. Lorn brought forth a memory of the Queen, focused, and touched the mirror once more. This time, the mirror's surface showed the True Queen of Between tearing across the Wasteland on her golden path, the Nightmare hordes close behind.

"Now *that's* a glorious sight," Medas said. "Look at her go!"

"She is a brave one, is she not?" Ash said admiringly.

"And fast," Trev noted.

"Very pretty," Lyssandra said.

"And strong," Alia said.

"Strapping. I approve," Dragma said.

"Well, that is a relief," Lorn said sarcastically. "How would I have slept at night without your approval?"

Dragma shrugged. "We were always going to like her better than the schemer and the biter."

"True," Ash conceded. "Your other options were rather bleak. I believe a toast is in order." He raised his glass. "To Lorn and the new Queen of Between."

"Here, here!" the other monarchs answered and sipped their mead.

"May she always run fast and far," Medas said with a grin.

Lorn snorted. "Odds are that she will do just that once she sees Between." He toasted the group and took a long drink.

The monarchs watched the Queen of Between run from the Nightmares a moment longer before Lorn tapped on the mirror, ending the vision.

"She is in great danger," Trev said quietly. "Dresden has a Scheme in place, and he will not allow an Earther to interfere."

Lorn nodded bleakly. "I need more eyes and ears in the Summer Palace. I need to know what the High King plans to do with her."

Ash sat back in his seat with an oddly satisfied smile. "Then your wish is granted. I have just been appointed to the High King's Fold."

Trev's eyes widened. "This is marvelous news!"

Medas pounded his fist on his armrest. "Yes! *Finally*, we have someone in the inner circle!"

"It's about time," Dragma said. "Way to weasel your way into Dresden's good graces!"

"Yesss—excellent weaseling," Lyssandra said.

There was an odd feeling in Lorn's chest—something unfamiliar and altogether positive. It took him a moment to recognize that it was hope and not a coronary.

"This means that, if there are plans afoot for the new Queen—" he began.

"—I should be one of the first to know," Ash finished with a grin.

"Speak ill of usss to the High King," Lyssandra said.

Trev nodded thoughtfully. "Sound advice. It would not do well for you to show any bias toward us."

"Go to town," Dragma said happily, gulping down another mug of mead.

"Just be your usual, disgustingly agreeable, charming self," Lorn said to Ash. "No one will suspect that you are, in fact, a spy and possible saboteur."

Ash sighed dramatically. "It is truly their own fault; I am criminally underestimated."

Medas raised his glass again. "This calls for yet another toast. To Ash." He turned to the prince. "May he cheerfully undermine the High King's rule."

"Hear, hear!" the monarchs answered and drank.

"And to us," Trev said, raising his glass again. "May we continue to conspire between us, and never against us."

"I will drink to that," Lorn said.

"I'll drink to anything," Dragma drawled.

And with that fine bit of treason, the *true* Gathering of the Summer Alliance Monarchs of the Lower Kingdoms came to a triumphant and somewhat raucous close.

BEWARE OF KINGDOMS BEARING GIFTS

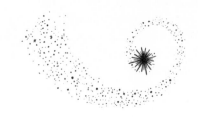

WHEN LORN RETURNED TO THE CASTLE AFTER HIS CHEERY BIT OF TREASON, he was stopped on his way to the Portal Chamber by one of the castle guards.

"The Heads are here to see you, Majesty," she said. "They're in your Less-Formal Meeting Chamber."

"I am surprised that they waited this long," Lorn said, turning on his heel.

When Lorn entered the Less-Formal Meeting Chamber, three people dressed in black robes—one tall and thin, one short and squat, and one dimpled and cuddly—rose from their seats and bowed. The Heads were the principals of the notorious Academy of Practical Arts—Between's premier educational institution, specializing in the instruction of what could be considered 'anti-social skills.'

Lorn smiled with true delight at the dissimilar trio and waved for them to sit down.

"Pardon, Your Majesty—we did not mean to intrude," Head-Fox Nevlyn, the Dean of Thievery/Procurement said as he squeezed his ample posterior into the narrow armchair, his feet swinging several inches from the ground. "But, given your schedule, it seemed easier for us to visit you rather than await your summons."

He smiled at Lorn, his trademark cheery, guileless smile; a smile that gave the impression that he was a jolly but simple, possibly even feeble-minded, man. In reality, Head-Fox Nevlyn was one of the shrewdest men in Otherworld. He could bargain the hide off a yak and was legendary for convincing a Vetch merchant to trade his caravan of precious metals for a bar of soap. "It was pine-scented," was all that Head Nevlyn would say—as if that explained everything—whenever the matter was brought up.

"I had planned to meet with you all," Lorn said, settling into his chair. "It was on my agenda."

"Item fifteen, from memory," Head-Raven Flynn, the Dean of Spying/Collection said as he folded his long, thin frame into his seat. Head-Raven Flynn was like a human shadow, usually unnoticeable, generally forgettable, and utterly silent. His spindly fingers flicked toward the pocket of his modest linen robe, reaching for that very list. But he visibly stopped himself and instead placed his hands on his bony knees, his frail shoulders hunched as if to protect all the secrets that he held within him.

Lorn inclined his head toward Head Flynn. "I am sure the Collection department knows better than I."

"But, of course!" Head Flynn said, affronted.

"Our congratulations, dear!" Head-Wolf Soren, the Dean of Assassins/Disposals smiled warmly at the King, her dimples on show. She was a motherly looking woman who gave off an air of home comforts: freshly baked cookies and stories before bedtime, hot soup on cold nights, and big hugs that warmed you to the bottom of your toes. It was disconcerting to think that she was, in fact, one of the deadliest people in Otherworld, and had once killed a man with a strategically placed bread roll.

"We were so very pleased to hear about the new Queen," Head Soren said, putting aside her knitting needles and garish yellow yarn. "We were especially pleased that it wasn't that Zadrian woman."

"That seems to be the consensus." Lorn's eyes narrowed. "Just out of interest, when did you learn that Between had a new Queen?"

Head Flynn pulled a small, leather-bound book from the black belt of his robe. He flicked halfway through before pausing and made a pleased sound. "Approximately four minutes after Her Majesty crossed the Wasteland."

"Four minutes." Lorn hummed under his breath. "Are we slipping?"

Head Flynn shrugged his pointy shoulders. "Our most seasoned students have just graduated; the new ones are still a little raw. We should be able to reduce information collection times considerably by next semester."

Lorn nodded. "Good. We cannot afford to let our standards slip."

"Of course not! We have a reputation to uphold."

"*Exactly.*"

"Are you pleased about this new development?" Head Soren asked Lorn. Her expression hardened. "You don't want the situation *remedied,* do you?"

Lorn shook his head. "Absolutely not. In fact, I want to ensure that Her Majesty lives a long and prosperous life. To that end, I want you to make sure that everyone in Otherworld knows that the new Queen of Between is to be protected at all costs. Any intelligence concerning her well-being is of the highest priority. The Crown will triple any assassination bounty posted for the Queen in exchange for her safety. All threats to her longevity are to be disposed of immediately. Is that clear?"

"Crystal," the Heads answered in unison.

Lorn nodded, pleased. "I would also like as many spies in the Summer Kingdom as we can spare—our best and brightest. The High King is *Scheming,* and we need to find out his plans for the Queen as soon as he makes them."

Head Flynn flexed his fingers, a rare smile touching his dour face. "Ah, a challenge! We already have our finest Ravens inside the Summer Palace. I will personally make the trip to see how we can integrate a few more."

"Do keep me informed," Lorn said. "I have some ... let us call them *reservations* about the High King's support for the new Queen."

At that, Head Flynn's expression became solemn once again. "I am aware. We shall get to the bottom of it."

Head Soren tsked. "Is it time to remove the High King? The poor dear seems to be making some terrible decisions of late."

"Tempting, but *no,*" Lorn said. "His crimes are primarily favoritism toward the Upper Kingdoms and tax fraud which are annoying but certainly not enough to warrant removal. And Midra knows that if he *is* removed, we in Between will be the first to be blamed. After all, we have a history of disposing of incompetent High Kings."

"Only because the other kingdoms are too squeamish to do it themselves," Head Soren groused. "They certainly benefited from it."

"They certainly did," Lorn agreed. "All restraints are removed, however, if the High King makes any attempts to harm the Queen."

Head Soren nodded, clearly pleased. "We've already put together a few disposal scenarios for the High King, just in case."

Lorn raised an eyebrow. "Such as?"

Head Soren reached into her gray sash and pulled out a notebook. She flicked through a couple of pages before pausing. "Here we are! We've planned a couple of 'tragic accident' scenarios, two 'act of gods' scenarios, and even a 'warning to others' scenario, which we probably won't go with since you want to keep Between out of it." She closed her notebook. "Unless we can find a way to pin it on one of our enemies."

"Two birds with one stone," Head Flynn mused, his fingers drumming restlessly against his knee. "I like it."

"*And* we use an actual stone in that scenario," Head Soren said, smiling. "A rather large one. Messy, but dramatic. A fitting end for a High King."

"Inspired," Lorn said.

"So, it appears that the Collection and Disposal departments will be kept busy—what do you require from Procurement?" Head Nevlyn asked. He fiddled with his orange sash, trying to arrange the luxurious fabric more comfortably around his ample belly. "I assume that Her Majesty will need provisions."

"She will," Lorn said. "Mainly supplies for the coronation and furnishings for her chambers. Maddox has drawn up a list."

The jolly man's eyes lit up. "We have just *acquired* several caravans of fine furnishings. They were headed to a rather esteemed establishment in Trundel ... that is, until they fell into a pothole."

"We really do need to see to those," Lorn said dryly.

Head Nevlyn grinned. "Indeed. We will reserve the best items for Her Majesty. Also, if I may suggest, two of our ex-procurement specialists have recently opened an interior decorating business. Perhaps they could assist you with Her Majesty's chambers."

Lorn raised an eyebrow. "Interior decorating? In *Between*—where most houses are furnished merely to withstand catastrophe?"

"It is true—Between is not the ideal market for their services. But they're hoping to work across Otherworld. I know they'd be happy to decorate Her Majesty's chambers to add to their resumes."

Lorn had a singularly terrible feeling about this. "You are suggesting that I allow two ex-thieves to decorate the Queen's chambers with dwarven furnishings which, if memory serves, are garish at best and tawdry at worst?"

Head Nevlyn waved his small hand airily. "It will be fine. Fine! Let them try. If they fail, you can swamp them."

"The proverbial silver lining. Very well. Send them to me."

"I shall do so immediately. Anything else you need?"

"Yes. A moment, if you will." Lorn took a piece of parchment and a quill from his desk and hastily drew up a list. "I require these and any similar supplies I may have forgotten."

He slid the list across the desk toward the Head of Procurement.

Head Nevlyn read through the list, his expression puzzled. "Art supplies?"

"*Professional* ones. Do not bring me back a child's paint set."

Head Nevlyn pursed his small, prune-like mouth. "It may take some doing, but I'm sure that we will find what you need."

"Anything else you need from us?" Head Soren asked. "I don't mean to rush things, but school finished up a while ago, and I'd like to be home for my young ones."

"Of course," Lorn said. He gestured to the knitting in her lap. "Before we finish, do you have news for us? Is there another little one on the way?"

Head Soren laughed heartily. "Dear me, *no*. Five is quite enough. I was trying to knit a belt that could double as a garrote." She held up knitted item and eyed it critically. "Problem is, I'm not sure of the tensile strength. I'll have to test it rigorously before use."

Head Flynn smiled at her admiringly. "Always perfecting your art."

"Truly, an inspiration to us all!" Head Nevlyn said, beaming.

Head Soren dimpled at the two men. "Well, in disposals, one cannot be complacent."

"Ah, words of wisdom," Lorn said. "I feel——" He stopped abruptly, his body shuddering.

Lorn, Shadow King of Between, we Summon thee, a woman's voice intoned.

A bell echoed through the chamber.

"Did you hear that?" Lorn asked.

"The bell?" Head Nevlyn asked.

"No, the woman. No," Lorn amended, recognizing the power behind the words, "the *witch*."

The Heads shook their heads.

Behind Lorn's navel, what felt like a fishhook caught and pulled at him, tugging him insistently toward the Portal.

"Are you alright, dear?" Head Soren asked. Her fingers strayed to her sash, where the hilts of two daggers glinted dangerously in the light of the chamber.

Lorn, Shadow King of Between, we Summon thee.

Lorn's clothing transformed into his ceremonial garb, the Cloak of Shadows appeared around his shoulders. "*Ah*—I believe I am being Summoned to the Earther Realm."

Head Soren looked critically at Lorn's attire. "You're not wearing your armor. I don't approve of you going into a strange setting without protection. Would you like me to come with you?"

Lorn shook his head and grimaced as the Crown of Blades settled on his head. "Many thanks for your kind offer, but I will be fine—I have my magic." He grimaced again as the fishhook sensation became stronger. "If you would all excuse me, I must be off."

"Go right ahead!" Head Nevlyn said. "We can show ourselves out."

"Here." Head Soren threw Lorn her homemade garrote. "Just in case."

"I'll want a full report when you return," Head Flynn said, his fingers straying to his notebook.

Lorn stuffed the garrote into the bottomless pouch at his waist, nodded to the Heads in farewell, and slipped down through the floor, emerging in the Portal Chamber.

"It seems that we no longer need to send a message to the Middleton Coven," his Shadow remarked in greeting. "A happy coincidence, is it not, that they just so happened to Summon you today?"

Lorn, Shadow King of Between, we Summon thee.

Lorn braced himself as the Summons shook his body once again. "Since when has any coincidence in Between been happy?"

The Shadow waved off his concerns. "Do not be such a pessimist! This bodes well, mark my words. The coven will assist you in the search, and we will have our Queen with us in no time!"

"Optimism remains one of the primary causes of death in Between," Lorn warned as he turned toward the Portal. Bright, gold light poured into the room as the door opened, ready and eager to lead Lorn to Old Middleton.

"Showtime," his Shadow said with a grin.

Despite himself, Lorn felt his stomach clench in dread. Walking through the Portal was one more step toward the complete upheaval of his world.

He took a deep breath. "Wish me luck," he muttered, stepping through the Portal, the Cloak of Shadows billowing behind him.

"Bring me back a queen!" his Shadow called jauntily after him.

❧

APPROXIMATELY FORTY MINUTES LATER, LORN STORMED BACK THROUGH THE Portal from the Earther Realm in a blaze of light, his expression dark and his jaw clenched.

"That," he bit out, as his ceremonial clothing disappeared, replaced by what he had been wearing before the Summons, "was an unparalleled disaster."

"Why are you so angst-ridden?" the Shadow asked his true form. "Was the coven uncooperative? Will Sasha be difficult to find?"

Lorn turned to his Shadow and allowed his memories to pass between them. The Shadow's eyes widened; it appeared that he was just as stunned at the revelation that the Queen was with the coven as Lorn had been.

"This ... this is *marvelous!*" the Shadow crowed. "Did I not tell you that this meeting would go well? Even so, the outcome is beyond my expectations! To think, Sasha was with the coven all along. This has all the hallmarks of *Destiny!*"

For a brief moment—when the Queen had stepped hesitantly out from behind the coven members, her shoulders braced beneath her green coat—Lorn had thought so, too. He had rejoiced at how uncharacteristically easy it had been to find her.

"Are you ready to leave?" he had asked, more as a formality than anything else. After all, she was standing in front of the Portal, clutching a bag and dressed for a journey. In moments, they would step through the Portal and life would return to a semblance of normali—

"No." The word had been as sharp and as sure as a slap and had echoed through the chamber. It was accompanied by a raised chin and a rather determined arch to her brow that did not bode well for Lorn and his plans.

So much for Destiny.

"You have a gift for only seeing the positive parts of my memories," Lorn told his Shadow. "Did you not see the part where she refused to come with me? Or when she enacted her first boon to ensure that she could stay in Old Middleton for six days? *Six days?*"

The Shadow waved away his concerns. "You found her—*that* is what is important. We can work with the rest. In fact, Sasha and her friend—"

"*Lyla*," Lorn said with a sigh. He had a feeling—an itchy, prickly, doomed sort of feeling—that this Lyla would be troublesome. *Continue* to be troublesome, he corrected. After all, she had started this whole mess by instructing the Queen to run toward the Nightmares rather than away from them; there was no telling what future catastrophes her advice had in store for Lorn.

"—should be commended," the Shadow continued. "Not only did they figure out that you owed Sasha three boons for crossing the Wasteland, but they used that knowledge to their advantage. Our lovely Queen is acting like a Betweener already ..."

"Yes, in the sense that she is causing me no end of trouble." Lorn rubbed a hand tiredly over his eyes. He had explained to the Queen about the dire consequences—to both her and their realms—if she did not accompany him to Between and yet, she had demanded to stay.

"If only she had asked for something else ... *anything* else," he said, shaking his head. "She could have asked for the contents of our treasuries, and I would have been honor-bound to give it to her. Riches beyond her dreams at her disposal and she chose *more time*—the one thing that I am not at liberty to give. If the High King demands that I bring her back to Between, then I will be caught between my Vow to him and this boon." He grimaced at the thought. "This is all becoming so wretchedly melodramatic ..."

"I blame you, of course," the Shadow said.

Lorn blinked. "Truly? What did *I* do?"

"You were too honest. You told her all about the thieves and the spies and the assassins and the cannibal ... and the cannibal is not even here yet! Why did you not tell her about the wonders of Between? The mountains—"

"Filled with wraith wolfs."

"—the lakes—"

"Filled with flesh-eating fish."

"—the fields of flowers—"

"Mostly poisonous."

"—and the wondrous creatures?"

Right on cue, thunder boomed right beside the tower, echoing through the Portal Chamber. It was answered by the roar of a blue and orange winged beast as it flew past the window in all of its dreadful glory.

The Shadow craned his neck. "Is that not the same creature that flew past the window the last time we spoke of this very subject?"

Lorn peered after the creature. "Yes, it is."

"You have to admit—the beast's timing is impeccable."

"What timing? That beast is always flying past this tower. All beasts fly past this tower." Lorn ran a hand through his hair, frustrated. "Between is a place of both infinite wonder and terror, but I would rather emphasize the terror to prepare the Queen for what is in store. If I told her only of the wonder, I would be selling her a pretty illusion; she would despise Between —and myself—for the lie. I had hoped that by preparing her ... that by being honest, she would one day see past the terror to the wonder beyond."

The Shadow considered Lorn's words, his head tilted thoughtfully to the right. "An excellent long-term strategy. Though, I must confess that I thought this would be easier. Sasha has a love of fairy tales and adventures —why would she not want to be part of one?"

Everyone here talks about Between like it's something out of a fairy tale, she had said. *But there are* good *fairy tales, and there are* bad *fairy tales...*

Lorn feared that the Queen's story was the latter. "We both know that this is a dark tale at best. I am no hero on a white horse, carrying her off to a shiny, white castle and a happily-ever-after. I am a reviled sorcerer dragging her against her will to a crumbling castle in a kingdom filled with sinkholes, fearsome beasts, and crotch rot."

"True. Then again, she is not a naïve blushing maiden. I thought the adventure would appeal to her."

"It is not an adventure of her choosing." Lorn knew all about being forced into a situation against his will. He could not blame the Queen for trying everything in her power to run away.

"Then we shall have to make it so. Try to be more charming next time you meet her." The Shadow looked at him slyly. "You could start by calling her *Sasha*."

Lorn's shoulders stiffened. *Caught.* "It is more respectful to refer to her by her title."

"Oh, please." The Shadow dismissed Lorn's words with a wave of his hand. "I know all about that ridiculous 'Queen Plan' of yours and your decision to ... what was it? ... refer to Sasha only by her title so as not to become too *familiar* with her?" He snorted. "As if calling Sasha 'the Queen' will make her any easier to ignore." His eyes narrowed. "Do you deny crafting such a ridiculous plan?"

"Not at all," Lorn said mildly. After all, it was pointless to lie to oneself, especially when that self had the ability to argue back. "You were saying?"

The Shadow rolled his eyes so hard that it was a wonder that he did not fall backwards. "Very well. Forget about being charming—it is clearly beyond your abilities. Instead, try to be more *alluring*." He looked critically at Lorn's attire. "Perhaps you should wear tighter pants."

Lorn looked down at his leather pants. "According to some members of the coven, my pants are already sufficiently alluring." He frowned, remembering the way that several members of the coven had stared at his chest. "Though, for some reason, they disapproved of my shirt ..."

"That is odd. It appears to be a perfectly fine shirt."

Both men looked at Lorn's shirt. "A perfectly fine shirt," the Shadow repeated. He shook his head, bemused. "I must admit, the coven was not what I was expecting."

"Nor I. *I* was expecting them to be more cooperative; they have Vowed to protect the Portal and yet, they would not allow the Queen to return immediately to Between."

The Shadow started to laugh.

"This is no laughing matter," Lorn said sternly.

"No, no—I quite agree. I was merely savoring your memory of those two sweet, old witches hugging you within an inch of your life when you admitted that you did not have loved ones."

Lorn groaned as he remembered being ambushed on both sides by the twin huggers. They may have been tiny, but they hugged with great vigor and were surprisingly hard to dislodge.

"Why does everyone insist on hugging me lately?" he asked. "It is disconcerting." He looked down at his sinister clothing. "Perhaps I should add some spikes to my attire."

The Shadow snorted. "Yes, because *that* is what you need—to appear even less approachable. Then again, those witches probably would have hugged you anyway; the coven was unexpectedly feisty."

"That is one way to put it. All I wanted was their assistance in locating the Queen. Instead, I was hugged, drugged, thwarted, denied—"

"Seduced. Well, almost. Let us not forget that bit. Normally, I would have chastised you for refusing the advances of that brazen, redheaded witch, but given that she was also the one trying to drug you with lust potion-laced lemonade, your actions were quite understandable."

Lorn rolled his eyes. "Many thanks."

"Moreover, Sasha was standing right beside you while she was making her advances. The entire situation was somewhat awkward." The Shadow shuddered delicately. "It is for the best that the lust potion did not work; the last thing we would want is to anger our lovely Queen." The Shadow paused, smiling at Lorn's memories. "She does not appear to be the least bit intimidated by you. So brave! Did you see her expression while she was giving that delightful speech demanding to know more about Between—"

"Do you mean the delightful speech where she accurately described Between as hellish?"

The Shadow ignored him. "Her eyes were blazing, her cheeks aglow, her lips full and lush, her chest heaving with emotion—did you see how well your amulet looked, nestled between her bre—"

"That's quite enough," Lorn interrupted.

Lorn had, indeed, noticed where his amulet nestled, but he abruptly cut short that train of thought, and the emotions that accompanied it.

"But—" the Shadow began.

"*Enough*," Lorn said firmly. He was uncomfortably aware of the fact that the Shadow had seen his memories, and probably knew exactly how Lorn felt about the Queen wearing something of his own—a symbol of his protection and care—around the her throat.

A Most Wretched Hug

As if to confirm his suspicions, the Shadow smiled—a very knowing smile.

Lorn's eyes narrowed. "I know what you are trying to do and it will not work."

"*Do?*" the Shadow placed his hand over his heart. "You make my motives sound so nefarious. I was merely trying to make you admit that Sasha Pierce is a beautiful, captivating, and brilliant woman ... and not at all burdensome." The Shadow shook his head, clearly disappointed. "I cannot believe you said that to our lovely Queen."

I am stretched to my limits with my duties as King, and I have no doubt that trying to engage in some form of marital arrangement would only add to those burdens.

Lorn recalled the words and cringed. "I am sure she will remind me of that grievous slip of the tongue for the rest of my days."

"If she does not, I shall. To make matters worse, it is a terrible lie. She will not be a burden; she will bring the light to this drab little kingdom. How could she not? She is simply *glorious*! Honestly, I do not know how you resisted the impulse to take her into your arms then and there, and carry her back to your kingdom."

"I am a man of remarkable restraint," Lorn said dryly. "Moreover, she did not consent to come, remember?"

"True," the Shadow reluctantly conceded. "Moreover, she was surrounded by a veritable wall of rather protective witches. Not that they would have posed any threat to you whatsoever. There was power there, true, but they each had only one or two Marks at most."

Lorn recalled the witches as they moved as one to surround Sasha, their expressions determined, their magic pressing against Lorn's in warning as sharp as needlepoints. "Do not underestimate them. There *was* power there —and experience." Lorn frowned as he recalled the coven. "Did it not strike you as odd that many of the witches were quite ...?"

"Old?"

Lorn nodded. "I always thought that the lives of magic folk were short. It was ... surprising to see that this was not the case in the Earther Realm."

"Well, Otherworld has a terrible habit of killing off its magic folk before they can die of old age. And I assume that the lifespan of those in the Earther Realm tends to be longer anyway: better nutrition, better potions, fewer rampaging fire-breathing beasts—"

"And, as you said, they only had one or two Marks." Lorn turned over his hands and stared at the white Marks on his palms and wrists. He tilted his hands toward the light and watched as the power beneath his skin rippled beneath the designs. "The greater the power, the shorter the life-span, regardless of the realm," he said grimly.

The Shadow contemplated his true form. "The greater the power, the more dangerous and impossible the feats that one is asked to perform with that power, is that not so? And it is those feats that cause magical exhaustion and death. Not the power. Do not be afraid of the power, Lorn. It is nothing to fear."

Lorn snorted. "Tell that to those who would happily burn me at the stake because of that power."

"Idiots always fear what they cannot control or understand. *They* would make much better kindling than magic folk. But that is beside the point—you no longer fear being burned. What you truly fear is magical exhaustion."

"And with good cause." Lorn pulled back the cuffs of his coat, revealing black patches that stained the pale skin of his forearms like spilled ink on parchment.

The Shadow contemplated the marks, his expression terribly sad. "What you need to remember is that exhaustion, magical or otherwise, is a function of doing too much and not accepting help. In six days, you *will* have help. Accept it."

Lorn pulled down his sleeves, covering the dark patches with even darker cloth. "How can she possibly help me? She knows nothing about this realm. She has no magic—she cannot wield the Portal or ward the city. I cannot see how she will be anything other than a burden ... that is, until she knows enough to rule." He snorted. "Assuming that she ever gets here. Six days. The Portal cannot remain open for that long. How will I keep her safe for six days, even with the coven's assistance?"

Suddenly, Lorn staggered forward. The Tether Mark between his shoulder blades flared white-hot, accompanied by an insistent pressure. In the back of his mind, Lorn felt the presence of Between, urgent and unrelenting.

"What is it?" his Shadow asked, concerned. "Is it Between?"

Lorn nodded sharply. "Between wants me to get her from the Earther Realm now. It does not want to wait six days." He looked over at the Shadow. "Could you please try and talk sense into it?"

The Shadow stared into the middle distance. After a few moments, he shook his head. "Apparently not. It seems to think that time is of the essence. It wants her here, right now, so that it can protect her."

"Well, she does not want *us* right now," Lorn said to Between. "She asked for time; it was her first boon. You must respect it."

The pressure on Lorn's back eased somewhat.

"Thank you, ever so," he said dryly.

The Shadow tilted his head, listening. "Between wants you to go to the Summoning Chamber. It wants you to retrieve its gifts for Sasha."

At that pronouncement, the pressure between Lorn's shoulders eased entirely.

Lorn rolled his shoulders and grimaced. "Why did it not tell me so?"

"It is far too excited. It wants too much—its thoughts and desires are all a jumble."

"Very well. I will go there momentarily ... as soon as I recover from being psychically pummeled by a sentient landmass."

Lorn felt Between apologetically brush against his mind.

"Yes, yes," Lorn said with a sigh. "A little gentler next time, if you please; it would not do to break your toys."

"Would you like me to come with you?" the Shadow asked.

Lorn considered his offer but shook his head. "Best if I do this alone."

"Good luck!" his Shadow called out as Lorn headed for the door.

"I have a feeling I will need it," Lorn said dourly and went to do Between's bidding.

～

In life, there are tasks that one must do that are less than agreeable. Some are too difficult, others are too taxing, and some merely take up time that could have been better spent doing something more pleasant, like drinking, or traveling, or enjoying an excellent slice of pie.

But there are other tasks that are, for want of a better term, *revelatory*. That is, by the doing, they reveal certain truths: secret desires, hidden talents, or, in Lorn's case, clues about the type of queen Sasha Pierce was Destined to become.

Needless to say, Lorn had a terrible feeling about all of this.

Please, he begged Between as he reluctantly walked down a series of narrow staircases toward the Summoning Chamber in the Large Treasury. *Just give her a couple of pretty trinkets.*

But even as he said it, Lorn realized that it was unlikely. The Queen had conquered the Nightmares in a dream. She had resisted the lure of power and had fought to retain her home and independence. Why would Between give such a formidable woman a pair of earrings or a necklace?

Very well, Lorn bargained as he spiraled deeper and deeper into the bowels of the castle. *Just try and select something non-lethal.*

The sound of stone grating against stone interrupted his thoughts.

Looking up, Lorn watched as the gargoyle above him—a terrifyingly realistic depiction of a dragon—began to shift and spread his wings.

"It is just me," he told the dragon fondly. "There are no thieves for you to devour tonight."

The dragon opened its mouth, baring sharp, stone teeth, and roared.

"Really?" Lorn laughed. "I am insulted that you are not happier to see me."

The dragon lowered its head apologetically and slithered down the wall until it was beside Lorn.

With a wry twist of his lips, Lorn patted the Sentinel's head affectionately. "That is better."

With a final pat, Lorn left the dragon, nodding to the other mythical creatures who awoke as he passed. Stone hydras, minotaurs, and griffins stretched luxuriantly, bowing their heads to Lorn as he crossed their path.

With a final nod to the Sentinels, Lorn found himself before an impressive metal door carved with serpents. At his approach, the serpents began to hiss and writhe, rising—fangs bared—ready to strike.

"Careful now," Lorn said mildly and placed his hands on the door.

The serpents retreated with a hiss and a bit of a leer, and the door to the Large Treasury creaked open.

As Lorn entered, torches across the cavernous hall burst into flame. He ignored the multitude of doors that lined the hall, some of which were open, and others bolted shut. He passed rooms filled with caskets that shimmered with precious stones, and others that contained sacks overflowing with golden coins; rooms filled with dangerous objects, and others filled with priceless artifacts. He also passed several locked doors, including one that rattled and shook as he approached. Lorn paid no mind to the treasures around him; instead, he moved swiftly to his destination, accompanied by the dry whispers of the Sentinels as they followed his progress across the chamber.

Finally, Lorn reached a small, golden door that opened silently at his approach. Unlike the Large Treasury, which was packed with crates and casks, this room was empty except for a circular dais that stood beneath a gold, domed ceiling.

Lorn looked at the dais and hesitated. The last time he had been in this room was on the eve of his own coronation. He had mounted the dais, prepared to receive ceremonial gifts fit for a king. A sword, perhaps. Or a scepter. Or possibly a wand to amplify and direct his magic, like the Wand of Infinity, which he had used as the High King's Left Hand.

Instead, Between had given him raw power.

Lorn's first gift had been a Mark on the back of his neck that stretched from his nape to the top of his spine and gave him the power to transform, not only objects, but his own form.

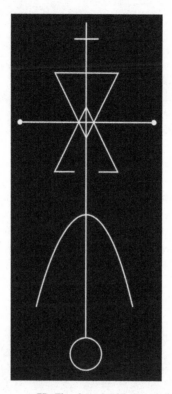

The Transformation Mark

He was suddenly free to soar the skies of Between as a bird, or to run across the plains as a wolf; to burrow beneath the ground, rabbit-quick, or to follow the streams, slick as a fish.

He was still marveling at this gift when Between Marked him again—a palm-sized Mark that spanned the base of his spine and magnified his powers. Lorn's eyes had widened in shock at this gift; it felt *extraordinary*—as if he had been hollowed out and filled brimful with power until raw current leaked from every pore of his body.

The Power Mark

For the first and only time of his life, Lorn felt drunk, intoxicated by the magic running white-hot and gold through his veins. He remembered standing on that dais and laughing at the wonderful shock of it all, while the voice of Between reverberated through his mind, speaking to him, reassuring him, *learning* him. He had never felt so joyous in his miserable life.

That is, until Between Marked him a third time.

The Tether Mark

This Mark felt like a brand between his shoulder blades. It immediately began to burn, began to *twist*, filling the space between his shoulders with a jagged, raw agony that rippled down his spine. Lorn felt something—something vital, something essential—being torn from deep within himself. His laughter turned to screams; his joy to pain and terror until mercifully, he passed out.

When he awoke—sprawled on his back on the dais, his throat raw, his cheeks wet with tears—he had looked up at the polished gold dome above him and saw himself looking back ... but *not* himself. *This* self had looked down on Lorn with great concern, then with pure joy when it realized that Lorn had awoken.

"Why, hello," this other self, this *Shadow* had said. "Am *I* happy to meet you!"

And this gift, this curse, this Shadow had explained that Between had given Lorn the power to draw upon the magical stores of Between itself.

"But," his Shadow told him sorrowfully, "there is always a price for power ..."

And the price Lorn had paid to Between for this wonderful, *terrible* power was a small sliver of his soul—now encased in a mirror—which tethered him to the kingdom such that he was unable to leave for more than three days without being called back to Between.

And so Lorn—who had lived his childhood as a slave, chained up by day and locked away by night—now found himself in a different type of cage.

Lorn shook his head, trying to clear away the memories and the emotions tangled around them. Was it any wonder that he was somewhat reluctant to find out what 'gifts' Between would bestow upon the new Queen?

"Remember—she is an artist," he said to Between in a last-ditch effort to sway the gift-giving process toward something pleasant and cheerful. "Surely, she would appreciate a lovely piece of art, an intricate frame, an instrument to help enhance her skills ..."

He listened, hoping for a reply.

"Ones that are not cursed," he added for good measure.

But there was only silence.

"Very well," he sighed.

Lorn reluctantly mounted the dais and looked up at the mirror-like surface of the dome. His own grim expression stared back down at him. With a heavy sigh, he read the inscription carved around the dome's edge.

Ask, but be prepared for all that you may receive.

"Easy for you to say," he muttered.

He cleared his throat and took a deep breath, readying himself. "I am

Lorn, True King of Between. I seek three gifts befitting Sasha Evangeline Pierce, the True Queen of Between, to serve her during her reign."

Lorn widened his stance, bracing himself for whatever would come his way. He raised his arms until they were outstretched at his sides and opened his hands.

A flash of gold flew out from the shadows and hurtled toward his left hand. Instinctively, Lorn caught it. He took one look at the sleek object, and his eyes widened in shock.

Before he could comment, the next object—a small bottle, its contents glowing cerulean-blue in the dim light—flew straight into his right hand.

Lorn looked down at the two gifts, his heart hammering heavily in his chest. "This is getting progressively worse."

Carefully, he placed the two gifts on the ground near his feet. He then stood, heart racing, for the third gift.

Despite bracing himself, the object that flew into his left hand forced him to step back under the power of its momentum.

"Bollocks," he said, staring at it in awe.

Somewhere in the chambers, the sound of a bell—clear and pure—rang out, as if a task of considerable Destiny had been fulfilled.

"Whatever have you done, Between?" Lorn whispered, staring down at the three gifts. "What have you gotten us all into now?"

Between made no reply. But beneath the echo of the bell, there was the dry sound of stone moving against stone. To Lorn, it sounded as though the ancient castle itself was laughing.

~

LORN LEFT THE SUMMONING CHAMBERS, GINGERLY HOLDING THE SILVER box containing the Queen's Coronation gifts and returned to his Less-Formal Meeting Chambers in a state that could be best described as shock—a state that was becoming all too commonplace for Lorn ever since meeting the Queen.

When Maddox entered the chamber a half hour later, he found Lorn staring pensively at the box, a half-full bottle of dwarven Red Gold whiskey sitting before him, and a glass nowhere in sight.

"You do realize that Red Gold has been classified as a cleaning product in every kingdom but Trundel," Maddox said, taking a seat opposite Lorn. "There is a good reason why they call it 'Red Death.' And yet, here you are, drinking it from the bottle. *Do* remember that you are a sorcerer, not a god."

Silently, Lorn opened the box and turned it toward Maddox so that he could see the contents. "Behold, the Queen's coronation gifts from Between."

"Fuck," Maddox said and reached for the Red Gold.

Lorn looked on in amusement as the older man took a long, deep drink. "My sentiments exactly."

Eventually, Maddox placed the bottle back on the table, coughing hard enough to bring up a lung. "This ... this is *quite* the development," he said when he was finally able to breathe, wiping the alcohol from his lips with the back of his hand.

"One that I would prefer *not* to become common knowledge; the less incentive the High King has to harm the Queen, the better."

Maddox looked toward the secret panels in the wall where the spies—and Terrance—resided.

But Lorn shook his head. "We can speak freely; I gave them the night off. I shall speak to Head Flynn about the matter personally."

Maddox nodded slowly, his eyes on the gifts. "No need—I will see to it."

"Marvelous." Lorn stared dully at the gifts before closing the box once again. With a sigh, he stood up. "I need to clear my head. I shall return momentarily."

"Very well." Maddox watched as Lorn crossed the room and stepped up onto the window-ledge. "But what of the box? Should I move it to a safe room?"

"No need—I have enchanted it. I did it while drinking that terrible whiskey, so Midra knows what would happen if you touched it." Lorn glanced at the box and shuddered. "I pity the person who tries to steal it." He gestured to the Red Gold. "Feel free to finish the bottle."

With a smart salute, Lorn stepped off the ledge into the empty air.

"Do not tempt me!" the older man called after him.

～

WHEN YOU ARE BESET BY CHAOS AND CATASTROPHE ON AN HOURLY BASIS, IT is important to have a refuge—a place where you can sit, undisturbed, for a few precious moments and gird your loins for what the rest of the day will bring.

Lorn had seven such refuges, the closest being an old broom closet in a forgotten wing of the castle, where he liked to sit—and sigh, or laugh a touch hysterically—when things were going worse than usual.

Typically, on Wednesdays.

Today, he decided to forgo the broom closet and head to his refuge on top of the highest peak in Between—a peak which was, incidentally, as far away from the box of coronation gifts as geographically possible within Between's borders.

It was also only accessible by flight, and if there was one thing that Lorn truly loved, beside granting Dreams, it was flying.

Even so, becoming a bird was never a particularly pleasant experience for Lorn. At the moment of transformation, he was subjected to an overwhelming rush of sensations—the reconfiguration of flesh and bones, the twist of ligaments and the binding of limbs, the sleekness of feathers and the softness of down—all accompanied by a gut-churning wrench as his very essence was molded into something smaller, something infinitely more fragile, something *other* than himself.

It was disconcerting, to put it mildly.

But flying made it all worthwhile. Soaring above his kingdom, Lorn found the dizzying sense of freedom that he could never hope to achieve on the ground. He made a series of lazy circles, taking advantage of the air currents, before landing on the peak with a hop. The icy air had cleared away most of the panic induced by the Queen's gifts, and the lingering effects of the Red Gold, leaving him clear-headed and relatively calm.

He was just beginning to savor the solitude when he heard the oddest sound—a sound completely out of place on a deserted, mountain peak:

"This is really awful," a voice complained. "Why can't you put me on a b-beach? Aren't there any b-beaches in this place?"

Wondering whether the mountain wolves had suddenly developed the power of speech, Lorn turned and there was the Queen. Even though her back was to him, he could see that she was shivering with cold, and dressed as inappropriately as ever in her pajamas.

"Unfortunately, not," he answered, his lips twitching. "Then again, you should be grateful that you were not deposited into one of our infamous swamps."

The Queen stilled for a long moment, and then looked at him over her shoulder. For some inexplicable reason, Lorn expected her to smile at him —that same, glorious smile she had given him when he came to rescue her in the Wasteland. But the Queen did not smile. In fact, the look she gave him—something prickly and vexed, composed of furrowed brows and narrowed eyes and tight, drawn lips—was so different from that smile that he was momentarily taken aback.

"Are the swamps warm?" she asked, her tone as chilly as the wind that whipped around them. She wrapped her arms around her torso and shifted from one foot to the other. "If so, they *are* the better option right now."

Lorn took one look at the vexed, shivering, non-smiling Queen and realized that this interaction had the potential for great disaster unless he swiftly remedied the situation.

Start by alleviating the shivering, he thought. *That is by far the easiest to fix.*

He quickly unclasped his cloak. "Forgive me—my chivalrous urges are somewhat rusty."

Lorn blamed the Red Gold for the strange sense of satisfaction that he felt as he clasped his cloak around the Queen's dainty throat and the warm flutter that spread across his ribcage when she smiled up at him in surprise.

"Thanks," she said, huddling into the folds of his cloak. She made a contented sound and looked up at him with such true gratitude that Lorn was momentarily taken aback.

"But what about you?" she asked.

The question made Lorn smile. Here she was, freezing on a frigid mountain peak, and she was concerned about *him*.

Suddenly, he wanted to do more for her. He looked down to where her feet were buried in the snow and reached for his tunic.

"Won't you be col—" She stared at him in wide-eyed alarm as he unbuttoned his tunic. "Hang on—I'm not *that* cold."

She quite literally threw herself at me during her first Dream and demanded that I seduce her, he thought to himself with amusement. *And yet now she objects when I remove my tunic.*

"Your feet may disagree," was all he said in return.

The Queen shivered and looked down at her feet. "They're okay."

"You are a dreadful liar." He laid his tunic across the snow beside her and held out his hand. "Something you will need to rectify if you are going to rule a kingdom filled with liars."

He gasped as his magic sparked beneath his skin, glitter-bright, the instant she placed her hand in his.

I must be slightly intoxicated, he thought, as he led her to stand on his tunic.

Even after she released his hand, he felt the echo of that sharp, bright magic skip through his blood, warming him in a way that cloaks and tunics could not. It was delightful but distracting; with great effort, he brought his full attention back to the conversation.

Which was just as well, as the Queen was staring at his chest as if it were a particularly tricky riddle. For a moment, he wondered if he had accidentally removed more than his tunic. But just as he was about to check, she spoke.

"How many layers are you wearing?" She tilted her head, as if different angle would solve the mystery. "It seems like a very complicated outfit."

"Do you wish me to keep disrobing so that you may find out?" he found himself saying.

He stilled. Was that ... flirtatious banter?

Good gods, he thought to himself in shock. *It was. When I return, I shall toss that cursed bottle of whiskey out the window ...*

He turned his full attention back to the Queen. She was frowning, her bottom lip caught between her teeth. "Hang on—was my question inappropriate?" she asked. "Dash it—it was, wasn't it?"

Lorn was about to tease her with a 'yes' when the oddest thought crossed his mind.

You are betrothed, the thought said. *There* are *no inappropriate questions between you, not anymore.*

And Lorn was suddenly struck by the full enormity of their betrothal. A Joining was a partnership in every sense of the word. There would be no topics off-limits or too personal to discuss. She would have his confidences and he would have hers, and together, they would work through all the problems that the world laid at their feet.

He was surprised to find that something in his chest—something bruised and tangled—felt lighter at the thought.

But he quickly brushed it away.

She did not choose this Joining, he reminded himself brusquely. *Nor did you. Stick to The Queen Plan.*

"Given that we are all but betrothed?" he said instead. "No, I believe not."

"And if we weren't 'all but betrothed'?" she asked.

"Then, I would have assumed that it was a strangely phrased invitation to engage in more intimate activities."

He almost groaned aloud. *More* flirtatious banter? What was *wrong* with him?

Thankfully, the Queen found it amusing. "Ha! No—definitely not my intention." She looked around the snow and shuddered. "That would lead to frostbite in the most awkward places."

"Truly, a dismal fate," he responded with a shocked laugh.

She grinned at him, as if delighted by his laughter, and then turned to admire the vista, an icy breeze blowing her curls around her shoulders.

As he answered the Queen's questions about the lands below, Lorn wondered about his odd behavior.

Flirtatious banter, chivalrous feats that would be the envy of any elf, public disrobing ... I must *be intoxicated. What other explanation could there be?*

Sorcerers cannot get intoxicated, a voice that sounded very much like the Shadow's whispered in the back of his mind. *Not even when they imbibe a liquid typically used to strip paint from barns. Which means—*

The voice paused, arrested by the sight of the Queen curling her toes into the velvet-soft fabric of his tunic.

Which means, it continued, clearing its throat, *that you—and only you—are responsible for this blatantly flirtatious conversation.*

"How did you get up here?" the Queen asked, thankfully interrupting his train of thought. "You don't look as though you've been mountain climbing."

His lips twitched. "I flew up."

"O-kay." Her brow furrowed. "But *how?*"

"I keep forgetting that magic is new to you," he mused, as she scanned the peak, looking for the source of Lorn's miraculous ascent. "You will need to brace yourself for a rude awakening."

The Queen opened her mouth to reply but instead awkwardly stumbled forward as if she had been pushed from behind.

"I'm waking up," she said, her hand flattening over her midsection. She grinned wryly at him, as if sharing a joke. "It was—well, fun, I guess?" She glanced away, still looking for his means of climbing the mountain.

It would be best for her—and for Between—if she lost her naivety about magic sooner rather than later, Lorn thought.

To that end ... "Until next time," he said. He waited until the Queen was looking at him before bowing to her with a flourish.

Then, he took two long strides backward and fell off the mountain.

"No!" Lorn heard the Queen cry from above him.

The bitter wind rushed up to meet him, holding him aloft as he folded himself into his bird form. Through the muffle of feathers and the twisting of bones, he could hear the Queen calling his name.

"Shadow King!" she screamed, her tone shrill and desperate.

Then, "*Lorn!*"

The sound of his name forced an answering cry from his throat. He stretched out his wings and flew back to her as quickly as he could until he was hovering above the cliff face.

The Queen stared at him, her expression stricken, her chest heaving.

"Bird," she said, addressing him as if he were a passerby, "did you just see a man dressed in black fall off the cliff?"

Lorn tipped back his head and laughed at the charming absurdity of the question, the sound coming out of his beak as a strangled caw.

The Queen was not amused. "You're a sorcerer," she said, figuring it out. "And a bastard." She began to float skyward, his cloak falling from her shoulders. "How could you scare me like that? You should be ashamed of yourself. *Bad bird!*"

She scolded him as if he were a naughty child in a schoolroom, not a sorcerer king with more raw power at his disposal than any of the magic folk in Otherworld. The idea of it was so preposterous that it made him laugh even harder.

"*Bad sorcerer!*" she cried, shaking her finger with gusto until she disappeared, leaving a shower of gold dust in her wake.

Lorn transformed back and looked down at the gold dust scattered across the snow, glittering away in the fading light.

"*Bad sorcerer?* She will have to improve her insults. Perhaps Felzik can coach her ..." He picked up his cloak and sodden tunic, his lips twisting into a reluctant grin.

Well, he thought, as he flew back to the castle, far more amused than he had any right to be at such a perilous time, *the new Queen certainly distracted me from my troubles.*

But the problem, Lorn realized when he returned to his chambers, was that he now needed something to distract him from his distraction. His cloak still held her fragrance—something floral and spicy, all warm notes like sunsets and summer evenings. He caught sight of his reflection in the full-length mirror in his dressing chamber and rolled his eyes.

"Sunsets and summer evenings? You utter *sop.*"

Lorn glared at his cloak as if it had committed a grievous offense and put it aside to be laundered. He threw his sodden tunic beside it, just in case it was similarly contaminated.

"She called me a bad bird," Lorn told his reflection with a wry smile. "And a bad sorcerer. No doubt 'bad husband' will follow shortly." He thought back over the scene and frowned. "She also called me Lorn."

Shadow King! Lorn!

He could still hear the Queen calling out his name, frantic and horror-struck, as he stepped off the peak. He felt a momentary pang of guilt, but he had not expected her to react in such a way.

"She tried to save me. Again. It is becoming something of a habit for her."

Lorn's reflection frowned, clearly puzzled by the Queen's actions. Which meant that he, too, was puzzled by the Queen's actions. Lorn was a schemer by nature—he spent his formative years amongst deviants in Between, and more time than was healthy amongst the backstabbers at the Summer Palace court. So, it was not surprising that his first thought was to ponder what the new Queen hoped to gain by such actions.

Then he dismissed that thought with a sigh.

"She appears to be kind," Lorn told his reflection, "with no ulterior motive to her actions. Which is dreadful—she will not last a day in Between with that attitude. Good gods, I shall have to watch her at every turn ..."

The thought of the Queen's kindness toward him elicited a strange mix of emotions in Lorn—a pinch of disbelief, a touch of despair at her naivety, and an odd sort of protectiveness that was so surprising, so unexpected, that it made him want to fly away again.

His reflection looked just as flummoxed as he felt.

Lorn cleared his throat uneasily. "Then again, perhaps she has realized that my untimely demise would result in her ruling this dreadful place alone. Truly a terrifying prospect. I am surprised that she did not hurl herself over the mountain after me."

And with that convenient—and utterly incorrect—explanation, Lorn put on one of the many sinister black outfits hanging in his wardrobe and left his chambers to finish the remaining tasks on his agenda.

12

A WRETCHEDLY MELODRAMATIC STATE OF AFFAIRS

Sunday, October 28th—When everything goes terribly wrong(er).

THERE WERE MANY UNWRITTEN LAWS IN BETWEEN. SOME REFLECTED BASIC manners and were taught to children at their parents' knee. (*Never touch another person's chicken. Do not disturb plotting goats. It's impolite to stab someone in the back when you're on a first name basis.*)

Others focused on ensuring one's survival and were quickly adopted to avoid a messy death. (*The Minotaur is not for riding. Let sleeping dog-dragon-hybrids lie. Never attempt to juggle flaming axes whilst drunk and standing in an ale barrel.*)

But the unwritten law almost universally upheld was: *Never utter the phrase, 'It could be worse'* within Between's borders. This was because the words were inevitably taken as a challenge by the Powers That Be and acted upon almost immediately.

But when it came to the Queen, Lorn found that the phrase did not even have to be uttered aloud; worst-case scenarios simply appeared as if Summoned.

Lorn's ultimate worst-case scenario regarding the Queen took place as he was attempting to nap between meetings. He had just settled back in his chair and closed his eyes when he felt the magical signature of his enchanted hand mirror alerting him that someone was about to call.

"Lorn!" Prince Ashlyn's voice called. "Where are you?"

Lorn opened his heavy eyelids and, sure enough, his hand mirror was glowing. Picking it up, he found Prince Ashlyn on the other side, a rare frown marring his handsome face.

Lorn yawned widely. "Please tell me that this is a social call so that I can end it immediately and return to my nap."

"I wish it were. Your Queen—"

"She is not mine," Lorn interrupted. "I believe she has full autonomy over her personhood."

"Well, you should tell that to the High King. I have just been ordered to go to the Earther Realm and escort Queen Sasha to the Summer Palace."

Lorn suddenly felt wide awake. "He ordered *you* to escort her to the Summer Palace?"

Ash snorted. "*Kidnap* would be a better word. But given that she is a queen, I believe the High King was being diplomatic."

Lorn shook his head. "But the Earther Realm is my responsibility—*I* am the Guardian of the Earther Realm. He should have ordered *me* to escort her to the Summer Palace."

Ash's lips flattened into a hard line. "I did remind the High King of your role and asked why you were not taking care of this matter personally."

"What did he say?"

"He said, and I quote"—Ash lowered his voice to a pitch-perfect imitation of the High King's dry baritone—"We are *all* responsible for the safety of Otherworld."

"So, he dodged the question?"

Ash nodded grimly. "He dodged the question. Regardless of whether it is a breach of convention or not, I have my orders."

Lorn felt as though the pit of his stomach was slowly filling with lead. This was all happening far too quickly. He thought that he would have a few days reprieve before the High King acted. Instead, it was not even a full day since Dresden had found out about the new True Queen of Between and he was already taking matters into his own hands.

Lorn sat back in his chair, resigned to see where this would all lead. "When is the wretched event to occur?"

"Tomorrow. We are to meet just after dawn."

So, so soon! Lorn tried to tamp down his growing unease. "Dawn is an obscenely early hour for a kidnapping; it is positively amateurish. Surely this cannot be Dresden's first kidnapping." A thought occurred to Lorn. "How is that he knows where she lives? *I* do not even know where she lives."

Ash shrugged. "I know not. We were told to find her at a boarding house."

"But no directions as to the whereabouts of the boarding house?"

The prince frowned. "No. Which, come to think of it, is odd. Unless the Summer Gateway deposits us in front of the boarding house, we will be required to ask Earthers for directions ... whilst wearing full armor."

"Well, that will be an adventure." Lorn tried to get his sluggish mind to think, to see the bigger picture. "It is not a stellar plan and certainly not as strategic as one would expect from the High King. It speaks more of desperation than cunning."

"There has been very little strategy applied to this plan," Ash agreed. "In fact, the High King did not even mention what Queen Sasha looks like."

Lorn raised an eyebrow. "*Interesting.* Well, do not spoil the surprise and tell him."

"Truth be told, I only saw Her Majesty for a handful of moments in your mirror, and she was moving exceptionally quickly." Ash sighed an exaggerated sigh. "I believe I shall be no help whatsoever in recognizing her."

"Marvelous. Did the High King say anything else about the Queen?"

"Only that she had a companion."

"Ah, yes. The notorious *Lyla.*" Lorn tapped his lower lip thoughtfully. "Her presence may work in our favor; you could simply kidnap the wrong woman."

Ash grimaced. "I would rather not kidnap anyone."

"How tiresomely noble of you."

Ash shook his head, his features pinched. "Nobility is only half the reason. When my father hears that I have kidnapped an innocent woman, he will have *strong words* with me. When my mother hears, she will cuff me around the ears." Ash winced. "She has such strong hands ..."

"So you have mentioned on numerous occasions. Very well, then—for the sake of your delicate ears there shall be no kidnapping. It is probably for the best; I doubt Otherworld is ready for Lyla. Did the High King say why he wants you to bring the Queen to Otherworld?"

"He claimed that her presence in the Earther realm was jeopardizing the safety of Otherworld."

"*Hmm.* I wonder if that is merely a palatable excuse for a dreadful deed, or if he knows that the Queen opens the Portal whenever she dreams."

Ash blinked. "She opens the Portal whenever she dreams?"

"Yes." Lorn ran a hand through his hair, frustrated by the whole ordeal.

"The Portal is trying to bring her back to Between to rule." His eyes narrowed. "That is a well-kept secret."

Ash mimed buttoning his lips closed. "One that will never leave my lips. Do you wish me to Vow it?"

Lorn noted Ash's earnest expression and snorted. "No need. You are disgustingly loyal."

The prince beamed. "Many thanks ... even though you say it as if it is a personal failing."

"It is. How does the High King intend to send you to the Earther realm? The only gateways to the Earther realm are in Between."

"My orders are to stand ready by the Summer Gateway tomorrow morning. I suspect that High Queen Orelia will use it as a passage to the Earther Realm; she *is* the Guardian of the Gateways in Otherworld."

Lorn balked at the very idea. "The power required to use the Summer Gateway as a portal to the Earther Realm would be astronomical. Even with the Wand of Infinity and her royal fae blood, the High Queen would suffer enormous magical exhaustion. Midra's sack—she would not be able to move for days." The thought of Orelia suffering in such a way, for such a ridiculous plan, made Lorn feel decidedly stabby toward her husband.

Ash's expression darkened. "This is not right. Kidnapping the rightful Queen of Between, and harming the High Queen to do it?" He shook his head angrily. "The High King is pursuing a most dishonorable Scheme."

"Well, we will simply have to hatch our own dishonorable Scheme to counter it. Tell me, will you be traveling alone?"

"No—Adies will accompany me."

Lorn groaned. "That sycophant. I was not aware that Dresden was able to pry Adies's lips from his buttocks long enough to send him on quests."

Ash grinned. "It is remarkable what can be accomplished in this Golden Age of Invention." His frown returned. "However, there is definite trickery afoot; *my* orders were to retrieve Queen Sasha and deliver her to the Summer Palace, but Adies was called aside after the meeting. I fear his orders may have been more nefarious."

Lorn swore under his breath. "Very well. Then we, too, shall have to be nefarious. We will have to incapacitate Adies using cunning methods."

"Shall I have his sword enchanted?"

Lorn nodded. "And whatever else befits the situation. Once the Queen Summons me, I shall take care of Adies myself. It will be over in a trice."

"I have no doubt that you will make quick work of the situation once you are Summoned. For my part, I am more concerned about what will happen *before* you are Summoned. If Adies has orders to maim or kill

Queen Sasha, then he will strike well before you arrive. I will, of course, do everything in my power to protect her, but I will have to tread lightly."

Lorn was barely listening to Ash. Three words kept echoing around in his skull.

... maim or kill ...

... maim or kill ...

... maim or kill ...

His heart began to pound viciously, accompanied by an emotion that fluttered against his ribcage and twisted around the pit of his stomach—something that reminded him uncomfortably of fear.

What in the Hell Realm was his body *doing?*

"I will need to find a way to help her," Ash continued, "without losing the High King's trust. I—" He stopped abruptly and leaned closer to the mirror, his brow furrowed. "Are you quite well, my friend?"

The concern in Ash's expression made Lorn feel itchy.

"Quite well," Lorn answered as calmly as possible.

"Is ... is there an *earthquake* back there?"

Lorn suddenly realized that he was gripping the handle of the mirror so tightly that it was shaking.

"Of a sort," he said smoothly, and relaxed his grip. "To return to the matter at hand, will you be able to keep the Queen alive until I arrive? Or will that prove too difficult?"

"Do not fear," Ash said, his tone solemn. "Queen Sasha is in good hands."

The twisty, fluttering emotion around Lorn's heart eased somewhat. "Yours or Adies's?"

Ash grinned. "Mine, of course! Now, I know you have been too busy to ask, but the answer is *yes*—I would be honored to stand by you as your best man at the Joining."

Lorn exhaled in a rush, happy to change the subject. "As you so astutely remarked, I have not asked you."

Ash ignored him. "Really, say no more. I accept."

"I had planned to ask Trev—"

"The honor is mine."

"Or perhaps Dragma—"

"It will be a privilege."

"Or Medas—"

The prince raised his hand. "Please, say no more. No need to convince me."

"Or Varran—"

"*Say no more,*" Ash said firmly.

Lorn sighed the sigh of a man who has been greatly inconvenienced. "Very well then, since it means so much to you."

Ash's smile was as glorious as the sunrise. "It does. Thank you, once again, for asking. I shall immediately prepare my ceremonial armor and my boldest cloak."

Lorn rolled his eyes. "Just make sure that the Queen is in one piece for the Joining, you peacock."

"I now have even more incentive to ensure it. Do not worry, my friend —we *will* triumph. Adies is no match for us ... and will be even less so after my wizard tampers with his sword. I shall do my utmost to ensure that Queen Sasha is safe until your arrival."

Lorn nodded. "Once I arrive, the situation will be swiftly remedied."

"You will see—victory will be ours." Ash grinned. "We will most likely be in and out of the Earther Realm in under an hour."

Such confidence!

Such bravado!

Alas for Lorn and Ash, it appeared that the Powers That Be were not particularly fond of those, either...

~

WHEN LORN AND ASH FINISHED THEIR SCHEMING, LORN LOOKED UP FROM his enchanted mirror and started.

Sitting opposite him was Head-Raven Flynn, his long, spidery frame folded neatly in the leather armchair opposite Lorn's desk, his expression as blank as a new piece of parchment. His ever-present notebook lay open in his hands.

Lorn placed his hand mirror carefully on the desk. "Head Flynn—I did not hear you come in."

"I would have been insulted if you had." Head Flynn bowed his head. "Forgive the intrusion, Your Majesty, but I had word from my Ravens in the Summer Palace that Her Majesty is about to be kidnapped."

Lorn gestured to the mirror. "I was just informed."

Head Flynn glanced at the mirror. "Yes, I know."

"Then you also know that the matter is highly suspect. *I* should have been contacted to retrieve the Queen, not members of the High King's Fold. *I* am the Guardian that stands between Otherworld and the Earther Realm. There is trickery afoot."

"There are always plots within plots in the Summer Palace."

"It is practically their motto," Lorn agreed. "I assume that you also know that Adies received additional orders?"

"Of course." Head Flynn consulted his notebook. "My Ravens informed me that Adies was instructed to retrieve not only Her Majesty but your amulet. The High King informed Adies that Her Majesty wears the amulet around her neck."

Lorn sat back in his chair and steepled his fingers together, his tired mind trying to see the bigger picture. "He noticed that I was not wearing my amulet during the meeting."

Head Flynn underlined a sentence in his notebook with the tip of one sharp fingernail. "So I heard."

"It is not unreasonable to assume that the High King guessed that I gave my amulet to the Queen. Still ..." Lorn frowned. "How could he possibly know how she wears it?"

"Is it true?"

Lorn was about to answer when, unbidden, the memory of the Queen wearing the amulet came to mind with startling clarity. He could see the pendant—*his* pendant—shining away within the folds of her garments.

Lorn blinked the memory away. "Yes. But how could he know?"

"An educated guess, perhaps?"

"I broke the chain when I gave it to Her Majesty. She could have put it in her pocket, or in her bag, or not carried it on her person at all."

A crease appeared between Head Flynn's brows. "The simplest answer would be that someone informed the High King that she wears it around her neck."

"Yes, but who? I am the only one who knows, and I certainly did not tell him."

Head Flynn's bony fingers twitched as if he could *feel* the High King's secrets. "Yet another mystery to be solved."

"We are getting a lot of those. Did the High King tell Adies why he wanted my amulet?"

"Possibly." Head Flynn's mouth twisted into a thin grimace. "While the High King was speaking to Adies, the Summer Palace guards began a drill in the hallway. There was too much noise—my Ravens could not hear the rest of their conversation." He bowed his head low. "My sincere apologies, Your Majesty; I fear that we failed you in this matter."

Lorn sighed—it was one problem after another. "It is inconvenient, but these things cannot be helped."

"Under the circumstances, it is more than inconvenient—we have missed crucial information." Head Flynn clenched his hands over his bony kneecaps, wrinkling his black linen robe. "For instance, we do not know what will befall Her Majesty once she reaches the Summer Palace, and that is unforgivable."

Something in the pit of Lorn's stomach twisted viciously.

It must be the oatcake I had for breakfast, he told himself. *It was probably rancid.*

"And there is more," Head Flynn continued, unaware of Lorn's gastrointestinal distress. "The High King's conversation with Adies was interrupted by his enchanted mirror. The person on the other side was a woman."

"I am sure that the High King has many mirror conversations with women. Why is this one of particular note?"

"He sent Adies away, so it was meant to be confidential." Head Flynn leaned closer to Lorn, a gleam in his dark gaze. "Moreover, during the conversation, my Ravens heard him mention both Adies and Prince Ashlyn."

Lorn blinked. "They spoke of the planned kidnapping?"

Head Flynn nodded. "The High King was agitated. At one point, he said, 'A small setback.' And then, 'I have this under control.' "

"*Interesting.* Anything else?"

"My Ravens were only able to make out a few words." Head Flynn consulted his notebook. "*Yellow, gate, rust, knights, lower, thrones, silver, lines, star, fall, time.* Unfortunately, there is not a lot of meaning to be derived from single words."

"*Hmm.* Was it not possible to read his lips?"

"No—he was facing away from the wall where my Ravens were situated."

Lorn grimaced. "The High King's meeting chamber requires more mirrors."

"That *would* make spying on him easier."

"The woman—do we know her identity?"

Head Flynn closed his notebook. "No. But we are working on it."

Lorn exhaled in a rush. "This situation is becoming quite vexing."

"It would be a truly delicious mystery ... if the stakes were not so high." Head Flynn inclined his head toward Lorn. "What are your orders, Your Majesty?"

Lorn rubbed the heels of his hands over his eyes. He wished that he was not so exhausted. This was a tricky situation that required quick thinking and clever strategizing, and right now he did not even have the mental capacity to scheme his way out of an open sack.

"We still do not know enough to act," he said eventually. "Prince

Ashlyn and I will handle the kidnapping attempt tomorrow. Have your Ravens find out how the High King knew of the location of my amulet, the identity of the mystery woman, and any other snippets of information that will help us to make sense of this entire situation. Keep me posted on what you find out—Her Majesty's protection is of the utmost importance."

Head Flynn uncurled his body from the armchair and stood beside Lorn's desk like a shadow. "Of course. You will know as soon as I hear anything."

"Excellent. Tell me, is the Kingdom of Dox still vying with Vetch for the High King's ultimate favor?"

Head Flynn's lips twitched. "On an hourly basis."

"Then send your Ravens to the Ambassadors' Eighth and start a rumor near the Dox embassy that the Kingdom of Vetch plans to provide the High King and Queen with mirrors for their meeting chambers. *Large* mirrors. Make up a reason—perhaps to provide them with more light or the illusion of space. Start a similar rumor near the Vetch embassy. Soon, the Summer Palace will be swimming in mirrors, and the High King will be honor-bound to accept them all—he will not wish to show obvious favor by selecting gifts from one over the other. Nor will he risk angering such prosperous kingdoms by discarding them all."

A small smile graced Head Flynn's dour face. "Cunning. An elegant solution to our lip-reading problem."

"If only all my problems were so easy to solve."

Head Flynn's expression turned solemn once more. "We shall get to the bottom of this, Your Majesty. We always do."

"Of course." Lorn straightened his posture, firmly pushing aside his misgivings. "We always prevail ... in our own terrible, disreputable way."

Head Flynn shrugged his bony shoulders. "That is the only way we know how."

"True." Lorn smirked. "Long live Between."

DESPITE LORN'S SHOW OF CONFIDENCE THAT HE WOULD TRIUMPH AGAINST the High King's plots, he remained uneasy throughout the rest of the day. The High King had a Scheme afoot—one that involved the Queen and the throne of Between—and Lorn's inability to figure it out made his brain positively prickle.

As he worked his way through his agenda, he tried to piece together what he had learned from Ash and Head-Raven Flynn to see the bigger

Scheme beyond. But it was impossible: it was like trying to solve a jigsaw puzzle blindfolded when half the pieces were missing, and the table they were resting on was on fire.

He was relieved to be interrupted by a sharp knock on the door.

"Enter," he called.

Lorn looked up and found three men, dusty and travel-worn, standing in the entrance. The first was part dwarf, short and densely muscled, with clever brown eyes and a smile as crooked as his nose. The second was the size of a small barn and composed primarily of muscles and tattoos, his exposed skin dark and oddly mottled. The third was tall and blond and saved from storybook handsomeness by features that were a little too pointed, and an expression that was far too sharp. He also possessed an impressive scar that ran, jagged and red, from the tip of his left temple to the point of his chin.

"*Ah*," Lorn said, smiling despite himself. "If it is not the Elite darkening my doorstep. Which fine tavern threw you out tonight?"

"See? I object to that assumption," the small man—Felzik, Commander of the Elite—said as he took a seat. "We left of our own prerogative."

"After being told to do so," Molven, the part-giant, said as he settled himself gingerly on the chair beside Felzik's. "In so many words."

"Those words were screamed by Maeve whilst she was waving a meat cleaver, so they were particularly persuasive," Sevastian, the scarred blond, said as he sat beside Molven. He stretched his long legs out before him and frowned at a streak of mud on his boots. "It was not the welcome home we had expected."

"True enough," Felzik said, his tone a little sour. "Especially since we rushed home as fast as we could. And do you know *why* we rushed home?"

Lorn raised an eyebrow. "You were being pursued by an angry mob?"

"Not this time," Molven said. "It made for a nice change."

"Let's not get off the topic," Felzik chastised. "No, we heard a rumor, didn't we boys? A rumor that the Boss—a confirmed, but not particularly active bachelor—had gotten himself engaged."

"Without consulting us." Sevastian placed his hand over his throat—the very picture of faux distress. "Frankly, I was hurt."

"See?" Felzik pointed to Sevastian. "Poor Sevastian took the news personally. So, we rushed back here—slept in our saddles, we did—to find out the truth for ourselves."

"Congratulations," Molven said to Lorn.

"Oh no, you don't!" Sevastian placed his hand on Molven's shoulder. "Let's not be premature with the congratulations. First—is it true, Boss?"

"Yes," Lorn said. "The rumors are true."

"*Oooooh*," the Elite crooned.

Lorn rolled his eyes.

"Unbelievable." Felzik tutted. "The boys and I are gone two weeks —*two weeks!*—and as soon as our backs were turned, you got yourself a queen. I mean, what's the world comin' to?"

"It's a sign that the end is nigh." Sevastian sighed dramatically, a twinkle in his eye. "We can't leave you unsupervised for a moment."

"Congratulations again," Molven said.

"Thank you, Molven," Lorn said dryly. "Now, what do you have to report?"

Felzik held up his hand. "Oh no, Boss—we want to hear *all* the details. People were a little hazy on just who the lucky lady was, so let's start with that."

"Please tell us it isn't the Zadrian woman," Sevastian said.

"The one that bites," Morven added.

Lorn raised an eyebrow. "You have heard of her?"

"We've met one of her ex-husbands—husband number six, I believe." Sevastian shuddered. "Not a particularly happy fellow."

"Well, he's a couple of inches smaller than he was before their nuptials," Felzik said with a grin.

Lorn winced. "Please, let us not get descriptive."

"And let us not get distracted," Sevastian said. "Your new bride— details, if you please."

Lorn leaned back in his chair. "A Dreamer. And, before you ask, well beyond the age of consent."

Morven whistled. "An Earther."

"Yes."

"So, why isn't Her Majesty here, gracin' us with her regal presence?" Felzik asked.

"She used her first boon to barter for more time in her realm," Lorn said.

"Smart move," Morven said admiringly.

"Agreed," Felzik said. "I don't know why she'd even want to come here in the first place. There are all sorts of wondrous things back there—plastic knives and forks, fountains that dance to music, towers as tall as mountains all covered in colored lights—"

"Sanitary hand soap," Molven added.

"It's always the sanitary hand soap with you," Sevastian said to his large friend.

Molven shrugged. "It comes in so many colors and flavors."

Lorn's eyes narrowed. "How is it that you know of such things?"

The Elite's expressions became curiously blank.

"Rumor," Sevastian said.

"Hearsay," Felzik said.

"We get around," Molven said.

Lorn's eyes narrowed even further. "A likely story. One day, we shall have to discuss your knowledge of the Earther Realm and its flavorful array of sanitary hand soaps. But for now, we have bigger problems—the Queen opens the Portal whenever she dreams. And before you ask, I do not know how, and I cannot stop it. But if she stays in the Earther Realm much longer, I fear that the Portal will open even when she is awake. And if it remains open, well … I shall allow you to imagine the horror that will befall both of our realms."

Sevastian whistled. "That's not good."

"It gets worse," Lorn said. "The High King is sending Ash and Adies to the Earther Realm tomorrow morning. They have been ordered to kidnap Her Majesty and bring her to the Summer Palace. I would like you to accompany me to the Earther Realm to stop this rather presumptuous event from taking place."

"Sure thing, Boss," Felzik said, suddenly serious. "When will it happen?"

"Just after dawn," Lorn said.

"That's a ridiculous time for a kidnapping," Sevastian said.

"Far too much sunlight," Morven said.

"I did point that out," Lorn said dryly, "but I doubt the High King wishes to take kidnapping advice from me. Stay in the castle and await my orders."

"Got it," Felzik said. "Can't wait to meet her."

"You will have plenty of time to make her acquaintance," Lorn said. "You will be training her."

Felzik rubbed his hands together gleefully. "Excellent! The boys and I were just sayin' that we're gettin' bored roaming around, lookin' for things to do."

"What kind of training?" Morven asked. "Elementary self-defense?"

"Elementary attack strategies, too, I would think," Sevastian said. "It's unlikely she'll need them sitting in the castle, but it'll keep her training balanced."

Lorn gestured to the silver box sitting innocently at one end of his desk. "As it turns out, she will need more than elementary training."

He summoned the box to him and turned it to face the Elite. With a grim flourish he opened the lid.

All three men stared at the contents, their mouths open, their eyes wide.

"Midra's filthy sack," Felzik swore. "Is that …? Are *those* …?"

"Why do you have three God Weapons in a box on your desk?" Sevastian asked, his tone shrill.

"*Stolen* God Weapons," Molven corrected. "They're supposed to be sitting in the Summer Palace vaults."

"Between saw fit to gift them to the new Queen," Lorn said. "The fact that they do not belong to Between does not seem to have been a consideration."

Morven slowly shook his large, bald head. "This is very bad."

"Catastrophic," Sevastian agreed.

"Most likely," Lorn said with a sigh.

"Now, now—I agree that it looks bad," Felzik said, unable to tear his gaze away from the box of weapons. "I mean, receiving *one* of them would have been alarmin', so receivin' three of them is … well … *even more* alarmin'. But on the upside, we have a Queen who's worthy enough to wield them, right?"

Morven nodded. "The gods don't just give them to anyone."

"That's right!" Sevastian said. "Think of the ones who've wielded them in the past: Vorchak the Good, Tara the Brave, Stelvik the Good and Brave. They were all good. Or brave. Or both, apparently."

"And often elves," Molven added.

Lorn stilled. "Good and brave and elf-like? Midra's sack, the new Queen is going to be insufferable."

"Maybe." Felzik grinned. "But we'll knock it outta her."

"Tara the Brave was a pirate before she fought the darklings with the dagger," Molven said. "Which means that the new Queen might be less insufferable than we first thought."

Lorn tapped his bottom lip thoughtfully. "I could tolerate a pirate wife."

"So, it looks like our new Queen *won't* be swanning around the castle decked out in jewels and furs, right?" Sevastian asked.

Felzik grinned his gap-toothed grin. "Nah—we're gettin' a warrior queen."

"Assuming you can train her to use those"—Lorn gestured to the box —"without killing herself, and all of us, in the process."

"We'll do it," Morven said solemnly.

"*The Warrior Queen of Between*. Has a nice ring to it," Felzik said.

"More like a death knell." Lorn stared at the box, struck once again by the utterly lethal ridiculousness of the situation. "Why, in Midra's name, would Between *need* a warrior queen? No one has attacked Between in centuries. No one even wants to *visit* Between; proper tourism is down to single digits."

"Maybe Between didn't know what else to give her," Sevastian suggested, his tone deliberately light. "Queens are notoriously difficult to buy gifts for—they already have a treasury."

"Maybe something is coming," Molven said quietly.

Lorn nodded, dread settling in the pit of his stomach. "That is what I fear."

The four men stared at the box in silence.

Felzik shook his head briskly, shedding the somber moment like a dog shaking off water. "Hang on now—we're gettin' ahead of ourselves, we are. Let's start by gettin' the Queen out of the Earther Realm. *Then* we'll worry about trainin' her up. We'll do a good job of it so that—Midra willin'—she'll be ready for whatever Destiny throws at her."

"A wise plan," Lorn said, making a mental note to revise The Queen Plan.

"Have you told her about her weapons yet?" Sevastian asked Lorn.

"No." Lorn's head throbbed at the thought. "I shall leave that inevitably awkward conversation until after the coronation. She will have enough to adjust to without adding a chest full of God Weapons to the mix."

Coward, he thought to himself.

He eyed the Elite hopefully. "Then again, *you* could break the joyous news to her during her training ..."

"Oh, no," Felzik said, holding up his hands. "We'll leave that one to you, Boss."

"It's better coming from you," Molven said. "She doesn't even know us."

"Agreed," Sevastian said. "The news that she has enough weapons to take out an entire realm should come from someone she knows."

Lorn snorted. "What is the use of having minions if they rarely do as you say?"

"I've always thought that bein' a king was a pretty terrible job," Felzik said. "Well, in Between."

"You have no idea," Lorn said. "Now, give me your report on what you found in the outskirts before I have you thrown into one of the swamps by your testicles for insubordination."

"And let the castle guard train the new Queen? Nah." Felzik grinned. "I think we're safe from a swampin'.'"

"For now," Lorn said darkly. "Just for now …"

THAT NIGHT, LORN DID NOT EVEN BOTHER DRESSING FOR BED. INSTEAD, HE took a seat at the desk in his chambers, took out his second favorite quill, and began to revise The Queen Plan in light of the events of the day.

After a few moments, he reread the list with a weary sigh.

Step one: Locate the Queen in the Earther Realm *(Done. Excellent work)*.
Step two: Protect the Queen from the High King during her time in the Earther Realm *(A work in progress. Start by keeping her un-kidnapped)*.
Step three: Bring the Queen to Between *(That poor, doomed woman)*.
Step four: Inform her that she is the proud owner of an arsenal of weaponry that could level Otherworld *(Try to delegate this step)*.
Step five: Teach her how to rule *(Try to delegate this step, also)*.
Step six: Ignore her as much as possible whilst she is in Between *(Find new hiding places; continue to refer to her only by her title)*.

And because it was a particularly terrible day, he decided to add another step.

Step seven: Flee this wretched place.

"My favorite step, by far," he said with a smile.

Lorn then took another sheet of parchment and tried to draw up all the possible motives for the High King's interest in the new Queen, and all the possible outcomes of his interest. At the end of the hour, Lorn looked down at the pages filled with his spidery handwriting and acknowledged that it was all bad news.

"Bollocks. The Revised Queen Plan is potentially doomed at step two."

He wrote *'potentially doomed'* beside step two. If he wished to get to step seven, he had to thwart the High King's plans—failure was not an option.

Lorn placed his quill on the table with a sigh and noticed a flash of silver hiding behind a piece of parchment. He moved aside the parchment and found the Queen's Dreamer volume.

"What are you doing here?" he asked the book. "Why are you not in the Vault of Dreams?"

The book ignored the question and glittered away coquettishly in the candlelight.

"*Hmm*, fearful of incriminating yourself? Clever thing."

He reached for the book. As soon as Lorn's fingers grazed the pretty, silver cover, he felt that same strange spark—like a cascade of lightning bolts skipping across his skin—as when he had first touched it. It felt familiar, he realized. In fact, it was the same spark that he felt whenever he and the Queen touched.

"Perplexing," he mused and opened the book.

As before, Lorn admired the endearing illustrations that told the Queen's life story. He turned the pages, smiling at the drawings that depicted their encounters: their first meeting on the Hill, both dressed in their pajamas; the two of them sitting at the border of the Wasteland after the Queen's run with the Nightmares, the sweaty Queen gulping water from his cup while he looked on, stunned; standing toe-to-toe by the Portal in the Earther Realm, the Cloak of Shadows binding them together; and finally, the Queen shivering on a snowy mountain peak, standing on his tunic and wagging her finger sternly at a large, black bird.

"You," he told the book, "are recklessly charming."

Lorn turned to the final page and found a picture of the Queen sitting in an armchair. The likeness was uncanny: the little drawing had a fierce chin and wild hair, a generous mouth and blue eyes that were just as bright and as kind as those of her real-world counterpart.

"You look so real," he said to the drawing. "It is as if, at any moment, you will come to life and call me a bad bird."

Lorn was about to close the book when suddenly, the queen-drawing looked up at him and smiled—a smile of such pure, undiluted joy that it made his breath hitch. It was the same smile that the real Queen had given him when he had appeared at the edge of the Wasteland.

"Who is it that you smile for?" he whispered to the book. "Surely— surely it cannot be *me?*"

But the queen-drawing did not respond. Instead, she merely tilted her head a little, contemplating him, and smiled even brighter.

Gently—ever so *gently*—Lorn traced the curve of that glorious smile, the tips of his fingers barely grazing the page. The drawing's eyes fluttered shut as if she found his touch unbearably wonderful.

Lorn was so shocked by her response that he looked up for the briefest of seconds and there, seated in one of his armchairs, was the real Queen.

"Hi," she said, oddly breathless.

For a moment, Lorn just stared at the real Queen. Had he somehow Summoned her? He looked down at the book.

The queen-drawing gave him a cheeky wink.

Lorn quickly looked back up at the real Queen. "Greetings," he said slowly.

And just as Lorn was beginning to regain his composure, the real Queen smiled at him—the same brilliant, sun-drenched smile as her drawing counterpart—and Lorn was more flummoxed than ever before.

"Sorry to have interrupted you," the Queen said, still smiling.

Lorn had a terrible, terrible thought. "How long have you been here?"

"I just got here." She cleared her throat. "Just now."

Lorn's relief was almost overwhelming. It would have been exceedingly awkward if the Queen had seen him talking to her drawing—even more so if she had seen him touching it.

"Good," he said briskly. "Excellent."

Lorn closed the silver book as nonchalantly as possible, and placed it on the table beside him, careful to hide the cover.

When he turned back to the Queen, Lorn noticed that she was wearing a strange ensemble, accessorized by a single boot.

"Apologies," he said. "I appear to have missed the dress code yet again."

The Queen looked down at her clothing and groaned. "Lyla interrupted me while I was getting undressed for bed. I must have fallen asleep before I finished the job." She glared at her single boot and wiggled the toes of her stocking-clad foot. "Dash it, I didn't want to be unprepared tonight."

"Clearly your plan was a spectacular success. A moment, if you will."

Lorn rose and strode briskly to his sleeping chambers, knowing that the Queen could disappear at any moment. As he picked up his robe from his bed, he caught sight of his reflection in the mirror. It took a few moments for him to recognize the expression on his face.

"Midra's sack," he muttered to his reflection, utterly scandalized, "are you *excited?*"

It appeared that he was.

"Well, that will simply not do," he told himself sternly. "Remember step six of The Revised Queen Plan: you will ignore her once she enters Between, so you must begin as you mean to continue. Be polite, possibly hospitable, but no more than that. Keep the conversation light, superficial even. No grand revelations. No deep and meaningful topics. No emotion. No attachments."

With a final nod to his reflection, Lorn left the room ... and then went and did the *exact opposite* of what he had promised.

It began so well, too.

The Queen sat as straight as a new arrow in her armchair, hands folded primly in her lap. "This is awkward, but I would like to apologize for how I acted ... when we first met," she began, her manner polite and painfully awkward as she gamely stammered out an apology for treating him like a lust object in her seduction fantasy.

But something about all that prim politeness brought out the very worst in Lorn. Before he knew it—before he could stop himself—he found himself teasing the Queen about her choice of seduction methods, the possibility of dragons hidden in his room and whether or not he had a lava pool in his *en suite*.

And as he teased, all that prim politeness fell away, and the Queen sparked to life, throwing herself whole-heartedly into the conversation.

"You know," she said, her eyes narrowed accusingly, "the only reason I thought that a lava pool *en suite* was an actual possibility is because *you* told me that this place was terrible."

"It is," he said, trying to keep his amusement in check. "Clearly, I have done an exemplary job of putting my point across."

She huffed and tucked a dark curl behind her ear. "Yes, mission accomplished. Don't strain your arm patting yourself on the back."

Lorn's lips twitched but he said no more. They settled into a companionable silence, the firelight dancing across the walls between them.

To his surprise, he found himself initiating conversation. "So, what scintillating topic of conversation shall we engage in tonight? Do you, perhaps, wish to know more about Between?"

The Queen sat up straighter in her armchair, a crease appearing between her brows as she appeared to consider the topic.

"Actually ..." She paused to drag her bottom lip through her teeth. "I'd like to learn more about you."

"You wish to know more about me?" A strange warmth crept through his chest at the thought. "I am hardly Between's most interesting inhabitant."

"Really?" She raised a brow. "You're a sorcerer; you open portals into other realms, you can turn into a bird, you wear clothing that has a mind of its own ... I'd say that was pretty interesting."

The warmth faded, replaced by a well-worn feeling of resignation. He knew where this conversation was heading.

Ah, here they come, he thought with a sigh. *The Questions.*

Lorn was rather sick of the Questions. Over the years, particularly during his time as the Left Hand, he had been constantly cross-examined about his powers (*Can you turn into a tick? How about a barn? Can you extinguish the sun, or pull down the stars? Will the oceans obey you? How about the sea creatures? Can you read my mind? Can you read the mind of my goat? Do you practice Dark magic? Or Forbidden magic? How about Gray magic? Can you stop Time? Can you raise the dead? No? How about the deeply unconscious? Or the really, really sleepy?* And so on and so on…).

But far worse than the Questions was the inevitable response to his answers: awe, distaste, *fear*. And for some reason, he did not wish to see those reflected in the Queen's eyes. Not now.

Not *yet*.

"Between has dragons. Hydras. A minotaur," he said, hoping to steer her away from the Questions. "My, my—are you truly unable to find a more exciting topic of conversation?"

The Queen crossed her arms over her chest. "We come from different realms. It's not as if we can talk about politics, sports teams, or the weather."

"Very well. Although I am sure to find the entire process excruciat-ing"—*So excruciating*, he thought—"we may as well proceed. But I warn you —speak quickly. I am in an oddly hospitable mood, but I doubt it shall last."

"You can keep your responses to two words or less," she said, clearly amused.

"Ah, conversation at its finest." He settled back in his chair and prepared himself to satisfy her curiosity about his abilities.

But instead, the Queen looked him straight in the eye and asked, "What's your favorite color?"

"Green," he blurted, taken aback. For some reason, he felt an odd desire explain, to tell her more. "Let me clarify. I like the green of the grass in the Summer Kingdom, not the green of the diseased swamps of Between, nor the green of pestilent boils."

The Queen appeared momentarily startled. "Ah, thanks. That was informative and way too visual. You could have just said 'the color of my eyes.' "

"You have noticed the color of my eyes?" For some reason, that made him smile.

The Queen sat up primly, a flush staining her cheeks. "They *are* right in front of me. Next question—"

Now she will ask the Questions, he thought.

"—favorite food?"

And at that precise moment, Lorn came to the startling realization that the new Queen was more curious about *him* than his powers.

She is just being polite, he thought, trying to crush the odd surge of satisfaction this realization brought. *The answers do not matter to her.*

But that was clearly untrue. When the Queen asked her questions, her brow furrowed as if the answers *did* matter to her in some inexplicable way. When he replied, she moved forward on her chair until she was almost at the edge of her seat, her entire being focused on his every word.

But of course, just as he was beginning to enjoy himself, it all went terribly wrong.

"We've done color, food ..." The Queen ticked off the questions on her fingers. "I think the next typical speed-dating question is star sign."

"Star sign?" he asked.

"Star sign. Astrology ... the twelve signs of the zodiac. Do you have those here? They correspond to the position of the sun at the time you were born. Hang on—" Her brow furrowed. "I think it's the sun. Maybe it's the stars?" She shrugged with a sheepish smile. "It's all just a bit of fun. I'm a Leo—the lion."

"Ah." *Of course,* she was a lion. "We have something similar in Otherworld. We call them celestial signs. There are no Leos or lions. Instead, we have Viggo, the disgruntled goat; Arturo, the obnoxious boar; Mort, the vindictive seahorse; Petrel, the inebriated unicorn—"

"Wait, stop!" she cried, laughing. She laughed with her whole body, her head thrown back, her shoulders shaking with joy. "You're joking, right?"

"I am afraid not," he said, pleased that she was so amused by the awfulness of it all. "We have twelve truly terrible celestial signs. As you can probably guess, the astrologer who discovered them was from Between, hence the dreadful names."

"Which one are you?" she asked, her smile impossibly wide.

His own smile fell away. *Not this,* he thought. *Not yet.* "I do not know," he said in his blandest tone.

The Queen appeared taken aback at his abrupt change of mood. "Hang on—what do you mean? Is it difficult to figure out? Do you need a chart?"

"No." *Leave it be,* he silently implored her. "Only a birthdate."

The Queen stilled. "Are you saying that you don't know your birthdate?" Her tone was so careful that it made Lorn's shoulders stiffen.

Just tell her, a part of him thought wearily. *After all, everyone in Otherworld knows that the Shadow King is an orphan who spent his childhood enslaved in the Dark, Dark Mountains. Why should she not know?*

But another part of him held back.

Yes—everyone knows, this part said bitterly, *and they judge you harshly because of it.*

Not so much the Betweeners, he conceded; they usually had their own secrets and dark pasts. But outside his kingdom, particularly in the Summer Palace—where the highest positions in court were granted on the basis of lineage—there were many who thought of Lorn as *lesser* because he did not know his parentage.

Or there were those like Derrek, who were more than happy to use his orphaned status as proof that he was an abandoned half-breed, more creature than human.

It is a lovely novelty, he thought wistfully, *to speak to someone who knows nothing of my past. Let her find out when she gets here.*

Decided, he spoke. "I am saying exactly that. And before you ask—yes, I can almost see the question hovering on the tip of your tongue—I am not trying to evade the question; I simply do not know the answer. I was not informed."

His tone was curt, *final.* The castle guards would have recognized that tone; they would have fled the room by now, bowing profusely.

The Queen, it seemed, was not intimidated by his kingly tones. "I don't want to pry …" she began, but then, with a series of gentle questions, she did just that.

"Are there lots of people who don't know their birthdate?"

"No," he answered reluctantly. "Only orphans. Even so, the caretakers of the orphanage usually provide them with a date … typically the date that they were gifted to the orphanage."

He could see the dawning awareness in her wide, blue eyes. "So … are you saying that you're an orphan, but that you didn't grow up in an orphanage?"

Technically, I grew up in a mine, he thought. *But you will know that soon enough.*

"Yes," he answered instead.

"Were you adopted by a family?" she asked. But there was something wary about her tone, as if she knew this tale would not have a happy ending.

Lorn allowed himself the briefest of moments to imagine it: a jolly mother, a kind father, perhaps a small cottage and a rambunctious pet … and his younger self, happy and whole—

Abruptly, he pushed the thought away as he had done countless times before. "No."

The Queen's eyes closed for a brief moment, as if she was wounded by the thought. "Did you grow up … did you grow up somewhere that wasn't safe?"

Safe? *Warning calls in the darkness, followed by the sound of crashing rock and agonized screams; cold, damp air that soaked through his rags to his very bones, leaving him gasping for breath; his heart pounding at the sound of claws scratching across the stone floors, as creatures—fanged and clawed and hungry—scoured the passageways, looking for fresh meat—*

"Yes," he answered sharply.

It wasn't safe *at all.*

The shadows in the room seemed to lengthen, matching his mood. Lorn braced himself for false pity or worse still, distaste.

But again, the Queen surprised him.

"Oh," she whispered, wrapping that tiny syllable in so much genuine compassion that the tension in Lorn's shoulders eased away.

She leaned forward in her chair, her hand lifting as if she wanted to reach out across the distance to touch him. "Is that a secret? Should I keep it a secret?"

Her gaze was so soft in the candlelight.

Too soft. It made something in Lorn's ribcage twist viciously.

Enough of this, he thought.

"Not at all," he answered, his tone deliberately light. He leaned back in his chair as if he did not have a care in the world … or something twisting away in his chest.

"It is common knowledge in Between," he drawled. "Everyone here is a terrible gossip."

That did it. The Queen sat back abruptly, her soft gaze replaced by something prickly and exasperated. "Then why not just *say that?* Why make me work for it?"

"I said I was feeling hospitable." He smirked for good measure. "Not gregarious."

She shook her head in exasperation. He was surprised that she did not shake her finger at him. "You're a terrible conversationalist."

This is better, he thought. *Her exasperation is easier to bear than her compassion.*

He mostly believed it.

As they continued their conversation, Lorn watched as a kaleidoscope of expressions—rolled eyes and pursed lips, frowns and furrowed brows, startled blinks and flushed cheeks, and at least three different kinds of smile —crossed the Queen's features. It was dizzying and rather delightful.

It was also worrying.

Her heart is on display for all to see, he thought, exasperated, *which—*

Lorn paused, momentarily distracted by the Queen curling her stocking-clad toes into his plush, white fur rug. He quickly looked away.

Which, he continued determinedly, *is utterly reckless of her. Did she not realize how easily she could—no, would be exploited—in Between if she displayed everything that she thought or felt at any given moment? She will be—*

"I'm going to be your almost-wife," the Queen announced, interrupting his thoughts. Her eyes widened, as if she could not believe what she had said.

Lorn could barely believe it himself. "Almost-wife?"

He watched as the Queen furtively crossed her fingers—for luck, he presumed—in the folds of his dressing gown and smiled despite himself.

"We're going to have a Joining ceremony, right?" the Queen said in a rush. "Which means that we'll be husband and wife in name only. I'll be your almost-wife, and you'll be my almost-husband."

Almost-husband. There was a certain practical whimsy about the term that he liked—as if he had approached husband-hood and not quite made it.

Very appropriate, he thought.

As the Queen continued to speak, Lorn contemplated being the almost-husband of a woman who was so attentive, so responsive, so guileless.

A woman who was currently bouncing in her chair with excitement over the idea of throwing him a birthday party to make up for his lack of birthdate, featuring something called a *piñata.*

"It's a hollow container," she explained, her eyes bright, her hands waving around, trying to convey the size and shape of it. "Usually in the shape of an animal—most often a donkey for some reason. You fill it with candy and trinkets. The birthday person gets blindfolded and beats it with a stick until all the candy comes out."

"You believe that *I* look like the type of person who would enjoy beating novelty livestock with a stick until it yields its hidden bounty of treats?" he asked.

"Honestly?" She swept her gaze from the tips of his boots to the top of his head. "Yes."

She is probably right, he thought, too diverted to care about the slur on his sinister dress sense.

"But we're getting off the point—" she continued.

"There was a point to this discussion?" he could not help but tease.

"—that you need to celebrate your birthday," she finished, glaring at him pointedly.

"Well, if I am to gain material possessions from the experience— including the innards of a donkey—then it might be pleasant to have a birthday party." He was surprised to find that he meant it. It was sure to be a disaster, but with a cake and a hollow donkey, it promised to be a different sort of disaster to the ones that he typically encountered. "After all, it shall be my first."

"You've *never* had a birthday party?" She stared at him as if he had uttered blasphemy of the highest order. "That's it—pick a day, and we'll celebrate."

It makes you feel dreadfully important, he thought, watching her smile giddily as she continued to plan his birthday, *to be the subject of all that unbridled interest and enthusiasm. It makes you feel so very* seen.

"See?" the Queen crowed, utterly radiant. "Answering all these questions wasn't so terrible, was it? You'll be getting a party because of them."

"No," Lorn answered. "Not terrible at all."

What was truly terrible was that he meant it.

It was only after the Queen returned to her realm, rising to the ceiling with her boot clutched to her chest, that Lorn realized that he had enjoyed himself immensely.

"Well … that went terribly *not* according to plan," he said to the Queen's empty armchair. He stood up, resolute. "What an unparalleled disaster. Let us never think or speak of this interaction ever again."

Lorn turned sharply on his heel and began to prepare for bed, determined to put the entire incident from his mind *forever*.

∾

Four and a half minutes later.

"Imagine the Queen wanting to know my favorite color," Lorn said to the reflection in his bathing chamber mirror. "Or my favorite food, or star sign." He splashed water on his face. "What use could this information possibly be to her?"

Unfortunately, the mirror in his bathing chamber was not sentient and did not answer him back, which was a pity because he could have used a second opinion.

Lorn picked up a hand towel and began to dry his face. "She believes that I am the kind of person who would enjoy beating a paper donkey until it expels treats. She is probably right, but how could she know that? What does she *see*?"

Lorn tried to look objectively at his reflection, as if he were a stranger —or an Earther queen, for that matter. He was too pale, he thought with a sigh, and a little too thin; he traced the sharp edge of his cheekbone with a frown. He gingerly brushed the dark shadows beneath his eyes with the pad of his thumb—shadows that were getting larger and darker by the day— and shook his head.

"She is quite right; I *do* look like the sort of person who would beat a donkey. This"—he gestured to his reflection—"is what happens when one foregoes sleep to put out fires and fix sinkholes." He resumed drying his face. "Then again, what does it matter? We are engaging in a Joining, not a Promising ceremony; there is no need for my almost-wife to find me attractive."

The idea was comforting ... but also a little brutal to his vanity. Lorn brushed that thought away.

"And besides, she will barely see me. If all goes according to The Revised Queen Plan, I will be ignoring her for the duration of our marriage."

But then ...

"She plans to give me a birthday party. With cake and gifts."

If anything, his reflection looked even more puzzled at that bit of information than Lorn felt.

Lorn replayed the memory, lingering on the Queen's smile as she positively beamed at the prospect of throwing him a party. "What an utterly preposterous idea."

Then, softer. "Why would she wish to do that? *Why?*"

His reflection's expression turned painfully wistful.

"This is all quite unacceptable," Lorn told himself harshly. "There will be *no* parties with tantalizing donkeys to beat. There will be *no more* fireside chats. Stick to The Revised Queen Plan. Protect her from the High King, instruct her on how to rule, and ignore her as much as possible. Escape or die, etcetera, etcetera."

Lorn quickly turned away from the mirror—balking at the thought of what he would see—and began to dress for bed.

He picked up his robe from where the Queen had discarded it on the chair and frowned. His robe seemed different. He opened his senses and immediately felt energy—energy very different from his own—imbuing the silk.

It was quick and lively, and warm.

So warm!

Before Lorn could pull away, he felt the Queen's essence wrap around his hand, friendly and eager to know him. And the *warmth*! It radiated along the length of his arm and across his body in waves of silver, rushing to fill that sliver of space in his soul that Between had taken away, leaving behind a radiance that made him feel ... made him *feel*—

Lorn dropped the robe as if it were infected with crotch rot.

"To the laundry with you," he said shakily, staring at the puddle of black silk. He could still feel the remnants of all that lovely, warm energy lapping away at his skin. "Or perhaps to the rubbish pile, should the corruption be permanent."

Lorn forced himself to walk away from the robe and head toward his bedchamber.

"I am already finding marriage to be intolerable," he muttered as he climbed into bed. "I have known my almost-wife a handful of days, and she has already entered my private domain, tainted my clothing, and cross-examined me about my parentage and party habits. Imagine how much worse it will be once we are in the same realm ..."

As Lorn drifted off to sleep, a stray thought began to wend its way past his exhaustion and the lingering memories of the day, until it reached the forefront of his mind ... where it slapped him forcefully into consciousness as effectively as emptying a bucket filled with live crabs down his breeches.

Lorn's eyes flew open. "Good gods." He lurched upright, his heart pounding. "I did not warn her about tomorrow."

He sat in the darkness of his chambers, stunned. Kidnappers—well, one true kidnapper and one faux kidnapper—were about to enter the Queen's realm and steal her on the orders of the High King.

And he had forgotten to mention it.

"*How* could you have failed to tell her?" he berated himself. "Was the discussion about party planning so scintillating that it completely removed all thought of tomorrow from your mind? How could such an important event have slipped your awareness—"

Stocking-clad toes curled in a plush, white rug ... a smile directed toward him, warmer than candlelight ... a hand lifted, just a little, as if reaching across the distance to touch him ...

Lorn ruthlessly pushed aside the images and the perplexing emotions they left behind.

"There is no need to tell her," he told himself firmly. "I have the matter well in hand." He settled back against the pillows and closed his eyes, ignoring his racing heart. "There is nothing to fear—I have a Plan in place."

Or so he thought.

13

STEP TWO OF THE REVISED QUEEN PLAN

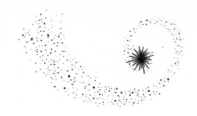

MONDAY, OCTOBER 29TH (THE LESS SAID ABOUT THIS ENTIRE DEBACLE THE BETTER).

IN RETROSPECT, LORN REALIZED THAT HE WAS FOOLISH TO BELIEVE THAT anything related to the new Queen would run smoothly or according to plan.

In fact, when he awoke well before dawn with a feeling of dread—more so than usual, thanks to the realization that he had forgotten to warn the Queen about the High King's plot—he should have taken it as a sign that the day would be an unparalleled disaster.

As Lorn went about his morning routine, his nerves felt stretched taut, his focus was scattered, and his heartbeat was faster than what any licensed healer would have considered normal. Or healthy. Or even humanly possible.

"You look wretched," his Shadow said, horrified.

"What do you mean?" Lorn asked. "I look as I always look."

The Shadow picked up a silver hand mirror from his table and word-lessly turned it to face his true form. With a roll of his eyes, Lorn crossed the Portal Chamber and looked at his reflection.

"Good gods! I *do* look wretched."

His skin was paler than usual, his green eyes were bloodshot, and— Midra's sack, was his eyelid *twitching*?

"Please," he implored his Shadow. "Put that away! It is enough to terrify small children."

The Shadow dutifully placed the mirror back on the table. "Shall we talk about the reason for your wretchedness? Or do you intend to retreat into denial as usual?"

Lorn felt a sudden desire to flee the room. He decided to pace instead, which seemed like a reasonable compromise. "I will not deny that I feel somewhat ... nervous ... which is perfectly acceptable. After all, I am about perform a dangerous feat."

"Ah ... denial it is then. But I will play along." The Shadow scrutinized the fruit bowl sitting on his side table and selected a crimson pear. "How many dangerous deeds did you perform yesterday?"

Lorn paused his pacing and removed yesterday's agenda from the bottomless pouch at his hip. He glanced over the items. "Twelve."

The Shadow sliced the pear neatly into two with a silver paring knife. "And how many before breakfast?"

Lorn checked the list once more. "Four ... and a half. I had an oatcake somewhere between the fourth and fifth task."

"And were you nervous before performing any of those tasks?"

Lorn frowned. He had not, in fact, felt nervous or anxious or even vaguely distressed before performing any of those tasks.

"Let me guess." His Shadow watched him shrewdly. "The answer is *no*."

"*This* situation is not the usual forest fire or beast infestation that I deal with on a daily basis. *This* is a kidnapping attempt."

"You have thwarted kidnappings several times before."

Lorn inclined his head. "That is true."

"Without ever feeling nervous."

"Surely, that cannot be true."

The Shadow contemplated the pear and then sliced each portion it in half once more. "I shall give you a moment or so to think back over those other kidnapping attempts."

Lorn reluctantly dredged up those memories and tried his best to recall how he felt before each one. And frowned again. He gave a grudging nod to his Shadow. "Well, that is disconcerting." He resumed his pacing. "However, *this* is a kidnapping attempt by the High King—a worthy adversary. A *dangerous* adversary."

"And yet, you and your merry band of Lower Kingdom monarchs delight in thwarting the High King at every possible turn." The Shadow picked up a slice of pear and looked at his true form almost pityingly. "Would you like me to tell you why you are so distressed?"

"Not at all. But you will probably do so anyway."

"You are distressed because the target of this kidnapping is not a stranger or a token peasant—it is Sasha, our Queen."

Lorn's heartrate accelerated, confirming the fact. But he refused to say anything to incriminate himself.

"And although you plan to ignore her and deny her name in accordance with step six of The Revised Queen Plan—which, by the way, is the most idiotic step of any plan ever concocted by a non-elf—you find her charming, and hence not as ignorable as you first thought. No, no"—the Shadow waved the piece of pear at Lorn—"do not even bother to deny it."

Lorn was about to do just that when, unbidden, an image of the Queen came to mind, one from the final moments of their latest encounter. She was floating toward the ceiling, her long curls a dark cloud around her pale face, her stocking-clad feet arched delicately in mid-air, one boot clutched to her chest like a doll. The sight was so delightfully odd, so whimsical, that he could not help but smile, just as he did the previous evening.

"And if you fail today," the Shadow continued relentlessly, "she will be at the mercy of the High King ... and whatever steps he deems necessary to close the Portal and protect Otherworld."

Lorn's stomach plummeted. The thought of the Queen—with her list of probing questions, and her wide smile, and her promises of paper donkey-beating parties—falling into the clutches of the High King was enough to make something in his gut tighten most disagreeably.

The Shadow looked at Lorn knowingly. "And *that* is the source of your distress."

Lorn exhaled sharply. "Nonsense. Ash and I have a Plan in place. She will be fine. She will not be taken to the Summer Palace against her will. She will not be imprisoned, or harmed, or maimed, or killed, or—"

"Your agenda is on fire," the Shadow said calmly and slipped a morsel of pear into his mouth.

"*Midra's sack!*" Lorn swore and dropped the flaming agenda.

The Shadow watched the parchment merrily burning away on the floor. "You were saying?"

With a snap of Lorn's fingers, the flames died away.

Several awkward seconds passed.

"Well." Lorn cleared his throat. "That was dramatic."

"*Quite.*" The Shadow wiped the tips of his fingers on a cloth napkin. "It has been years since you have lost control of your magic in such a flam-

mable fashion. But, of course, that has absolutely nothing to do with Sasha
—your *almost-wife*." The Shadow picked up the hand mirror again and
turned it toward Lorn. "Would you like to see your facial expression right
now?"

Almost-wife.

Lorn's heart clenched. "Put that away."

"No, really—you should see it." The Shadow fiddled with the mirror,
trying to position it at just the right angle. "If you turn any paler, you will
be transparent." He waved the mirror at Lorn. "Go on. Face the truth."

At that moment, Lorn was less concerned about the truth and more
concerned about his heart, which seemed to be trying to eject itself from
his chest. Against his better judgment, Lorn turned to the hand mirror.

"You had better be having a heart attack," he told his panic-stricken
reflection, "because any other explanation for this embarrassing display of
emotion is simply unacceptable."

And with that parting remark, Lorn stormed from the Portal Chamber,
leaving the smoldering remains of his agenda—and a Shadow, whose smile
was far too knowing—behind.

～

To Lorn's great disgust, his unease continued throughout the
morning, distracting him during his duties, including his meeting with
Maddox to discuss the preparations for the coronation.

"And after the ceremony, I propose that we gather together all the goats
hiding in the castle and string them together to create a goat flotilla to carry
you both, triumphantly, through the city."

Lorn looked up at his chief advisor in surprise. "A moment—did you
say *goat flotilla?*"

"Ah, so I have your attention again." Maddox closed his notebook.
"Many thanks. It was getting monotonous speaking to myself."

"Apologies." Lorn ran a hand distractedly through his hair. "My
thoughts were elsewhere." He stole a glance at the timepiece on his desk;
Ash and Adies would arrive at the Summer Gateway any moment now.

Maddox noticed. "Do not worry," he said. "Prince Ashlyn has the
matter in hand."

"Does he?"

"He has always been the reliable sort. Moreover, Her Majesty has your
amulet. She will Summon you the moment that she is in danger, and you
will swoop in and save the day. In fact, I can already see the scene in my

mind's eye. You will arrive in the nick of time—your cloak billowing dramatically behind you, the very elements at your disposal, et cetera, et cetera—and vanquish the villainous Adies back to Otherworld, thereby earning you the admiration and gratitude of Her Majesty, who will swoon in a queenly fashion at your feet. Then everyone will live happily-ever-after or some such thing …"

Lorn shot him a dark look.

Maddox ignored it. "Meanwhile, we have a coronation in a matter of days—an event that usually takes months to plan."

"You say that so reproachfully. We both know that we have little choice in the matter."

"True, but we are now in the unenviable position of hosting two events of considerable distinction with very little notice."

Lorn sat back in his chair and steepled his fingers together. "Then we must simply lower the scale and expectations of these events."

Maddox opened his notebook once more. "What do you envisage?"

"I wish the day to be elegant and tasteful … and free of stampedes and drunken brawls."

Maddox raised an eyebrow. "So, the exact opposite of your own coronation?"

"Yes," Lorn said dryly. There were parts of the castle that had never recovered from Lorn's coronation. The castle guards had sealed off these areas, and everyone had agreed to never speak of them again.

"*Elegant and tasteful.*" Maddox wrote the words in his notebook, grimacing the entire time. "I doubt that Between is capable of such an event. Nevertheless, we shall do our best for Her Majesty. First things first —invitations. I have taken the liberty of printing four potential versions. And before you ask, I used the absolute minimum number of words to save on printing costs—which, given the healthy state of the treasuries, is ridiculous."

"I know that we can afford it," Lorn muttered. "It is the principle of the thing. Their prices are utterly exorbitant, and I have no desire to give them the satisfaction of full payment. Printers are just thieves with a printing press."

"That is more accurate than you know—all of Between's printers went through the Academy."

Lorn snorted. "Of course, they did."

Maddox carefully set out four invitations in front of Lorn, each printed on expensive cardstock.

"The navy one with silver ink," Lorn said, pointing to the only non-white invitation.

"Ah, the sinister one. What a surprise…"

"It is the only one that does not look like a tax proclamation. What of the guest list?"

Maddox pulled a small stack of parchment from a leather folder and placed it in front of Lorn.

Lorn read through the names and groaned. "Could we not omit the Upper Kingdoms entirely? The tolerable ones will not want to come, and the ones that *will* want to come are not tolerable."

"Life is funny that way," Maddox mused. "But no, we cannot omit them; to exclude them would be a slight. Between is despised enough in Otherworld—why give people a true cause to dislike us?"

"Then again …" Lorn's expression turned sly. "What if the invitations were to arrive late?"

Maddox raised an eyebrow. " 'Late' as in *after* the actual event?"

Lorn nodded, his expression gleeful.

Maddox's lips twitched. "That could be arranged."

"Marvelous. That way, we are saving the Upper Kingdoms from having to fabricate a reason to decline."

"How magnanimous of us."

"And it ensures that we do not have to play host to a truly dismal group of bastards. Make sure that the Lower Kingdoms receive their invitations as soon as possible."

"I will send our swiftest Arrows to the Lower Kingdoms," Maddox said, making a note. "As for the Upper Kingdoms, I will tell the Arrows to take the long way to their destination."

Lorn nodded. "And be sure to send Fleet with the invitation to the Kingdom of Vetch."

Fleet—a lanky, good-natured fellow, with hair the color of mustard (the grainy kind)—had the dubious honor of being one of the most misnamed entities in Otherworld, second only to Pleasant Meadows, a small parcel of toxic swampland that had been named by an overly optimistic farmer. Fleet, as it turned out, was the son of the overly optimistic farmer, and was neither agile nor nimble, nor quick nor light-footed. Moreover, Fleet had a terrible sense of direction and a reputation for getting lost in his own home.

But in the Arrows, Fleet had found his calling; he was personally requested by the Shadow King whenever there was a message that needed to be delivered as tardily as possible.

Maddox nodded and made a note. "Very well. What of Her Majesty's friends and loved ones? Will they be attending?"

"Truly, I had not thought to ask her."

"Perhaps you should." ·

Lorn sighed. "Perhaps I should. I doubt she will be able to invite many. After all, the coven would have already sworn her to secrecy. Then again"—he tapped his finger against his bottom lip—"she has a troublesome friend ... *Lyla*. She will no doubt be invited. And the coven will also attend."

"I shall prepare their invitations." Maddox added Lyla and the coven to the guest list. "Should we ask Her Majesty to assist in the planning—to ensure that the events will be to her taste?"

Lorn shook his head. "The celebration is for her; she should not have to plan it. Moreover, I am sure that she has enough to do, what with packing up her entire life."

"Very well." Maddox closed his notebook and placed the guest list back into his folder amongst the other stacks of parchment and pieces of cardstock.

Lorn noticed the folder's bulging seams and grimaced. "I know that planning the coronation and Joining is stretching you to the limit. Prepare a list of tasks that must be performed, and we shall delegate them to the ministers, the Heads, and some of the more competent castle guards. Perhaps if we give everyone a single task, they will not make a complete mess of it."

Maddox looked at Lorn disapprovingly. "That sounds dangerously close to optimism."

"I prefer to think of it as *delusion*." Lorn glanced at the timepiece once more.

"All will be well," his advisor said calmly.

"Of course." Lorn tried to ignore his growing sense of dread. "All will go according to plan."

∾

ALL DID NOT GO ACCORDING TO PLAN.

∾

Several hours later, Lorn sat on a rickety chair in the dingy confines of the Sleazy Weasel tavern, nursing a tankard of ale and still in shock at just how *not* according to plan events had gone.

It should have been simple. Lorn should have been Summoned to the Earther Realm, where he would have quietly vanquished Adies with minimal effort, and then been home within twenty minutes—ideally without speaking to, or interacting with, the Queen in any way whatsoever.

Instead, the Queen and her friend Lyla had attempted to take on the kidnappers with a chain, followed by a mail truck—a scene that Lorn had watched with mounting horror via the Dreamer's Mirror, which had unexpectedly flared to life—and had finished the job by pummeling Adies's crotch with his own sword.

To top matters off, Adies—a member of the High King's Fold—was currently trapped against his will in the Wetlands in a manner that some narrowminded folk, including the High King, would consider treasonous.

Lorn stared at his tankard and frowned. There was not enough ale in the world to make this situation palatable, particularly Between's version of ale which tasted of pure evil and, oddly enough, cabbage.

Ash noticed Lorn's dour expression and nudged his arm. "Are you *still* brooding about today? It ended well!"

Lorn lifted an eyebrow.

"Eventually," Ash conceded. "After a great deal of horror. So, drink! Be of good cheer! There will be tales told of this great victory!"

"And probably a terrible ballad written about it, too," Felzik said, cocking his head toward the Sleazy Weasel house band, who were sprawled over a small stage, sleeping off their hangovers.

"Most likely one that contains a lengthy yodeling solo," Sevastian added with a grin.

"Maybe even two," Molven said hopefully.

"See?" Ash raised his tankard and toasted Lorn. "Much to be celebrated."

"I do not typically celebrate unparalleled disasters," Lorn said. "Otherwise, most of my reign would have been spent in this tavern."

"It wasn't a disaster," Felzik said, taking a handful of boiled nuts from a chipped bowl in the center of the table. "We survived—that's always a win in my book."

"It's good to set the bar low," Molven added.

Ash took a healthy sip of his ale, grimacing at the taste. "If I may—*agh!* Good gods, this ale is truly vile!" He coughed heavily, his eyes tearing up.

"Don't fight it," Felzik said, as the prince pounded his fist on the table.

"It is better if you just surrender," Lorn agreed, sipping his own ale.

Ash stopped coughing and gave a shuddering sigh.

"There you are!" Molven said. "You'll be fine now."

"Many thanks," Ash said, wiping his eyes on the edge of his cloak. He cleared his throat. "If I may ask, why ... why is it that it took so long for you to answer Queen Sasha's Summons?"

Lorn groaned. "The High Queen's spell. In order to transport you and Adies to the Earther Realm, Orelia must have linked the Summer Gateway to the Portal. When she opened the Gateway, she also opened the Portal, allowing you to travel through both before stepping into the Earther Realm."

The Prince's brow furrowed. "That explains much—it was an odd journey. It seemed to go on for much longer than usual."

Lorn inclined his head. "When the Summons came, we could not enter the Portal because it was already open. I was effectively trapped between the magic of the Summons and the magic holding open the Portal. It was —well, let us say that it was decidedly unpleasant."

Unpleasant was an obscene understatement. The magical backlash of being tugged back and forth by two opposing powers had been staggering. Lorn expected to feel the reverberations echoing through his bones for some time.

"You should have seen the Boss," Felzik said to Ash. "It looked like two giants were playing tug-o'-war with his body."

"One pulling on each arm," Sevastian said.

"Lots of wincing and grunting and shuffling to and fro," Molven added, shaking his head.

"A graphic but apt description," Lorn said. He took a long drink from his tankard.

Ash winced and patted Lorn's arm sympathetically. "That sounds excruciating, my friend. How is it that you managed to get to the Earther Realm at all?"

"The Summons won," Lorn said with a shrug. "It is old magic—a Binding of sorts. The fact that the Queen used my amulet to Summon me, which is linked to the Portal, no doubt helped."

"Well, I am relieved that you are in one piece." Ash gave a Lorn's shoulder a final pat. "All's well that ends well."

Lorn snorted. "Hardly. The True Queen of Between just vanquished Adies with a mail truck."

"Did a fine job of it, too," Felzik said admiringly. "I was a little hesitant when you told me I'd be trainin' her up, but there's a lot there to work with."

"She's bloodthirsty," Sevastian said with an approving grin.

"Resourceful, too," Molven said. "We can work with that."

"Ah yes—bloodthirsty and resourceful." Lorn shook his head. "What does it say about Between that it requires the sort of queen who can merrily hit a man with a mail truck?"

"Don't forget the bit where she beat his crotch with a sword," Ash added.

"That bit's important," Molven said, nodding.

"It was hard to miss," Lorn said dryly.

Watching his almost-wife wallop Adies's crotch in a fit of vengeance had made Lorn distinctly uneasy about the fate of his own genitals during their upcoming marriage.

"And to think we were worried that she'd be insufferable," Felzik said. "In fact—"

He paused as an impromptu wrestling match between four drunk goblins started at the table next to theirs. The tavernkeeper—a tall, broad-shouldered woman with fiery red hair and a jaw strong enough to crack walnuts on—vaulted over the bar. With mighty flex of her ham-sized biceps, she tossed the wrestlers out the front door without blinking an eye.

The tavern patrons cheered heartily.

The tavernkeep adjusted her apron and turned to the crowd. "The rest of you lot had better behave, or you'll be joining them, got it?"

"Yes, Maeve," the patrons said meekly.

"Beautifully done, my love," Felzik said, looking up at the woman adoringly.

"That goes for you, too," Maeve muttered to Felzik as she made her way back to the bar.

Ash shook his head. "Terrifying."

"Just how I like my women," Felzik said with a grin. "Now, as I was saying before the interruption, I think the new Queen will fit in nicely."

"I think there is some truth to that statement." Ash lifted the pitcher of ale from the center of the table and refilled their tankards. "After all, look at who Between chose as King: Sorcerer of the Highest Order, Master Thief, Master Assassin, Master Spy ..."

"True," Lorn said. "This place thrives on the disreputable."

"Speaking of which, what is to be done with our friend, Adies?" Ash asked.

"How was his tour of the Wetlands?" Lorn asked the Elite.

"Scenic ... but mostly traumatic," Sevastian said with a mock sigh.

Ash grinned. "Could not have happened to a nicer fellow. What now?"

"Now," Lorn said and put down his tankard, "we retrieve him from the Wetlands, get him completely drunk on Wraithspa—which, as Sevastian can attest, effectively muddles the memory—"

Sevastian shuddered. "I still don't remember what happened on my eighteenth birthday. Or the two weeks that followed."

Molven patted his shoulder.

Lorn inclined his head toward Sevastian. "Then we take Adies to a troll bordello and allow Ash to 'find' him as soon as he awakens."

Ash blanched. "I will not find him—how should I put this?—in a *disheveled* state, will I?"

"Not at all," Lorn said, with an airy wave of his hand. "The trolls are professionals; they would never dishevel someone without their consent. They would, however, be open to a bribe to drop hints to the contrary, if that is what you wish?"

"That's true," Felzik said. "A gold coin would have them swearin' till sundown that Adies walked into the bordello, dropped his breeches, and started singing folk tunes."

"No," Ash said quickly. "No dishevelment hints necessary. Many thanks."

"Then we will continue as planned," Lorn said. "We will put Adies in the waiting room, far from all the disheveledness—it is enough to find him in a seedy location that no knight in the High King's Fold should find himself in."

Ash looked inordinately relieved. "Marvelous! And if Adies should ask how he got there?"

"You will inform him that once you were both deposited in the Earther Realm, you found the Queen in my presence. I then invited you both back to Between to celebrate my upcoming Joining, where we indulged in a little too much drink. Sometime during the night, he wandered off in search of revelry—"

"That never goes well," Molven said.

"Well, certainly not this time," Lorn said. "The Wraithspa will remove his memory of events, and his unsavory environment will make him reticent to discuss matters with the High King. Moreover, given the unreasonable dislike that elves have toward trolls—"

"Thanks to centuries of land disputes," Felzik interrupted.

"That the trolls always won," Sevastian added gleefully.

"—he will be reluctant to discuss his adventures with his elven peers," Lorn continued. "He will also owe you a favor."

"Why?" Ash asked.

"Because you will promise not to speak of his intoxicated, troll bordello-frequenting tendencies."

"Nicely done, Boss," Felzik said.

"It's despicable yet elegant," Sevastian said.

"Diabolical," Molven said.

"I am glad you approve," Lorn said.

"Marvelous!" Ash said, laughing. "So, shall we go and pick up Adies and get started?"

"No need," Lorn said. "I have ordered a Fix-It crew; they will look after it all. In fact, they are already with him."

The Prince blinked. "I thought Fix-It crews were a myth."

"Nope," Felzik said. "They're as real as dragons."

"And just as deadly, though a lot more organized," Molven said.

"I spread the rumors that they were a myth," Lorn said. "One of my better ideas."

Ash started laughing. "Queen Sasha will fit *right* in. May the gods keep you both from plotting together to take over Otherworld."

Lorn snorted. "Who has the time for realm domination? I barely have time to bathe. Somehow, I also have to find time to plan a coronation and a Joining."

"Will Her Majesty's pretty friend Lyla be attending the coronation?" Ash asked, a little too nonchalantly.

Lorn's eyes narrowed. "She is blonde."

Ash inclined his head with a grin. "I had noticed that."

"The woman required to lift your curse must be red-headed. Which means you could only dally with Lyla and no more."

Ash opened his mouth to argue then shut it again with a sigh. "A pox on my curse," he said instead and took a long sip of ale.

Molven patted him on the shoulder and refilled the prince's tankard.

"Think of the bright side," Lorn said, trying to cheer his friend up … somewhat. "Would you *truly* want to dally with the best friend of a woman who did not hesitate to run down a man with a mail truck? A woman who was willing to beat your crotch to a pulp had I not intervened?"

Ash looked down into his tankard, his shoulders hunched forward, his expression decidedly gloomy. "You make several excellent points, and yet I cannot find it in me to care."

Lorn shrugged. "It is your crotch. Good luck."

"When are you goin' to give the new Queen her coronation gifts?" Felzik asked Lorn.

Lorn wiped a speck of foam from the lip of his tankard. "After the coronation."

Felzik turned to the Prince. "Then you'd best make your advances to her friend beforehand."

"Why?" Ash asked. "What gifts will the Queen receive for her coronation?"

"A box of pure terror," Lorn said with a sigh. "I recommend staying far, far away from her."

"Like I said—make your advances well before the coronation," Felzik said with a wink.

"Now I am more intrigued than deterred," Ash said. "Nevertheless, I shall keep that in mind."

Felzik picked up his tankard. "I think a toast is in order. To us, for defeating yet another Summer Kingdom plot."

The men lifted their tankards.

"And to the Warrior Queen of Between," Ash added, his good mood restored. "May she be more than a match for all that Between throws her way ... including the King."

Lorn rolled his eyes. "Where is a mail truck when you need one?"

LATER THAT EVENING, AFTER TOO MUCH ALE AND FAR TOO MANY SCHEMES, Lorn sat at his desk in his Less-Formal Meeting Chamber and pondered Ash's toast. He recalled the way that the Queen had wielded a chain and a sword and a mail truck and wondered whether she would prove *more* than a match for him.

He reached into his pocket and allowed his fingers to tangle in the slippery wrapper of the energy bar that she had given to him when he had been overcome with magical exhaustion. He pulled it out of his pocket and placed it on the desk in front of him.

"You were oddly useful," he told the wrapper. "Though utterly vile in flavor. I would rather lick the sulfur lakes of the Hell Realm than eat another bite." He flexed his fingers, remembering how his magic had returned after consuming the dreadful bar. "*Hmm*, helpful but disgusting—Gahil would approve."

He turned the wrapper over, noting the way that the material shone silver-bright when it caught the candlelight. "Still ... it was kind of the

Queen to care for me; after all, she was still suffering from the shock of her own Ordeal."

He recalled looking down at the Queen after she had assisted him, her hair disheveled, her clothing covered in dirt and grass, and could not help but marvel at how well she had not only risen to the challenge, but triumphed.

Like a warrior queen, a voice had whispered in his mind.

And in that moment, he had felt a strong impulse to ... what? *Comfort* her? Surely not. *Congratulate* her? That was more likely. He rubbed the silver wrapper between his fingertips, still unsure.

But one thing was certain—before his departure, he had found himself stepping toward her in a manner that many would interpret as an invitation to hug.

Including the Queen.

"Were you going to hug me?" she had asked him.

And then, worse still:

"Would you like *me* to hug *you*?"

It was not just the words that gave him pause—it was the way she had said it, with a glint in her eye and laughter in her voice, and a lift of her brows that seemed to say he would be a fool to refuse.

And if Lorn was honest with himself—which, when it came to all matters associated with the Queen, he tried to avoid at all costs—he would have admitted that, for the smallest fraction of a second, he had been inclined to agree.

The Queen must have sensed his moment of terrible weakness because, despite his denials, she had pressed the point.

"So that's a maybe?" she had asked, grinning madly. "A soft maybe?" And then, when he continued to refuse, "Well, it's your loss. I'm a fantastic hugger."

You should have tested the truth of that statement, a voice that sounded very much like the Shadow told him. *You certainly wanted to ...*

Lorn shook his head, trying to shake away the memory. "Nonsense," he muttered to himself. "I most definitely did *not* want to hug her."

Such self-delusion, the Shadow voice said with a sigh. *And yet, you reached out for her, did you not?*

And just like that, Lorn remembered how, almost without his volition, he had reached out for the amulet around the Queen's throat and turned it over, his fingers grazing the dark cloth of her jacket. He had felt the Queen's gasp of surprise through the fabric, the throaty sound causing his own breath to hitch. Under his fingertips, the amulet had glowed in recognition, the metal as warm as the look in her eyes.

"Perhaps ..." he told himself, suspended in that memory. "Perhaps I simply wished to give her reassurance." He cleared his throat and smoothed out the wrapper. "Which is the appropriate response when someone has almost been kidnapped and has had to defend themselves with heavy machinery. Or so I have heard."

To his great joy, his disturbing train of thought was interrupted by a knock on the door.

"Enter," he said gladly.

One of the castle guards poked his head around the door. "Majesty, the Fix-It crew said they're ready for you in the Swamp of Perpetual Suffering."

"Ah, excellent!"

Lorn pushed back his chair and crossed the room to the far wall, where a dusty tapestry of the constellations hung crookedly from a brass pole. Pulling the heavy fabric aside, he opened the secret door behind it and stepped into the Map Chamber.

Lorn ignored all the lovely objects scattered around the room: the carefully-sketched maps of Otherworld that hung on one side of the chamber, and the delicate, navy and silver star maps that were mounted on the other; the tightly rolled parchment maps tucked into the brass shelves; and the fragile, glass globes suspended from the ceiling that glittered and spun above his head.

Instead, Lorn made his way to the enchanted model of Between that dominated the room. It was larger than the model in the Portal Chamber but otherwise identical. It showed the same twisty little city, the same dark, squat castle, and the same cruddy little kingdom—all articulated in minute detail and enchanted to mirror the movements of the real Between, citizens and all.

A castle guard stood beside the model, staring at it with fixed concentration.

"Have you seen anything odd today, Joff?" Lorn asked, then reconsidered. "Let me rephrase that. Have you seen anything odder than usual?"

Joff bowed his head toward Lorn but kept his eyes on the model. "Nothing odder than usual, Your Majesty. Well, except for the elf touring the Wetlands with the Fix-It crew."

Lorn looked down at the model. Sure enough, there was a figurine of Adies sitting on a chair beside the Swamp of Perpetual Suffering. Four figures stood nearby, each carrying an oversized bag.

"Good. I shall go and check on that."

"Probably should," Joff said. "Just in case. Those elves can be slippery sorts."

Visualizing the spot in the swamp where Adies and the Fix-It crew stood, Lorn let himself sink beneath the stones of the Map Chamber and slip across his kingdom until he emerged in the Wetlands, right beside the Swamp of Perpetual Suffering.

As always, it was the smell that first assaulted Lorn—something vinegary and putrid-sweet that burned his nostrils and left a strange, sour taste in his mouth. Then, the ash. It fell from the sky like a snowstorm, settling on the ground, the trees, the rocks, even the creatures until everything was matte black as far as the eye could see. A large pit lay to his left, its black tar surface churning uneasily.

Lorn's magic itched beneath his skin, responding to the enchantments around him. The air itself was thick and moist and heavy; he could feel his lungs strain to take breath after breath of that terrible air. Above him, a creature with leathery wings and fangs screeched a song of hunger and loss.

In the midst of this dismal place was a cozy armchair, looking as out of place as a purple velvet armchair could look in the middle of a swamp. And on that armchair sat Adies in his silver armor, holding a half-full glass of misty, white liquid. He bore only a passing resemblance to the arrogant elf who had entered the Earther Realm earlier that day to kidnap a queen. Thick globs of tar were spattered over his armor, spoiling its lovely, silver finish. Black ash had settled in his long, white hair along with leaves, twigs, and clumps of mud; and his pale face was speckled green with Gahil's bruise paste.

And yet, despite his terrible surroundings and disheveled appearance, Adies looked happier than Lorn had ever seen him.

"Why hello, Lorn! I mean—Your Majesty," Adies called out. "How lovely to see you!"

Lorn raised an eyebrow. "Why hello, Adies. Lovely to see you, too."

"Come." Adies beckoned him over. "Come and join my friends and I." He gestured to the Fix-It crew, who bowed to their King.

"We just gave him a drink, didn't we Adies?" the crew boss said with a smile.

Adies blinked a little, then looked down at the glass in his hand. "So they did!"

"So they did," Lorn agreed. He crooked a finger at the boss, who obediently followed him until they were no longer within Adies's earshot.

"How is he?" Lorn asked quietly.

The boss looked back at Adies, who was still peering into his drink. "Gahil looked him over and patched him up," she said, just as quietly. "He had a bunch of injuries, but the worst of them was a nasty concussion and bruising around his man-bits."

Lorn winced. "Unfortunate, but not particularly surprising."

"Gahil gave him a bunch of potions that fixed him up a treat. Said he should be fine by morning."

Lorn watched as Adies sipped his drink contentedly. "Did he say anything about the kidnapping attempt?"

"Nah. He was too busy yelling the standard protests. You know—that he shouldn't be here, that we would all pay for putting him here, that the High King would hear about this, and so on and so forth. At that point, the swamp creatures attacked, so he was too busy screaming and fighting to maintain a conversation. Gotta say"—she gave the elf an admiring look—"he was a pretty good fighter. He almost took down a hydra."

Lorn eyed Adies speculatively. "*Hmm*, that *is* impressive. Say what you will about elves—they are formidable fighters. Is the hydra alright?"

"Yep. A couple of flesh wounds. It'll be fine by sunrise—you know how quickly they heal up." The boss looked up at the sky. "We shouldn't stay much longer; the really nasty stuff will be out soon."

"I will only need a moment."

Lorn returned to Adies, his footsteps disturbing the ash covered ground. He tapped the armchair, and it obediently expanded into a settee.

Adies smiled with childish delight. "Look at that!" He patted the now much larger chair. "Just like magic."

"Just like magic," Lorn agreed, sitting beside him. "How are you feeling, Adies?"

"I feel oddly *heavy.*" Adies gestured to Lorn's chest. "Do you feel heavy?"

"Not so much. Perhaps ..." Lorn placed his hand over Adies's armor. "Ah, yes—it is as I thought." He could feel the enchantment—dense and sluggish—that had been cast by Ash's wizard to weight the metal. With a twist of his wrist, he gathered up the magic and released it back into the earth. "Better?"

Adies sat up straight. "Oh, yes! That is *much* better. Many thanks!" He flexed his shoulders with a grateful sigh. "You know, I was having a wretched day. Nothing was going to plan—" Adies paused, his gaze unfocused. "At least, I *think* that nothing was going to plan." His gaze cleared, and he smiled broadly. "But then, I met these fellows, and now things are going very well." He began to lift the glass to his lips but stopped, his eyes wide. "Am I in a swamp?"

"Yes," Lorn said pleasantly. "Now, Adies, I need you to concentrate. The High King sent you on an errand today, did he not?"

Adies nodded sloppily.

"To visit Sasha Perse, correct?"

"Yes." Adies nodded again. "That is correct."

"What were his orders?"

"To bring her back to the Summer Palace."

"Alive?"

Adies nodded, his head lolling around on his neck.

Lorn's relief was ridiculous. He pushed it down and focused. "Tell me, what were the High King's plans for Sasha Perse once she arrived at the Palace?

"He did not say."

"*Hmm*, that is most unfortunate. Were you given any other orders?"

Adies squinted, clearly trying to recall. "Oh!" His expression cleared. "Your amulet. He wanted that, too."

"Do you know why?"

"To keep it safe. It could fall in the wrong hands, you know." Adies leaned conspiratorially toward Lorn and toppled forward until his face was resting on Lorn's shoulder. "Earthers," he mumbled into the dark fabric of Lorn's tunic.

Lorn grimaced in distaste; the last thing he needed was an elf drooling on his clothing. "Ah, yes—we must beware of those tricky Earthers. Was there anything else?"

Adies shook his head, dislodging bits of leaf and twigs resting in his hair. "Nothing more. Though, two orders from the High King are quite enough, do you not think so? They were both very important."

"So they were. Well, many thanks, Adies." Lorn gently pushed Adies off his shoulder and began to stand.

"I do not know what the woman wanted with Sasha Perse."

Lorn sat back down. "The woman? Which woman?"

Adies blinked owlishly. "The woman in the mirror."

Lorn stilled—the High King's mysterious mirror conversation with the unknown woman. "You overheard their conversation? I thought that the High King ordered you out of the room when the conversation occurred?"

Adies's cheeks flushed with color, turning his pale face a mottled, tomato red beneath the bruise paste. "I was not *eavesdropping* if that is what you are implying! I had a question for the High King and—"

"Yes, yes, of course—you are very honorable, Adies."

Adies exhaled in a rush, his shoulders relaxing. He moved a strand of hair from his eyes with a proud flick of his wrist, his cheeks still flushed. "Yes. Yes, I am."

"What did the woman say?"

Adies paused for a moment, as if trying to recall. "That Sasha Perse could be valuable ... though I cannot see how. She is just an Earther, is she not? Oh! I forgot—she is also the Queen of Between. By the way, I am *very* sorry that I tried to kidnap—"

"Yes, yes, I am sure," Lorn interrupted impatiently. "What else did she say?"

Adies blinked sleepily. "She said ... she said that, if we failed—Prince Ashlyn and myself—others would have to be sent."

"*Others?*"

"Others. And that this setback could not derail the Plan." Adies looked down at his drink. "I wonder what she meant by that?"

Lorn frowned. He did not like the sound of any of that. "I am not sure. What else did you hear?"

"Nothing." Adies rubbed his face sleepily with the back of his hand. "The conversation ... the conversation was obviously *personal,* so I left. It was not chivalrous to stay, and I am an elf ... who is chivalrous. A chivalrous elf. A chival-elf," he slurred.

Lorn rolled his eyes. "Do you know who the woman was?"

Adies yawned so widely that Lorn could see all the way to his tonsils. "I do not know. But she sounded like the one who promised us the world."

"Promised you the world?" Lorn asked incredulously.

Adies's head began to fall forward in slumber.

"Adies?" Lorn said sharply.

The elf sat up abruptly and blinked as if waking up from a long sleep. "Lorn!" he said brightly. "Why, hello!"

"And that's about all you'll get out of him," the crew boss said.

"I suppose it is," Lorn said with a sigh.

"Am I in a swamp?" Adies asked, looking around.

"You sure are," the boss said cheerily.

"Best get him out of here," Lorn said to the crew boss.

She nodded and beckoned to a member of her crew, who brought around a horse and cart, the horse's hoofbeats muffled by the ash.

"Your ride is here, Adies," she said, helping the elf to his feet. "Let's go on an adventure."

"Wonderful!" Adies said, leaning on the boss as they made their way to the cart. "I love adventures. I *am* a knight, you know …"

Lorn watched Adies stumble to the cart, and felt a migraine forming, needle-sharp, behind his left eyeball. He had so many questions about this entire debacle and speaking to Adies had given him even more.

"This entire affair is becoming more wretchedly melodramatic by the hour," he muttered to himself.

He was contemplating the best way to return to the castle—tunneling beneath the ground or soaring through the sky—when he felt an electric jolt surge through his entire body.

Shadow King! he heard the Queen scream, her voice—desperate and terrified—reverberating through his skull.

Lorn's heart began to beat wildly.

She felt close, *so* close. She was in Between and in trouble—*terrible* trouble.

He felt the Summons tug behind his navel.

"Take me to her!" he ordered Between. "NOW!"

The tug on Lorn's navel pulled him underground so fast that the breath left his body in a gasp. He felt himself hurtling across the land at a terrific speed, almost quicker than the ground could make way for him. Soil and rock crushed him on all sides, making it difficult for him to catch his breath.

Abruptly, he shot out of the ground like a cork from a champagne bottle, hovering high above the ground.

From his vantage point, Lorn looked frantically below for the Queen through the thick, white mists of the Swamp of Eternal Angst.

He heard her before he saw her.

"COME ON THEN!" the Queen screamed, her voice echoing across the swamp. "I WILL MELT OFF YOUR FACES! I WILL *END* YOU, ASSHOLES!"

The mists shifted, and there she was, one foot on the path, the other seemingly stuck in enchanted quicksand. Two gray robed men were advancing on her, one reaching for his dagger. The Queen faced them fearlessly, defending herself with only her leather bag and a bit of pink plastic.

The sight of her waving that bag so defiantly made something in Lorn seethe … and thrash … and finally, *burst*. Magic poured off him in waves, unleashing a tempest that emptied the trees of their black leaves and threw them skyward.

Lorn willed himself back down to the ground, landing just behind the Queen. As soon as his boots touched the wet soil of the swamp, the earth buckled and broke, sending fissures racing across the land.

The two men saw him and stopped in their tracks.

"That's right," he heard the Queen yell. "Now, step *back*!"

The men raised their hands and obediently stepped back, their eyes never leaving Lorn's. He read the fear in their gazes—their eyes wide, pupils blown—and something dark inside him, something that he usually kept well leashed, crowed in triumph.

Lorn stared back at the men and let his gaze promise dark and dreadful things.

"There's something really terrifying behind me, isn't there?" he heard the Queen ask the hooded men.

The hooded men nodded slowly, their eyes still locked with Lorn's.

"How terrifying?" she asked, her voice trembling.

"*Truly* terrifying," Lorn answered between clenched teeth.

It was one of the few moments in his tediously dreadful life that Lorn was grateful for just how truly terrifying he was. He barely heard her reply or paid attention to the conversation that followed; it took all of his focus to keep his power in check.

Apparently, the Queen did not find him terrifying at all. She turned to him, and granted him one of her glorious smiles, her entire body sagging in relief.

"I'm *so* happy to see you!" she said, staring up at him as if—as if he were a hero in a fairy tale.

That look shook him to his very core.

"I'm gonna hug you," she said, still giving him that devastating look. "A lot."

That was the final straw. He was so shocked by her look, her words, her smile, that he lost control of his magic. As if a lever had been dropped, the tempest ceased; the leaves and twigs fell abruptly to the ground, the gathering darkness fled into the white mists. The swamp was suddenly still, as if it, too, had been stunned silent.

"What a truly dreadful thing to say," he blurted out. He forced his shaking hands into fists and clenched them until his knuckles turned white. "I would prefer to have my face melted."

But he was forced to push his emotions aside as the Queen explained that this was yet another kidnapping attempt—one that involved two Death Cultists with a fire beast, and an open gateway straight to Old Middleton.

A kidnapping attempt that could have resulted in a murder.

"And there was another man, too," she said breathlessly. "In a white robe—he seemed to be their leader. He knew that the gateway would be open. He also knew that I open all the gateways when I dream."

Lorn's heart dropped to his toes. He had been focused—so focused!—on the Portal opening while the Queen dreamed of Between that he had not even considered that the other gateways might do the same. How could he have been such a *fool?*

He looked toward the open gateway, a cheery-looking yellow gate. "How could he possibly know that?"

"I don't know," the Queen answered as she rose from the ground, Summoned to the Earther Realm. "*I* didn't even know that! Oh! And he knew where I lived—he even had a map! The wizards said that a 'source' gave it to them."

The situation was getting worse by the moment. Proving this point, Lorn was horrified to realize that the Queen was about to put herself in even greater peril.

"Oh, hurry up!" she yelled at the Summons. "Mrs. Landshome is in danger! I need to save her!"

"Do be careful," Lorn found himself saying over the blood rushing in his ears. "You have been heroic enough for the one evening. Allow the coven to vanquish the wizards and share in the glory."

"We'll see," was all she said, her chin raised.

Lorn wanted to say more. He wanted to explain why fighting Death Cultists without magic was something that only those with a death wish would attempt. He wanted to point out that it was the coven's job to protect her, not the other way around. He wanted to persuade her to go to bed and live to fight another day.

But Lorn did none of those things. He could see that she had a Purpose and that nothing he could say or do would dissuade her.

Instead, he did the little that he could to help. He liberated her from the quicksand—her shoe, regrettably, remained behind—and sent a sincere plea to Midra, asking him to ensure that the coven vanquished the Cultists and their beast before the Queen awoke.

And then, the Queen repeated her dreadful threat:

"I owe you a hug."

But *now* she said it while smiling that wonderful/dreadful smile of hers and it looked as though she truly meant it.

The situation was a disaster on so many levels.

"I think not," he found himself saying as she floated above him. His gaze caught on her pale foot; her toenails painted the color of rubies.

With a heavy heart, Lorn watched her soar skyward toward her realm.

"Give them hell, Shadow King!" she called down to him with savage glee just before she disappeared into the mist, leaving gold dust in her wake.

"Imagine how intolerable she will be when she has the weaponry to support all that wretched heroism," Lorn mused, staring at the spot where she had disappeared.

He pushed aside that thought and turned back to the Queen's assailants. They were staring up at the sky in awe.

He cleared his throat. The men quickly turned their attention back to him.

"As you no doubt heard, Her Majesty instructed me to *give you hell*," Lorn began. "I am not sure if that is an Earther figure of speech, or if she wanted me to send you to the Hell Realm."

The men stared up at him with slack jaws, their expressions horror-struck.

"I would be happy to do the latter," Lorn continued, "except that it would require the intervention of multiple Elder Gods and the reactivation of the lei lines to unseal the realm which seems like an obscene amount of work at this time of evening. So, as an alternative, I suggest that we do this the Between way. You will be interrogated, most likely beaten, and then given a nocturnal tour of the Wetlands—"

A wolf's cry tore through the mist—a cry that was haunting and hungry and far too close.

The men's eyes widened.

"—which will consist of a great deal of running, screaming, and probably dying on your part. Then again, I may spare you that—"

The men exhaled.

"—and kill you myself for the impertinence of attempting to assassinate the Queen."

The men went back to looking petrified.

"Or ..." Lorn tapped his finger against his lip thoughtfully. "I *could* contact the Union of Most Excellent Assassins and inform them that you attempted to assassinate a queen without going through the correct procedure and paperwork. They will be most displeased and will probably vote to punish you. And they are so *creative* in their punishments when they are displeased ..."

"Please, Your Majesty, we didn't know who she was," one of the gray robed men babbled.

"And I'm not an assassin!" the other one cried. "I was just planning to knock her out and—"

Lorn held up his hand. "Enough. Spare me your trite excuses and lies. Who are you working for?"

The men opened their mouths to speak and grimaced in pain.

Lorn's eyes narrowed. "Let me guess—you are under a Vow?"

The two men nodded frantically.

"Of course," Lorn said with a sigh. "Because nothing about this matter is allowed to be simple or straightforward. Let us see how powerful this Vow is, shall we? What are your names?"

The two men opened their mouths and shut them again.

Lorn raised an eyebrow. "Where are you from?"

Again, the two men opened their mouths and closed them with a frustrated sigh.

"*Hmm*. Interesting."

Lorn slowly circled the kneeling men, the Cloak of Shadows swirling angrily around his boots, and carefully observed them. Both wore armor beneath their robes, but it was mismatched and ill-fitting. One had dirt caked beneath his fingernails and the sun-streaked skin of a farmer; the other had a hunter's dagger and soft soled boots.

Lorn was willing to bet the Small Treasury that these were not soldiers.

"If I could, I'd tell you everything," the farmer said in a rush. "I have no loyalty to—" He winced in pain, the Vow stopping his words.

"Same here," the hunter said quickly. "I want no part of this. I'm not here of my own free will. If you can find a way around it, I'll tell you anything you want."

"*Anything*," the farmer echoed desperately.

"I shall hold you to that," Lorn said. "But just to be sure ..."

He tapped his boot on the ground.

The earth beneath the two men opened up. With a shout, they slipped down into the swampy soil until just their heads remained aboveground. The dirt closed tightly around them, trapping their bodies beneath.

Lorn reached into the bottomless pouch at his hip and pulled out his hand mirror. "Maddox of Between," he ordered.

A few moments later, Maddox's face appeared in the mirror.

"Your Majesty?" he asked.

"Round up the Guardians and have them take their positions at the gateways immediately; all of the gateways open when the Queen dreams."

Maddox blinked. "I will do so at once. Anything else?"

"We have a situation in the Swamp of Eternal Angst." Lorn turned the hand mirror so that Maddox could see the two men, neck-deep in swamp soil. "These two tried to kidnap the Queen from the Earther Realm. They were accompanied by two Death Cultists and another fellow in a white robe—presumably their leader—who escaped. Tell Head Soren that I need her Wolves to scour the Wetlands and bring him back to me. Also, alert the Arrows. If they catch sight of him, they are to tell us immediately."

"It shall be done. And what of the two you have captured? Do you wish to leave them there for the swamp beasts to devour?"

"NO!" the men cried.

Lorn turned the mirror so that he was facing Maddox once more. "Perhaps in the future—for now, I want them questioned. Unfortunately, they are under a Vow; I need a vowsmith to break it."

"Of course. I shall send for the Goblin."

"Excellent. And an extraction crew—the best we have. I need the information as quickly as possible."

"Very well. Given that the two tried to kidnap Her Majesty, would you like the extraction crew to err on the side of *thoroughness* rather than care?"

"We're happy to cooperate!" the farmer yelled at the mirror.

"We'll tell you everything!" the hunter added.

"I would rather that the crew did not break them," Lorn said. "I may need them in the future."

The two men exhaled in relief.

Maddox nodded. "I shall pass on that information to the extraction crew. Anything else?"

Lorn's thoughts were racing. His anger had seared away his exhaustion, leaving behind a clarity that he had not felt for days. There was something about this kidnapping attempt that did not sit right. There was something that he was missing, something that he could not put his finger on, something that—

Lorn's eyes widened. "Call the Heads to the Less-Formal Meeting Chamber; I need to see them—and yourself—immediately."

Maddox bowed his head. "It shall be done."

14

THE SPY AND THE BIND

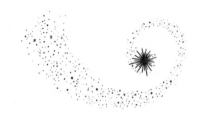

Ten minutes later...

Lorn stormed into his Less-Formal Meeting Chamber, where Maddox and the Heads awaited him.

They stood and bowed as Lorn made his way to his desk.

"We have a spy in our midst," he announced, placing the Queen's lost shoe on his desk. It was a credit to the Heads that they were not distracted by misplaced Earther footwear.

"There are many spies in our midst, Your Majesty," Head-Raven Flynn said. "Some are in the secret wall panel behind you."

"Hi, Your Majesty!" the spies behind the secret wall panel called out. Terrance let out a friendly roar.

"Not those," Lorn said. "This one is actively working against us."

The Heads shared a look.

"A rogue spy?" Head Flynn asked, his tone dark.

"But we control all the spies in Otherworld!" Head-Fox Nevlyn said, waving his hands expansively. "Even the ones that the other kingdoms believe are working for them. We've bound them all to Between with Vows and blood."

"And yet, the High King possesses knowledge that very few know," Lorn said.

"What does he know, dear?" Head-Wolf Soren asked Lorn.

Lorn held up his hand and ticked off each fact on his fingers.

"Someone told the High King that the Queen lives in a boarding house in Old Middleton, that she has a companion, that she wears my amulet around her neck, and that she holds open the Portal—*and* the other gateways—when she dreams of Between."

The Heads' faces drained of color.

"She ... she opens *all* the gateways when she dreams?" Head-Fox Nevlyn asked.

"Yes." Lorn turned to Head Flynn. "Did you know any of this?"

The Head of the largest spy network in Otherworld shook his head. "We knew that she opened the Portal when she visited Between, but not *all* the gateways. We knew that you had given Her Majesty your amulet, but not that she wore it around her neck. We did not know where she lived in the Earther Realm. How could we? We would—"

"—have to live there," the other Heads finished for him, eyes wide.

Lorn nodded heavily; the Heads had confirmed his suspicions. "The spy is in the Earther Realm. The High King had a mirror conversation with a woman—I believe she is the source of his information." He turned to Head Flynn. "*Yellow, gate*—those were two of the words uttered by the woman in the mirror conversation. Yellow is the color of the gateway in the Swamp of Eternal Angst where the Death Cultists entered Old Middleton."

Head Flynn's spidery fingers reached for the notebook tucked into his black waistband. "Which means that the other words may also refer to other nefarious plans for the Queen." He flipped open the book to the correct page. "*Rust, knights, lower, thrones, silver, lines, star, fall, time* ..." he read. He looked up at the King. "What could they refer to?"

"I am sure we will find out soon enough," Lorn said. "Though, I would rather find out *before* the next catastrophic event rather than after. When I spoke to Adies in the Wetlands, he said that the woman in the mirror mentioned that the Queen could be 'valuable'—valuable enough to keep pursuing should Adies and Ash fail their mission. She also mentioned 'a Plan' that could be derailed by the Queen's presence."

"I am beginning to dislike this woman immensely," Head Soren muttered. "We need to find out who she is as quickly as possible."

"I could not agree more, but it may not be easy," Lorn said. "Adies mentioned that the woman, 'sounded like the one who promised us the world.' Any ideas on what that could mean?"

"Could be a merchant," Head Nevlyn mused. "Merchants typically promise the world—the best prices, the finest products. Or a peddler—they're always promising that their trinkets and potions can perform miracles. Or it could even be a deity; I've heard that the lesser gods and goddess make lavish promises to build up a following."

"Or it could be nothing," Lorn conceded. "Our talk took place after Adies had experienced the joys of both Wraithspa and a concussion. His mental faculties may have been affected."

"Well, whoever this woman is, if we put a stop to her then we'll also put a stop to the High King's information," Head Soren said. "Two birds, one stone—so efficient!"

"I could not agree more," Head Flynn said. "But it may be difficult to put a stop to this woman if she is in the Earther Realm."

"Perhaps you should contact the coven," Maddox said to Lorn. "Alert them to the possibility of a spy in their midst."

"I thought of that," Lorn said, "but we may also alert the spy. For all we know, the spy could be the coven leader herself. We need more information before we can act. I have an extraction crew and a vowsmith working on two of the kidnappers."

"I'd like to supervise the extraction crew," Head Soren said briskly, cracking her knuckles.

"Nothing would please me more," Lorn said. "But do try to keep the fellows relatively intact; I may need them in the future."

Head Soren looked momentarily disappointed. "If that's what you wish, dear."

"Surely this will only be a problem while Her Majesty is in the Earther Realm," Head Nevlyn said. "Once she is in Between, the spy will no longer be close to her."

"Unless the spy comes with her," Head Flynn said.

Lorn nodded. "A definite possibility. Which is why we must identify the spy as quickly as possible and dispose of them immediately."

"Oh, good!" Head Soren said with a grin. "I shall begin the paperwork."

"So, what is the plan, Your Majesty?" Head Flynn asked.

Lorn sat back in his chair and steepled his fingers together. "I need more information. It appears that the High King, the King of Zadria, and … or … the Death Cultists wish to take over the throne of Between, whether through Challenges or by marriage. Either way, they appear to want sole rulership because both of those options inevitably lead to my death."

"Or genital disfigurement," Maddox added.

"The less said about that, the better," Lorn muttered. "What I need to know is *why*. Why do they want the throne? Or, more likely, why do they want the Portal? The presence of the Death Cultists seems to suggest that the Portal is their true goal. Moreover, what are their plans for the Queen? Will they use her to gain the throne? Or do they wish to dispose of her because she interferes with their plans?" Lorn ignored the sick feeling in his gut at the thought and plowed on. "There have been two kidnapping attempts on Her Majesty today, which is two attempts too many. The High King organized the first. But what of the second? Was it an attempt by Zadria or the Death Cultists?"

"Or are they one and the same?" Head Flynn asked.

Lorn sighed. "Yet another question we cannot answer. Either way, a line has been crossed—the Queen was almost killed. Summon Black."

Black was the codename for the finest spy in Between, summoned only for the most sensitive and delicate assignments. Black's identity was one of the true secrets of Between, known only to Lorn, Head Flynn, and Maddox.

Head Flynn hummed under his breath. "Excellent timing! Black has just finished an assignment and is standing by. What are their orders?"

"Have Black shadow the High King at all times," Lorn commanded. "Wherever the High King goes, whomever he meets, I want Black beside him."

Head Flynn bowed his head. "It shall be done."

"Are the gateways still unguarded?" Head Soren asked.

"The Guardians were summoned," Maddox said. "They are all at their posts."

"Good," Lorn said. "As added insurance, I want each gateway watched by one of your Ravens, Head Flynn. No one is to go in or out of those gateways without our knowledge from now on."

"Very well," Head Flynn said.

"My Wolves are in the Wetlands, hunting your white-robed leader," Head Soren said. "I will let you know when they find him."

"It is a long shot," Lorn admitted. "It is likely that he is long gone by now—or had the good sense to change his robe. Nevertheless, keep me informed."

"Is there anything you wish me to do?" Head Nevlyn asked Lorn.

"The usual—gather information. Instruct your Foxes stationed on the trade roads to report anything that they may hear about these matters. The idlest whisper about the Queen should be brought to my attention immediately."

"But of course! Consider it done."

"Don't worry, dear," Head Soren said to Lorn, "we'll get to the bottom of this." She thumbed the hilt of her dagger. "No matter the body count."

"We had better," Lorn said grimly. "This a terrible kingdom. It is beset by wild beasts, wild magic, and constantly teeters on the brink of pure chaos. But I will be *damned* if I will allow the little control that I wield over it to be undermined by the High King and a cult with a skull fetish."

"Here, here!" the Heads chorused.

Lorn stood up. "Now, if you will excuse me, I have to retrieve two Death Cultists from the Earther Realm."

$\sim$

As it turned out, retrieving Death Cultists from the Earther Realm was one item Lorn did not have to add to his agenda.

"The Middleton Coven has sent you a present," the Shadow said as Lorn entered the Portal Chamber.

Sure enough, not far from the Portal were two bound and gagged Death Cultists, slumped in an ungainly pile on the tile floor.

"Are they alive?" the Shadow asked, as Lorn crossed the room and knelt beside the wizards.

Lorn checked their pulses. "Yes, though unconscious."

The script on the Death Cultists' heads was still; their magic was silent. Lorn sniffed the air around them. They reeked of magic. Some of it was acrid and Dark, but there was also hints of purely elemental magic: Fire and Wind, if he was not mistaken—a mix of ash and ozone.

There had been a battle—and the Death Cultists had lost.

"It appears that they unsuccessfully challenged the Middleton Coven," Lorn said, noting the bruises that were beginning to bloom across the wizards' exposed skin.

"Ah, that explains their state; I did not think arms were supposed to bend that way. Or legs for that matter."

Lorn winced at the unnatural configuration of the wizards' limbs. "They will certainly feel that when they wake up."

The Shadow's grin was pure malice. "Could not have happened to two nicer fellows. It seems that the Middleton Coven is even feistier than we first thought. I believe they also left you a note."

Sure enough, there was an envelope addressed to the Shadow King pinned to one of the Cultist's robes.

Lorn took the note and read it through. It was just as he had thought;

there *had* been a battle. Not surprisingly, the coven was concerned that there would be more in the future. They warned Lorn about the open gateway and the growing number of creatures that were flocking to their realm.

Lorn ran a hand through his hair and sighed.

"Broken Death Cultists thrown through a Portal, secret love notes from a coven … my, my—what an eventful evening," the Shadow drawled. "Are you going to tell me what all this is about, or am I required to guess?"

Lorn looked over at his Shadow and made eye contact. "It has been an eventful evening."

The Shadow blanched as he experienced Lorn's memories of the Queen's brush with the kidnappers.

"How *dare* they!" the Shadow hissed. "How dare they try to take her! Try to *harm* her!" His expression became stricken. "Sasha must be brought here at once! Regardless of her boon, you must bring her here!"

Lorn carefully folded the note and tucked it into his bottomless pouch. "She does not wish to come here, clever woman."

The Shadow leapt up from his chair and began to pace the length of the mirror, his steps a sharp staccato. "But she is alone and defenseless in that wretched world of hers!"

Lorn remembered the Queen standing in the mist, ready to melt the faces off her enemies.

"She is not defenseless," he said. "Vulnerable, perhaps, but not defense-less—and certainly not alone." He gestured to the slumped forms of the Death Cultists. "She has powerful friends."

The Shadow stilled. "She would be safer here with you, under your protection."

There was a part of Lorn that thought so, too. But there was an even larger part that recognized the Queen's agency. She would be angry and hurt and devastated if he dragged her to this realm against her will.

"The Queen has chosen to stay in the Earther Realm. It is my task to ensure that she is safe to pursue her choice, not to remove all choice from her entirely." The Shadow opened his mouth to argue, but Lorn held up his hand. "You must admit, most of the terrible things that have happened to her have occurred in Between. There are far more dangers here than in a small village in the Earther Realm, especially now that I have ordered the Guardians to the gateways."

The Shadow slumped onto his chair with a sigh. "This is all so very vexing."

"And becoming more so by the day."

With a wave of Lorn's hand, the Death Cultists rose from the ground and began to float toward the door.

"Where are you taking them?" the Shadow asked.

"To a cell. Once they awaken, I intend to ask them a few questions ... in a rather forceful fashion."

"Excellent! Be sure to bounce them around the walls as you make your way through the castle."

"Of course," Lorn said, heading for the door.

"Also, while you are at it, you should get a present for our lovely Queen."

"Why ever would I do that?" Lorn called over his shoulder.

"Because, while rescuing her from her attackers in the swamp, you informed her that you would rather have your face melted off than receive one of her hugs."

Lorn stopped in his tracks. The Death Cultists, however, continued to float forward and bounced, with a rather large crash, off the door. "Surely not."

The Shadow studied his nails. "Allow me to refresh your memory. She said to you, 'I'm so happy to see you. I'm going to hug you. A lot.' And you answered—"

"*What a truly terrible thing to say,*" Lorn recited in horror. "*I would prefer to have my face*—oh, no. I actually said that."

"*I would prefer to have my face melted.*" The Shadow tsked and shook his head. "And the worst part is that it is not even true. You would *love* for her to hug—"

"*Enough,*" Lorn groaned.

The Shadow grinned. "Get her something fancy."

Lorn pinched the bridge of his nose.

"Very, *very* fancy," the Shadow said.

～

Tuesday, October 30th

When Lorn awoke the next morning, there was a moment—a blessed space between sleep and true wakefulness—when he was momentarily unaware of who he was or where he lived.

Then, it hit him like a turnip cart.

"*Agh,*" he groaned and smothered his face with his pillow.

"Let it go, Boss," the imp with the small notebook said, tugging at one corner of the pillow.

"Today might be okay," Setzl said as he tugged on another corner.

"Liars," Lorn muttered as the imps wrestled the pillow away from his hands.

"Yeah," Izzy said, "it'll probably be a terrible day."

Izzy was right. It *was* a terrible day.

As with all of the days since Between had forcibly acquired a queen, Lorn was required to perform a series of challenging tasks of escalating dreadfulness.

There seemed to be more paperwork than usual (the dull kind), more dignitaries to meet with (the tricky kind), and more problems to solve (the dire kind) than was typical for a Tuesday. Moreover, the castle was a complete disaster. The foyer ceiling was leaking fish (again); several castle guards found themselves, inexplicably, on the ceiling of the throne room without any way of getting down; and all the water in the courtyard fountains had turned a sickly shade of yellow and smelled of pickles.

Even magical creatures required his assistance. Terrance had caught a cold and was shaking the secret paneled walls with each sneeze; Tractor the unicorn was stuck, horn-first, in an ale barrel; and an irate griffin had tried to storm the castle's main entrance only to get caught in the doorway, leading to a sizable crowd of Betweeners on either side of the beast who were unable to get in or out of the castle.

After the beast tried to bite Lorn's head off during the liberation attempt, Lorn was tempted to leave him there.

Questioning the Death Cultists had proven to be an exercise in futility, primarily because they stubbornly refused to regain consciousness.

"Well, I have to hand it to the witches," Gahil said, examining the Death Cultists with a frown. "They were thorough. Even if these fellows wake up, I doubt they'll even remember their names, let alone what they were doing in the swamp last night."

"Well, that's inconvenient," Lorn said. "I suppose I will have to be patient and wait for them to awaken."

"I doubt that will be possible," Maddox said, entering the chamber. "Ambassador Zoth has requested their immediate release."

"How does he know that they're here?" Gahil asked.

Maddox shrugged. "We were not trying to keep it a secret. His Majesty bounced them off almost every wall of the castle before depositing them in their cell."

Lorn inclined his head. "This is true."

"Regardless of how he found out," Maddox continued, "Ambassador Zoth *does* know that they are here and would like them returned."

Lorn lifted a brow. "On what grounds?"

"On the grounds that these fine, upstanding citizens were apparently searching for a missing Zadrian betrothal party in the Wetlands on the orders of the King of Zadria."

"Really? And their trip to the Earther Realm?"

"A wrong turn in the mist."

"With a fire beast?"

"They were taking it for a walk."

Lorn felt a headache begin behind his left eye. "And what of their attempt to kidnap the Queen?"

"According to Ambassador Zoth, that never happened. Moreover, he pointed out that, technically, there is no Queen of Between—Zadria does not recognize uncrowned monarchs."

Lorn pinched the bridge of his nose. "I am going to stuff Ambassador Zoth into one of his horns."

"There is more. The ambassador went on to say that holding the Death Cultists against their will *could* be construed as a restriction of religious freedoms—a charge that they *could* bring to the High King's attention."

Lorn's eyes narrowed. "I wonder if Ambassador Zoth is aware of the fact that a sinkhole *could* appear beneath the Zadrian's embassy at any moment … while he is in it."

"Between is a wondrous and ever-changing landscape," Maddox said with a straight face.

Lorn looked up at the ceiling and took a moment to compose himself. He then turned to Gahil. "Are you sure they will not remember anything?"

Gahil pointed to one of the Death Cultists. "This one's head is *spongy*. Plus, they're probably up to their armpits in blood Vows. Even if you tried to question them, you'd get nothing out of them."

Lorn nodded, resigned. "Very well. Send for our legal advisors. Have them draw up a list of every law that the Death Cultists broke by entering Between—and the Earther Realm—with a fire beast and the penalties for violating each law. Then, prepare an invoice listing all the expenses that the Death Cultists have accrued while staying in the castle: food, water, potions, air and so forth. Send one copy to the Summer Palace for their records and another to the Zadrian embassy. We shall then send both documents along with the Cultists—properly gift-wrapped—in the ricketiest cart via the bumpiest road back to the King of Zadria. We shall request that all fines, fees, and expenses be paid immediately. After all, we are a poor kingdom, and every coin helps. If we cannot get information out of the Cultists, we may as well get reparations … and annoy the Zadrian ambassador."

"So it shall be," Maddox said, his lips twitching.

The day stubbornly refused to get any better for Lorn.

Even when he had ventured into the city for something to eat, problems seemed to follow him around. He had broken up two tavern brawls involving magical creatures, stopped the Minotaur from singing a new ballad that he had heard in Aurora, and redirected a pack of mountain wolves who had decided to venture into the city to find a bite to eat.

Even food was challenging. When Lorn finally got around to purchasing something for supper, he had foolishly allowed himself to be persuaded by the baker to try something new called a rock cake—which, Lorn thought as he chewed the gritty morsel, may have been made from actual rocks.

"Well, it certainly is authentic," Lorn said to Maddox, as he tossed the rest of the cake into the garbage pail.

"You were warned by the name. Between is a literal place."

Lorn sighed. "True. Are you *sure* it is not a Wednesday?"

"It only feels that way. Imagine what tomorrow will bring."

"I shudder to think. Any word from the extraction crew?"

Maddox shook his head. "It has only been a couple of hours. Give them time."

"Assuming we have time," Lorn muttered. "I would like to be ahead of the next kidnapping attempt."

"Perhaps you should give Her Majesty her coronation gifts now—at least she will be properly armed." Maddox looked over at the Queen's shoe, which sat on the silver box of God Weapons. "They may help her to keep her footwear during the next kidnapping attempt."

Lorn dropped his head on his desk and groaned.

Nevertheless, it was not long afterward that the vowsmith came to visit Lorn.

"Many thanks for your assistance in this matter," Lorn said as the ancient goblin huffed and puffed in his chair, trying to get comfortable "I know how busy you are."

It always paid to be polite to a powerful vowsmith—especially one that was not morally opposed to breaking Vows.

The vowsmith, known only as the Goblin, wheezed out a laugh, his thick, leathery lips shifting to reveal sharp teeth. "I always have time to work for Between—*you* appreciate craftsmanship." His mouth twisted into a bitter grimace. "Unlike those fancy folks in the other kingdoms. They're quick enough to condemn me in public for breaking Vows, even while they're secretly lined up to use my services."

"People can be exceedingly narrow minded," Lorn said. He thought of the people of Fisk. "And hypocritical. In Between, we reward those who have talent and an open mind." He pulled a small sack of gold coins from a hidden desk drawer and placed it on the desk. "Handsomely."

The vowsmith eyed the sack and grinned. "That's why I like this place."

"You would be the first. Now, let us discuss the two gentlemen that I liberated from the swamp. Did you examine the Vow that kept them silent?"

The vowsmith tore his gaze from the gold and looked up at Lorn with sharp, beady eyes. "A tricky case, that one. Tricky, tricky, tricky …"

"How so?"

"It wasn't just a Vow—it was something more."

"Something more? What do you mean?"

"A Vow twisted around a Binding."

Lorn's stomach clenched. "A *Binding*? Are you sure? They are Forbidden."

The vowsmith wheezed out a laugh. "To goblins, magic is magic. Light, Dark, Gray, Forbidden—those distinctions mean nothing to us. Those are mortal terms."

Lorn had heard that argument many times before. Magical creatures like goblins *were* magic—the nuances were beneath their notice.

Lorn inclined his head. "Fair enough. Were they formed at the same time?"

"The Vow was recent, fresh and green." The Goblin licked his fleshy lips. "The Bindings were older. The hunter had his for longer than the farmer; the magic around him was as tight as a vine."

"Could you untangle the Vow from the Binding?"

"Bindings are not my field—I don't like the way the magic *tastes*." The Goblin shifted uneasily in his seat, the leather creaking in protest beneath his weight. "And once they're mingled with a Vow, the Vow doesn't work in the same way. It becomes volatile. *Tricky*."

Lorn's heart sunk. He had been relying on the vowsmith to provide answers. This news was less than promising. "So … nothing could be done with the Vow?"

"I peeled away a few layers, enough to yield an answer or two. But I couldn't go too far. Remove too much, and the person goes mad. Remove it all, and the person is a person no more. Tricky, tricky, tricky …"

"Well, that sums up this entire situation—nothing about it is simple or straightforward. Did you recognize the workmanship? Did a vowsmith you know create the Vow?"

"No vowsmith was used. Just a scrap of magic to seal a series of promises. As for the Binding"—the vowsmith licked his fleshy lips again—"the magic tasted familiar. Like rust. Like vengeance."

"Marvelous," Lorn drawled. "For some reason, we have a farmer and a hunter, bound by Forbidden magic, taking a Vow to kidnap the Queen. Could the Death Cultists have bound the two?"

The Goblin snorted. "Bindings are powerful magic. To bind someone takes more skill and raw magical talent than Death Cultists are known to have. Most likely they handled the Vow; the magic tasted like theirs. Thick, like tar." He stared at Lorn with his clever, black eyes. "*You* could do them—Bindings—if you had a mind to do so."

Lorn barely suppressed a shudder. "Then it is lucky for Otherworld that I have no mind to do so."

The vowsmith grinned but said no more about it. Instead, he reached across the desk for his sack of gold.

"Bindings that powerful need to be anchored in flesh and blood," he said, hiding the sack within his cloak. "There will be a Mark somewhere holding it in place. Tell your crew to search for it. Find the Mark, unravel the Bind."

"You say it as if the entire process is as easy as eating a slice of pie."

The vowsmith grinned, all pointy teeth. "For some, it is."

"For gods and goddesses, perhaps. Or the dark fae—Bindings were usually their specialty. And there are not a lot of those running around in Otherworld."

The goblin's grin became even pointier. He leaned toward Lorn, bringing with him the scent of wet moss and dark earth. "You'd be surprised."

There was a glint in the goblin's eyes that Lorn could not interpret; something deeper than just amusement. It made Lorn uneasy.

"Thanks to Between, not much surprises me anymore," Lorn said. "I shall probably stumble on a knot of dark fae when I least expect it. Probably in an old closet, and most likely on a Wednesday."

The vowsmith leaned back in his seat, still grinning. "Maybe so."

Long after the vowsmith had fumbled and wheezed his way out of the room, Lorn continued to stare at the doorway, a sour feeling in his gut. It seemed that the more he learned, the worse the situation became.

He was debating whether or not to bring out the bottle of Red Gold, when he heard a gleeful shriek coming from the sky, followed by the beating of hundreds of wings.

Looking out his window, Lorn watched in horror as flocks of birds and more exotic winged creatures tore through the air, heading for the open window of the Portal Chamber.

"Oh, dear," he said with a sigh as the creatures poured through the window. "This does not bode well."

He was right—it did not bode well at all ...

15

FIT FOR A QUEEN

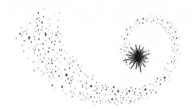

MOMENTS LATER

BY THE TIME LORN REACHED THE PORTAL CHAMBER, HE COULD FEEL THE Summons to the Earther Realm.

Shadow King! We need you back here! the Queen called.

"I am coming," Lorn muttered, grimacing at the fishhook feeling behind his navel.

The sooner, the better! the Queen yelled back.

Despite himself, Lorn grinned.

Within moments, Lorn found himself in sitting in a tree in the Earther Realm, laughing at the sight of the beasties of his kingdom cavorting with tiny Earthers. And oh, what charming chaos it was! The high-pitched screech of assorted flying creatures mingled with the delighted squeals of the children as they ran to and fro, chasing—or being chased by—brownies and sprites, goblins and pixies.

And at the center of it all was the Queen, charging forth, club in hand, rescuing her small charges with the sort of selfless heroism usually only seen in elves.

I wonder if she will use the same sort of ruthless efficiency when dealing with the miscreants of Between? he thought with a laugh as she batted several creatures over a fence.

But he did not have long to ponder that thought. Soon, the Queen spotted him, her eyes flashing with irritation.

"This is no laughing matter," she scolded from below his branch, her grasp tightening on her club. Something told Lorn that she would not be opposed to using it on him if he continued to laugh.

"Apologies," he said, trying to fold away his smile. "But I could not help but relish the fact that these creatures were making a mess of someone else's realm for a change."

The Queen began to reply but stopped as a terrible, mechanical screeching sound filled the air.

He turned toward the noise and saw a shabby little unicorn head-butting a shiny, red vehicle. Lorn's eyes narrowed. The unicorn was distressingly familiar.

"Tractor," he muttered under his breath.

"Hey!" the Queen yelled at the beast. "Hey! Stop that!"

To Lorn's surprise, Tractor stopped. The little unicorn obediently turned toward Sasha and belched so hard that it lurched forward a few paces.

"Is that pony drunk?" the Queen asked, transfixed.

"Unicorn, not pony," he stated, still impressed by the fact that Tractor had obeyed a direct order. Perhaps there was hope for him yet.

"*That* is a unicorn? Are you sure?"

Her skepticism was quite justified. It was hard to imagine a less impressive creature than Tractor; the little beast looked like an inebriated, mange-encrusted goat.

"Quite sure," he said. "I believe it came from the Goblin Kingdom, hence its less-than-majestic appearance. And yes, it is drunk. Though, I suppose it is a little early in the day to be intoxicated, even for him."

Tractor appeared to be the last straw for the Queen. "Would you please fix this?" she asked wearily, rubbing her eyes.

Lorn looked around at the lovely chaos below him and could not help but smile. "Yes. But it will happen again, and again, and again—as you well know."

He turned back to the Queen and his smile fell away. She was bracing herself for what he was about to say next, her shoulders stiff, her knuckles white around the handle of the club. And even though Lorn knew it was the right—no, the *only* course of action in the circumstances, he wished for her sake that there was another way.

"You made a promise to return to Between if the people of Old Middleton were in danger, Your Majesty," he reminded her, as gently as he could.

The Queen closed her eyes for the briefest of moments. "Before I—"

She stopped and cleared her throat. "Before I go, I need to ask one last time ..." She looked up at him and he stilled at the utter devastation in her expression. "Is there *any* way—any way at all—that I could stay?"

"None that I know," he answered quietly. He hoped that she could hear the truth in his words.

She must have because she did not look surprised, only desolate. "And —and after the trial run ...when I return to Old Middleton ..." A flock of creatures screeched by overhead. The Queen paused to watch them, her eyes wide. "Will the creatures follow me? Will the dark wizards follow me?"

"I will do all in my power to stop the dark wizards," he vowed. "But the Portal *will* open while you are in this realm. It opens to guide you back to Between ... to where it believes you belong."

She exhaled in a rush, her shoulders falling as if her breath had been the only thing holding her up. "Fine." She lifted her chin. "You win. I'll do it. Just call off your unicorn—that car cost me a fortune."

Finally! Those were the words that Lorn had been waiting to hear. He would no longer have to worry about open gateways and portals, or kidnapping plots that spanned realms.

And yet, looking down at the Queen, Lorn felt terrible. When he had first arrived at the scene, she had been aglow with passion and purpose, tearing across the playground with her club like a comet. But now ... now she looked beaten. Defeated. And he *hated* the sight of it.

She deserves better than this, he thought as she stared up at him, her expression bruised. *She deserves more.*

"When will I leave?" she asked, her voice as hollow as an echo. "I need to collect my things."

Lorn broke eye contact and made a show of brushing the gold dust from his gloves. "Tomorrow evening."

Then he stilled because he could not quite believe what he had just said.

Neither could the Queen. He glanced up—her blue eyes were wide with surprise.

"But—but the Portal!" she said in disbelief. "The *creatures*—and the dark wizards and the fire beasts and—don't you want me to leave right now?"

Yes, he thought to himself, exasperated. *What* about *the Portal and the creatures and the dark wizards and the fire beasts?*

"Do you wish to leave right now?" he asked her, half hoping she would say *yes.* "That *can* be arranged."

The Queen shook her head emphatically, her wild curls flying around her shoulders. "No. Not at all. Forget I even asked. Tomorrow evening is fine. More than fine. *Great*, in fact." She smiled up at him as if he had granted her the world.

It made his heart clench in a way that was both dreadful and wondrous.

"Sunset," he repeated firmly. Not only for her benefit but for his own; the last thing he needed was to lose his head entirely and give her an additional week.

"Sunset," she repeated, still beaming up at him in that dreadfully wonderful way.

And that was that. Before he knew it, Lorn was wrangling his creatures from the clutches of the children and performing a magic show that involved a ruby-red dragon.

It was, all things considered, a triumphant day.

"So," his Shadow said as Lorn emerged from the Portal holding a drion cub, his dark armor covered in soot. "How was the Earther Realm?"

Lorn released the little lion-dragon hybrid and made eye contact with his Shadow. Within moments, his Shadow was roaring with laughter.

"Oh!" The Shadow wiped a tear from his eye. "The delightful *havoc*! Earther children and beasties in the one place, cavorting together!"

Lorn collapsed into his customary armchair. "The children were completely enthralled by the beasties. They enjoyed themselves immensely."

"They also seemed to have enjoyed your magic show. The piece with Kyra was truly delightful. The Earthers were justifiably awed to see a dragon in the flesh."

Lorn recalled the act of pulling a very large dragon from a very small hat. "I believe Kyra enjoyed being the star of the show. She played her part beautifully." He smiled at the memory. "It was such a novelty to watch those children react with wonder and joy at magic ... rather than with pitchforks and flaming torches. It was how it should be. Perhaps, once this is all over ... when we are free ..."

The little drion butted against Lorn's hand until he scratched the top of its furry head. "You certainly enjoyed yourself. You even made a new friend —one abundant in candy and chaos."

"He was an odd little boy," the Shadow mused. "There was something about him ..."

Lorn remembered the tiny boy as he stared fearlessly at the wild creatures gathered around him, his eyes fiendishly bright even in the face of a terribly dangerous, fire-breathing dragon. "Yes. Yes, there was."

The drion pulled away and glanced toward the Portal, then back at Lorn and whined.

"I am afraid not," Lorn said gently. "You are in your realm; he is in his. Some things are not meant to be."

The little cub raised his chin and growled.

Lorn looked down at the small bundle of fur and defiance, and something in his chest ached; he knew all about bravado in the face of losing one's fondest wish.

He reached out and offered his hand, palm up, to the little beast. "Then again, the separation between Otherworld and the Earther Realm is not what it used to be. If it is in my power, I will let you be together. After all, Dreams are not just for Dreamers."

The little drion tipped back his head and roared with happiness, sending a small arc of flames above his head.

"Extraordinary," the Shadow said, watching the resultant plume of smoke drift toward the ceiling. "I did not know they were capable of fiery destruction; I always thought their lion ancestry was dominant."

"Use it well," Lorn told the drion.

The little beast turned toward Lorn's outstretched hand and licked it with his leathery tongue. He then ambled off toward the door, a strut in his step.

"What a strange little thing," the Shadow said.

Lorn stared after the creature and grinned. "Bunion is as unique as his name."

"*Bunion.*" The Shadow shook his head and sighed. "Well, regardless of his name, you have made one small, destructive beast happy."

"Two, if we count the boy." Lorn began to brush the soot from his armor but then paused. "Perhaps we should keep this between ourselves. I doubt that the Queen will be in favor of gifting a drion to her student."

"True. She did not seem particularly enamored of their friendship." The Shadow smiled suddenly, his eyes emerald-bright. "She is coming *tomorrow*. Oh, what a glorious day it will be!"

Lorn gave up on trying to remove the soot and sighed. The thought of the Queen's arrival invoked an odd tangle of emotions. To his great surprise, the feeling at the very forefront was something ... *positive*. He probed at it cautiously, trying to discern what this foreign emotion could be—

"Midra's sack—it is *excitement*," he said in disbelief. Lorn did not expect excitement. *Curiosity* would have been acceptable in this situation. *Interest* would have been tolerated. But *excitement*?

Excitement was wildly unacceptable.

"This will not do," Lorn muttered.

"Are you talking to yourself?" the Shadow asked. He tilted his head to the right, considering his question. "If you are, then this is a three-way conversation with yourself. Which is unnecessarily complicated, if you ask me ..."

"We are woefully unprepared," Lorn said, ignoring the Shadow. He stood up abruptly and began to pace the chamber, trying to crush his surge of excitement with each footstep. "Has Maddox made any headway on the preparations?"

The Shadow's glaze was all too knowing. Nevertheless, he did not comment on Lorn's odd shift in mood. "Maddox has gone to the Wetlands to deal with the Zadrian betrothal party."

Lorn paused his pacing. "Are they still wandering around in there?"

"Well, it *is* a vast and ever-changing landscape. Apparently, a second betrothal party arrived yesterday—"

"Are they also in the Wetlands?"

"So it appears."

"Soon there will be more Zadrians in the Wetlands than swamps."

Lorn crossed quickly to the model of Between. Sure enough, there were now two parties of gray and purple clad riders wandering hopelessly around the various tar pits, cesspools, and quicksand traps.

"True," the Shadow said. "Though, I am not sure which is more toxic. Maddox thought it was high time to round them up and put an end to their rescues and leisurely strolls around the swamps with fire beasts."

Lorn watched as a very large, winged lizard burst out of the shrubbery and began to chase one of the Zadrian riders. "He has a point."

"Did I tell you that she paid me a visit last night?"

"Who?" Lorn said, trying to find Maddox on the model.

"Sasha, our lovely Queen."

Lorn stilled. He ignored the fact that the lizard was now breathing fire and turned to the Shadow, shocked. "No. Why did you not tell me?"

The Shadow made a dismissive gesture. "It slipped my mind, what with the second kidnapping attempt, and the Death Cultists crashing through the gateway—"

"What did you say to her?" Lorn interrupted, his tone urgent.

"Nothing of consequence. Merely that I was your Shadow."

"*Merely that I was your Shadow?!*" Lorn stared at his Shadow in horror. "As if that does not lead to more questions, each answer more damning than the next!"

The Shadow held up his hands. "Calm yourself." He sat down in his armchair and made a show of getting comfortable. "For the record, Sasha figured out that I was not you almost immediately." He stretched out his long legs before him, pausing to admire the shine on his boots. "Imagine, she has only met you—what? A handful of times? And yet, she knew that I was not you exceedingly quickly. Such a clever, observant woman!" He glanced at his true form. "Do you not agree?"

Lorn simply stared at him, frozen.

"Of course, she had questions," the Shadow continued when it became apparent that Lorn was too stunned to speak, "but I told her to speak to you."

Lorn was barely listening. He had planned to hide his Shadow from the Queen—for his safety, for her own. And now, thanks to a dream, she knew his most dangerous secret.

Now she knows what an abomination I truly am, Lorn realized, more distressed by the thought than he could have possibly anticipated.

His Shadow pretended to be blissfully unaware of Lorn's turmoil. "For what it is worth, I think she likes me."

"Of course, she does," Lorn said, momentarily shaken out of his internal angst. "You tend to be my more palatable side."

"Funny, she thought so, too."

The beats of Lorn's heart began to mimic the footfalls of stampeding wildebeests, and frankly, it was not at all enjoyable.

Oblivious to the wildebeests in Lorn's chest, the Shadow continued. "She was *most* delighted by my response to her question."

"Which was?" Lorn asked as a mere formality; he already knew the answer. He had a second sense when it came to horrific situations.

The Shadow leaned back in his armchair. "Why, what *I* would have done if I had met her on the Hill that first night."

Lorn *knew* that he should not ask.

He *would* not ask.

He asked.

"What did you tell her?"

His Shadow laughed—a laugh of dark promise and seductive delight—and Lorn groaned because he recognized that tone and immediately knew what it meant.

"No." Lorn held up his hand. "I take it back. I already know what you said. You have made your opinion on what I should have done that evening quite clear."

The Shadow said nothing; he merely lounged in his seat, looking immensely pleased with himself.

Lorn, on the other hand, was in turmoil. He began to pace the room frantically. "What must she think of us? Of *me*? After all—what kind of man has a piece of his soul encased in a mirror?"

The Shadow waved away Lorn's concerns. "It is a very small piece— positively tiny, in fact—and it was not your choice to do so."

Lorn stared at his Shadow incredulously. "What does the size of the piece matter? Or whether it was my choice or not? Neither point reduces the dreadfulness of the situation."

"Power always involves a sacrifice. Yours was perhaps a little more literal than most. Perhaps if you explained it to her in full …?"

Lorn collapsed into his armchair and dropped his face into his hands.

"Come now," the Shadow said, "there are worse things. You could have been cursed like your friend, Ashlyn." He shook his head. "Poor fellow. Utterly doomed."

"Why is it that when someone is going through a crisis, people feel the need to bring up someone else who is going through a different, objectively worse crisis?" Lorn muttered through his hands. "It is neither helpful nor comforting."

"For what it is worth, Sasha appeared to take our meeting in her stride. She is a very practical young woman. I do not know why you are taking this so badly."

Lorn remained as he was, hunched over and miserable.

"Ah." The Shadow spoke softly, but there was a wealth of understanding in the small syllable. "You believe that now she has met me, she will think you a monster, an abomination. Something less than human. Something repulsive. But you are wrong. I assure you, she did not appear to be in any way repulsed."

Lorn's face stayed buried in his hands, his stance weary, *hopeless*.

"The thought of Sasha seeing you as something to fear or shun bothers you, does it not?"

Lorn finally lifted his head. "Of course, it does! I have had quite enough of that to last a lifetime, thank you very much."

The Shadow leaned as close to his true form as he could within the confines of the mirror. "Between saw fit to introduce us. Between wants her to know all sides of you—"

Lorn groaned. "And we both know Between's motives are dubious at best, and its actions are often relentlessly dreadful. I put no stock in Between's intervention in any of this."

"She met me last night. Did she speak to you any differently today? Has her demeanor toward you changed?"

Lorn thought back to their interactions at the Elementary School. "No," he said cautiously.

"Did she suddenly cower before you in fear? Or run from you in terror?"

Lorn snorted. "She hit me on the arm, ordered me around, and chastised me for bringing a dragon into an educational setting." He paused. "She may have had a point on the latter."

The Shadow smiled brilliantly. "There you are! Sasha was not at all upset when she met me. Cautious at first, but by the end, she seemed rather *delighted* by our interaction."

Lorn's eyes narrowed. "Why? I doubt your usual litany of lewd comments would have delighted her. You must have said something—what was it?"

"A handful of truths." The Shadow smiled at the memory. "That she was glorious. That Between was lucky to have her. That *we* were lucky to have her."

"Marvelous!" Lorn threw his hands in the air in horror. "*That* will not make matters between us awkward at all."

The Shadow blinked. "You are upset because I *complimented* her? Midra's sack, would you have preferred that I called her an ill-dressed hag?"

"Possibly. I could have worked with that. She already thinks that I am difficult and poorly mannered."

"Well, you had better work on your manners or the next time she pays me a visit, I will strip off and show her your best side. Well, your best *feature*. All sides of it."

Lorn's eyes widened in horror. "You—*you would not dare*—"

The Shadow laughed. "Oh, but we both know that I *would*. Consider it a standing threat if you do not try to make a better impression—you could start by using her name." The Shadow waved his hand airily. "Regardless, there is no time to fret about such inconsequential things. I believe you have a kingdom to wrangle into submission before she arrives tomorrow." The Shadow gestured toward the model. "And it looks as though you will have your work cut out for you."

Lorn reluctantly turned back to the model. In the time his attention had been diverted, four sinkholes, two fires, and a rampaging herd of feral goats had appeared. From their flailing arms and rapidly sinking figurines, it also appeared that one of the Zadrian betrothal parties had fallen into a pit of enchanted quicksand. The other betrothal party was on fire; the fire-breathing lizard watched as the Zadrians ran around, trying to extinguish their flaming pants and cloaks, satisfied at a job well done.

"This whole situation is a disaster," Lorn said.

"It is," his Shadow agreed pleasantly. "But soon, you will have someone to share it with."

As Lorn had feared, preparations for the Queen's arrival were going terribly.

His meeting with the interior decorators—referred by Head-Fox Nevlyn—had only just begun and he was already experiencing a familiar sense of foreboding.

"What am I holding?" Lorn asked as he stared at the shiny piece of cardboard in his hand.

"That would be our business card!" one of the decorators—a weaselly little man with a hooked nose and a jaunty peacock feather in his cap—responded proudly. "See?" He pointed to the card. "*Murgatroyd and Spetzelbrass—Interior Decorators of Distinction*. That's us."

"We paid extra for the shiny cardboard. Thought it looked classier," his partner said—an equally weaselly little man, whose skin was tinged a rather unfortunate shade of green. "We also had them make the top corner extra pointy, so that you can use it in a bar fight."

"You can never have enough shivs," the first decorator said, adjusting his peacock feather.

"That appears to be Between's unofficial motto," Lorn said. "Which one of you is Murgatroyd?"

"That would be me," the first decorator said, releasing the feather and raising his hand. "But it's also *not me* if you get my drift."

"I do not," Lorn said.

"We stole the names off ice fisherman we met in the Ranges," Spetzelbrass (but also *not*-Spetzelbrass) explained. "We thought they sounded artistic. Interior decorator worthy."

"They truly do," Lorn said with a straight face. He placed the business card, with its terribly pointy corner, carefully on the desk. "Now, if we may return to the matter at hand: have the Queen's chambers been furnished yet?"

"*Almost*, Your Majesty," Murgatroyd said. "We just … ah … *rescued* the furnishings from their tragic trip down a pothole."

"We really need to look into filling those up," Lorn said, with absolutely no intention of doing so.

"I'll volunteer to do it myself," Murgatroyd said, also with absolutely no intention of doing so.

"The caravan was full of rather artistic and unique pieces," Spetzelbrass said. "It's now just a matter of picking the right ones for the chamber."

Murgatroyd nodded. "The right pieces are key. So, to make sure we're all on the same page, we'd like to know what your 'vision' "—he made air quotes around the word—"is for the chamber."

Lorn lifted one eyebrow. "My vision?"

"You have to say it with the air quotes, Majesty," Spetzelbrass said. "It's a special interior decorator term."

"It's asking what you want the room to look like," Murgatroyd said. "Fancy isn't it?"

"Quite," Lorn said. "I am suitably impressed. Very well then. I anticipate that once the new Queen arrives, she will want to decorate her chamber according to her tastes. But until that time, my 'vision'—"

He made sure to air quote; the two decorators nodded at him approvingly.

"—would be a chamber furnished in the height of good taste. Nothing ostentatious or dramatic. I do not wish to see a replica of the Summer Palace bedchambers, with all those terrible murals on the ceiling and gold leaf dripping from the walls. The new Queen is unused to the trappings of royalty, and I do not wish her to feel out of place. Her room should be comfortable—a sanctuary from this terrible place." Lorn paused. "She may need an actual sanctuary. Perhaps we should fortify her room?" He waved away his remark. "Never mind—I shall deal with that."

"Let us know if you change your mind about that," Murgatroyd said.

"We can add some metal spikes around the walls and door," Spetzelbrass added.

"I will not change my mind," Lorn said firmly.

"What were you thinking for colors?" Murgatroyd asked.

"I would like a pleasant color palette," Lorn said. "Perhaps white? Or pastels? Something clean and fresh. Nothing black or gray—the room is ridiculously gloomy as is." He tapped his finger against his lower lip. "Then again … she *is* a Queen, so perhaps some subtle gilding here and there to add a regal tone."

The two decorators stared at him blankly.

"Was my 'vision' unclear?" Lorn asked.

Murgatroyd rubbed the back of his neck uneasily. "Well, there was a lot of it."

"You used a lot of words," Spetzelbrass clarified.

"You also mentioned several 'design concepts' "—Murgatroyd air quoted—"which we aren't familiar with."

"Which concepts specifically?" Lorn asked. "Pastel? Palette? Gilding? Gold leaf?"

"Yep," Murgatroyd said, nodding. "Those."

Lorn took a deep, cleansing breath. "Gentlemen, my patience—just like my sanity—is hanging from an incredibly thin thread. So, to ensure that I emerge from this mentally scarring meeting with both relatively intact, I propose that we keep this as simple as possible: decorate the chambers in a manner that is both elegant and tasteful. Can you do that?"

The two designers shared a look.

"We have a candelabra with squirrels on it," Murgatroyd said.

"It's rather tall," Spetzelbrass added.

Lorn pinched the bridge of his nose. He then reached beneath his desk for the button that activated the trapdoor beneath the interior decorator's chairs.

When he could not locate the button, Lorn remembered that the trapdoor was in the Formal Meeting Chamber and swore.

"Perhaps—" Murgatroyd began.

Lorn held up his hand. "A moment, if you please." He took a piece of parchment and wrote: *Install trapdoor in Less-Formal Meeting Chamber.* He then turned back to the decorators. "Where were we?"

"Squirrel candelabra," Spetzelbrass said helpfully.

"Damn," Lorn said and stopped himself from reaching for the non-existent button.

"Some would say that a squirrel candelabra is the height of elegance and taste," Spetzelbrass said.

"Those people would be liars," Lorn said. "Or suffering from some sort of terrible head injury."

"Taste is subjective," Spetzelbrass insisted.

"Not when it comes to squirrel candelabras," Lorn said.

"It's just that there isn't much call for elegance in Between," Murgatroyd said.

"Or taste," Spetzelbrass added.

"Our customers usually want flashy."

"And non-flammable."

"And by customers, we actually mean *customer*. Singular. We've only had the one," Murgatroyd confessed.

"My brother," Spetzelbrass said. "He tames fire-breathing lizards."

"Why does none of this surprise me?" Lorn asked. He steepled his fingers together and rested his forearms on his desk, leaning toward the two men. "Gentlemen, I confess that, after speaking to you, I actively fear for Her Majesty's chambers. In fact, despite this meeting, I have a terrible feeling that the 'vision' you will impose upon that poor, unsuspecting room is one that will have Her Majesty fleeing back to her home realm."

Murgatroyd looked over at his partner. "I have a 'vision' that we're about to be fired."

Lorn held up his hand for silence. "But, given that Her Majesty arrives tomorrow, time is of the essence. And as much as it pains me to say this—and I mean that quite literally—I have no other option but to keep you on."

"Phew!" Spetzelbrass said.

"You're desperate," Murgatroyd said knowingly. "We figured that's how we'll get most of our customers."

"Most likely," Lorn agreed. "Decorate the chambers in a manner that is the *exact opposite* of the chambers of your lizard-taming brother. Go completely against your instincts."

"Yes, Majesty!" they said giddily.

"And keep in mind that I will inspect the chambers tomorrow afternoon before Her Majesty arrives. If it is not up to my incredibly high standards, I will send you to the Wetlands."

"Like … on an all-expenses-paid holiday as a thank you for our fine services?" Murgatroyd asked hopefully.

Lorn stared at the designer. "No."

"That's what I thought," Murgatroyd said with a sigh. "But, say we do a good job—"

"I doubt there is a realm in existence where that is possible," Lorn interrupted.

"But, say we *do*," Murgatroyd persisted. "Could you give us a royal reference? That would do wonders for our business."

"Seal of approval and all that," his partner added.

Lorn continued to stare at the decorators. "If by some miracle, you do not bollocks this up completely, I will give you a royal reference and a barrel of ale. Now, be off with you both—time is fleeting."

"Woohoo!" Murgatroyd crowed, leaping from his chair and running out of the room before Lorn could change his mind.

"You won't regret this, Majesty!" Spetzelbrass yelled over his shoulder as he followed his partner out the door.

"Oh, but I already do," Lorn muttered.

Lorn's next meeting with the representatives of the castle guard only fueled his growing sense of foreboding.

"Have you practiced Her Majesty's welcome?" he asked, dreading the reply.

Jakobson nodded. "Yes, Majesty. We've practiced our greeting."

Lorn sighed in relief.

"And we're also going to play a welcome tune for the Queen when she arrives," Lennox said.

"I was unaware that the castle guard had a band," Lorn said.

"We don't," Jakobson said cheerfully. "But the Procurement department acquired some musical instruments the other day and asked us to carry them to storage. We looked at them and thought, why not start a band? I mean, how hard can it be to play a horn, right? It's just a matter of blowing into one end."

Lorn opened his mouth to argue and then gave up; he knew from experience that it was better to just let the guards learn the hard way.

"Well," he said instead, "there is certainly enough hot air in the castle guards."

"Exactly!" Lennox said.

"We'd also like your opinion on something." Jakobson cleared his throat, his prominent Adam's Apple bobbing nervously. "When we went with you to the Summer Palace last year, we saw how *their* castle guards greeted dignitaries. They were in formations."

"*Really* professional, like," Lennox added, her eyes round with wonder.

Lorn raised an eyebrow. "And?"

Jakobson took a deep breath. "We'd like to try a formation."

"You know—arrange ourselves so we're standing in a shape rather than a line," Lennox explained.

Lorn noted the guards' hopeful expressions and sighed. "Are you, perhaps, being a little too ambitious? The last time I checked, the Between castle guards could barely manage to walk together in a straight line. You have an Otherworld-wide reputation for falling over each other whenever you try to exit a room. Most of the injuries acquired by the castle guards are caused by tripping over each other while marching—"

"That's all in the past," Jakobsen interrupted firmly. "We've been working on that little problem since I was promoted in March."

"Falls are down by about twenty-percent," Lennox said proudly.

"Marvelous," Lorn drawled. "Otherworld will have twenty-percent fewer opportunities to mock us."

"Great, isn't it?" Jakobsen said, grinning widely.

"Go on," Lennox pleaded. "Let us give it a shot!"

Lorn sighed. "Fine. The day is bound to be an unparalleled disaster anyway—why not make it interesting?" He waited until the guards stopped cheering. "What type of formation were you thinking of attempting?"

"Well, we were thinking of a circle," Jakobsen said, "but some of the guards thought that was a bit too ambitious—it being our first time and all."

"And a square just seems odd," Lennox said. "I mean, would the Queen even be able to tell that we're standing in a square? It would just look like we're in a bunch of lines and we're *always* in lines. What we need is something that's like a circle but less complicated."

"Have you considered a semi-circle?" Lorn asked.

Lennox's eyes bugged. "That would look so classy."

"Do you really think we're at that level, Majesty?" Jakobson asked. "I mean, that's half a circle!"

"I believe in you," Lorn said, deadpan.

The guards looked at him in awe.

"Right, we'll try it then!" Jakobson said, his Adam's apple bobbing enthusiastically. "We'll do you proud, Your Majesty. Just you wait and see!"

"I am holding my breath in anticipation," Lorn said.

"You probably shouldn't do that—on account of your health," Lennox said, all seriousness.

Lorn was about to answer that odd bit of medical advice when he was distracted by a strange, guttural sound coming from below him. He and the guards exchanged puzzled looks, then simultaneously crouched down and looked under the desk.

There, lying on his back, his little legs sticking straight up in the air, was a small, drunk, sleeping unicorn.

Lorn rolled his eyes. "Jakobsen, could you please speak to the guards again about giving Tractor ale? The practice needs to stop immediately."

Jakobsen smiled fondly at the beast. "But Majesty, little Tractor here looks at us with those big, unicorn eyes of his, and we just can't resist."

"We're not made of stone, Majesty," Lennox added, rubbing Tractor's tummy. "I mean, could *you* resist the little fellow?"

At that moment Tractor belched, releasing a cloud of foul, ale-scented air that had Lorn and his guards scrambling out from under the desk in record time.

"Yes … yes, I could," Lorn said, coughing. He glared at the disreputable creature as it emerged blearily from beneath the desk. "This beast has drunkenly head-butted every mirror at eye-level in the castle, urinated on my throne multiple times, and has been in more bar fights than the entire castle guard combined." He remembered the unicorn gleefully head-butting the Queen's vehicle. "Not to mention the damage it caused in the Earther Realm. This beast is altogether *resistible*."

"Well, he seems to like you," Lennox said.

Sure enough, Tractor lurched over to Lorn and rubbed his muzzle on Lorn's leg, then staggered out of the room.

Lorn looked down at the mess of unicorn hair and snot on his leather pants and grimaced. "Fine. Get him cleaned up before the Queen arrives. He smells diseased."

The two guards grinned.

"Very well, Majesty," Jakobson said.

"We're on it!" Lennox said, as they bowed their way out of the room.

～

To Lorn's extreme dismay, the preparations for the coronation and Joining were faring even worse than those for the Queen's arrival.

"Tell me the good news first," Lorn said to Maddox. "Assuming there is any. Actually, I take that back—if there is no good news, make some up."

"I shall try my best to be both accurate and deceptive." Maddox looked down at his notebook. "The invitations are out, and the venues selected. As for the decorations, the procurement teams said that there were slim pickings on the trade roads this week. They only managed to liberate four caravans from the potholes. This is the best they could do."

Maddox handed Lorn a hand mirror.

Lorn tapped the surface. A medium sized storage room came into view filled with various objects, ranging from lanterns to napkins. He stared at the contents in horror. Everything was gray or purple, or purple and gray, and almost every piece bore a skull that appeared to be either grinning or screaming.

"These caravans—they were not Zadrian by any chance?" Lorn asked.

"Whatever gave it away?" Maddox asked dryly. "Was it the purple and gray, which happen to be the official colors of Zadria? Or was it the skulls, which happen to be the official symbol of Zadria?"

"So many skulls," Lorn muttered, shaking his head. "I know that their god is dead, but must they continue to mourn him centuries later with skull paraphernalia? It is exceedingly tacky."

"Indeed. Their deep-seated pain at losing their protector and spiritual guardian is truly an inconvenience to us all."

Lorn held up his hands in surrender. "You are completely correct. My apologies to the Zadrian people for making light of their spiritual plight." He looked back at the mirror. "But you have to admit—the skulls are terrible."

"Incredibly tacky," Maddox agreed. "And they make it needlessly difficult to sell the merchandise; customers tend to find skulls off-putting. Our best bet is to try and resell it back to the Zadrians." He peered at the mirror. "Still, do you see anything that we can use for the coronation or Joining?"

Lorn shook his head. "Not a thing. I will have to take a closer look but —hang on." He turned the mirror to face Maddox. "Why, in Midra's name, are there so many taxidermied animals?"

Maddox glanced at the mirror and shrugged. "They were also in the Zadrian caravans—taxidermy is something of a national pastime."

"That explains the animals. But why are they all wearing paper foil crowns?"

"The interior decorators you hired insisted upon it. It was part of their 'vision.' " Maddox's air quotes somehow managed to hold a wealth of sarcasm. "They thought it would make the animals appear regal."

"Yes, nothing says *regal* like a weasel wearing a paper hat."

"Well, the weasel is the official national animal of Between."

Lorn gave a long-suffering sigh. "I asked for tasteful and elegant. Is that truly too much to ask?"

"Yes, it is. This is not Vale—"

"Ah, Vale," Lorn interrupted, his tone wistful. "So tasteful. So elegant …"

"This is Between, where things are typically diseased and flammable. You are asking for something that goes against our very nature."

"True. It serves me right." Lorn tapped the mirror and handed it back to Maddox. "This will not do. Tell them to find decorations in silver or white, *not black*." Lorn noticed Maddox's pointed glance at Lorn's clothing.

"Yes, I know that black is our unofficial color but allow me to be the one sinister element on the day."

"Very well," Maddox said. "Though, I cannot help but wonder why you are trying so hard to make Between appear to be something it is not. I thought you warned Her Majesty that the place was wretched?"

Lorn leaned back in his chair. "Oh, I did. But I fear that Between may be far more wretched than she can imagine. I am merely trying to elevate it to normal levels of wretchedness. *Tolerable* levels of wretchedness—the sort of wretchedness that does not lead one to fear for their life."

"I shall leave you to your delusions. Now, the feast."

"Food," Lorn groaned. "Always a problem in Between."

"Yes. Unfortunately, this celebration will put quite the dent in our stores for winter."

"It will, but we have little choice in the matter. We will have to steal or buy items to replenish our stock before the winter storms. I would prefer it if we went with the former rather than the latter."

"Of course!" his advisor said, clearly affronted. "We have a reputation to maintain."

"Indeed," the Lorn said, grinning.

"And before I forget, the scribes have completed your Joining contract." Maddox handed Lorn two long scrolls. "One copy is for Her Majesty's representatives to look over—I assume that is the coven."

Lorn's grin disappeared. "Ah."

"Note the color of the ribbons," Maddox pointed to the neat, black-silk bows that bound the scrolls. "They are in mourning for your bachelorhood … and Her Majesty's."

"Very fitting," Lorn said approvingly.

He placed one of the scrolls in his pouch to give to the Queen. He decided to ignore his own for as long as possible—perhaps until the hour before his nuptials.

"Now," he said, trying to distract himself from the idea of marriage entirely, "before I attend to the next disaster, I shall ask you the eternal question: Have you found a way to free me from Between?"

"Yes," Maddox said.

Lorn blinked. "Did you—did you just say *yes?*"

"Yes. I did."

Lorn's heart began to race. He glanced toward the secret wall panel and surreptitiously touched his earlobe in a gesture meant to convey that *the walls have ears.*

Maddox also glanced at the wall but shook his head. "I dismissed the spies earlier. Terrence, however, remained too elusive to capture. We will have to swear him to secrecy."

From behind the secret panel, Terrence gave an agreeable whine followed by a sneeze.

"Bless you," Lorn said absentmindedly. He stared at his chief advisor. "How is the answer *yes?*"

Maddox reached into one of the many hidden pockets of his gray coat and carefully removed a small book bound in red leather. He placed it hesitantly on the desk between himself and the King. "When I heard that there was a new queen, I went to the Archives to learn more about our previous queens—as a means of preparing the kingdom, you understand."

Lorn stared at the book, his mouth dry. "Of course."

"As you well know, there have been very few queens in Between and even fewer True Queens. Almost every queen before now has been a witch or a sorceress. It seems that we have entered new territory. But I digress. In my travels through the Archives last night, I encountered this book. I could have sworn it was not there before—the cover, you see?" Maddox touched the red leather cover lightly with the tip of his index finger. "The color is very distinct. *Noticeable.* I would have remembered it." He slid the book across the table toward Lorn. "Let us just say that this book answers the eternal question."

Lorn picked up the book slowly, carefully, as if it were as fragile as a dream. "Many thanks," he said hoarsely.

Maddox stood up from his chair and crossed slowly to one of the windows. As usual for this time of year, it was raining. Thankfully, it was only raining water today—not flames, or fish, or rocks, or flaming fish and rocks.

"If I may say …" Maddox paused, staring out at the city below. "That is, if I may speak *candidly* … as if to my friend, not to my King—" He stopped abruptly and collected himself. "I know it is not my business, but if I may be permitted to say …"

Even amidst his emotional turmoil, Lorn was surprised to see his chief advisor so tongue-tied. He stared at Maddox's tense frame silhouetted by the window and waited. When it became apparent that the older man was not going to continue without reassurance, Lorn spoke.

"Maddox, I can rarely stop you from speaking your mind, and I always value what you have to say. Speak your worst."

Maddox turned back toward Lorn, his expression uncharacteristically open. "You have been an exemplary King—one of the best in Between's terrible history. I understand that fact is neither here nor there in this matter. But, Gold Feather or not, you were born to rule."

Lorn swallowed past the sudden tightness in his throat. "Your good opinion means a great deal to me, Maddox. But we both know that my reign—good or bad—is coming to an end. I will not survive it much longer."

Maddox looked down at Lorn's hands, a terrible pity twisting his features.

Puzzled, Lorn followed his gaze and noticed a smudge of black ink on the back of his knuckles. It reminded Lorn of his dark patches; clearly, his advisor thought the same.

"As I said—it is neither here nor there," Maddox said quietly, the sadness in his tone unmistakable. "But it should be said."

Lorn was suddenly desperate to leave the room. To see his usually stoic advisor so moved by emotion on his behalf …

It was unbearable.

But instead of fleeing, Lorn took a deep breath and carefully stowed the little red book into the bottomless pouch at his hip.

"Many thanks, Maddox. For everything. Your service—your *counsel*—is beyond the worth of the treasuries combined."

Before Maddox could reply, Lorn stood abruptly and, with a few quick strides, left the chamber, the weight of the book—and all it meant—heavy at his side.

∽

MADDOX WATCHED THE DOOR CLOSE BEHIND HIS KING, MORE DISQUIETED than he would ever admit. But he quickly put aside his feelings. After all, there was a castle to prepare, a Queen to welcome, and assorted catastrophes to avert.

When he opened the Less-Formal Meeting Chamber door, he was greeted by the sight of several castle guards running down the corridor. One of them spied the chief advisor and paused. "Some kind of lizard-dragon hybrid has just appeared in the west wing," he announced breathlessly.

"That does not sound too terrible," Maddox said.

"It's bigger than a turnip cart, covered in spikes, and appears to be spitting lava."

"And it's on the move," another guard said cheerfully before both guards returned to the important business of running away.

Maddox stared longingly at the retreating guards. Truth be told, he would rather confront a cart-sized, lava-spitting reptile than try to prepare Between for its new Queen.

He shook his head, shaking away that thought, and reminded himself of what was truly important: loyalty to the King, service to Between, and possession of a key to the Small Treasury. Patting the key reassuringly, Maddox went on his way to make mundane miracles.

16

THE RED BOOK AND THE WHITE RUG

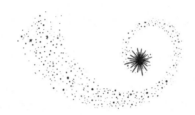

DESPITE THE PROMISES OF THE LITTLE RED BOOK—OR PERHAPS BECAUSE OF them—Lorn did not open the precious volume until late that evening when he was safely in his chambers.

He settled into his armchair, adjusting his posture until he was sitting comfortably. He rearranged the candelabras in the room until the light was just right. He Summoned a throw pillow.

Then, a glass of water.

Then, another pillow.

Then, he stoked the fireplace … and so on and so forth until he finally admitted to himself that he was stalling, the fear of disappointment momentarily stronger than the lure of freedom.

"Just open it," he told himself, rolling his eyes. "You have been disappointed before and will be so again. You will survive it."

Squaring his shoulders, Lorn opened the pouch at his hip. The pouch was truly bottomless—a pretty piece of magic that he had acquired for two oak buttons and a handful of gold dust from a crotchety old centaur at the Twilight Market in Faire. Although bottomlessness was imminently useful when storing objects, it was an utter pain when it came time to retrieve them. Lorn placed his hand into the pouch and visualized the book. Then, unleashing a sliver of magic, he Summoned the book to his hand.

The book came as soon as it was called, the leather binding smooth and cool against his palm.

"Why, hello lovely thing," he crooned as he pulled the small, red book free of the pouch. "Maddox believes that you hold the secret to freeing me from this dreadful place. Is he right? Are you my salvation?"

His breath caught—the means of his escape could literally be in his hands.

"Steady now," he told himself firmly. "It could be another dead end."

Lorn rolled his shoulders, conscious of the space between them where Between had Marked him—

Branded and yoked him.

Lorn pushed that thought aside. Instead, he focused on his accelerating heartbeat and took a deep breath to slow it, concerned by his optimism.

He closed his eyes and opened his senses, stroking the book's cover with his long fingers.

The book felt … *eager.*

Tamping down his anticipation, Lorn opened his eyes and turned to the first page, skimming the words as fast as he could. The more he read, the harder it became to hold back his growing excitement.

"Oh, Maddox," he whispered in wonder, "you *are* worth far more than the contents of the treasuries!"

As he reread the relevant passages, he marveled that all the elements for his escape would soon be in his grasp. It was so simple!

Too simple.

Which ... which was suspicious.

The timing of this discovery was almost *too* fortuitous—Midra knew his life was neither lucky nor straightforward. He knew that he should be on guard.

But still …

But *still.*

He had felt more hope in the last few moments than he had felt for years, and the feeling was intoxicating.

Lorn gasped out a laugh—a laugh that sounded incredulous and desperate to his ears.

"You are a treasure," he told the book. "You are worth your weight in sapphires and stars."

A breeze lifted the chamber curtains and moved swiftly into the room, ruffling Lorn's hair.

"Why, hello," Lorn said to the breeze. "Have you come for a visit? I should have sought you out; the imps told me that you tried to assist the Queen during her run across the Wasteland. You have my eternal thanks."

The breeze ruffled his hair, clearly pleased with the praise.

"For once, my mood is as joyous as yours. I have just had some wondrous news—Maddox has found a way to free me of this place." He gestured toward the book sitting open in his lap.

The breeze tore through the chamber, extinguishing the candle flames and upending the parchment on Lorn's desk, before circling back to Lorn's chair. It then ruffled the pages of the red book roughly, clearly agitated.

Lorn sighed and raised his hand; the candelabras flared to life once more. "Yes, I had the same thought. Given my terrible luck to date, it is most likely a trap. Or if not, then it will probably go terribly wrong. But right now, I am allowing myself the exquisite luxury of hope. Later, I shall fret and worry. But for now … *now*, I hope."

The breeze again played with the pages of the book, a little gentler this time.

"Soon, I shall be as free as you, my friend. Shall we adventure together?"

The breeze ruffled Lorn's hair, clearly pleased.

Lorn smiled. "Oh, what adventures we shall have!"

The breeze paused and moved to Lorn's desk where it flitted against one of the pieces of parchment. It picked it up and carried it across the room to Lorn, depositing it in his lap on top of the red book.

Lorn stared at the parchment and frowned—it was The Revised Queen Plan. He tapped the tip of his finger next to step seven.

Flee this wretched place.

"I may just accomplish step seven after all," Lorn told the breeze.

Which meant that step six—*ignore the new Queen*—was now imperative.

"She cannot become too reliant on me," Lorn explained to the breeze. "It will make things difficult for her when I leave." He ignored the traitorous thought that leaving would make things difficult for the Queen regardless of her reliance on him.

"I must keep my distance," he told the breeze—and himself—quite firmly. "I must make it clear that our relationship is simply that of two strangers unifying to perform the task of running a kingdom. I will be polite, professional, and most of all, elusive. *Extremely* elusive. There will be no room for sentiment or … or *smiles*."

Lorn nodded to himself, exceedingly pleased that he had a sensible plan in place for dealing with the Queen and the latest red book development.

And then—at that exact moment, in fact—the new Queen appeared on his rug and proceeded to ruin everything.

"Lyla," she called out, her eyes half-shut, "we need to get off the floor."

"This is an unexpected development," Lorn murmured to the breeze as he stared down at the woman giggling to herself on the floor. "Should we make ourselves known?"

The breeze fled out of the closest window, fluttering the curtains in its wake.

"Coward," Lorn muttered. He quietly took a seat on the footstool beside the rug and waited for the Queen to notice his presence.

The Queen, it seemed, was in no hurry to do so. She languidly stretched out her long limbs, her dark curls spread across the plush, white fur. She squinted up at the ceiling. "Huh. Were there always stars on the ceiling? Lyla? Seriously, who put the stars up there?"

Lorns lips twitched. It appeared that the Queen was roaring drunk. He sniffed the air; an over-indulgence of wine, if he was not mistaken. Something fruity and—

"This rug is nice," she announced, slapping at it clumsily.

—fairly potent, he thought, grinning.

If there was one thing that Lorn was well versed in, as both the only sober person in a variety of taverns and the ruler of a kingdom that brewed the fifth most dangerous substance in Otherworld, it was drunkenness in all of its forms. Pixies, he found, were typically aggressive drunks, and were known to start bar fights; whereas fairies were lusty drunks and were famous for their bawdy jokes and saucy advances. Goblins had a terrible habit of stripping naked during their drunken bouts, and trolls became eloquent after a few ales, elevating their drinking sessions to raucous poetry recitals. The imps were chaotic drunks, Prince Ashlyn was a generous drunk, Maddox a disgruntled drunk, Ambassador Zoth a bossy drunk, and the Minotaur was a morose drunk. The most hazardous of all were the fae, who were charming drunks, stealing hearts and wallets and possibly first-born children with their winsome drunken ways.

I wonder, he thought as the Queen praised the rug for being furry, *what sort of drunk the Queen will be?*

At first, she appeared to be the disgruntled sort.

"Oh, no," she groaned when she finally noticed Lorn's presence. "Not *you*."

Definitely disgruntled, Lorn thought, as she mumbled and grumbled and then wagged her finger at him for good measure. *Maddox will be pleased.*

"You know," she said, squinting up at him accusingly, "you have a lovely voice. It's all low and warm and handsome—"

He could not help but smile at the compliment. "Handsome?"

"—and it sounds the way that towels feel when they first come out of the dryer—"

That was less of a compliment. "I sound like dry towels? Marvelous."

Her eyes narrowed. "But *then* you use your lovely, dry towel voice to say all sorts of pointy things. A voice like yours isn't meant to say pointy things. A voice like yours is meant to say round things. Like ... like ..."

"*Round?*" he suggested helpfully.

"Yes," she said, trying to nod and failing spectacularly. "But even *rounder* words like *hors d'oeuvres*. Or *cinematography*. Or—or my name. My name is very round. Say my name."

She is also a bossy drunk, he thought, trying to hold back a smile. "Sasha."

"No," she commanded like the queen she was. "Say it *rounder.*"

"*Sasha,*" he said, as roundly as possible.

It must have been sufficiently round because the Queen crowed in triumph. "Yes! Just like that! That was lovely and round. Well done. Remind me to give you a sticker."

Bossy and disgruntled, Lorn thought as the Queen sighed happily at the roundness of it all. *Far better than naked, lusty, aggressive, or charming.*

"You have a round name, too, you know," she announced, interrupting his thoughts. "*Lorn.* See? Very round. *Lo—*" She quickly covered her mouth, her eyes comically wide. "I *can* call you that, can't I? *Lorn?* Or are you going to make me call you something fancy, like 'Shadow King'?" She removed her hand and grimaced as if she had sucked on a lemon. "Lyla wants me to call you 'Shadow King,' and I *can* do that, but it's going to be really awkward, especially over breakfast."

"Truly?" he asked. "How so?"

"Let me show you." She made a great show of clearing her throat before speaking in a truly fancy voice. "Pass the salt, *Shadow King.* Do these eggs taste weird to you, *Shadow King?* Here, lick this bacon, *Shadow King?*" She beamed up at him, delighted by her demonstration. "*See?*"

Bollocks, he thought, trying so very hard not to laugh. *She is a charming drunk. Midra save Between ...*

"You spoke the truth," he said hoarsely, when he was finally able to speak. "That was truly awkward and should be avoided at all costs."

"Told you. *Some* people make you do that, you know—call them fancy things ... like *Headmistress.* You can't just call them *Penelope.*" She squinted up at him as if she was trying to see him from a great distance. "Can I call you Penelope?"

Penelope? He frowned. Did he resemble a Penelope? "I would prefer Lorn to Penelope, if it is all the same to you."

"Deal! Lorn it is." She waved in his direction, her hand flopping around inelegantly. "And you can call me—" She stopped and stared at her floppy hand. "Should my wrist be bending like that?"

"I am not the right person to ask," he said, dutifully looking at the wrist in question. "My wrists often bend in odd ways. I believe yours is bending at an acceptable angle."

"Good to know." She gave her wrist one last suspicious look and then let it fall to the rug. "Hang on ... what was I saying? Before the wrist."

"You said, and I quote, 'You can call me—' and then you became distracted by your bendy appendage."

"That's right! You can call me..." She trailed off, her expression delightfully befuddled.

"Sasha?" he suggested.

Her expression cleared, replaced by an enormous smile. "Bingo! Got it in one."

And right then and there, Lorn realized that step six of The Revised Queen Plan was well and truly *doomed*. For who could ignore a woman with graceful hands and bendy wrists? A woman who raced across the Wasteland with monsters and hit elves with postal vehicles? A woman who was currently poking his calf with considerable vigor ...

"You have firm calves," she said, poking away.

He looked down at his firm calves in shock. "I beg your pardon?"

"You're welcome," she said, poking once more for good measure.

It appeared that she was also a curious drunk, because despite being intoxicated enough to compare Lorn's voice to dehydrated bath linens, Sasha still had sufficient wits about her to ask about his love life.

"Were you ever in love with someone?" she asked.

"I thought so," he found himself answering. "Very, very briefly, mind you."

He considered telling Sasha about Nina but thought better of it—Nina was far too complicated to learn about while drunk. Or sober, for that matter.

"But," he said instead, "it turned out to be a terrible case of mistaken identity."

Of course, Sasha was curious about the entire debacle.

"What do you mean?" she asked. "Was she really something else? Like an imposter? Or a spy? Or a horse?"

And then:

"Did she have different personalities—one nice and one evil?"

And then:

"Was she mean to you? Did she cheat and lie to you?"

"All the time," he answered, trying to hold back his laughter. "But I had assumed that there was a true fondness for me hidden beneath all the cheating and lying."

Nina's true fondness, as it turned out, was power—not the people wielding it. She was also rather fond of dwarven miniature horses—the mean kind—but that was beside the point.

"It turned out that I was mistaken," he continued. "Ultimately, I believed her to be someone that she was not—the fault of which was entirely my own."

Before his eyes, Sasha's charming intoxicated demeanor transformed into something outraged and vengeful. "Well—well—*screw her!*" she cried, as vicious as a pixie in a bar brawl. "I can't stand cheating liars! There's just no excuse for it. Shall we set fire to her house?"

He was momentarily blindsighted by how quickly that escalated. But as the surprise fell away, he felt oddly gratified that she was so quick to defend him in such a flammable manner. "In Between, we have outlawed arson unless you have a permit, and those are notoriously difficult to get. But I thank you for your support."

" 's no problem." Sasha clumsily patted his calf. "Don't worry. One day you'll meet a good woman, and she won't cheat and lie, and you'll live happily-ever-after."

"Excellent," he said, looking down at his calf. "I shall be sure to inform my wife of this fact."

"Oh." She blinked as if startled by the realization. "That's right—you're marrying me. My condolen—hang on—*I'm* not a cheating liar."

"Well, that is a relief."

Her brow furrowed. "But ... it's only fair to warn you that I get bored easily. And then I usually leave. And according to my last two—three—maybe four boyfriends, I'm too sexually demanding. Which is such a double standard." Her tone turned prickly and sour. "First, they're happy about it, and then it's, 'I have a headache, Sasha.' Or: 'We already did it three times today, Sasha.' Or: 'I think you broke me, Sasha.' The pretty ones break so quickly. No stamina." She looked up at him, her eyes narrowed accusingly. "*You're* pretty."

Lorn gave up. He buried his face in his hands and laughed and laughed. "*Sasha.* I believe you shall regret this conversation once you awaken."

"I regret nothing!" she cried. "It's the truth, the whole truth, and nothing but the truth." She reached out for his calf and held fast to it. "I want to be honest with you. I want us to be friends. Can we be friends, Lorn?"

Lorn removed his hands from his face. *I shall have to revise The Revised Queen Plan,* he thought with a sigh.

"I believe we shall," he said, resigned. "Whether I like it or not."

"Good." She yawned so extravagantly that Lorn had to stifle his own yawn in response. "I'm going to be moving to a new place soon. I'll need all the friends I can get."

"Have you ever been in love?" he blurted out and immediately regretted it.

Why ever did I ask that? he wondered. *Good gods, is her intoxication contagious?*

But Sasha did not appear to mind his question; she stared off into the distance, her brow furrowed in thought.

"Not with my whole heart, no," she answered eventually. "But I'd like to be. Wouldn't you like to fall in love with your whole heart someday?"

It was such a simple question, so easily asked. And yet, it hit Lorn like a meteor to the chest, leaving him breathless.

Wouldn't you like to fall in love with your whole heart some day?

Almost unbidden, he thought about his dream queen—the vision of the bold, vibrant woman that would come to him whenever he was at his most broken and vulnerable, giving him a tantalizing glimpse of true love.

True love. He almost laughed aloud. *Such things are not for the likes of me.*

"You can admit it, you know," Sasha said, interrupting his thoughts. "I'm drunk—you can be truthful when you're drunk."

"But I am not drunk." *Though, I am starting to feel as though I have a hangover,* he thought with a sigh.

"I'm drunk enough for the both of us," she reassured him with a floppy wave of her hand. "We're almost married which makes us partners—if I'm drunk, you're drunk. Would it be easier to tell me if my eyes were closed? I'll close my eyes so that it won't feel weird." She screwed her eyes shut. "Does that feel less weird now?"

"Remarkably so," he said, humoring her.

But she looked so serious, lying below him with her eyes closed, that he felt as though he owed her a reply.

He was about to say 'no,' when he was stopped by a thought.

Are you quite sure that true love is not for the likes of you? a voice that sounded remarkably like the Shadow asked. *After all, until this evening, you thought that leaving Between was quite impossible, and yet now there is a little red book sitting on your desk that says otherwise. Perhaps you need to dream bigger…*

Lorn stilled. Below him, Sasha waited for his answer, her eyes still closed tight, her arm wrapped around his leg.

You can be truthful, she had said.

You can be truthful, the Shadow voice urged.

"Very well," he said, his heart beating like a wild thing freed from a cage. "I believe I should like that, too."

"It's a deal then," she mumbled sleepily. She patted his calf and sighed sweetly. "One day, we'll fall in love with our whole hearts."

His breath caught in his throat, strangled somewhere between a laugh and a sob. With great effort, he swallowed it down. He stared at his almost-wife, both wanting and fearing to hear what she would say next.

But she said nothing more; her breathing slowed and deepened. Soon, her hold on his boot relaxed, her lovely hand falling away as she drifted off to sleep.

"Whatever am I going to do with you, Sasha?" he whispered hoarsely, as she began to disappear, leaving behind a rug covered in gold dust and a heartsore king.

∼

"SHE IS DE-LIGHTFUL!" HIS SHADOW CROWED. "INTELLIGENT, WITTY, adorable when intoxicated, ever so fair of face and form, and best of all—"

Lorn held up his hand. "Do not say it."

"—sexually demanding. *Sexually demanding!* Tell me, are there two sweeter words in the dictionary, especially when paired in this manner?"

Lorn ignored him and sat in his customary armchair. He instantly regretted talking to his Shadow about Sasha's latest visit. He knew it would make the Shadow excitable and he was right—the Shadow was practically prancing on his side of the mirror.

And yet, Lorn had still made his way to the Portal Chamber immediately after Sasha had returned to her realm.

He wondered if he had developed another concussion.

"You did hear her, did you not?" the Shadow continued. "She confessed it herself while she was lying on your rug, spread out like a gift, like an *offering.* And yet you did nothing but laugh at her. What were you *thinking?*"

"What did you expect me to do?"

The Shadow raised an eyebrow. "Truly? You have no idea? My, my—it *has* been too long since your last intimate encounter." He tsked. "Allow me to enlighten you. She called you pretty, Lorn—which was exceedingly gratifying—and then alluded to the fact that you would not be able to keep pace with her sexually. You should have taken up her challenge for the honor of pretty men everywhere. Have you no pride?"

"Have you no shame? No need to answer, it was a trick question." Lorn leaned forward in his chair, seriousness personified. "For the short duration of this marriage, I intend to act as I intend to go on—honorably and with restraint. I will be polite to Sasha and no more in her presence."

"*For the short duration of this marriage*? Whatever do you mean? You are not giving me that speech again about magic folk dying young, are you? Not with the Middleton Coven demonstrating how false that assumption truly is ..."

Lorn initiated eye contact with his Shadow and let the memories of Maddox's red book pass between them.

The Shadow saw it all—the spell, the possibilities. He even experienced the surge of hope Lorn had felt when he contemplated the idea of freedom.

The Shadow sat heavily on his chair, clearly stunned. "Maddox actually did it. He found a way out. And you ... you intend to go through with it. You intend to use the spell in Maddox's little red book to free yourself from this place."

It was not a question.

"I do." Lorn could still feel the hope fluttering, fragile and eager, behind his ribcage. "I have read the book. The spell seems easy enough—"

"Have you finally succeeded in becoming intoxicated?" the Shadow interrupted incredulously. "There is *nothing* easy about that spell!"

Lorn raised his hands. "Calm yourself. I only meant that it contains so few elements and all of them will be at my disposal next month. I would have thought that leaving this place would involve blood magic, or raising a new god, or some other complicated, impossible thing ..."

"Let us look at this foolhardy plan in more detail, shall we?" The Shadow leapt from his chair and began pacing in front of the mirror. "You first need to transfer me into another mirror so that I will no longer be part of Between."

"I have several ideas on how to accomplish this," Lorn said. "It is fortunate that I have an affinity with mirrors."

The Shadow raised an eyebrow and continued pacing. "Well, we are about to test that affinity because one wrong step and you will be no more."

Lorn snorted. "That is barely a disincentive."

"More importantly, one wrong step and *I* will be no more, which is the true tragedy here."

"Clearly," Lorn said dryly.

The Shadow stopped pacing and faced his true form. "If we put aside the fact that this book has appeared far too conveniently for it *not* to be a trap—"

Lorn stilled. "I had considered that."

"—you are assuming that Between will *let* you cast this spell. That lovely, intricate Mark between your shoulder blades links you—links *us*—to this very sentient kingdom. Do you *really* think that Between will just let you go?"

"Between will be too busy fulfilling the Dream of the Dreamer during the Lunar Crossing to stop us."

The Shadow sat back down in his chair. He stared at Lorn as if searching for something in Lorn's expression.

Whatever the Shadow saw did nothing to reassure him.

"So … there is nothing I can say to dissuade you from this foolhardy plan," the Shadow said eventually, his tone flat, his expression curiously blank. "A plan that may leave you dead, myself Midra knows where, and Between under the guidance of a magicless Earther."

Lorn stared at his Shadow, truly stunned. "Why would you want to dissuade me? The day is finally here! Between will have another ruler, and we will be free to roam."

"A lot has happened in the past seven years. As much as you wish to deny it, you have developed a fondness for this terrible place. Why leave?"

Lorn shook his head, utterly betrayed. "I cannot believe you. All that has kept me going has been the dream of leaving."

"What if Sasha is worth staying for?" the Shadow asked quietly.

Lorn's hands clenched into fists. Why was his Shadow not joyous at the news? Why could he not understand that *this* was the chance that they had been waiting for since Lorn's coronation?

Lorn felt the sting of his nails biting into the flesh of his palms and relaxed his hands. "As if I would exchange a certain and painful death for a pretty face."

"Do not diminish her." The Shadow's tone was like a lash. "Sasha is the True Queen of Between—she was chosen to rule by your side. She will be an asset to both you and Between … and more if you allow it. Please"—the Shadow waved away Lorn's remark—"spare *me* your lies."

Lorn crossed the room until he was almost touching the mirror. He stared at his Shadow, his expression raw. "I have to leave. This place is killing me. Look at me!" He tore open his doublet and shirt, exposing the pale skin of his chest mottled with black marks. "I am just patches and bones. As soon as these heal, more will take their place. Every day is a fight against elements that I cannot bring to heel. Seven years feels like *seventy*. There is nothing here for me except pain and exhaustion and death. And I am so *tired*. There is not a part of me that does not ache. I cannot—"

He took a trembling breath and rested his forehead against the cold surface of the mirror, defeated.

"I cannot keep this up," he whispered, his voice broken. He closed his eyes and shuddered. "No wonder so many of the previous kings went mad."

The Shadow's shoulders slumped. He closed the distance between himself and his true form, and rested his forehead against Lorn's, separated only by a pane of enchanted glass.

"I can feel your pain," the Shadow said mournfully. "I know that you are exhausted and demoralized and so, *so* lonely for the type of companionship that those around you cannot provide. That loneliness can leach away your strength just as much as tirelessly working toward an impossible task. You are beset within and without." He reached out and placed his hand against the mirror over Lorn's shoulder. "But I ask of you—no, I *beg* of you—to wait a month before you try to leave. Give Sasha a month to change your mind. Do not turn away from her companionship. Allow her the opportunity to ease some of your burdens."

"I doubt that Sasha's presence here will have any bearing on my burdens," Lorn said wearily. "If anything, they will only increase."

"Stay, and you will have the chance to find out. Allow yourself to see what it is like to have a true companion."

Lorn lifted his head from the glass. The Shadow mirrored his actions until they were standing toe to toe.

"You are assuming that she will want my companionship," Lorn said.

"Of course she will! Who else will she have here? Besides, she said she wants to be your friend. Good friends, from the sounds of it. After all, she was willing to help you burn down Nina's house."

Reluctantly, Lorn smiled at the memory.

As did the Shadow. "I am simply asking you to encourage the friendship, not push it away."

"Shall I use my dry towel voice?"

"If that is what it takes."

There was a long pause as Lorn considered the Shadow's proposal. "And if I still intend to leave? Would it not be kinder to maintain my distance?"

The Shadow stared at him incredulously. "If you leave her to run this terrifying kingdom by herself, she will hate you regardless of whether you are friends or not ... and with excellent cause."

Lorn's stomach dropped at the thought. He was momentarily surprised by the strength of his reaction. All at once, he was struck by a memory of Sasha—her dark curls fanned across his white fur rug, her grip on his calf surprisingly firm—staring up at him so trustingly.

I want to be honest with you, she had said. *I want us to be friends. Can we be friends?*

And then:

One day, we'll fall in love with someone with our whole hearts.

Lorn's stomach clenched to the point where it felt like a hydra was gleefully twisting his innards.

"And if Felzik manages to train her up with those God Weapons, Midra help you if you decide to return," the Shadow added.

Unconsciously, Lorn pressed a hand over his midsection. "She will run me through. And with those weapons, she will not miss."

"You have nothing to lose," the Shadow said. "Companionship, assistance, a queen. Perhaps not the kind of queen you had envisaged— whoever thought your queen would be battle-trained? But a queen nonetheless. A balm to your loneliness."

Abruptly, Lorn pulled away from the mirror. "You have an ulterior motive in asking me to befriend her."

"Several, in fact!" the Shadow agreed, not at all fussed to be found out. "But believe it or not, they are all in your best interest—I can act in no other way. Trust me when I say that there are glorious and unexpected things in store. But whether they come to fruition will depend on your willingness to bend."

Lorn felt torn. Both paths—stay or leave—were beset by complications, problems, and possible death. At this point, he was not sure which was the better option.

Perhaps they were both equally terrible but in slightly different ways.

"One month," the Shadow coaxed. "Give her a single month. You can always leave afterward."

"Assuming I have not died from exhaustion in the interim." Lorn pinched the bridge of his nose and sighed. "Fine. I will stay. Better the demon you know, et cetera, et cetera. But only for a month."

"I am sure that it will be quite the month," the Shadow said with a smile.

～

THAT NIGHT, LORN'S DREAMS WERE A TANGLE OF IMAGES THAT FLICKERED and flashed relentlessly before his mind's eye—white mists and yellow gates, enchanted weapons in a silver box, men in cowled robes of white and gray, crowds of goblins that snickered and wheezed, breezes and red books and maps stained with blood the color of rust...

But then there was a vision, clear as day, of dark curls scattered across a white fur rug and slender arms raised toward him.

Your whole heart, Lorn, the dream queen whispered, beckoning him closer. *Your whole heart.*

And then, she smiled.

Lorn awoke with a gasp and lurched upright.

Your whole heart, Lorn ...

Lorn rubbed his eyes with the heels of his palms. He turned accusingly to a small plate sitting on his bedside table, where the remains of a piece of hard cheese sat amongst cracker crumbs.

"Those dreams had better be your doing," Lorn said to the cheese.

The cheese, unsurprisingly, remained silent. Lorn had to admit that it looked rather innocent, but if the cheese had not led to that inappropriately pleasant dream, well ... Lorn refused to contemplate what it all meant.

"I should have chosen cake as my bedtime meal—cake would never have betrayed me in such a matter," he muttered, clearly in denial.

With a final glare at the dairy snack, Lorn settled back into bed and warily went back to sleep.

17

AWAITING THE QUEEN

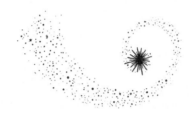

Whether Lorn—or Between—was ready or not, the day of the True Queen of Between's arrival had finally dawned.

Despite Lorn's best laid plans to inspect the preparations for Sasha's arrival, events conspired against him once again. There were traveling dignitaries to meet with, a mudslide to foil before it crushed a village, a territory dispute between four wolf packs to settle, and a drunk unicorn to liberate from yet another wall.

There had also been a present to make.

"Not a present," Lorn told himself, ignoring the Shadow's advice to buy Sasha something fancy. "A way to fulfill the requirements of Sasha's first boon."

Sasha had asked for a way to communicate with Lyla while she was in Between. Technically, Lorn could have instructed Sasha to write her friend a letter and then slipped it through the Portal during the Crossing.

But instead, he had enchanted a pair of hand mirrors.

Lorn stared down at his work, the silver mirrors aglow with new enchantments in the darkness of his chambers, and had a singularly terrible feeling about the whole enterprise.

"I believe I shall regret this dearly," he told the mirrors. "If history is anything to go by, the dreaded *Lyla* will encourage Sasha to act in ways that vex me on an hourly basis." He paused. "On the bright side, there are no mail trucks in Between ..."

Despite Lorn's affinity with mirrors, the complex, intricate magic had cost him dearly in dark patches. Magical exhaustion began to settle over his limbs like a lead blanket.

But at least he was prepared. Lorn pulled two oatcakes out of his bottomless pouch and a Vigor Draught from his bedside table and grimly consumed them all.

He had just finished the last drops of the Vigor Draught when the guards summoned him to his Less-Formal Meeting Chamber to meet with Head-Wolf Soren.

"The extraction is done," Head Soren said, dusting off her black robes.

"Did it go well?" Lorn asked, placing one of the newly enchanted mirrors carefully into his pouch.

"As well as can be expected in the circumstances, what with the Binding and all." She smoothed the black fabric over her ample lap, flicking away bits of dust and cobwebs. "I must say, they were the nicest fellows that I've ever had in my extraction chamber. So polite, so well behaved! They didn't scream or swear or insult my looks or parentage. Really, they spoiled me for all other extractions."

"I am pleased to hear that they were model extractees. But were you able to get any information out of them?"

Head Soren grimaced. "Not a lot. Bindings are bothersome." She pulled a piece of paper from the gray sash around her waist and placed it on Lorn's desk. "After we got the vowsmith to loosen the Vow—and gave the dears a few potions to loosen their lips—we were able to find out a little more about them. Long story short—you were right. One is a hunter from the village of Little Idle, the other a farmer from the outskirts of Aurora."

Lorn blinked. "They were both from Aurora?"

"They were indeed. Both had trained as Aurorean castle guards in their youth, but they didn't know each other before they met up in the Swamp of Eternal Angst—a bit of an age gap between them, so that's not unusual. Apparently, they were going about their daily business when they were Summoned through their Binding to Between. They didn't know it was a kidnapping; their only instructions were to guard the party."

"Hmm." Lorn tapped his finger against his lips, his mind trying to fit the pieces of the puzzle together. "I doubt this is an Aurorean plot. They were probably chosen because of their proximity to Between. Did they say who their leader was? The man in the white robe?"

Head Soren shook her head. "They didn't know who he was, and they didn't see his face. He kept it hidden."

"And let me guess—they could not tell you who performed the Binding?"

The Head of the assassins beamed at him. "An excellent guess, dear! They couldn't. They clammed right up and writhed around in pain when we pressed the point. Nasty stuff, Bindings. But, we did what your vowsmith suggested: we stripped them down and looked for a Mark. The dears didn't even object—such sweet boys. We found this."

Head Soren pushed the piece of paper across the desk to Lorn. On it was a strange symbol—a sort of crude compass of arrows with a diamond at the base.

"Both of them had it on the sole of their left foot," Head Soren added.

"Have you seen it before?" Lorn asked.

Head Soren shook her head.

Lorn traced the symbol with the tip of his finger. Even though it was just a drawing on a scrap of parchment, he could feel the power behind it. "Hmm. Neither have I, but there is something about it that looks familiar. What color was it?"

"A sort of brownish-red. The color of clay."

Lorn stared at the symbol. It was the key to this entire matter—he was *sure* of it. "We need to speak to someone who works with Bindings."

Head Soren's pleasant face crinkled into a frown. "They won't be easy to find, dear. You know Binding magic is Forbidden. There won't be a lot of people advertising the fact that they can do it. Or undo it."

Lorn remembered the Goblin's pointy, knowing grin when they spoke of undoing a Binding. "True. But then again, many things are Forbidden in Otherworld. Vowsmiths are not supposed to undo Vows, and no one in Otherworld is supposed to have contact with the inhabitants of the Earther Realm ... and yet, in Between, these occur regularly. If there is someone who can undo this Binding, the odds are that they reside here."

Head Soren smiled broadly. "Well, that makes it easier, doesn't it?"

Lorn inclined his head. "Easier but certainly not easy. And what of the white robed man? Were your Wolves able to locate him?"

"Not a trace of him, I'm afraid. There wasn't much to go on—white robes are everywhere."

Lorn was just about to agree when he felt the Summons to the Earther Realm.

Shadow King, Sasha called.

"Apologies," Lorn said, wincing at the fishhook sensation behind his navel. "The Earther Realm calls."

Head Soren waved away his concern. "That's quite alright, dear—we're done here anyway. Say hello to the Queen for me." She gestured to Sasha's shoe, still sitting on the box of God Weapons. "Best bring that with you—she's probably missing it."

~

"MIDRA'S SACK," LORN GROANED AS HE ARRIVED IN THE PORTAL CHAMBER. He slipped Sasha's shoe into his pouch. "Is it truly sunset in the Earther Realm already?"

"Yes," his Shadow said gleefully, not even bothering to contain his excitement.

Lorn stilled, his eyes going wide. "Oh, no. Today is Wednesday. Nothing good ever happens on a Wednesday."

"Well, perhaps today we shall break that curse. No—we *will* break the curse—I can feel it!"

As his dark armor unfurled over his body, Lorn could feel the weight of the Shadow's stare.

"What is it?" he asked as the Cloak of Shadows appeared at his shoulders.

"Your appearance." The Shadow shook his head tersely. "This is an important day! Do you really want our lovely Queen to see you so disheveled? At least *try* to look enticing."

Lorn took a cursory glance at himself in the Dreamer's Mirror. "I look as I always look." He winced as the Crown of Blades settled on his head. "I am not disheveled—I am as presentable as always."

"Yes, but not *enticing.*"

Lorn looked down at his armor. "I am encased in metal. How enticing could I possibly be?"

"Women love men in armor. How do you think the High King's inbred White Guard attracts women? It is certainly not their intellect or scintillating conversation. You are simply not trying." The Shadow made a frustrated gesture at Lorn's appearance. "Midra's sack! Just try not to bollocks this up."

Lorn gave the Shadow a quelling look and tried to contain the unexpected flutter of anticipation in his chest. "Bollocks what up? Regardless of what you may desire, this relationship between Sasha and myself is merely a Joining. She is the Queen … and possibly the means to our future freedom … and as such, I will afford her every courtesy but *no more.*"

The Shadow smiled slyly. "We shall see."

Lorn opened his mouth to retort, but the Summons pulled him toward the Portal.

With a burst of gold and silver light, the Portal opened and drew him through to Old Middleton.

To Sasha.

To Destiny.

"We shall see," the Shadow whispered.

EPILOGUE

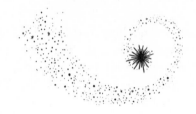

HIGH ABOVE OTHERWORLD, IN A TOWER BUILT BY AN ELDER GOD FROM stardust and bone, three powerful men conspired under cover of night.

"Well," said one, drawing his voluminous fur cloak tightly around himself, "you certainly bollocksed that up."

High King Dresden sat back in his chair and surveyed the fur-clad man with a look that would have terrified most Otherworlders.

"How so, Your Majesty?" he asked dryly, even though he knew the answer.

The King of Zadria seemed utterly unfazed by the High King's look. He was, after all, typically surrounded by Death Cultists, whose looks ranged from pure evil to utterly deranged. "You had a chance to take both the amulet and the bride, and yet your men came back empty-handed."

The High King inclined his head. "And yours did not come back at all."

The King of Zadria lifted his pointy chin until it jutted out from beneath the hood of his cloak. "I told you—"

"If it is any consolation, you both bollocksed it up," the third man drawled as he poured his fourth goblet of wine.

"Remember to whom you are speaking," the High King said sharply. "Or the favor that I show Vetch will be quickly transferred to the Kingdom of Dox."

King Laurent of Vetch held up his hands in mock surrender, the gold-tulle cuffs of his jacket cascading to his elbows in a whisper of froth and glitter.

"Peace, Your Majesty," he said, his tone languid. "I freely admit that *I* bollocksed it up, too. *All* of our recent plans have come to naught. Lorn refuses to be lured from the throne—or Between in general. The prince and the elf were unable to retrieve that inconvenient queen or the amulet. And the less said about that *other* excursion into the Earther Realm the better."

"That *other excursion* is why I called this meeting," the High King said. He looked pointedly at the wine puddled on the table around the King of Vetch's goblet. "I assume that you are sober enough to remember my message?"

"Yes, but I am well on my way to forgetting it." The King of Vetch lifted his overly full goblet and jauntily toasted the High King.

"Well, I hope this meeting actually accomplishes something," the King of Zadria said, his hooked nose twitching in agitation. "We need to move faster."

"Really?" The High King leaned toward the King of Zadria. "If you had sent the betrothal parties *before* the Challengers as I instructed, then perhaps Between would have a Zadrian queen by now, and Lorn would no longer be a threat to our plans."

The King of Zadria's eyes narrowed. "I am pursuing a two-pronged plan." He held up two gloved fingers. "*Two-pronged.* It will pay off in time, you shall see."

"Something had better pay off soon," King of Vetch said. "Otherwise we will be found out—before time, mind you—and tried by the good people of Otherworld for something tedious, like *treason.*"

"As I have said numerous times, we will *not* be tried for treason," the High King said, his voice echoing hollowly across the room.

"True." The King of Vetch sighed and took a long sip of wine. "It will probably be something much worse. Refresh my memory—what happened to the last treacherous High King? Was he not tied to a light-ning rod in the middle of a storm? Or was that one of the *other* treacherous High Kings?"

The High King stared at the picture of decadence that was the King of Vetch. "Everything I do is for the good of Otherworld."

The Zadrian King snorted. "I doubt the Lower Kingdom monarchs will see it that way—not once your plan comes into play."

"Well, it is not as if we can ask them what they think about it, can we?"

the King of Vetch said gloomily. "Not now and *certainly* not for much longer." He drank deeply from his goblet.

"Everything I do is for the good of Otherworld," the High King repeated firmly. "And to that end, I have chosen our puppets."

"But Between—" the King of Zadria began.

The High King held up his hand for silence. "The source told us that the new Queen of Between is leaving the Earther Realm—she will be in Otherworld soon enough, and we will take care of her then. But for now, our time is better spent fixing matters in our own realm." He pulled two pieces of parchment from his tunic and handed them to the kings. "These are to be destroyed in the fireplace before you leave, so read them thoroughly."

A bitter wind whipped through the tower, blowing the parchment from the King of Zadria's hands. With a muttered curse, he chased it across the room and grabbed it just before it reached the window.

"Why must we always meet in this drafty old tower?" he grumbled as he returned to his seat. He huddled further into his furs and moved his chair closer to the fireplace.

"Tradition," the King of Vetch said drolly as he poured himself another goblet of wine. "Most conspiring happens in towers. It provides the necessary atmosphere."

"This is the highest tower in Otherworld," the High King answered, ignoring the King of Vetch, "and it will only open for the High King." He gestured to himself. "We may speak freely here without fear of being overheard."

"It is a pity that there isn't a sauna or a thermal spring or even a nice, warm underground cavern that will only open for you," the King of Zadria grumbled.

"Come now, it is not *so* bad in here," the King of Vetch said, filling the King of Zadria's goblet. "It is just a little brisk." He placed the decanter back on the table and paused when he caught sight of his reflection from across the room. He tilted his head, pleased at how well the candlelight brought out the warm notes in his golden-brown complexion, and then turned back to the King of Zadria. "You are behaving as though we are in the middle of a blizzard."

"I come from a desert kingdom," the King of Zadria bit out. "We do not do *brisk*. We do not do *blizzards*. We do *scorching* and *blistering* and *fiery death by sand* ..."

"Gentlemen, can we discuss the weather another time?" the High King asked tersely.

He looked up at the fae-charmed clock that was suspended above the table. Three crowned wooden figurines stared back at him from the base of the clock's face—one in armor, one in furs, and one in gold. A word appeared below them in tiny, red letters.

Conspiracy.

The High King eyed the clock warily. "Time is truly of the essence."

The clock dutifully ticked louder.

"As if I want to spend a second more in this tower than necessary," the King of Zadria muttered.

"Dawdling is unattractive," the King of Vetch agreed, sipping his wine.

As the Kings huddled together over their parchment and their plans, the bitter wind rattled the window shutters and then slipped out the window, down the tower, and circled a slight figure that was suspended high above the ground.

Black—the craftiest of all the Ravens—sat beneath the window ledge in a leather sling that had been enchanted to attach itself to anything that it touched. Around Black's shoulders was a cloak that reflected its surroundings; if anyone thought to look up, they would have seen nothing but the bone-white tower awash with starlight.

As Black listened to the kings conspire, the spy grew more and more uneasy. For although Black had heard many plans while in the service of Between—dastardly plans and ruthless plans; simple plans and foolish plans —*this* was a plan that threatened the very fabric of Otherworld.

I must tell the King immediately, Black thought. *He will know what to do.*

When the kings finally emerged, one by one, from the entrance and headed furtively back to their kingdoms, Black made the long, treacherous climb down the tower.

Filled with dangerous knowledge and terrible purpose, the spy went off to save Otherworld.

THE END

COMING SOON

OTHERWORLD

Book 2 of the Chronicles of Between

by

L. L. Starling

More swords. More sorcery. More leather pants.

THANK YOU

Thank you, you marvelous reader, for picking up this book! There are so many books out there with pretty covers all vying for your attention; I am humbled and delighted that you chose mine. You are now my favorite human.

And yet another 'thank you' to those who took the time to write a review, because reviewing takes time and energy and *words*, like 'erinaceous' (which, according to *Wikipedia*, means: 'of, pertaining to, or resembling a hedgehog'). I read and appreciate every single one (*especially* those containing the word 'erinaceous').

If you enjoyed *Between*, please consider recommending it to a friend.

If you didn't enjoy *Between*, please consider recommending it to an enemy (take THAT enemy! *shakes fist at sky*). Damn enemies …

ACKNOWLEDGMENTS

BETWEEN took eight long (L-O-N-G) years to write. During that time, I tried the patience and sanity of many wonderful people who supported me enormously (and never once ran screaming from the room when I brought it up, even though it's likely that they seriously contemplated it).

My husband, Peter, was infinitely supportive and encouraging; I could not have done this without him. Even though he has never read a fantasy novel (he prefers to read about allergies and spine alignments and the stock market—odd, but true), he still offered to read Between, which, if you ask me, is a sign of True Love.

Louisa Gallie, developmental editor and artist extraordinaire, turned a series of bawdy jokes and half-written scenes into a novel. Better yet, a novel with a glorious, glittery cover. Without her brilliance, insight, artistic prowess, and beast-wrangling abilities, Between would have been nothing more than a coverless, blurb-less, forty-page description of Lorn's leather pants.

Melissa Findley, the copy editing queen and Knower-of-All-Things-Fantasy, fixed punctuation errors, plot holes, and made numerous brilliant suggestions that made this novel infinitely better. She also saved the day with last-minute illustration fixes. I could not be more grateful for all her assistance.

Rebecca Morse single-handedly made this book 187% prettier and at least 212% fancier by creating the gorgeous illustrations featured throughout. She managed to capture the characters in ways that words could not. I have spent hours staring at those lovely drawings in awe and delight.

Three of the bravest women I know—Corrina Wilson, Melissa Findley, and Rebecca Morse—read this book while it was still in draft form (those poor, poor women) and added in more jokes, more plot, and at least four new crotch references.

Alexandra Godwin used her magic (and some kind of software) to turn my terrible sketches into the Marks. Thank you!

Many people were kind enough to encourage and support me while writing this novel. If they had known the outcome, they might not have done so. Nevertheless, I am grateful for the fantastic cheerleading from my family, friends, and the fanfiction community, especially the fabulous deviants of the LFFL.

Last but definitely not least, this book was fueled by lots and lots and lots of coffee—probably enough to flood a moderately-sized village. I am forever grateful to the jolly baristas and the overly-generous Wi-Fi policies found in the following fine cafes: Colectivo Coffee, Ancora Coffee, Michelangelo's Coffee House, Crescendo Espresso Bar, Johnson Street Public House (all in Madison, Wisconsin); and Kafé Neo (tucked away in Kogarah, Sydney, Australia).

I have probably forgotten many others and will only remember them when this goes to print. Please imagine that I thanked you, profusely and repeatedly, for all your lovely support.

L. L. Starling

ABOUT THE AUTHOR

L. L. Starling is an Australian who lives in Madison, Wisconsin—right in the midst of the deliciousness that is 'America's Dairyland.' She loves small dogs and bucket-sized iced lattes, glitter and crowns of all sorts, Wonder Woman, Bowie, and the music of the 80s (especially the power ballads, which she sings into her hairdryer on the 'cool' setting so that her hair blows around in a suitably epic fashion). *BETWEEN* is her first novel.

If you have any questions about *BETWEEN*—say, you want to know Endora the chicken's favorite food, or what color leather pants Lorn will be wearing next Monday (hint: black)—or you'd like a sneak peek (or two) of the next book in the series, come and visit her on:

facebook.com/llstarlingwriter

instagram.com/llstarling

Made in the USA
Coppell, TX
15 May 2022

77799760R00437